A FIRE IN THE FLESH

ALSO FROM JENNIFER L. ARMENTROUT

Fall With Me
Dream of You (a 1001 Dark Nights Novel)
Forever With You
Fire in You

By J. Lynn
Wait for You
Be with Me
Stay with Me

The Blood and Ash Series
From Blood and Ash
A Kingdom of Flesh and Fire
The Crown of Gilded Bones
The War of Two Queens
A Soul of Ash and Blood
Visions of Flesh and Blood: A Blood and Ash/Flesh and Fire
Compendium

The Flesh and Fire Series
A Shadow in the Ember
A Light in the Flame
A Fire in the Flesh

Fall of Ruin and Wrath Series
Fall of Ruin and Wrath

The Covenant Series
Half-Blood
Pure
Deity
Elixir
Apollyon
Sentinel

Gamble Brothers Series
Tempting the Best Man
Tempting the Player
Tempting the Bodyguard

A de Vincent Novel Series
Moonlight Sins
Moonlight Seduction
Moonlight Scandals

Standalone Novels
Obsession
Frigid
Scorched
Cursed
Don't Look Back
The Dead List
Till Death
The Problem with Forever
If There's No Tomorrow

Anthologies
Meet Cute
Life Inside My Mind
Fifty First Times

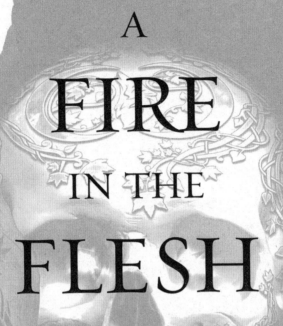

A
FIRE
IN THE
FLESH

#1 NEW YORK TIMES BESTSELLING AUTHOR

JENNIFER L.
ARMENTROUT

BLUE
BOX
PRESS

To see a full-size version of the map, visit
https://theblueboxpress.com/books/afitfmap/

A Fire in the Flesh
A Flesh and Fire Novel
By Jennifer L. Armentrout

Copyright 2023 Jennifer L. Armentrout
ISBN: 978-1-957568-43-0

Published by Blue Box Press, an imprint of Evil Eye Concepts,
Incorporated

ACKNOWLEDGMENTS

Behind every book, no matter how many written, is a team of people who helped get the book in your hands. Thank you to Blue Box Press—Liz Berry, Jillian Stein, MJ Rose, Chelle Olson, Kim Guidroz, Jessica Saunders, Tanaka Kangara, the amazing editing and proofreading team, and Michael Perlman, along with the entire team at S&S for their hardcover distribution support and expertise. Also, a huge thanks to Hang Le for her incredible talent at design; my agents Kevan Lyon and Taryn Fagerness; my assistant, Malissa Coy; shop manager Jen Fisher; and the hardworking team behind ApollyCon and more: Steph Brown, along with Vicky and Matt. Also, the JLAnders mods, Vonetta Young and Mona Awad who help keep the group a safe and fun place for all. Thank you all for being the most amazing, supportive team an author could want, for making sure these books are read all across the world, creating merch, helping with plot issues, and more.

I also need to thank those who've helped me procrastinate in one way or another—KA Tucker, Kristen Ashley, JR Ward, Sarah J. Maas, Steve Berry for story times, Andrea Joan, Stacey Morgan, Margo Lipschultz, and so many more.

A big thank you to JLAnders for always creating a fun and often hilarious place to chill. You guys are the best! And to the ARC team for your honest reviews and support.

Most importantly, none of this would be possible without you, the reader. I hope you realize how much you mean to me.

DEDICATION

To you, the reader. Yes, you.

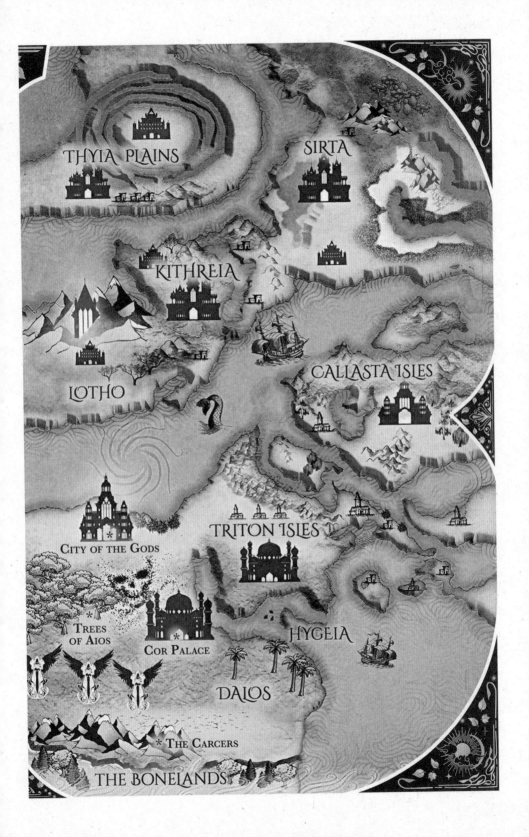

PRONUNCIATION GUIDE

Characters

Aios – AYY-ohs
Andreia – ahn-DRAY-ah
Attes – AT-tayz
Aurelia – au-REL-ee-ah
Baines – baynz
Bele – bell
Daniil – da-NEEL
Diaval – dee-AH-vuhl
Dorcan – dohr-kan
Dyses – DEYE-seez
Ector – EHK-tohr
Ehthawn – EE-thawn
Elias – el-IGH-us
Embris – EM-bris
Erlina – Er-LEE-nah
Ernald – ER-nald
Eythos – EE-thos
Ezmeria – ez-MARE-ee-ah
Gemma – jeh-muh
Halayna – hah-LAY-nah
Hanan – HAY-nan
Iason – IGH-son
Ione – EYE-on
Jadis – JAY-dis
Kayleigh Balfour – KAY-lee BAL-fohr
Keella – KEE-lah
King Saegar – king SAY-gar
Kolis – KOH-lis
Kyn – kin
Lailah – LAY-lah
Lathan – LEY-THahN
Loimus – loy-moos
Madis – mad-is
Mahiil – ma-HEEL
Maia – MY-ah

Marisol Faber – MARE-i-sohl FAY-berr
Mycella – MY-sell-AH
Naberius – nah-BEHR-ee-us
Nektas – NEK-tas
Nyktos – NIK-toes
Odetta – oh-DET-ah
Orphine – OR-feen
Peinea – pain-ee-yah
Penellaphe – pen-NELL-uh-fee
Phanos – FAN-ohs
Polemus – pol-he-mus
Queen Calliphe – queen KAL-ih-fee
Reaver – REE-ver
Rhahar – RUH-har
Rhain – rain
Saion – SIGH-on
Sera – SEE-ra
Seraphena Mierel – SEE-rah-fee-nah MEER-ehl
Sotoria – soh-TOR-ee-ah
Taric – tay-rik
Tavius – TAY-vee-us
Thad – thad
Theon – thEE-awn
Veses – VES-eez

Places
Callasta Isles – kah-LAA-stah eyelz
Cauldra Manor – kall-drah [manor]
Cor Palace – kohr pal-is
Dalos – day-lohs
Elysium Peaks – ihl-LEES-ee-uhm peeks
House of Haides – howz of HAY-deez
Hygeia – high-JEE-uh
Iliseeum – AH-lee-see-um
Kithreia – kith-REE-ah
Lasania – lah-SAHN-ee-uh
Lotho – LOH-thoh
Massene – mah-SEE-nuh
Pillars of Asphodel – [pillars of] AS-foe-del
Skotos Mountains – SKOH-tohs MOWNT-ehnz

Sirta – SIR-ta
The Carcers – [the] KAR-serz
Thyia Plains – THIGH-ah playnz
Triton Isles – TRY-ton IGH-elz
Vathi – VAY-thee
Vita – VEE-tah

Terms
Arae – air-ree
benada – ben-NAH-dah
ceeren – SEE-rehn
chora – KOHR-ah
Cimmerian – sim-MARE-ee-in
dakkai – DAY-kigh
demis – dem-EEZ
eather – ee-thohr
graeca – gray-kah
Gyrm - germ
imprimen – IM-prim-ehn
kardia – KAR-dee-ah
kiyou wolf/wolves – kee-yoo [wolf/wolves]
meeyah Liessa – MEE-yah LEE-sah
nota – NOH-tah
notam – NOH-tam
sekya – sek-yah
so'lis – SOH-lis
sparanea – SPARE-ah-nay-ah

I

The throbbing pain in my throat was fading, and I no longer felt the flames of red-hot agony burning through my body.

Despite the warmth and humidity of Dalos, the City of the Gods, I was now cold—colder than I'd ever been. I thought maybe *I* was fading because my vision was flickering in and out. I tried to focus on the open doors of the circular chamber I'd awakened in after the Shadowlands siege—in a cage and chained.

I had thought I'd seen a large wolf standing there. A wolf more silver than white.

A wolf I'd known in my heart and soul was him: the Asher, the One who is Blessed, the Guardian of Souls, and the Primal God of Common Men and Endings. The ruler of the Shadowlands.

My husband.

Nyktos.

Ash.

He'd never confirmed that he could shift forms, but I knew it was my Primal of Death. And when I saw the wolf, I'd thought he'd come for me. That I would see him, touch him one last time, have the chance to tell him once more that I loved him. That I'd get to say goodbye on my terms.

But I didn't see him in the doorway now.

He wasn't there.

What if he'd never been there?

The arms around me tightened, making my sluggish heart race. Kolis, the false King of Gods, still held me, likely reeling from the realization of who was in his embrace—who he'd fed on.

"Is it truly you?" Kolis's voice was no louder than a sigh. Tears dampened my cheeks. Were they mine? His? "My love?"

I shuddered. Gods, Ash had been wrong when he said I may feel fear but am never afraid. Because the sound of Kolis simply speaking brought an avalanche of terror. It didn't matter that it was only Sotoria's soul inside me. That I wasn't her, and she wasn't me. He terrified both of us.

Two leather-clad legs suddenly appeared in my line of vision. My gaze lifted, moving over the shadowstone daggers strapped to his hips. Light brownish-blond hair brushed the collar of a black tunic. The Primal of War and Accord had been facing the doors. The traitorous bastard who'd brought me to Kolis must have seen Ash if he'd been there. Right? In his wolf form, he was massive—larger than any wolf I'd ever seen.

Unless he'd never been there in the first place, and I'd hallucinated him.

My chest hollowed, and…oh, gods, the swell of sorrow was an unbearable pressure, threatening to crush me.

"Your Majesty." Attes twisted sharply toward us. "She's not well," he said. "She's close to death. You have to be able to feel that."

"You need to take those embers before she passes," another voice urged, one that carried a soft lilt. The Revenant, Callum. One of Kolis's *works in progress.* "Take them—"

"The embers are the least of your concerns," Attes interrupted, speaking directly to Kolis. "She is about to die."

There was no response from the false King. He just…gods, he just held me, his large body trembling. Was he in shock? If so, that made me want to laugh. Which meant I, too, was likely in shock.

"If she dies with the embers, they die, too—along with everything you've been working toward," Callum insisted, drawing my attention to him. He was blurry at first but then came into focus. The Revenant was golden all over: his hair, his skin, and the elaborately painted mask shaped like wings that swept down from his forehead to his jaw on either side. "Take them, my King. Take them and Ascend as the Primal of Life and—"

"She will be lost," Attes cut in. "Your *graeca* will be beyond your reach."

Graeca.

It meant life in the old Primal language. It also meant love. But I thought perhaps it had a third meaning.

Obsession.

Because what Kolis felt for Sotoria couldn't be love. Love didn't create monsters.

"That is not her," Callum hissed, his eyes narrowing behind his painted mask. "Do not listen to him, Your Majesty. This is a—"

Callum suddenly jerked forward, blood spraying the cage bars. His mouth slackened as he looked down at the shadowstone hilt protruding from the center of his chest.

My gaze shot to Attes. Only one dagger remained strapped to his body. He'd thrown that blade.

Why?

"Damn it." Callum stumbled and then hit the gold-streaked floor. Dead. But I didn't think he'd stay that way. However, I couldn't remember why at the moment.

I couldn't…

My chest spasmed. Shadows descended over my sight like a veil. Icy panic seized me as I fell into darkness, the brief moments of relief dissipating. No sound. No scent. No sight.

I didn't want to die.

Not now.

I didn't—

Liessa…

I jolted, hauled from the darkness. Images of what I saw pieced themselves together: the golden divan I'd been asleep on, the chain connected to the band I barely felt around my neck, the golden bars of the cage I was in, and the shadowstone dagger that had been in Callum's chest, which now lay on the floor. The Revenant was rising, standing. How long had I been unconscious? I looked past him, beyond the golden throne, and farther out to the open doors.

I saw the wolf again, this time partially hidden by the wide palm fronds swaying in the balmy breeze.

My right hand—no, the marriage imprint that had appeared during my coronation as Ash's Consort—warmed. The golden swirl across the top and palm tingled, and the embers of life in my chest started to hum, vibrating wildly. A sharp swirl of prickles broke out along the nape of my neck.

Kolis continued to rock as I sensed a storm of gathering power. My skin pimpled, and the tiny hairs on my body rose.

Attes turned to the doors. "Oh, fuck."

The wolf's head lowered, its eyes a luminous silver. One large paw pressed against the gold-streaked marble floor, his lips peeling back in a snarl.

A dark mist came from everywhere all at once. Shadows clung to the chamber ceiling where the chandelier's light didn't reach, then began pulsing and peeling away from the marble and limestone, slipping down the walls to race across the floor in smoky waves. My already too-shallow breaths snagged as the wolf leapt into the air and the churning mass of darkness. Tiny starbursts exploded all around him, and the center of my chest warmed—

The whirling shadows by the doors expanded and lengthened. Twin, sweeping arcs of shadow and smoke appeared behind the mass, and a shockwave swept through the chamber, making its way to the throne. The golden seat shuddered and then crumbled into nothing. The burst of power reached Attes, tossing him aside before lifting Callum, slamming him into the cage with a sickening crunch of bone.

Several rows of bars *shattered*. The chamber ceiling cracked and splintered, splitting open. The shadows and smoke solidified in the bright moonlight now pouring into the chamber.

The walls around us exploded, sending chunks of stone flying outward, leaving only a few feet of the structure standing as Ash rose even higher.

For the briefest moment, I saw him in his mortal form, the angles and planes of his face harsh and maybe even a little cruel, his skin a lustrous shade of golden-bronze, his hair reddish-brown in the moonlight falling against his broad cheeks. I caught just a flash of his strong, cut jaw, wide mouth, and full lips that had touched my skin in such decadent ways.

Then he slipped into his true form and hovered above where the throne had been, his flesh becoming a continuous swirl of midnight and thin, throbbing streaks of eather. The fresh, citrusy scent that was all his reached me, comforted me.

Ash was terrifying, his beauty vicious and breathtaking in both forms. And he was mine.

"*Kolis!*" Ash roared, his voice a thunderstorm reverberating through the air.

Without warning, a burst of light cut through the night sky, slamming into the floor before Ash as heat flared in my chest. The funnel of light burned brightly, momentarily blinding me. When my vision returned, I saw…

A crown of ruby antlers gleaming in the moonlight.

Another Primal had arrived.

Hanan, the dark-haired, pale, and angular-featured Primal God of the Hunt and Divine Justice, stood before Ash. He held a spear made of some sort of dull white material that reminded me of bone in his right hand.

"Walk away, Nyktos." Hanan's spear began glowing from within. "Before it's too late," he warned. But I heard the tremor in the Primal's voice, he who'd sent the Cimmerian to retrieve Bele instead of coming to the Shadowlands himself. I heard the *fear*.

Hanan may be a Primal, but he was also a coward.

"Before it's too late?" Ash's voice boomed, the power of it leveling what remained of the chamber walls. "It's already too late."

White light poured from Hanan as he rose into the air, drawing his arm back. Eather crackled from his spear right before he threw it. My breath caught—

Ash laughed. He *laughed* as his wings swept out and stretched wide, a violent mass of shadows and moonlight. Power sparked from the splayed fingers of the hand he lifted, and a bolt of stunning light erupted from his palm, hitting the spear in midair. A clap of thunder sounded just as light erupted in every direction.

Then Ash was in front of the Primal, grabbing him by the back of the head. He'd moved so quickly I didn't see his other hand until Hanan screamed, and I saw Ash jerk his arm back. A bloody, pulsing mass smacked the floor.

Ash lifted Hanan into the air, and someone shouted. I thought it might have been Attes.

Seemingly oblivious to it all, Kolis finally stopped rocking and lifted his head.

Ash gripped the Primal under the jaw, tearing—

My lips parted when Ash tore Hanan's head from his shoulders.

Something fell, and eather pulsed from Ash's hand.

The Primal embers of life hummed even more intensely in my chest, sending warmth to my hands. I knew what that meant, even before the crown clanged off the golden tile.

Ash had killed another Primal.

Was that how it was done? Ripping out the heart and destroying the head? It was a grotesque and barbaric method.

And disturbingly hot.

The crown of ruby antlers began vibrating as I heard a distant rumble. Beneath it, the tile split open, and the ground started to shake. White light appeared from within the ruby crown, bleeding out until the antlers could no longer be seen. The noise continued, coming from the sky and below, shaking even Kolis. Stone cracked in every direction. The ground outside the ruins of the chamber groaned and then split open. Palm trees shuddered and slid sideways, falling into the gaping fissure.

Hanan's crown pulsed and then vanished.

A deafening boom hit the air, and I knew…oh, gods, I knew the sound traveled beyond Dalos. It likely hit every land in Iliseeum and beyond, extending into the mortal realm.

But I also knew that somewhere in the Shadowlands, a new ruler of Sirta had risen as the Goddess of the Hunt. Not because Bele was the only god of Hanan's Court to have Ascended—and at my hands—but because I felt it in the embers of life.

And I knew Kolis had felt it, too.

The chain connected to the band around my neck clinked off the floor when Kolis lowered me. He braced my head with his hand, an act so unnerving in its tenderness that it seized my attention. My heart stuttered, and my gaze locked with his. Icy air whipped through the cage, sending the golden strands of Kolis's hair across his face as he laid my cheek against the gold tile. I flinched at the unsettling gentleness of his palm sliding over my skin.

A guttural, inhuman growl shook the cage. "Get your fucking hands off my wife."

Kolis smirked, and my skin iced over. He rose. "Oh, Nyktos, my boy," he said in his summer voice, glancing to where Hanan's crown had last been seen, past where Callum lay in a pool of blood, his fingers twitching. "I see you've been hiding how powerful you've become." Kolis looked up at Ash. "I'm impressed."

"Like I give a fuck," Ash growled.

"Rude," Kolis murmured.

I needed to get up. Had to help Ash and fight beside him. Kolis wasn't Hanan. False Primal of Life or not, he was still the oldest Primal alive. He was incredibly powerful.

I needed to help Ash.

My limbs felt weighed down, almost like they were attached to the tile. I struggled to roll onto my side, the simple act leaving me short of breath.

Kolis sighed loudly as if he were dealing with a petulant child. "Because we're family, I'm going to give you the grace your father never extended to me. A chance to walk away from this."

I frowned, and several strands of pale hair fell across my face. Kolis was just going to let Ash leave after killing another Primal? That made no sense.

Until it *did*.

Kolis couldn't kill Ash. If he did, the Primal embers of death would transfer back to him. Kolis would no longer be the Primal of Life or the King.

There'd *be* no King.

It would throw the realm of the gods into chaos.

"You will return to your Court, and if Bele is still there," Kolis continued, "you will advise her to appear before me and swear fealty."

In the distance, silver briefly lit the night sky—rolling flames of eather. Then, in the brief light extending along the horizon, I saw two massive, winged beings crash into each other.

Draken.

Oh, gods, was that Nektas? Another? I didn't even know if Orphine had survived the dakkais attack. I'd seen her fall. I'd witnessed so many fall.

I needed to get up.

"And you will order whatever forces followed you to stand down and leave Dalos's borders immediately." In the silence that followed, a muscle in Kolis's jaw spasmed. "Take this offer, Nyktos."

Arms trembling from the effort, I managed to lift myself halfway up, but that normally effortless task came at a price. My head swam, and I drew Ash's attention.

The eather in his eyes crackled as he looked at me, at the surely mangled skin of my throat and the band below Kolis's bite. He saw the golden gossamer gown I'd been dressed in, and I felt his rage. It fell like icy rain against my skin. I wanted to tell him that I was all right, but my tongue felt too heavy to speak the lie. I wasn't sure I would be okay.

And I think Ash sensed that.

His chest rose sharply, and his head swung back to Kolis. "I'm going to kill you."

The false King of Gods tipped his head back and laughed. "Now you're just being silly."

Ash moved as fast as an unleashed arrow, streaking forward. He came through the opening in the bars, the swirling shadows around him retracting. The air went utterly stagnant and turned thin just before Ash landed on the cage floor a few feet from Kolis. Tendrils of shadows whipped out from leather-clad legs. His eyes became pools of eather.

"Don't," Kolis warned, his chin dropping, "even think it."

"As I said before,"—static crackled from Ash, and dual bolts of eather erupted from his palms—"too late."

Kolis moved, becoming nothing more than a blur, but even as fast as he was, nothing was faster than unleashed Primal power. Ash's bolts slammed into Kolis with shocking intensity, lifting and throwing him back. He crashed into the bars. The gold gave way under the impact.

Shadows swirled across the floor and over my legs as Ash spun, reaching for his waist. I saw the glint of shadowstone when he unsheathed his sword and threw it.

The blade struck Kolis in the chest. The force of the hit threw him back until he had nowhere else to go, and the sword hit the exterior wall, embedding deeply and pinning the false King.

Dear gods.

Pounding footsteps thundered across the ruined floor. Guards in golden breastplates and greaves charged the cage, shadowstone swords raised.

Ash turned his head, looking over his shoulder at the newcomers.

The shadows, the very essence of the Primals, poured from Ash, shooting between the cage bars. The dark mist reached the armor of the guards' boots.

High-pitched, agonized screams tore through the space, shrieks that ended abruptly.

Wisps of night bled into the air around me as Ash knelt by my side, only a hint of his features visible in the swirling darkness.

Despite the dryness and pain, I swallowed, forcing my vocal cords and tongue to work. "That... That was...so incredibly arousing."

Ash froze for a heartbeat and then laughed roughly. "Keep your eyes on mine," he said, grasping the band around my throat. "And do not move, *liessa*."

Liessa.

Something beautiful.

Something powerful.

Queen.

My heart…gods, it melted at hearing him say that. It was such a silly thing to think, but it was true.

His churning silver gaze held mine. I heard the sound of metal snapping, and my entire body jerked. Chains hit the floor, causing me to topple over.

Shadows rippled across my chest and waist as Ash's arms surrounded me, catching me. The essence covered me like a cloak but caused no pain. It never had.

He pulled me to him. His hand, so incredibly cold but also welcome, cradled my head. He pressed me to his chest.

Inhaling his fresh, citrus scent, I shuddered. When Kolis's fangs had sunk into my skin, I honestly believed I'd never see Ash again. So to hear his voice? To be in his arms? Tears filled my eyes. Having this was overwhelming.

"I'm sorry," he rasped, quickly moving us from the cage. "I'm sorry I didn't get to you sooner, but I've got you now, *liessa*, and I won't let go. I'll never let go again."

His apology tore at my heart as he lifted us into the air. This was all on Kolis and his demented actions. It was on Eythos, Ash's father, for placing the embers and Sotoria's soul inside a mortal and never telling his son. "None of this is—"

Ash cursed, twisting his body. A startled heartbeat passed.

Something hot and heavy slammed into Ash's back. He grunted, and the air seemed to reach up and wrap invisible hands around us, rapidly pulling us down. Fear gathered in the back of my throat.

The impact was deafening as Ash hit the floor, still on his feet, taking the brunt of the landing. He staggered, going down on one knee, but he still held me. The shadowy essence around him thinned, and I saw the pain in the tight clench of his jaw.

"It's okay," he gritted, his bright, sterling eyes locked onto mine. "I've got you—" His head jerked back.

A hoarse scream tore from my throat when the tendons in his neck bulged. Ash held on, rising once more. He didn't let go. He wouldn't, just like he promised, despite the agony. No matter the cost.

"Ash," I whispered.

His eyes went wide, and he stilled for a moment. "*Sera*," he rasped.

Then something ripped Ash away from me.

My heart lurched, panic washing over me. There was a moment of weightlessness, and then I hit the floor. My head cracked off the tile, the burst of pain startling before the realm went black.

Silent.

Still.

The feral, brutal roar of Ash's fury rushed me back into consciousness. The moon. I saw the moon. I turned my head.

Kolis stalked forward, the wide, jagged gash in his chest dripping shimmery blood. Eather shone from his wound and poured from his palms, streaking across the chamber.

Ash was on one knee again but had both hands out now, shielding himself from the golden-tinged ripples of deadly essence.

"You really shouldn't have done that," Kolis said, followed by a sigh heavy with displeasure and even a bit of disappointment. "Now, I'm afraid you've gone and started a war."

Eather-laced shadows swelled from Ash, smothering the bolts of power until they fizzled out. He glanced back at me before refocusing on Kolis. "The moment you breached custom and faith," Ash seethed, rising to his full height, "*you* started the war."

"Have you forgotten yourself, nephew? Clearly, you have." Tendrils of eather flickered from Kolis's fingertips as the golden Revenant moved into sight behind him, once more alive and standing. "Because I am your King."

"You're no King of mine." Lightning streaked from Ash, slamming into the tile floor and Callum, throwing the Revenant back. The scent of charred flesh rose. "I could humor you by saying your sovereignty ended the moment you took her. But truthfully, you have never been my King."

Catching sight of several fallen shadowstone swords by the guards' twisted and mangled bodies, I ignored the dampness at the nape of my neck and rolled onto my side. It took even more effort than before.

"Bold words." Kolis stepped forward, a streak of eather whipping out toward Ash. "And surprising ones. I killed your father, and you swore fealty to me. I take your Consort, and you kill one of your brethren and attack me. Why is that, Nyktos? Is it the embers of life inside her?"

I rolled my eyes as I shifted my weight to my flattened palms. That had been Ash's plan, but once he'd learned what it would cost, it became the last thing he wanted.

Because taking the embers meant killing me, and he had chosen *me*, even though I was already dying, and it was foolish.

Still, it was beautiful.

"That's it, isn't it? You sought to take the embers from her and rise as the Primal of Life," Kolis accused, golden-tinged eather sparking from his fingertips. "You sought to hide them from me. To hide her. That's treason."

"Treason?" A deep, dark laugh rumbled from Ash, a sound I'd never heard him make before. "You killed my mother and the true Primal of Life." Shadows spilled onto the floor below Ash, billowing like smoke. "You're a fucking joke."

Kolis stiffened. "You want to know what's a joke? You thinking I had no idea what you've been up to. That I haven't seen through your false assurances and pledges and didn't know you've been plotting to overthrow me and take all that is mine."

Ash's fury lashed out, causing the temperature in the room to plummet as I began the slow crawl toward the bodies. "None of this has been yours. You stole it—"

"From your father," Kolis interjected, moonlight reflecting off the golden band around his biceps. "And I imagine you believe history has repeated itself, but you'd be wrong. The embers of life do not belong to you."

"*She* does not belong to *you*!" Ash roared.

The air thinned once more. I halted, arms trembling. Raw, violent energy drenched the ruined chamber, pimpling my skin.

"You think she belongs to *you* simply because you crowned her as your Consort?" Kolis's laugh caused my heart to clench. Golden swirls of eather began churning across his bare chest, where the wound Ash inflicted had already healed. "If she is who she claims to be, she was never yours to crown."

I needed to get to my feet and get my hands on a sword. And I needed to do it quickly. But my head still swam, and my legs felt strange, like I was disconnected from them. It wasn't because of the hit to the head, though that hadn't helped. It was blood loss. I'd lost too much. I could feel that in how hard my heart worked to pump what blood remained inside me, how fast it raced. And I had a feeling, some instinctual knowledge, that told me if I didn't have the embers, I'd already be unconscious or dead.

As I pushed onto my knees, I thought it was strange that what would inevitably kill me was also keeping me alive.

Kolis stepped forward, his too-perfect lips curved into a smile. "She was never yours, nephew. She has always been mine."

Ash's fury lashed out. The breath I exhaled formed a puffy cloud as energy charged the space once more. Ash rushed Kolis, taking to the air.

All I saw was a sneer from Kolis before wispy eather poured from the false King. He rose, slipping into his Primal form, creating a glow that was too bright and painful to look upon for any length of time.

Ash and Kolis met high above me, and it was like seeing the night and the sun crash into each other. The eather-laced shadows and the intense, gold-and silver-streaked light whirled at dizzying speeds, but the wind had stopped. The clouds had ceased their journey across the sky. Everything…everything else had gone silent and still as my chest constricted.

I squinted, catching glimpses of the two Primals between the shadows and daylight. Golden hair, then reddish-brown strands. Black tunic, then white linen pants. Silver cuff and golden band—one that appeared to flash white when the arm moved. Fists. Heads kicked back.

They were punching each other.

Then the swirling around them stilled, and the air began to vibrate and pulse. The embers in my chest hummed—

A bolt of eather burst from Ash, hitting Kolis and throwing the Primals apart. The false King caught himself and returned to Ash, his speed shocking. A harsh, low scream tore from my throat when Kolis slammed into Ash. Eather spat and crackled around them as they rose.

They came back down in a blur. I stared wide-eyed and couldn't make sense of it until one of them crashed into the tile, cracking several feet of the marble around them. Only when I saw the swirling black mist overtaking the brilliant glow did I know that Ash had driven Kolis into the floor.

Relief shuddered through me when the essence around Kolis dimmed enough for me to see Ash straighten. He stepped over his uncle, spitting a mouthful of shimmery blood onto the Primal before reaching down and grasping Kolis by the head—

The false King shot up like a spear, sending Ash flying back. Wind surged, blowing my hair in front of me. Lightning arced overhead. My head tilted toward the horizon, to the west. I saw no signs of the draken.

My heart lurched as Ash and Kolis battled with fists and bursts of Primal energy, their bodies rising and falling so quickly. I turned back to where the guards lay, the distance between them and me seeming insurmountable. But I needed to get to a sword. I wasn't sure what I would do once I had it, but I had to do something.

Hands suddenly landed on my upper arms. I let out a startled scream, and instinct took over. I immediately tried to break free. My mind knew how to, I'd been trained by the best, but my body wasn't responding quickly enough. I felt sluggish and disjointed, and all I seemed to do was wiggle like a dying worm.

"Stop," a voice hissed in my ear—one I recognized.

Attes.

Anger boiled as I jerked my body to the right. "Let go...of me, you...fucking traitorous bastard."

Attes's grip tightened, and he turned me sideways, bringing us face-to-face.

I got a really good look at him. And he didn't look well. Bluish-red blood trickled from his nose, eyes, ears, and the corners of his mouth. The shallow scar running from his hairline, across the bridge of his nose, and down his left cheek stood out starkly.

Godsdamn. That one blast from Ash had really done a number on him.

"Listen to me," he said, shouting over the wind.

"Fuck you." I pitched back—or *fell* back—kicking out. My foot glanced off his chest.

Attes halted, raising his brows. "You really need to conserve your energy, Sera. And listen to me."

Yeah, that wasn't happening. "You betrayed...us," I forced out, feeling dizzy. "After I helped Thad, you...betrayed—"

The ground shook as Ash and Kolis hit somewhere to our right, their bodies digging up tile and sending marble flying in every direction.

Cursing, Attes twisted and pulled me toward him, shifting us away from the rain of debris. I reached up, digging my fingers into his hair and yanking hard. It was a bitch move. I knew it, but it was the best I could manage at the moment.

Attes snarled through bared teeth—fangs. He jerked his head, and I felt a savage burst of satisfaction when I saw strands of golden-brown hair between my fingers.

"Damn it," he growled. "Stop—"

Fingers clawed, I aimed for that fucking dimple.

"I know what I've done." He caught my wrist, eather snapping in his eyes as Ash and Kolis returned to the sky. "There isn't time to discuss that or for you to seek revenge."

My mouth opened.

"Kolis will kill Ash," Attes said, our faces inches apart. "He won't mean to, and that's not because he doesn't want to. It's because of what will happen if he does." Something wet hit my cheek and then my arm. "Ash is not powerful enough to defeat Kolis and his draken, which will come this way the moment they sense that Kolis is truly in danger. Ash will die."

Panting, I stared at the Primal who'd strolled into Ash's office, seemingly without a care. The one who had flirted while delivering Kolis's message and teased as he asked about the movements of the Shadowlands' forces toward the borders of the Court he shared with his brother, Kyn. Ash hadn't trusted him completely, but there had been something between them. Not exactly a friendship but maybe a kinship.

And he'd fucked us.

He'd likely been in on Kolis ordering me to slaughter that poor draken, and had probably told Kolis that I brought Thad back.

The act the false King had been waiting for me to complete, as it was proof that the embers had matured enough to be transferred.

Something splashed off the hand Attes held between us. The drop was a shimmery reddish-blue color.

It was Primal blood.

I sucked in a startled breath.

"They need to stop," Attes insisted. "And the only person either of them will listen to is you."

I wasn't sure about that. Kolis didn't seem like the type to listen to anyone. And Ash was likely beyond listening. He was caught in a cyclone of fury that had been building for *centuries*. This wasn't only about me. It was about his mother, whom Kolis had slaughtered while Ash was still in her womb. It was about his father, whom Kolis had killed—whose soul he still held. It was for all the lives inked into Ash's skin that Kolis had taken from him or forced Ash to take.

But Attes, bastard or not, spoke the truth.

Kolis *would* kill Ash.

And the death of either Kolis or Ash would destroy not only the mortal realm but also Iliseeum and every Primal. Completely. I wasn't sure if the draken could even survive. Perhaps only the Arae—the Fates—would remain.

But I didn't care about any of them. Only Ash mattered to me. So, I had to try. But how? They were still going at it, trading blasts of eather. The glow swallowing Kolis had faded, making it so he was no longer painful to look at. The shadows had grown thinner around Ash. I didn't even know what I planned to do if I made it to one of the swords.

My gaze flew to the daggers at Attes's hips, and I thought... I thought maybe I knew how to get Kolis to stop.

I started to push up with legs that felt like the jelly my stepsister Ezra liked to smother her rolls in. "Help...help me stand." My cheeks warmed with embarrassment, which was so godsdamn stupid considering the situation. "I...I can't do it."

Features tense, Attes hesitated. It was clear he didn't trust me. And he shouldn't. Because if I lived longer than tonight, I would find a way to do terrible things to the fucker.

But also because I had lied—well, partially. I could stand, but I also knew the effort it would take, and that would wipe me out. I was doing what Attes had suggested: conserving my energy.

After a heartbeat, he tipped closer and shifted his hold from my wrist to my shoulders. He rose, bringing me with him. "You steady?"

I couldn't really feel the floor beneath my feet. "Yeah."

"Good." Attes's gaze searched mine, his features pinched with what looked like concern. I had to be imagining it. "So, what's the—?"

I moved as quickly as possible, which wasn't very fast at all. I was surprised I managed to grab the hilt of one of his shadowstone daggers before he could stop me. I'd just caught him off guard.

"Are you fucking kidding me?" Attes exclaimed, eyeing the dagger I took from him. "Was I not clear enough?"

"Calm down." I took a shallow breath, and my chest...gods, it felt weird. Like it was loose. "You aren't worth...the effort."

Surprise flickered across his face. He hadn't expected that response.

Feeling top-heavy, I turned to where the two Primals had landed. Their hands were on each other's throats, eather firing from their fingers.

I stepped forward, shouting, "Stop!"

Neither heard, or if they did, they ignored me. Their veins were lit from within, and if they hadn't been in the process of killing each other, I would've thought they looked oddly beautiful.

And I also knew there might not be enough blood getting to my brain.

Panic trickled through me as I yelled again and again, feeling myself swaying. Attes, the rat bastard, steadied me. My heart was slowing, and I suspected that wasn't good. Mainly because darkness crowded in at the edges of my vision. I didn't know how I, a mortal, could get two Primal gods to—

But I wasn't entirely mortal.

Not anymore.

The embers of life had changed that—the embers of Primal essence.

The back of my skull tingled, and my mind raced. The power the embers could manifest was connected to me feeling extreme emotion, just like a god or Primal as they grew closer to their Ascension. Ash had tried to get them to come out in me intentionally. It hadn't exactly worked then.

But it was strange. As I stood, my chest oddly loose, sort of feeling detached from myself, I suddenly knew why the embers hadn't flared.

I had been born with them inside me, but I'd never considered them *part* of me. I'd only been a vessel. Something to hide and store them. It was what Eythos, Ash's father, had intended.

But that was no longer the case. The embers were a part of me. And for right now, they were mine.

I hadn't truly understood that before. Hadn't believed it until now.

Taking a deeper, slower breath, I concentrated on the throbbing in my chest. The embers fluttered and then pulsed as I summoned the eather, tapping into it.

"Good Fates," Attes whispered.

What came next simply happened, almost like when Rhain told me about the deal Ash had made with Veses. Except this time, I was well aware of the essence coming to the surface. I controlled it. And when I used it, I didn't think about how. It was just instinct, ancient and primal.

Primal essence seeped into my veins, hot and smooth, and when I spoke, I felt the power in my words. *"Stop."*

I didn't realize what I'd done until both Ash and Kolis halted, the bolts of eather fizzling out mid-streak.

I'd used compulsion. On the two most powerful Primals alive.

"Good Fates," Attes whispered again hoarsely, clearly shocked. Ash and Kolis turned their heads toward me.

I was surprised, too. I hadn't expected that, but I shoved my astonishment aside because while I'd been able to do that, I could already feel the embers weakening. Yes, they were a part of me, but I was dying. So, *they* were dying. I had to be quick. I stepped forward and did the only thing I could think of.

Ash cared for me greatly. If he could, he would love me. He'd pretty much said that himself after we'd spoken with the God of Divination, Delfai. But he'd removed his *kardia*, the piece of the soul that all living beings had that allowed them to irrevocably love another not of their blood and enabled them to do anything for that person. The goddess Penellaphe had said it must've been incredibly painful for him to do so. To me, it was just so damn tragic. He'd done it in an attempt to protect himself and whoever he might come to love from his uncle.

Kolis was an evil, sick bastard, and I didn't think that what he felt for Sotoria was love. It was more like an obsession. But he was still in possession of his *kardia*, and he *believed* he was in love with her. If that were true, then he'd do anything for her.

Someone he believed was me.

Heart stuttering, I lifted the dagger to my throat.

"Fucking Fates," Attes snapped from behind me, his voice low. "That wasn't what I had in mind."

"Stop fighting," I repeated, ignoring the Primal of War and Accord. "Do this for me. Please."

I was focused on Kolis, speaking directly to him, but Ash reacted first.

The thinning shadows whirling around and inside him vanished. Blood leaked from his parted lips and nose. His jaw was already swelling, and his tunic was burned in places, revealing charred flesh beneath. But it was his eyes that caused my heart to lurch. They were wide and stark, the wisps of eather still.

Kolis was slower to respond, the golden glow only fading enough that his features became visible beneath it. He wasn't much better off than Ash. His chest was also a burned, bloody mess.

"Sera," Ash rasped thickly, his hands lifting halfway. "What are you doing?"

I swallowed, my stomach full of knots of anxiety, but my hand was steady. "Stop fighting, or I will slit my throat open."

Kolis's chin snapped down. "You will do no such thing."

I pressed the tip of the blade into my skin until I felt the prick of pain. Suddenly, Ash...gods, it seemed like he had no control over his body. He jerked back a step. "Yes," I said, keeping my gaze trained on their chests. I didn't trust either of them not to use compulsion. Though avoiding eye contact wouldn't prevent them from doing it. Not completely. "I will. And if I even *think* one of you is about to use compulsion, I'll do it."

"Sera," Ash said again. "Put the dagger down." He took a step forward, seeming to completely forget about Kolis as his scorched chest rose and fell rapidly. "Please."

I sucked in a sharp breath, my hand trembling. "I will—" I gasped, a sharp sting of pain slicing across my throat when someone ripped the dagger from my fingers.

Ash shouted, and the fear in his yell...gods, it was palpable. I immediately knew I'd made a grave mistake.

Oh, gods.

I'd underestimated what they would and wouldn't do. I'd thought I could distract Kolis. That he would be vulnerable to his love, his obsession for Sotoria.

But I'd distracted Ash, too.

The dagger I'd held to my throat was now in Kolis's hand.

The false King of Gods was so damn fast. He twisted, slamming the dagger into Ash's chest.

Right into his heart.

3

The blow Kolis landed knocked Ash back, and horror seized me.

The blade was just shadowstone. It should have little effect on a being as powerful as a Primal, but the numerous injuries marking Ash's body had weakened him. That much was clear.

Ash caught himself, reaching for the hilt of the blade as he staggered forward, his wide eyes fixed on me and the wet warmth I could feel dripping down my throat. He dropped…oh, gods. He fell to his knees.

"Run," he choked out, pitching forward onto one hand.

A high-pitched, terrified sound blasted my ears. It was a scream. *My* scream. The embers fluttered, briefly swelling before stalling. Pressure built in my chest and head, rapidly becoming an unbearable weight. I started toward Ash but didn't make it. My legs collapsed, and I hit the cracked floor. Starbursts exploded across my vision.

Snarling, Kolis grabbed a fistful of Ash's hair, yanking him back. The dagger was still in his chest, in his heart. "I offered you grace."

"Stop," I wheezed, my fingers pressing into the tile as I crawled forward on my belly.

Kolis threw Ash onto his back. "And you tossed it back into my face."

Arms and legs shaking, I pushed up onto my knees. "Please," I forced out, blood dripping onto the floor beneath me. "Stop—" My throat seized, cutting me off.

"You, of all people, should know better." Kolis swung his leg up and then brought his foot down on the dagger's hilt.

Ash's entire body jerked.

A hand smacked down on my mouth, silencing my newest scream. "Listen to me," Attes hissed in my ear. "Ash is still alive. A shadowstone blade will not kill him. He's just weakened from battling Kolis. But if you keep screaming, Kolis *will* kill him."

Kolis stomped his foot down on the dagger once more, and I felt it. I swore I felt the blow in my chest. My entire body shook.

Everything felt like it was rushing and spinning. The chamber. Attes's words. What I saw. I strained against the Primal of War and Accord's hold, desperately needing to get to Ash. Kolis was…oh, gods, he pulled the blade free and then thrust it into Ash's chest again. A spasm went through me, swift and sharp. I went boneless and limp. Lifeless.

Attes cursed under his breath as he shifted me in his arms. "Sera?" Bright tendrils of eather whipped through his eyes. "Sera?"

My mouth was open, but only the thinnest bit of air got in, and there was this godsawful thumping and a wet, fleshy sound. I struggled to breathe, to turn my head toward Ash.

All I saw was the rise and fall of Kolis's arm. Up. Down. Up. Down. A blood-slicked dagger glinted in the moonlight.

I screamed. I knew I did, even if there was no sound. I screamed and screamed, still shaking.

"Fuck." Attes's head shot up. "Kolis! She needs your help," he shouted, his skin thinning. "Godsdamn it, listen to me. Sotoria is about to die."

Thump. Thump. Thump.

"If you let that happen, you will lose her. Do you hear me?" Attes squeezed his eyes shut, and I thought I saw panic flash across his features. But I wasn't sure what I was seeing. My eyes couldn't focus. "You will lose your *graeca*."

The horrific thumping ceased.

"No," Kolis croaked. "*No.*"

The faint scent of vanilla and lilacs—*stale* lilacs—enveloped me, and then Attes was no longer holding me.

Kolis had me in his arms. He lifted me as he rose, my head lolling. "Put him in the cells," he said. "I will deal with him when I return."

If more was said, I didn't know. A rush of wind whirled around us, and I was vaguely aware of warm night air touching my skin.

I struggled to open my eyes, but they no longer responded to my commands. The darkness smothered me, suffocated. My breaths came in shallow gasps, and my heart raced before it stuttered. Time. It sped up and slowed down, leaving me to exist in those too-long gaps between the beats of my heart and the ceaseless roar of the wind.

I didn't want to die.

Not like this.

Not alone in the darkness with this monster.

I wanted to be with Ash, in his arms at my lake, as he'd promised we would be when my time came.

This wasn't right.

It's not fair, I swore I heard Sotoria whisper, her thoughts briefly mingling with mine.

The embers of life vibrated wildly. Panic surged like a wild animal trapped in a cage, desperate to break free, but there was no escape.

Death had always been inevitable.

I sensed that we'd stopped moving, stopped shadowstepping. A palm pressed down on the center of my chest, and my breath, my heart, snagged as a strange pins-and-needles sensation swept over me.

Then, there was nothing.

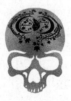

Ash.

That was the first thing I thought as I came to. The battle between him and Kolis, the blade striking him, moving up and down, up and down, stabbing into Ash's body.

My eyes peeled open, going wide. The sky above was drenched in starlight, and I gulped salty, damp air that turned into thin breaths that barely did anything to ease the constriction in my chest. The buzzing in my ears retreated, and I heard voices coming from every direction. Whispers followed us as I caught the vague impression of people lowering themselves to their knees, and glimpsed twinkling lights inside sandstone buildings and larger structures in the distance. I couldn't be sure, though. All I knew was that I was still being carried as I struggled to breathe.

Ash.

I didn't know where I was or where he'd been taken. I had a vague memory of hearing a cell referenced. And before that, a wet, fleshy, thumping sound and the flash of a blood-slick dagger.

Oh, gods.

The edges of my vision turned white. I felt like I couldn't breathe—

"Calm yourself," a voice full of bitter warmth and cold sunshine ordered from above me.

Startled, my gaze swung to silver eyes laced with golden flecks. Kolis's attention shifted, and shimmering sweeps and swirls churned beneath the flesh of his cheeks. A shudder rolled through me.

"You will live," Kolis stated, glancing down at me. "As long as you are who you claim to be."

Nothing about his words made it easier to breathe. With each passing second, it felt like my lungs shrank. My heart no longer pulsed listlessly. It raced, skipping beats. White static crowded the edges of my vision when I fought to remember what Holland had taught me, what Ash had shown me. Breathe in. Hold—

The ground moved under us, the soil turning to sand. Kolis's steps slowed, his hold shifting. A rhythmic sound reached me, the gentle rise and fall of waves lapping against a shore. My head slid, my cheek catching on the golden band around his biceps. For a moment, I forgot about suffocating as I stared at the rippling moonlight reflecting off the vast, midnight-hued sea.

Kolis had stopped at the edge of pearly white sand, but there was no gradual incline to the water like there was on the beaches of the Stroud Sea. This was a steep drop with no bottom in sight, but something in the water moved.

They swam in circles, over and under one another. Dozens, maybe even hundreds of them. Their powerful arms and sleek, bare bodies were half flesh and half scales, creating fierce currents beneath the surface. The tails of those closest to me were radiant in the moonlight—vivid, glittering blues, intense pinks, deep greens, and streaks of bright yellow.

My gods, they had to be the ceeren.

"Phanos!" Kolis roared.

I flinched as the shockwave of his shout hit the water, sending the ceeren scattering into the deeper parts of the sea. Their frantic flight stirred the tranquil waters. Small, white-tipped waves rippled across the surface and a form appeared amid the ceeren.

His entire body moved in a wave-like motion, propelled by the rapid swishing of the large fin at the end of his tail. Faster than the others, he swam toward the surface.

As he neared, a bolt of silver erupted from his hand, forming a long spear that came to three points at one end. A trident.

One made of eather.

Phanos, the Primal God of the Skies and Seas, erupted from the sea in a spray of water, the trident spitting sparks of amber against the warm, dark brown skin of his shoulders and broad chest. Beneath him, his undulating tail keeping him in place, the ceeren calmed enough for me to see there were smaller ones farther down. Children who still darted back and forth, appearing briefly before scurrying behind the older ceeren's tails.

Phanos's stare drifted over Kolis and then me. In the bright moonlight, the handsome lines of his face tensed. He bowed his head. "Your Majesty."

Kolis knelt. My calves slid over warm, rough sand. He didn't let go, he just held the top half of my body upright and against his chest. "I am in need of your assistance. She has lost too much blood."

Phanos glanced at me, his stare lingering on my throat. "Correct me if I'm wrong, but is that not Nyktos's Consort?"

"Yes," I gasped. Or I *thought* I did. I couldn't be sure. My tongue felt leaden and useless.

"That is irrelevant," Kolis responded.

"Perhaps to you. But I felt the loss of one of our brethren, and the rise of a new…sistren. All of us did." Phanos's gaze slipped past us, and I heard retreating footsteps. His gaze shifted back to me. "Is it because of her?"

"You ask too many questions," Kolis growled, his smooth voice roughening. "And I have very little patience for answering them."

"I apologize, my King." Phanos bowed his head slightly. "But I want no problems with Nyktos."

"My nephew is currently no threat to anyone," Kolis said, and my heart felt like it twisted until nothing was left of it. "However, even you should be more worried about inciting my wrath than Nyktos's," Kolis warned, cold bitterness filling his tone as gold-laced eather poured out of him. I winced when the essence glided harmlessly against my skin before spilling over to the sand. "Or do I need to remind you?"

Phanos eyed the tendrils of eather as they stopped short of reaching the water, where they lifted and coiled like vipers preparing to strike. I shuddered at the sight of them, having no idea what would happen if the eather reached the water. Whatever it was, I had a feeling it would be something terrible.

Phanos's nostrils flared, and then the trident collapsed and vanished from his hand. "No, you do not."

"Good." Kolis's voice was warm once more—gentle, even. The way he switched back and forth so quickly was unnerving. "She cannot die. I need you to make sure that doesn't happen."

Confusion arose. Between the blood loss and my worry for Ash, my addled brain was having a hard time processing everything, and many things were a blur. But even in this state, I had no idea how Phanos could assist.

"If you do not wish for her to die, can you not do what you've done to the others?" Phanos questioned. "Make her one of your Revenants. She is a godling, is she not? That shouldn't be a problem, should it?"

But I wasn't a godling—the offspring of a mortal and a god. However, it was how I *felt* to the gods and Primals because of the embers. Either way, Phanos clearly knew about the Revenants. Maybe all the Primals but Ash did. But Phanos didn't know about the embers.

I wasn't sure what to make of that. Was there anything to gain? But I hadn't even thought of Kolis turning me into whatever the Revenants were. Could he even do that? What would that—?

"That is only death reborn," Kolis answered, the warmth straining. "And I cannot risk her soul being stolen away in the process of the rebirth."

Two things happened at once. One, I realized that a Revenant had to die to become one. And the second thing? Phanos realized exactly why Kolis was here.

"Is that her?" he whispered. "Your *graeca*?"

A burst of anger lit my insides, temporarily replacing the coldness that seemed to have penetrated every part of me. Words scorched my tongue, and I wanted nothing more than for them to make it past my lips. I wasn't his *graeca*. Neither was Sotoria. We didn't belong to him. I willed my mouth to move, just as I had earlier when I yelled at Ash and Kolis, but the embers only sputtered weakly, and all I managed was a whimpering sound.

"She... I believe so." Kolis's fingers pressed into the flesh of my arm and hip. "I'm holding her soul in her body. I'm not sure..." He faltered, the weight of his words a whispered admission. "I'm not sure how much longer I will be able to do so."

I thought of the pins-and-needles sensation I'd felt when he placed his hand on my chest. Was that it? When he grabbed hold of my soul—*our* souls?

Shock rippled through me. The god Saion hadn't believed that Kolis retained enough power to summon a soul like Ash could. Did this mean there were still some embers of life in him? Or was this a byproduct of the true embers of death? I wasn't sure, but it explained why I was still alive—well, barely.

"You know what you ask of me," Phanos voiced quietly, wind whipping across the water and tossing the edges of my hair over the sand.

"I am not asking."

Small bumps of unease prickled my skin as Phanos tipped his head to the side. A muscle in his jaw throbbed. Then he slipped below the water. A moment or so later, the ceeren went still. The smaller ones, the children, swam deeper and deeper, disappearing from sight.

Phanos resurfaced less than a foot from the sand. Water coursed over the smooth skin of his head and streamed down his chest. Wordlessly, he extended his arms to us.

Kolis hesitated, not moving at first, and then he lifted me once more. "If she dies, I will destroy your entire Court," he swore, handing me to the Primal who hadn't approached neither Ash nor me during my coronation.

Once more, panic seized me as Phanos took me into his arms, and the embers in me briefly flared. My heart rammed against my ribs, but I thought I felt Phanos's chest rise sharply against mine. Warm, fizzing water lapped against my legs, and then everything below my chest was underwater. What thin breaths I managed seized. I loved being in my lake back in the mortal realm and enjoyed splashing around in Ash's pool, but I couldn't swim. And this...this was the sea a Primal was carrying me into.

"Nyktos once took what belonged to me."

My wide eyes and frightened gaze darted from the star-strewn sky to Phanos. He was speaking about Saion and Rhahar.

"I should be amused to see something of his taken from him."

With his featherlight voice, it was hard to hear him over the seething water. "But I find no joy in this." Wisps of silvery eather surged in his eyes. "I can sense your panic. There is no need. What would be the point in harming you when you're already dying?"

How in this realm and beyond was that supposed to be even remotely reassuring?

One side of Phanos's lips kicked up.

On second thought, I didn't think he'd meant what he said to be reassuring at all.

"You're in the water off the Triton Isles, near the coast of Hygeia," Phanos continued. "Do you know what that means? Of course, you don't. Most of the other Primals are not even aware, including Nyktos." Phanos drifted out even farther. "I wonder if he'd have already brought you here if he'd known."

I truly wasn't following most of what he was saying. All I could think about was how deep the water must be.

"Water is the source of all life and healing. Without it, even the Primal of Life wouldn't hold power...if that power was to be held." A wry, humorless smile appeared. "Those born here, the ceeren, carry that source within them. It's a gift that heals, just as the water does."

His eyes met mine, and I heard...singing—soft strains in an unfamiliar language. The eather had stopped whirling in Phanos's eyes, and I thought maybe I saw a shadow of sadness there. But I had to be imagining it. This was the same Primal who'd flooded the Kingdom of Phythe because he'd been insulted.

"For most in your...state, this would provide a cure. But for you? You are no godling, Consort. I felt them the moment our skin touched." Phanos's head lowered, and he whispered, "The embers of Primal power. Strong ones. Too strong for a mortal, and that's what you are." The bridge of his nose brushed mine. "Or *were*."

The suffocating feeling of helplessness rose, making me jerk. I had no idea what he would do. Any Primal could attempt to take the embers, just as Kolis had from Eythos, and what could I do to stop it? Nothing. My fingers, all that I could move, curled into my palms. I wasn't used to being unable to defend myself. The feeling made me want to scratch my skin off. Fury whipped through me, crashing into my panic until desperation choked me.

"You have embers of life in you. Which means Eythos dealt the final—perhaps winning—blow to his brother, did he not?" Phanos glanced at the shore, the tendrils of eather in his eyes burning as brightly as the moon. A low chuckle came from him. "Ah, you have always been his weakness, haven't you? I could take those embers myself."

I stared up at him, wondering if it would be better if Phanos did just that. Although considering how he'd flooded a kingdom in the mortal realm over the cancellation of a tradition meant to honor him, probably not.

"But then I'd be fighting Kolis *and* Nyktos, the latter likely to be as displeased as the former, at least based on what I saw at your coronation. I am no fool." He turned us in the water so his back was to the shore. His damp forehead brushed mine. "What truly ails you goes deeper than blood loss and cannot be circumvented, Consort. It can only be delayed, no matter how steep the price or how often it is paid."

A steep price? What—?

"When this is all done, and you still breathe?" The bridge of his nose brushed mine again. "Remember the gifts given to you tonight."

Before I could even process what he'd said, churning water rose over our heads, and we dipped below the surface. Phanos's mouth closed over mine, causing my entire body to go rigid at the contact. He didn't kiss me. He breathed into my mouth, the panels of my gown floating around me and my arms following as we sank. Phanos's breath was cool, fresh, and powerful, like swallowing the wind.

His arms relaxed around me, and I slipped free of his grasp. My wide gaze darted through the cloudy water, and I continued sinking until—

Hands folded around my ankles, dragging me down. My mouth opened in a scream that sent bubbles roaring upward in the water. Fingers pressed into my waist, turning me around. A woman was suddenly before me, her long, dark hair tangling with my much lighter strands. She leaned in, the scales of her tail rough against the skin of my legs. Her eyes were the color of the Stroud Sea during the summer at noon, a stunning shade like sea glass. Her bare chest pressed against mine as she grasped my cheeks. Like Phanos, she placed her mouth over mine and exhaled. The breath was fresh and sweet, pouring down my throat.

The ceeren let go and floated away from me, her eyes closing, and our hair separating. She didn't fall. She *rose*.

A hand on my shoulder turned me again. A man with the same blue-green eyes and pink skin took hold of my cheeks, bringing his mouth to mine as beams of brilliant moonlight washed over us. He, too, breathed that fresh, sweet, cool air into me, filling my lungs. His hands slipped away from me like the first, and then another caught me, this one with hair nearly as pale as mine. Her lips met mine, and her breath filled me, the two of us drifting from the light of the moon into the shadows. She floated up as another and another came. There were so many, and less and less moonlight reached us. I could no longer keep track of how many touched their lips to mine and exhaled, but with each breath, I felt different. The coldness inside me faded, and the tightness in my chest and throat eased. My heart skipped beats, then began pumping steadily. The erratic racing of my pulse slowed, and sound finally reached me. I looked around and saw the ceeren in the shadows of the dark water. It was them. They were singing like the ones on land had. I couldn't understand the words, but it was a hauntingly beautiful melody. The backs of my eyes burned.

A ceeren's smooth hands cupped my cheeks, turning my head away from those singing and toward her. She didn't appear much older than me. Her blue-tinged lips spread in a smile as her tail moved up and down, propelling us upward toward the now-dappled moonlight. Tears. I could see them, even in the water. They streamed down her ivory cheeks, and I closed my eyes against what I felt at seeing them. The urge to tell her I was sorry hit me hard, even though I didn't know what I was apologizing for. But her tears, her smile, and the song the ceeren sang…

Her mouth closed over mine, and she exhaled, her breath filling my chest. The embers of life thrummed strongly, vibrantly, as if reawakening. It struck me then that it wasn't their breath they breathed into me.

It was their eather.

We broke the water's surface, and my eyes shot open.

Different hands took me by the shoulders, ones I knew belonged to Kolis. He lifted me from the sea. Sparkling water streamed from my limbs and dripped from the hem of the gown and my hair, running into my eyes as he pulled me onto the beach.

I pitched forward, blinking water from my eyes and planting my hands in the warm, rough, white sand. My head no longer felt as if it were full of cobwebs. My thoughts were clear and already racing, preparing my muscles to fight or run. I started pulling myself free of Kolis's hold when the blurriness left my vision.

I froze.

Every part of my being seized as I stared at the surface of the water. I didn't see Phanos anywhere, but what I saw made my tingling lips part in horror.

Bodies floated, some face-up, others on their bellies. Dozens of them just...bobbed in the now-still waters. My gaze skipped over scales, no longer vibrant and vivid but dull and faded.

Suddenly, I understood the mournful song that no longer filled the air. The last ceeren's smile. Her tears. The sadness I'd seen in Phanos's eyes. *This* was the price he'd spoken of.

The ceeren had given me life.

At the cost of theirs.

4

I stared at the bodies gently bobbing in the moonlight-drenched water, so utterly shocked by what the ceeren had sacrificed that I was numb, deadened to the point where I felt incredibly empty.

Why had they done this?

But they hadn't been given a choice, had they? Kolis had demanded that Phanos assist, and this was how the Primal of the Sky, Sea, Earth, and Wind helped.

You know what you ask of me.

Kolis had.

But I hadn't.

If I'd known, I would've done everything in my power to prevent the unnecessary loss of life. Because it *was* unnecessary. Phanos had said it himself. What the ceeren had given their lives for was only temporary. I would still die. But even if I wouldn't? I wasn't okay with this.

"Why?" I whispered into the wind, my voice hoarse.

"Because I will not allow you to die," Kolis answered, speaking nearly the same words Ash had but...

When spoken by Ash, they had always sounded like a tragic oath birthed of desperation, stubbornness, and want—so much want. A tremor started in my hands and swept through my body. Kolis's words sounded like a threat and reeked of obsession.

My gaze skipped over the lifeless ceeren. I had never wanted anyone to lose their life because of me. Like those who'd perished during the Shadowlands siege.

Like Ector had.

The image of the god flashed in my mind, momentarily obscuring the horror in front of me. It wasn't how I'd seen him on the pike when Ash and I returned from the mortal realm. While that had been bad, I preferred it to how I'd last seen him; when he'd been nothing more than red, slick pieces. Ector hadn't deserved that. Neither had Aios, who I'd at least been able to bring back. But had she wanted that? I had no idea how long she'd been dead. Could I have ripped her away from peace? And that act had a ripple effect—ending how many other lives? The eather I'd used to restore Aios's life drew the dakkais and caused them to swarm those fighting in the courtyard.

Now, dozens of ceeren had died—were *murdered*—for me. And for what? This wouldn't stave off the Ascension. It was only a reprieve.

Instead of being rushed toward the end, I was now inching toward it. But it was still coming. There was no stopping that. Just like there'd been no changing what had been done to Ector. Or to the ceeren and countless others.

"I don't want anyone dying for me," I choked out.

"You do not have a choice," Kolis stated. "And if you are who you say you are, you should know that."

I flinched at the sickening truth of his words. Sotoria had never had a choice from the moment Kolis saw her collecting flowers along the Cliffs of Sorrow. And *I'd* never had a choice from the very second Roderick Mierel made his desperate bargain with the true Primal of Life to save his dying kingdom.

It wasn't fair.

It never had been.

Rage and panic swiftly swelled inside me, but I wasn't sure it was entirely mine. My fingers curled into the sand as my heart rate sped up. Raw, jagged emotions lodged in my chest and throat. I pushed to my feet, my breath coming in short, too-quick pants. And turned to Kolis.

The false King of Gods looked down at me, a curious pinch to his features. The wind lifted the flaxen strands of his hair, sending them against high, arched cheekbones. Golden smudges of eather snaked through the bronze flesh of his bare chest. There was no evidence of his battle with Ash. He was completely healed.

I spared a glance around us. We weren't alone. Others stood several feet back in the shadows of leafy palms. I only saw them because their shadowstone blades glinted in the moonlight. I didn't know if they were Kolis's guards or Phanos's, but they had weapons, and that was all that mattered.

"She had fewer freckles than you, and her face was shaped more like a heart. The hair isn't right. Hers was like…like a polished garnet in the sun." Kolis's voice was soft, almost childlike in its awe, but his words slithered along the sand and brushed against my skin. "But if I look hard enough…if I let myself see, I do see her in you."

I reacted.

There was no hesitation. No thought. I took off, darting past him and running hard and fast, my feet kicking up sand as the material of the soaked gown clung to my skin. I ran straight for the guards.

Surprise flashed across the face of a pale-skinned guard, his blue-green eyes luminous with eather widening a second before I slammed my palm into his chest. The god grunted, stumbling back as I reached for the hilt of his short sword.

"Fuck," he gasped, reaching for me when I yanked the blade from its sheath.

I'd caught him off guard. I was simply quicker than he was. I jabbed the elbow of my other arm out, catching him under the jaw and snapping his head back.

"Do not touch her," Kolis ordered as another grabbed for me. "Ever."

The other guard froze.

Spinning toward the false King, I firmed my grip on the cool iron hilt the shadowstone blade had been forged to.

"Leave us," he instructed. "Now."

I didn't dare look away from Kolis to see if the guards listened to him. I could only imagine that they had, which suited me just fine.

Kolis and I stared at each other in silence while I willed my racing heart to slow. I needed to be calm, careful, and purposeful. Because even though Kolis questioned what I claimed about Sotoria, he believed deep down. That was why he'd shaken so hard when he held me, and it created the awe in his voice that I'd heard only moments earlier.

That all meant he was vulnerable to me—only me—and this was my chance. Possibly the only one I'd get to end this.

"I expected you to run from me," Kolis remarked. "That's what she would've done. She always ran."

"Not always," I said, remembering what I'd learned about Sotoria.

She may have run in the beginning, but that changed.

Laces of golden eather swirled faster across his chest. "You're right." His chin lifted. A heartbeat passed. "Put the sword down."

That would not happen. "Make me."

"Come now," he said with a low chuckle, his wide mouth curling into a mockery of a smile that bordered on patronizing. He started toward me, the wind off the sea tugging at his linen pants. "What do you think you're going to do with that?"

Waiting until he was within reach of the blade, I showed him exactly what I could do. I thrust out with the shadowstone sword, aiming straight for the bastard's heart.

Kolis's eyes widened, and his brows lifted, creasing the skin of his forehead. The stunned look on his face was comical. It was as if he couldn't believe that I dared to do such a thing. I would've laughed, but he was a Primal.

And he was fast, his reflexes as insane as Ash's. But like with the guard, I had the element of surprise. Kolis didn't really believe I would attack, which cost him a fraction of a second.

The shadowstone blade pierced his skin, and my lips split in a savage grin.

The second the sword sank into his chest, he knocked the hilt from my grasp with such jarring force that I lost my balance in the unforgiving sand and fell to one knee.

The sword vibrated where it was partially lodged in his chest, a half an inch—if that—to the right of his heart.

Son of a bitch.

Shimmery blood trickled down Kolis's chest as he gripped the sword's hilt, tearing it free. The very moment the blade was out of his body, the damn wound immediately stopped bleeding.

Thick, dark clouds raced over the once-calm sky, blotting out the stars and moon. A stuttered heartbeat passed.

Lightning suddenly streaked above and energy swamped the air, slithering over my skin and causing the embers in my chest to flare. The weight of the soaking power was oppressive, threatening to push me into the ground.

Heart thundering, my head jerked up. Fury was etched into every line of Kolis's face and set the hard jut of his jaw. The veins in his cheeks lit up with golden-tinged eather. The embers in my chest responded, beginning to thrum wildly as the Primal essence turned his eyes into silver pools with flecks of gold.

"That is the second time tonight I've had a sword pierce my flesh." Light pulsed from his hand, and the shadowstone sword he held evaporated into nothing, not even dust. "I did not appreciate it before, and that has not changed."

My stomach hollowed as I shot to my feet. I'd stabbed Ash more than once and threatened to do so again too many times to count, but I'd never been afraid of him. Not even when he went full Primal on me in the Dying Woods after I accidentally hit him with a bolt of eather.

But I was afraid of Kolis.

I tried to swallow, but my throat seized. I took a step back.

Kolis swiped a hand over his chest and looked down at his blood-smeared palm. He tilted his head and lowered his hand. "That was very unwise."

"It was," I rasped. "I probably should've aimed for the head."

His gold-flecked silver eyes went flat. Absolutely dead.

I did the only sensible thing. Pivoting, I ran. This time, no guards stood in the shadows of the sweeping palms. My arms and legs pumped—

Kolis caught my hair in a fist, jerking my entire body back. Fiery pain erupted in my scalp as my feet slipped. I landed on my knees again. Knowing this put me at a dangerous disadvantage, I attempted to regain my footing while he dragged me through the sand.

Kolis hauled me up and whipped me around. "Now that, I am more accustomed to." He yanked my head back.

I gasped as pain traveled from my scalp down my spine. Grabbing hold of his arm, I tried to loosen the tension.

"The running-away part, in case you're wondering what I meant."

A tiny part buried deep inside me knew this was one of the moments I needed to keep my mouth shut and think before I did anything. Not only for my life but also the entirety of the mortal realm.

But I refused to cower before him. *She* refused to do it, no matter the cost. No matter how foolish it was. I was not weak, and I'd been wrong when I first heard the legend of Sotoria. She was not weak either.

"That sounds like something to be proud of," I spat, bringing my knee up fast and hard.

I'd missed his heart before, but I did not miss now.

My knee slammed into his groin. A roar of pain erupted from Kolis, and his arm cut through the air—

Agony exploded in my jaw and cheek. A metallic taste immediately filled my mouth. I went down, catching myself a second before I face-planted in the sand. I didn't even know what part of him had hit me. His arm? A fist? Whatever it was had my ears ringing. For a moment, the pain stunned me enough that I feared it was something Ash could feel if he was conscious.

Rocking back onto my knees, I breathed through the pain until the initial brutal shock of it lessened. I spat a mouthful of blood onto the sand, shocked that a tooth hadn't come flying out with it.

"Godsdamn it," Kolis snarled. "I didn't mean for that to happen." The white linen of his pants edged into my vision. "Are you all right?"

A spasm ran through me. He sounded…gods, he sounded genuinely concerned, and that sent a chill down my spine. "What do you think?"

"I told you not to push me," he reasoned, the sound of his breaths sharp and short. "But you're determined to make me into the villain."

"*Make* you a villain?" A wet laugh left me as I pushed to my feet. I lifted my throbbing head. "You're already that."

"I never…" Kolis's eyes tracked the blood running down my chin, and he flinched. The fucker actually *flinched* at the sight of the blood he'd drawn. "I never wanted to be that."

"My gods," I whispered. "You're unhinged."

In the moonlight, his cheeks deepened in color. "If so, then I am only what my brother made me," he snarled.

"Is there anything you don't blame your brother for?" I snapped.

Kolis shot forward so fast I sucked in a stuttered breath and jerked back a step. And I hated that I'd retreated, that I'd given him even an inch.

He halted, his chest rising and falling rapidly. A moment passed, then another. It was clear to me that he was keeping himself in check. Barely. "This is not what I want—us fighting."

"I don't care what you want!" I shot back, my stomach twisting. I wasn't exactly sure that had only been me who'd yelled the words.

His hands fisted at his sides. "Do not push me, *so'lis*."

So'lis? I had no idea what that meant, but I thought Sotoria might because her rage was palpable, and it was most definitely her that screamed what came out of my mouth next. "Fuck you!"

I didn't see him move before I felt his grip at my throat. My hands flew to his. I pried at his fingers, but it was no use. His fingertips pressed in, making it difficult to breathe.

"I warned you not to push me," Kolis accused, his nostrils flaring. "Yet you do exactly that and more."

Ignoring the fluttering panic in my chest, I met and held his stare.

"I think you've spent too much time with my nephew." Kolis smirked. "And I saw him give me that very same look tonight. I'm sure I will see it again soon enough."

"You touch him, and I—" I forced out the words amid gasps for air.

"You will do what?" Kolis cut in, faint wisps of eather beginning to stir in his eyes as his grip got even tighter. "What will you do for him? Because I saw what he'd do for you. He'd kill his brethren. Attack me. Start a war."

Some level of common sense returned, warning me that I needed to be smart when it came to Ash. It took no leap of logic to know that if Kolis suspected I was in love with his nephew, he would approach it as Sotoria being in love with him, and that wouldn't end well.

The image of the dagger rising and plunging flashed before me. I could still hear the wet, fleshy sounds.

My heart raced with fear—potent, numbing terror. Ash wasn't safe right now. He'd been weakened, and because of me, gravely injured.

"What?" Kolis demanded, his fingers digging into the bite he'd left behind as he lifted me onto my tiptoes. "What will you do for him that you will not do for me?"

"Just about anything you can think of, but that has nothing to do with him. At the end of the day, I couldn't care less about him." I forced out words that couldn't be more untrue. My chest felt as if it were shrinking with each passing second. Kolis's grip tightened, likely bruising, and I choked. "I would do anything for literally anyone else— a random guard, another Primal, a corpse, a piece of grass..." I wheezed.

"I think I get the picture." His lip curled. One fang appeared. "And I also think you're lying."

Alarm quickened my pulse. I realized I needed to distract him from thoughts of Ash, and the only way I knew how to do that was to direct his attention to me completely. "And I think you...I think you hit like a wanna-be Primal of Life."

Kolis's laughter filled the air like a hiss as he hauled me against his chest. The contact of his flesh against the too-thin gown sent a shudder of revulsion through me. "You are so incredibly foolish and reckless. Too bold and entirely too mouthy."

"You..."—I struggled for breath—"forgot one...thing."

"And what is that?" he asked. "Disrespectful?"

"Sure, but…I'm also soon…to be dead," I wheezed.

He raised a golden brow. "Is that so?"

"Yes," I croaked. "Since you're killing me…again."

For a moment, Kolis didn't move. He'd gone completely still. Then his gaze dropped to where he had me by the throat. His eyes widened in surprise. It was almost as if he'd had no idea he was choking me. He shoved me away from him.

Stumbling back, I barely managed to keep my balance. I bent at the waist, hands on my knees while I dragged in deep mouthfuls of salty air. A tremor coursed through me, and I swallowed, wincing at the soreness in my throat.

I could practically feel the bruises forming on the skin of my neck, but I learned something then. I laughed, the sound like nails against stone. It hurt, but as sick and twisted as it was, his love of Sotoria was a weakness in more ways than one.

"This conversation is over," Kolis said. Another laugh almost snuck free. He thought this was a *conversation*? "We are going home, and once you've calmed down, we will talk then."

"Home?" Slowly, I straightened, my disbelief, anger, and maybe a little of Sotoria's, getting the better of me. "Go fuck yourself, you nightmarish piece of—" I tensed, seeing his hand move this time, knowing it would hurt.

The blow never landed.

Kolis gripped my chin, and my heart stuttered. It wasn't his hold. The press of his fingers was firm but nowhere near as bruising as it had been on my throat. Still, what I saw caused my heart to continue skipping beats.

Primal essence sparked and ignited, spilling into the air around him. A bright, golden glow rose, arcing from his back like wings. The swirls of eather spread so rapidly over his flesh that, for a moment, he became as he had been when battling Ash: blinding, golden light and spitting eather that stung my skin.

But the light faded quickly, showing that his skin had thinned to the point where the bones of his arm were visible. A knot of dread twisted in my stomach as I lifted my gaze. I didn't want to see, but I couldn't stop from looking.

I saw the dull sheen of his cheekbones. His jawbone. The bones of his arm. And his eyes… They were just sockets filled with pools of black, swirling nothingness.

Kolis hadn't looked like this when he battled Ash, but I knew instantly that this was what the *true* Primal embers of death looked like.

And it was terrifying.

The wings of eather lifted and stretched behind him, then disappeared into golden smoke. The aura in his veins faded as his skin thickened, hiding what he truly looked like. "I do hope you are far more aware and grateful of the grace I've shown you than Nyktos was."

"Grace?" I exclaimed. "You—"

The whirling abyss of nothingness that had been his eyes flashed to silver and gold. "*You will not speak.*"

My body went rigid, the four words thundering through me. An aching pulse shot through my jaw, and my mouth clamped shut.

"*You will not talk back*," Kolis said, and his voice was everywhere, both outside and inside of me. "*Nor will you fight me.*"

My muscles obeyed him instantly. I lowered my hands to my sides. What I'd feared in the ruined chamber as I held the dagger to my throat had come to fruition. He was using compulsion.

"That is much better." Kolis smiled and drew me toward him with just the curl of his arm. He lowered his head, and his mouth was just an inch from mine when he spoke next. "Much, much better."

I felt his hand on my lower back and then his chest against mine. My heart lurched. I willed my mouth to open. Wished for my arms and legs to move, but nothing happened. All I could do was stand there. He could do anything to me. Fear blossomed at the loss of control.

"There is something you need to understand, whether you've spoken the truth of who you are or not." One by one, he lifted all his fingers but his thumb. "If anyone dared to speak to me as you have, I would have their flesh flayed from their bodies and fed to them."

Kolis wiped at the blood under my lower lip and then lifted his hand to his mouth.

I was going to be sick.

Hopefully, if I did vomit, I would do it in his fucking face.

He sucked on his thumb, drawing the blood into his mouth. The eather brightened in his eyes. "You saw what happened to Nyktos for daring to strike me." His head tilted, sending a lock of gold hair against a cheek. "So, if it turns out you are not my *graeca*, and this is some sort of elaborate ploy? There will be no limit to the atrocities visited upon you and everyone you've ever cared about before I take the embers of life." His lips grazed mine as they curved into a smile. "That, I promise you."

5

Kolis's compulsion lifted, and the moment he vanished, control over my body and thoughts returned.

But I stood where he'd left me, in what was yet another, much grander gilded cage—one I had a terrible, sinking suspicion was the one Aios had spoken of.

Seawater dripped from my hair and gown, leaving small puddles on the shiny black floor as a faint tremor coursed down my arm. The return had been a blur, but once inside the cage, Kolis hadn't left immediately.

He'd lingered for some time.

But hadn't spoken.

He had just looked down at me—at my face, my body—hands trembling on my arms, then my waist and hips. I could still feel his fingers pressing into my flesh and then curling around the wet, thin material of my gown, my skin crawling the entire time.

He'd shook as if overcome by some kind of extreme emotion or struggling with restraint.

And he'd shivered while terror lodged in my throat and helplessness slowly suffocated me. He'd quivered through each second, every minute, as I feared what was to come, what he would do while I stood there. That choking, smothering powerlessness had entrenched itself deeply within me, and it remained, even with him gone.

A shudder went through me, and my chest tightened. I hadn't been able to look away or move out of his reach. I couldn't even tell him to stop touching me, nor did I have the chance to regain some semblance of control. Nausea rose, turning my stomach.

I'd been helpless, absolutely powerless, and it had been so easy for him to ensure that. Four words. Just four fucking words, and he'd had complete control of me.

The back of my throat burned. The gold bars before me, spaced a foot apart, blurred. I managed one step, and then my legs stopped holding me up. I went down onto my knees and palms. I didn't even feel the impact. My too-tight chest constricted even further as I took rapid, too-shallow breaths.

Kolis could do that again at any time. He could seize my will, strip my power from me before I even knew it, and there was nothing I could do to stop it.

I was trapped here, with him, without control. I would die here, either at Kolis's hands or upon my Ascension, and there was no telling what would happen between now and then.

Actually, I did know.

Aios had spoken little about her time as one of Kolis's *favorites*, but I'd been able to fill in what she hadn't shared. He'd never touched his favorites, but I would eventually be different. I knew that. I'd seen it in his stare when he stood before me, his hands fisting the gown. It was the same kind of dark, twisted need I'd seen in Tavius's eyes more times than I cared to remember.

I leaned back, my heart racing. I squeezed my eyes shut, but my cheeks became damp. Pain flared across my jaw as I clamped my mouth closed, but the ragged sound still deafened my ears.

I smacked my hands over my face—fuck, that hurt—but the physical pain was nothing compared to the withering agony that would leave no bruises behind.

Kolis's promise of violent destruction of not only me but also those I cared about echoed in my mind, overshadowing the fear of assault. It was an oath I didn't doubt for one second.

My body was now the one that shook. Raw panic and anger crashed through me, pouring into the crack in my chest that had formed in the Dying Woods when I attempted to escape the Shadowlands and turn myself over to Kolis. Pressure built. My heart did that skipping thing that caused what breath I'd managed to take to catch repeatedly. The inside of my throat had to be shrinking as tears stung the tender skin of my lip.

The Primal essence stirred, pulsed. My skin prickled all over, the tiny hairs rising in response to the brief charge hitting the air.

In the back of my mind, I knew this wasn't good. I clearly remembered what had happened the last time I'd completely lost control. I'd almost brought Ash's palace down on us and sent myself into the Ascension I wouldn't survive. I'd end up going into stasis.

I couldn't afford to weaken myself and become truly vulnerable.

The embers in my chest vibrated, and I lowered my hands, opening my eyes. My breath snagged. Silver eather sparked along the tips of my fingers as the embers and my blood started to hum.

"Keep it together," I told myself, trying to slow and clear my thoughts.

But it was impossible.

Because it wasn't just what would happen to me, it was what would surely be done to Ash—what had already been done to him. And Kolis had him in a cell somewhere.

I knew what kind of state he'd been in, and it hadn't been good. Something struck me, then. I thought of the roots that had come out of the ground when I nearly sent myself into Ascension. Why hadn't the earth attempted to protect Ash? Although they hadn't tried to protect me or the embers inside of me either when I was so very close to dying. There had to be a reason for that, but my mind couldn't focus on it. It dwelled on what awaited Ash—what Kolis would do to him.

I jerked, my shoulders rising and falling rapidly as I tried to take in enough air between the ragged, shattered sounds still coming out of me.

I pressed my lips together, attempting to cease the quiver in them and silence the sobs. Ash had never been entirely forthcoming when it came to what Kolis had done to him in the past, but I knew enough. Gods, I knew plenty.

Ash was a Primal, but that didn't mean he couldn't be injured. He could be hurt badly. He could even be in stasis now, unable to defend himself.

Gods, thinking that wasn't helping. The embers throbbed more violently—

A low-pitched cracking sound drew my attention to the cage floor. Where my bent knees rested on the black tile, a small splinter appeared in what looked like shadowstone, forming a thin spiderweb of fractures.

Gasping for air, I looked at the bars above me. A faint cloud of dust drifted down. Something glinted at the center of the cage up high, where all the bars came together, but I couldn't focus on it.

My gaze moved to the chamber beyond. A buttery yellow glow from several chandeliers cast a soft light over shiny, obsidian walls. Shadowstone. I could see the cracks in the stone—fractures that were far deeper and impossible for me to have caused.

I saw a gilded seat. How many damn thrones did Kolis have? One in every room, it seemed—possibly even the bathing chamber.

But it wasn't the only item. Centered around it was a sitting area with several settees, a few low tables, and a couple of wingback chairs. To the left was a dining table and some other chairs. A dark, cherry-wood credenza was against the wall, stocked with numerous bottles of liquor and stacked glasses. All but the credenza and what it held was gilded.

Did Kolis hold meetings in here?

Fucking gods, I bet he did.

Several windows were near the ceiling, too high to reach and only a couple of feet wide and tall. So, unless I learned to fly and could contort my body to half its size, they wouldn't do me any good.

I could only assume I was inside some chamber within Cor Palace, but I had no idea for sure. I could be anywhere.

Ash could be anywhere.

The tile beneath my palm cracked.

Holy shit, I was breaking shadowstone, one of the strongest materials in both realms—if not *the* strongest.

Oh, gods, I needed to calm down.

I slid my trembling hands to my knees. I could do this. I could control the panic and the Primal essence, couldn't I? Even if it didn't feel like it, the anxiety came from my mind. I knew how to stop it. And the eather? I now knew that was a part of me, so much so that the embers couldn't even be removed without killing me. I'd controlled it earlier. I could do it again now. *The embers are yours for the time being*, I reminded myself.

And I could control them again. I could control myself. I was not weak. I wasn't helpless when it came to this. I wouldn't be. I refused.

So, I needed to figure this out.

Was the essence responding to my emotions? To the violent mix of panic and anger? Or was it reacting to the feeling of not being able to breathe? It wasn't the former. Yes, the eather always became more active when I felt something strongly, but it was the breathlessness and the feeling of not being attached to myself that was the cause. It was the spiral of feeling completely out of control as if I were capable of doing anything to myself, and anything could happen to me. That was doing this. Because it felt like dying. Like running full speed toward death.

But I wasn't completely out of control. I wouldn't do anything to myself. This wasn't like the night I'd taken too much sleeping draft. I didn't want to die. I hadn't really wanted to then, either. I'd just been lost. And I was breathing. Not very well, but I wasn't being choked by unseen hands. Air was still getting into my lungs. I just needed to slow down my respiration.

My fingers dug into my knees as I forced my aching jaw to open. I went with Ash's instructions because it made me feel like he was here, and I badly needed that. I conjured up the memory of his body bracing mine, and his arms wrapped firmly around me. Gods, I could hear him, his smoke-and-shadow voice.

"*You need to slow your breathing,*" he said softly. "*Put your tongue behind your upper front teeth.*"

I did as he'd instructed, pressing the tip of my tongue to the back of my upper teeth and keeping my mouth closed. Then, imagining that he was guiding me to do so, I straightened my back, removing any actual physical pressure from my chest.

"*Close your eyes and listen to me.*" I obeyed the command from the memory. "*Focus only on me. I want you to exhale to the count of four. Don't breathe in. Just exhale. One. Two. Three. Four. Now, inhale for the same count.*"

I did exactly that, breathing out and then in.

"*Don't stop.*"

I didn't. I kept going as seconds became minutes. I didn't regain control immediately. I had to fight for it. Needed to wait for my chest to loosen and my throat to expand. I had to fight for my breathing to slow and deepen. Fight for the embers to calm down.

So, I did what I did best. I fought.

I had no idea how much time had passed. Could've been a handful of minutes or hours, but the tears finally slowed. My breathing deepened and became steadier. The embers calmed, and the spiraling feeling faded until I felt present, attached to my body, and in control once more.

Blowing out a ragged breath, I rocked back and then pushed to my feet. The pain in my face and mouth alternated between a dull ache and a throbbing pulse as I shoved tangled, damp curls back. I carefully wiped at my cheeks, my stomach dipping at the red sheen I saw on my palms.

Tears of blood.

Tears of a Primal.

Gods.

I took another deep breath as I looked at my right hand. The luminous, golden whirls swept over my hand and slipped between my thumb and pointer finger, continuing in sweeping swirls across my palm.

Ash was alive.

I just needed to make sure he stayed that way, which meant I had to get the hell out of here and find him so he could take the embers. Then he would Ascend into what he was always meant to be: the true Primal of Life.

In my chest, the embers wiggled as if they…disapproved?

Gods, that was a wild thought. They were only energy. Power. They didn't have opinions or biases. They just were.

And once Ash was the true Primal of Life, the few embers of death that still existed in Kolis would force him to once more assume the role of the Primal of Death. That would stop the Rot from spreading within the kingdom of Lasania, and eventually the rest of the mortal realm. And with the ability to Ascend gods restored, as I'd done with Bele and Aios, Ash could kill Kolis and have a new Primal rise in his place.

"What was Eythos thinking?" I whispered, asking for what felt like the hundredth time.

He'd created a weapon by putting the only true embers of life inside me, along with Sotoria's soul.

But it was a poorly thought-out, imperfect one.

He clearly hadn't considered all the things that could go sideways after the deal was made. Perhaps he'd thought I would be born before he died, even though he knew Kolis would kill him. Or maybe he assumed Ash would follow through, taking me when I turned seventeen and therefore giving me a chance to kill Kolis before I entered the Culling. Before the embers could merge so deeply within me that a single drop of Ash's blood had made it so they couldn't be removed without my death. Perhaps he'd hoped his son would take the embers and be able to raise a god of the Shadowlands to assume the role of the true Primal of Death before Kolis's death wreaked havoc in both realms, which would happen if all the power had no place to go. But…

I slowly shook my head. There was no way he was foolish enough to bank on that. There was no way Ash could Ascend himself *and* raise another god before the energy Kolis's death would release did its damage.

I'd seen how fast the shockwave had left Hanan, and there was already another god—another vessel—ready to hold that power.

So, again, what the hell had Eythos been thinking? All he'd managed to do was keep those two true embers of life safe.

And Sotoria.

Until now.

Swallowing, I pressed my hand to the center of my chest. The gown was still wet, and it stuck to my palm. I didn't hear Sotoria's voice, but I knew she was there.

I could feel her like I never had before. It was as if she were a tangible entity that had woken up inside me.

And she was aware.

Of how much, though? Enough to feel what I did? Or just enough to know that she was trapped inside me? I wasn't sure, but I hoped her awareness was only the result of me being close to death and that she'd eventually return to being...well, what I wished for was something akin to being asleep.

Because I didn't want her to feel imprisoned. I didn't want her to be conscious of what would likely happen next. She had been through enough already.

But hadn't I been through enough, too?

A rising sense of hopelessness crashed over me. I...I couldn't do what needed to be done. Was there even a point to it now? I'd had my shot at killing Kolis out on the beach and failed.

I didn't care.

I *didn't*.

Besides, Kolis likely knew exactly what I had been trained for, even if he hadn't seemed all that concerned when I wielded a sword against him. The only option I had now was to escape and get to Ash.

Is it? whispered an annoying voice that sounded an awful lot like mine.

My heart turned over heavily as I stared at the golden marks on my palm. But that nitpicky voice needed to shut the fuck up because I had tried to do my duty.

But did you, really?

I hated that fucking voice. Because, no, I hadn't really tried. Stabbing Kolis out there had been an act of fear and opportunity. That was all. Trying meant...

Becoming his weakness.

Making him fall in love.

Ending him.

I closed my eyes, but that did nothing to prevent the truth from smacking me upside the head. I did care. I pressed my balled fists against my eyes. The truth was, I didn't want to do this.

I couldn't.

I didn't deserve to spend whatever time I had left forcing myself to seduce a being such as Kolis. Convincing myself that I had a choice in what I was doing with my body. That I was in control. Enduring his attention and touch. Lying to myself and hating every second of it. And all for what?

To stop the Rot? Save a kingdom that didn't even know I existed? The so-called greater good?

It wasn't right.

And I couldn't do it to Ash—to my love for him. More importantly, I couldn't do it to myself. I couldn't become an empty vessel again, a blank canvas. I was a person, not just a warm body created for manipulation, deceit, and the purpose of destruction.

"Fuck the greater good!" I shouted, my head jerking back as the scream echoed off the bars of the cage.

The answering silence was a whole different kind of agony.

A harsh laugh slithered out, and a storm of emotions raged within me. Flames of anger licked at my insides and stirred the embers as a deep, painful sorrow dragged me down, like a weighty anchor tugging me into the depths of despair.

Because the truth was, I didn't want to be the kind of person who sacrificed everything—their life, body, autonomy, and godsdamn soul—for everyone else. Everything I'd ever dealt with? My mother's coldness and the feeling that I was somehow responsible for my father's death? The fucking years of loneliness and having to carry the weight of a kingdom that didn't even know I existed, let alone my name? My duty and being oh so careful in catering to Tavius's fragile ego? The sense of bitter, festering failure? Everything I'd given up? Family suppers and kinship? Friendship and companionship? Knowing what it felt like to be wanted for who you were and not for what you could do for someone? Being known? Included? Spoken to and acknowledged? Having people actually know that I fucking existed and was real? I did all of that because I had to. Never because I chose to. I'd never had the choice to choose myself.

Now, I would.

I was choosing to fight.

6

Briefly closing my eyes, I silenced the voice that wanted to remind me this wasn't the way to go about things. That it was a really terrible, bad idea.

That voice could shut the fuck up.

I needed a weapon. Pushing to my feet, I turned sharply to the various chests lining one side of the cage. There'd been a few in the last one, but not like here, nor had they been as lavishly adorned with gold and what looked like shadowstone trimmings.

Giving the chamber beyond a quick scan, I hurried over to the first trunk. I had no idea when Kolis would return, but he would. He claimed we needed to talk.

Kneeling, I threw open the lid of a chest about two to three feet wide and deep. Books were stacked neatly inside, one on top of another. Running my fingers over the spines, I wondered how many others had done the same. The thought left me cold. I knew Aios's hands, when Kolis had kept her as one of his favorites, had likely touched these very books—not to mention countless other captives.

"No more," I whispered. "There will be no more *favorites* after me."

Because their lives had mattered, too—they still did. And once I got to Ash, and he took the embers, he could stop Kolis.

I quietly closed the chest and opened a slightly larger one on my other side. It was full of sheer, lacy slips used for sleeping. I moved on to the next one—the largest. It held more clothing. All gowns. I rooted through them, making sure I could touch the bottom to see if anything had been hidden there. Most of the garments were transparent enough that even the Mistresses of the Jade would've blushed wearing them, and they were all either white or gold, like the nightgowns. A few of them appeared as if they only provided the most basic level of decency. And there were no undergarments.

Gods.

I moved on to a fourth chest, the hinges creaking when the lid opened. More pale white and glittery gold gowns. Closing it, I scooted over to the smallest trunk. I went to pick it up, surprised to find it had some weight and something clunked around inside—several somethings.

Frowning, I knelt. Flipping up the lid, the hinges moved far smoother than the others. I found several strips of material inside, and just like the gowns, they were all white or gold. I picked one up. What in the world was it used for? Placing the ribbon back, I reached in farther. My fingers brushed something cool and smooth.

Shoving the material aside, I froze as I revealed what rested at the bottom.

They were glass...sculptures? Some were smooth and straight, cylindrical. Others curved slightly. A few were ribbed at the center. They ranged from six inches or so, and were one to two inches wide, in various shades of blue and red. A few were even wider and longer.

They couldn't be...

I picked up one made of deep blue glass and suspiciously shaped like...a cock.

All of them were—well, except for the ribbed ones, and that crimson-hued one as wide as my fist that seriously terrified me to even contemplate. But I thought I knew what these were. I'd seen similar ones in pleasure dens. They were glass cocks.

Aios had also told me that Kolis liked to sit with his favorites—talk with them and watch them. I knew that Aios hadn't told me everything about her time here, but I figured I'd found something Kolis liked to watch.

"Perverted bastard," I muttered, disgust churning. All of these had clearly been cleaned, but it was unthinkable to imagine how many hands had touched them. How many bodies...

I wanted to break every single one of them, shatter them to pieces. Damn, I wanted to do way worse with them, and at least one of those things involved shoving one of them through Kolis's eye.

A tight-lipped smile tugged at my lips as I studied the one I held. Likely the strangest weapon I'd ever considered, but it was better than nothing. Glancing at the closed doors, I got a feel for the weight. It was pretty heavy and sturdy, not easily broken, I would imagine, but I was strong.

Gripping the base, I slammed it onto the edge of the chest. The bang it made echoed through the cavernous chamber. The impact rattled my arm, and a crack split across half the width. Shifting back, I brought it down on the chest once more. The glass cock broke unevenly, causing the damaged end to be jagged and sharp.

Perfect.

Picking up the other half of the glass, I placed it back into the chest, then shut the lid and rose, the new glass dagger in hand. As close as I was to the bars, I noticed something I hadn't seen before. They weren't made of gold. They were painted. I saw that in the mild discoloration. Frowning, I stepped around the chest and reached out, placing my fingers on them—

A sharp, quick bite of pain danced over my fingertips, and a wave of silvery sparks briefly lit up the bars. Gasping, I drew my stinging hand to my chest as I stepped back. "What in the world?"

It had to be some sort of ward—magic fueled by Primal essence. Or something else? Whatever it was, it presented an obvious problem.

Turning from the bars, I faced a golden divan and the thick, white fur rug at its feet. The bed was piled with white and gold pillows and fur blankets and positioned directly at the center of the cage. My head turned to the chamber.

The throne sat directly in front of the bed.

Of course, it did.

After all, Kolis would want a perfect view to watch his favorites sleep or…entertain him.

Lip curling, I glanced over the round table and chair near the front of the cage, to the left of the bed.

Chains lay coiled on the floor, secured to the bedposts. My stomach hollowed as my hand moved from my chest to my throat. Much like the one Ash had broken on me, a golden band glinted in the lamplight. The taste of bile filled my mouth, and I dragged my gaze away. A privacy screen and a white chair were on the other side of the bed.

Having a good idea of what I would find, I crossed the cage and stopped beside the large, tufted chair. Behind the screen was a rather massive bathtub, a toilet, and a vanity, all secured to the floor.

The chair faced the tub.

"Fucking gods," I snarled, the embers humming. "Could he be more disgusting if he tried?"

One would hope not, but the answer was probably a resounding *yes*.

I wondered how mad he'd get if I shoved what used to be a glass cock down his throat.

I turned to the standing shelf filled with towels and numerous glass bottles. There were salts, lotions, and cleansers. My gaze flicked to the vanity. A comb lay on the marble sink, along with a brush for the teeth.

The sad thing was that the inside of the cage was nicer than what I'd had at home in Wayfair Castle.

But it was still a cage, no matter the luxuries provided inside it.

I took care of my personal needs and then started to leave the bathing area. My gaze snagged on that damn chair. The arms of it were thickly padded, but there was no mistaking the imprint of fingers.

A chill swept through me as I stared. How many times had Kolis sat in that chair, his fingers pressing into the arms like they had on my hips, to leave an imprint like that? How many did he watch, not even allowing them the most basic privacy?

I felt the flames rising in my chest, spreading through my veins like wildfire. My hand trembled as I clutched the broken glass, my knuckles turning white. Holding on to that rage, I stalked past the chair. Tossing the weapon onto the bed, I returned to the chests and opened one, grabbing a white, lacy garment with slits on either side of the skirt.

Quickly, I peeled off my still-damp gown and changed into the other. It was looser, and the sleeves sat off the shoulder, but it left little to the imagination.

It was clear that Kolis liked to dress his favorites for his viewing pleasure, treating them as one would dolls.

Highly sexualized toys.

Grossed out on so many levels, I retrieved my newly fashioned dagger and sat on the floor.

And waited.

Part of me knew how foolhardy it was. I had no real plan beyond finding Ash and escaping, but anything was better than sitting in the cage and waiting for Kolis to return.

Waiting for him to move beyond looking and touching while only the gods knew what was happening to Ash.

I didn't have to wait long.

Footsteps sounded outside the chamber. Quickly, I lay on my side with my back to the doors. I didn't like it, but it was the only way to keep the glass dagger hidden beneath my other arm while also allowing me to react quickly with it.

My heart beat fast as I heard the doors open and then the soft click of them closing again. I lay completely still, my grip tight on the glass. I didn't feel the stir of embers that alerted me when a Primal was near. So, it was either a guard or possibly a Revenant. If it was the latter, they wouldn't stay dead for long.

The length of my entire back tingled with awareness as the silence stretched. I thought whoever was in the room had moved closer because the faint, sweet-but-stale scent increased, but I couldn't be sure. Seconds ticked by but I held myself still, half-afraid I'd have to sneeze or—

"Seraphena."

Fuck.

Recognizing the voice belonging to the Revenant, Callum, I closed my eyes. I would have to do some serious damage to keep him down for any length of time if a dagger thrown by Attes and blasts of eather hadn't incapacitated him for long.

And why *had* Attes done that? Simply because Callum annoyed him? Or because the Revenant had continued to push for Kolis to take the embers while Attes obviously didn't want that?

Come to think of it, why was Attes so willing to believe that I spoke the truth about Sotoria?

The answer couldn't be as simple as the Primal God of War and Accord not wanting Kolis to rise to such power because that made no sense. Not when Attes had brought me to Kolis.

But none of that mattered at the moment. I needed to focus.

"Wake up." He sounded closer, and impatience crept into his tone when I didn't respond. "*Seraphena.*"

Picturing all the ways I planned to use the broken glass on him, I remained quiet and still. I needed him to come into the cage.

A moment passed.

Then another.

"Godsdamn it," he muttered. "How can anyone be such a deep sleeper?"

Why would he think I was asleep on the floor when there was a bed right beside me?

The clink of a lock turning was like a siren's song to my ears. I forced my aching jaw to loosen and my breathing to slow despite my wildly beating heart.

Callum was in the cage now, but the bastard was quiet. I didn't even hear his approach until I felt the tip of a foot nudge my leg.

"Shit," he grumbled, sounding as if he'd knelt behind me. "If you choked on your tongue or something..." His icy hand came down on my arm.

My heart slowed as honed instinct took over. He called my name again, rolling me onto my back.

I reacted without hesitation.

Eyes opening, I shot up. Gripping the front of his white tunic, I swung my arm around and nailed the fucker right in the throat.

A flicker of surprise rippled across his painted features, widening his pale eyes. His lips moved, but the only sound that came out was a gurgle.

Blood trickled from his mouth as I tore the glass free. He smacked a hand over his throat and stumbled back.

I didn't let him get far.

Aiming low, I kicked him, taking his legs out from under him. He hit the floor with a nice thud, blood seeping between his fingers and running down his arm and chest—dull, red blood that smelled of stale lilacs.

Knowing he'd probably recover quickly, I moved onto my knees and straddled him, lifting the broken glass above my head.

He reached for my arm, his movements slow and weak as I drove the glass down into his throat. Blood spurted, splattering the front of my gown, the length of my hair, and my cheeks. His body jerked, his blood-soaked fingers sliding off my skin. I slammed the glass down once more, grunting when it hit the floor beneath him. What remained of his neck were a few raw, bright pink tendons.

My lip curled in disgust as I rocked back. Callum was dead. For now. I knew it wouldn't last, so I figured the more injuries he had to heal, the better it would be for me.

Through the opening in his shirt, I saw no scar left behind from when Attes had thrown the dagger at him. But there hadn't been any signs on the Revenant called Dyses, either, and Ash had torn his heart free.

With both hands, I drove the glass through Callum's chest. Flesh tore, and cartilage gave way. The glass sank deep, slicing through muscle. I hit his heart and gave the dagger a nice twist with a savage smile. Then I got him in the groin.

Just because.

Wiping the blood from my face with the back of my hand, I

searched his pockets, finding a single golden key. I rose and stepped over the Revenant. Not knowing how long I had before Callum resurrected, I wasted no time. Blood dripped from the broken glass as I hurried from the cage.

Outside, I gripped the bars of the door. I hissed, fiery pain erupting across my hand when I pushed the door shut. Then, quickly, I shoved the key into the lock, turning it.

"Fucker." Sparing one last glance at Callum, I started to turn but then stopped, looking down at the key in my hand.

I moved to the side, in front of the bed, and carefully extended my arm through the bars. I flung the key into the cage, watching it slide deep beneath the bed.

"Just in case," I told myself as I spun. If I ended up back in the cage, I'd at least have a key.

The shadowstone was cold beneath my feet as I crossed the chamber. My mind quieted when I neared the doors. It was almost like donning the veil of nothingness because I felt nothing. No fear for my life. No fear of failure. That had been trained out of me, but unlike the times my mother had sent me to deliver her *messages*, I didn't feel like a monster.

I felt like vengeance and wrath come to life.

The embers in my chest hummed. Cleaning my hand on my gown, I curled my fingers around the gilded door handle. I doubted these were unguarded.

Opening it, I kept myself hidden and pressed against the wall. A second later, I saw that I'd been right. Through the crack between the door and wall, I saw a guard's white and gold armor.

I waited, knowing it was likely a god, and there could be more. There should be, but only the one entered.

One?

Kolis only had one guard stationed outside the chamber. Seriously?

I was kind of offended.

The moment the guard caught sight of the mess in the cage, he halted. "What the—?" He cursed, gripping the edge of the door and moving to close it.

I struck, pushing off the wall. Gripping the back straps of his chest armor, I thrust the glass into the base of the guard's skull as I leapt, driving my knee into the center of his back.

The god grunted, staggering forward under my weight and the unexpected blow. He went down on one knee, his hand reaching for the hilt of the short sword at his waist.

"I don't think so," I snarled, wrenching the god's head sharply to the side. The crack of bone was sickening yet satisfying.

I didn't think a broken neck would keep a god down for long, but shadowstone? That would. Leaving the fractured glass cock embedded in the back of the god's skull, I reached for the sword—

The air charged around me as I unsheathed it. I could feel it dancing across my skin when the god straightened his neck. The cracking of bone turned my stomach as he planted his palm on the floor. Bluish-red blood darkened his brown hair.

"You fucking bitch," he spat. "What in the fuck is in the back of my head?"

"A cock." I lifted the sword.

"What?" The god froze.

"A glass cock," I said with a smile, driving the blade down.

The shadowstone cut just below the bulge of glass protruding from the base of his skull, silencing whatever the god was about to say. The blade cleaved through bone and tissue with little resistance, ending the rapidly building power.

Stepping back, I ignored the warm pulse of the embers—the urge to undo what I'd done. To restore life, not take it.

But that wasn't going to happen.

Sword in hand, I turned to the door, finding a sunlight-filled hall—a breezeway of sorts. Closing the door behind me, my gaze darted to the leafy palms beyond the rounded archways. Ahead was another door, and to my left, a solid wall made of gold and marble. Fine cracks had formed webs all along the surface.

I didn't want to go farther inside if this was Cor Palace. But what if Ash was being held somewhere in there? Kolis had ordered Attes to take him to the cells. The House of Haides in the Shadowlands had cells beneath the sprawling structure. So did Wayfair Castle, my home in the mortal realm.

"Shit."

I probably should've attempted to question the guard first. Then again, that wouldn't have been wise. It would've only given the god time to use eather, and that was something I couldn't fight.

I had a choice to make, and I had to decide quickly. Go into the palm trees and see where that led, or travel farther into the palace.

Ash would not be in the palms.

Grip firming on the sword's hilt, I stalked forward. A warm breeze wafted through the opening, sending several pale curls speckled with blood across my face. I reached the door at the end of the hall and yanked it open.

It was a chamber—a bedchamber—darkened by drawn, heavy curtains. The smell of stale lilacs was strong here, and I had a sinking suspicion this was Kolis's room.

Situated against one wall was a large, unmade bed. Clothing lay strewn across the floor. White pants. Tunics. Bowls of fruit sat on a dining table. Crystal decanters were everywhere: on the nightstand, the table, and the end tables by a large sofa, some half full of amber-hued liquid, others empty.

Did Kolis overindulge to help him forget the atrocities he committed? I snorted. That would mean he actually felt bad about what he did, and from what I'd seen and knew, I didn't think that was the case.

I headed for the double, gold-plated doors and pushed one side open.

A wider, absurdly long hall greeted me, windows and alcoves lining one side and doors on the other. Either luck or the Fates were on my side today because the hall was empty, and no hot, breathy sounds came from the alcoves as they had when Ash and I had first come to Dalos.

I went forward, trying each door as I passed. Some were locked. Those that weren't were either completely empty spaces or contained only narrow beds, barely more than cots. Some rooms held four to five of them.

I didn't want to even think about what those chambers and beds were for.

I kept going, searching for any door that may lead to a stairwell, all the while afraid that it would be like the House of Haides, where the entrance to the underground level was near the study and close to the throne room.

Well aware that Callum could wake at any moment, I picked up my pace, trying door after door until I found one that opened into a narrower corridor. I entered, scanning the numerous wider openings framed by gold-plated columns on both sides of the hall. My skin tingled as I picked up on the whispering sound of cloth.

My steps slowed when I neared an opening to my left. I peered around one of the columns and felt the air leave my lungs in an unsteady rush.

I had to be right about being in Cor Palace.

Because all I saw was white.

White robes and veils that covered nearly every inch of those inside the sunny, airy space. There had to be dozens of them. They stood by windows, sat on thick, ivory-and-gold-tasseled cushions. If any of them spoke, they did so quietly.

They were the Chosen, brought to Iliseeum during the Rite to serve the Primals and their gods. Because they were the third sons and daughters, they had more essence of the gods in their blood than their siblings did, which allowed them to be Ascended into godhood—a tradition revered in the mortal realm and once honored in Iliseeum for the purpose it served. It replenished the realm of gods with those who remembered what it was like to be mortal.

But none of them Ascended. Not since Eythos ruled.

Now, the Chosen were ushered into a waking nightmare.

Gemma, one of the Chosen Ash had saved, said that many of them went missing. Most didn't return, but those who did? They didn't come back the same. They became something cold and starved, moving only in dark spaces. Holland had called them Craven, what I believed the poor seamstress Andreia had been turned into.

Something clicked into place as I watched them lift their veils, only enough to drink from crystal chalices. Could the Revenants have been Chosen at one time also?

I looked ahead, swallowing. The hall curved and turned as if it had been built while following a serpent. Would the Chosen help me? Could they be of any help? Probably not. The best thing for me to do would be to get past this chamber without being seen. But…

But these were Chosen.

Innocent mortals who were likely being abused. Or worse. And, gods, I thought about Andreia again. There *was* worse, and I could walk right—

A scream made my heart leap in my chest. My head cut to the chamber. A Chosen stood at the opening, gloved hands lifted to their veiled head.

"It's okay." I stepped forward. "I'm not going to hurt you."

More screams tore through the air as another Chosen spotted me. They rushed forward, grasping the one who stood near the opening and hauling them back from me. Not that I blamed them.

I looked quite…murderous, covered in blood and carrying a sword.

A door within the chamber swung open, and a silver-haired man shuffled out, clothed in gold robes. "What in all that is holy is going—?" Gray brows shot up, causing deeper creases in his skin as he got an eyeful of me. "My gods," he uttered.

"I'm not a threat," I began. "I'm—"

"Guards!" the man shouted, his robes swishing as he twisted around to the door he'd come out of. "Guards!"

"Damn it," I gasped.

Left with no choice, I took off running as fast as I could. My heart pounded in rhythm with my steps. I flew down the hall and then moved into another, the chambers on either side a blur. It was only then when it occurred to me that the guards weren't the only thing I needed to be worried about. The vicious, flesh-eating dakkais were pets in Dalos. Little too late to worry about that now.

Shouts erupted from behind me, but I kept running, darting into another hall, a different chamber—

I came to a complete stop. I couldn't process what I was seeing for a moment, even though I understood the soft, breathy moans and flashes of bare skin. It was all just so very unexpected.

People in all stages of undress were sprawled across the floor in groups of two, three...and, *wow*. My gaze danced over a woman riding a man, her heavy breasts swaying while another took her from behind, her hands and mouth full. She smiled around one cock as the man groaned...

Goodness, that took talent.

A man had another bent over the arm of a couch, his hips plunging while the other buried his head between a half-dressed woman's thighs. She had her mouth on another woman who reclined, legs spread. Some were on gold and sapphire silk-draped mattresses. Others on couches. Some merely watched the festivities, their hands pumping cocks or fingers delving deeply inside themselves.

Blinking, I shook my head. This wasn't the first time I'd seen something like this. After all, there were similar spaces back home at The Luxe, but these weren't mortals. Instead, the lust-laden eyes here glowed with eather. This was a chamber full of gods fucking. Fucking gods.

Slowly, I backed out and returned to the hall.

Without a single person seeming to notice me, I was running once more. Damn it. I didn't know where to go, and the place was a maze of halls and chambers. I skidded into yet another passageway, my breath coming out in shallow, short pants.

The area I'd entered was darker, with no windows to let any natural light in, and there was a strange smell in the air.

Metallic.

Bloody.

7

Unease snaked its way through me as I crept forward. Tapestries with gold brocade hung from walls and gently rippled, disturbed by some sort of breeze. I glanced up, spotting the spinning blades of fans along the ceiling.

I swallowed, pushing forward. Several chambers were empty, only full of shadows, but they… I squinted. They appeared damp. Wet. The rich scent of iron permeated the air.

There were sounds here, too, coming from candlelit spaces with shrouded archways.

Hungry, greedy noises.

I tightened my grip on the sword as I passed a marble statue of a man holding a shield in one hand, and a small child against his chest with the other.

Both were missing their heads.

Keep going, I told myself. *Just keep going.* There had to be a stairwell somewhere.

A shout exploded from within a shrouded chamber, one filled with pain and terror, not pleasure.

I stopped, turning to my right. A cry sounded, weaker and shorter. *Keep going.* My chest clenched as I glanced back to where I'd come from. I had no idea where the guards were, but the sounds, the greedy slurping…

Damn it.

Some days, I hated myself. Prowling toward the gauzy black curtain, this was one of them.

Shoving the barrier aside, I scanned the dimly lit space. There were no couches or chairs in here, just mantels full of lit, half-melted candles and a mattress on the floor—one with rust-hued stains.

And it was not bare.

A dark-haired woman was on top of a man, her face buried in his throat. She wore a shapeless white gown or robe, but I could still see her body writhing beneath the cloth. Under her, the man was half-dressed, his skin nearly as white as his shredded robes. His frantic, darting gaze collided with mine.

His lips peeled back over tightly clenched teeth and then moved, forming one word I didn't hear but felt to my very bones.

Help.

A different kind of instinct took hold as I rushed forward. The woman moaned deeply as the man beneath her jerked, his eyes squeezing shut so tightly the skin puckered at the corners. The woman was so caught up in what I figured was feeding that she was utterly unaware of me.

Reaching the side of the mattress, I grabbed a fistful of hair and yanked with all my strength.

I caught a glimpse of the jagged puncture wounds in the man's neck as I shoved the woman to the side.

Her head snapped in my direction, lips peeling back to reveal two bloody canines smaller than what I saw on the gods and Primals, but still sharp. She growled at me, and it once more reminded me of Andreia. This woman didn't have two fangs on the bottom row of her teeth, though, nor did she look…well, *as* dead as Andreia had.

My gaze flew to hers. Good gods, her eyes were pitch-black, so dark I couldn't see her pupils.

They weren't like a god's or a mortal's.

She moved quickly, getting into a crouched position, her knees jutting out from the sides of her gown.

I had a sick feeling that both of them were Chosen, but she was what Gemma had spoken of: the Chosen who went missing and returned hungry.

Because this bitch looked like she was *starving.*

Her head tilted to the side as she sniffed the air. "You smell…"

I frowned at the raspy, throaty voice.

"You smell of Revenant and god," she purred, moving fluidly, much like a pit viper. She moaned, and thick lashes fanned her cheeks. "And something else. Stronger."

"Thanks?" I murmured, keeping an eye on her as I moved closer to the man. He wasn't moving. "I think."

A soft hissing sound came from her before she pressed her hands to the waist of her gown. "I'm so hungry."

"Uh-huh." Keeping the sword level, I bent and touched the man's neck, feeling for a pulse. I found one. It was weak but there.

The woman angled her body toward me as she ran her palms up her chest. "You smell…"

"You already said that."

"Like life," she whispered, her lashes lifting. Pitch-black eyes faintly lit from within fixed on me.

"What the—?"

The woman leapt at me, full-on jumped like a large feline.

She was fast—faster than I expected—and crashed into me. The impact knocked the sword from my grasp. I stumbled back, tripping over the man's legs. I went down, my hands on the woman's shoulders. Hitting the stone floor was brutal, but the snapping fangs inches from my face were far more violent.

"Fuck," I gasped as I held her back, my arms trembling as she grasped my wrist.

"Let me have some," she cooed, her knees pressing into my hips. "Just a little bit. A taste. That's all. Please." She moaned, her hips rolling and grinding. "Please."

"What in the fuck?" I exclaimed. She was almost as strong as a god. "Get off me."

"I need it. I need more," she whined, her voice thickening. "I need—"

Pushing with everything in me, I thrust her to the side. I didn't stay on my back, realizing how damn fast she was. I popped to my feet and looked for the sword.

She flew at me, her movements frenzied and untrained, all arms and fangs. Was she biting the air? I shoved her back. If she were Chosen, I didn't want to hurt her. Maybe whatever had been done could be *un*done. I didn't know. "You need to calm down."

Not doing that at all, she launched herself at me once more. I dipped under her arms, coming up behind her. Twisting at the waist, I kicked out, planting my foot in her back. She careened forward, dropping to her knees. I turned, spotting the shadowstone sword lying on the mattress. Grabbing it, I spun. She ran at me at full speed. I stumbled as my arms bent—

The woman jerked, her head and legs falling forward, her back bowing. I looked down to see the sword's hilt flush with the white robes of the Chosen's midsection.

I looked up at the same time she did. Her lips parted on a soft exhale. My eyes locked with hers, and time seemed to slow as tiny cracks appeared in her cheeks. They spread much like the fissures in the walls had, traveling across her face and down her throat.

Her weight against the sword disappeared first, like she went hollow. Then her skin flaked off, turning to dust as it hit the air.

My mouth dropped open as she caved into herself, breaking and shattering until the sword I held pierced nothing but robes.

"What the fuck?" I repeated, frozen for a moment before shaking the blade clear of the robes and looking for some sign of the Chosen. A bone. Something.

There was nothing.

I swallowed, taking a step back. I hit the edge of the mattress and turned, looking down at the man. He was paler than before. His eyes were open, but they were glazed over and fixed. Glancing at the pile of empty robes, I knelt, touching his neck.

"Damn it." My chest squeezed. There was no pulse. I started to pull my hand back when movement caught my attention.

His fingers twitched. Then his arm. A ragged breath left me. I pressed more firmly on his neck, searching for a pulse and still finding none. "Shit." I looked at his arm. It was still.

Okay. I must have been seeing things.

I looked at all that remained of the woman: nothing but a pile of clothing. She hadn't been what Aios had once called a demis. That was when a mortal who was not a third son or daughter Ascended.

The heavy fall of footsteps echoed from outside in the hall, snapping my attention to the gauzy curtain. Several shapes rushed by.

One stopped.

A man with long, light-colored hair that fell down his back lifted his chin. He turned to the curtain of the room I was in.

Stepping over the Chosen, I lifted the sword.

"Found her," came an unfamiliar, gravelly voice.

Damn it.

Damn it.

Another appeared outside, his gold armor dull in the low light. The long-haired man thrust the curtain aside a heartbeat later, striding in.

I shot across the space. The man cocked his head, making no move to protect himself. That was fine. I leveled the edge of the blade to his throat.

"Move," I ordered.

Though his features were lost to the shadows, I could've sworn he smirked as he lifted his hands.

"Moving," he replied. "Your Highness."

Hearing the title was jarring. Somehow, amid all of this, I'd forgotten that a Consort held a status similar to a Primal.

"Back," I added, not having the time to wonder if this was a god or a Revenant. "Move back."

He did just that, exiting the chamber and entering the hall. "How far would you like me to move?"

Keeping the blade at his throat, I darted behind him. The man was freaking tall, several inches taller than me, but I grabbed hold of his arm as I forced him toward the guard.

"I want you two to listen closely because I won't repeat myself," I said, pressing the tip of the blade against his throat. "If either of you makes even one move I don't like, I will cut off his head. And I'm fast. You won't be able to stop me."

"How fast are you?" he asked, far too casually for someone who had a blade to his throat. "I'm thinking you have to be pretty fast to have made it this far."

My heart lurched and sped up. His skin? It was warm, almost feverish, and it felt either scarred or...ridged. The man turned his head to the side.

Several blond waves fell back, revealing his cheek. "But how strong are you?" he continued, and I looked up. "Because you're going to have to be really strong, Your Highness."

My stomach tumbled as I saw the ridges along his jaw and cheek. They formed a pattern of scales. Then I saw one ruby-red eye.

A draken.

I was holding a blade to a draken's throat.

Two thoughts occurred simultaneously: Had this draken wanted to bond with Kolis? And could a shadowstone blade kill a draken? I was about to find out, so I really hoped this draken was happy to serve Kolis and not doing so because he had no choice.

"Don't," the guard warned.

I jerked my arm back—

The draken turned, grasping my wrist and twisting. Pain shot up my arm, but I held on to the sword. It was my only weapon. My only—

He increased the pressure on my wrist, digging into the tendons there. I gasped as my hand spasmed open. The sword clanged off the floor as I kicked out, slamming my foot into his chest.

The draken didn't even budge.

"That's not very nice," he said, smirking. "But if it makes you feel good, please, by all means, continue."

"Fuck you!" I spat, angling my body away. I swung with my other arm, catching him in the chin as a thud came from somewhere behind me. I had no idea what it was, and I didn't have time to find out.

"Ouch," he grunted. A deep laugh came from him. The blow likely caused me more pain than it did him. "That was…cute."

Cute?

Cute?

Fury erupted from deep within me, mingling with the rising panic and stoking the embers. This was my only chance. If I didn't make it out now, I likely never would, and I *had* to. I must. The back of my skull tingled as the embers of Primal essence hummed.

They vibrated deep in my chest, reminding me that the sword hadn't been my only weapon. I had *them*.

And they were mine.

From deep within me, an ancient power stirred and stretched. Bright and hot, the eather hit my veins, filling me.

The draken's head tilted, his nostrils flaring. Shock widened his eyes as his grip on my wrist loosened.

Eather surged, and I didn't attempt to pull it back. I latched on to the power—*my* power. I *summoned* it, thrusting out both arms. Silvery sparks erupted from my fingers, and I slammed my hands into the draken's chest.

His feet left the floor, and he flew backward, hitting the wall across the hall with enough force to crack the stone. Then he fell onto his side, limp.

A strangled laugh left me. Holy shit, I'd just knocked out a *draken*. There was no time to be awed by my awesome strength, though. I spun toward the brown-haired guard.

Eather pulsed behind his pupils. "Shit."

I threw my hand out. Power erupted from my palm, and something happened. The crackling and spitting Primal essence took shape in my hand, stretching and lengthening, forming a *thunderbolt*.

My eyes widened.

"Good Fates," rasped the guard, stumbling back.

A low rumbling growl came, jerking my head to the side. The draken pushed off the floor, his skin thickening into scales and darkening to a crimson shade. His jaw opened, and his ruby eyes flashed a bright, shiny sapphire as smoke spilled from his nostrils.

I reacted out of an old instinct, one born of the Primal power I wielded. My arm cocked back as I prepared to throw the thunderbolt—

What sounded like the moan of the wind echoed from within the chamber I'd come out of. A low, howling noise that rose into a shrill cry, causing my skin to pimple. I looked over my shoulder.

Something bolted out through the gauzy shroud, crashing into me. Concentration broken, the thunderbolt collapsed into a shower of harmless sparks as I fell backward.

Grasping it by the shoulders, I hit the floor hard. Air punched from my lungs as the thing went wild, shrieking and snapping. But it wasn't a *thing*.

Even in my confusion, I knew it was the man who had been dead only moments before.

And he still looked dead.

His skin had taken on a ghastly gray pallor, and dark shadows had blossomed beneath his eyes—eyes that now burned coal-red. Pale, grayish-blue lips peeled back, revealing four long canines that hadn't been there before, two on the upper row and two on the bottom.

Just like the fangs that had appeared on the seamstress, Andreia.

"What the fuck?" I gasped, shoving him off.

I scrambled away, my heart thumping as he landed on his side. His body twitched, arms jerking uncontrollably, and head whipping toward me. The sound he made then was like the shrieks of a hundred souls sentenced to the Abyss, sending a chill down my spine. He launched to his feet, coming right for me like no one else was around.

I stumbled to my feet, bracing myself—

A shadowstone sword swept forward, catching him at the neck. His scream ended abruptly as the sword cleaved through, severing the head.

Stunned, I watched the body crumble, unable to process how the Chosen had gone from what I'd seen in the chamber to *this*.

"Fucking Craven," the guard muttered, and my gaze snapped to him. A lock of brown hair fell over his forehead as he nudged the head with his foot. "Abominations."

I'd been right.

What Andreia—what *this Chosen*—had become was a Craven. And the woman who'd bitten him had been something else.

"*Your Highness*," came a raspy whisper from behind me.

My shoulders tensed. How had I forgotten about the draken? My escape plan? The Craven and whatever the woman was fell to the wayside. I searched for the embers and found them. They throbbed to life, a little weaker than before but still there. I stepped forward and twisted, calling the essence. Heat hit my veins as my eyes locked with ones that flickered between crimson and sapphire—

A hand landed on the nape of my neck, warm fingers digging into the side of my throat. I tried to lift my arms and step away from the sudden pressure, but my muscles went rigid, and a dizzying whirlpool of darkness rose, pulling me into the vast nothingness without mercy.

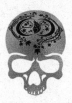

I dreamt of my lake and the cool, dark waters gliding over my skin as I swam under the bright stars.

Dreaming of it didn't surprise me. This place was a source of good memories, and I was relieved that my mind had decided to bring me here instead of someplace terrible, but I couldn't exactly remember what had happened before this. I had been somewhere in Cor Palace, hadn't I? I wasn't sure. Everything existed just out of my reach, clouded in mist. And besides, this…

I knew nothing bad could reach, scare, or disturb me here. Because I wasn't alone.

A wolf sat on the bank of my lake, one more silver than white. He watched.

And I knew I was safe.

8

When I opened my eyes, all I saw were bars above me and the fragmented glitter of light in the center of the cage's ceiling. And I felt the softness of a blanket beneath me.

My brows knitted in confusion. How did I get back here? I'd been in a dark hall, with—

"You're awake. Finally."

The warm, summery voice sent a rush of adrenaline through me. I shot upright and to the side, losing my balance on the narrow divan. I started sliding off the edge.

Kolis caught me by the shoulder, his hand flat against my bare skin. "Careful."

I jerked away from his touch, pressing into the back of the divan as I reached down beside me, my fingers scraping off nothing but the thick fur of the blanket.

Kolis knelt before me, his head tilted. "What, pray tell, were you grabbing for?"

My dagger.

Or the broken glass cock.

I'd been reaching for a weapon out of instinct and honed reflex. "I...I don't know."

"Hmm." A single brow lifted.

Stomach shifting unsteadily, I eyed him from behind several strands of hair that had fallen across my face—pale hair now stained crimson.

Fuck.

The attempted escape, what I'd seen in the darkened part of the palace, and my subsequent failure came rushing back. My gaze shot to the floor behind Kolis. The shiny tile was clear of blood and gore. I looked toward the chamber beyond—

"If you're looking for the guard you senselessly murdered with an object typically designed to bring pleasure—though I must admit that was somewhat impressive," Kolis observed. "You will not find him."

I stiffened, and the lingering cobwebs of sleep cleared. I focused on him. He was dressed much like before, wearing nothing more than the gold band around his biceps and loose linen pants.

"He has been removed," the false King continued. "And the chamber was cleaned."

Breaths coming in short, quick pants, I refocused on Kolis. "Senselessly murdered?" I winced at the hoarseness in my voice.

"What else would you call it?"

"Self-defense," I snapped.

His cool stare flickered over my face. "Did he attack you?"

"No—"

"Did Callum strike you?"

"No, but—"

"Then how is what you did considered self-defense?" he countered.

My lips parted in disbelief. Was he seriously asking that question? "You are keeping me prisoner. I do not need to be attacked to feel threatened."

"You're not a prisoner." His head straightened, sending strands of golden hair falling against his shoulder. "You're a guest."

"A guest?" I whispered.

"A troublesome one," he amended in that same flat, arid tone.

All I could do was stare at Kolis. Part of me wondered if I was still sleeping or if the guard who'd rendered me unconscious had caused some sort of damage to my mind. There had to be a reason Kolis sincerely appeared to believe what he said. Unless he was simply insane.

Which was likely.

But at least he wasn't referring to Cor Palace as my home anymore.

"You slept deeply," Kolis stated after a moment. "As if you were at peace."

I *was* at peace. I'd dreamt of my lake and the silver wolf—wait.

"How…?" I cleared my throat. "How long have you been watching me?"

"Long enough," he answered.

Disgust churned through me. "Do you have any idea how extraordinarily disturbing it is to know that you were watching me sleep?"

Warm light glanced off an arched cheek as his head tilted. "It bothers you?"

"Of fucking course it does," I snapped.

"Your language." His lips thinned. "It is far more uncivilized than I remember."

"And watching someone as they sleep is *civilized*?" I shot back.

A shadow seemed to fall over the false King, darkening the very air around him. His expression hardened, his jaw clenched, and a cold, steely look settled in his eyes.

Kolis shot forward, slamming his hands on the divan beside my legs, making me jump. He smirked as he leaned in, and boy did the Primal know how to give a cruel smile. It was a cold, brutal twist of such a lovely mouth and face. I forced myself to be still as he invaded my space, fighting the desire to kick his head back.

Kolis halted, inhaling deeply.

A prickly sensation rushed across my skin. "Are you…are you *smelling* me?"

"You smell of…" His nose brushed my temple, sending a chill of revulsion through me. He inhaled again, and my pulse raced. "You smell of damp soil."

Did I? All I could pick up was the stale-sweet lilac stench. My fingers curled into the cushion. But if he really smelled damp soil, it didn't make any sense. That was what my lake smelled like, and I hadn't gone past the breezeway.

Seconds ticked by as Kolis studied me with an unsettling, unblinking stare. Still, by the time he blinked, my fingers ached from how tightly I gripped the edge of the divan.

"I want to apologize to you," he said in a strained sort of way as his stare moved to my mouth and jaw. "For striking you. I am truly sorry. I did not intend to do that."

His apology lingered in the silence like a noxious, choking cloud as I eyed him. He sounded genuine, but so had my stepbrother Tavius on the rare occasions his father called him to the carpet on some inexcusable, wretched act he'd committed. So had the parents of the beaten children the Ladies of Mercy rescued. I'd seen enough abuse to know there were two types of those who hurt others: ones who felt remorse for their actions, and those who simply did not. I thought I knew which category Kolis fell into, but in the end, it rarely mattered if the apology and remorse were genuine or not because nothing justified the violence, and the abuser almost never changed.

Kolis could take his apology and choke on it, but I had enough common sense to keep that to myself. At least for the moment.

Kolis stayed where he was for several more seconds, then rose to his towering height. A ragged breath left me as a little of the painful tension in my legs and back eased.

"You're even more filthy than last we spoke," he stated. "When Callum returns, you will do as he requests, and you will not attempt to harm him."

Slowly, I lifted my head and looked up, my eyes moving over his large hands and arms, the golden band, and—my gaze darted back to it. I frowned. The cuff had looked white for a moment.

"Are you listening to me?" he snapped.

Blinking, I refocused on him and nodded.

"Then do you understand?"

"That's…that's it?" I placed my feet on the floor. "I tried to escape, and that is all you have to say?"

A faint, bemused smile appeared. "Should I say more? Should I be angry with you?"

"Uh, I would assume so."

"I am displeased, *so'lis*," he said, causing a shudder from within. "But I expected nothing less from you."

"Is that so?" I murmured, not trusting his seemingly ambivalent response.

"You've tried to escape me many times before." His stare sharpened on me. "That is, if you are who you claim to be."

Unease blossomed as I swallowed dryly. Kolis believing that Sotoria and I were one and the same was the only thing keeping me alive. "I…I don't remember any of that," I admitted, knowing that telling the truth whenever possible made the lies more believable.

"Is that so?" he parroted what I'd said.

I nodded.

"Then you don't remember what happens when you displease me," he said.

The back of my neck tightened as I held his stare. "No, but I'm sure I can guess."

Kolis laughed softly. "No, you cannot."

Ice hit my chest, and I shivered.

"I hope you do not rediscover that knowledge," he added, his stare moving over me.

"I don't need to rediscover it to know," I bit out. "I know what happens to those who fall out of favor with you. To others who've been your *guests*."

I saw small twitches in his jaw muscles and above his eyes as he stared down at me. "You speak of others I not only provided for, lavishing them with the finest silks and the richest wines and foods, but also protected without ever expecting a single thing from them other than companionship?"

I choked on a rage-filled breath. Did he really think keeping someone in a cage could ever be considered anything but keeping them a prisoner? "Were you protecting them once you grew tired of them and tossed them aside, allowing anyone to do anything to them? To assault and abuse them. To kill—"

Kolis snapped forward, bringing his face to within inches of mine. It took everything in me not to react. "You have no idea what you're talking about." His flesh began to thin as his chest rose with a deep breath. He slowly straightened. "But I know who has been talking to you. Aios."

I said nothing as I held his stare.

"Did she tell you why I grew tired of them? Why they were tossed aside? I'm sure she didn't. Each and every one of them was ungrateful. No matter what I gave them. No matter what I did. They were either morose or conniving, believing their lives were better without what I could provide." His chin lifted. "All I did was allow them to discover how false that belief was."

I couldn't believe what I was hearing—justification for not only kidnapping but also his role in their demise. And his tone told me he truly believed he'd done nothing wrong.

Kolis eyed me. "I can sense it."

"What?" I asked, wondering if my rage was so palpable it had forced him to develop an ability similar to Ash's.

"The essence in you." Shimmery gold pressed against the flesh of his throat. "The embers. They are even more powerful than before." His chin lowered. "That shouldn't be possible. You are, after all, mortal. Yet you not only harnessed it to strike a draken, but you also invoked compulsion on not one but *two* Primals."

"And?"

"And?" Kolis repeated with a soft laugh. "Only the Primal of Life can wield compulsion against another Primal."

My heart tripped. "I'm not the Primal of Life. Obviously."

"Yes, obviously," Kolis repeated. "Callum will be returning soon. Do not displease me. I would hate for there to be a need to station a dakkai in this chamber," he said, and my stomach hollowed at the thought. "Their temperament and stench don't make them good companions, *so'lis.*"

"What does that mean?" I asked, feeling palpable rage that wasn't mine erasing any concern regarding the dakkai. "*So'lis?*"

Kolis was motionless for several moments, then he smiled, and my body turned cold.

It was a beautiful smile.

He was beautiful.

But there was something wrong with that smile. It was...practiced, as if he'd studied many types to perfect one, but the emotion behind it wasn't there.

It wasn't anywhere in his perfect features.

"*So'lis* is the language of the Ancients and Primals," he said, the Ancients being the first Primals, the ones who prophesied a being that would wield the supreme power of both life and death. "It means one thing."

If that were true, it would be a first.

"And I'm sure you've noticed that it is similar to my name."

I had.

"*Ko'* in the old language can be translated to the word *our*. *Lis* is *soul*," he explained as my muscles began to lock up. "Ko'lis would translate to *our soul*. That is what my name symbolizes."

"How sweet," I remarked. "What does *So'* translate to?"

The gold slowed in his eyes. "*My*."

My chest hollowed.

My soul.

I paced the length of the cage, hands fisted at my sides as I waited for Callum's return. I'd been doing that since Kolis left.

My thoughts kept switching from what I'd seen in the darkened part of the palace to the future. I should've asked him about the Chosen I'd seen. It was important for Ash to know what Kolis was doing here.

Except how in the realm would I get that information to Ash?

I'd tried to kill Kolis.

And failed.

I'd tried to escape.

And failed again.

That left me with the reality of the situation. The only option.

That was always the only option. That annoying voice that sounded like mine had returned. Great.

My fists tightened as I picked up my pace, the stained gown snapping at my ankles. But I couldn't go through with it. I'd already decided that much. Just as I'd decided that I didn't care about the greater good. I wouldn't be a person who sacrificed everything.

But I *was* that person.

And I *did* care.

I couldn't fool myself into believing otherwise, no matter how desperate I was. If I weren't that kind of person, I wouldn't have stopped to aid the Chosen. I might not have escaped, but I would've made it farther.

What Holland had told me once resurfaced. It had been something he'd said in the years after Ash rejected me as his Consort. I couldn't remember exactly what had caused Holland to say what he did. I'd likely been bitching about not wanting to do something—that was common at the time.

"I know you feel like you've been given no choices in life," he'd said in that gentle way of his when he told me something he knew I didn't want to hear. *"But every day, there is a choice to keep going, to face the future head-on or not. Every day, there is a choice to be honest with yourself or to lie. One will be the hardest thing you've ever done, and the other the easiest, but there is always the opportunity for choice if you don't take the easiest path."*

He'd said that when he was Sir Holland, a Royal Knight trained to prepare me to complete my duty and defend myself. One who often liked to spout what I'd fondly considered nonsensical, philosophical bullshit. But he'd never been just Sir Holland. He hadn't even been mortal. He was an Arae. A Fate. His philosophical ramblings were never bullshit.

They were still mostly nonsensical, though.

However, I did get what he'd been saying. Maybe. But I *felt* what he'd meant…like there was no choice. I'd lived in that state since I could remember, and it was like that now.

But he was right.

There were many choices. To do nothing and let fate determine what happened to you. Or to face reality and make it hard for the Fates to dictate your path. There was also the choice to keep going. Once before, I hadn't made that choice. Either the Fates, luck, or possibly even the embers had prevented that decision from becoming my last, but it had been a choice. One I regretted to this day because it had been the wrong one.

And I knew if I chose to say fuck the greater good and attempt another reckless escape, it would be another choice I regretted for however long I had left. Trying to convince myself otherwise was foolish, but so was believing I had complete autonomy. That I somehow played an active role in the choices left to me. That was bullshit. The truth was that none of this was right or fair.

But the fact that this—all of this—was so much bigger and more important than me was also true.

Kolis had to be stopped.

Choosing to fight my way out of here meant choosing myself, and that would likely end in me dying before my Ascension. Kolis seemed to take my escape attempt and *murder* in stride, but he had less control over his anger than I did on a really bad day. And if that happened, all would be lost. Choosing myself wouldn't help gain Ash his freedom, and that…gods, that was more important to me than even fulfilling my duty.

Because I loved him. I was *in* love with him. And right or wrong, I would do anything for him.

I stopped, my eyes closing.

Shaking my head, I opened them again. How was I going to do this? Bitter sorrow rose, stirring the embers. They thrummed.

I knew how.

Folding my arms across my waist, I began pacing once more, giving my mind time to calm—well, to get as calm as my head would ever be. More like my mind was manageable and clear enough that I could face the reality of the situation and approach all of it logically, which wasn't exactly a skill of mine, but I knew there were two possible outcomes from here.

Either I found another more reasonable and thought-out plan to escape, one that actually included a strategy, and I managed to reach Ash so he could take the embers.

Or I was unable to escape and killed Kolis.

Both options required the same thing, and gods, didn't knowing that just make me want to vomit? It fucking hurt somewhere deep, felt like a dagger repeatedly plunging into my chest. But I couldn't let myself dwell on it. Instead, I breathed through it.

I had to.

Which meant I would have to exploit Kolis's love for Sotoria, and I knew what that would involve. The only difference now was that I didn't have to seduce Kolis into falling in love with me. That part was already done thanks to Sotoria's soul—as long as he remained convinced I was her.

I would only have to earn enough of Kolis's trust to gain some level of freedom to make my escape.

"Only." I laughed hoarsely.

Successfully escaping so Ash could take the embers was the option I was shooting for. It was the only way the Rot could be stopped from destroying Lasania, my home, and eventually, the entire mortal realm.

And even if the kingdom didn't know I existed, they still mattered. Ezra and her Consort, Lady Marisol—and every other living person— were worth any and all sacrifices I may have to make. Even my mother was.

A short, weak laugh left me. Okay, maybe she wasn't exactly worth it, but the mortal realm was, and the people there had no idea their doom approached.

And if I couldn't gain freedom from this cage? Then I would have to kill Kolis.

I needed to do better than what I'd managed on the beach near Hygeia.

Common sense told me that escaping was the least likely outcome, leaving me with killing Kolis. That wouldn't fix everything. It wouldn't prevent the catastrophic damage that would hit both realms or end the Rot, but it would stop him from hurting those who survived. It would end his tyrannical rule where he could force dozens of innocents to sacrifice themselves.

But maybe killing Kolis would slow the Rot. Another dry laugh left me. I knew better. The Rot had begun with my birth, which signaled the eventual death of the embers. If Ash didn't Ascend to become the Primal of Life, mortals were, well…fucked. But it may give Ash and the others time to figure out what, if anything, could be done regarding the Rot.

There had to be something. Because, eventually, it would spread from the Shadowlands to all of Iliseeum.

Until then, killing Kolis protected Ash and the people of the Shadowlands—Aios, Bele, Reaver, little Jadis, her father, Nektas, Saion, Rhahar, and so many others, including those in the city of Lethe. Even Rhain, who I still wasn't sure liked me.

They mattered.

They all deserved a life worth living. And Ash? Gods, he deserved to live without the threat of Kolis's boot on his neck, where his innate kindness was rewarded instead of punished. A life that hadn't made him fear falling in love so strongly that he'd had another Primal remove his ability to do so.

But there was something I had to accomplish as soon as possible.

I needed to gain Ash's freedom.

He could not remain imprisoned. It wasn't as if him being kept in a cell made him easier to reach. That required me escaping one cage to enter another—likely a well-guarded one. But even if it were easier, I couldn't bear the thought of him being held captive, subject to whatever cruelty Kolis devised.

Ash needed to be far away from the false King. He needed to be home with his people, especially if Kolis was serious about a war starting.

And I knew how to accomplish all of that.

My hand fell to my side as my heart kicked sharply. It wasn't the knowledge that I might fail in an escape attempt or that I needed something to actually kill Kolis with that made me feel like vomiting. It was the fact that I knew what I had to do.

I needed to become that blank canvas. The empty vessel. No emotion. No personal needs or wants. Only skin-deep. It was the only way.

My chest clenched, and my head fell back. I stared at the gold bars above me.

Resolve sank in, entrenching itself as I opened my eyes. Slowing my breath once more, I stopped again. "I'm sorry," I whispered to myself and Sotoria.

There was no answer.

Not from her or my annoying inner voice. I looked down where my toes peeked past the edge of the gown.

Wait.

My gaze lifted to the bed. The *key*. Gods, I'd nearly forgotten all about it.

Crossing the short distance, I lowered myself to the floor and peered under the bed. Relief swelled as I spied it. They hadn't seen it yet.

I wasn't sure how useful it would be now, but I couldn't leave it there.

Glancing at the closed doors of the outer chamber, I went down on my belly and scooted as far as I could. I stretched out my arm, trying not to think about the dreams I'd had as a child of monsters beneath my bed. My fingers brushed the cool metal. I grabbed it and quickly rose, looking around the cage. Where could I hide it?

The chests couldn't be that secure. Nothing in this cage was secure, except...

I thought of the one place very few men traversed.

Smirking, I hurried into the bathing area and knelt at the shelf. There were baskets on the bottom. I opened one lid, finding the feminine cloths used to protect the clothing during menstruation.

Speaking of menstruation, when was my last? Gods, I was always terrible at keeping track of them. I knew I'd had one...last month? Though I wasn't quite sure how long I'd been here. The sky beyond the windows near the ceiling was light, but that told me nothing since I knew the sun could shine much longer in Dalos than elsewhere. I could've been out for a day, but based on the *finally* Kolis had tacked on when I woke, it could've been longer. So, who knew?

It didn't matter.

It wasn't like I was having sex with anyone that could get me pregnant. Or sex at all.

I unwound the slim bundle of cloth and slipped the key inside. Once I was sure it was hidden, I rose and caught my reflection in the mirror.

"Gods." I winced.

Blood spotted my cheeks and forehead. The bruise on my swollen jaw was a lovely shade of purple edged in red. The split in my lower lip was raw. I could see the bruises, the imprint of fingers on my throat, even from where I stood. I looked over my shoulder at the arms of the white chair and felt sick.

It could've been worse, I reminded myself. Most didn't walk away from taking a hit from a Primal. I did. It wasn't anything to be proud of. It was just something to remember.

This had been nothing compared to the lashes Tavius had delivered. I was sure it was nothing compared to what Sotoria faced.

I thought of what Kolis had shared, and I couldn't help but wonder if Sotoria meant something like his name did.

Our soul.

Damn. I bet his parents would be so very proud. I snorted as I stared at my reflection.

Hers would translate into my...something. That was if *toria* actually meant anything.

So'lis.

My soul.

A shudder went through me. Gods, he'd called her his soul? No wonder that enraged her—

The doors to the chamber opened without warning, and my stomach plummeted.

I was no longer alone.

9

Warm, sweet-but-stale air seeped into the cage as I darted out from behind the privacy screen.

Callum stood before the throne, having entered the chamber so silently it was nearly as eerie as the fact that I'd seen him die at least four times now and last saw him with his head hanging on by only a few tendons.

The damn painted mask was in place, stretching from his forehead to the edges of his jaw. One quick look showed what I already knew. There was no evidence of the injuries I'd inflicted upon him, not even a faint red mark on his throat.

"Hello again." Callum spoke with a smile that would've been friendly on anyone else, but combined with the pale, lifeless blue eyes, and his inability to fucking stay dead, it gave me the creeps. "I didn't get a chance to ask before, but I'm not sure how I should address you. Should I call you Seraphena or Sotoria?"

Was he seriously going to stand there and talk to me as if I hadn't nearly severed his head and turned his heart and cock into mush?

"I believe Seraphena is more…fitting." His cold, dispassionate gaze flickered over me. I knew damn well he could see nearly everything beneath my gown, but he looked at me as if I wore a potato sack from head to toe. "But I suppose His Majesty will determine what you will be called."

My jaw tightened with irritation, causing pain to flare as I quickly looked past him to where the double doors remained open, revealing the breezeway beyond, flooded with sunlight.

"Either way, I'm going to attempt to complete what I intended when I entered the chamber yesterday," he continued. "You were in need of a bath then. That is now an understatement."

He spoke in a tone that matched his smile as he gestured to the privacy screen. Friendly. Conversational. He'd spoken like that when I first arrived in the cage, and it was just as unnerving now as it had been then. But I was more focused on what he'd inadvertently shared.

A day had passed.

And that meant Ash had been imprisoned for at least two days.

"Where is—?" I caught myself as my panic overrode intelligence. I'd almost said, "*Ash*." Using that name would seem too intimate. Too affectionate. "Where is Nyktos?" I demanded, knowing better than to ask Kolis. It probably wasn't much smarter to ask Callum, but I needed to know. "Is he still imprisoned?"

"Once you finish bathing, you will change into clean clothing." He went on as if I hadn't spoken. "If you'd like, I can choose something for you to wear."

Yeah, that wasn't happening.

Callum's head tipped to the side. A strand of blond hair that had slipped free of the knot at the nape of his neck fell against the gold paint down his cheek. "Do I need to repeat myself?"

My fingers curled inward, pressing into my palms. "Where is Nyktos?"

A faint smile appeared as if he sensed my rising frustration. "Once you're clean and dressed, you may eat if you'd like. If you're not hungry, you can rest. It's possible there will be time for both before His Majesty returns for you."

Anger boiled inside me as I clenched my hands tighter. I *may* eat. I *could* rest. It reminded me too much of my youth, where every minute and hour of my days was summed up by what I could and could not do.

He quietly moved closer, stopping to stand in front of the cage. "But what you will *not* do is stand there," Callum went on in the patient voice of a parent speaking to a young child. "In your filth, soiling your quarters."

"My *quarters*?" I let out a sharp, brittle laugh that caused the side of my face to ache. "You're calling a cage that?"

"I've been in your world many times. What you call a cage is better than what most have there."

Immediately, I thought of the cramped tenements in Croft's Cross. Unfortunately, he spoke the truth. Somewhat. "Yes, but most have their freedom."

His smile took on a patronizing edge. "Do they? One would think they were prisoners to their poverty and the rulers who care little for them." He paused. "Like your mother, my dear friend Calliphe."

I stiffened at the reminder of his past contact with my mother. After all, Callum had shared with her how a Primal could be killed, which, admittedly, made little sense. Because that kind of knowledge endangered every Primal, including Kolis. Still, neither had known about Sotoria's soul. They'd never considered me a threat.

"But she no longer rules, does she?" Callum tacked on, his smile growing until a hint of teeth was visible. "Queen Ezmeria, along with her Lady Consort, does." Speaking of my stepsister, he snapped a finger. "You know what? I haven't paid her a visit. I should so I can...congratulate her."

Every part of my being locked up as I stared at the Revenant. There was no love lost between my mother and me, but Ezra was one of the few people who had treated me like a person. I cared about her. Loved her.

"And just so you know,"—Callum leaned forward and lowered his voice—"I'm well aware of the wards Nyktos placed around your mortal family. Nice of him to do so, but rather pointless. I've already been invited inside Wayfair. No wards will keep me out."

It didn't pass me by that I'd just learned something new about the Revenants, but that didn't matter at the moment. I stepped forward, feeling the embers in my chest thrumming. "If you go near her, I will—"

"What will you do?" His brows rose, causing the painted wings across his forehead to crease as I slowly approached the bars. "Other than offend my senses with your stench. You smell of the ceeren, and the gods only know what else."

My chest clenched at the mention of those who'd given their lives in the water. "I will make you wish you stayed dead."

Callum chuckled lightly. "I'm not sure if you realize this or not, but in your current condition and situation, your words are not nearly as threatening as you may think."

I matched his smile. "How did it feel when I slammed that glass into your throat?"

"Wonderful," he replied. "Can't you tell?"

"I don't know much about whatever you are, but I have to imagine that coming back to life isn't exactly pleasant, especially when you have numerous injuries to heal."

His smile froze.

I was right. My lips curved more. "And I bet reattaching your head is painful, just as repairing your heart." I lifted my brows. "But your cock? How did *that* feel?"

"I have a question for you," he said. "How did it feel going through all that trouble, only to end up exactly where you were?"

My nostrils flared with a burst of anger.

"I bet it feels just as good as it did regrowing a dick," he said. "And by the way, that was totally unnecessary and brutish."

I rolled my eyes. "Disagree."

"And so like something His Majesty would do," he tacked on. "But you have always been more like him than you'll ever be willing to admit."

I stiffened. "If you think that, then you know nothing about me."

"I've watched you for years," Callum announced. "Kept an eye on you for Kolis."

My skin prickled with irritation. I was getting really tired of learning that I'd been watched. Ash had done it, too, although his reasons had been less…cringe-worthy. "I'm sure that was a stimulating task."

"Well, not particularly. But when you decided to start spending your time fucking instead of moping about, it became far more entertaining."

The heat of my anger simmered just below the surface. "You're such a fucking creeper."

"Perhaps. But I know everything about you, Seraphena," he said, the glow of eather flaring in his eyes, though fainter than a god's. "Every irrelevant detail of the insignificant, sad life you've led. I know enough to realize the only time you ever appeared to actually *live* was when you were killing."

He struck a nerve, and I glared at him. What he'd said wasn't true. I *always* felt like I was dying.

I'd felt as monstrous as Kolis.

I lifted my chin. "Yet you didn't know who I really was, did you?"

Callum's lips flattened.

I smirked. Just like with Kolis earlier, I knew better than to clarify that. "You watched me for years, and you never realized that I was the one thing *His Majesty*," I said, mockery dripping from my tone, "valued more than the embers of life. I bet that really pissed him off." I gave Callum my best sympathetic smile. "And worse yet, it likely made him so disappointed in you."

His jaw tensed.

Something occurred to me then as I leaned in as close to the bars as possible without touching them. "Does he know that you told my mother how a Primal can be killed?"

The Revenant went so still I didn't think he breathed.

Damn, that response told me there was a good chance that Kolis had no idea, which led to the question of why, exactly, he'd done it. "Don't worry. I won't tell him." I winked. "It'll be our little secret."

Callum moved damn near as quickly as a god, standing so only the bars separated us. It caught me off guard—anyone moving like that did.

"I would be very careful if I were you, Seraphena." His lip lifted enough that I saw he had no fangs. "I can see by your face that Kolis isn't completely convinced of who you are."

Was he suggesting that Kolis had never harmed Sotoria? What a fucking liar. He could take that lie and go fuck himself, taking Kolis's apology with him. "As if him believing that or not matters."

"If you were truly Sotoria, you would know that it does," he said. "But perhaps you've forgotten. Either way, I know how this ends."

"Oh, so you're also an Arae?"

"What I am is patient. I only have to wait. Eventually, Kolis must choose between love and...well, literally everything else." Callum grasped the bars. He didn't react. Either he was masking the pain I'd felt when I touched the bars, or they did not affect him. "So, he may humor this...whatever this is." His gaze swept over me with that cold-as-a-grave stare. "He may spend the next days, weeks, months, or even years convincing himself that you are all he's ever wanted or needed, but rest assured, you will eventually end up like all of his other favorites."

He pressed his forehead against the bars. "Because there is one thing he's wanted more than his *graeca*, and that is to be the most powerful Primal ever to exist. So, it's either something as intangible as love, or ultimate power over life and death."

He was talking a lot of shit, but the part about there being months or even years for Kolis to grow tired of me stood out. Exactly how could he delay the Culling for that long?

Callum let his fingers slide over the bars before stepping back. He clasped his hands. "In a few moments, servants will begin entering the chamber and then your quarters. You will move to your left and not speak to them," he instructed, nodding toward the divan and the chests. "You will allow them to complete their tasks without interruption. And just to be clear, that means you will behave yourself. So, no attempting to murder anyone."

I breathed through the flaring pulse of red-hot anger. "And if I don't?"

"I know you want to fight, Seraphena." That godsawful pleasant smile returned. "I know your first response to any situation is to attack, just as you did before. But I strongly advise against trying that again."

"Like I give a fuck what you advise," I hissed, losing control of my temper. Attempting to earn Kolis's trust did not extend to Callum.

"Be that as it may, you should know what will happen if you decide not to give a fuck about my advice. If you attempt to attack me, it will not be you who pays the price. It will be a servant."

My mouth dropped open.

"You speak to one of them? I will kill them. For each minute you delay them, one will die," he told me, speaking so damn casually. "And just so we're perfectly clear, their lives are in your hands. When *they* die, they do not come back."

A cold sweat broke out across my forehead as I stepped back from the bars. He couldn't be serious.

"They mean little to me," Callum added with a shrug. "I suppose we will see how much they mean to you."

My gaze shifted to the open doors. Figures in white robes and veils appeared in the sunlight-drenched hall.

The Chosen.

My heart thumped as they entered the chamber, walking in a single, neat line. Each one carried a large bucket. Were they the same as those I'd seen in the other chamber the day before?

As the Chosen approached the cage, Callum sighed and then moved—so damn fast—to stand behind the first Chosen.

I hadn't done as he ordered.

Shooting to the side of the cage, my feet slipped on the tile. "No. No—"

Callum smiled.

His hands went to the sides of the veiled head—

Bone cracked like dried branches snapping in the wind.

I jolted at the clang of metal hitting tile. I didn't want to believe what I saw as the Chosen's legs collapsed, and they slumped to the floor. I shook my head in denial, but the embers of life throbbed in response to the death, pressing against my skin, demanding that I use them to restore life to the Chosen. Horror swamped me as I stared at the crumpled pile of white. Dimly, I became aware of my hand lifting halfway as if that could fend off what I'd witnessed.

Or do something else. But what? I couldn't restore life without touch.

"You...you didn't have to do that," I said shakily. "I can bring them back."

Callum slowly turned to me, his brows rising. Then he moved to stand behind the second Chosen—

"Don't!" I hurried toward the divan as nausea rose. "I'm moving. Look! I'm doing what you asked. You don't have to hurt them. Please."

Callum's eyes locked with mine, and my stomach pitched. A second passed. Two. Then he moved away from the Chosen, his haunting smile never fading.

Trembling with barely restrained anger and disbelief, I watched him approach the cage. He fished out a key as the Chosen waited behind him.

Did Callum not realize the key he'd used before had gone missing?

The cage opened, and I curled my arms around my chest, stopping myself from rushing the door and launching myself at the fucking Revenant.

My gods. I was going to do terrible, permanent damage to him one of these days.

Just not today.

I focused on the Chosen. None of them had reacted to the murder. Not a shout or a jerk, yet they'd screamed when they saw me. It was likely these were different Chosen, ones too familiar with this kind of violence.

Sickened, I stood by the divan, my stomach twisting and turning as my toes curled into the thick, soft rug. One by one, they entered, disappearing momentarily behind the screen and then returning with their pails in hand. They didn't look at me. No one spoke. The only sound was the whisper of robes across marble.

By the time the bucket that had hit the floor earlier had been refilled and added to the water in the tub, the embers in my chest had finally calmed. Callum locked the cage door as the last Chosen left the chamber. The approach of heavier footsteps drew my attention.

A dark-haired guard appeared in the hall, crossing the room in his knee-length, white tunic and gold greaves. The bright light of the chandelier reflected off the sigil engraved on the golden armor: a circle with a slash through it. His face was painted the same as Callum's.

But I recognized him.

It was the guard who'd been with the draken, the one who'd knocked me out.

As he neared the fallen Chosen, his head lifted just a bit. Amber eyes lit by the glow of eather glanced over me as he lifted the body. Then, without saying a word, he left. The guard was a god, yet he'd used none of his godly abilities against me yesterday.

Neither had any other guards, and the draken had only appeared close to attacking me once I hit him with that bolt of eather.

The reason was suddenly clear to me in light of Callum's actions. It was likely the guards and Kolis's loyalists had been warned not to harm me. I could exploit that.

To a point.

Because Callum had shown exactly how he would ensure my cooperation.

"Make use of your bath," Callum said, drawing my attention to him. "If you do not do so, I will bring another Chosen in here, and they will meet the same fate as the other."

I turned to where he once more stood before the cage. "I'm going to kill you," I promised.

Callum laughed softly. "I suggest you bathe and change. Kolis will be most displeased if he finds you in this state."

"Fuck Kolis," I snarled, once more losing control of my temper.

"He would enjoy that, I'm sure." Callum winked. "Your bath water is growing cold."

Whatever caustic response I had died on my tongue as Callum bowed and turned. I stared numbly as he left, the wide, heavy doors swinging shut behind him. The click of several locks followed.

Callum hadn't touched those doors.

Either that was something the doors did on their own, or Revenants had some of the same abilities as a god.

An unkillable god.

That potentially made the Revenants as dangerous as a Primal, and that was yet another problem.

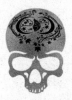

Worry gnawed at me. Kolis could return at any moment, but I still hesitated at the tub, my hand pressed lightly to the base of my throat. Just the sight of it full of water caused a knot to swell in my chest.

Having been nearly choked to death in a bathtub had kind of tainted what used to be a luxury I enjoyed.

Even to this day, I still felt the sash coming around my throat from behind, cutting off my airway before I even realized I'd taken my last breath. Damn, the memory was even fresher now.

I didn't want to get into the tub, but it was too deep for me to dunk my head like I had been doing in the Shadowlands until Ash noticed I wasn't using the tub to bathe. Instead of making me feel foolish, he'd understood the trauma and sought to work around it. He'd brought me into his chambers and stood guard in his quarters so I felt comfortable bathing.

That wasn't the only thing he'd done. My skin briefly warmed at the memory of him climbing into the tub, leathers and all…

But Ash wasn't here to have my back and help me feel safe.

I had to do it for myself and had a lifetime of practice doing just that. Today would be no different. At least, that was what I told myself.

A tremor started in my legs as I shifted from foot to foot. I needed to get over this. No one would choke me. Hopefully. What *would* happen was retaliation from Callum if I didn't bathe.

I was a quick learner—contrary to what my mother believed. It had only taken once with Callum. I disobeyed, and someone died.

I peeked around the screen and gave the chamber beyond the cage a hard scan. I knew no one was there, but I needed the reminder. Once I had it, I hurried behind the screen again and peeled off the bloody gown, wishing I could set fire to it as tiny bumps appeared all over my body. The feeling of hundreds of unseen gazes pressed upon my flesh.

"Stop it," I hissed. No one was watching me.

That I knew of, anyway.

I rolled my eyes. I really needed to learn how to be more reassuring.

Cursing, I stepped into the warm water. The knot in my chest expanded as I gripped the sides of the tub. Focused on my breathing, I lowered myself until I could sit.

The water reached just below my breasts, and my sore muscles immediately got on board with the whole soaking idea, but I wasted no time. I bathed as quickly as possible, using one of the pitchers filled and left by the tub to cleanse my hair. Only a handful of minutes could've passed when I stepped out of the tub and pulled the plug at the bottom that allowed the water to flow down the drain beneath it. Grabbing one of the towels, I dried off as I stepped onto a rug, my toes curling into the soft material. I turned, looking at myself in the mirror.

Wide, green eyes stared back at me, and without the blood splattering my face, the freckles dotting my cheeks and nose stood out in stark contrast.

But something else snagged my attention. I leaned in closer, my mouth parting with a sharp inhale. "What the...?"

A faint silvery glow of eather formed an aura around my pupils.

How long had it been like that?

I hadn't noticed it the day before. Granted, I'd been distracted by the state of my busted face.

I swallowed, drawing back. Did this mean that despite the ceeren's sacrifice, I was even closer to my Ascension?

To death.

"Damn it," I whispered, wrapping the towel around me. There was nothing I could do about it now.

It wasn't like I was unbothered by the fact that I was close to dying as I left the bathing area of my *quarters*. Death was as common to me as it was to those Chosen.

I'd spent my entire life accepting that it would find me. That I wouldn't have a long life, and there was no escape. It had only been that short span of time between when Ash had shared his plans to remove the embers and we'd learned what would happen that I had begun to think of a possible future.

I wasn't thinking of that now—at least one that involved me.

Once more kneeling at the chests, I took a bit more time searching for something close to what I'd typically wear.

I searched some more.

There was nothing, but I already figured as much. I had just been doing...wishful looking.

Disgusted, I grabbed a white frock. The halter style of the gown left my shoulders and arms completely exposed, and the material was some sort of gossamer and lace fabric. But at least it was loose-fitting at the bust and below the hips.

Weary, I sat on the divan and began working the tangles out of my hair with the comb I'd retrieved from the vanity. The monotony of the act calmed me, allowing me to think more clearly about the idea of, well…everything, including Kolis delaying my Culling.

Kolis may not know the embers could not be removed without my death—something not even Ash had been aware of. After all, Primal embers had never been inside a mortal before.

However, from what I'd been told, not even gods always survived the Culling. And godlings, which I was the closest to, were even more at risk of dying during the process.

So even if Kolis could Ascend me, there was a high probability I wouldn't survive. That was why he'd stopped. He could've tried right then to take the embers without killing me. He hadn't.

Either way, there was a good chance Kolis had no idea that only Ash could Ascend me. Even more importantly, though? I didn't think Kolis *could* Ascend me, even if I hadn't taken Ash's blood.

I thought back to the injuries I'd received when Veses freed the entombed gods in the Red Woods. I'd been pretty torn up. Ash's blood had made it like those wounds never happened. Clearly, Kolis's blood didn't have the healing properties Ash's did. He wouldn't have had to take me to the ceeren if it did.

But what the ceeren sacrificed for me? Had it done more than just save my life? Had it also slowed the Culling? If so…

Could something like that be done again…and again? Basically, delaying my Ascension for months or even years?

Using the essence of others—their life force—to keep me alive didn't seem all that impossible because I felt fine. Better than, actually—well, except for the ache in my face and throat. Other than that, there was no headache or weakness. I didn't have that bone-deep exhaustion that had plagued me before.

But if I stayed alive, that meant the embers—

"No." I shut down that line of thought before it could grow. I wouldn't even consider the idea of sacrificing lives to save others. There had—

A strange noise startled me, causing my head to jerk up. A resounding whoosh from outside echoed into the silent chamber. The sunlight in one window suddenly disappeared.

The comb slipped from my fingers as a...a *hawk* flew in through one of the windows near the ceiling—an enormous silver hawk with a wingspan the width of my arms.

I figured I had to be hallucinating as I watched the bird dive right for the cage. It angled its body sideways at the very last moment, gliding between the bars. My lips parted as it circled above and then swooped down, its dark talons latching on to the top of a bedpost.

Keen, sharp eyes a vivid, intense shade of blue locked onto mine— eyes full of wisps of silvery eather. Tucking its wings close to its body, the hawk pushed off the bedpost—

And shifted. All at once, I felt the warm pulse of awareness in my chest as a burst of thousands of tiny, silvery stars swallowed the bird's body. I recognized the feeling as the dazzling explosion of light lengthened and took the shape of a man—a Primal.

I shot to my feet, my hand going to my thigh out of reflex but coming up empty as the spectacle of lights faded. A broad chest with golden-bronze flesh replaced feathers. My gaze shot up as brownish-blond hair settled against a cut jaw and a...scarred left cheek.

The Primal God of War and Accord stood before me.

IO

A surge of pure, red-hot anger coursed through me as Attes took a step toward me. "Seraphena—"

I reacted without hesitation, and this time, I wasn't slow or weak. Swinging at him with every ounce of strength I had in me, I caught him in the jaw with my fist.

Pain erupted across my knuckles as Attes grunted, his head snapping back. I cursed, shaking my throbbing hand.

"Fuck," Attes bit out, pressing his hand to his jaw as he lowered his chin. His chest rose with a deep breath. "I suppose I deserved that, but godsdamn, you *can* hit."

"You deserve worse than that." I started toward him.

"I'm sure I do." Attes held up a hand, sidestepping me. "But you make a move against me one more time, and you will bring out my most basic Primal nature," he warned, his eyes blazing with fiery eather. "And you do not want that."

I wasn't so sure.

The embers throbbed fiercely in my chest, pressing against my skin. They wanted out—wanted at him. Or, more likely, they were simply responding to what *I* wanted.

However, some level of common sense prevailed. I knew I wouldn't win a fight against the Primal of fucking War and Accord.

I forced myself to back down. "You betrayed us."

"You already said that." Watching me warily, he lowered his arm. "But you're wrong."

"I don't think so," I spat.

His eyes narrowed. "What I did was save lives, you little hellion."

"Save lives?" I let out a scathing laugh as I stepped back even farther in an attempt to cling to my rapidly waning common sense. "Exactly how did you accomplish that by launching an attack on the Shadowlands alongside your brother?"

"I launched no attack against the Shadowlands. If I had, they would be nothing but ruins." Eather crackled in his eyes. "And my brother had no choice. When Kolis had you kill Thad, it forced Kyn's hand. Just as Kolis planned."

My stomach twisted with nausea as I thought about the young draken Kolis had forced me to slaughter as punishment for Ash not seeking his permission before announcing that he was taking me as his Consort. "I brought Thad back."

"I remember. But Kyn didn't know that. He still doesn't, for obvious reasons," he reminded me. "Kyn was supposed to capture you, but not before he leveled the Shadowlands, leaving only the road to the Abyss and the Vale remaining. When I took you, I stopped that from happening."

I inhaled sharply, thinking about the people in the city of Lethe, both mortal and god. I felt a little dizzy. "Was that what Kolis ordered?"

"In a roundabout way. He told Kyn to make a statement." Attes's shoulders tensed. "You don't tell a Primal of War or Vengeance that and not expect utter devastation."

I swallowed down the knot of fear building in my throat.

"The attack ended as soon as I took you," Attes said. "I swear."

"You give your word?" I sneered, heart thumping. "As if that means anything."

He sighed. "You don't trust me."

"No shit," I snapped.

Attes studied me for a few tense moments. When next he spoke, his voice was lower, calmer. "Kolis has known about you for a very long time."

"I know." My hands curled into fists. Fury surged at the painful reminder that Kolis had been aware of me since the night I was born, and had only been waiting for the embers to mature and me to use them. And everything Ash sacrificed? The deal he'd made with that bitch Veses, allowing her to feed from him to ensure my existence was kept secret? It had been for nothing.

The embers in my chest throbbed, responding even more now. Static raced down my arms, startling me. Lifting them, I saw that the fine hairs there had risen.

Attes's stare sharpened on me, almost as if he sensed the energy ramping up inside me. Maybe he did. Either way, I needed to calm myself. That was easier said than done, though, when I normally existed in one of two states: restless or ready to murder someone. Most of the time, there was no in-between.

And I really wanted to murder Veses.

Badly.

However, I was in a fucking cage, talking to Attes, and Veses was hopefully still imprisoned in the House of Haides, so that wouldn't happen.

"Then you know there was no stopping what happened," Attes said. "Kolis would've taken you one way or another. The only thing that could've been prevented was the unnecessary mass loss of innocents."

"Am I supposed to thank you for that?" I nearly shrieked.

"I don't need your thanks but would appreciate it if you kept your voice down," he ordered. "There are guards outside this chamber. And while shadowstone is thick, it's not completely soundproof."

"What will happen if they discover you in here?" I asked, giving him a cursory glance. "Naked?"

"Does my nudity bother you?" The fucker grinned until a godsdamn dimple appeared in his cheek.

Fuck common sense.

Bending, I picked up the comb I'd dropped and threw it right at his face. "No," I growled as his hand snapped out, catching the comb an inch from his nose. "But I bet it will bother Kolis."

The grin disappeared as he tossed the comb onto the bed. "Yeah, it would." His gaze dipped to my mouth and jaw. "But you would likely pay a far steeper price for it than I."

Cheeks warming, I realized he was looking at the bruises. I stiffened. "As if you care."

"You have no idea what I care about or don't." His jaw tightened as he looked at the closed doors.

"You're right. And, frankly, I don't care."

"You need to." A moment later, he waved his hand, and a pair of black leather pants appeared out of thin air, encasing his legs.

Reluctant jealousy rose. If I had that talent, I'd conjure something that constituted clothing. I started to ask him to do that for me but realized wearing something that didn't run the risk of flashing a nipple would raise questions.

"We likely do not have long for this conversation," he continued. "So, I need you to understand that I'm not here to betray Nyktos or you—especially you. After all, I have saved your life before. More than once."

"What?" I scoffed. "You're going to have to refresh my memory—" I cut myself off. Attes had stopped Kolis when he was draining my blood to get at the embers. It wasn't like I'd forgotten that. My anger at Attes's betrayal had sort of blocked out that little fact. "You intervened when Kolis was feeding on me. I wouldn't go as far as to say you saved my life."

A quick grin returned to Attes's lips. "But that wasn't the first time."

A frown tugged at my brows, then they lifted as I finally saw—or acknowledged—what had been right in front of me, having flown in through the window. "That was you? The hawk in the Dying Woods?"

A slight grin appeared. "It was."

As Attes's confirmation landed like a fist to the chest, my mind suddenly blanked for several seconds. And then I remembered what Ash had said about hawks—that they were a symbol that belonged to his father, along with the wolf. Kolis used the same representations, except his were golden, while... "Eythos's hawks were silver," I murmured.

Attes frowned. "They were."

I blinked. "Did Eythos shift forms?"

"He did. All Primals can."

"And was his a hawk?" I surmised. "Or a wolf?"

"A wolf," he confirmed. "Though, he always wished to fly with the hawks."

I started to ask why he hadn't chosen to take the form of the bird of prey, then, but did that matter? No. "And Kolis? What does he shift into?"

"A hawk," he said with a wry twist of his lips.

I blinked. Why in the realm would Eythos and Kolis—nope. Not important. "If that was you in the woods that night, why didn't—?" I almost said "*Ash*" again but using the name only a few called him by in front of Attes didn't feel right. "Why didn't Nyktos know you were there?"

"Primals cannot sense one another when we're in our *nota* forms—

when we take the shape of the animal we find ourselves most connected to," he explained. "Just as Kolis didn't sense him in his wolf form."

And I hadn't felt Attes until he shifted. "Why?"

His bare grin returned. "Because when we're in our *nota* forms, it is us but...not."

Well, that just explained everything, didn't it?

"Seeing you in the Dying Woods that night was luck. I was snooping when I came across you there." The light glinted off the silver cuff encircling his biceps as he rubbed a hand over his chin. "I'm half-afraid to ask what you were doing."

I wasn't going to get into that. "What about in the Red Woods? Before then?"

"That wasn't me, but it *was* one of my many unique hawks. I felt its death and then sensed it come back to life. That was how I knew Nyktos had brought you to the Shadowlands."

My thoughts raced as I ended up asking probably the least important question. "What do you mean by unique hawks?"

"They're what we call a *chora*. They're basically an extension of the Primal that takes the *nota* shape. They are created from our blood and are very much alive," he said, his words becoming draped in a shroud of sorrow. "Iliseeum used to be full of *chora*. It was once a tradition, a way to honor our *nota*, as was the Primal *notam*—a bond formed with those we take the shape of. It was common when Eythos reigned, but impossible under Kolis. Most of the Primals have lost all of theirs, but the *chora* that still exist can do so for centuries and longer, even if the Primal they are bonded to enters Arcadia."

Well, that was all kinds of weird. "So, this is yet another thing that has died out with Kolis?" My head jerked to the side. "How you've all gone along with what Kolis has done is beyond me."

Attes's body locked into place, tensing like a coiled spring. "With Eythos's death, and Nyktos having no Primal embers of life, we had no choice."

No choice? I almost laughed. If my often-irrational ass could realize there was always a choice, there was no excuse for the Primals not to have come to that conclusion after living for hundreds if not thousands of years.

Something Attes had said moments before came back to me as I smoothed my hands over my hips. "Wait a minute. This *chora* of yours I saw in the Red Woods, it was doing the snooping for you?"

"It's not an *it*, Seraphena. It's a hawk, flesh and blood, which you should know."

"Whatever." My patience was thinning. "Exactly why were you snooping before you even met me?"

"Because I already knew of your existence." Attes's gaze locked with mine. "I've known longer than either Nyktos or Kolis."

I...I was at a loss for what to say.

"I knew what Eythos did before Kolis or Nyktos figured it out. Eythos and I were brothers in a way that he and Kolis never were. Friends," he shared, his voice changing. It now carried the bittersweetness of the pain and joy of knowing and then losing someone. "And I was one of the few entrusted with the knowledge of what Eythos did."

Backing up, I sat on the edge of the divan. Ash believed that Attes had been testing me that day in the study at the House of Haides, trying to feed into my emotions. And Ash became concerned, because when it didn't work, he knew the Primal of War and Accord would realize something was up. But if Attes spoke the truth now, he'd actually been testing how strong the embers had become.

If he was speaking the truth.

His knowledge of what Eythos did explained why he'd been so quick to believe my claim regarding Sotoria. He must have known.

I looked up at him, finding the Primal watching me closely. He made sense, but I only trusted a small handful of people, and he wasn't anywhere near that list.

"If you knew about the embers, why were you so surprised when I brought Thad back?" I asked.

"Honestly?"

"No, tell me a lie," I retorted.

Attes grinned. "Because I have not seen life restored—*real* life, with my own eyes—since Eythos. But more than that? I never thought his plan would work." A bit of wonder seeped into his tone. "Restoring life to a hawk is one thing, but a draken?" His eyes wandered upward as he shook his head. After a moment, he exhaled softly, and his gaze returned to mine. There was a sense of wonder in his expression. "Eythos was under the impression that the embers would protect you and maybe give you some ability to restore life, but not to that extent. Even before the embers he stole from Eythos died out, Kolis couldn't bring a draken back."

"Then why was I able to?" I blurted out.

Attes's gaze went to the floor as his head moved from side to side once more. "I don't know. But if I had to guess based on what I've seen and heard about, including your recent escape attempt?"

My eyes narrowed.

"The embers are bonding with you, allowing you to access more of the essence." He shrugged. "It happens when gods near their Ascension, just as it does with Primals."

I swallowed, clasping my knees as I processed everything I'd just heard, which felt slightly impossible at the moment. "Why didn't you tell Nyktos any of this? And I don't want to hear anything about how the knowledge would've endangered him. That's bullshit. It's not like he would've run off and confronted Kolis, revealing what he knew. He's not foolish." I leaned forward, anger sparking. "And if you think that, then you and Eythos underestimated Nyktos. *That* is what endangered him. If he knew about the embers from the beginning, so many things could've been done differently. It would've prevented me..."

Brow creasing, Attes knelt. "Prevented you from doing what?"

From taking that tiny bit of Ash's blood that had inevitably put our lives on a collision course with death. My death.

"You should've told him," I said instead of sharing that with him.

A long beat of silence passed as Attes stared at the tile. "You're right, but Eythos had no choice but to keep silent. Nor did I. When he put the embers in your bloodline"—tension formed brackets at the corners of his mouth—"and put Sotoria's soul with them? He fucked with fate in a major way. And the Arae do not like to be fucked with."

Thinking of Holland, I grimaced. "I know all about the Fates."

"Do you?" he asked, his head tilting. "Then you know they are the ones who prevented Eythos from telling his son what he did?"

I tensed. "I know one of the Arae. He didn't say anything about that."

"Of course, not. Because he probably didn't want a comb thrown at his face."

I glared at him.

The brief teasing glint vanished from his eyes. "You see, when you mess with fate and think you got away with it, you quickly find out you didn't. Every action has a reaction, one that becomes either a reward or a consequence. That creates balance. And if that balance is undone in the minds of the Arae? They will reset it in the most fucked-up ways imaginable," he said. "And in this case? They prevented Eythos and anyone else from telling Nyktos what was done. Because in their minds, that balanced things out."

Disbelief flashed through me, leaving me feeling like I was caught in a surreal dream that no amount of pinching or shaking could snap me from. "How is what Eythos did such a huge upset to the balance when you have Kolis running around stealing embers and killing Primals?" I demanded. "How does that not mess with fate?"

Attes's laugh was quick and harsh. "Who's to say that Kolis got away with fucking with the Fates?"

"Looks to me like he's doing pretty damn well for himself," I declared.

"Is he?" Attes tossed back. "To get what he's wanted, he'll have to risk killing the only person he's ever loved."

I snapped my mouth shut. Attes had a point there. It seemed like Eythos's actions had created the punishment for Kolis.

My foot tapped the floor as I realized Holland hadn't been entirely forthcoming. I knew it wasn't like he was the only Arae, and I also recognized that he had to walk a fine line between advising and interference, but I wanted to do worse than throw a comb at his face the next time I saw him.

If I did.

I exhaled loudly. "Okay, so if everything you say is true, then get Nyktos out of Dalos."

"I would if I could."

"If you *could*?" I rose, anger lodging in my chest. "You're a Primal who flew in here as a hawk."

"That doesn't mean I can fly out of a cell as a hawk *with* Nyktos." He stood cautiously, almost as if he expected me to throw another punch. "You see these bars? Have you touched them?"

"Yes." I began pacing. "It didn't feel that great."

"Of course, not. They are bones of the Ancients." He jerked his chin at them. "They're chock-full of eather and powerful wards."

Bones? My lip curled as I noted the discoloration in the gold once more.

Ew.

"Those bones, when wielded as a weapon? Prick even the skin of a god? Dead. And because of the embers, if I try to take you through them and you get nicked? Dead. They can even put a Primal into years-long stasis," he told me. "Nyktos is just as imprisoned by them as you are, and he's far more guarded."

Slowly, I faced him as an image formed—the weapon the Primal of the Hunt and Divine Justice had held. "Was that what Hanan's spear was made of?"

He nodded.

"Then, clearly, the bones of the Ancients *can* be destroyed," I said.

"Only by two Primals: the Primal of Life and the Primal of Death."

Great.

I crossed my arms. "But can they kill a Primal with more than just a few embers?"

"They can kill a fledgling Primal, depending on where they are struck, like one who is just coming out of their Culling. They'd be susceptible to that for many years until they fully harness their eather. But if any Primal, fledging or not, is impaled by a bone, they would remain incapacitated until it was removed."

Well, that was the first helpful piece of information he'd shared. But in the moments of silence that followed, I realized there was something else I wanted to know.

"Can you...?" *Breathe in.* My chest constricted. *Hold.* "Can you tell me how Nyktos is?"

"You're not going to like this answer, but I can't." He tracked the short path I was making in front of the divan. "I wish I could, but I haven't seen him since I took him to the cells."

He was right. I *didn't* like the answer. "Was he conscious then?"

"No," he said quietly.

Breathe in. I squeezed my eyes shut against the rising swell of panic and helplessness. *Hold.* Caving to that wouldn't help either of us. *Breathe out.* "Where are these cells?"

"Was that where you were trying to escape to?"

I didn't answer.

There was no need.

Attes let out a weary breath. "You would never make it there, even if you had managed to get free. I wouldn't even be able to get you there and past the wards in place—at least undetected."

"Where are these cells?" I repeated.

"They are in Dalos, but nowhere near the city," he said. "They're in the Carcers."

Even though I figured Ash wasn't being kept within reach, the disappointment still hit me hard. "The Carcers?" I asked, my voice hoarse.

"There's a mountain range south of the City of the Gods, second only to Mount Lotho," he said, speaking about Embris's—the Primal of Wisdom, Loyalty, and Duty—Court. "Those are the Carcers."

My lower lip stung as I pressed it against my upper one. "What... what are the Carcers like?"

"You don't want to know."

Stopping, I faced him. "I want to know."

Something akin to respect flickered across his face. "What are mortal prisons like?"

"Terrible."

"Imagine that, but much, much worse," he said, and a chill hit my spine. "I believe you would only find a more forbidding locale in the Abyss."

Gods.

The weight in my chest increased as if an unseen hand pressed upon it. *He won't be there long*, I reminded myself. He won't. I looked over at Attes, thinking about my key. "If I could get out of this cage—"

"If you were able to escape this cage, I'd take you." Eather pulsed in his eyes. "I'd get you out of here and take you someplace safe."

I wasn't sure if I could trust that. "But you couldn't take me to Nyktos, right?"

His gaze searched mine. "I wouldn't even risk it, knowing the wards wouldn't fail."

"Because you'd be punished?"

"I'm not worried about me," he replied. "I'd be more worried about what Kolis would do to you or Nyktos."

"Right," I murmured. There was no point in gaining Attes's help in my escape. I was also worried about what Kolis would do in retaliation once he realized I'd left in an attempt to free Ash.

Kolis hadn't even asked why I'd tried before. He hadn't been surprised. I imagined it was because Sotoria had attempted to escape so many times—as he'd alluded to.

"If you're not here to help Nyktos, then why are you here?" I asked. "To assuage your guilt?"

"My conscience is long past that."

"Then what?" I demanded. "To tell me you're secretly loyal to Nyktos, despite your actions?"

"I'm loyal only to the true Primal of Life." His head cocked to the side. "That was Eythos, and now it is you. Yes, you only have two Primal embers," he added quickly, "but that still makes you, for all intents and purposes, the true Primal of Life, as long as those embers remain inside you."

The embers warmed in response, and I decided to ignore it. "You have a real fucked-up, unhelpful way of showing your loyalty."

He huffed out a laugh. "You do wonders for one's self-worth, you know that?"

"Well, what I'm about to say won't help in that department. I think you're a fool." Anger thinned my voice. "I think all of you Primals are fools if you blindly serve another based on some embers or stolen titles."

"Blindly serve?" He chuckled under his breath. "Sera—may I call you that?"

"No."

A wider smile appeared, hinting at a dimple. "Only those destined for war serve a King or Queen simply because they carry embers or claim themselves a ruler. I would know." He paused. "*Seraphena.*"

My nose scrunched. "That sounded very philosophical and nice, and I bet it made you feel clever, but in reality, you said nothing."

"See this scar?" He pressed a forefinger to the shallow slice on his cheek. "Kolis put it there. Do you want to know why?"

Based on what little Ash had been able to tell me about Attes, and what I'd picked up on, I thought I'd be better off not knowing. That would make me a coward, though, so I nodded.

"Eythos wasn't the only one who paid the price for Kolis losing Sotoria. The cost for Eythos was Mycella's life." Wisps of eather stirred violently in Attes's irises. "But many others were caught in that rise of violence—friends, parents, lovers, favored draken." His lips thinned, and his features tightened with the kind of pain that never really went away. The word he spoke next was low, sounding as if it came from the depths of his soul. "Children."

Oh, gods. A tremor went through me.

"When I tried to stop him... This?" He gestured to the scar once more. "This is what a bone of an Ancient wielded by a Primal of Death can do."

I'd suspected something like that had happened. The loss of a lover or even a Consort. But... I had a feeling what Kolis took from Attes had been a part of him. "I didn't know."

"How could you?" he asked. "Our losses are our stories to share. Nyktos, being born of that kind of loss, would've respected that."

My heart twisted as my gaze tracked over the scar. The ones I couldn't see were likely far deeper. Godsdamn, my heart hurt. "I'm sorry."

"So am I." He closed his eyes. "Is that a good enough reason for you?"

Clearing my throat, I blinked back tears. "Yes."

The eather in his eyes had slowed when he reopened them. "I've never stood with Kolis. Not truly."

"Then I have a question for you." Anger returned to my voice. "Has it never occurred to you to share this with Nyktos?"

"Why would I do that?" he countered. "I've never known where Nyktos really stands when it comes to Kolis."

My brows shot up. "Are you kidding? He hates—"

"Hating someone doesn't mean you will cease serving them, especially if doing so benefits you," he cut in. "Confiding in him without knowing his true thoughts and intentions was a risk to my Court and everyone who relies on me."

Indignation rose. I couldn't believe what I was hearing. "He never would've turned you over to Kolis."

"You think that?"

I met his stare. "I *know* that."

Attes laughed softly. "You have no idea what any of us has done or what we are capable of if backed into a corner. And that includes Nyktos."

I started to argue, but thought about that one decent bone Ash claimed to have that belonged to me and only me. I knew he had far more goodness in him than that. What he did for the Chosen he could save, the young Pax, who he'd rescued from the streets, and countless others were proof of that. But there *was* a cool ruthlessness to Ash. I'd seen it.

"There used to be a time when we trusted one another," Attes said, his voice taking on a distant quality. "When we Primals worked together for the betterment of Iliseeum and the mortal realm. That time has long since passed. And while Nyktos's dislike of Kolis was clear to anyone who remotely paid attention, he was still loyal when it came down to it."

"He did what he could to make a stand against Kolis," I hissed. "But he had no choice but to serve him."

"Exactly." Attes threw up his hands in frustration. "None of us has had much of a choice, Seraphena."

I looked away. His reasons for not confiding in Ash were valid... and yet not good enough for me. "So, what's different now?"

"You," he said. My fingers pressed into my arms. "You are the reason things are different now."

"Because of the embers?"

"Because within you resides the only one who can kill Kolis. The one who can end this. And everything must be done to protect her."

Tension poured into my body, causing the embers to hum. I shouldn't be surprised to hear concern for literally anything but me. Usually, it was my duty or the embers. It was never me.

Until Ash.

A sharp slice of pain hit my chest, but I breathed through it, focusing on what Attes had said. Or rather what he *hadn't*. "You mean I am the only one who can stop Kolis."

"No, Seraphena," he said, his tone heavy. "I do not."

My body flashed cold as I stared at Attes. "What are you saying?"

"I'm saying that Eythos's plan didn't work as he intended. And, yeah, I didn't think it would work at all in the first place, but that is neither here nor there." His shoulders rose with a heavy breath. "Let me ask you something. Are you and Sotoria one and the same?"

A great sense of foreboding seized me. "Why are you asking that?"

"Because I know." His voice dropped. "I know you're not her. Not really."

My heart lurched as his features blurred in a hazy fog of disbelief.

"There's an uncanny resemblance between you and Sotoria. So much so that I don't know how Kolis didn't see it immediately. I don't think he could let himself," he continued, almost cautiously, his words low and measured. "But if you were Sotoria reborn, you would look just like her. You don't. And you would not have been able to speak as her like you did."

A wave of shock swept through me as my arms uncrossed, falling to my sides. Attes was possibly the first person to say that and sound like he believed it. I couldn't even say for sure if Ash truly accepted I wasn't Sotoria. I didn't think it mattered because I was always Sera to him.

But I thought of what Ash had said about the Primal Keella during the coronation. Keella could follow the souls of those she captured who were reborn. Ash had not believed that Sotoria was reborn—no, that wasn't what he had said exactly. He'd only said that he hadn't been sure if Keella could follow Sotoria's soul because her return hadn't been a rebirth.

"You know what I'm saying is true. You don't want to confirm it. I get it. You know that Kolis believing you are Sotoria is the only thing keeping you alive, and the embers of the Primal of Life safe. That's smart." Attes crossed the cage. "But there is no point in lying to me, Seraphena. I know Eythos's plan did not work as he intended."

I stood rigidly, my thoughts racing. Even knowing what had caused

Attes's scar, wariness still invaded all my senses. I shifted from foot to foot, glancing at the closed doors. I knew I had to make a choice. Trust Attes, or not. If I did and was wrong, I would die, and Kolis would have the embers. But I didn't... I didn't think he was here spying on Kolis's behalf. That just didn't make sense when he'd apparently covered for me and stopped Kolis when he attempted to take the embers.

I took a deep breath, knowing I wasn't risking only my life. "Is there a difference between rebirth and being reborn?"

"The phrases are often used interchangeably, along with rein-carnation, but a rebirth usually involves the souls of those who have not truly lived," he said, referencing the babes Ash had spoken of. "Those who are reincarnated may have memories or even dreams of who they once were, and that's as rare as the act itself, and is usually reserved for *viktors*."

"And being reborn is like starting over," I murmured. "Having no memory of who you once were." I glanced up at him. "So, having a soul placed alongside another is...?"

"I have no clue," he admitted with a biting laugh. "It's not supposed to happen. But it could be the result of what Eythos tried to do—something impossible. Or the Arae intervened."

I thought back to what Attes had said about the Fates. "But you said the Arae ensured Eythos's silence, as well as yours, as a way to balance what Eythos did."

"Yes. But I never said it was the only thing they did," he countered. "I don't know why they did this. Then again, one of them put the idea of taking embers from another in Kolis's head to begin with, and who really knows why anyone would share that knowledge?"

He had a point there. Delfai, the God of Divination Ash and I had spoken to, had said the same.

I shook my head. "What is the point of this? Sotoria's soul is in me. Does that not make me her for all intents and purposes?"

"A soul is nothing like embers, Seraphena. Two should never be in one."

A great sense of unease rose. "And what happens if there are?"

"It means that Sotoria's soul is..."

I watched him look away as he shoved a hand through his hair.

"She's trapped in me?" I asked.

"Basically."

I closed my eyes as a shudder rocked me. *Trapped.* I thought I knew what that felt like, and I did. But I couldn't imagine what it must be like for Sotoria.

"That bothers you."

Opening my eyes, I found Attes's gaze on me. "Of course, it does. I can't even let myself really think about it without freaking out," I admitted. "I don't want that for her."

"Neither do I." A muscle ticked in his jaw. "And it also means that when you die, Sotoria's soul dies with you."

"Well, I figured that, but wouldn't that be the case if her soul were simply reborn or whatever, too?"

"If Sotoria's soul was reborn, you would be her. She would be you. And when you died, your soul would move on. But that is not what happened here. Her soul is in you, so when you leave the mortal coil, she will be trapped in your body until her soul is destroyed, and then she will continue in this...state. Unable to move on. Unable to live or die." His eyes closed. "She would just be."

My lips parted in horror. I could practically hear the wailing often heard in the Dark Elms. "She would be like a spirit?"

"Worse. She would become lost." He came forward again. "Does anyone else know this?"

"No."

"Not even Nyktos?"

"I...I don't think so. He's always made a point of telling me that I am Seraphena, but how would he have any way of knowing?"

"He would if he looked," Attes said. "He is, after all, a Primal of Death, retaining the abilities lost to Kolis. He can see souls, but I'm not even sure he would understand what he saw if he got the impression of two souls."

I sucked in a sharp breath. Had Ash looked? I didn't know. "But Kolis said he held on to my soul, keeping it inside me until he took me to the Triton Isles. Wouldn't he have felt two?"

"I'm surprised he could even do that. So, it's doubtful he knew exactly what he held. He *could've* grabbed her soul, which kept you alive. It's anyone's guess. Either way, do you understand what all of this means?"

My earlier unease multiplied, forming knots in my chest. "Based on your tone? Apparently, not."

"Sotoria's soul is in you, but you're not her." Attes's gaze met mine. "And even if Kolis never realizes that, it means you're not the weapon Eythos believed he created."

II

You're not the weapon...

I staggered back, bumping into the divan. Attes couldn't be insinuating what I thought he was. "I'm still able to fulfill my duty."

"Maybe," Attes replied, eather pulsing in his stare. "But you're not her, and we have no way of knowing if that matters. If I had to go off my gut feeling? It does. Which means you won't be able to kill him."

I sank onto the plush divan, my head shaking in fierce denial. Attes's words pelted me like stones thrown against a fortress of adamant refusal instead of providing respite.

I felt no solace.

And shouldn't there be? I didn't want to do what it would take to fulfill my destiny. I should be celebrating this news, but there was no relief.

How could there be when it meant I'd never been able to save my kingdom? Everything I'd suffered and given up, all the sacrifices I'd made throughout my life for a kingdom that didn't even know me. Not to mention the choices my family faced. They were all for nothing. All those years of grueling training and pushing my body and mind to the brink of collapse meant nothing. There'd been no need for me to learn what it felt like to be so godsdamn empty, what it took to be so, and what it stole.

Accepting that truth was unbearable, intolerable. It meant my life, my entire *existence*, had been a lie.

No.

I couldn't accept that I wouldn't be able to stop Kolis if I failed to escape. That he would survive, continuing to hurt Ash and others. There would be more favorites, and Sotoria…good gods, she would be trapped once I died. That was inevitable. I would not allow others to die to keep me alive.

No.

Attes's gut instinct had to be wrong. Wouldn't the Fates have known this? Holland? And if so, why had he spent so many years training me? Why did it matter if Kolis believed the one thrusting a blade through his heart was the one he loved? Perhaps it didn't.

Because there was no way that everything I had given up— everything Eythos and Kolis caused—was for nothing. That it was all fucking pointless.

"You have to be wrong." My shoulders squared. "You have to be."

"I hope I am." The Primal's gaze was now focused somewhere above me, his fingers curled at the base of his throat.

"Nothing has changed," I told him.

"Except if you attempt to kill him, and it doesn't work?" His chin lowered. "What do you think he will do to you?"

"What he's already done," I said. "I stabbed him earlier. I missed his heart by an inch, and I'm still alive."

Attes blinked.

"He was angry," I amended, flattening my palms against my knees. "But he didn't kill me. Obviously."

The Primal stared at me for several moments. "You managed to stab him?"

"Yeah."

"With what kind of weapon?"

"Not one made of the bones of an Ancient," I muttered. "Shadow-stone."

His eyes widened. "And that pierced his skin?"

I nodded. "He healed up pretty quickly."

"Shit," he whispered, surprise evident in his tone. "He's weaker than I thought. Even with the embers he stole long since faded, he's still the oldest Primal. Shadowstone shouldn't have pierced his skin."

"Well, that's a good thing, right?"

"It's an *interesting* thing," he corrected. "If he hadn't healed immediately, *that* would've been a good thing."

I started to frown.

"It just means the playing field may have been leveled a little," he added. "But just because he didn't end up killing you before, doesn't mean he won't do it later. And if you die? And her soul is lost—"

"Yes, I get it. Her soul is the most important thing," I snapped. "She dies, everything is lost."

Attes's head tilted. A moment passed. "You matter, too."

A bitter laugh left me, even as my cheeks warmed with embarrassment. "You don't need to lie."

"I'm not."

Irritation rose. I knew better, which left me even more frustrated. I should be used to that by now. But also? Her soul *was* important. "So, what are you saying? I shouldn't attempt to kill him?"

"I don't think it's worth the risk," he shared.

"Then what am I supposed to do?" I demanded. "Nothing?"

"That's not what I'm saying. Kolis doesn't know the truth, and that means you're still his weakness. You can use that to our benefit."

"*Our* benefit?" Tension returned as I curled my fingers into my gown. "Funny choice of words."

Attes ignored that. "Nyktos needs to be freed as soon as possible if there is any hope of preventing the kind of war Kolis spoke of," he warned. "And we're already racing toward it. I can sense it." His eyes searched mine. "You can change that, at least."

"I know." I straightened my fingers. "I have a plan."

"You do?" His brows lifted. "Already?"

"Yeah." I frowned. "Why does that surprise you?"

"You were only just taken." His eyes searched mine. "No one would've faulted you if you weren't of clear enough mind yet to develop a plan."

"Yeah, well, this isn't the first time I've found myself in a situation that doesn't allow for a whole lot of time to break down."

He stared. "What kind of life *have* you lived, Seraphena?"

I laughed, but there was no humor in the sound. Not when I felt like my body was caving in on itself. "Then what? I gain Nyktos's freedom, and what happens next? You think Nyktos will simply return to the Shadowlands and pretend like nothing happened?"

"If he's wise, he will." His gaze held mine. "And you know that's true."

My heart skipped a beat. It was. I'd prefer if Ash did exactly that, but he wouldn't. "He cares for me," I said quietly. "He feels responsible for me. He won't do that."

"I think he feels you are more than a responsibility," he quipped with a smile that caused a dimple to wink to life.

The breath I took scorched my lungs. It hurt because I'd spoken the truth. Ash did feel responsible for me. He cared for me. He was fond of me. But he could not feel what Attes was clearly suggesting.

It took a lot for me to breathe past the burn and focus beyond it, but I did. Because I had to. "Then how will this prevent a war?"

"I didn't say you were preventing a war," Attes corrected softly. "I said you would be preventing the kind of war Kolis spoke of. There is a difference. While I know Nyktos is capable of many terrifying things if pushed, it pales in comparison to what Kolis will do. With Nyktos free, he'll be able to protect his people and gather support."

"Is there support to be gained?"

"There can be."

My hands fell to the cushion. "That's not good enough."

"Look, news of what Kolis has done is spreading. It will make others uncomfortable, even if Kolis thinks it won't stir up too much unrest," he said, and I immediately thought about Phanos's response upon seeing me. "But Kolis likes to forget that Nyktos comes in as a close second in the top three Primals that no one wants to piss off."

"Let me guess. You're number three?" I remarked dryly.

"You're very clever." That dimple was back.

And I was unimpressed. "Has anyone told you that you're so very stab-worthy?"

A low chuckle radiated from him. "I've been told that a time or a thousand."

I snorted. "Figured." Easing my death grip, I stood. "What about you and your support? Will you back—?" I stopped myself, looking at the Primal. I remembered what he'd said. Attes claimed only to be loyal to the true Primal of Life.

And as he'd said, for all intents and purposes, that was me.

I inhaled deeply, or at least thought I did, but the breath filling my lungs felt disappointingly shallow. My chest constricted with anxiety like a fist squeezing my heart with every beat. "You will back Nyktos on whatever he chooses and aid him in gaining allies," I began, my voice trembling slightly. Making demands such as these wasn't something I was accustomed to. "He will have your full support and that of your Court."

Attes's head tilted. "Is that an order?"

My heart raced. At the end of the day, I was still just a mortal ordering a Primal to do my bidding. But the embers in me hummed intensely. I lifted my chin, swallowing. "It is, even if you find yourself standing opposite your brother."

Wisps of eather whipped through his eyes and lit up the veins beneath the skin of his cheeks. He angled his body toward me.

"You will swear it," I added, knowing a Primal could not break a promise once made.

Energy ramped up, charging the air. For a moment, I thought I might've overstepped a smidgen.

Or a lot.

Probably a lot.

"Very clever," Attes murmured, then stepped forward and lowered himself onto one knee. Placing one hand over his heart, he bowed his head. "With my sword and my life." Eather-laced eyes lifted to mine. "I swear to you, the One who is born of Blood and Ash, *the* Light and the Fire, and *the* Brightest Moon, to honor your command."

My title…the one Ash had bestowed upon me. I inhaled sharply as another charge of energy rippled through the air, skating down my spine. I could feel it. I felt the power in commanding such an oath. It caused the nape of my neck to prickle, and the embers to thrum fiercer. His words carried the strength of an unbreakable oath etched into his bones and mine—into the very soil of the realm itself.

And that sudden power? It was as unnerving as it was emboldening. It was also a little awesome.

Attes waited, and I nodded for him to rise, only because I had no idea what I was supposed to respond with and had seen my mother and King Ernald do something similar.

As Attes rose, I cleared my mind and tried to focus. "What will be done about Sotoria's soul?"

"I've been searching for a way to safeguard it, and I will continue to do so." There was no trace of humor or charm to be found, and when he spoke again, he did so somberly. "I know what it will take for you to gain Kolis's trust and garner Nyktos's freedom. It's the same thing you'll have to do to stay alive."

Growing uncomfortable with the direction of the conversation, I shifted from one foot to the other.

"And I…" A muscle ticked in his temple. "I'm sorry."

I looked away, my aching jaw tight. Gods, he sounded as if he meant it, and I didn't know what to do with that when I preferred he *not* know what it would take.

"I need to leave," he said, clearing his throat, but a thickness lingered. "Staying so long without being discovered is luck I should not continue to push."

Nodding, I faced him as something I'd wondered about earlier resurfaced. "Can I ask you something first?"

"Of course."

"Does Sotoria's name mean anything in the language of the Ancients and Primals? I know that *so'* means *my*," I explained when the skin at the corners of his eyes creased. "And I just thought that perhaps her name meant something. Like it's two words joined together."

"Like Kolis'?" he asked.

"Yes."

"It does. Or *did*." He exhaled heavily, dragging his thumb over the base of his throat. "It's from the oldest of our language. *Toria* had a few meanings. One meant garden. Another could be loosely translated into pretty flower." He smiled then, but no dimple appeared, and I couldn't help but think of what Sotoria had been doing when she died. She'd been picking flowers. "But a more exact translation is poppy."

"Like the mortal flower?" I thought of the ones that had started to grow again in the Shadowlands. "Or the silver ones?"

"I believe it once referenced the mortal flower, but it could've been describing either."

My brows lifted. "So, Sotoria's name could be translated into my pretty..." A strange shiver curled its way down my spine. "My pretty poppy?"

Attes nodded. "Or my pretty garden."

"Oh," I whispered.

He studied me. "Does something about that translation bother you?"

Yes, but...

"No." I shook my head, unsure where the feeling of unease had come from or why. "I do have another request for you."

"Anything."

I smiled wryly at that. "Find me a weapon made of the bones of the Ancients."

His head tipped to the side. "Seraphena..."

"I am not going to take any unnecessary risks. I swear."

The purse of his lips said he doubted my oath.

"But if there comes a time when the only thing left is to take a risk? I want to have something that can kill him, or incapacitate him at the very least," I said, and could tell he knew what I meant. "It doesn't hurt to try, does it?"

"No, I suppose not," he said. "But you have to be careful with such a weapon. And I say that not because I think you cannot handle one," he added when I opened my mouth. "You cannot touch the bone itself without causing pain. A hilt would need to be crafted, which isn't a problem. What *is* an issue is where you would hide it on your person."

Considering the transparency of my clothing, he had a point. "I can hide one here."

He exhaled through his nose. "Do you think they won't check for such a weapon, especially after your escape attempt? Especially one of a size that would be useful for what you intend?"

My jaw clenched. I hated all the logical points he made. "Okay."

Attes turned to the bars, then stopped. "Do you feel her now?" His throat worked as his gaze found mine. "Sotoria's soul, I mean."

His question was strange to me, but I lifted a hand to my chest. I didn't hear her as I had previously, but there was a flicker of something that wasn't an ember. An awareness of someone there, watching and listening. "Yes."

Emotion flickered across his face, too fast for me to determine what it was or even be sure I'd seen anything.

"Then I hope she hears this," Attes said, swallowing once more. "I will save you this time."

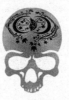

I was restless after Attes turned himself back into a hawk and flew off, which was as bizarre as it sounds. Left to nothing but my thoughts, I did what I normally did.

I trained.

Finding nothing to tie my hair back with, I braided the length, then gently knotted the ends, knowing I'd likely regret it later. Calling on as much memory as I could recall, I imagined myself sparring with an invisible partner and went through the motions Holland had taught me.

As I moved from jabbing with an imaginary dagger to shadow-boxing, my mind wandered instead of emptying.

Attes.

Picturing his face, I swung my closed fist into the air above me and only felt a little bad.

Obviously, I had a hard time trusting him, but that oath? Either I or the embers had felt it. He couldn't break it. And how he spoke about his scar? The pain evident in his voice and on his face was too real, as was the thread of agony in his words when he vowed to save Sotoria this time.

I dipped, moving as fast as I could in the gown. Something Attes had said finally occurred to me after he left. It was so damn obvious. But in my defense? A lot had been—and still *was*—cycling through my mind.

Attes had mentioned how much I resembled Sotoria but knew I didn't look exactly like her. Based on that, and what he'd said before he left, Attes had known her.

And, man, I had so many questions about that. But I realized something else once he was gone.

Sweat dotted my brow as I rose from a crouch and spun, swinging out with my arm. I repeated the move over and over as I thought about how Attes hadn't mentioned Nyktos taking the embers. He probably figured it was something assumed and unnecessary to say.

You're not the weapon…

My steps slowed and then came to a stop, my chest rising and falling from exertion. I rose from another crouch, my arms dropping to my sides. Holland had said that I was Sotoria. So had the goddess Penellaphe—or at least that was how I'd interpreted what they said.

But what if Holland hadn't known? I wiped the back of my hand across my forehead. It wasn't like every Fate was all-knowing. Another could've done something without Holland's knowledge. Or he had been unable to tell me without interfering.

But why did he train me? What was the point?

Unless Attes's instincts were right, and Holland had actually trained me to keep Sotoria's soul and the embers safe. Was it about that instead of killing Kolis?

And if it was?

Letting my head fall back, I stared at the bars above. Gods, I sort of felt like a huge part of my identity had just been shattered, and it was so damn frustrating.

I'd hated that part of myself, loathed what it had cost me. Yet I still didn't feel relief. The resolve to stop Kolis hadn't faded. No part of me attempted to latch on to it as an excuse not to try. And maybe…

Maybe that was because I didn't know who I was without my duty. Maybe it was because it was the one thing I could do before I died that would make a difference. And I just couldn't let that go.

The thing was, whatever the reason, I couldn't dwell on it. If I did, I would lose it.

Turning, I went into the bathing area and picked up a small towel. Using the pitcher of fresh water that had been left behind, I wiped the sweat from my forehead.

My pretty poppy.

A tremor skated over my body, sending shivers of unease cascading down my spine. What bothered me about that? It was the absolute least concerning thing Attes had shared.

Tossing the towel onto the vanity, I returned to the divan and removed the blanket this time, letting it fall to the floor. I plopped down and wiggled into the corner. Drawing my legs up, I tucked them under my gown.

My gaze traveled over the bars, landing on the glittering center of the cage ceiling. With the chamber lights turned down, I could see it clearer. I squinted, realizing the source of the fractured light I'd noticed before. It was a diamond. Or maybe a cluster of them?

I rolled my eyes.

I sat there for a while in silence, my thoughts continuing to jump from one thing to the next. Like so many times before, my mind latched on to one of the most random things.

I suddenly thought about the kiyou wolf I'd seen in the Dark Elms as a child.

I'd been collecting rocks for some bizarre reason I'd long since forgotten when I spotted the wolf. Its fur had been so white it could've been silver, and I'd always been surprised that it hadn't immediately run off or attacked, especially since the kiyou were notoriously averse to mortals. The only other one I'd been close to was the injured wolf.

I was sure I knew why now.

When Ash and I had been at the pool beneath the House of Haides, he'd admitted to checking in on me in the past. I realized now that it had been him all those years ago. There wasn't a single part of me that doubted it.

Chest squeezing, I dropped my chin to my knees. Gods, I missed him, and I was so damn worried about him. What if my dream had given me some insight into his condition, and he was in stasis? That would heal his wounds, but he'd be completely vulnerable.

I needed to get him out of there.

Closing my eyes, I decided it was time to try my hand at being more reassuring. Instead of stressing myself out to the point where I wanted to either scream or throw myself face-first at the bars, I pictured Ash free. Of course, I skipped over exactly *how* I'd manage to free myself from the cage and Dalos and, well…everything else. I went right to the good stuff. Seeing Ash. Feeling his arms around me. Hearing his voice. For real. No dreams.

We wouldn't have long together before Kolis came for us, but I would take the time to make Ash swear he wouldn't blame himself for my death. That once he Ascended and took care of Kolis, he'd find a way to restore his *kardia*.

The back of my throat burned as I buried my face in my knees. I would make Ash promise to live—to *really* live. And that meant eventually opening himself to learning what love felt like and being loved in return, as much as it made me want to set fire to the entire realm.

Because I wasn't that good of a person. I already hated the unknown individual who would one day have the honor of loving and being loved by Ash. I absolutely loathed them.

But I still wanted that for him.

I suppose love made you capable of that: wanting happiness for another, even if it meant them finding it with someone else.

When I opened my eyes again, it was to the sound of rushing water and the feel of cool, damp grass against the length of my body.

Immediately, I knew I was dreaming.

Besides the obvious fact that I wasn't capable of shadowstepping myself free of somewhere deep within Dalos to the mortal realm, something was off. Something that had nothing to do with there not being a stitch of clothing on me.

I wasn't swimming.

In the last couple of dreams I remembered, I was always swimming while the wolf watched me.

Dark waters spilled off the cliffs of the Elysium Peaks. It was my lake, and like my dreams before, no stifling heat clung to the air, but it was different.

While the lake was always dark due to one of the biggest deposits of shadowstone found in the mortal realm, there was no movement. The water was utterly still and smooth, like a black mirror, even where the waterfall poured from high above. My lake had never been like this in my dreams.

I looked down to where my fingers splayed against grass the color of midnight. I lifted my gaze, looking past sweeping elms full of onyx-hued leaves, and branches the color of shadowstone, to the sky that was neither completely night nor day. Vivid and intense stars cast radiant light down on the lake and me. I searched the sky, finding no sign of the moon.

It reminded me of the Shadowlands, but there were no lakes there. Not anymore.

My fingers curled around the blades of grass. I could feel the ground beneath me, cool and prickly. I felt the faint breeze drifting over my legs and glancing off my cheek. There was none of the fuzziness that clung to dreams, even when I swam. Everything was sharp and clear, from the stars above to the rich scent of the damp soil.

This didn't feel like a dream.

As I stared at the star-kissed sky, a humming warmth suddenly came alive in the center of my chest. My skin pimpled. Slowly, I became aware of heat against my back, someone behind me when there had been nothing there upon me opening my eyes.

I wasn't alone.

A hand came over the flare of my hip, warm and heavy in a deliciously familiar way. My stomach started spinning. I breathed in deeply. A fresh, citrusy scent I'd recognize anywhere surrounded me.

My breath snagged as my entire body locked into place. I couldn't move, too afraid that my mind was about to trick me.

A soft touch against the nape of my neck startled me. A silkier sensation followed. Lips brushed the curve of my shoulder, sending hot, tight shivers coursing down the length of my body.

"Liessa."

12

That voice, the shadowy whisper of midnight that never failed to send a myriad of shivers through me, was all his.

Ash's.

My eyes closed. It was his voice. He was behind me. I knew that in my bones and heart but dreaming of my lake instead of falling into any nightmarish scenario was already a blessing. Dreaming of him? Finding him here, even in my dreams…that felt impossible.

Like a miracle.

The hand on my hip firmed, easing me onto my back. Fingers slightly calloused from decades of training with weapons trailed over my cheek, the touch so reverent that my breath caught.

"Open your eyes for me, *liessa*. I need to see them." His breath danced over my lips. "Please."

I responded as if compelled to, but his words held no compulsion. It was just how I reacted to him. Only him. My eyes opened, and I found myself staring into twin pools of molten silver.

Ash.

My heart fluttered out of control as a storm of emotions rushed through me, every fiber of my being swept up in the onslaught. All I could do was stare in a heady mix of disbelief and joy as the breeze lifted the edges of his chestnut hair, tossing the strands against the bronzed skin of his jaw.

My gaze tracked over his wide, expressive mouth. His lips parted, and he looked down, his eyes full of wispy strands of eather, brighter than I'd ever seen. This was only a dream. I knew that, but I still searched the strong slashes of his brows and striking features for any signs of his battle with Kolis. There were no bruises. I looked down.

And *my* lips parted.

Nothing obscured my view of the delineated lines of his chest. Except for the faint scars that had been there before, there was no evidence of the dagger that Kolis had repeatedly plunged into his chest. No signs of wounds across the tightly packed muscles of his abdomen. My gaze skipped lower, running over the fascinating indents on the insides of his hips—

My breath hitched once more. Like me, Ash was completely naked and fully, gloriously aroused. A deep heat spread through me. Gods, I had no idea how my mind could replicate every part of him in such startling detail.

But I was happy about it.

My gaze lifted. One side of his lips quirked up in a half-grin that tugged at my heart. Ash had smiled freely in the mortal realm but less in the Shadowlands. That had begun to change, though. More of his teasing nature had started to resurface, but then...

I didn't want to think about any of that. Not now. What I wanted was to touch him. Desperately so. But my fingers curled into the grass. I feared that if I did, he would vanish on me and collapse into nothing.

And if that happened? Even in a dream? It would be an unbearable loss. Because we didn't have much time, and this counted. It had to.

Ash's head tipped back and to the side as his gaze left mine and glided down. The intensity of his perusal was like a physical touch. My skin tingled, and the tips of my breasts tightened. Liquid heat pooled low in my stomach as the other side of his lips rose in a mischievous quirk. His gaze lowered more, running over my stomach and then between my thighs. His stare was blatant and all-consuming, branding my skin. The tips of his fangs appeared as he drew his lower lip between his teeth.

"*Liessa*," he repeated in that smoke-and-shadow voice of his, sliding his hand across my lower stomach, leaving a trail of liquid fire in its wake. His eyes returned to mine. "Is it really you? Come to taunt me in my dreams?"

"Your dreams?" I said, watching his eyes close briefly at the sound of my voice. "More like you're in *my* dream."

Ash chuckled, and I sucked in a reedy breath. That rough, low laugh created heat in my blood. Gods, no one else could make such a simple thing sound so hedonistic. "Even in my dreams, you argue with me."

"I'm not arguing with you."

"You're not?"

"No." I totally was.

That laugh came again, teasing my lips, and then his mouth was on mine. There was no pain from my split lip, but I was dreaming. Of course, there'd be no pain. But nothing could've prepared me for the feel of his mouth against mine. It came as a shock to the senses because it felt so damn real. I didn't think any memories could capture the soft-yet-unyielding firmness of his lips.

But then I wasn't really thinking anymore because Ash's kisses obliterated all thoughts. They always had. It was just us. His mouth, and how he kissed like a man dying of thirst, taking from me, drawing my tongue in to duel with his, and sipping from my lips. The slower, more languid kisses were electric, sending sparks of desire dancing all over my body. In that moment, my senses were overloaded, and it was hard to think of anything but the sensation of his lips on mine. I was breathless by the time he drew back.

"I dreamt that I could hear you calling my name." He caught my lower lip between his teeth. I gasped at the quick nip. "I dreamt that you were in need of me."

I listened, my heart racing as his hand swept up, curving around my breast. My back arched.

"But I shouldn't be able to dream," he said. I wasn't sure what he meant, but then his voice changed, taking on a velvety quality, smooth and rich like the sweetest chocolate. "Touch me. Touch me, *liessa*, so that I know you're real. Please."

Gods, there was no way I could do anything but what he demanded, what he pleaded for. Hands trembling, I pressed my fingers against his cheeks. I trembled at the contact. His skin was hard, warm, and so very real. As his mouth moved over mine, I drew my hands down his chest, marveling at the feel of him. My fingers skimmed the tight ridges of his stomach.

Ash moaned against my lips, and the sound heated my blood even more. I could feel him against my thigh, hard and thick. His mouth left mine, and my eyes fluttered open. He was looking down at me once more, his gaze slowly tracking over my face for several seconds. "Thirty-six."

My freckles.

My heart swelled so swiftly and strongly that I wouldn't have been surprised if I floated right off the grass.

"I had to count them." His hand came to my jaw. "Just to make sure they were all where they're supposed to be."

Dreaming of him counting my freckles made sense. His tendency to do that was something that made my heart melt. But the rest? What a strange thing for me to have dreamt him saying.

Ash's lips captured mine once more, giving me no time to dwell on that. And when he kissed like this, as if I were the only thing in the world that could sustain him, I could do nothing but happily drown in those kisses.

And I did.

I kissed him back, saying everything I felt without uttering a single word, conveying a depth of emotion that words could never do justice to. I kissed him like it might be the last chance I'd get.

And it really could be.

A knot of sadness threatened to form and ruin the moment, but I refused to let it. I clasped his shoulders, feeling the slightly raised skin under the ink that had been driven into his flesh.

Ash shook, breathing raggedly as he pressed his forehead to mine. His hand splayed across my cheek, and that trembled, too. "I miss you," he whispered hoarsely. "I don't...I don't know how much time has passed. A day? Two? A week? Only a few hours? I don't know, *liessa*, but I miss you, even as I sleep so deeply."

Something about what he said caused my skin to prickle. A feeling, or maybe a memory, prodded me, but I couldn't figure it out.

And I didn't think it mattered right now. "I'm here, Ash."

He shuddered.

"So don't miss me." I touched his jaw, feeling the slight stubble there. "Love me instead."

"I do," Ash swore. "Fates, Sera, I do."

I lifted my head, bringing our mouths together, even though his words reminded me that I was dreaming, that all of this was me creating what I *wanted* to feel and hear. And, gods, I wanted nothing more than to hear Ash say that he loved me. That he was capable of it. And if I could only get that in a dream, I'd take it without shame. My tongue parted his lips, and his answering groan was the sound of pure bliss.

Ash's palm returned to my breast. A breathy moan left me as he dragged the rough pad of his thumb over the hardened nipple. I sank a hand into the soft strands of his hair, curling my fingers around them as his hand skated down my stomach and then between my thighs. The feeling of him there, his fingers slipping through the dampness and into me, was another shock to the senses. I cried out, the sound caught by his kiss. My hips rose at the wicked, torturous pressure of his finger sinking into me. I ground against his hand, tension spinning, and…gods, I'd *never* felt something like this in a dream before. Never anything this intense.

I felt the sharp tip of one fang against my tongue and shivered. His bite never caused pain, only sensual, decadent pleasure. Not like—

My hand tightened in his hair. There was no space for that. Not in my dreams. Not when I was living in a state I didn't want to wake from.

But I knew I would.

That knowledge filled me with a keening, desperate yearning. I pulled on him, wanting to feel his weight on me. Needing to. "I need you." I gripped his arm with my other hand, feeling his muscles jump. "I need you, Ash. Please."

"You have me, *liessa*." Ash, thank the gods, obliged without hesitation. He shifted, his large body coming down over mine, caging me. The coarser hairs of his legs teased mine as he settled between my thighs. "You've always had me." The tip of a sharp fang dragged along my lower lip, creating tiny knots of pleasure as the hot, hard length of him pressed against my core. "I've always had you."

The feel of him sparked a pulsing twist of pleasure that ignited frenzied need because he felt…gods, he felt better than a memory.

A deep sound rumbled from Ash. His hand returned to my hip, and he pressed into me as his kisses turned fiercer, deeper, and rougher. With each drugging, tugging brush and pull of his mouth, tiny fires erupted through me. Then, with one thrust, he seated himself fully.

My cry was lost in his hoarse shout as a jolt of surprise swept through me, causing me to lock up. I could feel the little bite of pain from his size and the pulsing pleasure of him filling and stretching me.

I could *really* feel him.

Pulse racing, my eyes flew open, and my gaze collided with Ash's. His body had stilled, too, but the bright-as-the-moon eather in his eyes whirled wildly. Neither of us moved or spoke for several moments as the embers in my chest started to hum.

"You feel…" Ash shook his head, his voice thick. His eyes were wide, the hollows under his cheeks starker as I felt him jerk inside me. "You feel as if you're here."

As did he.

I inhaled deeply, catching the faint scent of lilacs—*stale* lilacs. My heart turned over heavily, and fear coursed through me. Was I waking up? My already-pounding heart sped up. No, I wasn't ready for that. I would never be.

"Love me," I ordered—begged, really. "Love me."

"Always," he rasped.

Tears dampened my lashes. I squeezed my eyes shut against them, not wanting to feel the hopelessness they evoked. I didn't want a sorrow-filled experience in my dreams.

I wanted to burn.

Ash's head dipped, his mouth closing over the tip of a breast. He drew my nipple into his hot mouth. I gasped as a new wave of pleasure rolled through me. His hips began to move, and my gasp quickly turned to a moan.

He lifted his head, nuzzling my neck under my ear. "You're so beautiful. Damn it, Sera, you're so fucking beautiful."

A shaky breath left me. I couldn't feel more beautiful than I did right then.

"Tell me," he murmured against the skin of my throat. "Tell me you love me, and I'll show you my gratitude. I swear to you."

"I love you," I guided his head up, his eyes meeting mine. "I love you so much, Ash."

Another tremor ran through him. He said something too low and quick for me to understand, but he did exactly as he swore he would.

The plunges and retreats picked up speed, moving faster and going deeper. We were all teeth and tangled limbs, greedy and desperate. We moved together, his hips thrusting down and mine surging to his. Pleasure spiked, making me dizzy and breathless in a way that conjured no fear, only want and need.

The muscles of his arms flexed, then he grasped my hip, lifting me until my ass was off the ground. I clasped the back of his neck, wrapping my legs around his waist. Gods, the angle…

Hot, tight shudders racked my body as his moved in a furious rhythm. The release came fast and hard. I fractured, his name falling from my lips and whispering against his flesh. He followed with a shout, driving me into the ground, bolts of pleasure arcing, leaving both of us panting and breathless, our skin slick with a sheen of sweat—

mine warm, and his…

Ash felt *cold*.

Like he did when he needed to feed. I didn't know why my memories decided to capture him that way now, but my thoughts scattered at the sound of his throaty laugh.

"Fates." Ash's cheek dragged against mine when he turned his head. His kiss was featherlight and tender as he eased from me, shifting so he braced the bulk of his weight. "How can this be a dream?"

"I don't know." I sighed as his nose touched mine. That too had cooled. A moment passed, and I let out a shaky breath. "It feels…"

"Real." Ash nipped my lower lip once more, and when I gasped, his curled upward. "That felt real, didn't it?"

I grinned, loving the sight of his smile. "Yes."

His tongue flicked out, soothing the sting of his bite. "You feel real, Sera. So much so that I almost think we're…"

Waiting for an answer, I searched his features. "What?"

His throat worked on a swallow, and he drew his fingers over the freckles on my chin. "I don't know." He smiled then, but it didn't reach his stunning silver eyes. "But I feel as if the Fates have rewarded me."

"*You* feel like that?" I laughed quietly. "This is such a strange dream—a good one, but strange."

"I've never dreamt of anything better."

"Neither have I," I whispered.

Ash's lips found mine, and my heart fluttered as if it had grown wings. The unrelenting need to hold on to him and cherish every moment spent in his presence surged through my entire being.

And I did.

I thought we lay there for a while, his forehead resting against mine, and our bodies still pressed tightly together. It felt like that—like the real passing of seconds and minutes.

But I'd never felt time in a dream before.

"Sera…" He spoke my name against my lips. "You have no idea how I wish this were real."

"I do." I found his mouth and kissed him. Even his lips were cold now.

He lifted his head, and his chest rose sharply against mine. "*Sera.*"

The way he said my name had my pulse spiking. My eyes fluttered open. His were wide.

"What happened?" His gaze darted wildly over my face. My concern rose. "Fucking Fates, did I hurt you?"

"What?" I frowned. "Of course, not."

The eather pulsed brightly. "Your lip is split, and your jaw…it's swollen. It wasn't like that before."

A shiver tiptoed down my spine. I managed to wiggle an arm between us and touch my lip. I winced at the flare of pain.

Ash moved quickly, catching my wrist. He pulled my hand away. "Don't poke at it." He drew my fingers to his mouth, dropping devastatingly gentle kisses on their tips.

Confusion swirled as I lifted my gaze to his. "It hurts."

His skin thinned until I saw the dark shadows of eather beneath his flesh. "I can see that it would."

"But it stopped hurting the moment I started dreaming…" I trailed off.

"Are these injuries real?" Ash's eyes had gone as flat as I'd seen Kolis's turn before. He cursed. "Did *he* do this?" Frost dripped from his tone. "Has Kolis hurt you?"

"I don't…" I slammed my eyes shut. "I don't know why I would dream this."

"This isn't your…"

My brows pinched together. His skin had gotten even colder. The next breath I took carried that sweet-stale stench again as I opened my eyes.

"My fear," he said, cursing.

"Your fear?"

"Yes." Shadows stained the skin under his eyes where none had been before. Hollows had formed under his cheekbones. His lips were tinted blue. "Even in sleep, my fear for you consumes me."

I stiffened at the sight of him. He was changing right before my eyes. His normally golden skin lost its color. Then the edges of Ash's face blurred. My chest spasmed. His shoulders did the same.

"*Liessa?*" His head jerked at the sound of a…footstep?

My skin pimpled all over. A sudden pressure spread along the nape of my neck. My gaze flew to where my fingers were pressed tightly into the skin of his arms. "I can't feel you." My throat dried as I held on tighter. Or thought I did. I could barely feel his skin beneath mine anymore. "I can't feel you any longer."

"It's okay," Ash told me, his voice rough.

But it wasn't okay. The tall, sweeping elms above us collapsed into smoke. The breeze vanished. Bone-deep desperation rose as I looked up at him.

"I don't want to wake up," I whispered, my heart cracking. I grabbed hold of him, but I couldn't feel him. "Please, don't let me wake up. I don't want to leave you. *Please.*"

A noise came from Ash that sounded as if it had been dragged from the depths of his soul. "Sera—"

I jolted awake, my eyes flying open. I dragged in a ragged breath and tried to ease the pressure clamping down on my chest. My eyes burned with tears, causing the bars to blur just as Ash's face had.

It had been a dream.

I knew that, but it had *felt* real. I could still feel Ash—his touch and kisses, the weight of him against my body. I could even feel that now, the fullness of him inside me and the dampness between my thighs. My hands *still* tingled with the feeling of his flesh against mine. It all felt so damn real. Still did.

But it couldn't be.

Because there were no bright stars above me, only bars. And beneath me? The softness of the divan I'd fallen asleep on. There was no tranquil quiet—the distant, guttural howls of the dakkais could be heard.

I was once more caged.

The Chosen arrived sometime later. It could've been hours, or another day could've passed, I couldn't tell. But there were fewer Chosen than before under Callum's watchful gaze.

I made sure I remained at the divan while they collected the used towels, replaced the water in the pitchers with fresh, and then set the table with what appeared to be a carafe of water and a tall, slender, capped bottle and four glasses.

"I'm relieved to see you're a quick learner," Callum commented after the last Chosen had left the chamber.

I looked over at him. "My life is complete knowing that."

The Revenant smirked. "I'm sure it is."

Rolling my eyes, I looked away. My heart was beating fast, mostly out of concern that somehow Attes's visit would be discovered.

But Callum said nothing. He just silently stood near the cage.

Frustration stoked my temper as I focused on him. "Do you need something?"

"No." That polite smile appeared.

"Then why are you just standing there, staring at me?"

"Does it bother you?"

"Who wouldn't be bothered by it?" I replied, unfolding my legs.

"I wouldn't."

"Well, I don't really think your opinion counts."

The golden paint shimmered when he lifted his head. "Why is that?"

"I can't imagine you're right in the head." I scooted to the edge of the divan, letting my feet touch the floor. "What with dying multiple times and all."

He laughed. "At least I come back. You—"

"I know. I won't." I raised a brow. "Not exactly a clever insult, considering I'm mortal."

Callum shrugged as I glanced at the doors. They weren't completely closed. I could see the glint of golden armor through the gap.

My fingers tapped the cushion as my gaze slid back to him. I thought about what I'd seen in the dimly lit part of the sprawling structure. "I...I saw other Chosen."

"I was under the impression that when you made your poor attempt at an escape, you saw *many* Chosen," he replied. "And frightened them."

I almost laughed. Yeah, I'd likely been a terrifying figure, but I knew I wasn't what truly scared them. "I'm not talking about them. I saw one feeding on another."

Callum said nothing.

"And she killed him," I continued. "But he came back. Not like you. He was—" The embers suddenly pulsed in my chest, jerking my attention to the doors.

"You feel him?" Callum asked. "I can see that you do."

My palms turned clammy as I rose. "Then why do you ask?"

"Because," he answered, much like a rotten little child.

The doors swung open, and I couldn't prevent the immediate burst of fear upon seeing Kolis enter the chamber. It invaded all my muscles, causing me to go rigid. Even after I forced myself to relax, it lingered like a dark cloud.

Intrigue flickered across Kolis's features as he approached the cage. "What are you two discussing?"

I opened my mouth to lie with who knew what, but Callum, the bastard, beat me to it.

"She was asking about the Chosen she killed," Callum shared, retrieving the key from his pocket. "And then the one who returned. She was sharing her astute observation of how Antonis wasn't a Revenant."

Antonis, I repeated to myself. So that was the name of the Chosen who'd come back to life and tried to attack me.

"Of course, not." Kolis frowned and looked at me as if I were somehow supposed to know what he was. "Some would call him cursed. A once-mortal, now-decaying body plagued with an insatiable hunger. Craven."

A flurry of nerves churned in my belly as Callum unlocked the cage door. The soft creak of the hinges sent shivers down my spine. I told myself that he must not know about Attes because I doubted we'd be talking about Craven if he did.

"They are nothing more than an unfortunate…side effect."

"Side effect of what, exactly?" I asked, watching Callum step aside.

"Of creating the Ascended. They are the product of maintaining balance and giving life." Kolis smiled then, ducking as he entered the cage.

Fear collided with my already-frazzled nerves, unleashing a surging tide of potent emotions I battled to restrain. I gritted my teeth in a desperate attempt to keep them at bay, ignoring the flare of pain it caused. "The Ascended? I don't think I understand."

"The woman you spoke of? The one I was told you killed." The smile faded as the door was closed behind Kolis. "She was an Ascended. My child."

I drew back in surprise. "You don't mean that in the literal sense, right?"

"I played a role in the creation of her new life," he replied. "Does that not make her my child?"

I wasn't so sure. I didn't know what he meant by *playing a role.* "How?"

"By Ascending her, just as my brother did with those before."

A jolt of incredulity surged through me. Everyone had said that no Chosen had Ascended since Kolis's reign began.

With keen discernment, Kolis's observant stare flitted across my face. "That surprises you to hear? Did my nephew not explain how the Chosen are made into gods? It's through Ascension."

I tensed at the mention of Ash.

"Whether or not he did, I can see you don't believe me." His jaw clenched, and the gold flecks brightened in his eyes. "You think I cannot give life just because I cannot make a god like my brother did?"

Oh, damn. I'd hit a nerve. "I—"

"It does not matter." His hand cut through the air in a curt wave.

"This is not what I came to speak to you about."

A heavy thud resounded from within my chest. Maybe I had been too quick to think he hadn't learned about Attes's visit.

"Leave us," Kolis bit out.

Outside the cage, Callum said, "Yes, Your Majesty."

Kolis crossed the cage, going to the table. "You didn't answer my question."

I blinked rapidly. He'd spoken?

"I asked if you've been resting." A glimmer of gold swirled beneath the flesh of his cheeks. "Since I last saw you."

Did he actually think I'd been relaxing? My mouth opened to ask him that, but I stopped myself.

The plan.

I had a plan.

Ash was far more important than the momentary satisfaction of speaking my mind. I took a deep breath and held it, forcing my mind to clear. Years' worth of training I wanted nothing more than to forget pieced themselves together, reminding me why I needed to be a blank canvas.

It was the only way to adapt to his needs, allowing my personality to become painted with what he wanted and all he approved of. It was a part of the art of seduction the Mistresses of the Jade had taught. *Pay attention to what is said and what is not spoken. Movements and actions.* Knowledge of a person could always be gained.

And used.

I already knew that Kolis didn't like cursing. Apparently, he also didn't enjoy being called out when he was being a creep, which was unfortunately often. What did he like? I already knew from my few interactions with him that he didn't enjoy others arguing or fighting back. He was nothing like Ash. Kolis wanted meekness. And I would bet that, above all else, he desired submission.

My fingers curled into the skirt of my gown as I cleared my throat. "I have been resting."

"Good." He gestured at the table. "Would you like something to drink? It will be disappointing if you decline."

Irritation buzzed through my veins, and I wasn't sure if I was more frustrated with his small manipulation or myself. He wanted me to drink, so I drank. He wanted me to stand on my head, I would stand on my fucking head. That was what it would take. I *knew* that.

"Yes." The word fell from my lips like dead weight.

Kolis smiled, flashing straight, white teeth and fangs. That smile… it was momentarily startling because it was strange. I still couldn't put my finger on why, but it was a nice smile. For all the Primal's horribleness, he was a beautiful being. That couldn't be denied.

And neither could his crimes against both mortals and gods.

I watched him make his way to the table and lift the stopper on a decanter. He didn't walk as much as he *glided*. His bare feet barely skimmed the floor, as if the air itself carried him forward. He was dressed as he had been when I briefly saw him in the Sun Temple the day of the Rite. A fitted white tunic and loose linen pants. Both were speckled with gold. His hair was down, tucked back behind his ears, and from the side, there was no mistaking how nearly identical his features were to the painting of his brother Eythos that hung in the House of Haides' library. There were slight differences. Kolis's jaw and chin were broader, and Eythos's brow was stronger, but they were still twins.

And it was impossible not to see parts of Ash in those features. The angles and planes of Kolis's face were more refined, less raw and wild than Ash's, but the similarities were unnerving, nonetheless.

Kolis poured a glass of clear liquid that formed tiny bubbles that raced to the surface of the slender flute. "Callum told me you asked about my nephew."

Motherfucker.

I was also a motherfucker because I had been desperate enough to ask Callum about Ash.

"He said you wanted to know where he is," he continued, picking up the glass and bringing it to me.

I was surprised by how steady my hand was when I took the flute. "I did," I answered, knowing better than to lie about it.

"Sit," Kolis instructed.

The order raised my hackles, but I sat on the divan as I glanced down at the strange drink. Giving it a sniff, I detected soft, fruity notes. "What is this?"

"Water infused with strawberries and lemon. It is a drink my brother used to make," he said, and my gaze shot to him. "He was good at creating all manner of things, be it life or refreshments."

I wasn't sure what to make of that tidbit of information, but there was no bitterness to his tone. Thinking it wasn't likely that he would poison me, I took a tiny sip. I sat straighter as the water danced on my tongue, taking in the sweetness of the strawberries and the faint tang of the lemon.

"What do you think?" he asked.

"It's good," I admitted, taking a longer drink. "Really good."

Kolis gave a curt wave of his hand, and the dining chair slid across the tile like a hound answering its owner's call. He sat directly in front of me.

"Why do you want to know where my nephew is?" he asked.

Any hope I had that he would move on from the topic fizzled out like the drink I held. "Curiosity."

Kolis chuckled, and the sound was bright yet cold.

I decided the best course of action was to direct the subject to something else. "Did the Shadowland forces you spoke of earlier leave the borders of Dalos?" I questioned, realizing I had not thought to ask Attes that.

"No, they have not," he answered. "They remain in the Bonelands."

"The Bonelands?" My brow knitted.

"Eythos named it," Kolis said with a shrug. "It's to the south of Dalos, along the coast, beyond the Carcers. A rather uninhabitable stretch of sand dunes and overgrown, forested lands full of forgotten Temples once belonging to the Ancients, and rocks that vaguely resemble the bones of giants. My brother believed them to be actual bones of dragons slaughtered by the Ancients." He scoffed. "Perhaps he was right."

Why were the Ancients killing dragons? The answer to that wasn't important, but hadn't Attes said that Ash was being held in the Carcers? "You haven't...attacked them? Forced them back from your borders?"

"Should I have?" he countered.

I wasn't exactly sure how he expected me to answer that question, but I went with the obvious. "Yes?"

"Truly?"

"If they were forces encroaching on my lands, I would," I answered objectively.

"But if I do that, then it would escalate tensions, possibly to the point of no return." He lifted his glass. "Contrary to what you may believe about me, I have no desire to start a war. Engaging with his forces would do exactly that."

My lips slowly parted as his claim hung in the space between us like a heavy fog of a whole lot of bullshit.

"You look surprised."

"More like confused," I said. Attes hadn't said that Kolis wanted war. He'd only said that the false King would fight a war his way.

"And why is that?"

"You said you wanted to rise as the Primal of Life and Death," I explained, carefully choosing my words. His cunning gaze centered on me. The gold should've warmed his eyes, but his stare was so damn cold. "And that those who don't relinquish their Courts and kingdoms to you would die."

"I did say that."

"You're speaking of Primals, gods, and mortals alike, correct?" When he nodded, I stated what I thought was pretty obvious. "Would that not cause a war?"

Kolis's chuckle was a low hiss like a serpent's, full of superiority and amusement bordering on mockery. "I suppose I should've been clearer. I have no plans of starting a war that I would not win or one that would leave much of both realms an uninhabitable mess, which is what would happen if a war began," he said. "Once again, you look surprised."

I bet I did look like that when I could feel my jaw hanging open like a broken gate. I wasn't even sure why hearing what he said surprised me so much. Kolis wanted to be a supreme ruler, which meant there would need to be land and people to rule over.

I suppose it was because I thought of Kolis as an unhinged, chaotic mass murderer.

And who would blame me for that? The way he'd behaved when I first woke in Dalos had backed up that belief. But he wasn't that.

Well, he was for sure an unhinged mass murderer, but he was far more logical than chaotic. Or maybe as logical as he was chaotic. Either way, the realization made him all the more frightening to me.

"Besides," he said. "Such a war would most certainly spill into the mortal realm, and while they have become far too complacent, they cannot worship us as they should if they're dead."

"Complacent?" I questioned.

"In their lives. But that will soon change, as I plan to take more of an active role."

My mouth had to be hanging open again, and it had nothing to do with what he meant by *an active role*. "I'm not sure how much time you spend among mortals, but the vast majority don't have the luxury of being complacent in their lives."

He fixed his stare on me. "Perhaps if they served Iliseeum better, they would have that luxury. However, their time spent in worship and prayer has steadily waned. Their pledges to the Temples continue to dwindle, while their tithes become less and less impressive."

Even as scary as he was, my mouth would not stop moving. "It's likely because most of their time is spent trying to survive."

"And as I just said, perhaps their prosperity would improve if they proved themselves worthy of it," he countered. "As it stands, their losses and struggles are of their own making."

Anger flashed through me so hotly, Kolis would be drowning in it if he had Ash's abilities. I had to move past this subject of mortals because if I didn't, I'd likely lose my temper. "Won't taking me, the Consort of the Shadowlands, further escalate things?"

"Nyktos started things by attacking me, but I am giving him time to rethink his actions, as acts of war can always be walked back," he said, and the only part I really latched on to was him saying that he was giving Ash time. "Taking you could present challenges, but only if the other Primals feel you are worth going to war over."

My lips pursed as I thought about what Attes had shared. "Or if they fear this act will embolden you to break tradition further with them?"

"They should already fear that," he replied, smirking. "Most do. Either way, they know what they could lose if they decide to take up arms against me. I will destroy everything they care about and send their Courts into ruin before they find themselves imprisoned right alongside Nyktos."

A shiver danced on the back of my neck. He sounded so very confident, but I'd caught what he'd said moments earlier. He'd basically admitted that there was a chance he could lose a war in his current state. Attes's reaction to learning that shadowstone had pierced Kolis's flesh flashed through my mind. Just how weakened was he? And why?

"You didn't answer my question," Kolis reminded me. "Why did you ask about my nephew?"

"I told you. I was just—"

"Curious. That is what you said, but I have ears and eyes, *so'lis*. I heard your scream when I took him down. Saw the terror in your expression and eyes." He shifted, hooking one leg over the other. "You have never screamed in terror for me."

I blinked, my mouth opening again.

"Careful," he murmured. Tension crept into my muscles. His smirk returned. "I have not known this version of you long, but I can already tell when you're about to say something very unwise."

Snapping my mouth shut, I winced at the flare of pain in my jaw. Across from me, brackets framed Kolis's mouth. He looked away, a lock of hair falling across his cheek just as…as Ash's hair was apt to do.

I took another drink, careful to avoid the tender skin of my lip as I quickly thought about what to say. Once again, I knew I needed to be smart when it came to speaking about Ash. My thoughts raced, thinking about what Kolis could already know. He wouldn't believe that I felt nothing for Nyktos, but I also knew I couldn't let him know how deep my feelings for him ran. I had no idea exactly how Kolis would respond if he learned that I was in love with his nephew, but I knew it wouldn't be good for Ash or me.

"I'm…fond of him—"

A roll of thunder echoed from outside, drawing my gaze to the ceiling as the walls of the chamber shook. Okay, maybe that was a bad way to start.

"Speak," he demanded, his eyes aglow with eather as the air in the cage became thick and heavy. "Or are you unable to do so because you seek to speak a lie?"

Anger bubbled up like the fruity water in my glass, but displaying that would get me nowhere. I lowered my gaze. "No, it's just that you scared me."

A moment passed, and the oppressive energy seemed to lift from the space around us. "That was not my intention."

Words crept up my throat. I knew what to do. Be understanding. Smiling would also be good. I should apologize. Above all else, I needed to reassure him that he'd done nothing wrong.

But the words that made it to the tip of my tongue didn't make it past my lips. I couldn't even manage a smile.

Damn it, this was easier said than done.

"As you were saying?" Kolis persisted.

"I was saying that I have a fondness for him. He's been kind to me," I added quickly. "And he kept me safe."

Kolis's flesh started to glow from within. A heartbeat passed, and then the empty flute shattered in his hand, turning to nothing and causing me to jump.

Good gods, this Primal needed to get a grip.

"I do not want to see him harmed because of that," I forged on. "But he…he never wanted me."

"Never wanted you?" he queried softly. "I've never known Nyktos to be possessive of anyone or anything. Until you."

"It's because of the embers," I said, knowing I was taking a huge risk. A major one. "And what his father did."

"Do tell."

I took another sip of my water, willing my heart to slow. "Nyktos didn't know what his father did, how Eythos placed the embers in my bloodline. He didn't even know that his father had taken an ember of life from him."

Kolis's unwavering stare latched on to mine. "I would prefer it if you didn't lie."

"I'm not," I said, frustration seeping into my tone because that was the truth. "All he knew was that his father made a deal with a mortal King, agreeing to save his kingdom in exchange for a bride from his bloodline. He didn't know why. And he was never told."

Kolis said nothing.

After a moment, I decided that the lack of response meant it was okay to continue. "But he was drawn to me—to the ember," I amended quickly. "The part of him that is in me. It connects us, and I suppose it can make one feel a...a certain way. But he doesn't want me. He never did." What felt like a gaping wound opened in my chest. "What he feels for me is based on duty and honor."

The Primal sighed. "Has he fucked you?"

I inhaled sharply, my muscles coiling with tension. What he asked was none of his business, but I knew better than to say that or lie. Still, speaking the truth wasn't any smarter. There was no good way to answer that question.

"Yes." I forced a casual shrug. "We are attracted to each other, but he's not the only person I've been attracted to—" The clap of thunder came again, much louder this time. "Or that I've been with. It's not like he loves me."

"See," Kolis drawled, the churning eather slowing in his flesh. "I'm not so sure about that. You do not kill for another unless love is involved."

I frowned. "People kill for every reason and no reason—"

"Mortals kill for every reason and no reason," he corrected. "Not Primals."

"Really?" I couldn't keep the dryness from my tone.

That strange smile of his appeared. "Every life I've ever taken, I did so because of love."

"And that is the only thing love has ever inspired in you?" I asked before I could stop myself. "Death?"

Deep grooves appeared between his brows. A moment passed. "Yes."

"I…" I fell silent. Was he serious? I thought he was. Gods, that was so damn messed up and sad—tragic, actually. I felt an unsteady sensation in my chest because it made me think of what I'd done for my mother. I loathed the woman, yet I loved her, and all I ever did for her was kill. I imagined if that were my only experience with love, I would think the same.

Damn.

It struck me then that until I met Ash, my views on love were less demented than Kolis's, but they hadn't been that much different.

Glancing over at him, I sighed. "Then I'm sorry."

Something like surprise flickered across his face, smoothing out the creases between his brows. "You have never apologized to me."

I stilled, half-expecting to hear Sotoria's voice, but she remained quiet.

"So, why would you do so now?" he asked.

"I…I don't know much about love, or anything really," I said, and that was also the damn truth. "But love should inspire one to indulge in more than just violence and death."

He watched me in silence for several moments. "You're right."

I was?

I *was*.

Swallowing the rest of the fruity water, I sort of wished it was liquor—hard whiskey.

"But," he said, causing my pulse to speed up even more, "I know that love inspires great acts of reckless violence, much like the kind my nephew engaged in."

"I know what you're getting at." I bent, placing the flute on the tile beside my feet. "But Nyktos cannot love me."

"What are you saying? That you're unlovable?" He lifted a brow. "Based solely on your mouth and disagreeable temper, I wouldn't argue against that assessment."

My eyes narrowed. "Well, that was kind of rude."

A half-smile appeared, and I realized he was teasing me. Shivers broke out across the nape of my neck, and the knots of discomfort grew. "But,"—I forced myself to continue—"that wasn't what I was going to say."

"What *were* you going to say?"

"Nyktos is the one who is incapable of loving anyone," I shared, the sinking sensation in my chest now joining the knots. I hated speaking any truths about Ash to Kolis. It felt like a betrayal, but considering what I would likely have to do, it was the least of my worries. "He had his *kardia* removed."

Kolis leaned back in his chair, his jaw loosening. "Come now." He shook his head.

"It's true." I clasped my knees. "He cannot love."

A heartbeat passed. Then another. A godsdamn tense minute went by while Kolis stared. "Why would he do that?"

"I don't know," I lied smoothly. "You'd have to ask him."

"Well, that might be a problem."

I flashed cold, then turned hot. "Why…why is that?"

"Because my nephew is currently unavailable for anything beyond taking up space," Kolis said as a low-level buzz filled my ears. "He's in stasis."

14

Denial crashed into concern as my worst fear was confirmed. Ash had been *that* weakened by battle. I needed to get to him. He was completely vulnerable.

My chest began to tighten. *Mostly*, I reminded myself. He was protected. I clung to that and asked, "So, he's…been taken to ground?"

"He has."

Aware of his keen stare fixed on me, I didn't allow myself to show even the minuscule amount of relief I felt. The ground would protect and heal him. I swallowed, looking over at Kolis as a thought occurred to me.

"Why didn't the earth attempt to protect him in the other chamber?" I asked. "I was under the impression that it happens pretty fast if a Primal is weakened."

"It normally does. That is if the Primal isn't killed outright." He jerked his chin at the floor. "You see these tiles? They're made of shadowstone. Do you know how shadowstone was created?"

I shook my head.

"Dragon fire. Not the draken, but their ancestors. Shadowstone is what became of any life form burned by dragon fire—from trees to mortals, even the Ancients. Perhaps even a few Arae." He laughed, clearly amused by that idea.

Meanwhile, my stomach churned as I thought about all the shadowstone in just this one chamber, let alone throughout Iliseeum and the deposits in the mortal realm—like my lake and the Shadow Temples.

Wait.

The floor of my lake was originally trees or people?

More importantly, the entire exterior of the House of Haides had been constructed from it, as was the grand staircase in the foyer, the walls of many of the chambers, and even some of the floor.

Well, that was something I could've gone my entire life not knowing.

"That's...a lot of melted-down people," I murmured, my lip curling.

His laugh was lighter. Friendly, even. "It actually doesn't take that much to have a rather large deposit of shadowstone. Once the living creature is, as you put it, *melted*, they in essence become slag, soaking into the soil and sometimes spreading into rivers and streams. Once that cools, everything the slag touches becomes shadowstone."

"Oh," I whispered, thinking that explanation didn't make the fact that my feet were resting upon the slag of people easier to swallow.

"There are only a few things in either realm that can penetrate shadowstone," he said. "And the earth is not one of them. There only needs to be a few slivers in a floor or area, and the roots will not be able to break through."

I frowned, only knowing of one thing shadowstone *was* vulnerable to, and that was shadowstone itself.

I bet the bones of the Ancients were the second thing.

"I may have gone a bit overboard in here." Kolis gave the outer room a scan, then shrugged. "The walls and ceiling of the chamber and your quarters are constructed of pure shadowstone, but it was my brother who built the House of Haides, what good that did him." His silver-and-gold gaze returned to me as he slowly unhooked one leg. "Shadowstone also weakens eather—the Primal essence—although it does not block it completely." Really? Surprise flickered through me. If that were the case, I hadn't expected the embers in me, a mortal, to be strong enough to get past the shadowstone. I glanced at the faint cracks I'd created in the tile and walls. Did he notice them? And if so, assume they were due to him and Ash battling? Ash had said the hit of eather he'd taken from me was strong.

"How does that work?" I asked, my curiosity getting the better of me. "How does the shadowstone weaken eather?"

"It absorbs the energy, just as it does light, and doesn't allow us to pull as much of the essence from the environment," he stated as if that explained everything. "I believe you, by the way."

I stopped thinking about shadowstone immediately. He did? Holy damn, I was so surprised, a breeze could've toppled me. "Good," I said. "Because I'm telling the truth."

"About Nyktos?" His chin dipped as his smile became tight.

"Yes."

My relief vanished in an instant, almost like it never was. The unease doubled, and it suddenly struck me that it wasn't just my response to Kolis. It was also Sotoria's. The feeling was stronger now than it had been when Attes was here. She was more than aware. Maybe actively listening in. I...I instinctually knew I was right, and I also knew she was wary. Very much so. A great sense of foreboding slithered up my spine like a slow-creeping vine.

"I doubt you'd have known that removing the *kardia* can be done." Kolis stood. "And it sounds like something Nyktos would do."

"It does?"

He nodded. "You see, I know my nephew better than he knows himself."

I doubted that, but I wisely kept my opinion to myself.

"He's likely convinced himself that removing his *kardia* prevents me from hurting him by striking at someone he loves." The kind of smile I was familiar with returned, and, gods, there *was* something off about it. Like it was an expression he'd learned but didn't quite understand. "What do you think?"

I pressed my fingers into my knees. "I think...I think what happened to his parents would've drawn him toward such a conclusion."

Kolis's laugh was short and flat. "Possibly, but it's not the real reason, my dear." He knelt. "It's because he fears turning into me."

The breath I drew in got stuck. Nektas had said something similar.

Kolis's gaze tracked over the tangled length of my hair. "And he fears that because he knows he would do the same as I did if the one he loved were taken from him." He lowered his voice. "He knows he would be capable of worse."

Maybe Kolis was right. If Ash still had his *kardia*, perhaps he *would* be capable of worse. But he was also wrong in a big way.

Sotoria had never been his to lose.

That was the godsdamn crux of the whole issue.

"Do you know how I know he fears becoming me?" His tone turned sly as if he were sharing a secret. "I made sure of it."

Fury surged through my veins and poured into my chest, stoking the Primal essence. It hit me so hard and fast there was no tamping it down. My skin tingled, seething—

"So, yes, I believe what you said about Nyktos." That hollow smile remained. "Calm yourself."

I jolted, only then realizing I had stood.

"Pull it back in." He spoke softly as a fine sprinkle of dust and plaster floated from the ceiling. "Now."

Looking down, I saw the glow of silver filling the veins of my hands. My heart stuttered with trepidation as my gaze flew to Kolis.

"Sit," he ordered.

I sat, my heart pounding as I struggled to rein the power back in.

"The eather is a part of you." His voice had thinned, the smile fading. "Show some restraint and will it back in."

Show some restraint? He had no idea the level of *restraint* I was already displaying. My chest rose with a deeper breath, and I told myself to, well, to knock it off. The essence was a part of me. I could control it.

After a moment, the glow faded from my skin.

"Good girl."

My narrow-eyed gaze shot to his before I could stop myself.

Kolis chuckled. "As I was saying," he said with a smirk, "I believe what you said about Nyktos, but what I don't believe is what you've claimed about how you feel. I know for a fact you're lying, and it's not only your behavior just now that confirmed it."

"I—"

Kolis was suddenly in front of me, causing me to gasp and jerk back. I didn't make it very far. He grabbed my wrist, lifting my hand so he held it between our faces—my *right* hand.

"This," he sneered, forcibly turning my hand so the golden swirls of the imprint faced me. "This tells me you feel far more than fondness for my nephew."

Oh, shit.

My heart started banging all around my chest. I hadn't even considered the imprint.

"Only a union formed out of *love* can be blessed." The wisps of eather slowed in his eyes. "You love him."

Pressure clamped down on my chest. I didn't know what to say.

My thoughts raced, but nothing my mind spewed provided a way out of this.

"So, tell me something," he said, that cold bitterness seeping back into his voice. "What are we going to do?"

"I…I don't know what you mean."

"With you. My nephew." He paused, looking down at my hand. "With *this*."

I swallowed thickly, the word *fuck* on a constant loop in my mind.

"Cutting off your hand won't change how you feel."

My eyes went wide. Had he seriously considered that?

"So, tell me, what am I to do?"

Acid churned in the pit of my stomach. "I don't know how this imprint happened. It wasn't something I decided on," I said in a rush. "It just appeared."

"Whether it was a conscious act or not is irrelevant."

A tremor started deep within me, birthing an icy fear that had little to do with my safety and more to do with Ash's. The only thing I could think about was the truth—and I thought I could make it work. "I don't know you."

He frowned.

"I don't remember you or…or anything from my past lives, only what I've been told," I continued. "But I know Nyktos. I got to know him. And, yes, I do love him, but…" My chest ached with what I was about to say next. "I'm not in love with him."

Kolis's eyes searched mine. "There's a difference between the two?"

I hesitated, seeing that he truly didn't know there was. "Yes, there is a whole realm's worth of difference between the two."

"Explain," he demanded.

"It's hard to put into words—"

"Then think very hard so that putting it into words will not be so difficult."

"Loving someone isn't…it isn't less than being in love. It's just not as strong or as irrevocable. Loving someone can change," I rambled, my heart thumping as he listened closely. "It can grow into being in love, and it can fade. Being in love…it doesn't do that. It only gets stronger, and you would do anything for that person. *Anything*." My throat thickened as I thought about the dream I'd had. "Being in love is…it's unbreakable."

Kolis fell quiet and looked as if I'd spoken an unfamiliar language to him. Then again, this was the very same person who believed a prisoner could become a companion.

My anxiety ramped up. I felt as if I were standing on the edge of a cliff, my toes curling into the abyss. I had a plan to free Ash, and I knew what it would take to carry it out.

Breathing shallowly, I counted. *Breathe in. Hold. Breathe out. Hold.* And as I did, I shut it down. All of it. My concern. The fear. My *rage.* Everything. Just as I'd done so many times during my life until Ash.

Doing so now caused a suffocating sense of sorrow to settle in my throat and chest, but it had then, too. I breathed past it, though. I shut it all down as I exhaled, even my awareness of Sotoria, breathing long and slow as I became nothing.

An empty vessel once more.

A blank canvas down to my bones, suitable and ready to become whoever I needed to be. Strong but hollow, and whatever Kolis *wanted* me to be.

The racing of my heart slowed. The trembling ceased. The embers quelled. I was just like his smile. Learned but hollow. "If…if you don't know the difference between the two, then how can you claim to love me?"

Kolis sucked in a sharp breath, dropping my wrist as if I'd burned him. He rose, his movements shaky. "I love you—" His eyes shut, his large shoulders tensing. "I'm *in* love with you."

"Then prove it," I whispered.

His eyes flew open.

"Release Nyktos."

The madly whirling eather stilled in his eyes. "And why in the fuck would I do that?"

"Because I asked you to."

"Let me repeat myself." His voice grew thick with fury, each word spat like a venom-tipped arrow. "Why in the fuck would I do that?" A muscle in his temple throbbed. "When your demand proves what's so plainly visible on your hand and in your behavior."

"I ask for his freedom because it doesn't make sense for you to do so. He's your enemy. My husband." I lifted my chin at the low snarl coming from him, allowing myself to only feel a smidgen of fear. I could control that. My tone. Him. The eather. The learned instinct was like slipping on a gown that only felt a little too tight, and it was so obvious to me then that I hadn't fully become nothing until right now. "My husband, whom I love but am not in love with. I wouldn't do *anything* for him, but will you do anything for me?"

"I think that should be obvious," he spat. "Considering I killed my brother to bring you back to life and then spent what has felt like eons searching for you."

"But I don't remember any of that."

His nostrils flared. "Do you remember me not killing you after you stabbed me? Should that not be proof enough?"

"No."

Kolis's eyes went wide. "And why not?"

"Because not killing someone you love is the bare minimum. That's not doing anything for them," I told him, thinking this was something I'd never thought I would actually have to explain to someone. "No matter what you have to gain from their death."

He snapped his jaw shut.

"But freeing Nyktos?" I picked up my glass and rose.

Kolis took a step *back* from *me*.

I could barely hide my smile. "That is something you don't want to do, but you would be doing it simply to please me."

"And why would that please you?"

"As I said, I love him. I don't want to see any harm come to him," I reasoned, more calmly than I'd ever done in my entire life. I crossed to the table and boldly turned my back on Kolis. "I don't want to have to worry about him, and I will. And that has nothing to do with love."

I picked up the decanter and pulled out the stopper. "He protected me, even before I became his Consort." I filled a glass for myself and then poured Kolis one. Hopefully, he wouldn't destroy this flute. "You've endangered me."

"I have done no—"

"But you have." Holding the glasses, I faced him. Kolis hadn't moved from where he stood near the divan. "But you also didn't know who I was. I didn't either, not for a long time." I offered him the glass.

He hesitated but then took it.

"Anyway, I don't think I can fall in love with another if I'm worrying about the one I do love," I said, taking a sip of the fruity water.

"And why would you be interested in…falling in love?" Kolis demanded, the hollows of his cheeks flushed.

"Because I've never known what it's like to be in love and to be loved in return—" My voice cracked, as did the vessel I'd become. Closing my eyes, I turned my head and waited until the burn of the truth eased. The sting didn't fade completely because what I'd said was true, and no matter how empty I made myself, I could still feel that agony. "I would like to know how that feels."

There was silence, and then the air around me stirred. My heart skipped a beat as I opened my eyes.

Kolis stood less than a foot from me. "This feels like a manipulation," he said. "But the pain I just witnessed was real." A moment passed, then his voice lowered. "Why would you want to love me?"

Man, wasn't that a damn good question? A very loaded one, with so many reasons why I could never, *ever* love him.

But Kolis didn't want to hear that.

It wasn't what he *needed* from me.

I watched the bubbles in the water fizz as I racked my brain for what I knew about Kolis. It wasn't much, but I did know why he'd frightened Sotoria so badly that she fell from a cliff in her attempt to escape him.

"*Relate to him,*" the Mistresses of the Jade had instructed. *"Form a shared commonality. Be sympathetic, but do not show pity."*

"I…I was never wanted as a child, not beyond what my mother believed I could do for her kingdom," I said slowly, hoarsely. "You likely already know that, but I was an outcast in my own home and avoided. Some even feared me. No one wanted to touch me."

The glass I'd given Kolis sat untouched on the table. He watched, not even blinking.

"I suppose we have that in common," I said. "And maybe from that commonality, love can blossom."

His head twisted sharply to the side, away from me. "But only if I first release the man you already love?"

"Yes."

Kolis's chin dipped an inch, his voice a whisper of nightmares. "Do you think I'm a fool?"

A niggle of fear found its way in, but I squashed it. "If you weren't, then I'd know you're not in love with me. Being in love with someone makes you do incredibly idiotic things."

"Idiotic enough to forget that you tried to kill me already?" he asked.

"I've stabbed Nyktos," I shared. "So…"

Kolis blinked. "You stabbed Nyktos?"

"Yep. Held a dagger to his throat, too." I took a drink as the false

King openly gaped at me. "I've also threatened him more times than I can even begin to recall."

He gave a slow shake of his head. "You are…not what I expected."

I snorted. "You aren't the first to say that."

His frown deepened. "What will happen exactly once I free Nyktos? What will that change?"

Hope sparked, but I would not let that little fucker grow. "I won't fight you."

"Explain," he ordered impatiently.

"I won't try to escape." That was a lie. "I won't run from you."

He inhaled sharply. "You will…submit to me?"

The feeling of thorns pricking my skin went up and down my body. I tried to get my mouth to form words, but I couldn't. Well, I'd been wrong again. My canvas wasn't as blank as I needed it to be. Apparently, even I had my limits. "I will not fight you, Kolis." I finished off the bubbly water. "Do we have a deal?"

The false Primal of Life studied me intently and a little warily. "We do."

Relief almost took me to my knees—*almost*.

"But only if you speak the truth about Sotoria and how you feel. I will find out. All your truths." He smiled. "And if you're lying?" He retrieved his glass. "I believe you know what will happen."

My throat dried. I remembered what he'd said. "There will be no end to the atrocities committed upon me and those I care about."

Kolis's smile spread. "In both life and for you in death," he said. "I will take your soul, and it will be mine."

15

It was the following afternoon—or was it early evening? I couldn't be sure. Sunlight had filled the windows when I fell asleep, and it was there once more upon waking.

I hadn't dreamt of Ash again or the lake. I hadn't dreamt at all.

Now, I was seated at the small dining table, staring at the platters of food. A bowl of soup and a heaping plate of eggs and crisp vegetables had been brought to me earlier, but an entire feast had been laid out now—beef, chicken, and roasted duck, sitting among bowls of vegetables and fruits dusted with sugar. There were also pitchers of three different types of refreshments. Another line of quiet, veiled Chosen had served the food while Callum supervised. Then, the Chosen left.

Callum did not.

He sat in the sitting area outside the cage, reading a book, and all I could think about was the Chosen he'd so callously and cruelly murdered.

My fingers tightened around my fork as I pictured myself plunging the sharp tines deep into his throat. A small smile tugged at my lips. Harming Callum wouldn't help me gain Kolis's trust, but I had told him I would kill him.

And I *would* honor that promise somehow.

As I forced my hold on the fork to loosen, I thought of what Aios had said about how Kolis's favorites were treated. Few were allowed to interact with them. For Callum to be in here several times now—alone—it had to signify something about him. No other Revenant spent any time in here.

My gaze flicked from the Revenant to the doors. When they were open, I'd seen two guards framing the entrance. I recognized the dark-haired one.

I had no idea where Kolis had disappeared to after reiterating his promise to make my life—and apparently, my afterlife—a living nightmare.

He'd promised to take my soul, just as he'd done with Eythos.

As I shuddered, I couldn't help but wonder where, exactly, he kept his brother's soul. Probably somewhere disturbing.

Either way, I wasn't foolish enough to hope he'd freed Ash while he was away. The deal only went into play once he was sure I hadn't lied. How he planned to go about determining that was anyone's guess.

I picked at my food, my normally voracious appetite nearly nonexistent. My stomach was still churning, and dealing with Kolis had been like messing around with a caged pit viper. It was exhausting.

As was becoming the blank canvas and staying that way. Both had played a role in how easily and deeply I'd fallen asleep again. I'd slept on the divan once more, unable to bring myself to sleep on the bed.

"You should eat," Callum advised, breaking the silence. "It will please His Majesty."

I rolled my eyes, wishing the meat hadn't been precut and a knife was available. I would've thrown it at the Revenant.

Which was likely why there were no knives.

"This is far too much food for one person to eat," I pointed out as I plucked a bread crumb from the lap of the ivory gown I'd found in the chest. It was constructed the same as the one I'd worn yesterday, except it included a golden rope as a belt.

"Is it?"

Eating a piece of broccoli, I looked over at him. "I think the answer to that is obvious."

Callum only shrugged in response.

I watched him as I chewed the buttery vegetable. "Do Revenants not eat?" I frowned, remembering I'd seen no pointy teeth on the bastard. But from personal experience, I knew fangs weren't needed to drink. "Or do you need blood?"

Callum flipped the page of his book. "That's a rude question."

"Is it?" I parroted his comeback from earlier.

A faint smile appeared. "Revenants do not need food or blood."

I ate a piece of chicken seasoned with some sort of spice. "So, if you don't need food or blood, what do Revenants need?"

"Revenants are in need of nothing."

"Nothing? That doesn't..." I trailed off, understanding dawning. "It's because you're already dead."

"Well, that was also a rude assessment," he responded. "Do I look deceased to you?"

He looked rather healthy. "No."

"Then there's your answer." He returned to reading.

"That's not an answer."

He sighed heavily as he turned another page. "Are you unable to see me?"

I frowned. "That's another question that should have an obvious answer."

"I ask because you must be experiencing vision issues," he replied. "Since you clearly cannot tell I'm trying to read."

Smartass.

My fully functioning eyes narrowed. "What are you reading?"

Callum's lips pursed as he looked up from his book, his head listing to the side.

"If you answer my questions, I'll shut up." I picked up a chalice full of fruity water, wondering exactly how mad he or Kolis would be if I threw it at the Revenant's head.

"That seems highly unlikely."

It was. "To become a Revenant, you must die—like the soul leaves the body and all that. Correct?" I pressed. "That's why Kolis didn't attempt to save me by turning me into a Revenant."

"That would be correct."

Wait. The way he'd been answering these questions... He'd only referred to himself once, asking if he looked dead, but when he answered the other questions, he never referred to the Revenants as *we*. "Were you once Chosen?"

"Was I a Chosen?" Callum's nose wrinkled as if he smelled something rotten. "Not exactly."

What did that mean? "The woman I saw feeding. She was a Chosen, though."

"I believe that has already been established."

"But you're not like her."

Callum's laugh was airy. "Obviously."

"Are all the Revenants like you?" I asked.

Callum scoffed. "There are no Revenants like me."

I rolled my eyes then. "How many are there?"

He said nothing.

Frustration rose, but I changed tack. I was more likely to get an answer if it was directly related to him. "I was under the impression that very few would be allowed in here without Kolis in attendance, but here you are."

"Because I'm special."

"Really," I replied dryly, extending the middle finger of the hand that held the flute.

Callum grinned. "I am the first."

I halted, the glass halfway to my lips. I hadn't been expecting that, and I wasn't even sure why. Everything had a first. "And how did you end up so lucky?"

"You ask a lot of questions, don't you?"

"Wouldn't you?" I countered.

Closing his book, he set it aside as he laughed under his breath. "No, I would be smart and stay quiet."

"Ah, yes, not asking questions and keeping oneself in the dark and without any understanding of those around them is so very clever."

Callum smirked. "Well, we will see just how clever you are shortly."

The tasty water soured in my stomach. "And how is that?"

"When Kolis discovers whether or not you are who you say you are." Callum leaned back, crossing one leg over the other. "If you're not, I imagine your death will be a painful one."

"And if I am?" I challenged. "Then what do you imagine?"

"You already know what I imagine."

I did. "Eventually, Kolis will grow tired of me. Whether it takes weeks, months, or years."

He nodded. "You're only an inconvenience."

"I'd rather be that than an ass-kisser."

"Charming," he murmured.

"Thank you." I smiled at him in the way I did that used to irritate my mother, wide and brightly. Based on his stiffness, I knew it had the same impact on him. Hiding a grin, I leaned back in my chair, deciding I was in the mood to be annoying. "So, what's up with the masks?"

"What about them?"

"Why is it always painted on your face and the other Revenants, those not as *special* as you?" Ash had told me the wings were silver when his father was the Primal of Life, but I hadn't gotten the impression that everyone ran around with the masks painted on their faces when he ruled. "And on the guards."

He stretched an arm over the back of the settee. "They are symbolic."

"No shit," I muttered, quickly swallowing. The tender beef tasted…different. I couldn't put my finger on why, but yuck. I washed the lingering taste away with a gulp of water.

"It symbolizes that we serve the true King of Gods and are created in his image." His fingers tapped.

"And who would that be?"

He chuckled. "Cute."

I ignored that. "I'm guessing the golden wings are supposed to mimic Kolis when he is in his true form?"

Callum nodded.

"But I've seen him in his true form," I said. "He's nothing but bones."

The Revenant's fingers stilled.

"I'm also guessing that's due to what remains of the last true embers of death in him," I surmised.

"You've seen him like that?" Callum asked.

I nodded.

A slow smile spread across his lips, one that caused my skin to prickle with wariness. "Then you've seen death," he said. "True death. No one sees that and lives very long afterward."

My stomach twisted as our stares locked. "You don't scare me."

Callum laughed. "But he does."

When Callum returned on what I could only assume was the following day, a bath had been prepared. Which was routine, but after I bathed, a

Chosen entered the cage with a swath of sheer material that shimmered like liquid gold in the chandelier's light.

The quiet Chosen had dressed me, then brushed my hair until it gleamed, sweeping it up with delicate pearl pins like my mother often wore in hers. Rouge was then applied to my cheeks and lips.

Then, she left.

And Kolis arrived.

While he was dressed as usual, a crown I hadn't seen on him when Ash and I came to Dalos now sat upon his head. It was so golden and bright I couldn't make out much detail at first, but the longer I stared, the more I saw.

The crown of gold was fashioned into a row of nine swords, each tip bearing a glittering diamond. The center spike was a sun made of more diamonds.

The Primal of Life's crown was the opposite of the Primal of Death's, yet they were identical. Day and night. Life and Death.

It was hard not to stare at it and think how it should rest on *Ash's* head. Yet seeing him in such, even in my imagination, didn't feel right.

Kolis's crown wasn't the only thing on display.

So was I.

There'd been no more talk of discovering my secrets as he'd warned. He hadn't mentioned Ash, and there hadn't been time for me to even ask.

All he'd said to me was, "Do not engage with those who enter the chamber," which was a clear warning. After that, between conducting the businesses of the King of Gods from where he sat upon his throne while staring at me—*at certain parts of me*—he was occupied.

Which was why I was dressed as I was, my hair styled in a way that provided an unobstructed view of everything the gown revealed.

The same brown-haired guard I'd seen during my escape attempt escorted the gods into the chamber. I'd discovered his name was Elias. I remembered it because he was the only one whose gaze never strayed in my direction.

The gods who were brought in often looked, no matter their gender, as they informed Kolis of the requests being made at the Sun Temples. Many of their stares were full of curiosity. Some carried the glint of *want* I was beginning to recognize in Kolis's eyes.

It was nothing like what I saw in Ash's gaze. His had been full of want and need, but there had also been tenderness, yearning, and much respect, reverence, and passion. A fondness and devotion that could've grown into love if he had his *kardia*.

The gods' stares reminded me of my stepbrother's—full of the desire to consume. To dominate without deference. To have for the sake of having because I'd been prepared to be pleasing to the eye and displayed in a gilded cage.

I hoped their eyes exploded from their heads.

Along with Kolis's.

The only reason I sat through it all like a quiet, caged bird was because of Ash. The deal. Once Kolis was convinced that I was who I said I was, he would release his nephew. But I needed to be careful. While Primals couldn't break their oaths, they often found ways to make you regret gaining their promises. There were things Kolis could do while still honoring what he'd pledged. But I couldn't let myself think about that or allow my imagination to run wild.

Because I realized something as I sat there. I hadn't been clever enough to clarify what *state* Ash should be in when he was released.

As Callum would say, I *behaved* myself as the meetings went on, and Kolis began to change.

He grew tense, fidgety, even. His stares became...*more*. Longer. Heavier. His grip on the arms of the throne got tighter, the ick-factor of his gaze stronger.

Which was why I ignored Kolis and the leering gods for the most part, so bored out of my mind that I spent an ungodly length of time staring at the cluster of diamonds at the center of the cage bars, wondering why Kolis would even put them there. Like, what was the point? I had no idea.

I learned that each of Kolis's gods represented different cities within the mortal kingdoms. And every time a new one entered, I paid attention just long enough to learn where they were from. None had come from Lasania.

I looked up as the god before Kolis droned on about offerings. My eyes narrowed slightly when I found his gaze on me. His stare held the same qualities as the ones who'd come before him. Want for the sake of wanting, which could also be translated into taking for the sake of it. Sighing, I shifted my focus to the open doors. I could only see Elias's shoulder and the arm of another guard. What was his name? He had only stepped foot into the chamber a few times, and when he did, he had a certain stillness about him that reminded me of Callum.

I rose, going to the table where I poured myself a drink of the bubbly water. Today, it carried a hint of pineapple.

"Do you find her distracting?" Kolis asked suddenly.

I stopped, pitcher half-lowered, and looked up to see the sandy-haired god jerk his attention back to the Primal.

"You've been paying more attention to her than you have to me." Kolis's grip on the throne arms loosened. "I don't believe you've taken your eyes off her since the moment she rose."

"I apologize, Your Majesty," the god replied, clearing his throat. "I have been distracted."

"By her?" Kolis prodded.

The god glanced at me again and nodded.

Kolis's head cocked. "What is it about her that you find so distracting?"

The handle of the pitcher dug into my palm. Could it be that my gown was transparent?

"She is...interesting to look upon," the god answered.

"Interesting?" Kolis questioned. "Please elaborate, Uros."

The god's stare lowered, lingering on my chest. "She is pleasing to the eye."

"Which parts?"

I flipped my stare to the Primal. Was he seriously asking that?

"Many parts," Uros answered, looking at Kolis before continuing. "Her shape."

Do not engage with those who enter the chamber, I reminded myself as I placed the pitcher back on the table before I launched it through the bars—something I didn't think Kolis would appreciate. Plus, it would be a waste. The water was tasty.

"And?" Kolis smiled at the god, but there was an edge to it. A tension that hardened his jaw.

Uros looked me over as he drew his lower lip between his teeth. "Her hips. They're full and appear soft. The shadowy area between her thighs."

My mouth dropped open.

Kolis raised his brows. "What about it?"

"I bet it is equally soft." Uros' stare was full of heat, and not in a good way. "And wet."

"What the fuck?" I spat before I could stop myself.

Uros' eyes widened. He obviously hadn't expected me to speak. And I probably shouldn't have. My question would likely be considered an act of engaging. But come *on*.

However, Kolis only chuckled. "I believe you may have offended her."

Uros said nothing to that, not that he needed to. His thoughts were clearly visible to me in the slight curve of his lips. He didn't care if I was offended and likely didn't believe I was worthy of worrying about such a thing.

"Are you?" Kolis asked, and it took me a moment to realize that he was speaking to me. "Are you offended?"

Who wouldn't be? But if I were insulted by this god, then it meant his words or opinions mattered to me.

And they didn't.

"No." I took a sip of the water as I met the god's gaze. "Mostly, just unimpressed."

Kolis snorted as the god's cheeks bloomed pink. I turned, heading back to the divan.

"The thing is," Kolis began, "you have offended *me*."

I turned to sit at the wrong time. Or maybe at exactly the right time. Regardless, doing so at that moment gave me a front-row seat to what happened next. Kolis turned his head to Uros and flashed that tight smile again.

He then lifted his right hand and flicked his wrist.

Uros *imploded*.

It was like he was sucked into himself. His face caved in, the bones there crunching and then collapsing. His chest deflated as if air, blood, and all the necessary things held within the cavity had suddenly been removed. The tunic he wore slipped down the chair as his shoulders and arms disappeared, pulled into the vortex of where his body used to be. The legs went next, and with one last meaty snap, nothing but bloodied linen and a few pieces of runny tissue remained.

It all happened so fast that the embers in me didn't have much chance to do anything but pulse weakly at the death. My hands didn't even warm.

Kolis looked over at me. "Do you find him more impressive in this state?"

I plopped down onto the divan, my mouth hanging open.

"I do." Kolis raised a brow. "Simply because he takes up less space."

"You...you just turned him into goo," I said.

"I did," Kolis responded without hesitation. "Does that bother you?"

I blinked slowly. I'd seen Ash do something similar, but this was different. *This* was done merely over words spoken, ones Kolis had goaded the god into speaking. "He was only looking at me."

Kolis went still. "Did you *like* him looking at you?"

"Not even remotely, but he wasn't the only one to do so," I said, trying to wrap my head around what had just happened and that incredibly idiotic question. "Many of the gods gawked at me."

"But they were wise enough not to make it so obvious." He tilted his head. "They may look at you, but they shouldn't speak on it."

"You *made* him talk about it."

"I simply asked him questions," he reiterated. "He chose to answer."

That wasn't exactly what had occurred. Kolis had basically hounded the god into answering. I glanced back at what was left of Uros, my stomach churning as the scent of iron and charged air reached me.

"That is so…gross," I murmured.

"No hysterics?" Kolis remarked. "Only statements. That's impressive."

I was definitely disturbed by what I'd witnessed, so the lack of screaming and fainting upon seeing someone turned to goo should have probably concerned me.

"Elias?" Kolis called.

The god entered, his steps halting as he got an eyeful of the mess. He recovered quickly, though, faster than I, which could only mean he was accustomed to things such as this.

"Please, let Callum know the Sun Temple in…" Kolis frowned. "Wherever Uros was speaking of, is in need of a replacement."

Elias nodded. "Yes, Your Majesty. Would you like me to send someone in to remove the mess?"

The mess?

I would call that more than a mess.

"Unnecessary." Kolis waved his hand, and the chair and goo went the way of Uros, except this time, there was nothing but a faint cloud of dust swirling over the shadowstone tile afterward. "Send the next one in."

The god who entered kept his eyes trained solely on Kolis. Obviously, after the last one didn't exit the chamber, this one had put two and two together when he came upon the empty spot. He halted for a moment, his throat bobbing on a swallow. Wordlessly, he sat on the settee.

I perched on the divan, the drink in my hand mostly forgotten as I stared at where the chair had been. Having been raised to commit the most fatal sort of violence, I was used to it. Some part of me wished I weren't, that something like what'd just happened impacted me more, but I didn't see it as a weakness. It was a strength, especially now. But the way Kolis had gone about things left me unsettled.

It was all a manipulation.

Kolis had me on display, taunting those to look from the moment they entered the chamber. There was no rhyme or reason behind his opinions on how long was too long for them to do so. Uros *was* disgusting, and his comments crossed so many lines, but they would not have been made if Kolis hadn't manipulated him into doing so.

And why had he?

Did he have an issue with the god? Had he done it to prove a point and remind the other gods what he was capable of? To remind *me*? Or was the reason the same as why Uros and the others found me so pleasing?

I wasn't *that* extraordinary to look upon, especially in the realm of the gods. Sure, some found my shape attractive and my features fine. Others felt there was too much of me and that my freckles were distracting. Either way, these gods took interest simply because they saw me as Kolis's newest favorite and knew I was untouchable. They wanted what they could not have. They desired because they could.

And Kolis had killed that god because *he* could.

Who would tell him he was wrong? After briefly speaking with him about it, I could see there would be no point in doing so. He did what he wanted and thought little of whether it was right or wrong.

I stared down at the delicate glass I held. What I didn't get was the purpose of...*this*. My claim of being Sotoria hadn't been confirmed yet. Still, did he think dressing me this way, putting me on display, and then murdering a god would aid in fostering my love for him?

Then again, Kolis didn't know what love was.

I'd been warned about what he and his Court were like. In fact, I'd already experienced it when Ash and I were here, so I shouldn't—

"Prayers for a bountiful harvest and a calm winter were made. I know, a complete and utter surprise." A goddess with long, dark hair and deep brown skin read from a parchment, her inflection as she spoke making what she said far more interesting than any of those who'd come before her. As did what had to be her additions to the requests. "Whiskey that I believe only tastes slightly like horse piss was left as an offering, as was a white bull that I suspect may have been painted to appear as such."

Wait. What?

"There was also a branch from an oak tree." Her pointy chin lifted, and light glanced off the gold shimmer of a sharp cheek. "I am not sure what one is supposed to do with a branch, other than mourn the senseless violence against the tree." She paused, glancing over at the Primal.

Kolis was, yet again, staring at me.

She cleared her throat. "Kraig, with a…" She frowned. "With a K, wished only to speak poetically and at great length about his devotion to His Majesty, leaving a—"

"Enough," Kolis barked, startling both the goddess and me. "Excuse me." He rose, looking at me. "I will return shortly."

The goddess turned from where she sat perched on one of the chairs, watching Kolis stalk from the chamber. Then she looked at me.

I shrugged.

Long, glossy hair slid over her shoulder as she cocked her head. Drawing her plump, red lip between her teeth, she glanced at the open door, and a hint of mischief flickered across her pretty face. Her form-fitting gown slid down the length of her long legs as she stood. Lowering the parchment to her side, she approached the cage. Well, *approached* was too tame a word to describe how she moved.

The goddess *prowled*, clearly aware of how well the gown complemented her curves.

She came to a stop a foot from the bars. Under the softer glow of the light where I was, I saw that her gown was about as good at concealing her body as mine and all the gowns I'd seen the other goddesses wear.

And I could safely say that her breasts were quite perky.

She grinned as she saw where my attention had gone. "Do you like them?" she asked, her tone softly teasing. "I like yours. Perhaps not as much as dear Kraig with a K likes His Majesty, but I do find them quite enjoyable to look upon."

I raised my brows, oddly entertained by the goddess. Her amber eyes were light, and she didn't stare at me like the others.

Not that she didn't look at me as if she wanted some alone time with no bars between us, because she did. But she didn't leave my skin feeling like it was trying to detach itself from my body.

I quickly glanced at the doors, not seeing Elias or the other guards stationed out there. "What kingdom was this Sun Temple in?"

Surprise flickered across her face. "Oh, she speaks," the goddess remarked, and my spine stiffened. "None have done so before."

At the mention of Kolis's other favorites, my amusement rapidly began to fade.

"But you are…different," she added, lowering her voice. "There are rumors about you, you know. That you are the Shadowlands' Consort."

A prickly sensation rippled over my skin as I stared at her. This was the first indication beyond Phanos and Attes that others knew who I was, or what they may be thinking regarding my presence here. I wasn't sure others were even aware of me, especially those who hadn't seen me when I attempted to escape.

"The Sun Temple is located in the kingdom of Terra," she answered in the silence.

My breath caught. Terra was a neighboring kingdom to Lasania, one that Ezra was in talks with. With the exception of the Undying Hills, much of Terra was farmland. How had I missed this? I leaned forward. "Do you have any news about Lasania? Have you heard anything about them?"

Delicate brows furrowed. "You speak of the kingdom that makes me think of tasty, layered noodles and cheese?"

"It's not pronounced—" I stopped myself with a curt shake of my head. "Yes, I'm speaking of that one."

"Not particularly."

Disappointment swept through me.

"Though several of those who left offerings at the Sun Temple were from Lasania," she said. "They mostly asked for good fortune with their work within Terra."

Could that mean that Ezra had successfully strengthened the relationship between the two kingdoms? It must. Because while Terra had land, they didn't have the labor Lasania did. A shudder of relief swept through me. "Thank you," I said, sitting back.

The goddess started to speak.

"Dametria." Elias filled the doorway, one hand resting on the hilt of his sword. I silently mouthed her name, committing it to memory. "Out."

My eyes narrowed on the guard.

"I'm leaving," the goddess said, returning her attention to me.

"It does not appear as if you're doing so," Elias pointed out. "His

Majesty will return soon."

"Yes. Yes. He will when he's done pleasuring himself."

"Fucking Fates," Elias muttered, and my lip curled in disgust.

"At least that is what I expect he's doing based on what I saw." Dametria's voice lowered. "By the way, I know the rumors are true."

I stilled.

"Dametria," snapped Elias.

The goddess stepped back, her next words barely audible. "I was there when you were crowned."

16

I would not think about Kolis pleasuring himself as I made quick use of the cage's bathing chamber. I would focus on the knowledge that Ezra had likely successfully negotiated a deal with Terra.

It wouldn't save them if Ash didn't get the embers out of me, but it would help them survive for as long as they could.

A platter of cheese, fruit, and bread had been served, and I ate a few pieces of each in silence, mulling over what Dametria had shared. She'd been at the coronation. So, did that mean she served within another Court? Or was she a member of the Court here, in Dalos?

I didn't know, but she'd seemed so unlike the others, especially when she finally strutted from the chamber, tapping the rolled parchment off Elias's armored chest.

Any thoughts about her slipped to the back of my mind when Kolis returned.

The false King looked a bit more at ease as he seated himself on the throne again, lending some credence to what Dametria had alluded to.

And that was far more disgusting than anything Uros had said.

A few more gods entered, but the sudden pulsing of the embers in my chest had me paying attention.

I saw no god beside Kolis as I turned to the doors. Then a tall, broad figure appeared, wearing deep brown leathers and a black tunic beneath armor that bore the emblem of a helmet.

I recognized the sandy-haired bastard immediately.

After all, the Primal of Peace and Vengeance was identical in appearance to his brother, except his features bore no scar.

Kyn was responsible for Ector's death and many more. A rush of anger went through me as I tracked his movements.

"Kyn," Kolis acknowledged, inclining his head.

The Primal bowed. "Your Majesty."

"I assume you have news for me?"

News? My ears perked right up.

"I do." Kyn stopped where Uros had ended up as slime on the floor.

"Then have a seat." Kolis extended a hand toward the chairs and settees as the Primal of Peace and Vengeance finally looked in my direction.

Resentment was evident in his eather-filled eyes and the hard press of his lips.

Kyn did not like me.

I could understand that, even though his feelings were misplaced. Kolis had forced me to kill Thad, one of Kyn's young draken, as punishment for Ash not seeking his approval for my coronation. I'd brought Thad back to life, but Kyn didn't know that. Maybe if he did, his raging dislike of me would change.

But *my* seething anger would not. The embers throbbed in my chest as I held Kyn's stare, more in tune with the Primal's vengeance than life. I didn't care if he had been manipulated or what his orders were. He'd attacked the Shadowlands. Killed those I'd come to care about. Whatever understanding existed in me had ended there.

"Perhaps this conversation is better held elsewhere," Kyn stated, sending me a scathing glare that lingered. "As it has to do with the Shadowlands."

A bolt of tension shot through me.

"Of course, it has to do with my least favorite Court at the moment," Kolis replied dryly. "We can discuss the Shadowlands openly in her presence. She is not going anywhere."

This was one of those moments when I had to remind myself to keep my mouth shut.

Kyn hesitated for a moment, then nodded. "May I?" He inclined his chin toward the dark cherry-wood credenza.

"Of course," Kolis murmured, his fingers beginning to tap idly. "Help yourself."

"Thank you." Kyn went to the sideboard, his long legs eating up the distance. "I spoke with one of Nyktos's commanders regarding their presence along the Bonelands' coast."

I racked my brain, thinking about who he could be speaking of. It had to be one of those close to Ash.

"They are unwilling to heed commands," Kyn continued, pulling the glass stopper from a large decanter full of amber-hued liquid. "They refuse to move their forces until Nyktos is released."

Pride surged through me, and I had to fight not to show it because I could feel Kolis's gaze on me.

"I expected that," Kolis said. "Are the draken still with them?"

Pouring himself a glass of whiskey, Kyn nodded. "Yes. Three of them."

"Nektas?"

"Yes." Kyn replaced the stopper.

My heart began thumping as I waited for him to say the others' names.

The Primal took a drink, his lips peeling back, I had to assume from the bite of the liquor. Even from where he stood, I saw the size of his fangs. They were massive.

"Nektas being there and them refusing to leave the Bonelands does not bode well for negotiations," Kyn said, turning. His gaze flickered over me. "You know how the draken are with lands they believe sacred."

Kolis hadn't mentioned that.

The false King sighed. "If they thought of every land containing the remains of those fallen in past battles thus, every piece of land would be sacred."

"Yes, but the lands west of the mountains bleed into the mortal realm," Kyn said. Was he speaking of the Skotos? "Where the Ancients—"

"I know what is in that land," Kolis interrupted. "There is no risk of them encountering a mortal there. None have crossed the Skotos and entered the Bonelands in eons."

So, this land existing between the Skotos and another mountain range was actually in the mortal realm? It made more sense than what the mortals believed, which was that the realm simply ended east of the Skotos.

Kyn made his way back to the sitting area and took a seat. "They use the sea and skirt the mountains, which puts them within range to attack Dalos."

"I'm also well aware of that."

"We must make sure Phanos can assist if such a situation arises."

"That won't be a problem."

The fact that Kyn, a Primal of Vengeance, would even ask meant it could be a problem.

"That is a relief to hear." Kyn's stare moved over me and then darted away, leaving my skin prickling. "Only half their forces are in the Bonelands. The other half is at my border."

"You mean your and your brother's," Kolis corrected, his fingers still tapping. His gaze slid to the other Primal. "Unless they are positioned to the north of the Black Bay, where I believe your encampment lays."

As far as I knew, they were east of Lethe, and that was Vathi—the brothers' Court.

"They are at our border and have been," Kyn said, not elaborating beyond that. "That is all that matters."

"Have they attacked?"

"Not yet, but I imagine it is only a matter of time before they seek their vengeance."

Part of me hoped they did. The other understood what that would lead to: an escalation of violence. War. Death.

Kyn's gaze swept over me again, his upper lip curling slightly before he refocused on the false King. "Something must be done."

A faint smile played on Kolis's lips. "I'm sure you have suggestions."

"I do." Kyn leaned forward. "Let me take my forces and remove the threat to our east. I will destroy them, leaving their bones to rot with those who came before."

Kolis laughed softly. "You said Nektas is with them. If you attempt that, you and your forces will do nothing but burn."

Tension poured into Kyn's body, charging the air. "Then allow me to finish what I started." Silver eyes drilled into me, causing my muscles to coil like a spring. "Let me take the Shadowlands."

"You had your chance to do that," Kolis retorted, the reminder of how close the Shadowlands had come to destruction sending a whisper of cold dread over the nape of my neck.

"All I need is permission to take the chance again," Kyn insisted. "I will not waste the opportunity a second time."

My stomach hollowed as my gaze bounced between the two. Attes claimed Kolis had forced his brother to turn on the Shadowlands, but Kyn sounded far too eager to have another go at it for his actions to be rooted solely in the recent loss of one of his young draken. Either Attes didn't realize this, or he didn't want to acknowledge it.

"You wanted a clear message sent. It can still be done." Again, Kyn's stare drifted over me. "And right now, a message is likely needed due to *that*."

An ache began settling into my fingers because of how tightly I clenched my glass.

"And what does your brother think?" Kolis queried after a moment. "Does he feel a message should be sent?"

"My brother favors accord over war—that and fucking."

"As if you are any different when it comes to the last part," Kolis pointed out. My brows rose, and I...

I thought about why Attes had killed his brother's guards. He said they'd been taking the young, those years away from their Culling, and bringing them back to their encampments. And as Attes had said, it wasn't to protect them.

"With Nektas in the Bonelands, my draken and men will be able to make quick work of what forces remain in the Shadowlands," Kyn reasoned.

Tangles of dread spread through my stomach as my tenuous hold on my tongue slipped and then disappeared altogether. "Then what?"

Two pairs of eather-filled eyes settled on me. Kyn's were wide with surprise. I could detect nothing from Kolis's stare nor tone when he asked, "What do you mean?"

My heart was somewhere in my throat as I repeatedly slapped myself in my mind. "If orders are given to destroy the Shadowlands," I said, knowing I needed to proceed with caution given this was not my mother I was speaking to, "then what comes next? The forces in the Bonelands, including Nektas, will be even more motivated to strike Vathi."

Kyn's lip curled as he eyed me, but he said nothing until Kolis prodded, "And what do you have to say about that?"

"I'm not that worried about Nektas," Kyn replied, taking a drink.

Unable to stop myself, I laughed.

Kyn lowered his glass. "Did I make a joke?"

"It sounded like one to me," I replied. "No one in their right mind *wouldn't* be worried about Nektas."

"Never said I was in my right mind."

"Obviously," I muttered under my breath.

Kyn's eyes narrowed.

Resisting the urge to flip him off, I focused on Kolis. "You said you didn't want to start a war. Destroying the Shadowlands will do exactly that." A sour taste filled my mouth as I continued. "What we discussed before? Between you and me?"

Kolis's fingers stilled as his entire focus zeroed in on me.

"How will any of that be possible if the realm goes to war?" I reasoned. "How will *anything* be possible then?"

The false King was silent as the other Primal's eyes thinned into glowing slits. Seconds ticked by as fury and dread ate away at me.

"You're brave, Kyn," Kolis began. "And you're loyal. For both, you have my gratitude."

"You have more than that from me." Kyn turned to the false King. "You have my army and my command."

Kolis nodded. "Things have changed since we last spoke. Plans...have adapted."

The look on Kyn's face gave me the impression he knew exactly what had changed. "But you need those embers," the Primal replied. I was a little surprised that Kyn knew I had them. "Because the reality of what must be done or what is to come remains the same."

Kolis nodded slowly. "I haven't forgotten."

Exactly what were they speaking of? Kolis wanted the embers so he could Ascend to become the Primal of Life and Death—a being with unfathomable power. If successful, he could wipe out all the Primals and rule over both realms. He wanted power—ultimate, unending power. Knowing the stability of the realms would no longer be impacted by their deaths, why would any other Primal support that?

"I've maintained the balance all these years," Kolis said. "There is no reason that will cease to be sufficient anytime soon."

The balance? What had he said about that before? Maintaining balance and giving life. He'd said the cold-eyed Ascended were the product of that.

"We will not make any further moves against the Shadowlands unless provoked," Kolis instructed, pulling me from my thoughts with a wave of relief.

"And if provoked?"

Kolis leaned back, his fingers once more drumming on the arms of the throne. "Then I will do what must be done." He glanced at Kyn. "I'm relieved to see you don't look too disappointed by my decree."

The Primal smiled. "I'm not."

"And why is that?"

Yes, why *was* that?

"Nyktos will likely be in a provocative mood once released." He shifted his focus from Kolis. "Unless you plan to imprison him for a small eternity, he will be a problem."

Kolis huffed out a dry laugh, causing me to tense. "He won't be a problem."

Oh, Ash would definitely be a problem. I felt my lips twitch—

"She draws the eye, doesn't she?" Kolis drawled.

Oh, gods, not this again.

Kyn gave a noncommittal grunt behind the rim of his glass. I doubted whatever the Primal said would end the way it had for Uros, but one could hope.

Kolis eyed the other Primal for several seconds.

"My dear?" he called, causing the muscles of my back to bunch. "Why don't you come closer?"

I hesitated, and that odd smile of his faltered. Knowing I'd pushed my luck by engaging not once but twice with those who'd entered the chamber, I reminded myself of *who* was at stake. I took a breath, clearing my mind so I could become nothing again.

Empty.

Unaffected.

Then, I rose.

Too aware of their stares, where they lingered, and knowing I'd been able to see through Dametria's gown in the light, I slowly walked toward the bars. I knew why Kolis had summoned me closer.

He wanted Kyn to look.

Just as he'd wanted Uros to do.

My heart started pounding. I couldn't remember in the moment if this was something he'd done with his favorites—showing them off. Enjoying the knowledge that others wanted what he'd claimed as his. It had to be, considering he'd been well aware of how many of the gods had looked upon me. And he hadn't said a word to them.

Well, except the one he'd *killed*.

But Kolis looked more pleased than murderous as Kyn lowered his glass and his gaze.

"What do you think now?" Kolis asked politely as if speaking about a painting.

Kyn's jaw tightened as his perusal swept over me.

Holding myself still, I wanted to feel absolutely nothing, but that wasn't the case. There was still too much of me present, which meant I hadn't become a blank canvas. In truth, Kyn was ogling my chest to the point where I wouldn't be all that dismayed if my breasts withered and fell off.

"She does draw the eye," Kyn muttered.

"I know," Kolis said. "You don't want to think that, but you do."

My gaze darted back to the false King. A glow of eather pulsed around him, and as it had with Uros, his attention was fixed on the other Primal.

But he seemed different this time. The tension was gone. He appeared relaxed.

"What would happen if she wasn't in that cage?" Kolis let that question linger in the silence between them. "If she weren't mine?"

The Primal's chest rose with a deep breath, and his lips parted. Clearly, he could imagine it.

And I was imagining slitting his throat to the bone.

Kolis watched the other Primal, a sort of feverish look settling into the flesh of his cheeks and the gleam of his eyes. "You'd be between those lovely thighs or in that equally lovely ass of hers."

Kyn smirked as I inhaled sharply. Like hell, he would. If I weren't in this cage, I would have *both* their cocks lying bloody on the floor.

Holding that image in mind, I returned Kyn's smirk.

The Primal's eyes went bright as he stiffened. "If she's not who you believe her to be? Your *graeca*?"

My nostrils flared. So, Kyn *was* aware of who Kolis believed me to be. Exactly how many knew about Kolis's obsession? Everyone?

"If she's not?" Kolis's fingers tap, tap, tapped… "You can have her when I'm done with her."

A wave of prickly heat swept over me as I stared at the Primal of Peace and Vengeance. The nothingness in me swelled. It wasn't embarrassment over them discussing me as if I were nothing more than cattle, nor was it fear.

It was rage.

"Yeah." Kyn's smile widened, showing his fangs as the embers thrummed. "Yeah, I'll take her."

He wanted to.

There was no mistaking the lust in his gaze and the few words spoken since Kolis had begun this game once more, but there was also a lot of loathing, and I knew in an instant what would happen if Kolis discovered the truth about Sotoria's soul and I survived all he'd do.

I *wouldn't* survive what Kyn would do.

I wouldn't want to.

And Kolis knew that.

"Good." Kolis's gold-flecked gaze swept back to me. "It's a deal."

"Honored," Kyn murmured. "Your potential…gift moves me, Your Majesty."

I hoped Nektas burned Kyn to a painful crisp.

Turning to Kolis, the Primal of Peace and Vengeance smiled. "I'm glad I came with one to give you."

Kolis's brow rose. "You did?"

"One moment." The Primal twisted in his chair. "Diaval," he called, setting his glass on a small table. "I hope you don't mind that I had your draken assist me."

"Not when it involves a gift," Kolis replied.

My brows knitted as my gaze shot to the door. A heartbeat passed. Then another.

A tall draken with long, wavy blond hair entered. A jolt of recognition went through me. It was the one I'd tossed across a hall, the one who'd knocked me out. But at the moment, I couldn't care less. Every part of me focused on his *gift*.

Diaval's hand clasped the bound arm of someone whose head was covered in a burlap hood. The man's black leathers and tunic were torn in several places, revealing slivers of bloodied flesh.

My heart thundered as they drew closer.

"Here you go." Diaval shoved the captive forward.

The man stumbled. I held my breath. He went down, his knees cracking off the shadowstone tile. He made no sound as he swayed forward, his chest rising and falling in quick, shallow breaths.

"My gift…" Kolis cocked his head. "Is quite battered and bloodied."

Kyn rose. "It required some convincing."

The false Primal smirked. "I can see that."

I knew—gods, I *knew* as Kyn rose and walked behind the kneeling man that this was no gift.

It would be a nightmare.

Kyn gripped the back of the burlap sack and ripped it off, revealing a shock of reddish-gold hair matted with dried blood.

My heart stopped.

It was Rhain.

The rising dread constricted my chest, stifling the breath I took as I stared at the god.

I barely recognized Rhain's boyish features beneath the blood caking his face, but it was him. His nose was crooked, clearly broken. His lips were split and ragged. Only one dark brown eye was open. Barely. The other was swollen shut. And his neck…

Rhain had been bitten, but it looked like an animal had done it. If he weren't a god, there was no way he'd still be breathing.

"He attempted to follow me when I left the Bonelands," Kyn explained, smirking as he looked down at the beaten god. "When I caught him, he demanded to be taken to Nyktos." Kyn laughed, and my chest squeezed. "I'm not sure what the idiot thought would happen."

Gods, Rhain was an idiot—a brave, loyal idiot.

"I know this one," Kolis commented, sliding his hands along the arms of the throne. "It's Rhain, correct?"

Blood dripped from his chin as Rhain lifted his head, angling it toward the cage. I froze as the one eather-lit eye focused on me.

"That is his name," Kyn confirmed.

Kolis studied the god. "Rhain, a god of the Callasta Isles," he said, sending a bolt of surprise darting through me. He'd originally served Veses? I'd never known which Court Rhain came from. "And son of

Daniil. You look so much like your father." He rose. "Well, you resemble your father the last time I saw him."

I sucked in a sharp breath, his meaning clear.

"Fuck you," Rhain spat.

Kyn reacted without hesitation. I flinched when his booted foot slammed into Rhain's back, knocking him to his stomach.

I jerked forward when Rhain groaned, turning his head so his one good eye was visible. He spat out a mouthful of blood.

"I'm sure your father said the same thing," Kolis replied. "I'll tell you what I told him. No, thank you."

Panic seeded itself deep inside me, taking root. Feeling as if the chamber had shrunk in size, I stepped to the side toward the locked door. My hands opened and closed at my sides, the embers in my chest throbbing.

"Did you...did you tell him?" Rhain rasped, the words warped. "Why you were...going to murder him?"

"He already knew." Kolis approached him. "He committed an act of treason. Like father, like son, I see."

"Conspiring?" A wet, broken laugh rattled from Rhain. Seemingly with sheer strength of will, he managed to get his knees under him. "My father...only refused to...become a murderous henchman."

I hadn't known any of this—or anything about Rhain, really. It wasn't like we'd chatted often and got to know each other. The god had been wary of me from the moment I arrived in the Shadowlands. And after he learned that I'd planned to kill Ash, he understandably hadn't been fond of me.

"What you call a murderous henchman, I call a loyal servant." Kolis stopped in front of Rhain. "Ah, look at you."

Rhain struggled to stand, his chest heaving with the effort, but he got his feet under him. His hair was even darker now, sweat mingling with the blood. But, gods, he *stood*. "You...you don't know what loyalty...is."

"And you do?" Kolis asked softly. "Your father thought he did. He was wrong." He looked over at the other Primal. "What do you think, Kyn?"

"I said what I think." The Primal of Peace and Vengeance crossed his arms. "He's a fucking idiot."

"Fuck you," Rhain spat.

Kyn stepped toward him.

The false King held up a hand, stopping the Primal. Growling low in his throat, Kyn backed off.

Rhain *smirked*.

And a huge part of me respected that. It was something I'd do, but I could also be a fucking idiot. I glanced at the cage door again, thinking about the hidden key. There was no way I'd get to it and get out. Even if I did, then what? I didn't know, but I had to do *something*.

Because what I felt? And what I saw clear as day in my mind? It was like a prophetic vision. There was only one reason Kyn would bring Rhain to Kolis alive. Pressure clamped down on my chest. I knew what was about to happen.

Kolis was going to kill Rhain.

"So, you followed Kyn in hopes he'd lead you to Nyktos?"

Rhain didn't answer as he swayed unsteadily.

"See, I have questions about that," Kolis continued. "You'd truly have to be an idiot if you thought you could follow Kyn without being caught."

The other Primal's smile was smug.

"But I know something he doesn't." Kolis leaned forward.

The corners of Kyn's lips straightened.

"Your father was an excellent tracker, able to move as a wraith, unseen and unknown. Until it was too late. It was why I wanted him to handle a few...errands for me," Kolis said. Only this madman would call murdering someone an errand.

Actually, he had that in common with my mother. Go figure.

"I'm sure he passed those talents on to you. He did when it came to his eldest son, Mahiil."

I jolted. Rhain had a brother? I had a horrible feeling that *had* was the keyword there.

"And I also know that my nephew wouldn't surround himself with idiots," Kolis added. "What I think is that you allowed yourself to be caught."

My lips parted as I stared at Rhain.

"And I also think being led to Nyktos wasn't your only goal or hope." Golden eather swirled across Kolis's bare chest. "So, I will only ask you this question once, and unless you wish to end up like your father and brother, I suggest you answer truthfully."

My gods, my suspicions were correct. Kolis had also killed Rhain's brother. So many of those close to Ash had suffered because of Kolis. Too many—

Seraphena.

I stiffened, my stare swinging to Rhain. His voice. I'd sworn I heard it in my mind.

"Were you attempting to discover Nyktos's location?" Kolis pressed.

Seraphena. Rhain's voice came again. *Listen to me.*

My throat dried. Either I was hearing him, or I was losing my mind.

"Or *hers?*" Kolis asked.

My heart stuttered. One brown eye locked onto mine.

"See? I think it's the latter." Kolis was less than a foot from the battered god. "And Kyn didn't just bring me a gift. He gave one to you."

My gaze darted to the other Primal. He was frowning.

Remember what you did when you learned what Veses had done?

Okay. I had to be hearing him because that was a weird thing to think.

When you saw her with Nyktos?

"Because I know something else that he doesn't." Eather whirled faster across Kolis's flesh.

Use the essence, Rhain's voice whispered amid my thoughts. *And bring this entire palace down—*

Kolis shot forward, grabbing Rhain by the throat. I cried out in surprise.

"Silence," Kolis warned, shooting me a look before refocusing on Rhain. "I know what your father was capable of. I also know what he passed on to both of his sons."

Rhain gasped for air as Kolis lifted him off the floor.

"Only a few of Veses' gods are capable of...what did she call it?" Rhain gagged, and Kolis smiled broadly. "Thought projection?"

"What the fuck?" Kyn snarled, his arms unfolding.

Holy shit, I *had* heard Rhain's voice. But what he asked of me? When I'd lost control? I didn't know how I'd made the House of Haides tremble. Though even if I did, it wouldn't kill Kolis. Rhain had to know that.

"It's a one-way street, but still effective." Golden essence throbbed around Kolis. "Especially when it comes to communicating things to others. Those before them." His grip tightened, causing Rhain to wheeze. "And even long-distance. The question remains. Exactly how talented are you? Like your brother? He could project his thoughts to those if he made eye contact."

All those times I'd seen Rhain, and he'd been quiet, yet those he was with seemed to know what he needed or thought before he spoke it... Like when he'd been with Ash and me beneath the palace. *Do it.* Rhain had told Ash as he tore another root free. *Do it now.* Rhain hadn't said what could be done to stop me aloud, but Ash had known what Rhain referred to.

"Or are you as skilled as your father was?" Kolis sneered. "Able to project thoughts to those he carried a token of?"

Rhain was starting to turn a chalky, bluish-white. He couldn't answer, but Kolis wasn't really giving him a chance. He gripped the front of Rhain's tunic, where the scrolling brocade came together, and ripped it down the center, revealing a small, black pouch hanging from his neck on a smooth, black rope.

"Just like your father." Kolis laughed, grabbing the pouch. The rope snapped with one tug. "Hid the tokens the same way."

Kolis tossed Rhain aside. The god rolled across the floor, stopping a foot from the cage.

Shaking his head, Kolis tugged the laces on the pouch and turned it over. As Rhain rolled onto his side, Kolis dumped the contents onto his palm.

I saw it then. The *token.*

It was the thin, delicate silver chain I'd seen Aios wearing and always fiddling with.

"Who does that belong to?" Kyn demanded.

Rhain's leg curled as he shuddered. "I...I don't know what you're talking about."

Kolis turned to him, his head tilting.

It was like invisible strings had been attached to Rhain's shoulders. He rose into the air. I stepped back when his back bowed, his mouth open in a silent scream. The veins of his throat started to glow with eather.

"It's mine!" I shouted.

Kolis looked at me.

"It's my necklace. It was given to me years ago," I lied, speaking in a rush. "I don't know why he has it. I didn't even know he could do the thought-projecting thing."

"My dear," Kolis purred. "Come now."

"That's the truth! I didn't even know that was a thing."

"How could you *not* know?" Kyn bit out.

"*You* didn't even know," I snapped, and his eyes filled with a pulse of eather. "And it's not like Rhain would share such information with me. He doesn't even like me."

Kolis frowned as the eather retracted from the veins of Rhain's mangled throat.

"He doesn't!" That was another truth.

Rhain managed to turn his head toward me, then Kolis said, "And why is that?"

"Probably because I stabbed Nyktos," I reminded him.

"You *stabbed* Nyktos?" Kyn asked.

I ignored him. "I'm also mouthy. I cuss too much. I'm temperamental. I start arguments. I'm pretty sure I threatened him—"

"I get it," Kolis said, glancing at Rhain. "I would agree with many of those things. Especially the mouthy and cussing-too-much parts."

I *fucking* prayed to the *fucking* Fates that he *fucking* died a slow, miserable *fucking* death.

But I sincerely didn't think Rhain had been attempting to feed information back to Aios regarding me. He'd been hoping to learn Ash's location.

I took a deep breath. "Maybe he thought to communicate with me, but he hasn't. And what would be the point of him attempting to talk with anyone else about my location?" I rushed on. "I'm sure everyone already knows I'm at Cor Palace."

"That's the thing, my dear," Kolis drawled. "You're not at Cor Palace."

I blinked. "I'm not—?" That didn't matter. "Rhain didn't try to communicate with me."

Kolis eyed me closely. A heartbeat later, Rhain dropped to his feet. He stumbled but kept himself from falling, then bent over, wheezing.

"So why did he have this?" Aios's silver chain dangled from Kolis's fingers, and I *hated* seeing it.

I swallowed. "Maybe he's not as good as you think." I forced a shrug. "And Rhain needed the necklace to do it, thinking I could tell him where Nyktos is."

"As if you wouldn't have," Kyn accused.

My head whipped to him. "No one asked you, asshole."

Kyn stiffened, and eather crackled to life along the flesh of his cheeks.

"My dear." Kolis laughed. "Didn't I tell you not to engage those here?"

"Then he needs to stop engaging me." I took a deep breath at the rise of Kolis's brow. "I'm...I'm sorry. As I said, I have a bad temper."

Rhain blinked his one good eye at me.

"But I'm not lying."

"I believe you," Kolis said, and before I could even feel relief, he turned to Rhain. "And because of that, your death will be quick."

"No!" I shot forward, grasping the bars. Sharp, hot pain stung my palms. I gasped, jerking my burning hands back. "You don't have to do this."

Kolis raised that brow again. "I don't? In case you missed the part of the conversation about avoiding the Shadowlands' forces, he is part of that open rebellion. And that is treason, a crime punishable by death, even in the mortal realm. He was also caught attempting to gain information. In other words, he was spying. Yet another crime punishable by death—"

"He is only loyal to Nyktos," I interjected, my neck muscles tensing as I heard Rhain's voice in my thoughts again.

"He should only be loyal to me!"

Shit. That had been the wrong thing to say. "I only meant that he is worried about Nyktos. All of them are. And you should be thrilled by that."

The Primal of Peace and Vengeance sighed loudly, almost overshadowing Rhain's voice inside my head—him repeating my name, reiterating what he'd said earlier.

Kolis frowned. "Why would I be thrilled by that?"

"That's a good question," Kyn muttered.

If he didn't shut up... "Because those who serve in the Courts of your Primals should care for the Primal they serve. If they don't," I continued quickly as Kolis opened his mouth, "how can they care for their King?"

Kolis stared at me.

So did Rhain from his one good eye.

"If they're not loyal to the Primal they serve," I went on, my heart pounding. I heard Rhain in my head again. "They cannot be loyal to you."

Kolis's brow knitted as he cocked his head. "I don't think that's how loyalty to one's King works."

"It's exactly how it works," I exclaimed. "In the mortal realm, the people are loyal to lesser nobles, which proves their loyalty to the Crown because those nobles are extensions of that Crown."

The false King had returned to staring at me.

"And when the people react based on their loyalty to those nobles, they shouldn't be punished—"

"They should be rewarded?" Kolis interrupted.

"No." I willed my temper to calm, then continued spewing utter bullshit. "I was going to say they shouldn't be punished by death. *Or*,"—I stressed—"torture."

"Then how are they punished?" Kolis demanded. "With a smack on the hand?"

Kyn snorted.

"They are usually sentenced to a reasonable length of time to think about how they should've handled the situation better," I explained, knowing that sounded absolutely ridiculous, even though it would be a better punishment than what was typically carried out in most kingdoms.

The look on Kolis's face said he thought it was ridiculous, and my fear for Rhain increased as I heard him too clearly.

It's okay, he said. *I'm prepared to die.*

But I wasn't.

I knew if I couldn't convince Kolis there was an alternative, Rhain would die, and it would be a horrible death.

It would also be another drop of blood Ash would have to ink onto his flesh.

I absolutely refused to allow that.

Resolve filled me, sealing the cracks in my blank canvas. *Become his weakness.* Even if Kolis wasn't convinced yet of who I was, he *wanted* me to be Sotoria. He wanted his precious *so'lis.* I was already his weakness.

"There is another option." I walked to the right, closer to where Kolis stood. "Release him."

"You've got to be kidding me," Kyn groused.

"Releasing him will only benefit you. It proves that you can be a benevolent ruler. A smart one," I said. "A King worth someone's loyalty. More so than any Primal ruling a Court."

"Worth?" Kolis whispered.

"Just because you believe someone should already find you worthy doesn't mean they do. Killing them won't change that," I said. "But releasing him will. It's not like he's accomplished anything but getting his ass beat."

"Well," Kolis remarked, "that part is true."

"And it sends a message. Release him in the condition he's in. They will know you can be fierce *and* giving, just as a King should be." I came as close as I could to the bars. "And releasing him will prevent further escalation."

Several seconds passed before Kolis spoke. "I see what you're suggesting, but I am not sure why you think I'd care if those who rebel against me find me fierce or giving."

Shit.

"I don't," Kolis continued. "I am only worthy of those who already see me as such."

Well, that made absolutely no sense whatsoever. I tried to swallow, but my throat was too tight.

It's okay, Rhain's voice came again. I *am ready—*

I blocked him out because I knew what he claimed, but I couldn't let it happen. I couldn't allow Ash to lose another person who was not only loyal to him but also cared about him.

And I couldn't watch Rhain die.

"Let him go," I said. "I'll do whatever you want."

"Seraphena," Rhain rasped out loud, his head loose on his shoulders as it turned to Kolis. "Just kill me. Just fucking kill—"

Kolis threw out his hand, and Rhain...he just dropped. He hit the floor like a sack of potatoes.

"What did you do?" I exclaimed.

"He's fine." Kolis walked forward. "What were you saying? That you'd be willing to do anything for him?" Kolis asked quietly—too quietly. "Why?"

Staring at Rhain's crumpled form and unable to see his chest rise or fall, I reminded myself that I would've felt it if he'd died. "Because... because if you kill him, there will be war. He's important to Nyktos." My insides burned, shriveling a little at the knowledge that Kyn was hearing this. "And as I said before, how can we start over if there's war? I'm willing to do anything to have a chance to..." My throat thickened. "To know what love feels like."

A small eternity passed as Kolis stared at me. "Anything?"

My heart stopped its ceaseless racing as finally, *finally* that veil of nothingness settled into place again. "As long as you promise that Rhain will return to the Shadowlands, no more harmed than he is now," I said, having learned from earlier that I needed to be as clear as I could in our agreements—something I hadn't done in our deal regarding Ash. "Anything."

The eather calmed in Kolis. "So, another deal?"

"Yes." I gave a half shrug, knowing how the movement pulled the gown against my chest and would draw his attention. "What can I say? I have a fondness for deals." I smiled. "After all, everything that has led to this moment is the result of one."

Something I'd rather not acknowledge flashed in Kolis's stare. "Deal."

I nodded, relieved.

"You're no longer needed," Kolis said to Kyn. "Rhain's transport will be handled by another."

"As you wish, Your Majesty." Kyn bowed. As he straightened, he looked at me with a blade-thin smile and a look…

A look that said exactly what he knew would happen.

Even though he was unconscious, I couldn't look at Rhain. So, I busied myself with pouring a glass of water as Kolis called for Elias to send for Callum. They took Rhain from the chamber in silence. I didn't know how long he'd be out, but I hoped it was long enough for him to be taken from…well, wherever I was in Dalos.

Kolis and I were alone.

He watched me. "Anything?"

I took a long drink and then faced him, but I wasn't me. I wasn't truly here anymore. So, it didn't matter when I nodded.

Kolis positively glowed. "Then, tonight, we will share the same bed."

Shortly after what I could only assume was suppertime, the Chosen once more prepared a bath for me. I didn't think about anything as I bathed, likely on Kolis's orders. Nor did I think about anything when I saw the slinky, ankle-length, gold nightgown on the bed.

The bed.

I hadn't slept in it yet.

I sat on the divan and waited, hollow and blank, until Kolis returned. He was alone, dressed in those loose linen pants with damp hair. It appeared he, too, had bathed.

Kolis crossed the chamber and entered the cage, finally speaking. "If you are who you claim, you are far bolder than you were before."

"How so?" I asked, even though I had a good idea what he meant.

"You never spoke your mind or shared your opinion, at least not at first," he explained.

Sotoria's presence stirred as a little surprise flickered through me. "I imagine a lot of that has to do with the times being different."

"You imagine?" His head tilted. "But you don't know. Because you cannot remember."

I shook my head.

Kolis didn't say anything for a long moment. "Is what I requested of you a surprise?"

Was it? No. Not in the way he likely meant.

"Will you not be bold now and speak your mind?" he asked.

I could be far bolder than his imagination could conjure because this wasn't me. I looked up at him. "You offered me to Kyn, so your request was a bit surprising."

"I offered you to him only if you are not who you say you are," he replied. "If that is not the case, then it should be of no concern to you."

He really thought that made a difference? Whether or not I was Sotoria, I was still a person—I stopped myself. He did think that made a difference, and it...it didn't matter.

Several more moments passed. "What you said earlier..." His chin lifted. "It was wise advice. Releasing one of Nyktos's men does show that I'm reasonable and fair."

A laugh bubbled up in my throat, but I proved that I was wise by not letting it break free.

"And that I am...how did you put it? Worthy of loyalty." Eather sluiced across his features. "You will be happy to learn that I've been advised Rhain has made it back to the Shadowlands, no more harmed than when he left."

The only thing I allowed myself to feel then was relief. "Thank you."

"I hope I do not regret this if what you've said ends up being a fabrication," he said. And he would when that happened. I couldn't regret it, though. Rhain lived. "And that my benevolence is remembered," he continued.

"It will be," I lied smoothly. I was nothing *but* lies now. This wasn't me anymore. I wasn't really here. Nothing I said or did mattered.

Kolis was quiet and still for a moment, then he extended an arm, gesturing to the bed. "The divan will not suit us."

I rose on steady legs, passed him, and sat on the bed, feeling the soft mattress.

He watched me like a hawk. "Lie down."

This isn't me. I reclined. *I'm not here.* Easing onto my side, I stared ahead. *None of this matters.*

Kolis remained standing. Seconds ticked by. I closed my eyes, not wanting to catch any hints of what he was thinking. Time continued to pass. I didn't hear him move. I only felt the bed dip, and the heat of his presence.

I squeezed my eyes closed until I saw stars bursting behind my lids.

His chest touched my back.

This isn't me.

His arm went around my waist. A shudder went through him.

I'm not here.

His presence, the stale lilac scent, and the feel of him, tainted my skin and stained my bones.

None of this matters.

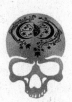

I watched Callum from where I sat at my little table. He was stretched out on the couch, his feet resting on an arm as he caught the dagger he repeatedly tossed into the air.

With his eyes closed.

I was reluctantly impressed...and also reminded of Bele doing the same as the seamstress fitted me for my coronation gown. That felt like a lifetime ago. Yawning, I toyed with the edge of a napkin.

"Did you not get much sleep last night?" Callum asked.

"Tons," I lied.

Kolis and I had shared the bed.

And that was all we'd done.

Well, all *I* had done. Kolis had slept, and he'd done so peacefully. I, on the other hand, had only slept for about an hour. And only after Kolis left in what I assumed was the morning. I'd pretended to be asleep. Having spent the entire night tense with my eyes wide open, my body caved to exhaustion the moment he left the cage.

It was hours later, and I still couldn't believe nothing had happened last night. When Kolis made his request, he had meant it in the most literal sense.

Share a bed.

I shook my head slightly. Perhaps he wasn't attracted to me.

I wished that were the case.

Unfortunately, I knew better. I'd seen how he looked at me the day before.

My focus shifted to the plate of barely touched sliced meats and fruits in front of me. Kolis hadn't even held me all that tightly throughout the night. Not like Ash. Not even like he had when he hadn't intended to—

I didn't want to think about Ash and sharing a bed with Kolis. My palms dampened, and I wiped them on the napkin. I didn't want those two things to ever occupy my mind simultaneously. Because despite nothing occurring last night, I still felt...gross.

Gods, I didn't want to think about that either. I focused on Callum. He was still entertaining himself with the dagger. I had more important things to dwell on. Like whether Rhain had been able to communicate anything to Aios.

I reached up, touching the delicate silver chain encircling my neck. When the Chosen woke me as they entered the chamber, I'd discovered that Kolis had left something for me on the pillow his head had rested upon.

Aios's necklace.

I hoped I had a chance to return it to her.

I *would*.

I truly didn't believe Rhain had been attempting to find me. He was loyal and brave enough to risk his life for Ash. Not for me.

"You're quiet today," Callum commented.

"I forgot you were even here," I lied. It was impossible *not* to know he was there as he snatched the dagger out of the air just before the blade was about to sink into his chest.

"That hurt my feelings."

"Uh-huh." I pushed from the chair and rose. "I learned something yesterday."

He tossed the dagger again. "That you're capable of whoring yourself out to get your way?"

My eyes narrowed, and I didn't think about what I was doing. I just did it as a ripple of hot anger swept through me. The embers throbbed as my gaze flipped to the dagger rising into the air. I pictured it speeding downward, faster than gravity would take it, straight for his eye.

And what I saw became my will.

The dagger had just flipped above Callum when a burst of energy left me. The blade jerked a foot to its side and then fell with the speed of an unleashed arrow.

"Fuck," gasped Callum as he rolled. His knees hit the floor a heartbeat before the dagger slammed into the arm of the couch where his head had been resting.

He whipped toward me.

I smiled sweetly at him. "Careful there, Cal, you might hurt yourself."

"Don't call me that." Glaring, he rose. "What did you realize?"

"I learned that I wasn't in Cor Palace."

"It took you that long to realize that?" He yanked the shadowstone dagger free.

"How was I supposed to know I wasn't there? What I've seen of the grounds reminded me of the palace." I watched him take a swig of his drink. "I know I'm still in Dalos."

"If you didn't know that, I would have grave concerns about your intelligence."

I arched a brow. "Where am I, exactly?"

"You are at the Vita," he said, sheathing the dagger to his hip. "It is a sanctuary built by His Majesty, replacing the existing Council Hall."

The Council Hall in the Shadowlands was in Lethe, an amphitheater holding a second set of much larger thrones. If the Council Hall was the same as the one in the Shadowlands, then that meant...

"I'm in the City of the Gods?"

"Maybe I don't need to worry that much about your intelligence," he quipped.

My gaze flew to the narrow windows. I'd only seen the sparkling city from a distance.

"You seem troubled by the knowledge."

Only because I had a feeling it would be harder to escape a whole damn city than one palace. "I didn't think the city was in use."

"And exactly why did you think that?" Placing his dagger on the low table, he sauntered to the cage. "Let me guess? Nyktos told you such?"

Actually, he hadn't. He'd just told me that many had taken to calling it the City of the Dead. I just assumed that meant it was vacant and no longer in use. But before I could respond, the embers suddenly hummed in my chest. My attention shifted to the doors. A Primal was near.

The gown swayed around my feet as I took a step back from the bars. The doors opened no more than a few heartbeats later, proving that I had been right about the feeling.

Kolis entered, his crown in place, and he wasn't alone.

A woman wearing a green silk gown followed him, her skin a medium shade of brown, her hair dark and chin-length.

"Your Majesty." Callum bowed as they drew near.

Kolis nodded at the Revenant as the attention of the one who followed him fixed on me. The silvery glow of eather pulsed behind dark eyes. She was a goddess. Her gaze quickly darted away.

A nervous goddess.

Kolis glanced over the table of food. "Did you enjoy your supper?" he asked warmly.

"Yes," I answered, softening my tone.

Callum's head snapped in my direction, his eyes narrowing behind his painted mask.

"Good." Kolis snapped his fingers, and the Chosen entered from the hall.

They approached the cage as Callum came forward to unlock the door. Clasping my hands together, I stepped back several feet, not wanting to incite any of them to hurt one of the Chosen.

"Leave the drinks," Kolis instructed. "I believe we will be in need of them when we're done."

The Chosen neither nodded nor spoke as they carried out his command. Within a minute or two, they had left the chamber, and the doors were once more closed.

But the one to the cage remained open.

That sweet and stale scent increased as Kolis entered, followed by the goddess. "I would like to introduce you to someone. This is Ione. She serves in the Court of the Primal Keella," he said, a bit of disdain tainting the Primal's name.

I wasn't surprised to hear that, as I didn't expect Kolis to favor the Primal of Rebirth, who'd aided Eythos in hiding Sotoria's soul. But what was one of her gods doing here?

Ione gave a curt bow as she folded one arm over the black rope at her waist. "Your Highness."

"Come and sit," Kolis said to me, gesturing to the divan.

Aware that those in the chamber watched, I went to the couch and sat on the edge.

"Ione is unique to the gods of the Thyia Plains," Kolis said, speaking of Keella's Court, while the goddess appeared to find something fascinating on the floor. "Not many are left that can do as she can."

Warning bells started to ring. My gaze shot to Callum. The bastard was grinning now, and it dripped with…feral anticipation.

"What…" I swallowed. "What can she do?" I asked.

"See into your thoughts," Kolis answered.

My heart began pounding. No, no, no. My muscles locked.

"She can see your truths and lies," the false King continued. "See all that is needed."

18

At once, the façade of my blank canvas began to crack.

My gaze swiveled from the Primal to Ione as I rose from the divan. Good gods, how could I have forgotten about Taric and not think about there being another god like him? One who could see right into my mind—and my memories.

Foolishly, I hadn't prepared for this, and there was no time to do so now.

Dread took root, dampening my palms as the reality of the situation hit me with the force of an out-of-control carriage. This was bad, really bad.

"It will not take very long," Kolis explained, that fabricated smile plastered across his face. "Ione will be quick and efficient."

Pressure clamped down on my chest. Not only was I mere moments from Kolis discovering way too quickly that I was manipulating him, I also clearly remembered how painful it had been when Taric flipped through my memories as casually as Callum had turned the pages of his book.

"Sit down," Kolis instructed, "so we can be done with this."

I didn't move. Outside the cage, Callum's smile grew even wider. That bastard knew what was about to happen. Whether it was just his distrust of me or something else, I had no idea, but he looked like he was about to witness all his dreams coming true.

The weight of the burgeoning fear was suffocating, threatening to crush me. My stomach twisted as the consequences of my lies being exposed loomed before me like a curse. I wouldn't gain Ash's freedom, and if Ione saw anything having to do with Sotoria's soul and how I wasn't truly her? I was as good as dead.

"*Sit*," Kolis snapped, his patience already running thin.

I felt Sotoria then, near my thundering heart. I felt *her* fear and anger, and it joined mine, forming a combustible mix. The embers started to thrum.

"You seem...nervous," Kolis remarked, his features stoic but his fingers curled inward.

I most definitely was.

The gold flecks in his eyes had stilled. "Why is that?"

My pulse pounded, and my mouth dried. *Think*, Sera. *Think*. "I am afraid," I admitted, my thoughts racing. I could only come up with one thing to say. "A god did this to me before, and it hurt."

Kolis's forehead creased as he eyed me.

"Taric," Callum surmised, his lips pursing as he walked the length of the cage. "Well, I suppose we now know for sure what happened to him when we last learned he was somewhere near or in the Shadowlands."

Kolis's mouth tightened. "Taric found you?"

"It wasn't just him. Cressa and another called Madis were with him," I said, hoping this delay would allow me to come up with something else to say. "Why did you...?" I glanced at Ione, unsure how much she knew, and then deciding it wasn't my problem if she wasn't supposed to know. "Why did you have him searching for the embers if you already knew where they were?"

"Because I didn't have him searching for them. Obviously," Kolis said in a slow, deliberate drawl as if explaining a complex idea to a child. "He was supposed to be searching for my *graeca*."

His love.

I wasn't the only one who'd assumed Taric and the others had been searching for that. Even Veses had.

"Did the others feed from you?" Kolis asked.

I shook my head. "No, it was only him. I...I didn't know yet about who I was, but he seemed to already know it was me when he looked at me. I didn't think he needed to feed. He just wanted to."

A muscle twitched in the Primal's jaw. "So, he fed from you but did not tell either you or Nyktos what he saw?"

"He really didn't get the chance," I told him.

Ione raised a brow as she continued staring at the floor.

Kolis's chin lifted. "Well, we will see if that is true, won't we?"

My heart lurched, and I swung my head toward Ione.

"It does not need to be painful," she said, looking up. "Though it is not entirely comfortable. You will be tired afterward and perhaps have a headache, but it should not feel like any unimaginable pain."

Yeah, well, the problem wasn't the pain. I could deal with that. Still, I latched on to the excuse. "I can't go through that again. It was horrible." A tremor coursed down my spine, and it was more genuine than forced. "I won't—"

"*Seraphena.*"

I locked up at Kolis's whisper. Or had he yelled? I couldn't be sure. Whatever it was, his voice felt like it was everywhere.

Oh, gods.

A compulsion. He was using compulsion again.

"*Look at me,*" he coaxed, his tone soft and lilting yet heavy and laden with power.

His voice washed over me like a rising tide, seeping through my skin—

No.

My fingers twitched.

No. No.

The muscles in my neck spasmed as I fought, and the embers hummed wildly in my chest. If he gained control, there'd be nothing I could do. Nothing. *No. No—*

"*Seraphena.*" Kolis was suddenly in front of me, his fingers on my chin.

I jerked back, starting to close my eyes. I could fight this, couldn't I? I had Primal embers in me. I could fight this with…with—

"*Look at me,*" Kolis demanded, and a wave of power hit me hard. "*Now.*"

I tried…gods, I tried to resist. My muscles spasmed painfully. Air punched out of my lungs, and my eyes lifted past his mouth. His nostrils were flared with irritation. My gaze locked on his, and I felt it then, the compulsion seeping into my muscles, relaxing them. His power wrapped around my mind. I wanted to scream, but I couldn't.

I could do nothing but obey.

Golden flecks whirled in his eyes, slipping under and over the wisps of silvery eather. "You will sit, and you will not attempt to fight Ione. Do you understand?"

My lips moved, forming one word. "Yes."

"That's a good girl," he murmured, running his thumb beneath my bottom lip, avoiding the healing skin there as I...

I stood still, unable to even shudder.

"Sit," he repeated.

Like a puppet, I sat.

Kolis turned to the goddess. "Do what needs to be done." He was silent as Ione moved closer. "And do it as quickly as possible." He glanced at me and then away. "I do not want her to feel any unnecessary pain."

He said as much now, but that would soon change.

"Of course, Your Majesty." Ione knelt before me. Dark eyes lit with eather met mine. "You seem to be aware of this, but to be clear, I will need to take your blood."

I did know that. I fucking remembered that part clearly.

Ione blinked, seeming to remember only then that I could not respond. She picked up my right hand, her touch cool. She halted, her brows lifting as her gaze flew to mine.

"Is there a problem?" Kolis demanded from where he lingered a foot—if that—behind the goddess.

Ione cleared her throat. "No."

"Then get on with it."

She hunched her shoulders and carefully lowered my right hand to my lap and lifted my left. I thought that was strange, but I couldn't really focus on that. My mind filled with what was to come. Would I have to react? To summon the embers and at least attempt to get free? I didn't know.

Ione's warm breath against the inside of my wrist was my only warning. A second later, the sharp tips of her fangs pierced my skin. I jerked, not even the compulsion able to prevent that.

The burning sting traveled up my arm, causing every muscle in my body to clench. Ione drew deeply on the wound, and that sting hit my neck. I wanted to tear my arm free from her light grasp, but I couldn't move. I couldn't—

Then I felt it.

A scratching like fingers against my mind, slowly sinking in instead of digging in with claws like Taric had done. The tendons in my neck cramped, and I felt my mind open.

Ione was inside me, in my mind, slipping in easily. It wasn't painless as she delved into my thoughts and memories. The supper I'd eaten was peeled back, revealing the dreamless sleep, the conversation with Kolis, and my lies—all my lies. She kept searching. Images of a sky full of stars but no moon flashed, then small waves crashing beneath the House of Haides. Those quickly blended into others. I saw the woods and heard myself telling Ash that I loved him. The flashes came in rapid succession as Ione saw what I'd seen. Heard what I'd said. She saw the truths. All of them. She saw the lies, too. Sweat broke out on my brow. A tremor rolled through me as sharp, stabbing pain shot through my head and ran down my spine.

I felt myself shaking on the inside, tears filling my eyes as the ebbing agony became a fire. My skin felt like it stretched, thinned. My vision blurred.

Not as painful? Ione had lied. I felt like I was burning from the inside, and there was no retreat. Nowhere to hide. Pressure built in my skull, sparking a fiery pain that settled there and took root. I *shook*, and a metallic taste gathered in my mouth.

Oh, gods, could Ash feel this, even in stasis? I didn't want him to be aware and unable to do anything.

I couldn't allow that.

I *wouldn't*.

The embers swelled beneath the pain, and I latched on to them. *Stop*. I focused on Ione, forcing her features to clear. *Stop*, I screamed as I…pushed. I *pushed* with my mind.

The goddess's head snapped back. There was a brief glimpse of wide, dark eyes, and then she was skidding backward on her knees across the shadowstone. She caught herself before she hit the cage bars, her chin jerking up. Blood trickled from the corner of her lip.

"Well." Callum sighed from outside the cage as I slumped forward, breathing raggedly. "That was inappropriate."

Trembling, I smacked my hand over the bite as my muscles twitched and contracted, over and over. The fire was slow to leave, just as before.

"What did you see?" Kolis demanded, his voice close. Too close.

"Much," Ione rasped, rising unsteadily to her feet. I tried to push through the lingering agony. "The embers in her are powerful."

"I already know that," Kolis stated. "Is she my *graeca*?"

My neck felt weak and loose as I lifted my head and saw Callum's eager face. I called on the embers, and they fluttered much like my heart. Godsdamnit, I didn't have time for them to weaken on me. I would have seconds, if that—"

"She carries the soul of the one called Sotoria," Ione answered, smoothly wiping the trickle of blood from her chin. "She is her."

I froze.

Everything froze.

Even Callum's *stupid* face.

"Truly?" whispered Kolis.

"Yes." Ione nodded, clasping her hands together. "It is her."

But that…that wasn't true. And Ione knew it.

Callum pushed back from the cage, his head swaying to and fro.

"And does she…does she love Nyktos?" Kolis's voice faltered and then steadied. "Is she in love with him?"

"She cares for him," Ione answered, her eyes locked on mine. "But she has never truly loved…nor been loved in return." Ione broke eye contact and turned from me. "She wants to, though. She will do anything for that."

My gods, the goddess was truly lying about *everything*. Well, except for that last part. I did want to be loved by Ash, and I would do anything for that. But the rest? Straight-up lies.

Stunned, I watched her walk to the table. While she filled a slender glass with the bubbly water, I tried to wrap my head around the fact that this stranger had just saved my life.

"It's really you." Kolis's voice was a gruff whisper, tearing me from my thoughts.

My gaze shot to the Primal. He looked at me as he had when I'd first said I was her, when he likely heard her voice in mine. I realized then that it was the only time I'd seen him show any real emotion beyond anger. Everything else had been a reproduction. A copy of what he'd seen in others. But like then, his features came alive with a tangible sense of wonderment, his eyes widening with awe.

"I didn't…" Kolis trailed off, not allowing himself to finish whatever it was he had been about to say.

The pain was almost gone from my head, but my body tensed with each passing second that Kolis's stifling stare remained on me. It was clear to me that he hadn't been a hundred percent convinced.

Now, he was.

It was yet another thing I should feel relief about—and I did. But his stare… I shifted, suddenly wishing I could put a whole realm's-worth of distance between us.

"This has to be some sort of lie," Callum said, sounding almost *spooked*.

"I do not lie," Ione cut in, the eather pulsing in her eyes, turning them from night to day. "I have no reason to."

Oh, but she most definitely did. I couldn't know for sure why the goddess had done it, but I could only assume that, like the Primal she served, she was not a Kolis loyalist.

Even so, this was a huge risk for her. More so than it was for Attes. Ione had just lied straight to Kolis's face about Sotoria, running the risk of another god coming in, reading my memories, and contradicting her.

Unless Ione and Taric were truly unique and the last of those who could do that.

"But she does not look like Sotoria," Callum argued.

Two things occurred to me at once. The Revenant had just confirmed part of what Attes had claimed. That if I truly were Sotoria, I would look like her. But, more importantly, Callum must have known Sotoria.

"That means nothing," Ione stated, and I had a feeling the goddess was lying again. "The rebirth of a soul is not common enough to know exactly how it will appear."

My mind raced as the two argued. The first time Sotoria had died...gods, it had been hundreds of years ago, if not close to a thousand, back when Kolis ruled as the true Primal of Death, and his brother the Primal of Life. So exactly how old was Callum? Had Kolis created Callum even before he stole the embers from Eythos?

Or had Callum known her decades later, after she'd been ripped away from the peace of the Vale and brought back to life—after Kolis stole the embers and brought her back? No one knew exactly how long she had lived that second life. But still, even that was hundreds of years ago.

Callum was clearly *old*, and Kolis could have been able to create Revenants before he stole the Primal embers of life.

"You should drink." Ione offered the glass to me. "It will help settle your mind."

Hand trembling slightly, I reached out and took the glass from her. Our eyes met. "Thank you," I said, hoping she knew it wasn't just the water I was thanking her for.

A faint smile appeared on her thin lips, softening her sharper features. "You're welcome."

I took a sip of the fruity water and then gulped as Ione turned back to Kolis. His hands continuously opened and closed at his sides.

"I am happy that you have found your *graeca*," Ione stated, and I nearly choked on my water, my eyes and throat burning. "You must be overjoyed."

"I...I am," Kolis murmured.

I thought maybe he should sit down since he appeared as if he were close to falling over.

"Is there anything else you need of me, Your Majesty?" Ione asked.

"No." His hands stilled. "Your assistance is appreciated and won't be forgotten."

Ione nodded as she stepped back, bowing to Kolis before facing me. She smiled, the eather now a faint pulse behind her pupils. It was quick. I saw it. Kolis didn't. His attention was fixed on me. I could feel it, like I was being suffocated in a too-heavy, coarse blanket.

"Good day, Consort." Ione inclined her head.

I mumbled something in response.

"Ione," Kolis called out, and my fingers twitched around the glass. The false warmth in his voice immediately caused warning bells to go off.

The goddess stopped at the cage door. "Yes, Your Majesty?"

I lowered the glass to my lap, watching Kolis's lips curve into a tight grin. "You addressed her as Consort."

"Yes, I..." Her arched brows knitted. "Was I not supposed to?"

"No," Kolis answered. "You were not."

Ione's wary gaze darted between us. "I...I apologize. I'm—"

"It's okay," I interjected. "That is my title."

Kolis's head turned toward me, his eyes as still and flat as the waters of my lake, causing the hairs on the back of my neck to rise. "It is no longer how you are to be addressed."

A sudden wave of dread flooded me, and I struggled not to show it on my face. It took everything for me to slip on that veil of nothingness again.

His stare held mine. "Your coronation was not recognized nor approved by me."

My mouth parted in incredulity. That was a bald-faced lie.

"Therefore, the coronation itself was invalid," he continued. I couldn't believe what I was hearing as he turned his attention back to the goddess. "Do you understand?"

"I...I was unaware of this." Ione lowered her gaze and nodded. "I do understand."

I was nowhere near being the blank canvas I needed to be now as I clenched my teeth. My fury had nothing to do with losing my perceived rank in some ridiculous class structure; it was the message that he was sending to the other Primals. That any accusations of Kolis breaking tradition by taking me could be discredited.

Only the Primals Attes, and his brother Kyn, had been present when Kolis gave Ash and me his permission. The latter would likely back up whatever Kolis claimed, but Attes...

He had sworn an oath to me.

However, the false King wasn't aware of that. Just as he had no idea that Ione had lied to him.

My anger cooled as Ione crossed the chamber. Attes would have to support Ash, and that included telling the truth about Kolis giving his permission. Of course, the other Primals could choose not to believe Attes or Ash, but Kolis's plans weren't as clever as he thought they were.

"Your Majesty," Callum began once Ione was gone.

"I know what you think, Callum. I understand it is hard to believe. And accept," Kolis said, the flatness leaving his gaze, and the golden flecks burning brightly. "And you're right. She looks different, but the similarities are there. I can see them."

Callum said nothing, but he too stared at me.

Gods. One was bad enough, but both of them scrutinizing me? I wanted to gouge their eyes out.

"But it is her," Kolis continued. The expression on Callum's face grew increasingly more disturbing, reminding me of how I knew I'd looked at Tavius. "After all this time, my *graeca* has returned to me."

Dragging my gaze from Callum, I looked up at the false King and felt my lips curve into a smile—a real one that had nothing to do with his words. His conviction meant only one thing I cared about. "I was telling you the truth before."

"I can see that." Kolis's stare softened, bringing life to his features once more. "I will honor my side of the deal," he told me. "And you will honor yours."

My stomach hollowed, but I felt myself nod and smile.

His chest rose with a deep breath as he looked at me. A second passed. Then several. My smile began to fade. "Callum, I will find you later."

The Revenant bowed stiffly. "Yes, Your Majesty."

As a kiss of unease bore down on the nape of my neck, I watched

Callum leave the chamber, closing the door behind him.

"When you smile, you look more like I remember," Kolis said, his voice thicker.

My gaze shifted back to the false King.

Was he closer?

I hadn't heard him move, but it felt as if he were. And as he stared, his features lost some of that softness, turning thinner, starker. My unease grew at the clear change that had occurred upon my smile. Tiny goose bumps spread across my flesh. The embers stirred, but something else moved restlessly in my chest near them. It was an awareness, one that warned me I was not safe being alone with him.

I started to recognize the look in his eyes. I'd seen it in Ash before—a predatory *need*—but it didn't even remotely evoke the same response coming from Kolis. My body didn't flush hot with desire. I turned cold to the very core.

Fuck. I shouldn't have smiled at him—

Wait, what was I thinking? I shouldn't have smiled? I had only fucking *smiled* at the Primal. That was all. It was not an invitation, and I wasn't ready. I was nowhere near the blank canvas I needed to be.

You will never be ready for that, a voice whispered, causing me to jerk, and my pulse to stutter. Had that…had that been Sotoria's thought? Could she actually talk to me? Or was I losing my mind? The latter was likely, and I really needed to pull it together because I needed to figure a way out of this.

Despite believing that Kolis wanted more than to just share a bed with me yesterday, I wasn't ready for what I saw in his stare now.

It was different than what I'd seen the day before. It was fiery. Alive. More potent. He'd needed me to be Sotoria. Now, he fully believed that I was her, and that changed things.

I stood suddenly, mouth drying. Kolis showed no reaction to me moving. "I am feeling quite tired."

"I have spent centuries waiting for you." He spoke as if I hadn't, and the almost guttural sound of his voice sent chills down my spine.

"That's a long time," I began, struggling to keep the creeping panic from my voice. "But—" I gasped.

Kolis was suddenly in front of me, causing me to take a step in retreat and battle the natural urge to force him to back off. "I have filled similar spaces with countless imitations of you."

I cringed.

"I'm sorry. I shouldn't have tried to recreate what I felt for you," he said, taking my glass from my numb fingers. "But I was lonely."

He'd really misunderstood my reaction to that statement.

His eyes closed. "I have been so damn lonely, *so'lis.*"

My muscles cramped with the effort it took to hold myself still instead of using my years of training on him. "And I'm sorry for that."

Kolis pulled me to him, wrapping his arms around my stiff body so tightly that I felt his heart pounding against my chest. I had no idea what he'd done with my glass. "Not as sorry as I have been," he murmured, cupping the back of my head.

Arms pinned to my sides, my fingers splayed. "Kolis—"

"You don't have to worry about Kyn or anyone ever again. I have you now." His head dropped to mine, and he inhaled deeply.

My eyes widened. Was he fucking smelling me again? I attempted to gain some space, as the horrid gown was no barrier, but his hold was immoveable.

"I need you," he whispered.

All the muscles in my body went rigid. And, dear gods, revolting images flashed in my mind, threatening to flood the waning emptiness I'd crafted inside myself.

"I just need to hold you." Kolis shuddered.

I blinked.

Okay, once again, that wasn't where my horrified mind had gone, but I wasn't sure if it was any better. I didn't want to be held by him.

Either I hadn't given him an answer in a timely enough manner, or he simply didn't wait, because he was suddenly sitting on the edge of the bed, and I was in his lap, my godsdamn feet dangling in the air.

His hand tangled in my hair as he continued to breathe me in. He was still shaking, and my entire being was in the midst of a frozen rebellion, barely able to force a wisp of air into my lungs. Inside me, near the embers, a scream built. One only I could hear.

I struggled to stay calm and searched for a way to take his mind off me. "Will you release Nyktos now?"

He pressed his forehead against mine. "What?" he asked with a laugh that sounded uncertain.

My heart thudded heavily. "We made a deal," I reminded him. "You promised to release him if—"

"I know what I promised," he cut in, his voice changing, becoming thinner. "I cannot believe you would bring him up as I hold you."

I suddenly became aware of how still Kolis had gone, and how hot his body had become.

"That you would even speak his name." He drew back, and I saw then that his flesh...fuck, it had thinned. There was no golden aura of eather, and I saw the faint gleam of bone beneath his skin. Considering the last time I'd seen something like this, it wasn't a good sign.

My fight-or-flight response kicked in. I jerked back as far as I could. Our gazes locked. It was just for a heartbeat or two, his eyes pools of golden-flecked eather.

Then he struck like a pit viper, sinking his fangs into my throat.

19

A jolt coursed through my entire being. The sudden shock of agony ramped up the screams coming from within. I couldn't breathe, couldn't move as my gaze swung upward.

But I welcomed the pain, held on to it tightly as his mouth moved against my throat. My hands spasmed and then fisted. I stared at the gleaming gold bars, the searing fire coursing through my veins like a thousand knives pricking my flesh. Darkness crept into the edges of my vision—

The embers pulsed wildly, pressing against my skin. The shadows crowding my eyes vanished in a flash of silver. I sucked in a whimper as Kolis's head shifted. His fangs eased their brutal hold on my throat, and the agony…oh, gods, the pain was fading. *No. No. No.* My chest rose with a too-short breath as unwelcome warmth crept into my veins.

No. No. No.

This wasn't happening. It couldn't. My nails dug into my palms, the little sparks of pain lost in a grotesque, twisting pulse as he sucked on the wound.

I didn't want this.

The…the screaming had stopped. I felt the presence in my chest go quiet, while the embers pulsed and flared, responding to my disgust, whirling fury, and rising desperation to stop this.

The essence swelled, pressing against my skin, and the near-instinctual drive to tap into it began to take hold. My skin started to hum as the cage and chamber became drenched in silver—

No.

Fighting the instinct to tap into the embers, I willed them to calm. I had to. My heart thudded. If I used them against Kolis, it would anger him, and Ash…he was still imprisoned. I couldn't risk him. I wouldn't. He was too important. I could deal with this, just as he had when Veses came to him to feed.

Focusing on my breathing, the essence calmed, though my heart thundered. I desperately tried to pull together the tattered remains of the veil of nothingness that used to be like a second skin to me. I could do this. I could deal with this. I'd spent years preparing for something like this.

But that was before Ash.

Nausea churned in my stomach, even as a disturbing heaviness settled in my chest and lower. Kolis groaned, his arms tightening as he drank from me. This…this was nothing like before. I clamped my jaw shut, my gaze fixed on the grouping of diamonds above me. They seemed to throb, like some light within them moved rapidly. Kolis sucked deeply from my vein, his hips jerking against my backside—

Oh, gods, I was going to vomit. I was going to fucking vomit.

How far would this go?

Not that far.

Fear pierced the undesired haze. *Breathe in.* I knew—oh, gods, I knew then that I couldn't do *anything* to gain Kolis's trust. *Hold.* There was no fooling me. If this escalated even further, I didn't know what I would do, but it would be bad. *Breathe out.* I could feel that in the violent hum of power within me. *Hold.*

One of Kolis's hands skimmed down my side, clasping my hip and leaving a trail of unwanted shivers. This wasn't happening to me. I wasn't here. This didn't matter—

That wasn't working.

I squeezed my eyes shut against a rush of tears, losing concentration as my thoughts careened wildly. I hated him. I hated Kolis, and I hated Eythos for creating this situation. I hated the Fates for preventing Eythos from telling his son. And I fucking loathed how this reminded me of Tavius and how he'd held me down in my bedchamber.

I was trapped.

The embers stirred again, responding to my maelstrom of emotions.

I kept my eyes closed and thought of Ash. His features pieced together in my mind, and I recalled the night we'd fallen asleep together on his balcony. That had been a first for us. For me. I clung to that memory, erasing Kolis. I wiped him from this experience. I *removed* him. He wasn't here. Nor was I.

I was back in the Shadowlands, tucked against Ash, safe and happy. That was where I retreated and stayed until Kolis finally stopped feeding and moving against me.

He grew impossibly still once more, his body as rigid as mine. My fingers and palms ached from how tightly I'd clenched them. I counted the seconds silently ticking by, barely breathing as I did.

One.

Two.

Three.

Four.

Five.

Kolis's arms loosened and then fell away. I shot to my feet like an arrow released, my hands and legs trembling. The back side of my gown was fucking damp.

Bile climbed into my throat. I took a step back and lifted my gaze to Kolis, feeling the embers pressing against my skin once more. A jumble of emotions roared through me, leaving me panting. Rage mottled my skin, and something I shouldn't even feel pricked at my flesh, leaving hundreds of brutal cuts as part of me—a foolish, somehow naïve part—couldn't believe what had just happened.

Kolis sat there, a curtain of blond hair shielding his features as he looked down at his lap and the blotch of acutely visible wetness. A shudder ran through him.

"I'm sorry." His head lifted abruptly. "I…I have shamed myself," he stammered. "I've shamed you."

The back of my neck crawled.

"I lost control." His eyes closed, his features tensing. "I…I didn't mean to."

All I could do was stare at him.

"I wanted this time to be different. I didn't want to frighten you with my passion and jealousy. You must forgive me," he fretted. "I was just overcome with emotion. I've waited so long for you."

I couldn't hear him. The screams in my head drowned out his

excuses. They were Sotoria's and mine, full of rage, disbelief, and pure hatred. They sounded sad, and all the while, he...he fucking sounded *agonized.*

Kolis suddenly stood, taking a step toward me.

I tensed.

His eyes closed once more, his features drawn. "That will never happen again." He took a deep breath, lifted his lids, and fixed his gaze on me. "Do you understand? You do not have to fear that."

I counted the seconds again.

One.

Two.

Three.

Four.

Five.

I felt myself nod, but I didn't believe him.

Kolis swallowed. "Please..." He cleared his throat. "Please say something."

"A bath," I said, my voice strangely steady. "I would like a bath."

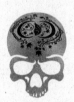

I sat in the tub, my knees tucked to my chest. The hot water the Chosen had brought in mere minutes after Kolis left the chamber had long since cooled.

I didn't know how long I'd sat here. Minutes? Hours? All I knew was that I had no fear when it came to bathing. The moment Callum and the Chosen left the chamber, I'd stripped off the disgusting gown and all but dove in. The horror of the incident that had occurred beyond the privacy screen I now stared at had replaced that fear.

There were so many more things to dread now.

Things every woman worried about, whether mortal or god. Things I knew Kolis was capable of the moment I learned what had been done to Sotoria. Things I knew I would have to face. From the moment I'd told him I was Sotoria, I'd known I wouldn't be like his other favorites. He wouldn't be content only observing. I knew those *things* would happen. It was one of the reasons I'd tried to escape and screamed fuck the greater good.

But from the moment I decided to use his love for Sotoria to my advantage, I'd known what would happen. And knew I might even have to initiate it.

I'd told myself I was ready. That I could do it. I'd convinced myself. I'd *known* this could happen. But the foolish, naïve shock still lingered. I didn't understand. I couldn't. Or maybe I *wouldn't*. Because I'd prepared for the likelihood that I'd have to seduce Kolis to gain his trust and Ash's freedom. And while it wasn't like I was okay with that, I at least had some semblance of control.

I'd had no control a bit ago.

None.

And I'd had no choice.

I really hadn't. Because choosing not to risk Ash or my physical well-being was not a fucking choice. I had been wrong earlier. Holland had been wrong. Choices didn't always exist. Not real ones.

Reaching up, I tentatively touched the bite on my neck and winced. He could've at least closed the wound. Dropping my hand, I dug my chin into my knees, the muscles in my body tense despite having soaked in hot water. Yet I felt numb. Detached. I closed my eyes.

I was lucky. This time. It could've been worse than him getting off while he fed. It could've gone further than that.

I didn't feel lucky, though.

I felt disgusted. Enraged. Desperate. Shamed. And angry at myself for even feeling that because I knew better. I felt *weak*. And I wasn't that. With or without the embers, I was fucking tough. Physically. Mentally. I'd cracked a little before, but I was not weak. Still, I felt that way. I felt everything as I sat in the tepid water.

But at the same time, I felt absolutely nothing.

20

Shortly after breakfast was served, the silver hawk flew in through the narrow window, arcing gracefully as it glided past the chandelier.

Leaving my glass on the table, I took a step back. I assumed it was Attes, but Kolis could take the form of a hawk, too.

Staying quiet, I watched the hawk tuck its wings in close, careful not to brush the bars as it flew between them. The feathered creature circled near the cluster of diamonds and then dove. At the same moment, starlight swallowed the hawk, and the embers hummed. I relaxed when I caught sight of brownish-blond hair.

Attes stood before me. "Meyaah *Liessa*." He folded an arm over his chest and bowed.

I arched a brow at the greeting. "That's not necessary."

"But it is." He straightened. "You are the—"

"I know. Whatever. You're naked." I paused. "Again."

A half-grin appeared, softening the scar on his face with the faint appearance of a dimple. I was willing to bet the combination of the three bewitched many.

As I reached for a pitcher, he summoned clothing. "I'm jealous of that talent," I admitted. "I would manifest actual clothes."

"I could comment on that," he drawled. "However, your husband would likely cut out my tongue and eyes and feed them to Setti."

Your husband. A pang lit up my chest. Two words I'd never thought would affect me so. Two words I'd never thought would apply to me.

Clearing my throat, I lifted the pitcher. "Would you like a drink?"

"Thank you, but I cannot stay long. Kolis is, well…his movements have been unpredictable of late."

I snorted.

"I'm sorry I couldn't come back sooner," he said. "But I do have news for you."

I faced him. He was entirely covered from his ankles to his throat in black. He must truly be worried about Ash learning about his nakedness because that was a bit excessive.

"I hope it's about the husband you're clearly afraid of."

Attes was quiet, so much so that I thought I might not have asked the question out loud. I lifted my gaze to his, about to repeat what I'd said, when I saw what he stared at.

My throat.

I stepped back, turning my head as if that could somehow undo what he'd seen.

Heat crept up my cheeks. "Do you have—?"

"Kolis?" he snarled.

I stiffened. "No, it was two very large mosquitos." My joke went over like a ton of manure-smeared bricks as eather pulsed in his eyes. "I'm okay."

"Seraphena—"

"I am," I stressed. "All he did was feed from me." I lifted my chin. "Do you have news about Nyktos?"

It took a moment, but Attes's chest finally moved with an exhale. "He is being awakened from stasis," he said. "It's taken longer than expected."

Pressure clamped down on my chest, and my mind became a whirlwind of fear for Ash. It cracked a bit of the veil I'd donned. "Do you know why?"

"I don't for sure, but…" The angles of his face sharpened. "I have my suspicions."

I stepped forward. "Tell me."

He hesitated for a second. "I think he was incapacitated with a weapon made of the bones of an Ancient."

My hand trembled as I heard what he'd said to me before about such a weapon. *They can even put a Primal into years-long stasis.* "But he's no longer incapacitated?"

Attes shook his head.

Relief swept through me, and I squeezed my eyes shut. This was good news. Great news.

"The only reason I can think of for why Kolis would do such a thing is because he plans to free him," Attes said. "I'm taking that to mean you've made progress with your plans."

"I have." I opened my eyes. "Kolis has promised to release him."

Now, Attes's lashes swept down. "Thank the Fates."

"Don't be too thankful yet," I advised. "Not until he's released. Until then…" I turned, walking to the bars facing the closed chamber doors. "Until then, I'll have to be careful not to give him a reason to find a loophole."

"I can only imagine how hard this must be for you."

"Actually, you *can* imagine." I dragged my thumb across the rim of my cup.

There was a brief silence. "Is this deal like the one you made to free Rhain?"

Tension crept into my shoulders. "I'm guessing Kyn told you about that." The corners of my lips tightened. "Your brother is a dick, by the way."

I heard a heavy sigh behind me. "Yeah, he is," he said. "Though he wasn't always."

I turned to him. "I find that hard to believe."

"I can't blame you for that, but if you'd known him a couple hundred years ago? You would've seen a different side of him." Attes dragged a hand over his chest. "A peaceful one."

My brows rose. A couple hundred years ago? "I suppose I'll have to take your word for it."

A wry smile appeared. "Did Nyktos tell you anything about why a Primal would either enter Arcadia or go into a deep stasis?"

"He mentioned it," I told him. "Something about them entering Arcadia when they were ready."

"When they're ready." He laughed roughly. "That's a nice way of putting it. Granted, some probably were simply tired of this existence and ready for what awaits in Arcadia, but others weren't ready by choice, Seraphena. They either had to enter Arcadia or go into a deep stasis because they were changing, becoming the worst of what their powers could do."

Something about what Attes said was familiar. I wasn't sure if it was something Ash had shared with me, or what the embers knew.

"How each of our essences influences mortals and gods does eventually affect us. For example, Nyktos's is rooted in death, but benevolent death—a just ending of one beginning. There is another side to that. One more malevolent that seeks death for the sake of death," he explained. "Maia can evoke love in others and herself, but it can turn dark, obsessive, and destructive. Even the essence that resides in Keella, who sees to the rebirth of all life, not just mortals, can turn wrong. The essence tied to each of us Primals is capable of great good but also terrible malevolence."

I thought I understood where he was going with this. "So, the vengeance part of Kyn's essence has a greater hold on him?"

Attes nodded, lowering his hand. "Just as accord will no longer suit me someday, and I will be driven by war. It happens to all of us, and all we can do to prevent it is either enter stasis to quell that side of us, or pass into Arcadia, where we would remain."

"If it happens to all of you, why is Keella not a raging bitch?" I asked. "Why are you not consumed by war? You and Kyn are the same age."

"Both Keella and I have entered stasis more than once over the years," Attes shared, surprising me. "But that doesn't mean it's not a struggle to keep from caving to the more toxic side of our abilities. It's like an infection slowly invading our flesh and blood."

"So, that's why Kyn is a dick?"

A wry grin appeared. "Partly. He's always been a bit difficult. But when Kolis did what he did? That didn't help. Any of us. The taint spread." His features tightened and then smoothed out with a sigh. "None of that is an excuse, obviously. I just wanted…" He frowned as if he wasn't sure *what* he wanted.

But I thought I might know. "You just wanted to let me know that your brother wasn't always this way. I understand." I took a small drink. "Going into stasis helps? Like if your brother went to sleep, would he awaken…less dickish?"

Attes's gaze flickered to mine, but he didn't answer for a moment. "I hope so. I hope it hasn't progressed that far in him."

And if it had? "How will he respond to Nyktos taking his rightful place as the Primal of Life and the King of Gods?"

His hand fisted at his side. "I can only believe that he will respond wisely."

As in he couldn't allow himself to think otherwise, because Attes knew what that meant. Once Ash had the embers of life, he could

Ascend another to rule in Kyn's place.

"I should leave," Attes said. "If I learn of anything else, I will do my best to let you know."

I nodded, resisting the urge to ask him to stay. It was nice having someone to talk to whom I didn't want to murder, even if we discussed things that left me feeling a bit hollow.

Attes turned, but like last time, he stopped. I waited for him to ask about Sotoria. "Are you okay, Seraphena?"

Surprised by his question, it took me a moment to answer. "Yes. Of course."

Attes exhaled heavily and nodded. He gave me one last look before starbursts swept over him, and he returned to his hawk form.

My eyes closed the moment he left the chamber, but I still saw the look he'd given me. It had been quick, yet I knew…

I knew he hadn't believed my answer to his question.

The diaphanous golden gown trailed behind me as I paced the length of the cage.

As always, I wasn't alone.

The Revenant stood a few feet from the gilded bars, his arms crossed over his tunic. Today, he wore black. Somehow, that made the thickly painted, golden mask even creepier.

I looked toward the closed doors, my stomach twisting with knots of anxiety. At least a day had passed since Attes visited, and it'd been two since Kolis agreed to free Ash and the *incident* happened.

I picked up my pace as I twisted Aios's necklace between my fingers.

I hadn't seen Kolis since he left that day, and the most fucked-up thing was that it was the same as learning I would likely be unable to kill Kolis. It hadn't filled me with any relief. I was too worried about Ash to appreciate Kolis's absence—and, hopefully, his all-consuming humiliation.

What if Kolis had changed his mind? *He can't*, I reminded myself.

He'd made an oath, and Attes had said that Ash was waking up. Had something else happened? Had Rhain managed to launch some sort of attack, accidentally stalling Ash's release? I closed the fingers of my right hand, pressing them into the golden swirl on my palm.

"I don't believe you," Callum stated.

I shot him an arch look. "About what?"

"As if you don't know what I'm talking about."

I had a few guesses. "Pretend I don't and enlighten me."

His pale gaze tracked my brisk movements. "I don't trust that you won't attempt to escape the first chance you get, nor do I believe that you're seriously open to loving Kolis."

Well, he would be right about both things. "Okay."

He cocked his head.

"What?" I challenged. "Think whatever you want. You're insignificant to me."

"You should care," he replied, and I rolled my eyes. "Kolis will realize that you're lying."

I *was* worried about that, because if that *thing* happened again, I didn't think I'd be able to stop myself from reacting.

And that wouldn't bode well for me.

"And he will realize it," Callum added. "Because you're not Sotoria."

My heart skipped with unease, but I didn't show it. The veil of nothingness was back in place. Mostly. "And why do you think that? Because I don't exactly resemble what you recall?"

"That's part of it."

Curiosity got the better of me. I stopped in front of him. "If you knew me from before, you have to be old."

A narrow smile appeared. "I am old."

"How old?"

"Very old," he replied. "And I did not know *you* from before."

A trickle of unease that didn't feel entirely mine tiptoed down my spine. "Clearly, Kolis favors you. You're important to him."

He raised his chin, and there was no mistaking the air of smugness in his voice when he said, "I am."

"So, you know what I think?"

"Can't wait to hear it."

Coming as close to the bars as I could without touching them, I mirrored his close-lipped smile. "I think you're worried I will replace you."

His laugh carried an undertone of uncertainty. "I'm not worried about that."

Knowing I struck a chord, my smile grew. "Sure, Cal."

He narrowed his eyes. "Don't call me that."

I smirked.

Callum exhaled noisily, his normally unaffected demeanor starting to show stress. "What I'm worried about is the destruction of the realms due to the charms of a charlatan."

"Charlatan? What a fancy word." Pausing, I met his stare. "*Cal.*"

More of that blasé attitude cracked. "You think you know everything, but in reality, you know so very little of the truth."

Did he really expect me to believe that he was concerned about the realms when he not only supported Kolis but had also been created by him? *Come on.*

"You have nothing to say to that?" he challenged.

Having grown tired of him the moment he entered the room, I resisted the desire to reach through the bars and punch him. "What is the truth, then?"

"Kolis is trying to save the realms."

I blinked blandly at him.

"Or he was," Callum amended. "Now, he's more concerned with his supposed great love returning to him." He shook his head. "See, even now, you can't hide how much you loathe him."

He was probably right about that since I could feel my face tightening. "My agreement with Kolis doesn't mean I'm on board with what he tried to do to me or what he would've done to the realms," I told him, proud of my response. "You were there when Kolis stated very clearly what he planned to do with the embers. At what point between becoming a Primal that's never existed before, and killing any who refuse to bow to him, does saving the realms happen?"

"Life must be created," Callum answered. "No matter what."

I stared at him, thinking of what Kolis had shared about the Chosen I'd killed. He'd Ascended her. Did that count as creating life? The false King apparently thought so. "Is that what Kolis is doing with the Chosen?"

"That doesn't matter."

My frustration rose. "I disagree."

"You're just trying to change the subject."

I threw up my hands. "You're the one who brought it up!"

He shrugged. "I did not."

"Oh, my gods." Turning from him, I started pacing again. "Do you not have something better to do?"

"Not particularly."

"Great," I grumbled, my attention shifting to the doors. I wasn't in the mood for this.

However, Callum *was* in the mood. "His Majesty may have only stated his…personal reasons for wanting to Ascend as the Primal of Life and Death. Blood and Bone," he said. "But it was not the only reason."

Since I didn't believe for one second that Kolis cared about the realms, I wasn't even going to bother arguing about it.

Callum watched me, his normal pleasant half-smile returning. "It'll only be worse for you later when Kolis realizes the truth."

"Sure, Cal," I muttered. "In case you've forgotten, you were standing right there when Ione confirmed that I was speaking the truth."

"She lied."

My chest knotted as I made another pass in front of Callum, my hand pressing against the golden rope belt at my waist. The goddess *had* lied, and dear gods, if Kolis ever discovered that? I doubted she would live long. But I nibbled on my lower lip and reminded myself that Ione knew the risks. She had to either know what had been done courtesy of the Primal she served, or she was one of the many spies loyal to Ash spread across the Courts. It was quite possible that he'd mentioned her name before and I simply couldn't recall it.

"I think you're in denial," I said finally.

"I'm not."

"You must be if you think any god would risk inciting Kolis's wrath."

"You'd be surprised how foolishly the gods can behave," he remarked. "I know you're not her."

I sighed, walking to the table. There were multiple unused glasses. New ones were brought in daily, and I had to assume it was done to prepare for a visit from Kolis. Resisting a shudder, I poured myself some of the bubbly water.

"And you're right. *Charlatan* is far too fancy a word for you." His gaze lowered to my throat. "I can think of another."

I stilled. My hair was down, but it had fallen over my shoulder, baring the side of my neck with the fading bite.

"Perhaps whore is more to your liking?"

Grip tightening on the pitcher's handle, I carefully placed it back on the table. "Do you remember what I promised you the other day?"

"Probably not," he said after a beat of silence. "You're as insignificant to me as you claim I am to you."

Glass in hand, I faced him. "I promised to kill you."

"Oh." Callum laughed, the sound light and airy. "Sure, *Sera.*"

I walked back to the bars, a storm of anger building inside me just as it had when Kolis held me in his arms. "I will. One day, I will discover how you can be killed, and I will make your death the thing of nightmares," I swore, and this time, I zeroed in on the hum in my chest, and I didn't shove it back.

Summoning the embers as I had before, I let them come to the surface. Silvery essence sparked from the skin on my arms as the chandelier above Callum began to sway. And then...then, something else happened.

It was almost as if the embers took control, or maybe the knowledge held within them did—ancient wisdom that I tapped into on some unconscious level, like when the lightning bolt had briefly appeared for me.

My chin dipped, and my lips curled as a white mist seeped in at the windows. It flowed across the ceiling, thickening and spreading, becoming clouds—rapidly darkening, ominous clouds.

A *storm.*

A storm to mirror what I felt inside.

Lightning streaked from cloud to cloud, charging the air. A clap of thunder followed, causing Callum to jump. He whipped back around.

The storm I had created quickly dissipated, leaving a dull throbbing in my temples and my heart pounding. Closing my eyes, I took a sip of the fruity water.

Tapping into that power probably wasn't wise, especially after Kolis's feeding. I didn't know exactly how much essence I could use before I weakened myself, or exactly what the embers would decide to do. But when I opened my eyes, I saw that I'd accomplished what I wanted.

Callum had stopped smiling. The skin below the golden mask was pale. Our gazes locked, and I felt the embers hum.

The doors swung open. Neither of us turned, even though my stomach suddenly shifted unsteadily. We both knew who'd entered.

"Why," Kolis began, "is it that you two look as if you're seconds from committing some atrocious act upon each other every time I enter this chamber?"

That had to be the most accurate observation I'd ever heard.

As Callum turned to him and opened his mouth, I beat him to it this time. "He still doesn't believe I'm Sotoria."

Callum's jaw tightened, and he took a step back as Kolis strode forward. Making sure I felt nothing, I looked at the Primal and then focused on the important things. I searched for any sign that he'd been around Ash. There was none. He looked just as he had when he'd been here before. Then again, what kind of sign would there be? Still, a tempest of disappointment brewed within me, much like the storm clouds I'd summoned moments earlier.

"He's just in denial," Kolis answered, approaching the cage. I sipped the water.

Watching Kolis unlock the door with a wave of his hand, I could almost feel the oppressive weight of his arms around me. My hand trembled slightly as I lifted my glass, and my back stiffened.

Kolis stopped at the cage door. "It's not every day that one learns their sister has truly returned to them."

21

Sister?

Choking on the water, I spit some out as I coughed, staring wide-eyed at the false King.

Kolis's mouth spread into an untried, lopsided smile. "Are you all right?"

"No," I wheezed, flapping my hand in front of my wide, stinging eyes. There was no way I'd heard him correctly. No way. "What did you just say?"

Kolis's forehead creased and then smoothed out. "Ah, you don't remember. He is your brother, your younger brother."

My stare remained fixed on the false King, so paralyzed by the shock of his revelation that I wasn't even thinking of that *thing* he'd done to me. "You can't be serious. He's not..." I couldn't even bring myself to say it. The fact that Callum was Sotoria's brother and not mine didn't matter.

"I'm not what?" Callum demanded.

"Sane?" I snapped. "Likable? Reasonable? Not vomit-inducing or the opposite of a murderer?"

"Charming yet again," Callum retorted. "She's Sotoria but doesn't know I'm her brother?" His lips pursed. "She recognized me the last time we met."

"She does not remember those lives," Kolis told him as he entered the cage, his eyes…gods, his eyes fucking *twinkled*. "Souls reborn don't have memories."

"She did last time," Callum countered.

"That was different, and you know it," Kolis said. "Her life was restored. She was not reborn."

"Whatever," Callum muttered, glaring at the opposite wall. And, man, if looks could kill, that wall would be, well…it'd still be a wall, but the Revenant looked…

He looked as disturbed as I felt.

Dear gods, could this really be Sotoria's brother?

That palpable unease in the center of my chest near the embers that wasn't entirely mine told me he was.

"Holy shit," I whispered, taking a step back. I placed the glass on the table before I dropped it. "You really are…" I *still* couldn't say it. "Good gods, what is up with there being such an abundance of terrible brothers?"

"What is that supposed to mean?" The golden strands of Callum's hair whipped out as his head cut toward me. A faint twitch in his nostrils hinted at his rising annoyance. "Wait. Do you think to compare me to the mortal trash known as Tavius?"

"I can't argue with that descriptor," I said. "But if the shoe fits, lace that bitch up and wear it."

Callum's mouth dropped open, and he looked positively *aghast*.

"You're siblings," Kolis remarked dryly. "You two argue just like Eythos and I once did."

We both fell silent as we turned to him.

Kolis smiled broadly.

"And look how that turned out," I murmured under my breath, needing liquor. Hard, mind-numbing, and memory-destroying alcohol. But something occurred to me then. I turned back to where Callum stood. "I asked if you were Chosen. You lied."

His chin went up a notch. "I didn't lie."

"Bullshit." I stepped forward. "How else—?"

"He was not lying," Kolis interrupted, drawing my gaze to him. He was less than a foot from me.

I couldn't stop myself from taking half a step back from him. I hated the reaction. I hated how my heart started pounding, and I especially hated how he frowned. It was as if he had no idea why I'd do such a thing.

As if he'd forgotten how he'd *shamed himself*.

"You had two siblings. An older sister named Anthea, and a brother." He nodded in Callum's direction. "When you left me, I visited your family."

Pushing the *incident* as far as I could to the back of my mind, I refocused. I assumed he meant when Sotoria died the first time after being frightened by him. But she hadn't left him. She'd run from him.

"I wanted to apologize," Kolis shared, a distant look creeping into his features. "And to explain to them that I petitioned my brother to return their daughter to the realm of the living." His jaw flexed. "But that was as fruitful as speaking with Eythos. Your parents..." He sighed, his eyes narrowing on the bars. "They were frightened of me, too. It didn't matter how many times I said I wasn't there to cause harm, they cowered in the corner of their small home, shrieking and wailing in their mourning clothes." A muscle throbbed in his temple. "Only your brother wasn't afraid."

I glanced at Callum. He'd now turned his death glare on the shadowstone tile.

"He spoke to me. Answered my questions about you," he continued, the skin between his brows creasing. "He admired you greatly."

"Really?" I drawled.

"*Yes.*" Callum's head shot up, his pale eyes burning. "Sotoria was kind and fierce. She *always* looked out for me, taking on my chores if I overslept or wasn't feeling well. She never grew annoyed with me. I loved—" His breath hitched. "Yes, I admired her."

I didn't know what to say to that as I closed my fingers around one of the silky tassels on the gown's belt.

"He grieved your death deeply," Kolis said. "Felt responsible."

I looked between them. "Why would you feel responsible?"

Callum didn't answer.

Kolis did. "He was supposed to be with you when you were picking flowers for Anthea's wedding. Instead, I believe he was fucking the baker's daughter."

Callum turned his head, and my brows inched up my forehead.

"He believed he could've prevented the tragedy if he had been there," Kolis said. "Could have calmed his sister."

Could he have? Possibly. "But how did he become a...Revenant?"

"Before I took my leave, he asked me to take him to Sotoria to apologize. I explained that was not possible. Mortals who have not passed judgment are not allowed in the Vale. He became distraught."

Weight constricted my chest, thinning the breath I drew in, and I knew that what I felt was Sotoria's sorrow—and maybe even a little of mine—because I…I thought I knew where this was heading.

"He withdrew a small knife from his belt and slit his throat," Kolis said quietly.

"Gods," I whispered, rubbing the center of my chest.

"I held you as you died." Kolis's voice thickened, filling with the heaviness of anguish carrying the sharp, bitter edge of regret. "And then, days later, I held your brother as he, too, took his last breath."

I sealed my lips together with a firm press, not wanting to be affected by the emotion in Kolis's voice—by the tragedy. It was hard not to be, though. Back then, it was quite possible that Kolis wasn't yet such a monster. He had merely been Death…

Well, Death with obsessive tendencies and poor interpersonal relationship skills. Like *really, really* poor interpersonal relationship skills.

But he wasn't what he was now.

"I couldn't allow him to die, and knowing Eythos would not intervene on my behalf, I did what was forbidden of Death." A wry, humorless smile appeared on Kolis's features. "I gave life."

"You…you Ascended Callum?" When Kolis nodded, I frowned. "But he's not like the one I saw, the one you called an Ascended. She had pitch-black eyes. And he wasn't a third son—"

"Because they are not the same," Kolis answered.

My thoughts raced as I eyed Callum. If he wasn't… "Revenants are demis then?"

Based on how dramatically Callum rolled his eyes, I was going with no.

"No, my dear, they are not." Kolis smiled, and my skin felt like it was coated in slime. "We will discuss this more later when we don't have other pressing needs to take care of."

Needs.

Everything revolving around Callum fell to the wayside. My body locked up with both dread and anticipation, the latter hoping these needs dealt with Ash, and the former… The bite mark on my throat just above Aios's necklace burned.

I didn't want to think about the former.

"Please, go ahead, Callum," Kolis instructed.

Stomach twisting, I almost did the unthinkable and shouted for Callum to stay as I watched him bow and then stalk from the chamber.

"*So'lis?*"

Lowering my hands to my sides, I searched for the veil of nothingness. It took too long for me to find it, but I did. When I felt nothing of myself, I shifted my gaze to him.

"I wanted to speak with you about the deal we made." He was watching me. "He has not been released."

My stomach hollowed.

"I am not reneging on our deal," he added quickly. "My nephew was still in stasis. That is currently being resolved."

This was what Attes had been talking about. "What does that mean?"

"My nephew is young for a Primal, but he is quite powerful."

Pride surged through me. Damn straight, Ash was powerful.

"He awakened briefly from stasis right before Ione came," he explained as he turned to the table. Something about that tugged at me. It was the same sensation I'd had when I dreamt Ash returned. "I had to ensure that he behaved himself while I decided what to do with him. That was before we struck our deal."

The odd feeling vanished as I gripped the tassel on the belt. "How did you ensure that?"

Please don't let it be what Attes suspected. Please. Please.

He poured himself a drink. "If I tell you, I believe it may upset you."

"Not telling me will make me...worry more," I said, choosing my words carefully.

He drank from his glass. By the time he faced me, my anxiety had my nerves strained and stretched taut. "To ensure that he caused few issues, I had him incapacitated. He will need to recover from that."

I stared past Kolis, my breath snagging. Attes had been right. My hand flattened against my stomach as it twisted. Gods, I felt sick.

"It is not easy."

My eyes snapped to him.

"Seeing you so affected by another," he said. "The worry practically seeps from your pores."

Warning bells rang in the back of my mind. "I told you that I care—"

"I remember. It's all I think about when I look upon him." Silver eather tinged in gold pulsed through his rapidly thinning flesh. The bones of his jaw and cheeks became visible, sending a chill down my spine. "I spent the last two days looking upon him while he returned to stasis," he said, his voice dropping and losing its warmth. "Knowing that you care about him."

My body went cold. So that was what Kolis had been doing since I'd last seen him? Staring at Ash? Every time I spoke to Kolis, I believed it would be impossible for him to disturb me more, and each time he proved me wrong.

"I wonder what it is about him that inspires such emotion in you." His lips had begun to draw back, losing color and then the flesh itself, exposing his teeth and fangs as the tissue around his eyes, his eyelids, and the skin below began to sink in, leaving nothing but the bone behind. "And what it is about me that incites fear from you."

A sour taste gathered as a near-hysterical laugh choked me. Was he seriously asking that? While he was turning into a godsdamn *skeleton* right in front of me?

"It makes me want to hurt him," Kolis snarled. "Destroy him."

Everything in me froze.

"But I won't. I *won't*. There must be balance, one way or another," he said as if reminding himself. And holy fuck, that wasn't reassuring. A shudder went through him, and the shape of his lips filled out. His eyelids returned, shielding the unholy burn of eather. "Without it, there is nothing."

I stared at him, wide-eyed.

"There are no realms. No me," he said. "No you."

"Uh-huh," I murmured.

Those eyes opened. Several moments passed as Kolis became more...fleshed out. "You were afraid of me before, when I first lost you and brought you back. It wasn't until the end of our time together that it changed." He exhaled long and slow. "But this time, you've shown very little fear of me, even if you've felt it. That's changed."

Looking upon Kolis now, after watching him lose his hold on his temper and let go of the façade that hid what he was, all I could think about was how Tavius had physically changed when he grew angry or was about to do something particularly heinous. He hadn't flushed or become erratic. When that darkness in him took hold, he'd grown very still, almost lifeless, except for the gleam in his eyes. That fevered, crazed look I'd seen once before in a dog that had become sick, causing it to foam at the mouth and bite at the air.

Kolis had the same gleam. "You showed it when I last left you," he said, the eather receding from his skin. "And you show it now. I don't need my nephew's talent for reading emotion to know that, nor my brother's foresight."

"Foresight?" I asked, unable to stop myself. "Eythos could see the future?"

"Not in the way you would think," he said. "Eythos was given…heightened intuition. Knowledge of what should not be known to him." A smirk twisted his lips. "He didn't always utilize the ability or listen."

Clearly.

"But I understand why I would frighten you now. I spoke of wanting to harm someone you care about. You saw me as I truly look— as I really am beneath the beauty and gold of the very last of the embers of life. You saw me as I was before and will always be. Death. That would terrify most," he said. "But you were afraid before all of that. Uneasy from the moment I entered, in a way you weren't before the last time we were alone. That, I don't understand."

One thing I'd never managed to learn when dealing with Tavius was how to proceed with caution when he got that glint in his eyes. I had a sinking suspicion I was about to repeat that mistake as my mouth opened. "You truly don't understand why I'd be uneasy after what you did?"

A muscle ticked at his temple. "I apologized and promised it would not happen again."

As if that erased what happened?

Kolis stared at me, waiting.

Apparently, he believed his apology and meaningless promises *did* change everything.

They didn't.

But I had to say something. I cleared my throat, my mind racing. Of course, I knew I should accept his apology. Tell him it was okay. Say I'd enjoyed it, even though I clearly hadn't. But I…I couldn't. I couldn't bring myself to say anything but the truth. "You…you did frighten me." My fingers curled inward. "I wasn't expecting that."

The skin between his brows puckered. "I apologized," he repeated.

"I know," I said. "And you promised that it wouldn't happen again. Neither of those things makes what happened okay."

"Then let me repeat myself once more. I told you it would not happen again," he said, frustration sharpening his tone. "Which you *just* acknowledged."

My control slipped. "You forced yourself on me."

The corners of his lips turned down. "I know the display of my love for you was intense."

Love? He called that a display of love? It had been a show of jealousy-and-anger-fueled punishment—one he ended up enjoying.

"I lost control," he said as the churning moved up my throat. "That is all."

For a moment, I was struck silent by his response. "You didn't just lose control," I said, a part of me unable to believe that I had to explain this to a more-than-grown-ass man. "You bit me *again* without my consent, and you found pleasure while doing so. An apology and promise will not make that okay."

"What will make it okay?" he demanded, his cheeks deepening in color. "I wish to start anew with you. Tell me how I can make that possible."

I stared at him, trying to understand how he could think this was something one could make okay. Like what experiences had he lived that gave him the impression that one could start anew after violating someone? Yes, he was a Primal god, and they operated under rules and norms I would likely never understand, but that didn't excuse his behavior now or before with Sotoria. That wasn't a good enough reason.

But then it struck me. And it was plainly obvious. There was no excuse. Just as with Tavius, this was simply how Kolis was. And maybe something in his past made him this way, but I couldn't give an actual fuck about what it might be, because no reasons were good enough. Mortals and gods alike had all been through horrible *things*, but not all of them turned into this. Aios was a good example. So was Ash.

So was I.

But what I did care about was Ash, so I tamped down my rage and gave Kolis what he wanted. Mostly. "I need time."

"Time?" he repeated, his brows lifting.

Taking a deep breath, I nodded. "I need time to trust that you will honor your promise."

"My word should be good enough," he stated flatly.

My gods, I was two seconds from losing my shit. "I don't know you—"

Kolis was suddenly right before me, eather crackling in his eyes. "I am the King of Gods. You know that. It should be enough."

He was out of his mind.

I held myself still, even as my heart hammered. "*This* is not helping."

Several long, unsettling moments passed, then he stepped back.

"You're right." The essence faded from around him. "I will give you time."

I didn't believe that. If he couldn't understand the wrongness of his actions or chose not to, he wouldn't respect my request for time. He wasn't capable of doing so. And that wasn't a justification or an excuse. It was the terrifying reality of who he was, whether he was all the beauty and gold of the embers he'd stolen or Death.

"I will give you time to feel more comfortable around me," he continued. His shoulders bunched in my silence. "Say something."

Go fuck yourself. I wanted to say that. Or *I hope you die a slow, terrible death that lasts thousands of years, you sick motherfucker.*

"Okay," I forced out instead. "Thank you."

"Good." Some of the rigidness eased from him, and that well-practiced smile instantly returned as he placed his glass on the table. "Nyktos is coming out of stasis and should be in a position to be released in the next couple of days."

There was no mistaking how he attempted to downplay what he'd done to Ash with his word choice. It wasn't a change in position. It was a change in his *health*.

A demand to see what kind of state Ash was in rose to the tip of my tongue—one that would surely make things worse for Ash. Because I'd heard the struggle in Kolis's voice when he reminded himself that there must always be balance. It was something he was very much capable of forgetting.

But it would also make things worse for me. Asking to see Ash before had...well, I knew how that had ended. A tremor went through me as Kolis adjusted the pitcher so the handle faced toward the chamber.

Kolis then turned to me. Several moments passed, then he looked upon me. My skin began to crawl as if a thousand spiders swarmed me.

"I am...sorry, *so'lis,*" he said, the skin twitching at the corner of his mouth. "For whatever distress I have caused you."

I said nothing, only able to muster a nod of acknowledgment.

Kolis lifted his hand and cupped my cheek. I didn't flinch. I didn't move away as he drew his thumb over the fading bruise on my jaw. I didn't don the veil of nothingness. This was different as he touched me. It was like I was here, but not. "What did I tell you about using the embers?"

I jolted, having forgotten all about that. I opened my mouth, but Kolis pressed his finger to the center of my lips, silencing me. "That was a rhetorical question, my dear." He smiled, and it reminded me of suffocating, sweltering heat. "I felt the essence. I know it came from you. I warned you not to use it lest you wish to be punished."

Every single part of me flashed hot with rage. I wanted to break the finger against my lips. Better yet, I wanted to bite it the fuck off. "I'm sorry. Callum—"

"I'm sure he provoked you. He can be quite vexing when he wants to be. But that is no excuse." His fingers curled at my chin, tipping my head back as his lowered.

Heart stuttering, I locked up as his mouth neared mine. Panic snaked through me, tightening my chest and taking my breath. This was not giving me time. I desperately tried to empty my thoughts and erase who I was, who I wanted to be, and who I wanted.

His lips halted less than an inch from mine. "The essence does not belong to you. It is not yours to use."

The embers throbbed in denial.

"And to be clear, this has nothing to do with what we discussed moments earlier," Kolis said. "This will be your last warning, *so'lis*. Do not use the essence again."

Kolis left then, and there was nothing but silence. Closing my eyes, I exhaled roughly as I made myself the same promise I had when it came to Callum. One way or another, I would see Kolis dead.

And I knew then that the moment Ash was free, if I didn't escape, I would not live long—no matter how important the embers were. Because I would become Kolis's worst fucking nightmare.

22

Sometime later, after several veiled Chosen cleaned the bathing area, I checked the wadded cloth to make sure the key was still in place.

It was.

Pressing my lips together, I returned it to its hiding spot before allowing myself to start thinking reckless things.

Then I paced until dinner was brought in, too restless to sit still. It was a larger meal, one containing two types of meat, vegetables, and glazed strawberries for dessert. I ate what I could and *behaved* myself while Callum oversaw the veiled Chosen as they removed the plates.

Then I found myself walking the length of the cage once more, trying to burn off the restless energy that had been building all day and attempting to escape all the things I didn't want to think about.

But no amount of pacing could prevent my mind from going there. It could not stop what I started to realize was coming.

My chest tightened. I was moving, walking back and forth, but my body felt still—too still. I was slow to realize that the restlessness wasn't only from being caged. It was also a warning sign of the discomfiting moods that seemed to come and go on a whim. One was on its way now.

"Shit," I muttered, picking up my pace as I knew the stillness always seemed to make them worse. This was the last thing I needed now or, well…anytime. But especially not now.

Quickly braiding my hair, I started to go through my training exercises, but my mind was too fragmented. I shadowboxed for a few moments and then discovered that I'd stopped and was just standing still again. Too still. Thinking about Ash. Consumed by my worry for him.

What kind of state had he been in—was still in? I had a hard time keeping track of the days here, so I had no idea how long he'd been forced back into stasis. My stomach churned, and my fists clenched. Part of me wished I hadn't known about how the bones of the Ancients could be used to keep a Primal sedated. The knowledge made me sick.

But Ash wasn't the only person I was worried about. I'd been forcing myself not to dwell on so many others because it only made me feel helpless. Had Rhain fully healed? And how was Aios truly doing? Mid-swing, I stopped and touched the necklace. Obviously, she was alive. I'd been able to restore her life, but I had no idea how she was processing that. She was only the third person I'd done that to, and her injuries...gods, they had been bad. I didn't know how long she had been gone before I'd brought her back. Could've been minutes. Maybe longer. How did she feel about that?

Then there was Orphine.

I gave up on training and returned to pacing. Thinking about the draken made my chest hurt because all I could see was the dakkais swarming her, their claws and teeth more than capable of tearing through the draken's hard flesh.

I was worried about Bele. I could only assume that her Ascension made her more powerful, but none of us had any way of knowing if that meant she could go head-to-head with a Primal. Was she still in the Shadowlands, or had she gone to Sirta? If she hadn't left, she couldn't hide in the Shadowlands forever. I didn't think she'd even try.

Then there was everyone else: Saion, Rhahar, Nektas, and more. So many more. Had they been wounded before the battle stopped? How were they dealing with the loss of Ector? Was little Reaver okay? Jadis? Was she even aware of what was happening around her, or was she too young? I hoped she was naïve enough to be blind to all of this and was happily setting fire to chairs. But Reaver? He probably knew what was going on, despite what everyone was likely keeping from him. He was still just a child. A youngling. But his eyes said he'd already experienced several lifetimes of loss and pain.

There was also Ezra.

A ragged breath left me, and I glanced at the windows along the ceiling. It had sounded like she'd been able to negotiate a deal with the kingdom of Terra, but had the Rot spread even farther? How was she handling the overwhelming stress of ruling Lasania—something she had never planned for and maybe didn't even want?

I hadn't thought of that when I'd told her to take the Crown.

Guilt settled on my shoulders, weighing me down and joining the worry as I fiddled with the necklace. The dread rose, too. The helplessness. My knuckles started to ache as my mind decided to revisit all the little things I'd done, the choices I'd made that'd seemed so insignificant as they happened but had all led up to this very moment once combined.

I *should've* confided in Ash the moment he brought me into the Shadowlands—told him what I had been trained for. If I had, I *would've* known then that he'd never been who I was supposed to kill. I could've changed so much.

I should've tried harder to get to Kolis. Even if I ended up not being able to kill him, I would've saved lives. Gods knew how many, but I could've saved Ector. He would still be alive. Aios wouldn't have experienced death. Rhain would never have been captured and beaten to within an inch of his life.

I should've acknowledged my feelings for Ash sooner instead of being too afraid. I would've been happy more than sad—sad and angry. I could've lived more in the time I had with Ash. Loved more.

I should've been smarter when Ash came for me. If I'd been thinking, I would've known that attempting to distract Kolis would also be lethal to Ash. I could've aided him instead of being a hindrance.

I should've stayed focused when I freed myself instead of being distracted by the violence in the dark chambers. I would've made it farther. I could've escaped.

Should've. Could've. Would've.

There were so many. Too many to list as I stopped at the foot of the bed and looked at it. I swore I could still see the imprint of where Kolis had sat. That was ridiculous, days had passed.

But I could see it in my mind.

Could hear his voice.

Feel his arms.

I should've taken control of the situation. I'd been trained to seduce and use every weapon—including my body—to perform my duty and achieve my goal. If I had, I would've prevented myself from feeling like I'd done something wrong. As if I'd brought it on myself. Like I would never forget that he'd made it feel good. That if he hadn't found release when he did, I would've found it no matter how badly I hadn't wanted to. I could've convinced myself that it was just a part of doing what needed to be done. I felt the awareness in my chest, Sotoria's presence, as I stood there, staring at the damn bed.

"I'm sorry," I whispered.

I should've fought back harder. I was a fighter. A warrior. I would've been able to stop him if I had. I could've prevented Sotoria from having to experience anything like that again. I could've—

Spinning around, I raced behind the privacy screen and dropped to my knees at the toilet with a low whimper. I heaved, expelling what I'd consumed that day and then some, tears stinging my eyes, my throat burning. Clasping the sides of the seat, dry heaves racked my body, causing the sides of my stomach to spasm painfully. It felt like it would never stop.

I didn't know how long I knelt there, panting as I willed my nausea to settle. Minutes? Hours? At some point, air drifted over my arms. My cheek. I cracked open a watery eye. Nothing was there. I listened for the sound of someone entering the chamber. There was nothing, but that coolness remained, reminding me of the soft press of a cool hand. Eventually, the tension leaked from my body, and the chilled air vanished, leaving me so damn tired. Closing my eyes, I counted the beats of my heart until I no longer felt like an overcooked noodle.

Pushing wearily to my feet, I went to the sink and used water from a pitcher to clean my teeth and wash my face.

Once done, I changed into a robe and felt sort of normal. My stomach still felt a little weird as I passed the bed, but I believed I was done with the vomiting. Hopefully.

I went to the divan, curling onto my side as I tucked my feet under the soft blanket at the foot of the low sofa.

I told myself that Ash was okay. So were Aios, Bele, and everyone else. Rhain would recover. Jadis *was* happily causing mayhem, and Reaver was hiding somewhere she couldn't reach. Orphine hadn't perished. Ezra was doing her best. She was smart. Strong. Resilient. She had Marisol. Even my mother wasn't alone. I hadn't been able to save Ector, but I *would* save others. I would save Ash. One way or another, I would make sure no one else occupied this cage. I would not be powerless again. Most importantly, I would not blame myself for what Kolis did.

I would not let that stain set in.

Opening my eyes, I saw the still, dark waters of my lake and knew I was dreaming.

But it was different.

I wasn't swimming. I was sitting cross-legged on the bank, naked as the day I was born, able to feel and sense everything as if I were truly there. Nothing was dulled as dreams often were. The grass was cool against my skin. The scent of rich, damp soil filled every breath I took. Above me, the elms swayed in the breeze.

But like the times before, it was my lake, yet not.

Through the thick branches, I saw no moon, but the stars were bright and large, reflecting off the surface of the water like a thousand twinkling lights. The wind that stirred the branches tossed the tangled curls of my hair against the sides of my face, and my arms and waist didn't carry the choking humidity that plagued Lasania well into what should be the cooler months. And my lake? There were no ripples, even with the water tumbling off the Elysium Peaks.

As I sat there, I realized there was a contrast between when I had been swimming and when I was not. When I was in the lake, a little bit of the fuzziness of dreams remained, a sensation of floating and just existing. But there was none of that now. There was a surreal realness when I was not in the water.

But I was alone.

Closing my eyes, I turned my face up to the cool air, fighting back the swell of rising disappointment. I was grateful to be dreaming of my lake again, but I needed…gods, I needed to see Ash, even if only in my dreams. I needed to see him. Hear his voice. Feel his presence. His touch. Ash's image would erase the others. His voice would replace the sound of Kolis's. His mere presence would overshadow everything else. Ash's touch would exorcise the reminder of *his* like one would cut away the rotten flesh of a festering wound.

I *needed* to see him.

Because even if it was only a dream, I could tell myself he was okay. I could convince myself that *I* would be okay.

My chest swelled with my breath. "Please," I whispered—pleaded, really—as a tide of agony rose. "I need you. *Please.*"

Nothing but silence greeted me. The wind nor the water made any sound. There were no soft bird calls. Nothing.

My cheeks felt damp.

Pulling my legs to my chest, I rested my forehead on my knees and began idly rocking. *It's okay. It's okay. It's okay…*

The air stirred around me, cooler than before. Still, there was no sound. No—

I stopped swaying as I *felt* the air thicken. Awareness bore down on me. My skin pimpled. Tiny hairs rose. My fingers curled inward, digging into my palms as I slowly lifted my head and looked to my left.

Eyes like pools of molten silver framed by a heavy fringe of lashes and set in features savage in their beauty, locked onto mine.

"Ash," I whispered, afraid to believe my mind had successfully conjured him.

Those eyes swept over my face, and his bare shoulders loosened with a heavy exhale. "*Liessa.*"

A tremor went through me, and then I sprang into motion, all but throwing myself at him because this was me. I was here with Ash, and it didn't matter that it was a figment of my mind and nothing more than a dream.

Catching me, Ash let out a rough laugh as he pulled me onto his lap and against his chest. I buried my face in his neck, inhaling deeply. I shuddered at the scent of citrus and fresh air, soaking in the feel of his arms around me. In his embrace, there was no other sensation, no one else.

"I was… I was nowhere, *liessa*. Nowhere." Ash's fingers tangled in my hair as he held me so tightly I felt his heart beating against my breast. "Then I heard your voice. You were calling to me. I thought I'd woken up. I thought I was going to—" He stopped himself, his voice thickening when he spoke again. "I still found you. That's all that matters."

I squeezed my eyes closed. He was right that it was all that mattered. "I'm glad…" My voice cracked as tears stung my eyes. "I'm glad you did."

Ash's chest rose sharply. Sliding his hand to the side of my face, he drew back. I fought against him lifting my head.

"Sera? Let me see you." His thumb smoothed over my jaw. "Please." *Please.*

I could never deny him.

My eyes remained closed as I stopped resisting, letting him lift my head.

"Oh, Sera." His fingers brushed under my cheek. "Don't cry."

"I'm not."

His chuckle was strained as if a heavy weight bore down on him. "*Liessa*." He pressed his lips to my forehead. "I see your tears. Feel them."

"I don't mean to."

"It's okay," he assured me. "Just tell me why."

I lifted a shoulder. At this moment, there were too many reasons. I went with the easiest one. "I thought I was going to be alone."

"I'd never allow that—not awake or in my dreams. Never." He drew the backs of his fingers over my other cheek. "Open your eyes for me."

Taking a breath, I did as he requested. Tears clung to my lashes.

His gaze searched my face as intently as it did when he counted my freckles. Except there was an edge to how he traced every inch of it, almost frantically. The wisps of essence pulsed in his eyes and then calmed. "It's odd."

"What is?"

He caught another tear, and this time, I saw the faint smear of red staining his finger. "I'm dreaming."

I thought it was strange how he spoke as if this were his dream. He'd done that last time, too, and I still couldn't understand why my subconscious had him doing that. Something tugged at the back of my mind again. It was the same sensation I'd had the first time I dreamt of him. It was as if I should know why, but that didn't make sense, and the feeling fluttered away as quickly as it came on.

"Yet I can still sense your emotions," he continued. "You're feeling so much—the woodsy, refreshing wash of relief, and the heavier, thicker weight of concern. There's something...sweet in the midst of it all, too." His brows knitted, and I wondered what the sweetness meant to him. "But there's so much anguish—tangy, biting anguish."

Another tremor went through me. "I've missed you."

Ash smiled faintly, but it was closed-lipped and didn't reach his eyes, didn't turn the silver into warm sterling. "It's more than that. I *know* it is." The crease between his brows deepened. "My mind feels...disjointed. Unsettled. But I think I was awake for a period of time." His jaw hardened. "I remember struggling against chains—ones I'd created. I remember hearing *his* voice."

My breath snagged as shadows appeared beneath his flesh. "Kolis?"

I flinched as I said his name.

The shadows darkened. "His. Others." His hand glided over my cheek again as his stare bore into mine, and then his hand kept going, brushing back the curls from my shoulder, my neck. His gaze dropped.

I stiffened in his arms. Was he looking for the bite? Was it even visible in a dream? The injuries he'd seen last time hadn't appeared until I was about to wake up.

His expression didn't give away what he saw or didn't. I had no idea why I would dream such a thing, but I hoped to whatever higher being was listening that he saw nothing.

"Tell me," he said, his gaze returning to mine, but as he spoke, it was almost as if he didn't see me. Like he saw the faces of those he'd heard when he was awake. "I remember hearing…"

"What?" I whispered, half-afraid of what my mind would cause him to say.

The distance retreated from his gaze. "Tell me what has been done to you."

A spasm hit me. I opened my mouth, but nothing came out.

"Has he hurt you?" His eyes closed then, the skin creasing at their corners. When they reopened, they were bright. "I know he has."

"What…what do you mean?"

"I remember what I saw in my last dream." The shadows slid along his temple, throbbing and separating, almost forming a design of sorts. One that reminded me of the vines I saw on the doors of the throne room and the gods' tunics—on Rhain's tunic. "I *remember* what I heard. What Kyn said. What Kolis claimed. And you…you *flinched* when you spoke his name."

I couldn't breathe. There was no panic or crushing suffocation like when I was awake, but I couldn't breathe. "Kyn?"

He nodded, his eyes flat. His skin was ice-cold, and the hand on my neck, where the bite mark would be, was steady. The arm around me was firm, but a storm of violence brewed beneath the surface when he got this still.

"Sera?"

I opened my mouth to answer but couldn't get any words out. Not even a denial. It didn't make sense. This was a dream. I could say anything. I could lie. I could tell the truth—one that wasn't all *that* bad. Right? So many people had experienced worse than I had. The man I looked at, the one my mind had called forth from memories, had. But the thing crawling up my throat now wasn't words. It was a scream that burned me as I fought it back. I didn't even understand why. I was dreaming. I could scream if I wanted to.

But I didn't want to.

I didn't want to think about any of this.

Because I was *me* here, and I was *her* there.

"Sera," he said quietly. "Please."

"I don't want to dream about this." My voice cracked. "I can barely deal with this when I'm awake." The words tumbled out of me like the water rushing over the rocks. "I don't want *that* in my dreams. I don't want any of that near us because this is me with you. I'm here, and nothing else—"

"It's okay, *liessa*." Something cold flashed in his eyes, something feral that even sent a chill down my spine before he tugged my cheek to his chest. "It's okay. We don't have to talk about any of that now." A tremor went through him then, causing my chest to hitch. He held me in silence for several moments, the hand on the back of my head tangling in the strands of my hair.

I let the feeling of his body calm the racing of my heart. His hands were cold, but the rest of him was wonderfully warm. I soaked him in because a part of me knew this could be my only chance, real or not.

"You're so brave. Do you know that? So godsdamn brave and loyal." His chin rested on the top of my head as he dragged a hand up my spine. "You are more than worthy of the swords and shields of the Shadowlands."

Seraphena will be a Consort more than worthy of the swords and shields each of you will wield to guard her.

That was what he'd said before, and a new wave of tears pricked my eyes.

"There is no one like you, Sera."

"Stop being sweet," I murmured, not even caring that I was basically telling myself these things. Or it was my subconscious speaking them. And it made sense because, right now, I needed the pep talk.

"I'm not being sweet." His hand made another soothing sweep across the center of my back. "I'm only telling the truth. You're the strongest person I know."

I smiled, snuggling closer.

"And even when you feel fear?" He managed to somehow pull me closer to him. "You're never afraid. There is a difference, remember?"

"I remember."

"Good." He dipped his head, this time pressing a kiss to my temple.

"There's something I need to ask you, *liessa*."

I exhaled, long and slow. "Okay."

"Do you have access to any weapons?"

I blinked. Okay. I hadn't expected my mind to come up with that, but I could deal with this line of questioning. "No." I thought of what I'd found in the chest. "Well, I did find something that I managed to use as a weapon."

"Was that when you tried to escape?"

How did he know...? He didn't. I did. My mind was creating what he said.

"What did you find?" he asked.

My lips pursed. "I believe it was a...glass cock."

Ash went still against me. "I'm sorry. I believe you misspoke."

"I didn't." My lips twitched. "There's a chest, and in it are a bunch of what appear to be glass cocks. I think they were..." I shook my head, my stomach twisting as I thought about what their presence signified. "I don't even know if they're still in the chest. I haven't looked, but I imagine they've been removed."

Ash didn't say anything for a long moment, but then he gently guided my head back. As our gazes connected, I detected the faintest scent of stale lilacs.

I tensed, the back of my neck prickling. There was a sound, a distant murmur. I started to turn my head.

Ash stopped me. "I need you to listen to me, okay? Have you told Kolis about what will happen once you begin the Ascension? That only I can Ascend you?"

I frowned. "No, I haven't."

"He believes you're Sotoria."

How did he...?

"You need to tell him that you will die without me," Ash said. "You are his weakness. He will do anything to keep Sotoria alive—to keep you alive. Even release you to me to prevent that."

"What?" I laughed. "Kolis will think it's a trap. He won't believe that. I wouldn't believe it."

"But he will believe the Fates," Ash insisted. "He knows they cannot lie."

I wasn't so sure about them not being able to lie. They had a knack for stretching the truth.

"Listen to me, Sera. I cannot summon the Arae. Neither can Kolis." Ash lowered his head so our eyes met. "Only the Primal of Life can. And for all—"

"For all intents and purposes, that is me," I finished for him. "Ash…"

"He's going to release me, Sera. Once that happens, summon the Fates." His features had sharpened, becoming more hollow. Shadows blossomed under his eyes, and those murmurs…

They were *voices* that didn't come from my lake but elsewhere.

I would wake soon. I wasn't ready. I wanted to stay here.

"Do you understand?" Ash implored. "Promise me you will do this. That you will tell Kolis the truth and then summon the Fates. All you have to do is call for them. They will answer."

"I…I promise." Confusion rose as I clasped his wrists. "But how will I know you've been released? Kolis could lie to me. He—"

"You will know. Trust me. He'll make a grand show of it," Ash said with a faint grimace.

"What I'm about to say next doesn't change what I told you before." The eather swirled in his eyes. "You're brave, strong, and resilient. You don't need anyone to fight your battles. You never have. You don't now."

My chest rose and fell rapidly as I listened to him.

"But I *will* fight for you. I will free you. And if that takes me laying waste to everything and everyone in Dalos, then so be it," he swore as my heart stuttered. "Nothing will stop me."

If he did that, there would be a war. "Ash—"

His mouth closed over mine in a hard, fierce kiss that was its own kind of oath. I felt it all the way to my bones.

"I'm nothing without you, *liessa*," he whispered as he started to slip away, and the embers hummed in my chest. "And there will be nothing without you."

I awoke with a start, and much like I had the last time I'd dreamt of Ash, I couldn't believe the interaction wasn't real.

The feel of him. His voice. Eyes remaining closed, I dragged in a deep breath. I could still smell my lake and him, citrus and fresh—

"Who were you dreaming of?"

Sucking in a gasp at the sound of Kolis's voice, I jerked upright and nearly knocked into him.

Kolis knelt by the divan.

Heart pounding, I pressed my hand to my chest. Good gods, had he been watching while I'd dreamt of being in Ash's arms? Anger and disbelief crashed together, forming a combustible mix. "You were watching me sleep? *Again?*"

His brow furrowed. "I can see the knowledge of me watching you still bothers you."

"No shit," I snapped.

His lips thinned as traces of gold swirled across his cheeks. "Do you want to know what is more troubling? How disturbing yet fascinating it is to watch someone find pleasure as they sleep."

Find pleasure? A chill of revulsion went through me, curling my upper lip as anger boiled. "What are you even talking about?"

"You were smiling," he said. "I saw your breath catch."

Dear gods, exactly how long had he been watching me?

"So don't lie to me."

Either this man had absolutely no idea what one looked like when they experienced pleasure, or he was out of his mind. "I didn't—"

Kolis snapped forward, slamming his palms down on the divan. He leaned in and inhaled deeply. I tensed.

The false King drew back with a frown. "Mountain air and citrus."

My heart may have stopped as I stared at him. Did he scent Ash on me? Because that's how Ash smelled to me. Like fresh air and citrus. But that was impossible, wasn't it? Thoughts collided with one another like ships tossed about at sea. How could I smell like Ash? The dream... I couldn't smell like him because I'd only *dreamt* of him.

"I will ask you one more time," Kolis said, snapping me from my thoughts. "Who were you dreaming of?"

Oh, a huge, irresponsible, and petty part of me wanted to scream Ash's name in Kolis's face. However, I knew better. "I don't know." I tensed as the gold flecks faded from his eyes but still pulsed under his flesh. "I don't remember my dreams. I don't even know what I was dreaming about."

Kolis fell silent while I hoped my years of lying were paying off.

Finally, the traces of eather slowed in his flesh and then disappeared. He rocked back and stood. "I've...upset you."

I said nothing as I gripped the edge of the divan. His gaze flickered to my throat where the puncture wounds were a faded pink.

"That is not what I intended to do. I just…" Trailing off, he closed his eyes. "We've made a promise to one another. A vow to start anew."

I didn't quite recall stating it like that.

"We will start fresh," Kolis said, opening his eyes. "We *will*."

His words made me think of what I'd dreamt. *I will fight for you. I will free you.* But that wasn't all I'd dreamt Ash saying. There was something about the embers and telling Kolis the truth.

"How can I make this happen?"

I frowned, refocusing on him. "Make what happen?"

His head tilted. "Make it easier for us to start anew."

Had he not asked me a similar question before, and had I not told him I needed time? Though it wasn't like I believed he would actually give me that. "I… I'm not sure—"

"Anything. There is no limit to what I will do for you."

Nausea churned in my stomach.

"Would you like a new gown? A necklace made of rubies instead of silver? I could have dazzling rings fashioned from any jewel you want," he offered. "Is there something else you desire? I can have books brought in from any kingdom. Would you like a pet? I can—"

"I would like to leave here," I blurted, my mind fully waking up.

His eyes narrowed.

"You asked," I said, struggling to keep the frustration from my voice. Getting out of the damn cage and seeing exactly where I was in the City of the Gods would be excellent. "I would like to see something other than this space."

Kolis's expression smoothed. "I assumed—never mind." He cleared his throat and then gave me an uneven smile. "You would like to spend time with me."

That wasn't at all what I was suggesting. Like, not even remotely.

"I would like that, too." He stepped back. "I will have breakfast sent in and give you time to ready yourself."

As Kolis started to turn, what I had dreamt of Ash saying, or at least what I'd thought was a dream, came back to me. "Kolis?"

He'd made it just outside the cage before stopping. "Yes, *so'lis?*"

"I do have something I need to ask."

He nodded for me to continue.

"What…what are you going to do about the embers inside me?" I pushed to my feet, curling my arms over my chest. "Kyn…he spoke to you the other day about the embers—"

"You don't need to worry about that."

"But I do." I stepped forward, swallowing. "When you two spoke of them, you also talked about maintaining the balance. It didn't sound like whatever was being done now would work forever."

"It won't." His jaw tightened. "I will need to take the embers once you've begun your Ascension, but not a moment before then." He inhaled, his chin lifting. "Then, I will Ascend you."

My heart thudded heavily. He...he *didn't* know I was already well on my way to Ascending, nor was he aware that he couldn't just take the embers and then Ascend me. I wouldn't survive. I wouldn't even make it if I listened to my dream and told him that only Ash could Ascend me. But...

"Ascend me?" I whispered, catching up to that part. "You would turn me into what? A Revenant? An Ascended?"

"Revenants are not who they were before," he said, his brows furrowing. "I have not been able to replicate what I did with your brother."

Brother.

Ugh.

"But that is neither here nor there," he continued. "You would not become a Revenant."

"Then I would become an Ascended?"

He nodded.

What I had seen of that woman flashed before me—eyes pitch-black and full of hunger. "What I've seen of the Ascended doesn't resemble anything mortal."

"That's because you haven't seen many," he answered. "The Ascended are who they were before." He paused. "After a time."

After a time? Well, that was reassuring.

"But, like I said, this is not something we need to concern ourselves with yet," Kolis said. "Okay?"

I nodded absently, but I was very concerned with a whole lot of it. "But what happens after you...take the embers?"

"I will Ascend as the Primal of Life and Death," he said. "But you already know that."

"Yes, but what does that mean for the realms, other than...?"

"Ensuring loyalty from my Courts?"

In other words, killing anyone who didn't agree. Which he could do, being a true Primal of Life and Death. He'd be able to Ascend a god to

The perfect lines and angles of his face lost all their summery warmth. "How do you figure that is all I've done?"

"What happened with Evander—"

"That was your choice."

That was such bullshit, but if he wanted to play this game...fine. "You allowed me to do it, knowing that he was not causing Jacinta harm. That doesn't foster endearment or even fondness. All it did was prove a point that could've been told to me instead of shown."

Kolis went completely still.

"Then you broke a god's legs and neck for simply calling another god a cheat?"

"No, my dear, there was nothing simple about what I did," he said as if speaking to a naïve child. "I sentenced him to death for disloyalty and disrespect."

"Exactly how is calling another god out for cheating a sign of disloyalty and disrespect."

"It was not that but rather his lack of displayed loyalty and respect before me." His tone hardened. "This is not a question of a god being loyal to another Primal, therefore loyal to me. It is about maintaining control and balance both here and in the mortal realm."

Oh, I saw exactly how this was about maintaining control. "How does any of what has occurred at Court today maintain balance?"

"It shows that every action has a reaction," he replied.

My gods, I truly believed Tavius could've come up with a better response than that.

"Just as the action of questioning my choices, a sign of disloyalty and disrespect would be met with reaction." His hold on the throne firmed. "One that means immediate death."

The back of my neck prickled as I told myself to focus on donning my veil of nothingness. To be quiet.

Unsurprisingly, I did not listen.

"Am I to be sentenced to death, then?" I noticed Elias shifting where he stood behind the throne. "I have questioned your choices many times."

"You have. Perhaps you should cease reminding me of that." The gold brightened in his eyes. "But you are different. I will not punish you for doing such."

At that moment, I almost wished he would try.

"Stand," he commanded.

I blinked. "What?"

"Do I need to repeat myself?"

Having no idea what he was about to do, I stood.

Kolis's lips curved into one of his fake smiles. "Come forward."

I inched toward him, stopping at the arm of the throne. The chalice he'd held had disappeared somewhere.

"Sit."

My brows furrowed as I started to turn back to the pillow.

"Not there."

The prickling along my neck picked up as I slowly turned back to him.

"Sit with me," he stated softly. He did not ask. He ordered.

My heart rate picked up. "I don't think there is enough room for both of us, Your Majesty."

The forced smile spread as that gleam entered his eyes. "Silly girl," he murmured, causing my spine to go rigid. "I am not asking that you sit beside me."

I knew that. I was just hoping he wasn't demanding that I sit in his lap while he held Court.

That smile of his began to fade. "*So'lis,* do you refuse me such a simple request?"

Yes!

I wanted to scream that until my throat bled. There was nothing simple about it. Only disgust. But if I refused him? Especially while his guards and Revenants were so close? While the gods and Primals watched? While Attes watched? Who knew what he would do?

Donning that veil of nothingness and holding it close, I stepped between his legs. My gaze briefly met Elias's as I turned, sitting so I was perched on Kolis's knee—

His arm snaked around my waist, hauling me deeper onto his lap. Stomach churning, I stared ahead, not allowing myself to feel anything.

"As I was saying," Kolis began, his voice low as he spoke directly into my ear, "you will not be punished for questioning my past decisions. But continuing to do so?"

My hands balled into fists as I held them in my lap.

"That will make me rethink the deals we struck. Both of them."

My breath snagged in my chest.

"I will not break them," he said, drawing his hand across my waist. "But…"

Kolis let the word hang in the air between us. I knew what came after. He could recapture Rhain—technically, he would've still fulfilled his deal. He could also delay releasing Ash. There were so many ways out of his agreement that I hadn't been wise enough to foresee.

Yet another failure.

Worse yet was the knowledge that him simply mentioning the deals we'd made gave him the upper hand.

And why would he ever want to lose that by fulfilling the one that carried the most weight?

Releasing Ash.

Kolis's nose brushed the side of my face. "Do you understand, *so'lis?*"

"Yes," I answered, my nails digging into my palms.

"Good." Kolis patted my hip. It took everything in me not to give in to the chill of revulsion. "And I'm capable of more than just death."

Lies.

"I will prove it to you." He leaned back just enough that I no longer felt his breath on my skin. "You will see."

I closed my eyes, not giving a damn about him being able to create life when his unspoken threat choked me.

Kolis didn't need to break his promise. He could simply continue finding reasons not to release Ash. Panic started to unfurl as I opened my eyes and looked at the blurred faces of those who remained in the Hall. Chest tightening and thrumming, I scanned the crowd, catching sight of the cold, harsh lines of Attes's features, and his brother...

Kyn was seated in one of the alcoves near the dais, a drink in one hand, and the other under the gown of a woman in his lap. Her head was buried against his throat, and based on the way her arm moved between them, she, too, had at least one hand full.

Kyn wasn't paying attention to her. He was staring straight at me, a smirk fastened on his lips.

I hated him.

And I fucking hated Kolis.

Chanting that in my head, I pulled my gaze away, skipping over red and gold before landing on Attes. He pushed off the pillar, his jaw tightening. Wait.

That red...

It was the shade of blood.

And that gold?

My head swung back. I searched those on the floor below, looking for that sheen of polished stone and gold...gold hair. My breath left me as I realized it wasn't some fancy headpiece I'd seen.

It was a *crown*.

One shaped like a small jade tree carved from stone the color of blood and streaked with gold.

And it sat upon golden hair that fell in cascading ringlets.

A cluster of gods at the center of the floor parted as the female strode forward—more like glided—toward the dais. She wore a lacy ivory gown that clung to a lithe figure, showcasing an impossibly narrow waist while revealing the large swells of her breasts.

My heart pounded as I lifted my gaze to full lips the color of dewy apricots, and a delicate nose set in a smooth complexion that was only a little paler and less creamy than I remembered. Disbelief thundered through me.

No.

There was no way.

But it was her, walking toward us, her slim hips swaying.

The Primal Goddess of Rites and Prosperity.

Veses.

26

Veses was free.

Worse yet, the fucking goddess who had extorted Ash into allowing her to feed from him, who had touched him, likely forcing him to feel unwanted pleasure in the process, and who had kicked Reaver, nearly killing him, didn't look all that bad for someone who'd spent time in a dungeon.

Other than the pallor of her skin, Veses looked as beautiful as ever.

Pure, unfettered rage erupted within me, flooding every part of my being with an indomitable force as Veses halted before the dais. Silver eyes darted from the Primal behind me to mine. Our gazes locked. Her nostrils flared as she scrutinized me.

Then the corners of her lips tipped up.

And the bitch smiled.

In my mind, I heard her say, *"There had to be a reason he'd be willing to do anything for you."*

Common sense clicked off. I was nothing but a storm of violence that wanted to destroy her. The embers sparked to life. Fists unclenched and muscles throughout my body tensed as I prepared to unleash a tempest of fury. I was going to rip that crown from her head and shove it through her chest instead of her eye as I'd done with the dagger before.

Feeling the Primal essence swell inside me, I leaned forward and started to rise—

A presence stirred near the embers as the arm at my waist dug into my stomach. Breathing heavily, I froze. A sudden rush of anxiety flooded my system—a nervousness that, for once, didn't belong to me.

Sotoria.

I was feeling her apprehension and…*fear*. Why would she…?

Slowly, I remembered the obvious. Where I was. Who I was with. I was in the Council Hall, surrounded by gods and Primals, sitting on the lap of the false King, seconds away from tapping into the embers.

I warned you not to use it lest you wish to be punished.

Shit.

There was no doubt in my mind that Kolis had felt the surge of power within me, and Sotoria—oh, gods, her unease. She'd likely been aware when Kolis spoke about how he hoped I didn't remember what'd happened when she displeased him in the past.

She clearly remembered.

Double shit.

Willing myself to calm down, I focused on my breathing. I wanted to inflict a disturbing amount of pain upon Veses badly enough that I doubted any punishment *wouldn't* be worth it, but I couldn't think of just myself. There was also Sotoria. I needed to get myself under control.

A hundred different thoughts raced through my mind as the Primal goddess bowed so deeply I half-expected her breasts to make an appearance. How had she gotten free? Had anyone been harmed in the process?

"Your Majesty." That throaty, sultry voice of hers was like dragging nails against stone.

"Veses," Kolis acknowledged. "Come forward."

Light glinted off the blood-red crown as the Primal goddess straightened. My fingers twitched as the skirt of her gown parted with each step, teasing at long, toned legs. Her gaze didn't stray to mine as she neared. She was focused entirely on Kolis.

"I have not seen you in a while," he stated, the fingers resting on the arm of the throne tapping slowly. "Where have you been?"

Oh, that was a loaded question.

I gave no reaction, even though my stomach dipped. I had no idea how she would respond or what Kolis's response would be if she spoke the truth.

"I was…inconvenienced," she answered.

"Is that so?"

She nodded. "There was trouble in my Court that required my attention—a group of godlings and gods I learned were plotting a coup."

Veses was lying straight through her pearly white teeth and fangs.

Surprise flickered through me, then faded in sudden understanding. Veses had sensed the embers of life and had come at me, believing that Kolis would be enraged that Ash had hidden me. As much as it killed me to admit it, she *had* been trying to protect Ash from Kolis's wrath.

I'd hated acknowledging it before, but Veses cared for Ash in her own twisted way. The fact that she would lie now was further proof of her desire for him, fueled simply by the fact that she could not have him. And it had actually grown into some sort of fondness.

Yet she supposedly wanted Kolis.

Who didn't want her.

I smirked.

"Traitors? The realm seems to be filled with them these days," he remarked. "And what has happened to these traitors?"

"They have been dealt with but were questioned first. That is what occupied my time. I wanted to make sure their plotting did not extend into other Courts," she lied—so damn smoothly. "Some were reluctant to talk, but in the end, I'm confident no others were involved."

"Well, it is a relief to hear that a coup has ended before I even became aware of it," he remarked. "You are such a dutiful servant."

Veses stiffened, having heard what I did: a hardening in his warm tone.

"Yet you somehow still managed to fail me," he tacked on.

Veses' delicate, pale brows furrowed. "Failing you is the last thing I will ever do."

She actually sounded like she meant that.

Kolis's fingers kept tapping. "But you did."

I glanced to where I'd last seen Attes. Another god now occupied the pillar the Primal had been leaning against. I scanned the alcove as my heart kicked against my ribs. I didn't see him.

Pressing my lips together, I refocused on Veses. I wasn't sure if the other gods were paying attention. More drinks had arrived. Some of them were the purple radek wine, and there was a lot more...activity in the alcoves. Phanos was paying attention, though. He watched the drama play out with a bemused expression.

"Then I apologize for however I have failed you," Veses said.

"You apologize before asking *how* you've failed me?" Kolis chuckled, and the sound caused tiny bumps to spread across my skin.

Veses' throat worked on a swallow as she smoothed her hands across the waist of her gown. I had no clue what Kolis was getting at, but it was clear that she was treading into dangerous waters. Her nervousness bled into the air.

"How have I failed you, Your Majesty?" she asked, her gaze flicking to me.

That didn't pass Kolis by. "Do you recognize her?"

"I'm not sure," she said.

"She lies," I said, unsure why as her stare shot back to me. I smiled.

Actually, I was lying to myself now. I knew exactly why I'd spoken up. Veses wasn't just lying to protect Ash. She was also safeguarding herself. After all, the deal she'd made with Ash was to keep my existence unknown to Kolis in exchange for Ash allowing her to feed from him.

"Do tell," Kolis murmured.

It would've been wise of me to keep quiet. Exposing Veses could expose Ash, but my pettiness and spitefulness had their claws in me. "She saw me in the Shadowlands."

"Really?" Kolis drew out the word.

"More than once," I confirmed. "The first time was shortly after I arrived."

Veses inhaled sharply, and my smile kicked up a notch.

"Interesting." Kolis's chest brushed my back as he leaned forward. "What task did I entrust you with?"

Her lower lip quivered. "Keeping an eye on Nyktos."

My entire body flashed hot. This was new.

"And how well have you been keeping an eye on him? No—" Kolis held up a hand. "Don't answer. It's obvious to me that it's not nearly close enough."

Unfortunately, he was wrong about that.

"You were aware of her presence in the Shadowlands, yet you did not share that information with me," he said. "Why is that?"

Better yet, why was he even asking that question? He'd known about me long before Veses ever did.

"I…I didn't think her presence mattered." Her upper lip curled. "She was just some mortal."

"You are so incredibly wrong in your assumptions." Kolis's voice rumbled with excitement.

He was enjoying himself.

That was why he was asking irrelevant questions. It was a game to him, inquiring about things he knew one could be backed into a corner with if they weren't careful enough with their answers. Just as he'd enjoyed manipulating me into killing Evander, he derived pleasure from the power he wielded as the King—power over me and the other Primals and gods.

"I know you haven't been able to sense Ascensions in quite some time," Kolis continued. "I find it hard to believe that you could not sense what is within her when you were keeping such a close eye on Nyktos. When you were aware of Primal energy being used."

"Why would I ever think a mortal would have anything to do with that?" she countered.

I could barely resist rolling my eyes. This conversation was so pointless. Kolis had known I carried the embers since I was born. Veses also knew I had them. She'd suspected I was the one everyone had felt. I'd later confirmed it by healing Reaver. So, both were lying.

And one of them was getting pissed off.

Kolis's fingers stilled. "You must have thought something if you didn't tell me about her at all."

"Her presence simply slipped my mind." Eather brightened in her irises. "There isn't much about her to remember."

I did roll my eyes then.

"You are by far the most beautiful of our kind, even more so than Maia." Kolis's compliment brought color to Veses' cheeks, a pretty pink flush of appreciation. "And yet I've often wondered how one as beautiful as you can have such a cruel tongue."

Her chest rose sharply, and whatever earlier fear had resulted from his disapproval was gone. "You know why."

My brows lifted as I suddenly felt like I was on the verge of witnessing a really awkward conversation.

"Do I?" Kolis leaned back. "You will need to refresh my memory."

Ringlets brushed her waist as she stepped closer to the throne. "You truly forget?" In Kolis's silence, she let out a soft, melodic laugh, reminding me of the Veses I'd interacted with. "Come now, why must you taunt me so?"

Kolis remained quiet.

She pulled her plump lower lip between her teeth as she knelt at our legs. "It's the same reason I agreed to keep an eye on Nyktos," she said, the words practically vibrating out of her.

"Agreed?" Kolis repeated softly. "I do not recall giving you a choice."

She lifted a slender shoulder as she bent forward. My eyes dropped to her chest, able to see the pink of her areolae, and if I was looking,

Kolis had to be. I didn't care what he'd claim. "You are right. There was no choice when I would do anything for you."

"Out of duty and loyalty."

"Out of the need for your approval," she purred, and I might've puked a little in my mouth. "Your attention." Red-tipped fingers toyed with the scalloped lace along the swells of her breasts. "And your love."

Damn it, I was right.

This was getting even more awkward, really fast.

"I'm not sure you know what love is, Veses."

Good gods, the irony of him saying that...

"I do." Thick lashes fluttered. "Love is why I would do anything for you, Kolis." She paused. "*Anything*. If you asked me to cry tears of gold for you, I would find a way to do so."

"I know." Heat radiated from Kolis. "If I asked you to take a blade to your throat, you would do so without hesitation." He sounded way too pleased by the prospect. "If I told you to suck my cock, you'd wrap your mouth around it before I could take another breath."

Gross.

Apparently, Veses didn't find that as disgusting as I did. Moaning, her eyes became hooded. "Happily."

As I stared at her, watching her all but grope her breasts, I couldn't help but acknowledge how incredibly messed up all of this was. Veses cared for Ash, but if she spoke the truth, she knew what love led one to do. She very well might love the false King, who was also in love with another who wanted nothing to do with him. Or perhaps that was why she believed she was in love with him. Veses was known to covet and fixate on what she could not have.

Either way, it was like being stuck in a toxic circle of rejection and unrequited love.

Eather shone from the thin slits of her eyes. "Ask this of me, Your Majesty, and I would do so right here before the Court."

"Well, that would be somewhat difficult at the moment, wouldn't it?" I said before I could stop myself, half-afraid that it would happen despite Kolis's professed love for Sotoria—and by extension, me. I would seriously vomit all over both of them.

Kolis chuckled.

"Unfortunately." Her eyes narrowed on me then. "Why are you even here?" She turned her attention back to Kolis. "I was under the impression that she was crowned as Nyktos's Consort."

"You would be wrong yet again if you believe that."

My jaw clenched.

Veses' lashes lowered as she glanced at me. A moment passed. "So, you didn't give your permission?"

"I did not."

The Primal goddess also knew that was a lie. "Then can I assume her presence is punishment?"

"Quite the opposite," he said, and I could hear the eager smile in his tone. "She is here because this is where I want her."

"For what?" One brow rose. "To keep your lap warm? I'm sure I could find you something not so…crushing."

My eyes rolled once more, this time so far back I wouldn't have been surprised if they got stuck.

"There's that dagger-sharp tongue again."

She lifted a shoulder in response, looking me over.

"Apologize."

Her chin jerked. "I'm sorry, what?"

"You were rude. You do not deny that." That hardness had crept into his voice again. "Apologize to her, Veses."

The Primal goddess couldn't look more…flummoxed. "Why would I do that?"

"Because it is my *graeca* you speak to," Kolis said, delivering a staggering blow that left no room for doubt that he had knowledge of Veses' feelings for him.

Veses' lips parted as she drew back. "She's…" Ringlets bounced as she shook her head. "That's impossible." Wisps of eather burst wildly through her eyes. "Is that what she told you? If so, it is a lie."

"It's not, Veses. It has been confirmed." His hand firmed on my waist, causing me to stiffen. "My love has finally returned to me."

Veses flinched as if he'd slapped her.

"Now, apologize to her."

What color had returned to her complexion had since drained, and I wanted to feel bad for her. Kolis knew exactly what his words would do to her, and he enjoyed it. But I didn't feel sorry for her. Not at all.

"Veses," Kolis warned.

"I'm sorry," she said, blinking rapidly. "I'm sorry if I insulted you."

If? The woman had never been anything but insulting.

She rose, the gown settling around her. She took a step back, her hands opening and closing. Her features shifted, going through an array of emotions. "I am—" She cleared her throat. "Happy for you, Kolis."

Now it was I who surely looked *flummoxed* as Veses bowed her head and started to turn.

"Veses," Kolis called out, waiting for her to face him again. His fingers tapped once more. "I do believe you are forgetting something."

She frowned, the crown she wore seeming duller now.

"You did fail me," he reminded her. "That will not go unpunished."

Veses stilled.

"Kyn?" the false King summoned.

There was a moment as the Primal of Peace and Vengeance disentangled himself from whoever had been in his lap and approached the dais when Veses and I realized what was about to occur at the very same second.

I knew because of what Kolis had offered to Kyn before. Her knowledge possibly stemmed from past experience. My heart started thumping as Kyn climbed the steps. The scent of liquor and sex wafted off him.

He held his chalice. "Your Majesty?"

"Veses will serve as this evening's entertainment," Kolis announced. "I assume you will ensure that occurs?"

Oh, gods.

Kyn turned to a silent Veses, eyeing her as he took a drink. "This will be fun."

My stomach churned as Kyn slid an arm around the Primal goddess's waist, his lips glossy from his drink.

Tossing his arm off, Veses sneered. "You and I have vastly different ideas of fun."

Kyn laughed as he took hold of her arm. "You and I have exactly the same idea of fun, darling."

I had to be wrong.

I kept telling myself that as he escorted her off the dais. That what I thought would happen, wouldn't. Veses wrenched her arm free of his hold, but she took the chalice when Kyn offered it to her. She drank greedily of whatever was in the cup. Holding his stare, she dropped the empty chalice onto the tray of a servant who rushed from the shadows and then scurried away again. Veses said something to Kyn that garnered another loud laugh somewhere between cruel and amused.

This wasn't happening.

Kyn looked at the dais, at Kolis, and whatever he saw brought a tight, harsh smile to his face. He stepped closer to her. Heads angled toward them. Bodies turned to watch. Veses didn't retreat as Kyn reached up and grabbed her crown. It snagged in her hair, causing her head to jerk. Thin, golden strands hung from the stone and gold.

The Primal tossed the jade tree headpiece to the floor.

My mouth dropped open as it skidded across the golden tile, ending up near the still-sleeping Naberius.

I didn't know much about Primal etiquette, but even I could see the utter disrespect in that.

Oh, gods, this *was* happening, and I wasn't sure why I was so surprised. I'd heard what Kolis did to his favorites after he grew tired of them. He basically tossed them to the vultures. He'd offered me to Kyn in the event that he wasn't convinced of who I was. But yet again, knowing what he was capable of was different from seeing it.

I hated Veses with every fiber of my being for what she had forced Ash into and for hurting Reaver. I would love nothing more than for my hand to replace the one around her throat so I could choke the life from her. She was a twisted, sick being who hurt others. In no way did I think Ash's soul was the only one she'd darkened. Veses deserved what came to her.

But this?

My wild gaze shot around the Council Hall. Not everyone was watching. Some had turned their backs. Most of Kolis's guards watched. Elias didn't. Dyses was gone, and Callum looked on with a curl of distaste on his lips.

Kyn circled Veses. A low-backed chair slid across the floor as if tethered to the Primal by an invisible string. He shoved Veses toward it. She bent over it, her face shielded by all those golden curls.

Kyn approached her, planting a hand on the center of her back and drawing it down. Someone hooted. Another catcalled. This time, it was I who flinched with every sound that came from those watching.

No one deserved this.

Kyn gripped the sides of her gown—

"Stop!" I shot to my feet, breaking Kolis's hold. Everything stopped. The sounds. The jeers. Kyn's hands. "Stop this now—"

"You," Veses spat, having moved faster than I could track. Standing upright now and facing the dais, she pointed her finger at me as if she were about to curse me with misfortune. The flesh of her beautiful face had thinned, exposing a dull gleam of red similar to her crown. "You will not interfere on my behalf. It is not needed."

I shook my head in disbelief. "This—"

"Nor wanted." Veses' eyes burned with the same silver fire that flared inside me.

"*So'lis,*" Kolis spoke quietly as onlookers shifted their attention to the newest drama unfolding. "Exactly what are you doing?"

Chest thrumming, I turned to him. "This isn't right."

Kolis stared back at me, his features impassive.

My hands shook. "Please stop this."

His fingers had ceased their tapping. "And if I don't?"

The embers pulsed more intensely inside me, pressing against my skin. "You will."

His chest stopped moving.

"Because this is wrong." I took a deep breath. "Because stopping it is the right thing to do."

A long, tense moment passed, and then Kolis rose, drawing the attention of his guards and Callum. He didn't speak until he reached my side. "It's time to return to your quarters."

"Stop this first—"

"*Silence,*" he hissed, his fingers curling around my jaw as his will snapped out, wrapping around me and sinking deep, seizing control. "We will return to your quarters, and do so in silence."

A silent scream of fury thundered in my head as I glared at him. I started to push against the compulsion, fueled by rage and ancient instinct—

Golden swirls erupted across his chest as a faint mist seeped out from somewhere under him. "Do not even think it."

The embers continued to swell, goading me to do more than just think it. They wanted me to act upon the rage and power building inside me.

"Your Majesty?" Phanos interrupted.

"What?" Kolis bit out, his gaze never leaving mine.

"I assume Court has ended for the evening," he said as, from the sides of my vision, I saw others peeling away from the shadows of the alcoves, some in states of disarray, their clothing wrinkled and hair tangled as they crowded around Veses and Kyn. "But I need to speak with you."

The mist faded around Kolis. "I have something I must take care of first. Then, I will return."

"Of course," Phanos remarked, his tone indecipherable. "I'll be waiting."

Chest rising and falling rapidly, I seethed as Kolis released my chin and took my hand. He guided me toward the doors we'd entered through, Kyn's laugh echoing in the Hall.

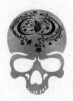

"What did I tell you?"

Kolis towered over me as we stood in the cage, his nostrils flared. I couldn't answer. His compulsion still had me in its grip.

But I didn't think he wanted an answer.

"I warned you not to question me, and within the hour, you not only did so again, but also in a very public manner." Golden swirls raced across his face at dizzying speed. "I warned you not to use the essence, and you did so twice in the same span of time."

Damn it.

He *had* felt it.

"I can see it even now." He grasped the sides of my face, tilting my head back. "The essence that does not belong to you, fueling your stubbornness. Your temper. I deserve neither of those things from you."

I would've laughed if I could have.

"I defended you against Veses' insults, and you proceeded to interfere with her punishment," he said, angling his body to the side. Beyond him, I saw Callum. He paced silently. "And this is how you repay me? With disobedience and ungratefulness?"

My gods, he was...he was demented.

"You repay me by siding with the woman who would have my cock in her mouth in five seconds if I allowed it?" His eyes were wide. "Have you no honor?"

I could not believe what I was hearing.

The fury faded from his features, from his voice. His eyes slammed shut. "Why did you have to disobey me? Not once. Not twice. But three times." A shudder ran through him. "I had such high hopes for today. Plans."

So fucking demented.

"I wanted to show you all I was capable of." His voice dropped, his eyes opening. The glow behind his pupils was almost too bright to look upon. "I wanted to show you what I'm risking for you."

What he was risking...? My gods, there were no words, even if I *could* speak.

"But now, today ends like this." He breathed in deeply through his nose, releasing the sides of my face. "You...you are my soul, but I am your King. You need to learn that you cannot question me, and you cannot use those embers."

A trickle of fear broke through my anger. Not for me, but for Ash. For Rhain. Kolis had told me what he'd do if I disobeyed, and I'd done it—without even thinking about the consequences.

Kolis stepped back. The compulsion lifted, unlocking my jaw as my shoulders slumped. "You will be punished."

I lifted my head. Callum had stopped pacing. "And?"

"And then we will see." His eyes...they shone. "We will see if further action needs to be taken."

Before I could speak or process the tears I saw gathering in his eyes, chains rattled.

My head swung toward the sound. They unclasped from the bedposts and slithered across the floor like serpents. A knot lodged in my chest as I tensed.

It happened so quickly.

Shackles clamped around my wrists, yanking my arms up. The chains wrapped around the ceiling of the cage, near the cluster of diamonds. My arms were pulled tight, stretching the muscles. A shout of surprise left me as my body rose, lifting until only the tips of my toes touched the floor. Cool metal clamped down on my ankles, anchoring me into position with my arms and legs spread.

Kolis stared at me, his face pale. "I want to hate you for making me do this," he rasped. "But I can only love you."

"This is love?" I gasped, already beginning to feel the burn in my arms.

"You disobeyed me repeatedly, yet you live. No one else would. So, yes. This is love," he said hoarsely as a thin line of crimson streaked down his cheek.

Kolis wept.

27

"I almost feel bad for you."

Opening my eyes, I didn't bother lifting my head or responding to the golden-haired Revenant. It would take too much energy and focus away from trying not to scream, which I'd been doing since Kolis left with crimson tears streaking his face.

I wasn't sure what was more messed up: everything else about Kolis or the fact that he could choose to hurt someone and then cry about it.

"You have to be in so much pain," Callum went on.

"I've never felt better."

"That is such an obvious lie."

What was evident was his unnecessary observation. The burn of my stretched muscles had disappeared. My arms were numb now. I couldn't even feel my hands anymore, but the stress of being suspended with only the tips of my toes holding my weight had moved into my shoulders. They felt as if they were on fire.

I had no idea how long I'd been hanging here. Had to be hours at this point. Callum no longer remaining quiet made it feel so much longer. When it was silent, I'd contented myself with thinking about all the ways I would cause Kolis unimaginable pain.

I'd discovered I had a vast imagination.

"If you were actually my sister?"

Gods, not this again.

"I wouldn't have allowed this to happen."

"So, if you believed I was your sister, you would think this is wrong?" I asked.

Callum stood just a few feet from the cage. "Of course."

A harsh laugh left me, causing the pain in my shoulders to flare. "The fact that you need to believe you're related to someone to see the wrongness in this tells me that every poor thought I've had of you is more than justified."

"You would think that because you do not know me." He crossed his arms over his chest. "Because you are not my sister."

"Whatever," I muttered, too damn exhausted to attempt to convince him otherwise.

Callum was quiet for several blissful minutes. "You were right." He paused. "About what was happening in the Council Hall."

Wearily, I lifted my head. My neck muscles cramped as my gaze fixed on the Revenant.

His chin was lowered, gaze focused on the floor. "That particular type of punishment is wrong." His shoulders tensed. "It's below Kolis. He's better than that."

"Yeah? Like when?"

"Before Eythos died."

Surprise shot through me. I hadn't really expected any answer, let alone that.

Callum looked up with a smirk. "What? You thought I'd say it was when Sotoria died her second death? Yeah, that had an impact on him, but he…" He clamped his mouth shut, a lock of blond hair falling over his face as his gaze returned to the floor.

Wincing, I shifted slightly to straighten my toes. "But what?"

"He loved Eythos," he said quietly. "Even then. Even after everything."

I stared at him, somewhat dumbfounded. I knew that Kolis had loved his brother at one time, but Callum was speaking of after he'd taken Eythos's embers and killed his wife. I didn't believe that was possible, and I sure as hell didn't think it was now.

Have you no honor?

He'd questioned my honor when his idea of punishment was ordering the rape of another. And even if Veses had gone along with whatever Kyn dished out, that was exactly what had occurred in the

Council Hall. It didn't matter that she was guilty of the same behavior.

Damn it. As much as I hated the woman and would gleefully celebrate her death, even I could understand that it wasn't right.

But not Kolis.

His treatment of Veses had little to do with defending me against pathetic insults that didn't even inflict a scratch upon my skin and everything to do with Veses' supposed failure with something utterly irrelevant.

Kolis's actions were all about reminding everyone he had the power.

And his reactions were all about being the wronged party—the victim. It was almost like he thrived on it.

A muscle flexed in Callum's jaw. "He never would've allowed such a thing before Eythos's death, nor would he have kept his...pets," he said, speaking of Kolis's favorites. "He didn't do that until after Eythos died." The Revenant's gaze returned to mine. "You don't believe me."

"Maybe you're speaking the truth," I said after a moment. "But he's like that now. And he's *been* like this, right? With the other gods and Primals? With the favorites he grew disappointed with—?"

"With you, once he realizes this is one great façade?" he interjected.

Anger stirred. "With *me* right now."

Callum's lips smashed together.

"And you know what? You're no better," I bit out. "You know what happened in the Council Hall and the gods only know how many other times is wrong, yet you stood by and did nothing."

"Unlike you?"

I glared at him.

"No one else spoke up. Those who were not thrilled with what was occurring left. You're better than them? Gods, Primals, draken, and Revenants alike?"

"Yes!" I said without hesitation. "Anyone who would at least attempt to stop that is better than the lot of them."

Callum smiled. "I'm sure Kolis would be thrilled to hear you say such treasonous things."

"And I'm positive you'll tell him," I hissed. "Like the loyal lapdog you are."

"I am loyal. I will always be loyal to him. He forgave me for failing to keep my sister safe."

"That wasn't your fault," I blurted. It was the truth. He hadn't caused his sister's death.

Callum stiffened. "It was my fault," he stated. "And he did forgive me. He also gave me eternal life."

I rolled my eyes.

"And he's the only thing keeping this realm together."

"For fuck's sake," I muttered. Callum had likely been decent before his unfortunate run-in with Kolis, but now he was... "You're just as delusional as he is."

His nostrils flared. "I'll make sure he's aware of that, too."

My head jerked up, sending a frenzy of pain across my shoulders and down my spine. "And I'll make sure he knows that his precious first creation is the idiot who told my mother how a Primal could be killed. I bet he'll be real...disappointed to learn that."

Callum's mouth snapped shut.

"Yeah." I smiled through the pain, baring my teeth. "I haven't forgotten that. Though I wish you would explain *why* you would do something so...reckless."

"I wasn't being reckless, you insignificant gnat." He snapped forward, clutching the bars. They didn't seem to affect him. "I was—" He sucked in a deep breath, then peeled his hands away, one finger at a time. "Do you want to know why you are being punished? Because, deep down, Kolis knows you're not Sotoria."

A kernel of unease unfurled. "Do you know how repetitive you are? It's exhausting."

His smile returned. "He would never treat Sotoria this way."

Another dry, aching laugh left me.

"I'm not sure what I said that would cause you to find humor."

"I'm not laughing at what you said," I told him. "I'm laughing *at* you."

Callum's eyes narrowed.

"You're an idiot if you think that. He killed her—"

"Her?" The painted wings lifted along his forehead.

Shit. I'd slipped up there. "Yes, *her*. I don't remember any of that," I said, recovering as best I could. "And that's not the point."

"But that *is* the point." His smile returned. "If you were her, you would know."

"Can you—?"

"You would know that he never killed Sotoria."

Now it was I who shut their mouth as her presence stirred restlessly in my chest.

"Yes, he scared her the first time, but that was an accident. He didn't know how easily Sotoria could be startled," he said, the skin beneath the painted wings softening in a way I hadn't seen it do before. "And he didn't kill her the second time either." His lower lip quivered. "Eythos did, and that was the second and last time I failed her."

Callum had finally quieted, having decided to sit morosely on the sofa. What he'd shared lingered in my mind.

It was always suspected that either Sotoria died by starving herself or Kolis lost his temper and ended her life. But Eythos? I couldn't believe it, even though Callum had very little to gain by lying about it.

Then again, what did Eythos have to gain by killing Sotoria? Well, other than revenge. Though, given what I knew of Eythos, he didn't strike me as the type to seek revenge by harming an innocent.

My thoughts eventually turned to worries as time ticked by. How had Veses escaped? Was anyone harmed? Would Kolis seek to punish me further by refusing to release Ash or turn his attention to Rhain? More concerns preyed upon my mind while I could do nothing but hang in pain.

How much time did I have left? Could I get to Ash? Would I somehow find The Star, and would it even work when it came to Sotoria's soul?

How could I continue to tolerate Kolis's presence?

And would Kolis come to realize that Callum was right? That I really wasn't Sotoria? My thoughts flashed to Veses and the Council Hall. If so, I wouldn't live long enough for him to make good on his offer to Kyn. He'd take the embers, killing me and effectively dooming Sotoria.

More time passed.

When Kolis finally returned, smelling of some sort of sweet smoke and staleness, my shoulders had gone numb. He said nothing as he took me by the waist and released the shackles.

I couldn't keep quiet when he freed my arms. I cried out, my sore muscles screaming.

"I'm sorry, *so'lis*." Kolis gathered me in his arms. A fiery, pins-and-needles sensation erupted, leaving me panting with discomfort and pain, unable to protest his embrace. "I'm so sorry."

He repeated those three words as he held me, rocking slightly. The Chosen brought in hot water, and new scents wafted through the cage: chamomile and peppermint.

Kolis rose then, carrying me behind the privacy screen and setting me on my feet. A veiled Chosen remained at the steaming tub, silent with her gloved hands clasped.

"She will assist you with your bath," Kolis said, speaking to the top of my head. I really couldn't lift it. "You will rest, and then...everything will be better, I promise."

I bit the inside of my cheek to stop myself from laughing. If I started, I didn't think I'd be able to stop. Ever.

He released me, and the Chosen drifted quietly toward me, reaching for the clasps on my gown that I couldn't even begin to lift my arms to unhook. My legs shook. The bodice slipped, pooling at my waist, and with my skin feeling as if an army of fire ants swarmed it, I could not care less if Kolis saw even an ounce of my nudity.

But he didn't.

He'd halted at the privacy screen, his back to us. The gown hit the floor at my feet as the Chosen's gloved hands gently cupped my elbow, helping me step into the tub.

Kolis cleared his throat. "I just want you to know that I ceased Veses' punishment when I returned to the Hall."

A laugh spilled out of me as I sank into the hot, minty water.

And the laughter didn't stop.

28

I slept without dreaming of my lake or Ash. When I woke, things were better. Mostly. I was still sore, but the worst of the pain was gone.

And I was no longer laughing. That alone was a vast improvement.

What wasn't good was that I wasn't alone. Callum once more sprawled on the sofa. He'd been there since breakfast, but he was far less talkative as I forced myself to walk the length of the cage. I had to get the soreness out. Sitting wouldn't help, but I wasn't sure moving helped with the other pain.

The ache that had taken up residency in my temples.

That was a bad, bad sign.

I quickly shoved what it signified to the back of my mind when Kolis entered the chamber. I stopped, immediately emptying myself of everything that made me who I was.

Because I knew what I had to do.

It was something I'd thought about while forcing myself to eat and as I walked.

After everything, it was harder than before, but I had to. I needed to convince him to free Ash, which meant I had to behave as if nothing had happened the day before. That he hadn't manipulated me into killing Evander. Or forced Veses to do who knew what before finally putting an end to it—an act I'd bet he believed erased everything that came before it. Like all abusers and users.

But that was okay.

Because I would be smarter than before.

As the false King approached the cage, Kolis's smile told me I'd won the wager I'd made with myself. "How are you feeling, *so'lis?*"

I clasped my hands like the Chosen often did, ignoring the tightness in my arms. "Rested."

"I'm relieved to hear that." His gaze swept over the golden gown I wore as he unlocked the cage. "You look lovely."

"Thank you," I said, my tongue withering as I recalled the Mistresses' lessons. *Become what they desire.* With Kolis, it was more than being meek and submissive. I knew that now. It was all about making him feel justified in his actions. Most of all, it meant becoming what Callum had: a loyal lapdog whose sole purpose was to shower their owner with affection and gratitude. "There is something I wanted to say."

He halted at the open cage door. "Yes?"

"I…I wanted to apologize for yesterday."

Kolis stared.

So did Callum.

"Everything has been quite overwhelming for me," I began, seeing Kolis's expression smooth out while Callum's eyes narrowed. "A lot has happened—has *been* happening. All of this is so unfamiliar to me. I'm not sure what I should or shouldn't be doing, but none of that is a good enough excuse for how I behaved yesterday."

"Your behavior is understandable, *so'lis.*" His eyes shone as Callum slammed his hands onto his hips. "You have been through a lot."

"But you have given me such leeway." I dutifully lowered my gaze. "And I have been disrespectful. I'm sorry."

"It's okay." His close voice was the only warning I got before I felt his palm on my cheek. He lifted my gaze to his. "Your apology is accepted."

Behind him, Callum appeared as if he were a second away from running headfirst into a wall.

I fought a real smile. "Truly?"

"Yes. Truly." Approval had settled into his features, causing his smile to become lopsided and more genuine. "Come. Let's walk."

Considering how yesterday had gone, walking anywhere with him was the last thing I wanted to do.

But it was what *he* wanted.

And I would become that.

So, I joined him without protest. When he looped his arm through mine, I said nothing. As we left the chamber, Callum and Elias falling into step behind us, I nodded and smiled, my actions and reactions as hollow as his.

Kolis didn't notice, though.

He was practically vibrating with joy when we crossed the breezeway and accessed the path that led to the colonnade. We entered the sanctuary, eventually passing alcoves full of breathy, heated sounds.

Kolis led us down the maze of halls, none looking familiar to me. We ended up passing through a pillared entryway and into a large sitting chamber of sorts with many ivory tapestries hanging on the walls.

"Sit." Kolis extended an arm toward one of the gold satin divans.

Like a very good dog, I did as he instructed and took a seat, crossing my feet at the ankles.

Callum followed, staying near the entrance. He still looked like he wanted to run headfirst into something.

"There is something I want to show you," Kolis announced as he entered. "I'd planned on doing it yesterday, but...well, yesterday no longer matters."

As if he could simply decree such a thing.

"Iason. Dyses?" Kolis called out.

I twisted toward what I had thought was a tapestry but was, in reality, ivory curtains shielding an archway. The dark-haired draken I'd spotted in the Council Hall came forward with the Revenant. Between them was a Chosen.

Wait. What had he said yesterday? That he'd planned to show me he was capable of more than just death?

My stomach dropped. I suddenly understood what he was about to do.

"You don't have to prove anything." Breaking with my dutiful hound act in a heartbeat, my overused muscles screamed in protest as I shot to my feet. "I believe you."

With a quick twist of his neck, Kolis cast an even, empty smile at me from over his shoulder. "You lie."

I did, but that was beside the point.

"I do not fault you for believing such," he added. "That is why you must know."

"You could just tell me how they're Ascended." My heart lurched because I knew what he was going to do: create life by nearly ending it.

Because this wasn't the same as what Eythos did. "You don't have to go to any trouble."

"It's no trouble."

Pressure clamped down on my chest as my head swung back to the three. My thoughts raced. I had a plan to free Ash: earn Kolis's favor and trust. With my failed escape attempt and literally everything else that'd happened, I was doing a really shitty job at that. I needed to be careful and not incite Kolis's displeasure, which I kept doing.

"This really isn't necessary." I tried again, hands spasming at my sides as I held myself back. The clap of Iason's and Dyses' boots against the stone, and the silent steps of the Chosen, were now like thunder. Dyses looked somewhat bored, but the draken...

Iason stared straight ahead, almost as if he saw no one. Once more I thought of how many draken in Dalos had been forced into bonding with Kolis. Was Iason one of those who, unlike Nektas's cousin, would've chosen *not* to serve Kolis if given a choice?

"But it is." Kolis turned to the Chosen. "Come," he coaxed, beckoning warmly.

Breathe in. My body went rigid. The Chosen crossed the remaining distance, gloved hands clasped before their waist. *Hold.*

"Unveil yourself," Kolis instructed.

Breathe out.

The Chosen lifted the veil, gradually revealing the fine features of a young man who couldn't be much older than me. *Hold.*

"Jove," Kolis spoke. A cowardly part of me didn't want to learn his name. "How are you?"

"I am fine, Your Majesty." Jove smiled, and gods, it reminded me of my smiles whenever my mother sent me to deliver her messages: practiced but empty. Just as I had been.

Breathe in.

"Today, you will be blessed," Kolis said, cupping the man's cheek. "Given new life."

Jove bowed his head. "It is an honor."

No. No it wasn't. Because I heard his voice tremble. I saw the increasing thinness of his smile and the wideness of his deep brown eyes.

He was afraid.

I stopped with the breathing exercises and stepped forward. "Kolis."

The false King's head cut in my direction. "Yes?"

"You don't have to do this," I repeated as the embers thrummed in my chest. "I…I thought when you said you wanted to walk, it was to spend time with me. Alone."

"We will." Kolis stared at me for so long, I thought maybe he'd changed his mind. "But there are things I must see to. This is one of them."

Jove stood completely still, his hands clenched tightly as dread flooded my heart.

"This is an honor," Kolis said, and I didn't know if he was talking to me or the Chosen. "Life can still be created, even if imperfect. And it must be. For without it, the very fabric of the realms would rip apart."

I blinked. "W-what?"

"Close your eyes, my son." Kolis fully shifted his attention to Jove.

The Chosen obeyed without hesitation. Kolis tilted the man's head back, exposing the length of his neck.

He was going to bite him.

My hand went to my throat as the memory of the pain burned through me. I couldn't stand here and allow this.

Instinct took over, and I was suddenly moving toward Kolis and the Chosen before I was even fully conscious of what I was doing. Crossing the space, the essence built inside me as I reached out—

I gasped as Kolis's other hand snaked out, capturing my wrist. "I understand," he said softly, his flat, cold stare locking with mine. "You've always had a kind heart, *so'lis*."

I shuddered.

And then *she* shuddered.

"Even now, under this sharp, rough, and often abrasive exterior, your heart is soft," he continued, my skin crawling from his touch. "You are a good person. I admire that. I always have."

Kolis was wrong. I didn't have a soft or kind heart. Nor was I a particularly good person. If I were, I wouldn't have been able to do all the things I'd done how I'd done them. I couldn't just stand by and watch this. There was a difference.

"You need to understand why this is important. What is and has always been at risk," Kolis said. "He is either recreated in the image of the gods, or he gives life to another who will be. That is up to you."

It took no leap of logic to know that giving life to another meant death for Jove.

"But make no mistake," Kolis said, drawing me to his side with just the curl of his arm. I swallowed hard, but it did nothing to ease the rising bile of the contact with him and the knowledge of what was to come. "Balance must be maintained."

There he was again, going on about his obsession with balance.

"That is more important than anyone in this space, including you." He held my stare. "Even me. Because without balance, there is nothing."

What he said made little sense. I inhaled a mere wisp of air. "Can you...can you make it not hurt?"

The eather stilled in his eyes, and his skin thinned. Coldness drenched me.

Saying nothing, he let go of my wrist and thrust me away from him. I stumbled but caught myself as he turned his head back to Jove. A heartbeat passed, and then Kolis's lips peeled back. I saw a flash of his fangs, and then he struck, piercing the flesh of Jove's throat.

My body jerked at the exact moment Jove's did. I tipped forward as the Chosen went rigid, his eyes and mouth opening wide. A tremor started in my legs. I knew what kind of excruciating agony he was likely enduring. Frantically, I swiveled around, scouring my surroundings for a weapon. My gaze landed on the swords of those who remained as the embers flared to life, reminding me that—

A moan swiftly yanked my attention back to Kolis and the Chosen. *The sound...* My gaze went to where the Primal fed deeply from Jove. The Chosen's lips were now only parted, his features slack and slightly flushed. I hadn't heard a moan of pain.

It was one of pleasure.

Breathing raggedly, I pressed my hand to my stomach. A spasm jolted Jove as he exhaled another heated groan. Kolis wasn't causing pain.

I watched, caught between surprise and agitation, as the Chosen gradually grew limp in the false King's arms. I had known Kolis was capable of feeding without pain, but I also knew he was not kind. He'd shown that over and over.

But the Chosen wasn't in pain. Ecstasy soaked his features. Still, this... I swallowed down the bitterness of bile. This didn't feel right. I took a step back, somehow even more disturbed by what I witnessed now than I would have been if Jove *had* been screaming.

I'd asked Kolis not to cause pain.

He'd done this for me, but all I could think about was what I'd thought when I first saw Orval and Malka and what I had been led to believe with the god from Keella's Court and Jacinta. All I could think about was how the last thing I'd wanted to feel when Kolis bit me was pleasure.

Oh, gods.

I'd asked Kolis to do this, and I knew this wasn't okay, even if my intentions had been in the right place. I just didn't know how wrong it was. In this case, did the *means* justify the end? I couldn't answer that.

Arms shaking, I backed up until I was nearly behind the pillow. My fingers curled against my stomach as my hands started to warm.

Jove was pale. He was dying.

Kolis jerked his head back without warning. "The process is fairly simple," he said in a thickened voice that reminded me of the overbearing summers in Lasania and how he spoke of his need. "The blood must be taken from the Chosen right up to when the heart begins to falter." He paused, catching a drop of blood from his lower lip with his tongue. "Then they must be given the blood of the gods."

The act of Ascension for the Chosen *was* the same as Ash had spoken of. A transfer of blood.

"Your Majesty."

Startled by Elias's voice, I turned sideways.

"Come, Elias," Kolis answered.

The guard passed me, not looking at me as he went to Kolis's side. Without saying another word, he lifted his wrist to his mouth and bit into his vein, drawing shimmery blood.

My gaze flew to Kolis as understanding dawned. Kolis couldn't give the Chosen his blood, which was what I'd figured when he took me to the ceeren instead of healing me himself.

But what I didn't know was exactly why he couldn't. Ash was a Primal of Death, and his blood healed. Could it be because Kolis was *the* Primal of Death?

I stood still as Elias placed his bleeding wrist over Jove's mouth. The Chosen's head was turned from me, but after a few moments, I saw his throat bob in a swallow.

Shivering, I folded my arms around myself, barely feeling the sore pull of my muscles. I didn't know how much time passed, but at some point, Elias had lifted the limp Jove into his arms.

"That was and is how it is done," Kolis said.

As if coming out of a daze, I blinked. Elias carried Jove toward the curtained archway.

"Come." Kolis didn't give me a chance to respond, just took my hand. "I'll explain more."

Every part of my being rebelled against his touch as he led us back through the doors. We returned the way we'd come in silence, arriving at the cage in what felt like heartbeats.

Kolis and I were alone.

"When my brother did the Ascensions, the Chosen Ascended into godhood." Kolis's upper lip curled, and then his expression smoothed out. "Without the embers of life, they simply become the Ascended, as I told you before."

Raising my hand—my left hand—to his mouth, he pressed a dry kiss to the top. "Those who are like gods but not. Sickness no longer plagues them. They may consume food, but it is not necessary. And they will survive most mortal injuries, susceptible to only a few manners of death," he told me, his voice carrying a hint of pride. "But I've been working on a few drawbacks."

"Like...?" I trailed off as he began leading me across the chamber, my heart spasming as we neared the bed. We passed it. He sat me on the divan, and I cleared my throat. "Like what?"

"They can become as strong as a god if given time, but so far, they have not been able to harness the eather." He walked over to the table. New glasses and fresh pitchers had been brought in during our absence. "They have a strong aversion to sunlight."

I thought about how Gemma had said the Chosen who returned remained indoors during daylight hours. My gaze flicked to the doors. Was that why the part of the sanctuary I'd seen the last Ascended in had been so dark? "But the sun is still out, and Jove was—"

"The aversion is not immediate. It takes a few hours." he cut in, running his fingers over the linen draped across the table. "While they do not need food, they *do* need blood, and their hunger is...insatiable in the beginning. It's difficult for them to control. Some do not learn such restraint. Any blood will suffice, but that which carries even a few drops of eather is preferred. It can help them manage the hunger."

The dull ache in my head returned, pulsing at my temples. "And if they cannot manage their hunger?"

From where he stood on the other side of the table, his gaze lifted to mine. "They are put down."

The way he said that, without any emotion, was more than unsettling.

Gods.

"That bothers you." He spread his fingers over the linen. "It shouldn't. It is for the greater good."

Gods, my two most hated words, but hearing Kolis speak of the *greater good* was, well, so absurd it was actually amusing.

"Gods have been unable to control their bloodlust, too. They were also put down under Eythos's rule," Kolis said, a hint of defensiveness creeping into his tone. "The only difference is that neither he nor those the god served bloodied their hands."

"It was you?" I figured.

"I was the Primal of Death, after all," he answered with a hollow smile. "Who else would carry out such distasteful deeds?"

He was still the true Primal of Death, and he knew it. But even I could admit that being tasked with such an act must have been terrible.

"Like Eythos, I'm creating life, not death. And an Ascended left uncontrolled is exactly that: Death. I give them a chance to restrain themselves. I do," he repeated, his shoulders rising sharply. "But if they fail? They will glut themselves on blood. And once they've fallen into bloodlust, they are almost always lost. They will kill indiscriminately, draining their victims, and what becomes of them then is nothing more than the living dead..." He pursed his lips. "It is not an act I enjoy, contrary to what others may believe. But I do not pawn it off on others. An Ascended who has given in to bloodlust must be killed, and it should be done by their creator."

There was a whole lot of stuff there to process, starting with the fact that Kolis actually sounded as if he believed what he said: that he was creating life. And it seemed he truly *cared* about that life. There was also the idea that he thought of himself as the creator of these Ascended. But was he? He'd drained Jove, but Elias's blood would ultimately Ascend him. However, what he said happened to those the Ascended fed upon and killed prompted my next question.

"How is an Ascended different than what you spoke of before? The Craven."

"Well, one is still alive, and the other is not. They are like the Gryms," he explained, and an image rose of the waxy-skinned once-mortals who had summoned a god and then offered their eternal lives in exchange for whatever they believed they needed so badly. "But one whose bite spreads a very different kind of toxin. An infection of sorts that will turn whomever they bite or scratch into the undead—if they survive the attack."

My mouth dropped open. "That's a pretty big drawback."

"Yes, especially since those who are mortal—or more mortal than god—are susceptible to turning Craven." A muscle ticked in his jaw.

"Which means newly-turned Ascended are a danger to the Chosen."

"If they are so dangerous, why was an Ascended left to feed on a Chosen?" I demanded.

Kolis's eyes reverted to their cold, lifeless stare, sending a surge of alarm through me. "Well, because it's not a danger we're entirely unaccustomed to. What do you think happens if a god drains a mortal? Something similar. You could say it's an even more virulent infection."

I thought about the seamstress. Madis had left her place right before I found her dead. The problem was, she hadn't *stayed* dead. And she also hadn't looked like the one I'd seen here.

"And newly made Ascended are always under watch," he continued in a tone that sounded like each word was chiseled out of stone. "However, a certain someone attempted to escape."

Me.

He was totally talking about me.

"And those responsible for watching over the Ascended were drawn away," he said. "Ironically, if they'd remained at their post, the Ascended wouldn't have killed, and you still would've been captured. But they have been dealt with."

I had a feeling *being dealt with* didn't mean they'd simply been reprimanded. I should probably feel a little bad about that, but I couldn't muster the energy when I still didn't know how to process what had been done to Jove.

He wouldn't die, but he hadn't chosen to live as an Ascended either. It had been decided *for* him. Maybe he would've chosen to live no matter what, but he could've decided to die instead. I would never know. But what if he was one of those who couldn't control his hunger? And were the Ascended good or bad? Somewhere in the middle?

My brows knitted as I thought of something. Ash could go longer than he probably should without feeding. Was it the same with these Ascended? "What...what if an Ascended chooses not to feed?"

"They will weaken over time, becoming akin to mortal once more."

I felt a skipping motion in my chest. "So, in a way, this kind of Ascension can be undone?"

"No." His head tilted as he frowned. "Being akin to mortal is not the same thing. If they take no blood, their bodies eventually give out. The process of that is..." His frown deepened. "Admittedly, quite disturbing."

Clearly, it was something he'd seen before. "There have been

Ascended who refused to feed?" I surmised, the ache increasing.

"There have."

"Why?"

Deep grooves formed between his brows. "They were not grateful for the blessing bestowed upon them."

I stared at him, somewhat dumbfounded.

He straightened, drawing his hand from the table. "What? It is clear you're thinking something. I want to know."

I really needed to learn how to control my facial features. "It's just that... Well, I was thinking that maybe they weren't grateful because they didn't want to become something that could turn into an indiscriminate killer."

He laughed under his breath. "All gods are capable of becoming thus, *so'lis,* and mortals are no different." He sent me a long, knowing look. "And from what I know of your life this time in the mortal realm, you were no different."

My shoulders stiffened at the truth of his words. He was right. I'd been no different.

I still wasn't, which was kind of funny, considering the embers within me.

"Everything that is created or born has the potential to become an indiscriminate killer," he tacked on.

I saw what he was trying to get at. "Okay."

His eyes narrowed. "It's not okay."

"I said it was."

"I may not always be able to tell when you lie, but most of the time I know," he remarked, and I stiffened. "While I am not the Great Conspirator spoken of in the prophecy, I am a Deceiver, a teller of lies. I recognize many of yours. This is one of them."

He was the only being who *could* be the Great Conspirator, and maybe he could sense my lies, but as long as he didn't recognize the really important one...whatever. My head hurt. "All right, then," I said, taking a breath. I could deal with a headache. "I see what you mean about everyone having the potential to be a killer, but—"

"There is no but. I am right."

I took a deep breath. "Never mind, then."

He stared at me, his head lowering. "No, continue."

"There is no point in continuing if you will automatically dismiss what I'm saying before I even finish saying it." I took a breath. "Gods were born knowing they would Ascend one day. They have their entire lives to prepare for it. The Chosen do not."

"They don't?" His brows rose. "They are given to the Temples at birth and raised as Chosen. They spend their entire lives preparing to serve in Iliseeum and to Ascend. The only difference is they do not Ascend into godhood."

First off, that wasn't the only difference. But not all of them were being Ascended. Some were being killed or turned.

But I could argue until I was blue in the face, and it wouldn't change what Kolis believed, nor would it answer what I wanted to know.

"And you have to do this because of balance," I said. "What exactly is this balance?"

"The balance is everything, *so'lis*. Without it, there is nothing."

"I know." I beat back my rising frustration. "You said that. But you haven't—"

"The balance is everything," he repeated. "And there is balance *in* everything. Or that is what the Fates say, at least. I tend to think their idea of balance is a bit...unbalanced." Anger crept into his features. "Did you know the Primal of Death is expected to remain distant from anyone whose soul may one day pass before them for judgment?"

My eyes widened.

"Of course, you wouldn't know that. The Primal of Death is not to have friends, confidants, or lovers among anyone who may need to be judged. The Arae believe that forming close bonds could ultimately skew judgment," Kolis stated. "That means any being that is not a Primal or a draken."

I hadn't known that. Did that also play a role in why Ash kept a wall up between him and Rhain, Saion, and all the others? Why hadn't he shared this with me? Then again, there hadn't been much time for me to learn the more intricate details of his duties when I spent half the time I'd been with him attempting to keep myself from growing close to him. It reminded me of when I'd asked him about his armies and plans. He hadn't keyed me in on any of it because, at that point, I hadn't expressed any real interest in becoming his Consort. Regret surged through me, joining what was sure to become a long list.

"And yet, this was not expected of the Primal of Life," Kolis continued. "There were no limitations, as if being in the Primal of Life's favor couldn't lead to poor judgment, even though the Primal god's abilities were a collection of the other Primals'—a medley of the others' *goodness* that could be exploited. Do you know how?"

I shook my head.

Kolis's smile was more of a smirk. "My brother could bring rain to lands parched, but he could not wash those lands into the sea as Phanos can. He could help foster love between two individuals, but he could not twist it into hate as Maia is wont to do. He could capture souls, but he could not direct their path as Keella can." His nostrils thinned. "He could grant fortune but not curse those with misfortune like Veses can. And he could ensure that a hunt—be it for animal or the missing—was successful, but he could not weaken the bow or hide what one seeks as Hanan was able to do. When asked for advice, Eythos could stir duty within the most slothful character, but he couldn't inspire blind loyalty as Embris can. He could breed peace and accord, but not war and vengeance."

Kolis tipped back his head. "He could change any mortal's or god's life for the better if he wanted to, in whatever way he saw fit. But the Fates did not see that as something forming bonds with them could influence."

"That doesn't sound fair," I said after a moment. "It actually makes no sense."

Kolis eyed me, some of the eagerness easing from his features. "Then you and I are in agreement."

That was a disturbing thought.

"But to the Arae, it does make sense, and ensuring that emotions would never sway me was how they believed those who hadn't earned their paradise or punishment would keep from being rewarded with such. To them, eternity was far more important than what they saw as a temporary life, despite how shortsighted that belief was."

More like how *long*-sighted it was. It was like looking upon the forest and being unable to see all the trees within it. "And neither you nor Eythos could talk to them about this?"

"For what purpose? To change their minds?" Kolis laughed, the sound bordering on mocking. "You do not change the Fates' minds."

Okay, maybe he was right. What did I know? Absolutely nothing when it came to any of this. "But what does this have to do with what you just did with that Chosen?"

"Because that, too, creates balance. One designed only to be known by the Arae, the true Primal of Life, and the true Primal of Death," he said. "A balance that was established when the Ancients created the realms."

Headache forgotten, I stared at him. "I thought Eythos created the realms."

Kolis's smile was harsh. "He created some, but he didn't create *the* realms—all the lands and oceans that allow life to foster and grow. The Ancients did. And contrary to what is told and believed, the Ancients were not the first of the Primals, nor will any Primal become an Ancient, no matter how old they become."

I opened my mouth, but then it struck me. If the dragons—the ancestors of the draken—were here, something had to create them. It hadn't been Eythos since they already existed when he'd become so fascinated by them.

"And they also decreed that there must be death and vice versa. Just as every action has a reaction, one cannot exist without the other. And it would not be as simple as there only being life if there was no death, or only death if there was no life." Kolis's eyes flashed. "So, there must always be *the* Primal of Death and *the* Primal of Life, even if nothing more than a spark of embers remains in them. Even if they are in stasis or…" His gaze flickered over me. "Or hidden within a mortal bloodline. As long as the embers exist in some fashion, and life is created and taken, the balance is maintained."

"Oh," I whispered, staring ahead but not seeing him.

He studied me. "I see you now understand the importance of life, even if it is undesirable to you. And that you see what I personally risk by not taking those embers."

I nodded, but he mistook my shock. I'd always known what would happen if the embers of life were extinguished. It was what he'd unintentionally shared that shook me.

Kolis couldn't be killed.

29

The realization that Kolis couldn't be killed occupied my thoughts long after he left, only allowing me a few hours of restless sleep—if that.

Kolis was *the* Primal of Death. *He* carried the true embers of Death.

Ash was *a* Primal of Death. He did not carry the true embers of Death.

And since Kolis had ensured that none of his Court were left to Ascend to the Primal of Death after he stole the embers from Eythos, he was it.

I couldn't believe it.

With a dull throbbing in my temples that spread to my jaw every so often, I paced restlessly while Callum read from whatever book he had in his lap. Glancing at the porcelain pitcher on the table, I debated launching it at his head for no other reason than it would make me feel better.

But only temporarily.

Frustration dogged me as I made another pass in front of the door. Ash may not know who'd truly created the realms, but he and everyone else, especially the Fates, had to know that Kolis couldn't be killed.

So why in the whole wide realm had Holland, a Fate, spent years training me to kill the Primal of Death? Why would Eythos put Sotoria's soul in with the embers, positioning her, through me, to kill him? Especially when doing so would wreak havoc and destruction throughout the realms.

I had to be missing something.

Rubbing my temples, I walked from one rounded corner of the cage to the other. First, I'd learned I couldn't kill Kolis because Eythos's plan had gone sideways. Now, I'd learned that Kolis couldn't *be* killed—

Stopping, I looked up at the diamonds in the center of the cage.

The Star diamond.

It could hold Primal embers. After all, The Star had been created to contain the embers of a fallen Primal.

I lowered my hands from my aching temples as I stared at the strange, almost milky light the diamonds reflected. My stomach soured. If I could get a hold of the Star diamond—and that was a big *if*—I doubted it could be used to hold a soul and the embers simultaneously.

But unless I'd spent my entire life training for something utterly pointless, the Arae must have believed they could get their hands on The Star again. It was the only thing that made sense.

"What are you doing?" Callum asked.

Tearing my gaze from the diamonds, I started walking again. "Praying."

"Really?" came the dry response.

I turned to him. "What are—?" The embers in my chest suddenly thrummed. A Primal was near.

I took a deep breath, preparing myself for whatever Kolis had in store today while hoping he would bring news of Ash's release.

You need to tell him that you will die without me.

My mouth dried as dream-Ash's words floated through my thoughts.

Callum frowned, following my sudden shift in attention to the doors. "You feel a Primal?"

Unfortunately. "Yes."

"That makes no sense." Callum flipped his book closed. "Kolis is occupied."

My brows rose as I eyed the doors. Interesting. "What is he doing?"

"If he wanted you to know, he would've told you." Callum rose, picking up the dagger lying on the cushion.

Throwing that pitcher at his head was becoming more appealing with each passing second.

"What do you think you're going to do with that dagger?" I asked.

"The same you would do with it." Callum shot me a sideways look. "Just because you can't kill with it doesn't mean you can't make it hurt."

He had a point.

A muffled voice came through the doors, possibly belonging to Elias or another guard.

I looked again at the shadowstone dagger Callum held. "Should I be worried?"

"Every Primal knows better than to come near this part of the sanctuary." The Revenant strode toward the doors. "Unless you misread what you felt, this Primal appears not to know better."

"I didn't misread anything," I said as I glanced around the cage for a weapon even more useless than the dagger he held.

The truth was, if a Primal meant to do me harm while I was stuck in a cage, I was already dead.

The embers pulsed in my chest, almost as a reminder that I had them.

And I did.

Except, I didn't think using them was all that wise given the head-aches I'd been having.

Callum reached the doors just as they swung open, smacking right into him. He staggered back, cursing as a trickle of blood leaked from his nose. A startled laugh left me, but it faded quickly when I saw a stunning vision in off-white cross the threshold.

Veses.

Anger pounded through me, causing my muscles to tense. Faint twinges of pain radiated through my limbs. The crown was absent, and her blond ringlets were swept up and pinned with rubies, but she looked even better than when I'd seen her in the Council Hall, her color completely returned to her cheeks.

The Primal goddess glanced in Callum's direction. "Oh." Taking in the bloodied Revenant, a light brown eyebrow arched as I caught sight of a thin-lipped Elias outside the chamber. "You were standing behind the doors." Her attention shifted from him to the cage—to me. Her full lips rose in a smile. "My apologies."

"Apology unnecessary." Callum dragged the back of his hand under his nose. "If you're looking for Kolis, he is not here."

"I'm not looking for him." Smoothing a hand over an ivory-clad hip, she took a step forward. For once, her gown was more modest than the one I wore. I couldn't see even a hint of her breasts. "Hello."

"Fuck you," I replied.

Her throaty laugh grated on my skin as she took another step.

Callum shadowed her. "Why are you here?"

Slowly, she turned her head to Callum. The air charged, sparking over my skin. Callum felt it, too. His spine stiffened, but he didn't back off. Reluctant respect flashed through me, but it was brief as he sheathed his dagger. "Again, why are you here, Your Highness?"

Her smile deepened. "As I already told Elias, I came to speak with Seraphena."

"That's not—"

"And as I also informed Elias, denying me would be seriously unwise."

Callum held his ground. "It would be seriously unwise for you to defy His Majesty's orders."

Veses' features tightened as she raised one hand. The doors swung shut in Elias's face. She focused on Callum, and for a moment, I wasn't exactly sure who I'd root for in a fight between them.

"I do not intend for Kolis to know I'm here." Veses placed a finger on Callum's lips, one with a black-painted nail instead of red. "Which means I do not intend for you or any of his guards to run and tell him. But I don't think you will. I also believe you will ensure his guards don't."

"And why would you think that?" I asked, walking toward the chests. "Callum is an...ever-faithful servant."

Veses smirked as her gaze flicked to me. "Because, unbeknownst to Callum, he and I share something in common."

"Being obnoxious pieces of shit?" I smiled.

Callum's head whipped to me. "Silence."

I lifted a hand and extended a middle finger.

"She's so classy, isn't she?" Veses purred, facing me. "But no, my dear, that is not what I was referencing."

"What do you have in common, then?"

Her syrupy-sweet smile returned. "Loyalty."

I stared at her, stuck somewhere between disbelief and revulsion. And gods help me, a little bit of pity rose because if she truly were still loyal to Kolis after the events in the Council Hall, and was still in love with the false King, then she hopelessly hated herself.

"I know you're loyal to Kolis," Callum said, stepping closer to her. "But you still cannot be here, Veses. Even if I said nothing to him about this visit, he could find out. And that would not end well."

"He will not harm you." Veses kept inching forward. She was close enough now that her rose scent reached me. "You're like a son to him."

For some reason, that disturbed me as much as her loyalty to Kolis.

Callum's jaw tightened. "I'm not worried about me."

My gaze shot to him. Was he...? He worried about Veses?

"That's sweet of you." Veses touched his cheek this time, just below the golden paint. "But I can handle Kolis and his punishments."

His chest rose sharply. "Can you?"

A pink flush stained her cheekbones. "I can." She withdrew her touch. "And, actually, that is what I wanted to speak to her about."

He stiffened. "Veses..."

"I'm not going to hurt her." Her chin lifted. "I'm not foolish."

His pale eyes widened. "I wasn't suggesting you were. That is the last thing you are."

Besides the fact that Veses was very, very foolish, Callum did not seem concerned for her. And he obviously harbored some level of fondness for the awful—albeit pretty—monster. I didn't know what to think about any of that. Actually, I simply didn't have the mental capacity for it.

"Look, I just want to talk to her about what happened. You know why I would want that. You were there, after all." Thick lashes lowered. "All I want to do is speak to her about..."—her delicate shoulders shuddered—"about *that* in private."

My eyes narrowed. Yeah, I didn't think that was why she was here at all.

Callum's lips pursed as he glanced in my direction. "Fuck." He shoved a hand through his hair. "You have ten minutes."

"That's all I need." Veses smiled brightly, taking his hand and squeezing it. "Thank you."

Shooting me one last look, he cursed again and then left the chamber.

Leaving me with the Primal who had already tried to kill me once.

Not that he knew that.

The door snicked closed, and Veses said, "Just so you know, I'm not here to thank you for attempting to intervene the other night."

"It didn't even cross my mind."

"Good. Because I actually enjoyed it," she said. "Kyn has a certain...sadistic edge to him that just gets me..." She shivered. "Wet."

"Sure."

"What? You don't believe me? That wasn't the first time I've been punished in such a way. If one can call it punishment." She trailed a finger over the neckline of her gown. "If you really anger Kolis, and he's in the mood to be entertained, he'll give you to one of his draken for the evening." She drew a plump, pink lip between her teeth. "And trust me, when their claws and scales come out, they fuck hard." She laughed softly. "Normally, Kolis likes to watch, and I enjoy it even more. When I come, it's while looking at him. Sadly, whatever you said put an end to things before they got real nice and—"

"Convincing me you speak the truth seems really important to you," I interrupted, not wanting to hear any more. "Or are you trying to convince yourself that you liked it?"

Her finger halted in the center of the bodice.

"Maybe you did." I stepped close to the bars. "I'm sure Kyn's sadistic roughness speaks to *your* sadism. *That* is what makes you wet."

Veses' nostrils flared.

"But I also know what I saw in your face when Kolis summoned Kyn. You may have gotten off, but you did not want it at first." I held her stare. "I'm sure both mortals and Primals call that the same—"

"Don't," she warned, her lips peeling back, "even finish that sentence. It was nothing, and I owe you no gratitude."

"I wouldn't want it even if you did." I looked down at her. "How are you even here?"

She let loose a delicate yet still-somehow-attractive snort. "I could ask you the same question."

"I think it's obvious why I'm here."

Her stare turned shrewd. "Perhaps."

My eyes narrowed on her, unease building.

"But to answer your question, I had to…chew myself free." She lifted her slender arms as my brows shot up. "If you're thinking I had to chew through my muscle and bone on both arms, you'd be correct."

I gaped at her, my mind immediately filling with grisly images. "Really?"

"How else do you think I got free of shackles made in the same way this pretty little cage of yours was?" Veses glanced down at her arms. "Growing these back from the elbow down took some time."

"That is…disgusting."

"You should've seen me when they were just mangled stumps," she replied. "Still, I was far more attractive than you."

I rolled my eyes.

"I'll admit, it was extreme, but when I felt Hanan's death, I just knew it was our dear Nyktos who'd done it," she said, and my teeth started to grind at the *our-Nyktos* part. "That's what woke me from stasis, if you care to know."

"I don't."

Veses smirked. "Anyway, no one else would dare do such a thing. But as I said to you before, Nyktos can be so…deliciously unpredictable in his anger. I figured Hanan had gotten his hands on you, you were dead in one way or another, and it was best if I made myself as scarce as possible before Nyktos returned and blamed me for something I had nothing to do with."

"Are you forgetting that he imprisoned you because you tried to kill me?"

"That's irrelevant."

I stared at her.

"But imagine my surprise when I arrived in my Court only to be told that Kolis had a new pet who also happened to be the recently crowned Consort of the Shadowlands." A glow of eather pulsed behind her pupils. "It was nearly as shocking as hearing Kolis call you his *graeca*, the same freckled mortal Nyktos sought to keep hidden, who happens to have the Primal embers of life stowed away inside her."

"Did you mean to say disappointment instead of surprise?" I retorted.

She eyed me. "Disappointed cannot even begin to adequately describe what I felt. Devastated? Heartbroken? Yes."

"Exactly how *devastated* could you be when, not that long ago, I saw you grinding on another man's lap?" I countered.

"Just because what I want has been out of my reach doesn't mean I cannot take what *is*."

But she had taken what was not within her reach.

"So, in the last day or so, I did some digging," she continued. "Oh, the things I've learned. Nyktos's imprisonment is not at all surprising. After all, he did kill another Primal—one known throughout the realms as brave and formidable." She pressed her hand to her neck. "If I had pearls, I'd be clutching them."

"Uh-huh."

"I detect a hint of sarcasm." Dipping her chin, she grinned. "You'd be right to suspect my sincerity. Hanan was a weak, sniveling coward who'd outlived his worth. Good riddance."

Apparently, Hanan and Veses hadn't been on good terms.

"I also learned that the Shadowlands are on the verge of invading Dalos." She shivered. "Now that will be entertaining. Should liven up the humdrum of everyday life."

"Was having to chew your arms off not exciting enough for you?"

Veses chuckled. "It was short-lived."

No part of me was surprised that she found the idea of people dying entertaining. And that was exactly what would happen if the Shadowlands' forces invaded—there would be losses on both sides.

She watched me. "I also learned about the deal you made for Nyktos's freedom."

"And by *learned about* the deal, do you mean you spoke with Callum?"

"I'll never tell." She winked. "But you know what the most interesting thing I learned was?"

"The better question is do I care," I said. "The answer is no."

"You *should* care," she replied, the edges of her fangs dragging over her lower lip. "Because there is some...how should I phrase it? *Doubt* concerning who you claim to be."

I forced myself to show no reaction. "Gee, I wonder who the source of that doubt is."

"If you think it's just Callum, you're wrong," she replied, and I tensed. "You see, all of us Primals who were alive when Kolis first became the Primal of Life remember what Sotoria looked like. And while you share similar features—"

"The hair color is wrong, and I have more freckles," I said. "I know. That is evidence of nothing."

"Except other reborn souls appeared as they were in their previous lives."

"And how many of those souls were also placed with the embers of life?" I reasoned, rather proud of my fast thinking. "Has it occurred to you or anyone else that had some impact?"

"Oh, I'm sure it's occurred to some," she said, tilting her head. "Mostly those who have no interest in whether or not you are Sotoria."

"But you? You have a vested interest in simply not wanting to believe that I am her," I said. "That way, you would be...less devastated."

Her lips thinned.

"But I'm beginning to think you like feeling that way," I continued. "After all, you are beautiful, Veses."

Her lips turned up.

"At least on the outside," I added, and the curve disappeared. "Either way, you could have almost anyone you want, gods and mortal alike, yet you seek the two most ineligible beings in both realms."

A muscle began ticking in her jaw. "I think it's funny you believe they are ineligible."

"What I think is funny, is that both you and Callum seem to assume I won't say anything to Kolis about your visit."

"I've assumed nothing. Callum? He's a charming boy, but he doesn't always think things through." She lifted a shoulder.

Callum? Charming?

"But I don't think you're going to say anything," she added.

I crossed my arms. "And why is that?"

She shrugged again, slowly walking from the side of the cage to where I stood. Eather crackled from her eyes. "You won't tell Kolis."

"You're far too confident in that."

"I'm not confident. I just know I'm right." She moved as close as she could without touching the bars. Only a foot separated us. "You won't tell him because you know how he'll react. And despite what I say, you wouldn't put me in that position because you're such a good and decent mortal."

Tension crept into my shoulders. "You're right."

Her smile turned smug.

"But you're also wrong. I'm neither good nor decent since I'd rather see you dead than punished."

Veses' laugh was like wind chimes. "I see jealousy makes you say terrible things."

The embers stirred in my chest as anger continued to flare. "I know."

Her head tilted. "About?"

"About the deal you made with Nyktos."

Veses' smile faded.

Mine returned. "Kolis seemed disappointed in you for not telling him about my presence in the Shadowlands. How do you think he'll feel knowing that you made a pact with his nephew to keep any knowledge of me hidden from him?"

Astonishment briefly lit up her features. "He told you?" Her eyes met mine as a cunning smile replaced her previous astonishment. "Did he tell you how eager he was to strike the deal? How much he enjoyed—?"

"Spin all the bullshit you want about yourself." A rush of rage caused the embers in my chest to go crazy. "But don't even try doing that to him, you sick bitch."

Veses sneered, baring her fangs. "How dare you speak to me in such a manner?"

"How *dare* I? What in the gods' names is wrong with you?" I struggled to keep the pulsing embers down. "There is no way you don't know how disgustingly wrong what you've done is. You cannot be that demented." The moment the words left my mouth, I realized that Kolis was that demented, so Veses likely was, too. I shook my head. "Clearly, what happened the other night in the Council Hall wasn't the first time. You know what *that* feels like."

"I already told you, I enjoyed—"

"I don't care what you claim!" I shouted, and her eyes widened as a burst of energy left me, blowing Veses' skirt back and causing the chandelier to swing. "You know what it feels like, and you still did it to someone else—someone you were once friends with. Yes, I know you two were close at one time. But that didn't matter, did it?"

Her eyes widened as her gown settled around her feet. A moment passed. Then another. "It's not like I hurt him."

"You didn't...?" My hands curled into fists. So help me gods, I was going to kill this bitch. I would find a way. "What did Kolis say? That despite how beautiful you are, you say such ugly things?"

Her chest rose with a deep inhale.

"He was right." My body trembled with rage. "He just forgot to mention how ugly you are on the inside."

Silvery essence poured into her veins. "You know nothing about me, little girl."

"*Little girl?* I thought I was the fat girl," I retorted. "And I know enough about you, Veses, to know just how depraved you are on the inside."

"I've tried to protect Nyktos!" she shot back. "And I've done so at great risk to myself."

"You tried to protect him by forcing him to allow you to feed off him? By getting off on it?" My heart thundered as I tried to rein my anger back in before I lost control completely. The last thing I needed was for Kolis to sense me using the embers. Damn it, he could've already noticed. "You're a godsdamn mess."

"And what are you?" Veses demanded, eather snapping into the air around her. "That's a rhetorical question. I know what you are. A whore."

I huffed out a dry laugh. "You really need to work on your insults, Veses. They're truly pathetic."

"It's not an insult when it's the truth. You had Nyktos. Was he not good enough? You had to take Kolis?"

"*Take* Kolis?" I cut myself off before I said anything she could use against me. I briefly closed my eyes. "Why are so many of you out of your minds?"

"That's an offensive question."

Head aching, I let it fall back. I stared at the bars above me. "I don't understand most of the Primals, but you? I think I understand you the least."

"You're likely not intelligent nor worldly enough to even begin to understand me," she quipped.

I sighed. "Again with the silly insults. You can do better." I met her stare. "You want Kolis, but since you can't have him, you go after his nephew—who also wants nothing to do with you. You seize the first opportunity to turn whatever friendship or companionship you once had with him into a nightmare, yet you claim to protect him? As if you care for him?"

"I *do* care for him," she argued, her cheeks flushing. "He hasn't had the easiest life for a Primal."

"And you really did your level best to make it worse for him, didn't you?" I had to count to five before I continued. "Is it because they share similar features, and you can pretend you're with the one you really want?"

Veses looked away, her jaw flexing.

Dear gods, could it really be that? What Ash had claimed? Telling her she was messed up didn't even capture what was going on in that head of hers. "That is even more pathetic than your insults, and I actually mean that in the most unoffensive way possible."

Veses' head snapped back to mine. "I can't wait to see you die."

I didn't even acknowledge that. "Since Kolis has no idea about the deal you made while you were supposed to be keeping an eye on Nyktos, it's not because you want to make Kolis jealous."

"Kolis may not know about the deal, but he believes I've kept a very, very close eye on his nephew for him. He thinks we've been intimate." She smiled tightly. "Something Nyktos hasn't made any effort to deny."

"So, it *is* to make Kolis jealous."

She shrugged. "You have nothing to say about Nyktos not swaying Kolis's belief?"

"No."

"Come now, you may be in this cage, and Kolis may call you his *graeca*, but I know where your interests truly lie."

I arched a brow. "I know why he wouldn't attempt to change Kolis's mind."

"And you would know that because you love him," she said, her stare unflinching. "Kolis may not know any better and may even believe that you just harbor a fondness for his nephew..."

Fucking Callum.

He hadn't been in the chamber when I struck the deal, but he'd somehow found out, either by eavesdropping or from Kolis himself.

"But I know better."

"You don't know anything," I sneered.

"Did you forget that I was there when you had your little breakdown after seeing Nyktos and me together?"

All the air went out of my lungs.

"Nyktos and Rhain were far too focused on getting to you and thought I'd left as ordered. Of course, I didn't, nor did I fully realize it was you causing the entire palace to tremble at first. But once I saw you use the embers, I knew it had been you." Her eyes gleamed. "And no one who harbors just fondness for another reacts that way. I would know. I leveled nearly half my Court when Kolis brought Sotoria back to life."

My lips parted.

"So, our...violent reactions regarding the ones we love is something we have in common."

There was nothing I could say to that.

"So, whether you're really Sotoria or not doesn't matter. Your heart already belongs to someone else," she said. "And once Kolis realizes that? You'll know just how sadistic Kyn can be."

I inhaled sharply. "You sick bitch."

"I'm not sick, Seraphena." Her chin lifted. "I'm just tired."

"Then go take a fucking century-long nap," I snapped.

Veses' laugh was far too sultry for our discussion. "I could never rest that long. I am too afraid of missing out on whatever is happening in the realm of those awake."

I shook my head as the ache moved down the sides of my face. "I'm almost positive your ten minutes are up, so what is the point of this conversation? Other than to be a living, breathing annoyance."

"It's to warn you."

"Of course." I sighed.

"I will not lose Kolis to Sotoria again," she said, her voice low. "I'd rather see him alone than have that."

"Guess you *weren't* telling the truth when you said you were happy for him," I muttered dryly.

"Make all the snide comments you want. It doesn't change the fact that I'm going to do everything within my power to wake Kolis up to what is so clearly evident to most of the realm," she said. "That your heart, no matter who you really are, belongs to another. And I will not regret what becomes of you after that truth comes out."

"Shocker."

"But what I will regret is what it will do to Nyktos. What it is *already* doing to him." The mocking, vindictive smile left her face. "Once Kolis realizes you're in love with Nyktos, he will find a way to keep him. He won't release him until Nyktos accepts it's time for him to move on and you're effectively dealt with."

My stomach twisted into knots.

"Or you could just find a way to take yourself out of the equation," she suggested. "Sacrifice yourself for Nyktos."

Or I could make sure Kolis freed him before Veses managed to convince him of anything.

"Just something to think about." Rubies glittering in her hair, she stepped back and swept her gaze over me. "I'd look better in that gown, by the way."

"I'm sure you would," I replied, speaking the truth. She would look better in a burlap sack.

Watching her leave, I remembered what Aios had said about Veses and Ash's mother. That they had been friends, and Veses had been good at one time—well, as good as any Primal could be.

Veses wasn't *good* anymore.

Maybe Kolis stealing the embers of life and Eythos's death had aided in changing her. Or perhaps she wouldn't be like this if she had rested for any real length of time. It was quite possible she could have remained decent if she hadn't fallen in love with Kolis.

What had Holland said about love? Basically, that it was as equally awe-inspiring as it was horrifying.

I was so glad that my love for Ash meant I'd gotten a taste of what the awe-inspiring bit felt like. I couldn't help but feel a little smidgen of pity for both Kolis and Veses, who only knew the awful side of it.

But Veses was right. Our love did make both of us capable of violence.

"Veses?"

She stopped at the door but didn't look back.

"I just want you to know that...I am sorry for what was done to you in the Council Hall."

Her back stiffened.

"But that doesn't change that I will do everything in my power to see you burn before I die."

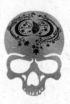

Weary, I found myself without much of an appetite when the Chosen served supper, but I forced myself to eat what I could, knowing I needed to keep up my strength.

Because I had a feeling I should keep from taxing my body further.

I wouldn't think about that, though. I already had enough on my mind after Veses' visit.

As I readied myself for bed, I hoped I dreamt of Ash again. Holding that desire at the forefront of my mind, I walked from behind the privacy screen, my tired gaze moving from the darkened chamber beyond to—

Wait. The chandelier had been on when I went behind the canvas screen. Hadn't it? I started to turn.

Kolis lay in the center of the bed, an arm thrust back, supporting his head. He had his long body stretched out, his ankles crossed. He looked as comfortable as a bug snug in a rug.

Choking on a scream of surprise, I jerked back a step as my hand flew to my chest.

"I startled you," Kolis said with a smile.

My heart pounded. "You're so observant."

That practiced smile faltered but quickly returned. "It is one of my many skills."

I didn't care about any of his skills. "What are you doing in here?"

One eyebrow rose. "You're asking what I'm doing in here, within the sanctuary I had built?" His head tipped to the side. "Surely, you're not asking that."

Keep your temper in check, I reminded myself as I folded an arm over my still-unsettled stomach. Especially with Veses' newfound purpose in life. "I just wasn't expecting you." I glanced at the screen. How long had he been in here? While I'd made use of the privy? Undressed. Gods, I had to add that to the ever-growing list of things I could not think about. "I didn't even hear you."

"Being quiet is another talent," he teased.

The hand at my side tightened. "It's an impressive one."

He practically beamed.

I forced my tone to be light. "I'm very tired, Kolis."

"That's perfect." He reached over with a hand, patting the space beside him. "As am I. I know no deals have been struck, but I so enjoyed the last time we slept together."

"I'm relieved to hear that," I murmured, thinking it was ironic that he took such joy in something that haunted me. Or maybe it was more disturbing than ironic. "Speaking of deals—"

"My nephew is being prepared for release," he interrupted. "It will happen very soon." Golden eather swirled across his bare chest. "That is unless a reason arises for that not to happen—or more of a reason than what you have already given me."

Visions of Veses' gloating face danced in my head.

His eyes locked with mine. "Join me. I would be so...disappointed if you didn't want to."

I stiffened. What he didn't say came across loud and clear. If I displeased him, it would become another reason to delay Ash's release. My fingers curled against the material of the robe as I resisted shouting that he should go find Veses, who'd be more than glad to share a bed with him.

"You hesitate," he stated flatly. "Do you not wish to be in my company?"

"It's...it's not that." I hated him. Gods, I *hated* him. "I'm just nervous."

He raised a brow. "About what, *so'lis?*"

"About what you expect from me. We have yet to get to know each other—"

"I only wish to sleep beside you, as we did last time." The eather slowed in his eyes. "The virtue you cared little for when it came to my nephew and whomever else is safe with me."

The implication of his words stung my cheeks.

And he knew it.

Saw it.

Because that tainted smile returned. "Unlike them, I am a gentle-man."

A laugh crawled up my throat. A very unwise one, but I didn't get a chance to let it free.

"But do not think it doesn't anger me that you were not as faithful as I, spreading those lovely thighs for whoever caught your eye," he said. "It does. But I have chosen to forgive such missteps. You have no memory of who you were or what you meant to me."

Okay.

There was a whole lot of *what the fuck?* in what he'd just said, but my mind skipped over the chauvinistic insults and latched on to one thing he'd said. "What do you mean you've been…faithful?"

"There has been no one since you."

My mouth opened, but I had a hard time finding the right word, let alone processing what he'd just said.

Kolis chuckled. "The disbelief in your expression is endearing. I didn't say I was a virgin, only that I have been with no other since I met you."

If Kolis hadn't been with anyone since he'd met Sotoria, which was a really long time ago, far more than just two hundred years, he might as well be a virgin.

Honestly, my shock had nothing to do with the virginity bit. Ash had been one when we met. Granted, the length of life he'd lived so far was not even a drop in the bucket compared to Kolis.

What stunned me was how deeply his obsession with Sotoria ran for him to stay faithful to someone he'd literally scared to death and then traumatized.

Was that what Veses had meant when she'd said she would rather see Kolis alone than with Sotoria? Because she knew that he'd truly been faithful?

Good.

Fucking.

Gods.

He and Veses were meant for each other.

"You should be honored to know this," Kolis remarked, a hard edge creeping into his voice. "I would've been honored if I had learned you had remained chaste."

Blinking, I snapped out of my stupor with a rush of anger. Ash's response to my lack of chaste behavior couldn't be any more different than Kolis's.

"Have my words insulted you?" he asked. "I have only spoken the truth."

"No, they have not." And that was true. His words meant very little to me beyond the sting of initial disbelief and the anger his chauvinistic opinions generated.

Not saying another word, I went to the bed and lay down, my back to him.

A couple of moments of silence passed. "Do you normally sleep this way?" he asked. "On your side?"

"Yes."

"On that side?"

I could sleep on either side, but I did favor my right. That was how I'd slept with Ash. With Kolis? I didn't want to look at him, and I wanted my dominant hand free, just in case. I didn't have to be concerned about that with Ash, not even before I realized I didn't need to worry.

The bed shifted behind me, and I closed my eyes, bracing myself.

Kolis's arm came around me. Another moment passed, and then his chest touched my back. His legs curled against mine, and I lay there, no longer focused on finding Ash in my dreams again. Instead, I fantasized about all the many, varied, and bloody ways I would hurt both Veses and Kolis before I died.

The problem was, those fantasies were difficult to make clear. It was unlikely I would accomplish both things before then because I...

I was on borrowed time that was quickly running out.

30

I stood in front of the vanity, staring at the pinkish-red streaking the clusters of foam.

My gums were bleeding.

Hand shaking, I reached for the cup and rinsed my mouth, then used the rest of the water to wash away the evidence of what Phanos had warned would happen. Whatever the ceeren had done for me was wearing off.

Either it was bound to happen, or there were other reasons. The injury sustained when I tried to escape? How long I'd slept afterwards? Using the embers? Kolis feeding on me? Regardless, I was once more barreling toward my Ascension.

I numbly pushed away from the vanity and changed into the first gown I retrieved from one of the chests, giving up on searching for a somewhat decent one.

As I walked to the table and picked up my glass, I eyed the platter of sugared fruits the Chosen had left after all the other plates were cleared. My appetite still hadn't returned. I couldn't recall my hunger being affected before, but Kolis's recent *punishment* had likely played a role in what I knew was true, as did worrying about what Veses was up to. I was further along in my Ascension now, and all the other symptoms made sense. The headaches. The tiredness. I just hadn't wanted to connect them because it meant time was running out.

I would go through my Ascension, and I wouldn't survive. Sotoria would be lost, and the embers…

There would be no hope for the mortal realm.

Surprisingly, my mind didn't linger there—on the most serious of the consequences. I didn't even think about Ash. My thoughts went to the Ascended.

If I started to die and was still here with Kolis, he would take the embers and attempt to Ascend me.

I drifted closer to the bars, thinking about what Delfai had said: that the embers had melded with me. I'd have to be entirely drained for someone to remove them. My heart would stop. According to Kolis, the Ascended never died like the Revenants did. I'd forgotten that in my initial panic upon hearing Kolis's plans.

There was some relief in remembering that. At least I wouldn't come back as a being swept up in bloodlust.

Hopefully.

Because there was so much I didn't know. Like what Kolis had shared about the Ancients, or the fact that Kolis's blood could give life—I thought about Callum. Well, it sort of could. Even if there was only a sliver of a chance that Kolis could somehow pull off what he planned, it was a chance.

I took a sip, swallowing water that tasted like mixed fruit today. About to refill the glass, I heard the sound of footsteps. A moment later, I felt the embers pulsing in my chest.

Focusing on my breathing, I emptied my thoughts and became no one as I stepped back from the bars.

Kolis entered the chamber alone, his white linen pants hanging loosely from his hips, but I could see the shoulders of the men standing guard in the hall.

"*So'lis*," he greeted with a warm, breezy smile. "You look lovely today."

"Thank you," I replied, my tone matching his. At least two days had passed since Veses visited me. I hadn't seen Kolis at all yesterday, not until whatever constituted night here fell, and he showed yet again to demand that I sleep beside him.

He'd held me even tighter last night than the one before.

I had no idea where he'd been in the meantime or if Veses had gotten to him.

Strangely, I also hadn't seen Callum since her visit.

Kolis's steps slowed as he approached the cage door. "Though you do look quite tired."

I blinked slowly at the criticism creeping into his voice.

"Did you not sleep well last night?"

I knew better than to tell the truth: that I'd only managed to doze and was unable to sleep deeply with him present. "I slept fine. I'm not sure why I look tired."

"Then perhaps this will help." He unlocked the cage. "I thought you might like to go for a walk."

Go for a walk.

Like a dog.

If he were anyone else, I would've kicked him in the throat. Instead, I smiled. "That would be nice."

And it would be. Any chance to leave the cage was an opportunity to see more of my surroundings.

"Good. Come." He motioned me forward.

I did as he ordered, taking note of the guards. Elias was there, as always. This time, the other was the Revenant, Dyses. His eyes looked even paler in the fading sunlight.

"Where has Callum been?" I asked.

"I sent him away for a few days to handle something important for me," he said, not elaborating on the task. "I figured you two could benefit from some space." He looked down at me, his stare suddenly sharp. "Perhaps be less inclined to disobey me."

Disobey him…?

Damn it, he had felt me using the embers when I'd spoken to Veses. Except he believed it was a result of my interactions with Callum.

Which meant that he remained unaware of Veses' visit. It could possibly even mean that Veses hadn't begun her campaign against me.

Despite how demented she was, Veses was smart enough not to launch an all-out verbal attack against me. She'd immediately arouse Kolis's suspicions, and not in the way she wanted. But I was willing to bet she'd already been whispering in his ear, laying the groundwork.

Something else struck me as Kolis led me down the same path we'd taken to the Council Hall. The color of the Revenants' eyes could only be described as a lifeless shade of blue. Emphasis on *lifeless*. I'd seen the eyes of the dead before, how they first fixed on the beyond and then glazed over. I'd seen the color change, or at least appear to. A film of sorts settled over them, the color a milky, bluish-gray.

Almost identical to a Revenant's.

Was that because they had died?

I glanced behind us, relieved to see that only Elias followed. What I wanted to ask seemed sort of rude to ask in front of Dyses. "Can I ask you something about the Revenants?"

"Of course." Kolis walked slowly, allowing me to keep pace beside him.

"Callum explained to me that Revenants are not in need of food or blood," I began.

"They aren't," he confirmed as we passed under the palms' broad leaves. "They have no need of anything that sustains either mortals or gods. Not even sleep."

My brows knitted. "Then what of less-tangible things? Like companionship?"

"As in friendship? Love? Sex? No."

Dear gods. "That sounds…"

"Wonderful?" He smiled. "Their lives are no longer tethered to the needs of the flesh or the wants of the soul. They're driven only by the desire to serve their creator."

Yeah, I wasn't thinking *wonderful* at all. More like horrific.

"You don't think so?" he asked as we approached the diamond-encrusted wall. The sparkling buildings of the city came into view.

I knew better than to breathe too deeply. The scent of decay was in the air.

"I…I just can't imagine not wanting anything." I honestly couldn't as we turned toward the colonnade. "Not feeling anything."

"I imagine it's rather freeing," he remarked as we climbed the short, wide steps.

I could barely keep my expression blank. While I'd wished I didn't feel anything many times in my life, I couldn't imagine a near eternity of feeling nothing. The mere thought of it caused my chest to constrict.

Forcing my breathing to even out and slow, I considered what Kolis had shared as we entered the hall of what I assumed was the main part of the sanctuary. The Revenants may be reborn and able to walk and talk and *serve*, but they were without wants and needs, and that was nothing more than a poor imitation of life.

Kolis had called the Craven the walking dead, but in reality, the Revenants were such.

Which was why Kolis hadn't wanted to turn me into one of them. What came back had no soul. Revenants were just reanimated flesh and bones.

Gods, I felt sorry for them. I probably shouldn't, because if there truly were no souls in them, then they weren't people. They were just *things*—something that shouldn't exist—but I did.

The hall was much quieter today, with only a few faint moans echoing from the shadowy alcoves. "But Callum is different," I said, remembering both he and Kolis saying as much.

He nodded as we stopped by one of the curtained recesses. He drew the covering back, revealing a door. "Callum is full of wants and needs," he replied dryly. "Just as you and I."

So, Callum at least *lived*.

"And you truly don't know why he turned out differently than the others?"

Kolis opened the door with a wave of his hand. "I don't, but..." He sighed loudly before looking over my shoulder at Elias. "You can wait here."

"Yes, Your Majesty."

Unnerved that I would be alone with him, I waited for Kolis to elaborate as we came upon a narrow, spiral staircase.

Luckily, he was feeling chatty. "I believe motivation plays a role. The why behind the creation of the Revenants," he explained, making his way up the staircase. "And I think it's because of what my brother said once about creating life. That there is a little bit of magic in creation."

Trailing a hand over the smooth marble banister, I eyed his back. It was always odd to hear him speaking of Eythos without bitterness or anger and instead with wistfulness.

"A part that was unknown and unplanned. Magic of the realms—in the eather of it all," he said, the statement reminding me of something Holland would say. "Eythos claimed that whatever the creator felt at the time of creation often shaped it. That even a hint of joy, sorrow, desperation, or anger could mold the life of the creation before it even began," he said, following the winding path of the staircase as a faint sheen of sweat broke out on my forehead. "When I create the Revenants, I feel only duty. But with Callum, I felt...I felt everything. Desperation. Anger. Sorrow. Even joy at being close to one who shares your blood."

My lip curled.

"Eythos would say what I felt when returning life to Callum is why he's different. That my emotions brought who he was back when I restored his life."

Up ahead, the light of dusk filled the landing. "But I don't think that's right."

"Why?" My leg muscles cramped, either from lack of use or from the tiredness Kolis had commented on.

"Because I have made myself feel those things when creating other Revenants," he explained, reaching the landing several steps before me. "And none have become like Callum, no matter what I feel or think at the time."

My lips pursed. He truly didn't know why. It was so obvious to me. What he felt when resurrecting Callum had been real. The other times? Emotions could only be faked to a point, and even if one managed to convince others of it, even themself, it didn't make the emotion real. I knew that better than anyone.

But Kolis? He may have understood emotion at one time, but he didn't now.

"Either way," Kolis said, facing me, "I suppose it is a blessing. I prefer my Revenants the way they are."

Of course, he did.

"You are tired," he noted as I finally reached the landing. "And out of breath."

Gods.

"It's unnecessary to point that out," I muttered. "I hate stairs."

The golden flecks in his eyes glowed. "You weren't a fan of them before, either."

Most weren't.

"But I hope you will enjoy what I have to show you." He walked out of an archway, dipping his head.

If he'd had this sanctuary built, did he not consider his height and massive head? I rolled my eyes.

Legs feeling like jelly, I followed him out onto what appeared to be a terrace—one elevated above the sanctuary wall.

Aching muscles forgotten, I crossed the patio floor and went to the waist-high balcony. I could see much of the city: the stunning crystalline towers, the circular structures with their sweeping pillars, and the shorter, squatter buildings that glittered in the fading sunlight. I looked down. Even the streets glinted.

Wordless, I turned to look behind us. There, I saw more of the glimmering buildings, the domes of Cor Palace, and eventually, the tops of the statues guarding the city and the patch of the golden trees of

Aios. That wasn't the only thing I saw, though.

Beyond the statues and trees, where a barren stretch of sandy land gave way, a thick mist smothered much of the ground that led to the mountains. A range that made the Elysium Peaks look like nothing more than hills in comparison.

It had to be the Carcers.

My breath caught as my gaze swept over the steep, slate-gray cliffs and deep, dark green, heavily forested ridges. I saw no roads in the mountains, but I caught glimpses of something darker through the trees blanketing the sides and plateaus. Patches of emptiness that absorbed what light penetrated the forest, turning those spots into abysses that glinted.

Shadowstone.

A bone-chilling screech drew my attention upward. Perched on one of the cliffs, a pale brown draken stretched its long neck, snapping at another who flew too close. Farther up, near the crest of the Carcers, two more circled.

I exhaled heavily, returning my attention to the pitch-black spots. That was where Ash was. My heart started pounding with relief and also frustration. Just witnessing where he was being held shook me, but seeing what it would take to reach him if he weren't freed was devastating.

"What do you think?" Kolis asked.

Clearing my throat, I dragged my gaze away from the mountains and back to the city—its silent buildings and empty streets. "It's beautiful," I whispered. "It looks like it's made of glass." Taking a deep breath, I looked up at him. "You said the Fates killed most who lived here?"

Kolis nodded.

"Why would they do that?" I pressed when he didn't explain. "I was under the impression they couldn't intervene in that way."

He snorted. "They can do as they please, whenever they want, especially when they believe the balance has been unsettled." His eyes tracked across the top of my head and then down my face. "And their methods of righting things can be extreme."

Thinking of what Attes had said, I looked over the narrow roads constructed of diamonds. "What were they attempting to return balance to?"

"When I took the embers of life and the crown, I gave the gods who lived here," he said, extending an arm, "within the City of the

Gods, a choice. They could serve me faithfully and loyally and live. Or they could refuse and die."

I stared at him.

"Half of them refused. I killed them," he stated, giving a slight cough as if to erase a thickness gathering in his throat. "It displeased the Arae, so they wiped out those who pledged their loyalty to me."

My stomach twisted. I would never understand how the Arae went about righting what they believed wrong, but something in his voice left me uneasy. "Do you...do you regret killing those who didn't pledge their loyalty?"

Kolis didn't answer for a long moment. "I could've sentenced them to imprisonment. Given them a chance to rethink their decisions." A muscle ticked along his jaw. "I could've given them time. I do believe life is important. I acted rashly. One would say I'm often wont to do that."

I was still staring at him. "Well, acknowledgment is half the battle," I murmured, unsure what to think of any of what had been said as I returned my gaze to the city, Cor Palace, and the Carcers.

Maybe Kolis regretted killing those gods because of how the Arae had responded. Perhaps he truly wished he'd done things differently, no matter what. Either way, he sounded as if he valued life.

And yet, I'd seen him kill so easily. That told me he didn't.

Or could it be the malevolent side of the essence of Death that caused his rashness to result in death, overriding the benevolent part? I didn't believe he had been born this way. He'd *become* like this. I would probably never know all the things that'd fed into how and why he was the way he was now, but I had a feeling going into a deep sleep would only make things worse.

I felt he was beyond reverting back to who he'd been.

And even if he could? It wouldn't undo what he'd done.

"There are times when I look at you when I see parts of how you once appeared."

My head swung back to him.

"The way you smile. The sound of your voice. Your mannerisms. Your eyes." His intense stare lowered. "The shape of your body."

Bile rose to my throat.

"But it's like all I remember was amplified. Your smiles are smaller, tighter. Your voice thicker. You are more confident in your speech and quite a bit freer with what you say. You move that way, too. There are more freckles." His gaze drifted across my chest. "More everything."

The bile increased.

"I find parts of the new you pleasing," he said, his stare lifting to my hair, and I had a sinking suspicion that I had been right about Veses already whispering in his ear. Why else would he bring that up? "Other parts, not so much. Despite what I said to Callum, I thought you would look just as I remembered."

I tensed.

He sighed heavily. "I wish you did."

I was so *fucking* glad I didn't, but that didn't stop my reaction. My brows lifted in surprise. He'd basically just told me, the one he believed was the love of his life and the person he wanted to start anew with, that he wished I looked like someone else.

Gods, and I thought I was bad when it came to interacting with people.

No one was worse than Kolis.

The skin of his forehead creased as a warm breeze carrying the stale scent of decay lifted the strands of his hair. "I believe I may have insulted you."

"Uh…"

"I'm not sure why," he said. "I didn't say I found you unattractive."

I looked back at the city. I didn't have it in me to even begin to explain all that was wrong with what he'd said.

"I've upset you." Kolis shifted closer. "How can I make it up to you?"

Gods, not this again.

"What would you like? New gowns? Books? Jewels? A pet?" He caught a curl that had been tossed across my face. His lips thinned as he tucked it back. Was *he* offended by the color? "Tell me, and I will get it for you."

I started to tell him that I wasn't offended and didn't need gowns, jewels, books, or a pet—wait.

What kind of pet?

It didn't matter. It was the other thing he'd offered.

Jewels.

The Star diamond.

My pulse picked up as an idea rapidly formed—a really poorly thought-out idea, but one nonetheless.

I turned back to the railing, placing my palm on the smooth marble. "Do you know why I find the city so beautiful?" My stomach and chest fluttered as I spoke. "It's the way it glitters. All the different shapes, some smooth, others irregular." Aware of how intently he was listening and watching, I smiled. "My mother had many jewels, mostly sapphires and rubies. Bright, perfectly polished ones. Completely unflawed—unlike me."

"How so?"

My mother did have many jewels, but most of what was coming out of my mouth now was completely made up. "The freckles." I lowered my voice, playing off what he'd said. "She found them to be too many. After all, she preferred smooth, unblemished beauty. Still, she had this one diamond that was rough-edged and irregularly shaped. It always fascinated me—all diamonds do. Is it true they were created from tears of joy?"

"Most of them."

"I wanted to wear it," I lied, having absolutely no desire to wear any jewelry. "But she would never let me touch it."

"I could retrieve it for you now," Kolis said quickly. "Tell me where it is."

Oh, shit. "I'm not sure where she keeps it now."

Determination settled into his jaw. "I can make her tell me."

Double shit. This was going sideways fast. "I'm not even sure she has it anymore." I angled my body toward his, desperate enough to get him off the idea that I placed my palm on his chest.

Kolis went completely still.

So did I, but for different reasons, as I did everything not to acknowledge how his skin felt beneath my palm. "You don't have to go to that kind of trouble, Kolis." The bile crowding my throat was back, the lump bigger than ever as I drew my fingers over the slab of muscle, stopping at the center of his chest. "Another diamond would suffice."

Kolis's chin lowered. He stared at my hand as I wondered if I'd lost my mind.

"Obviously, not one from any of the buildings." I could feel how fast his heart beat. "I would be sad if they were damaged in any way. But something large and unique would work."

"Exactly how large?" His voice had roughened. "And unique?"

How big was this Star diamond supposed to be? All I remembered was that it was jagged and what I'd heard about the color. "Well, the size doesn't matter so much as its uniqueness," I decided, feigning a sigh. "And that it has a silver sheen. Hers was so very silver and jagged." I tapped my finger against his skin and then withdrew my hand. "It doesn't matter. I don't need anything." I started to turn away.

"I know of one. It's large and irregular," he said. I might've stopped. breathing. "I believe it also has a silver sheen. It's a…rare diamond."

Slowly, I faced him. "You do?"

"Yes." He was still staring at my hands.

I returned my palm to his chest. "Can I…can I see it?"

Whirling gold and silver eyes lifted to mine.

I bit my lower lip. "I would like to see it. Hold it." I made my tone turn breathy, likely sounding ridiculous compared to how Veses naturally spoke. "Touch it."

The swirling of his eyes went crazy. "Will it make you happy?"

"Yes." I nodded, withdrawing my hand again. I clasped them at my waist. "It would."

"Then come. I'll take you to it."

My chest and stomach were still wiggling as I followed Kolis back into the sanctuary. Part of me was lost in disbelief. Could he truly be this easy to manipulate? Really?

But Ash hadn't known about the diamond. Attes had never mentioned it.

Delfai had said it was not to be known to *any* other than the Fates. Obviously, an Arae had shared the knowledge with Kolis. I'd asked Delfai how a Fate could've done that since they weren't supposed to interfere, and he'd claimed that when Primals started to feel emotion, so did the Arae. Therefore, they could be exploited, too. Who knew? Other Primals could know of its existence and what it was capable of, but there was a good chance it wouldn't even cross Kolis's mind that I was asking to see The Star.

That was if he was actually taking me to it.

I began to seriously doubt that when we ended up back outside, Elias trailing behind us on the pathway. When Dyses came into view, my hands fisted.

The door to the chamber opened, and Kolis led me inside. When he passed his throne and unlocked the cage door, my steps slowed.

"I don't understand," I said. "I thought you were showing me a diamond."

"I am." He stepped inside the cage, waiting for me at the threshold.

Forcing myself forward, I joined him. He didn't leave much room for me. My body brushed his as I passed him.

The door swung shut as he came to stand behind me. Like *right* behind me. "Look up."

Anger simmered as I did what he said. I looked up. "Yes?"

"You see it, don't you?" Kolis said.

"I don't see..." My gaze landed on the cluster of diamonds at the center of the cage. "That's a cluster of diamonds. And the sheen isn't silver." It was a strange, streaky, milky color.

Kolis chuckled. "It appears that way now, only because I've willed it to be so." Reaching around me, he lifted an arm and opened his hand. "*Vena ta mayah.*"

Recognizing the words as the language of the Primals, my lips parted as the cluster of diamonds at the ceiling of the cage started to vibrate, making a high-pitched whirring noise.

They shuddered free of the gold, and I realized that it wasn't a cluster of several but only one. The shape *changed* as it floated downward, pulsing with a milky streak of light and silver.

When it reached Kolis's hand, he held a single diamond the size of his palm, its irregular shape vaguely forming the points of a...

I couldn't believe it.

The damn diamond had been above me the whole time.

31

I stared at The Star in silence, absolutely shocked that the all-powerful diamond had been above my head for weeks.

"What do you think, so'lis?" Kolis asked. "Is this more or less than the one you once coveted?"

"More," I whispered as he turned the diamond in his hand. The sharp angles glimmered silver. "It looks like a star."

"That is what it is called," he said. "The Star."

"Oh." I feigned surprise. "It's a fitting name."

"That it is."

The heat of his chest bore down on my back as I turned slightly. "How was such a diamond created?" I asked, already knowing the answer, but I was interested to see how Kolis would respond.

"From what I understand, it was created by dragon fire." As he spoke, he drew his thumb over the diamond, and I could've sworn the sheen of silver retracted from his touch. "Long before Primals could shed tears of joy. I came upon it by pure chance."

That was exactly how Delfai had said it was created, but I knew Kolis hadn't *stumbled* upon it. "It truly is beautiful." I watched the milky light ripple through the diamond as he turned it once more. "Why would you change its appearance and keep it here, where it's hidden?"

"Because where else would I place such a beautiful stone than where

I keep what I cherish the most?"

My stomach churned at his response, but I managed a smile. "May I hold it?"

"Of course," Kolis purred.

I swallowed the sourness gathering in my mouth as he moved the diamond closer. My fingers folded around it—

A jolt danced across my fingertips the moment my skin came into contact with The Star. The rush of energy flowed over my hand and up my arm as the embers in my chest immediately thrummed to life, humming and buzzing so fast I couldn't stifle the gasp or hide how my entire body jerked.

The intense current bordered on painful as it pumped through me, forcing my hand to tighten around the surprisingly warm stone. A tremor started in my arm as the diamond heated. I tried to force my grip to loosen, but I couldn't let go of the stone, couldn't look away as its sheen intensified. The light I'd seen hadn't been a reflection. The streaks of milky, silvery-white light were *inside* the diamond. They now expanded, filling the entire stone—

Images appeared in my mind without warning, rapidly forming and flipping as if a tome of paintings. I saw a lush forest—a heavily wooded area atop a mountain—and a man caught in a windstorm with long, whipping strands of dark hair around features partially covered in russet-hued ink. And his eyes...

His eyes.

They were the color of the realms—blue, green, and brown, with stars filling his pupils. He yelled at the sky, his words lost to the wind.

Hot, violent air came from the open jaws of a massive, winged beast. A *dragon* the color of the ground and the pines its breath toppled.

Red sparked from inside the dragon's mouth, along the sides. Bright flames erupted from the majestic being, a funnel of fire that swamped the man on the mountain. And the flames kept coming, obliterating the entire crest of the peak until nothing remained where the man had stood.

Nothing but scorched earth and a diamond that sank deep into the ground, burying itself—

The images rapidly changed again. The mountain and the dragon were gone, replaced by another man, a black-haired one this time, who held the diamond just as I did, tightly, his knuckles bleached white. His arm shook as mine did. His entire body trembled as he lifted his head, shock filling his silver eyes and flickering across his broad cheekbones, slackening his wide mouth and strong jaw, paling his golden-bronze skin.

He stared at the man across from him, one with golden hair who shared his features.

I knew who I saw now.

"Nothing can erase the past," Eythos rasped.

A hand the same shade as Eythos's closed over his. "I have no interest in erasing the past. I will change the future," Kolis swore.

Their stares locked as lightning erupted above them. "Not the way you think you will," Eythos pleaded, his large body trembling as he struggled to lift his other arm and clasp the back of Kolis's neck. "Listen to me, brother. It won't bring anything but pain to the realms—to you."

"As if I don't already live with nothing but pain!" Kolis shouted. "That is all there has ever been for me."

Tears filled Eythos's eyes. "I wish nothing more than for your life to have been different. If I could change it for you, I would. I would do anything—"

"But you had your chance to make me happy. You had a choice to do anything for me, yet you refused," Kolis snarled. "And now look at us. Look at where we are!"

"I'm sorry." Eather crackled from Eythos's skin. "I am. But it's not too late to stop this. I swear to you. I can forgive you. We can start anew—"

"Forgive me?" Kolis laughed roughly as thunder roared. "Come now. You speak as if you're still capable of looking upon me as your brother. As if you could after Mycella. You've never forgiven me for her loving me."

Eythos drew back. "Never forgiven...? Brother, she once held a tender spot for you—"

"She was only with you because I wouldn't have her."

Anger flashed in the Primal's face. "Why must you say things like that?"

"It's only the truth."

"No, it's the truth you've decided to believe," Eythos shot back. "Mycella may have loved you when we were younger, and she continued caring about you until the moment you slaughtered her."

Kolis looked away, his jaw tensing.

"But she loved me, Kolis. She did not choose me because she could not have you. That is not love. What we had? What grew between us? That was love. She loved me, and I never held what she may have once felt for you against you."

"Fucking liar."

"Never!" shouted Eythos. He took a deep breath, visibly attempting to rein in his temper. "Yeah, I wasn't happy about it at first. Who would be? But I never blamed you."

Kolis scoffed. "You just cannot stop yourself from playing the role of the better one—"

"It is no role!"

"Bullshit," Kolis shouted. "You're not as good of a liar as I am. You never were. There's no coming back from this—any of this."

"But there is. There has to be. We are of the same flesh and blood. Brothers. I love you—"

"Shut up!" Kolis screamed, his other hand thrusting out.

Eythos jerked, his eyes flaring in disbelief. He looked down at a rod of dull white penetrating his chest, entering his heart.

Time seemed to stop.

The swirling wind. The building storm. Everything ceased as pure, unadulterated energy ramped up.

Kolis snapped his hand back—his bloodied hand. His mouth parted.

"I knew... I knew you were capable of this." A shudder rolled through Eythos as he lifted his gaze to his brother's. Shimmery blood leaked from his lips. "But I...I hoped I was wrong. I always...had hope."

"Eythos," whispered Kolis. He shook his head, denial etching into his features. "No. No!"

Kolis caught his brother as Eythos's legs went out from under him and then held him as energy exploded from his twin, filling the air and the realm.

The...vision or whatever it was faded away. I was still holding The Star, still staring at it, but all I saw was the red flowing down Eythos's chest. The red streaming from Kolis's eyes.

A wave of incredulity swept over me because I knew—*I knew* two things at once. "You cried."

"What?" Kolis demanded, and before I could answer, he gripped my arm and whipped me around so I faced him. Silver wisps of eather erased the flecks of gold. "What did you say?"

Oh, damn, I shouldn't have said that. Shock had gotten the better of me. "I...I don't know what you mean—"

"Don't lie to me."

"I'm not." A hiss of pain went through me as his grip tightened on my arm, stoking the already thrumming embers.

His wild stare dropped to the diamond I still held. He sucked in a sharp breath and lifted the arm of the hand that held the diamond so it was in my face. "What did you see?" Kolis shook me, causing my head to snap back and then forward again.

A burst of sharp pain radiated down my spine. My already too-tight skin prickled as I gripped his arm.

He reached across the arm holding me and pried the diamond free from my grasp, throwing it into the air. My eyes shot to it, my gaze following The Star as it returned to the cage's ceiling, once more becoming the cluster of diamonds.

The milky streaks of silvery light throbbed down upon us.

I shuddered.

Because I now knew *what* was in that diamond.

What had witnessed everything that had happened in this cage.

The center of my chest throbbed as Kolis shook me like I was nothing more than a rag doll.

Fangs protruded below his fleshless lips. "Me? The King of Gods. And you? A once frightened maiden turned whore?"

My grip on his arm loosened as I stared at him. The blank canvas was nowhere to be found as the embers inside me swelled. There was nothing but messy rage—hot, powerful fury. The edges of my vision turned white. I thrust my hands out, slamming them into his chest as power flooded my veins.

I saw a flicker of shock on Kolis's face that echoed through me before he released me. I fell to the floor, almost toppling as he skidded backward from the blast of eather. He caught himself before he slammed into the bars. There was a brief moment when I realized that I shouldn't have been able to do that to him in here, surrounded by shadowstone and the bones of the Ancients.

I shouldn't have been able to summon that storm to frighten Callum, either, but the embers…

Chest heaving, Kolis lifted his head. Through the curtain of blond hair, I saw that his eyes had turned into pools of endless nothingness, and his skin had thinned, revealing the bone beneath.

"Then you've seen death," Callum had said when I'd told him I'd seen Kolis's true form. *"True death. No one sees that and lives very long afterward."*

Panting, I took a step back, bumping into the wooden column at the foot of the bed.

"What did I tell you about using those embers?" he seethed.

Warning bells went off, kicking off instincts that told me I was in danger. My gaze flicked to the closed cage door. I pushed off the column—

Kolis was on me before I took an actual step, his hand at my throat again. Gasping for any breath possible, I clutched his arm as he abruptly pulled me away from the column and lifted me into the air. My eyes went wide as my feet dangled.

"I want you to remember one thing." There wasn't a strip of flesh left on his face. "Do not blame me for my actions. You caused this."

Suddenly, the pressure around my throat was gone. There was a moment of confusion as I found myself suspended in the air, then I went flying backward.

I hit the bed hard, the soft mattress doing very little to lessen the impact. Air punched from my lungs, momentarily stunning me into immobility as Kolis *levitated*, the bones of his chest and arms becoming visible beneath the crackling eather.

Instinct took over. There would be no pacifying him. No manipulating him with kind words. I knew at the very core of my being that I needed to get away from him.

Flipping onto my stomach, I rose onto my knees, making a mad scramble for the other side of the bed. The distance wouldn't do much, but—

I shouted as Kolis was suddenly behind me, shoving me flat onto my stomach. There was no time for me to react. He grabbed hold of my hair, yanking my head back so far that I thought my spine would crack. I saw The Star above me, silvery light racing across it. Fury crashed into the building panic as Kolis forced my head to the side. I tried to get my hands under me and push up, to move him off me, but he was too heavy and strong.

"Get off me!" I screamed.

His weight kept me flat, and the feeling of him against me, against my backside, was unbearable, robbing the breath from my lungs. I couldn't breathe.

Panic exploded in my gut then, so all-consuming and intense that the golden cage around me vanished for an instant, replaced by the bare stone walls of my bedchamber in Wayfair. It wasn't Kolis bearing down on me, it was Tavius. I was *there*. I was *here*. Trapped. Unable to breathe. Unable to do anything to protect myself against my stepbrother or against Kolis as his breath coasted over my exposed throat. I knew his fangs would soon tear into my skin. And I also knew it wouldn't stop there. Not this time.

There was nothing I could do. I was weaponless. Powerless. Nothing I did would change that. No amount of training or preparation would help. But those embers...

They belonged to the Primal of Life.

And they now belonged to me.

They were powerful enough for Rhain to tell me to bring the building down. They were formidable enough to restore life, to break through the negating effects of shadowstone. My wild gaze landed on the bars.

"Clearly, the bones of the Ancients can be destroyed," I'd said to Attes.

"Only by two Primals."

The Primal of Death.

And the Primal of Life.

My heart thudded as Kolis twisted my head back. I saw The Star once more.

The embers of the Primal of Life were capable of so much, but my will…

My will was capable of *anything*.

Because I was not weak.

I was not powerless.

The embers hummed. The sharp glide of Kolis's fangs scraped my throat. I wouldn't let this happen. I refused to.

I didn't lose control.

I fucking *took* it.

Summoning the essence to the surface, I welcomed the heady rush of power as it poured into my chest and veins. I embraced the all-consuming rage that I'd pushed down when he held me at night, when I realized he'd manipulated me into killing Evander, when I smiled at him and thanked him for his hollow compliments, when he offered me to Kyn, when he bit me and found pleasure doing so, and so many other times. I let in the fury that had been building in me for the days, weeks, months, and years that had ticked by, and the centuries that didn't belong to me. As my vision turned silver, I felt Sotoria rise inside me, and it was she who screamed, "Get off us!"

Kolis froze against me.

The burst of power rippled out from me in every direction, throwing the false King off me. I heard him hit the bars this time, his grunt of surprise giving way to a sound of pain.

Energy and essence pumped through my muscles, lighting up every cell in my being, and I knew then that I was truly more than just a few embers.

I was them.

They were me.

What I wanted. What I thought.

It became reality.

In the blink of an eye, I was on my feet, but I didn't run for the door. Slowly, I turned to where Kolis now stood. He was more bones than flesh.

Death stood before me.

But I was Life.

"Us?" he whispered.

Eather roared to the surface of my skin, spinning down my arms. Screaming, I threw my hands out to either side. Another blast of energy left me, evaporating the divan and the table. The bed rose as an area rug and stacks of untouched books crumbled. The privacy screen collapsed as everything not bolted down in the bathing chamber took to the air. I caught sight of the damn key I'd hidden away but never had a chance to use. It disintegrated. The gilded bars exploded, sending shards flying outward.

"I am done with this," I whispered—or screamed, I couldn't be sure. However loud it was, eather filled my voice, and it sounded like air that carried the winds of time, rushing beyond the half-destroyed cage and speeding into the chamber beyond. The throne Kolis had sat upon shattered into dust as the essence—as my *will*—poured from the narrow windows along the ceiling.

Kolis stumbled, the abyss of his eyes sparking gold and silver, but I didn't see him. He wasn't important as I held on to my will, picturing the silvery strands of eather stretching above the sanctuary and whipping outward, racing through the empty streets and between the sparkling buildings, past Cor Palace and the glittering wall of diamond and marble. I saw the winged statues guarding Dalos, and because I was feeling petty, I turned them to dust. Then I saw the mountains I'd looked upon earlier. I focused on the spots of darkness—the shadowstone—as I summoned the tendrils of throbbing power. They blanketed the foot of the Carcers like a silvery web before spreading up the sides of the mountain and winding their way through the maze of trees, finding the targets of shadowstone and blowing straight through them—through all the walls, floors, ceilings, and the chains within them.

At the end of the tendrils of eather I sent out, I saw eather-streaked silver eyes snap open.

And I smiled.

Kolis's head jerked to the right, his jaw clenching as if he sensed what I'd done.

Who I'd freed.

His stare whipped back to me, and, yeah, he knew who was coming. Kolis had to feel the ice-drenched rage hit the air high above Dalos, fueling an unthinkable power, because I could.

A drop of blood hit the bodice of my gown as I shifted my focus to Kolis. The back of my skull tingled as the essence throbbed through what remained of the cage. Chests toppled. Gauzy gowns of white and gold lifted into the air, whirling around us like dancing spirits.

Kolis's flesh reappeared as he returned to his mortal form. "*Us?*" he repeated.

"Shut up." Eather surged, and I latched on to the power—*my* power. Crackling and spitting eather erupted from my fingertips, taking shape in my hand, stretching and lengthening into the thunderbolt I'd created before. My fingers closed around the humming mass of energy.

Kolis's eyes widened. "Don't."

"Fuck you." I threw the bolt as if it were a dagger.

And I rarely missed when I threw a blade.

I didn't this time, either.

The lightning bolt struck true, knocking him off his feet and throwing him through the hole in the cage behind him. He hit the floor and rolled several feet.

I walked forward, lifting my hands. What remained of the gilded bones rose into the air all around me, mostly just tiny shards with a few the length of my hand or slightly longer.

Kolis shot to his feet, the skin of his chest charred and smoking. His lip curled as his chin dipped. "You don't want to do this."

I glanced to my left. "But I do."

His gaze followed mine to the shards. "Fuck."

He darted to the side, escaping the full brunt of what I sent at him, but several embedded themselves in his stomach and thighs. His head lifted as he grabbed one in his stomach, his face grimacing from the pain. "Stop this now."

"Stop?" I laughed as a draken's roar ended in a yelp in the distance.

"Yes. It's not too late—"

"Do you swear that to me? That you can forgive me?" As I stepped out of the cage, silky material swirled around me, snagging on the shredded bones. "That we can start anew?"

Confusion flickered across Kolis's features as he blinked. "Yes."

I laughed as a thunderous roar of rage neared. "Come now, you speak as if you're capable of still looking upon me as...*her*," I said, changing only that in what he'd said to Eythos. "You're not as good of a liar as I am."

Kolis went still.

"You never were." I walked through the spinning gowns. "There's no coming back from this—any of this."

Disbelief gave way to a mess of emotions I'd never seen on his handsome face before. Horror. Sorrow. *Regret.* "You saw..."

A longer piece of bone flew forward. Kolis lurched to the left, but his shock cost him. It got him in the shoulder, dragging him down to the floor.

My hand snapped out, catching one of the bones. The contact burned my hand as I prowled toward him, but I held on. The pain was worth it. "You didn't believe Eythos when he said he loved you."

Kolis struggled with the bone jutting from his skin, his wild gaze darting to the one in my hand.

"That is why you stabbed him. You didn't think it would kill him. A wound to the heart wouldn't have done that—not even with one of these." I kicked his hand away, then slammed my foot onto his arm, pinning it down. "But he was weakened, wasn't he?"

Kolis stared up at me as if I was a spirit he'd known had been haunting him but hadn't been able to see until now. "I...I didn't know he had removed the last embers from himself. If I had—"

"If you had, you wouldn't have...what? Killed him by accident?"

A heavy breath shuddered from Kolis. "I...I didn't mean to." His eyes were so wide, so full of gold, that for a moment he didn't look like the false King of Gods, but a man who had made many mistakes. "Because how could he love me?"

"Good question. I suppose your brother was a much more forgiving being than the rest of us. Definitely better than me," I said, kneeling so I hovered over him but kept his arm pinned. "I want you to remember one thing, Kolis."

Understanding dawned in his features, his gaze going to the bone I held.

"I want nothing more than to kill you."

Kolis went completely still beneath me. He didn't attempt to throw me off or defend himself. There was a flash of something akin to acceptance, and in the back of my mind, I thought maybe he wanted this. That he finally knew his actions had caused him to lose who he believed to be Sotoria, and death would now come as a relief.

It would've been sad if he weren't such a bastard.

I drove the bone down onto his chest, into his heart and against the floor, jerking his entire body. I tore it free and thrust it down again and again, turning his breaths into nothing but gurgles. I counted as I had after he'd bitten me and kept stabbing Kolis. I counted as I had when I'd sat in that bath as I drove the bone into his throat, head, and stomach.

One.

Two.

Three.

Four.

Five.

Blood covered my hands and spotted my arms and cheeks as I slammed the bone into his heart again. My arms shook. My body trembled.

Then I felt *him*.

Sucking in a few too-shallow breaths, I yanked my aching hands free from the bone, leaving it buried deeply in what turned out to be a highly sensitive part of him. I crawled off Kolis, scooting back against the floor until I hit the legs of a chair, the still-spinning gowns falling all around me. I stared at the closed chamber doors.

Why hadn't Kolis's guards entered?

It didn't matter.

Pain pierced my temples and lanced across my jaw, slowly fading into a dull ache. Panting, I closed my eyes and focused on the embers. The eather throbbed inside me, in my veins and bones, no longer contained to just my chest. They were weaker than before—way weaker—but I pulled on them as I struggled to breathe. I wanted to see him. I needed to because the feel of the hot essence in my veins was likely significant. Final. A spasm ran through me as I remembered what Ash had told me about the essence. That it was my will.

So, I used it to give me what I wanted.

A weightless sensation settled over me, almost as if my consciousness were leaving my body. I became a wraith that floated through the windows in the ceiling and drifted across the empty breezeway, through Kolis's chamber and into the corridors, tethered to the wispy fingers of eather that searched and searched—

Until I found him.

Ash.

He stalked the halls of the sanctuary, his leather pants tattered and hanging low on his hips. His skin was ashen, those savagely beautiful features—broad cheekbones and strong brow—sharper than ever before. Dirt smudged his abdomen, where the packed muscles stood out more starkly, proof that he hadn't eaten anything substantial in weeks.

But Ash had been feeding.

Blood dripped over the defined lines of his chest, drenching his throat and smearing his wide mouth.

A guard raced out from one of the halls, charging the Primal, the gold of his armor glinting in the fading sunlight.

Ash caught his arm before the sword blow could land. "Where is she?"

"Fuck you," the guard snarled, but he quaked as he did so, his body revealing his fear.

"Wrong answer." Ash snapped his arm in two.

The god howled as the sword clanged off the floor. Ash was as fast as the crack of a whip, tearing into the god's throat. He drank deeply and fast before lifting his head.

I supposed that was...fast food?

Two guards spilled into the hall. Someone threw a shadowstone short sword.

Ash twisted, using the guard he held as a shield. The god's body jerked as he took the blade in the back.

Flipping the god around, Ash tore the sword free, letting the body fall to the floor. A bolt of eather streaked through the hall as another guard rushed him. I saw a flash of pale blue eyes. A Revenant. Ash shadowstepped to his right, avoiding the blast of energy. He threw the sword, striking the god in the head as silvery streaks of eather fizzled out. Spinning, Ash caught the Revenant by the throat, tearing the dagger from its hand. "Where is she?"

The Revenant grunted something I couldn't make out. Whatever it was, Ash wasn't impressed.

He slammed the dagger into the Revenant's chest, then tore out his throat, ripping the *spine* out through the gaping hole. He tossed the still-twitching body aside.

"Where is she?" he repeated over and over, leaving a trail of armored bodies in his wake, some that would wake up, others that wouldn't. He passed quiet alcoves, their golden, gauzy curtains rippling gently.

Several guards appeared. Shadows rose from the floor, swirling around Ash's leather-clad legs. "Where is she?"

"Back in the north wing, beyond his chambers," a god answered, dropping his sword. "You follow this hall. You'll enter His Majesty's personal chambers. That is where she is kept." He lifted his hands as he took a step back. "We didn't—"

"I don't care." Ash turned his head toward him. That was it. Just a look, and the god halted. His back bowed, his body going rigid. He rose into the air, and his mouth stretched open as cracks appeared in his flesh. Eather poured from the suspended god as Ash shifted his attention to those ahead. The god shattered into shimmery dust.

Several other gods began backing away.

"Run," Ash spoke, his voice calling the shadows from the walls and the alcoves. "But you won't get far."

The gods spun and ran.

Whatever circumstances had led to them siding with Kolis or any remorse these gods felt wouldn't save them. As Ash had warned, they didn't make it far.

The whirling midnight mist whipped out, racing across the floor. All around, gods rose to the ceiling, their arms outstretched, and heads thrown back. Armor exploded from their chests and calves. From the center of their midsections, a silver glow pulsed as they hung in the air like paper lanterns. Then they fell like stars.

A swarm of dakkais erupted from a corridor and entered the hall, their gaping mouths full of blade-sharp teeth. Either drawn by the eather or sent due to Ash's presence, they shoved into one another, growling and snapping at the air as they raced toward Ash.

There wasn't even time to feel concern because Ash was very, *very* well-fed at the moment.

Tendrils of shadowy eather lifted once more, streaking out from Ash and slamming into the dakkais, piercing their bodies. Sharp yelps ended suddenly, one after another, until there was nothing before Ash.

Startling sharp pain flared once more, shaking my concentration. It severed the connection, and I suddenly no longer felt as if I were floating.

I pitched forward onto my palms as I heaved, dragging up nothing but air and the faint taste of something metallic. Through the tangled strands of my hair, I stared at my hands—my left one looked as if the pores had filled with faint silver light. Nausea rose, and I gagged, my stomach clenching. Though my eyes were closed, the chamber felt as if it were spinning.

I didn't feel right. My head. My body. I felt too loose, yet too tight. There was a strange hollowness in my chest, one that felt *final*. My arms and legs trembled from the effort it took to keep myself upright. Sweat dampened my skin as if I had a rising and breaking fever.

The embers suddenly hummed in my chest as my right hand *warmed*. Blinking stinging tears from my eyes, I looked down. The swirl across the top of my hand shimmered brightly.

He was almost here.

My arms gave out. Suddenly, my cheek was plastered against the cool shadowstone tile, and gods, it felt good against my hot skin. My eyes drifted shut as I thought I heard shouts, but I couldn't be sure. My heartbeat was in my ears. A loud crash came from somewhere, the sound of doors slamming into walls and shattering. Charged air stirred around me, then blissfully cold fingers touched my cheeks. I was lifted and brought against something cool and solid. Safe. The scent of citrus and fresh air enveloped me, and a breathy sigh left me.

"*Liessa*," Ash spoke, his rough voice a balm. "I've got you. Everything will be all right now. I've got you."

32

I've got you.

Three short, simple words, yet they shook me to my core.

"Open your eyes, *liessa*." Ash pulled me tighter to his chest as he rocked back.

Fighting the bone-deep exhaustion, I opened my eyes. Everything was blurry at first, but my vision soon cleared. Crimson stained the lower half of his face, but the blood did nothing to mar the striking lines and angles of his features. The harsh shadows under his eyes weren't so unforgiving, having faded between the time I'd lost my connection through the essence and now.

"There you are." Ash smiled, but it was tight and strained as he brushed strands of my hair back from my face. I saw his lips move before I heard him speak. It was as if my mind was on some kind of delay. "Talk to me."

I swallowed, wincing at the dull ache in my throat. I struggled to concentrate on him. "You—"

A roll of rumbling thunder came from outside—somewhere close. I stiffened. The sky beyond the narrow windows flashed an intense silver. That wasn't thunder and lightning.

"It's okay," Ash assured me as distant shouts turned to quickly silenced screams. "It's Nektas. He felt it the moment I got free."

Nektas was here? Who was he burning—?

A high-pitched yelp came, causing me to flinch. The entire sanctuary shook as something large landed nearby.

I now knew what Nektas was burning.

Other draken.

"You're safe." Ash caught my wide stare. "Talk to me, *liessa*. Please."

"You found me."

"Always." Eather-laced eyes swept over my features before they slammed shut. His chest rose, and then he looked at me again. "I will *always* find you, Sera."

Tears immediately rushed my eyes, stinging them. Drawing in a breath filled with his scent, I lifted a tingling arm and grasped the back of his neck, catching strands of hair between my fingers.

"But I didn't find you." Ash dragged his thumb over the curve of my jaw. "You found me. My beautiful, strong Consort. You ended this nightmare."

I had, hadn't I?

But didn't that sound too good to be true? That I'd stopped Kolis before he...destroyed me in ways I wasn't sure I would recover from? That I finally understood the full extent of how powerful the embers were and freed Ash from his prison?

My breath hitched.

I could see and feel him, but everything felt surreal—from the moment I'd touched The Star until this very second. It didn't feel real.

What if this—all of this—was one of those too-real dreams? Panic slithered up my spine. What if I hadn't stopped Kolis and had instead retreated far into my mind? Heart tripping, I turned my head to the side. My gaze skipped over small shards of gilded bone, swaths of fine cream and gold silk, and a wide pool of shimmery red-blue blood.

Kolis lay on the floor, his arms widespread. His face and throat were a mangled mess. So were other parts of him. A gilded bone jutted from his chest—from his heart—but that wasn't where my stare lingered. It shifted back to his arms.

Arms he hadn't lifted to defend himself. He'd gone still when I said I was going to kill him. I thought I'd seen...*acceptance* settle into his features. Maybe even a glimpse of...*peace*.

That couldn't be right. It sounded like something my imagination would cook up. I sucked in a shallow breath as a draken's growl grew closer.

"Is this...?" I rasped, my throat scratchy and hoarse. "Is this a dream?"

"No, *liessa*." Ash guided my attention from Kolis with a gentle press of his fingers against my cheek. Tension bracketed his mouth. "This is not a dream. It's real. I'm here. We're not at your lake."

A shudder of relief coursed through me as Ash's confirmation scattered the remaining fuzziness from my mind. So many things rushed me at once—stuff I needed to be concerned about, but the only thing I cared about was *him*. "Are you okay?"

"Am I...?" A shaky laugh parted his lips as he shook his head. "I can't believe you're asking if I'm okay."

"You've been imprisoned," I pointed out, drawing in another deep breath. I didn't feel like I needed to vomit, but the exhaustion remained, and I thought—

No, I *knew* what that meant.

I did.

A strange sense of calmness descended over me. My chest loosened. Resolve filled me. I needed to get up. We had to get out of here because someone, or multiple someones, were bound to arrive. And if someone removed that bone from Kolis, he would awaken. And then...

Everything would get really bad, really fast, because Kolis would know the truth—that I wasn't Sotoria.

Even if that didn't happen, Nektas's fight could end up on top of the sanctuary, and there were innocent people like the Chosen here. I tried to sit up, but Ash's arms were like steel bands around me.

"And you haven't been?" Ash's hand slid to the nape of my neck. The coolness of his fingers was pure bliss against the tight muscles.

"I've had it much easier," I said, though the talk of imprisonment made me think of another. "Veses is free. I don't know how."

"With me being in stasis, the wards on the cells would've weakened," he said. "Are you sure you're fine?"

"Yes," I assured him as he tilted my head back. "But what if she hurt someone—?"

"You are not fine." His nostrils flared.

The air in the chamber suddenly thinned, charging with energy. The tiny hairs on my arms lifted as the embers in my chest thrummed faintly in response to the power pouring from...

"Ash?" I whispered.

Shadows appeared, whirling beneath his flesh in a dizzying rush as his eyes filled with tendrils of crackling eather—eyes that were focused not on mine but on my throat.

My heart thudded heavily. The memory of Kolis's fangs scraping against the skin of my throat sent a wave of revulsion through me. He must've broken the skin. That would explain the dull pain there.

Ash's head lifted, his attention shifting beyond me to where Kolis lay. His lips peeled back, revealing his fangs. He started to lower me to the floor. "I'm going to destroy him."

My breath snagged in my chest. With the eather lighting up the veins of his, cutting through the whipping shadows there, and the darkness gathering on the floor, I thought there might be a good chance he could, in fact, do that, especially given Kolis's state. As Kolis himself had said: His nephew was very powerful. But...

But Kolis couldn't die.

I'd known that when I drove the bone through his heart. My hold on Ash tightened as I willed myself to be, for once in my life, the smarter, more logical one. "Let it go."

Ash tensed against me as a thick mass of midnight whipped around us. "What?"

"Let it go," I repeated, tugging on his hair until his gaze returned to mine. I could barely see the pupils in his eyes. "He's not worth it."

"Worth what, exactly?" he snarled. "Because right now, anything and everything is worth ending the bastard's existence."

"The end of the realms?" I reasoned.

His eyes narrowed. "I don't give a fuck about the realms."

A quick, hoarse laugh left me. "Yes, you do." I took a deep breath to clear my mind more. "You care about the realms."

"You give me too much credit, *liessa*," he said. "You think of me too kindly."

"You don't give yourself *enough* credit," I shot back.

Two clouds of shadowy eather rose behind him, taking the faint shape of wings. "I've told you this before. Any and all decent bones I have in me belong to you."

"And I've told *you* before, that isn't true."

"Do not argue with me, Sera." His body hummed with vicious power as the shadows in his skin melded. Somewhere in the chamber, something cracked loudly. "Not about this."

"I'm not arguing with you!"

He glared, and I could've sworn he was counting to ten. "I don't think you understand what the word *argue* means."

"I don't think *you* understand what it—"

"He bit you!" Ash roared, causing my body to jolt as the shadow wings slammed down onto the floor, shaking the entire chamber.

I sucked in a sharp breath, resisting the urge to touch my neck. "He didn't. I stopped him this—" I stopped myself before I said more and made things worse. "I stopped him."

"This time?" Ash's voice dropped to a whisper of such cold death that even I shivered. "That is what you meant to say."

"No."

"Do not lie to me."

"I'm not lying," I lied.

Shadows spread up his throat, cresting his jaw. "Do you think I don't know what has been done to you?" The air turned freezing. "What he's done?"

I locked up as I felt the blood racing from my face. Every muscle had gone rigid, and it had nothing to do with the iciness of the chamber. "No," I said, and I wasn't exactly sure who I was saying that to. Him? Me? Both of us? Either way, he couldn't know. I needed to believe that. Ash only suspected things based on his knowledge of Kolis.

Ash shuddered as he stared down at me. "I'm going to *eviscerate* him," he swore in that icy, shadowy whisper that I bet whipped through the Abyss. "I will tear his head from his shoulders and rip him limb from limb, scattering what remains across the realms."

My brows knitted as something occurred to me. "Actually, that doesn't sound like a bad plan."

"Then do not argue with me, *liessa*." His arms loosened around me, and my rear was once more touching the floor.

I gripped his shoulders. "That's not what I meant."

Those smoky wings swept up again. "Do you think I cannot see?"

"I'm thinking that's a rhetorical question since you obviously can."

"I can," he confirmed, and I rolled my eyes. "I see how he has you dressed."

I rolled my eyes right back at him.

"I see what state you're in."

What state...? Looking down, I saw that the fragile material of the gown had torn at the neck. By some miracle, my chest wasn't exposed—well, *more* exposed than it already had been.

"Do you think I don't know what it must've taken for you to tap into the essence like that?"

"If you ask me one more question that you clearly think you know the answer to..." I muttered.

"To wield it to such an extent, do this to him, and free me?" he continued, ignoring me. "And did you forget that I could feel you? Sense what you were feeling?"

Oh.

Oh, no.

My lips parted as he confirmed my worst fears.

"Every time I was conscious, I felt you. Your pain. Your fear. The panic. The fucking *desperation*." The walls rattled as that frosted whisper circled the chamber, falling against the floor like hail and sleet. I knew it wasn't Nektas or any other draken doing that. "Your anger? I felt it all. Tasted everything you were feeling until I was drowning in it. Until I tore at my flesh to get to you." His voice cracked then, and so did the wall behind him. "And I could do nothing—fucking *nothing*—to protect you. To take away any of the horror you were experiencing."

Pressure clamped down on my chest. Oh, gods, I hadn't wanted him to feel that—any of it. It was the one thing I'd believed the stasis had prevented. My skin suddenly felt too tight, and I wanted to close my eyes and crawl inside myself. But I couldn't look away from Ash.

I stared at him, realizing I'd been wrong when I believed I'd seen those Primal embers of death come out in him before. I really hadn't. Not until now. I'd seen glimpses of them when he killed Tavius's guards and the gods who came into the Shadowlands for me. I'd seen hints of it when he battled the entombed gods in the Red Woods. And later as he struck the draken, Davon, from the sky and *laughed*. I'd seen some of it when he killed Hanan and fought Kolis, but I *truly* saw it now.

Ash didn't do that freaky turn-to-a-skeleton thing that Kolis did. He didn't need the dramatics because each word he spoke carried the weight of a thousand cold, empty graves and the promise of endless death in the Abyss.

Once more, I realized there was a good chance Sotoria wasn't needed. Ash could take out Kolis, but without there being a true Primal of Death? Whether or not Ash took the embers, the balance Kolis had harped about would be upset in ways that would result in unfathomable destruction.

So even though I wanted nothing more than to cave to the pressure and desire to get up and run, putting as much distance between what Ash possibly knew and me, I couldn't.

This was bigger than me. More important. I had to pull it together because we didn't have much time. I could feel that, despite doing my level best to ignore it. I counted as I'd done before.

One.

Two.

Three.

Four.

Five.

I lifted a trembling hand from Ash's shoulder and touched his cheek. Nothing of the golden-bronze flesh was visible now, and his jaw was hard as granite beneath my palm. "I want nothing more than his death," I said. "But he can't die. You have to know that, right? This whole time, you had to know he couldn't be killed. Not by anyone. Not even Sotoria."

Ash said nothing as the wings behind him thickened, but I knew I was right. He had to know the Primal of Death must always be. Just as the Primal of Life must.

"I know you care about the realms," I told him. "Even if you didn't, I *do*. I care about my sister and Marisol. The people of Lasania, and the rest of the mortal realm. Even my mother."

His head straightened. "Your mother?" he snarled. "Fuck her."

My lips twitched, but I stopped myself from smiling. I didn't think that would help things at the moment. "We need to get out of here, Ash." I swallowed again, but it did little to end the soreness in my throat. I glanced at Kolis's still body.

There were many reasons we needed to leave, starting with Ash's wrath toward his uncle. It was so intense it would lead to nothing but ruin, and if he let himself cave to it, he would regret it. He didn't think that now, but I knew he would, and I couldn't let that happen. I refused to allow another regret to stain his soul.

But that wasn't the only reason.

"We need to get somewhere safe," I continued. "And you need to take the embers before it's too late."

The muscle along his jaw throbbed under my palm. A long, tense moment passed, and then the shadows began to break apart, scattering to disappear beneath his flesh. Something I'd said must have gotten through to him.

"Okay?" I said.

Ash nodded as the shadow wings faded away, but his gaze left mine and returned to Kolis. I thought I heard something then.

Footsteps? Before I could look, Ash's arms clamped down on me. One second, I was sitting on the floor, loosely held in his embrace. The next, I was on my feet, his arms holding me up and close to him. The movement had my stomach turning as his head cut toward the door. A low growl rumbled from his chest.

"Your Majesty?" came a voice it took me a moment to recognize. Elias.

Willing my stomach to stop rolling, I twisted toward the doors as they swung open, one side falling half off damaged hinges.

Elias drew up short, his golden eyes flipping from Kolis to Ash, then to me. "Is she okay?"

All that rage directed toward Kolis shifted to the god in the entranceway. A low rumble of warning came from him. "What did you ask?"

"I mean her no harm," Elias insisted, stepping back. But based on what I'd seen Ash do in the halls of the sanctuary, I knew that would do the god no good.

Shadows spilled from Ash, slipping over me harmlessly as they rose, preparing to strike at Elias. The god would not survive that. One of the tendrils snaked across the floor. I didn't think Ash intended for Elias to survive, but...

"Don't." My fingers pressed into Ash's chest. "Don't harm him."

Ash pulled the smoky eather back, but he didn't take his attention off the god. "Do you make this request because you wish to have the honor of doing so?"

"That's actually kind of sweet of you to think," I said, patting his chest.

The painted wings above Elias's brows seemed to lift.

"But, no." I stared at the god. The shadowstone sword he held was slick with shimmery blood. My gaze lifted to his painted face. I thought of the advice he'd offered instead of how he'd knocked me out.

Before any of us could respond, I saw a flash of deep gray scales, and the entire chamber trembled as Nektas landed outside. At the other end of the breezeway, guards spilled out from the doors to Kolis's chamber. The one spiked tail whipped across the breezeway as only half of Nektas's horned head came into view, his massive jaws opening.

A funnel of silver fire erupted, streaming over the guards. They lit up like dry tinder, dropping their swords as their screams pierced the air.

"Or perhaps you'd prefer that Nektas burn him?" Ash suggested, his frozen-over stare still focused on Elias.

"Uh, no to that, too." I cringed as one of the gods flailed about, swallowed by the silver flames. "At least, not yet."

"And what is your reasoning for this, *liessa*?" Streaks of eather lit up the veins of his cheeks. "The realms will not suffer the loss of one more god."

Damn.

I glanced at Ash, feeling an almost unfamiliar rush of heat. He was...*savage* when angry, and I found it, even amidst all of this, really arousing.

For once, I didn't think that should disturb me as Ash *finally* pulled his attention from Elias. He looked down at me. One of his brows rose as warm wisps of eather stirred in his eyes. Realizing he likely sensed my desire, I found I wasn't embarrassed. I was...gods, I was so relieved to feel that warmth swamping my veins. So damn ecstatic. Because in this moment, as I stared up at him, I felt normal.

Well, as normal as I'd ever felt. And it was because of him... Ash helped me feel that way. My chest swelled with emotion, momentarily filling the gnawing hollowness growing there.

"I love you," I whispered.

The change in Ash was swift. His features softened as his chest rose against mine. "*Liessa...*"

Eyes stinging, I looked away before I started sobbing all over him. There was no time for that. I refocused on Elias, who looked slightly confused and also a little relieved. I then looked past him to Nektas. There had to be a reason he wasn't charbroiling the god. "Do you...do you serve Kolis, Elias?"

"I serve the Primal of Life," Elias answered.

"There's your answer," Ash stated, his brief warmth dissipating. "He will die, too."

"I misspoke," Elias amended as he lowered himself to one knee.

My heart thumped heavily in my chest. "Not this again."

Ash frowned.

"I serve the *true* Primal of Life." Crossing his sword over his chest, he bowed his head.

"It *is* this again," I muttered as Ash eyed the god.

"With my sword and my life." Elias lifted his head. "I swear to you, the One who is born of Blood and Ash, *the* Light and the Fire, and *the* Brightest Moon, to honor your command."

Ash stiffened. "You're pledging yourself to Seraphena?"

Elias nodded.

"It's just the embers," I explained, the dull ache returning to my temples as I wondered if Elias was working alone against Kolis, with a Primal like Attes, or possibly even Keella, who clearly was not a Kolis fan. "That's what he's swearing his allegiance to."

"No." Ash's brows knitted, then he angled his body toward me. His gaze swept over me. "It's you."

I opened my mouth, but I didn't get a chance to argue the semantics of the god's loyalty. Ash dipped his head, kissing me, and honest to gods, the entire chamber disappeared around us because his mouth was on mine, and I didn't care that I could taste the blood of those he'd fed on. I'd feared I would never feel this again. That I would leave Iliseeum, never to experience the touch of his lips on mine outside of a dream again.

Ash lifted his mouth from mine, whispering, "Tell him to rise, *liessa*."

Feeling even more weak-kneed, I blinked. "Huh?"

His lips curved against mine. "He's still kneeling."

"Oh." I cleared my throat. "You can rise."

There was a hint of a smile on Elias's face as he stood. "I've sent word to Attes," Elias said, answering my question of who he was working with. "He is coming—"

The center of my chest lit up as Ash tensed beside me. "I think he's already here."

Elias sighed.

"Of course, I'm already here," came the Primal's voice from outside.

A second later, he crossed into view, the breeze lifting his sandy-brown hair as he skirted Nektas. The draken tracked his movements, his crimson eyes alert.

As Attes drew closer, I saw that blood stained his armor. "I got a bit held up." He passed Elias, looking at Ash and me. "I know you two would probably like to continue this reunion, but I suggest we make haste and get out of here. I'm confident one of the gods shadowstepped their ass to Vathi to alert Kyn, and those fucking Revs you got are doing their reanimation thing. Basilia has Diaval and Sax on retreat, but that won't last long, especially if Naberius decides to..." He trailed off, coming to an abrupt halt as he got an eyeful of Kolis.

I had no idea who Basilia or Sax were, but since Attes had mentioned Diaval, I felt it safe to assume that Basilia was one of Attes's draken. Sax must be another of Kolis's.

Attes swallowed thickly as he stared at Kolis. "I was right."

Aware of the frigid air blowing off Ash, I said, "You were."

Ash's gaze cut to the false King and the gilded bone protruding from his chest. He inhaled sharply, and I figured what he saw and what it meant had finally caught up to him.

Storm-hued eyes swept to mine. "I knew it," he whispered.

"That I wasn't really her?" I asked.

"Those questions need to wait," Attes interrupted, and Ash's expression became emotionless. "You really need to get her out of here, Nyktos. She cannot be here when my brother arrives."

Ash glanced at Attes and then dipped his head, speaking into my ear. "You okay?" When I nodded, he pressed his lips to my temple. "Stay put. We'll leave here soon."

I started to frown as he released me. My legs felt a little wobbly, so it took some effort to keep that from showing as Ash strode away from me.

Attes faced him. "Nyktos, I know you likely don't trust me, but I have never been loyal to Kolis."

"Is that so?" Ash said, his voice soft.

Warning bells immediately went off. When he spoke like that, things got bloody.

"Your father was like a brother to me—even to Kyn at one time. I would never truly stand behind Kolis after that. I did everything I could to run interference and protect what your father planned. You have to know that deep down—"

That was all he got to say before Ash's fist slammed into the Primal's jaw. My eyes went wide as Attes staggered back.

"Uh," I murmured as Elias shifted nervously by the doorway.

I wasn't sure what propelled the god's anxiety more: the two Primals or Nektas's entire head right behind him. Smoke wafted from the draken's nostrils as he blew out a breath.

"Fuck." Attes spat blood. "Okay. I deserved that."

Tendrils of eather-laced shadows gathered at Ash's feet as he grabbed hold of Attes's breastplate, dragging the Primal to him. They were nearly eye to eye, and I thought I should intervene, but Attes was right. He *had* deserved that, but...

"Attes can be trusted," I said.

"He had better hope so," Ash said, and I heard the smile in his voice. It wasn't a friendly one. "You and I?" There wasn't even an inch of space between their faces. "We're going to have a little chat."

Holding Ash's glare, Attes nodded. "Yeah, we will, but not here. If Kyn arrives, he'll—"

"I know what he'll do," Ash snarled, and my knees locked. "So you know what I'm going to do."

"I do." Attes's voice had roughened, and his gaze darted to where I stood.

My knees unlocked, and I started toward them. "We should—" A wave of hot dizziness hit me, immediately causing a fine sheen of sweat to break out across my forehead. The entire chamber seemed to tilt, and I squeezed my eyes shut as my stomach churned.

"Dear Fates," Attes rasped.

Ash was at my side in a heartbeat, one hand on my shoulder to steady me. "Sera?" His cool palm cupped my cheek. "Talk to me."

I clamped my jaw shut, fighting the rise of nausea as I focused on the relief his cold touch brought forth.

"Is it your breathing?" Ash's voice dropped to a whisper, and he stepped into me.

Gods, the fact that he'd even thought of that and made sure only I could hear him... I inhaled through my nose as the nausea receded. "No, I...I was just dizzy." I opened my eyes to see his concerned stare latched on to me. "I'm fine."

"No, you're not." Attes's voice was closer.

Ash's head snapped to him. "Do you want to get punched again?"

"Not particularly," the Primal responded, his skin blanching. "You saw what I did."

"What did you see?" I demanded, glancing between them. Neither answered. "What?"

"You appeared as if you were shifting," Elias answered as the distant, angry roar of a draken sounded.

"Shifting?" I said while Nektas pulled his head from the breezeway, scanning the sky. "Into what? Someone wearing more clothing?"

A dimple appeared as Attes cracked a grin. It was probably a good thing Ash hadn't seen that.

"We could see the embers." Ash tucked a strand of my hair back. "In your flesh. But only for a few seconds."

"Oh," I whispered, thinking of the tiny dots of silvery light I'd seen in my skin.

"You... You looked beautiful," Ash said, a flicker of awe crossing his features before concern settled in his gaze. "We need to leave."

Wordlessly, I nodded as I glanced over at Attes. The concern was evident on his face, too, but I knew it wasn't reserved only for me. I swallowed, searching for Sotoria's presence. I... I felt her where the embers *had* been, quiet but aware.

"But we also need time," Ash went on. "As much time as possible with Kolis out of commission."

Elias jerked his chin at Kolis. "I can get him out of here. Hide him and make his recovery a bit more...taxing." A brutal smile appeared, and I had a feeling a *taxing* recovery involved growing back limbs. "His loyalists will be concerned only with finding him. That will give you some time."

"Not a lot," Attes warned.

My heart turned over heavily as I thought about everything I wanted to do in this *not-a-lot-of* time. All I wanted to experience. A knot lodged in my throat. This was yet another thing I couldn't think about.

"Is that what you want done?" Elias asked.

Silence greeted him as I waited for Ash or Attes to answer, but they were looking at me. So was Elias.

My brows flew up. "You're asking me?" I squeaked hoarsely.

A faint smile tugged at Ash's lips. "You are the Primal of Life he swore his allegiance to," he reminded me. As if I'd forgotten.

"I'm your Consort," I reminded him.

"Actually," Attes began, then stopped himself. "Never mind."

I sort of wanted to know what he'd been about to say, but we needed to leave. "I have no idea what we should do with him."

"You know my answer," Ash said. "But you were right to stop me—as much as I wish you were not."

"You and me both." I ran a hand over my arm, ignoring the stickiness of the blood there. "Could we take him with us until we can figure out what to do with him?"

"That would be ideal." Attes had moved closer to Kolis and knelt. He cursed. "But I'm not sure that would be wise."

Ash's attention shifted to the other Primal. "What is happening."

"The bone shard didn't go nearly deep enough to stay in on its own. You can't even get it that deep," he explained, rising. "His body will start pushing it out soon." He turned to us. "He'll awaken."

"And there's nothing else we can do to keep him down?" I asked.

"Not unless we get our hands on a bone blade," Attes said.

I tried to keep the frustration down. "You can't take your brother's?"

Attes shot me a bland look. "I don't think he'll give his up without a major fight."

"One you perhaps don't want to start," Ash bit out.

Attes's stare flicked to Ash. "You would be correct. I want to avoid that for as long as possible." His jaw flexed. "Because I know it will end with either my death or his."

My stomach twisted. No part of me would mourn Kyn's death, but his passing, without another to rise to take his place, would cause more upheaval. I looked at Kolis.

And Attes shouldn't be the one to kill his brother if it came down to that.

"So, that leaves us with what again?" I asked.

Ash kept his arm around me as he turned to Elias. "You really think you can get him out of here?"

Elias nodded.

"That will give us some time," Ash said. "Do it."

"But can you do it safely?" I tacked on. "Like without getting killed?"

"My safety is of no concern to you, Your—"

"Don't call me that," I cut in. "And your safety *is* a concern, or I wouldn't have asked that."

Elias glanced at Ash, then swallowed upon seeing whatever look Ash sent him. "I am honored that you would be concerned for me. I can do this safely." He looked at Attes, a gleam lighting up his amber eyes. "If you lend me something big enough to haul his ass out of here with and fast. Like perhaps Setti?"

"I think you just want to ride my horse," Attes remarked, dragging his fingers over the cuff encircling his biceps. "But yes."

A thin stream of mist drifted from Attes's cuff, rapidly spreading and taking shape, solidifying into a massive horse the size of Odin with a glossy, shadowstone-hued coat. Setti shook out his mane, making a soft, low-pitched nicker.

"I will never get used to seeing that," I murmured, my gaze moving to the cuff on Kolis's arm.

I thought of the weird milky reflection I'd seen there. I hadn't seen his steed—

Wait.

Milky-white light.

Eythos.

"Wait!" I shouted as Attes took hold of Setti's reins. The warhorse stomped hooves twice the size of my hand. My heart pounded. "My gods." I twisted toward Ash, my eyes wide. Gods, his father... "I almost forgot."

"Forgot what?"

"The diamond." I slipped free of Ash's hold. Or tried to. He moved with me, his arm at my waist. "The Star diamond."

Attes stepped around Setti as Ash straightened, asking, "You found it?"

"Yeah. Yes. Do you know what it is?"

Elias shook his head, but Attes nodded. "Eythos told me about it."

Ash stared at him, a whole lot of stuff likely beginning to click into place.

"You're not going to believe this." I twisted around. This time, Ash let me go. Even though my legs felt as if only thin tendons held them together—barely—they were thankfully steady. "It's here. It's been here the whole time."

I shuffled toward the ruined cage. "I don't think I destroyed it. Hopefully." I peered inside, relieved to see the cluster of diamonds still at the center of the cage. "There it is. In the ceiling. Kolis had it hidden there."

Ash joined me, a muscle in this temple throbbing as he surveyed what was left of the enclosure and what remained inside it.

"Up there," I repeated softly, not wanting him to think about anything else he saw. "I don't have much time to explain all of this, but we need that diamond."

His shoulders squared as he lifted his gaze. "You sure that's it?"

"He summoned it. And when he did, it changed shape, becoming a diamond that looked like, well...a star."

"How did he summon it?" Attes asked, coming to our side.

"He spoke in Primal, I think." I wiped my damp palms on my gown. "Do you think The Star could hold Sotoria's soul?"

Attes rubbed his jaw as he eyed the cluster of diamonds. "I don't see why not when it can hold embers."

"I feel as if I'm missing vital information," Ash remarked.

"You are." Quickly as possible, I filled him in on the part about Sotoria's soul. "Kolis said something like...like *vene ta meyaah* but not."

Ash repeated what I said back, his brows furrowing. "Do you mean *vena ta mayah*? It translates into come to me."

"Yes!" The translation made sense. "Do you think it will work if someone else says it?"

"It's like some kind of ward," Ash said, his gaze dropping to the bed. His chest rose. "If so, neither Attes nor I will be able to summon it." He met my gaze. "But you could."

"Because of the embers," I surmised.

He nodded. "But I don't want you to do that."

Attes stiffened. "We need to get Sotoria's soul out of Sera before anything else happens."

"You may need that," Ash corrected, eyes flashing a vivid silver. "But what I need, what Seraphena needs, is to not use those embers."

My stomach twisted at what Ash *wasn't* saying. That using the embers would push me over the edge, completing my Ascension.

"You don't understand," Attes argued. "We may not be able to kill Kolis yet, but one day, we might, and only Sotoria will be able to do it."

"I don't give two shits about *one day*," growled Ash. "I care about right now, and what using those embers will do."

"It's not just that." Eather laced Attes's eyes. "Sotoria's soul will be trapped here when—"

"Don't"—a storm of fury blew off Ash—"even think of finishing that sentence."

Attes stepped back, thrusting a hand through his hair. "I'm sorry—"

"Don't finish that sentence either." Shadows bled beneath Ash's flesh.

Neither sentence needed to be finished. We all knew what wasn't being said. Sotoria's soul would be trapped here if I Ascended, which wouldn't happen. Or if I died, which was happening. That was the strangeness I felt in my body, the hollowness in my chest. Because the embers were no longer there.

They were *everywhere* now, becoming a soft hum in my blood and a faint vibration in my bones.

Whatever the ceeren had sacrificed for me had either run its course, or what I'd done to put Kolis out of commission and free Ash had used it all up. Attes knew I was dying. That was what he was apologizing for. And Ash...

Ash knew, too.

But Sotoria wasn't the only reason I needed that diamond. Taking a deep breath, I stepped into the cage.

"Sera," Ash snapped, suddenly beside me. "I don't want you in this cage ever again." Eather streaked his cheeks as he clasped mine. "Not for one second."

Gods, I loved him.

"You need to conserve your energy," he said, tension gathering in his body. "And we need to leave. Now."

Sensing that he was about to pick me up and shadowstep to the gods only knew where, I wished there was another way to share what I'd discovered with him. "It's not just about Sotoria." I spoke past the emotion clogging my throat. "It's about your father. His soul is in The Star."

33

Ash stared down at me, his lips parting. "What?" he rasped.

"Are you sure?" Attes demanded, his voice nearly as rough as Ash's.

I nodded. "I'm positive. When I touched it earlier, I...I knew his soul was in there."

Ash's entire body jerked. He stepped back, almost as if out of reflex.

I didn't take my eyes off Ash's. His were so bright I could barely see his pupils. "I need to get The Star for him, too."

His throat worked on a swallow as his gaze flickered to the ceiling. "My father..." He shook his head as his gaze returned to mine. Tension bracketed his mouth, and his voice lowered as he said, "I don't want you using the embers."

"Ash—"

"Not for him. Not even for me. I will not have you risking your health and—" His voice...gods, it cracked. And so did my heart. Eather whipped through his irises. "I will not risk you."

Shock rippled through me. "It's your father's soul, Ash."

"I know. Fates, I know." A tremor ran through him. "But I will not risk you."

My chest swelled even as that fissure in my heart widened. Because how could Ash not be capable of love? His desire, his need to keep me safe, felt like something one would do when they loved another.

It was what I would do for him.

Which was why I had to do this.

"I'm okay." Like the Great Conspirator, I was a good liar when I needed to be.

"Sera—"

"I'm okay," I repeated. "I feel like I did before. I can do this." I stretched up, guided his head down to mine, then kissed him softly. "I'm going to do this."

Kissing him once more, I settled on my feet and then turned. Luckily, I didn't stumble or sway. I lifted my hand as Kolis had done, concentrating on the embers. "*Vena ta mayah.*"

The essence thrummed weakly throughout my entire body, but it was enough. My temples throbbed, and the cluster of diamonds vibrated, making that high-pitched whirring sound.

Ash cursed from behind me. "Will you ever listen to me?"

"I'm sorry." My heart skipped, and not in a pleasant way. It caused my breath to hitch. A faint tremor ran through me as I breathed through a rush of dizziness.

"No, you're not." Ash came up behind me, circling an arm around my waist.

There was a grounding, soothing quality to the feeling of him touching me that I'd missed so terribly. And it...it wasn't fair that I experienced it again only now.

The glittering cluster morphed as it neared my palm, forming one diamond shaped like a star.

"I've got it," I said, just in case either he or Attes thought to reach for it.

I didn't know if they would see what I did, but I didn't want anyone else witnessing it. Especially not Ash—not without any warning.

The diamond landed in my hand, sending a charge of energy up my arm. There were no sudden flashes of images this time, but that milky light—the soul—pulsed.

"That's it?" Ash peered over me, clearing his throat. "The light? I can't feel or sense anything."

"I think so." I knew we didn't have much time, but there were some things I needed to know. "How...how do you think we can put Sotoria's soul in this?"

"I can't answer that," Attes said.

Ash's arm tightened around me. "Keella would know."

"You think she'll help?" I asked, suddenly remembering how she'd questioned Kolis. "She will." Or at least I really hoped she would after what I'd done to Evander. I looked at Attes. "Can you get her?"

"Of course," he said solemnly. "I'll help Elias get Kolis out of here and then retrieve Keella."

I held the diamond tightly. "Do you think she will also know how to *retrieve* a soul from the diamond? I'm guessing it's not like pulling them from other things." I paused. "Or people."

"If it's different, she may know, but I imagine it's the same as with anything. I would be able to draw it out. Kolis would be able to." Ash shuddered. "And you. You would be able to."

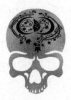

After Attes helped Elias haul Kolis onto Setti's back, Ash folded his arm around me again, drawing me against his chest. The gown was no barrier against the coolness of his flesh, and the contact did what it always did; it elicited a sensual shiver that curled its way down my spine. I turned my head slightly, seeing the bed. Gods, I'd been so afraid I would never feel this again.

"Are we going to shadowstep?" I asked, holding the diamond tightly in my grasp.

"It's faster." He cupped his hand over the back of my head and dipped his, pressing his cheek to mine. "Just remember to breathe."

"I will."

The air charged, and Ash's body began to hum. White mist poured out of him, thick and laced with streaks of midnight. I exhaled, then held my breath as the mist spun around us.

"Hold on," he whispered, then kissed my temple as I heard the rush of air stirred by Nektas taking flight.

I held on as what remained of the cage, and then Dalos, fell away.

It felt like only a heartbeat—possibly two—passed before I inhaled again and caught the scent of fresh air not tainted by the smell of death or staleness. What I breathed in was damp air and sweetness. Lilacs? There was also the sound of tinkling water.

Ash's fingers curled in my hair as he held me to him. A moment passed. Then another. Neither of us moved as I let the tension out of my body. We were free. Both of us. Safe—at least for right now. And we were together.

Keeping my eyes closed, I felt the mist falling away from us as I soaked in the feel of Ash. Breathed him in. Even though I should be, I was in no rush to part from his embrace. I'd been too long without it.

"You okay?" Ash asked, his breath stirring my hair.

I nodded, the edges of the diamond digging into my palm. "Are you sure this isn't a dream?"

"Yes, *liessa*." He kissed the top of my head. "We are awake. We are together."

A shudder went through me. "It feels like one. I didn't think…" I trailed off, shaking my head.

"What?" he questioned softly.

Words tiptoed to my lips and then just stopped there. Speaking the truth about, well, anything had always been hard. But when it came to talking about how I felt? How I *really* felt? What I'd been afraid of, or my weaknesses? I didn't have much experience. Like, at all. I hadn't been taught that. I'd been groomed to feel nothing and share only lies. So, the fear of saying something wrong or not the right way caused near-crippling anxiety. Even now, with Ash, who I knew wouldn't judge me, wouldn't laugh. After all, it wasn't like he had a lot of experience with this stuff either. Still, it was hard.

Yet according to Holland, the hardest things reaped the greatest rewards.

He was correct.

Hard wasn't impossible.

And keeping my eyes closed helped. "I…I told myself I would get to see you again. It was how I…" I shook my head slightly. "It was how I did what I needed to…you know, survive."

Ash's hand flexed at my hip and then slid to the center of my back. "I know."

I squeezed my eyes shut harder. "But I was so afraid. And I know you say I'm never truly afraid, but I was. I was terrified that I wouldn't get to see you. That I wouldn't be strong enough to deal with everything and *ensure* I saw you."

"Strong enough?" Ash dragged his hand up my spine. "You're the strongest person I know."

"I don't know about that," I murmured.

His fingers tangled in my hair more. "You freed me, Sera. You took

Kolis down."

I bit the inside of my lip. "And I could've done that anytime. I could've freed you days or weeks ago. I could've—" I stopped myself from going *there*. "I should've realized I could do what I did."

"Fates, Sera." Ash lowered his head so I felt his breath against my brow when he spoke. "Even if you realized it earlier, you wouldn't have been able to free me. I would've been in stasis," he pointed out. "And then what? I have a feeling you wouldn't have done the right thing."

"I would've gone to the Carcers and woke you from stasis," I told him. "That is the right thing."

"The right thing would've been making a run for it," he said softly. "Instead of risking being recaptured."

"Would you have made a run for it, or would you have come for me?"

"I would've come for you, but we're not talking about me."

I frowned.

"You also freed me from stasis," he went on. "You got Kolis to wake me."

Some of the tension began slithering its way back into me. "He told you that?"

His hand made another pass up and down my back. "He did."

I turned my head, pressing my forehead against his chest. I wanted to ask exactly what Kolis had said, but I also didn't want to know.

Ash was quiet for a moment. "That allowed me to escape. So, yes, you're the strongest, bravest person I know," he said, and my eyes started to sting. "I thought I was going to save you. Each time I woke, it was all I focused on: getting free and getting to you."

I thought about what he'd said, how he'd torn at his flesh to get free. The sting behind my eyes increased.

"And I should've been able to do that. I should've gotten you out instead of going after Kolis," he said, his voice flattening. "I should've been smarter."

"Don't." I tried to lift my head, but his hand kept me in place. His skin was cool and hard beneath my palm. "Don't put that on yourself. You came for me. You fought Kolis, and I distracted you."

"Sera—" A breath shuddered from him. "None of that matters now. You're not there anymore. We're here."

He was right. All that could've and would've had no place here. Not anymore.

I slowly tilted my head back and felt the damp air on my face.

Somewhat confident I wouldn't start sobbing, I dared to open my eyes, finally seeing where we were. There were branches, or perhaps vines, full of large, funnel-shaped blue and purple blossoms. Lilacs. I lifted my gaze, my lips parting. The flowers crawled up the slab-gray walls and across what I could see of the ceiling, lacing together to form a canopy.

I felt a twinge in my neck as I leaned farther back. Dappled sunlight penetrated the flowers, sending narrow streams of light down onto a…

Ash's hands slid away from me, and he allowed me to turn. Wisps of steam drifted up from an earthen pool and danced in the slivers of light.

Based on what limited descriptions I'd heard of the Bonelands, I didn't think we were there.

"Where are we?"

"We're in the mortal realm." Ash stayed close behind me. "This is a hot spring I discovered once. I figured we could both use a couple of moments of privacy and to clean up."

My gaze crawled over the water, lingering where it churned around the outcroppings of rock. I didn't need a mirror to know I looked as equally disturbing as Ash.

"I know it's not your lake, but we're not that far from the Bonelands. We're just on the other side of the Skotos." He paused. "What do you think?"

I blinked. "This is…it's beautiful." I shook my head in wonder, taking in the lilacs hanging in clusters from the cavern's ceiling and the steaming water that glimmered in the slivers of sunlight. "I never even knew such a place existed."

"It's pretty hidden away." Silvery eyes pierced mine as I looked over my shoulder at him. "I'm not sure a single mortal has ever stumbled upon it."

Holding on to the diamond, I twisted back to the rock pool. "What about Attes? Nektas?"

"They can wait."

But could we? Could I? The hollowness in my chest hadn't spread, and my stomach had settled. The ache in my head was manageable. I was tired but not falling down. "Attes will probably need time to find Keella, right?"

"Yes," he said. "And Nektas knows I'm fine. He can sense if I'm not."

I nodded, somehow forgetting that a bonded draken could sense when their Primal was in danger. "Does he know about this place?"

"No. No one else does." His fingers grazed my arm as he scooped the hair clinging to my already-damp skin. "We don't have much time."

No, we did not.

"But we have enough."

There was comfort in knowing that no one would interrupt these stolen moments. A heavy, long breath left me as I looked up through the blossoms to the pinpricks of sunlight. Then I looked down at the diamond. It was warm against my palm, and I could feel it pulsing.

"See the large rocks there, in the center?" Ash pointed to the ones the water lapped against. "As long as you don't go too far past that, the water will only come to about your shoulders. Beyond that, it does get deeper."

Tears rushed to my eyes once more, and I blinked them away. Gods, he was so damn thoughtful.

Swallowing, I turned to him. Half of his face was cast in shadow. "How are you feeling?" I glanced down at the diamond. "About this?"

Ash tipped his chin back. "Honestly?" He turned his head. "I don't know." His brows knitted. "It's hard to even think about—if he's aware in there, knows what is going on outside the diamond." His jaw flexed, and I hoped—gods, I prayed—that he wasn't thinking about where The Star had been positioned and what Eythos could've seen beneath him. "What it could feel like being trapped in there?"

"It's...it's unimaginable."

He swallowed. "Yeah."

I glanced down at The Star. The milky light inside had calmed—or at least was no longer zipping back and forth. "I think he's aware."

"What—?" Ash cleared his throat, briefly looking away. "What makes you think that?"

"It's just a feeling. Like maybe the embers of life recognize his soul or something. I don't know. But the way that light inside moves? It changes speed, becoming...almost frenzied. Now, it's calm."

"That light is a soul." He looked down, almost as if he were finally letting himself do so, and then stepped in closer. His blood-streaked chest rose with a deep breath. "I still don't feel anything, but that's what a soul looks like—a good soul. A pure soul would be more intense—a brilliant, blinding white light."

The light in the diamond—the soul—seemed to float close to the surface of the stone. I wondered what Kolis's soul would look like.

Gray like the Rot, I imagined. But then I wondered what *my* soul looked like. My gaze lifted to Ash's. "Did you know that I wasn't truly Sotoria?"

His stare met mine. "I couldn't be sure, but I assumed that what Holland and Penellaphe believed was correct." His forehead creased as his gaze dropped to the diamond. "When you kept insisting you weren't her, I did search for an additional imprint of a soul in you, but I never sensed anyone's presence but yours. That could simply be because your soul is stronger or it's what I fixated on."

I had no idea why I was flattered by the fact that he'd fixated on *my* soul, but I was.

"But it also never mattered to me."

My breath caught then.

"I didn't care if you were only Seraphena, or if you had, at one time, been known as Sotoria." A strand of his hair slipped forward, coming to rest on his cheek. "It didn't matter to me. You were always Seraphena, no matter what."

I...I'd been right when I'd thought it hadn't mattered to Ash either way. Pressing my lips together, I felt tears gathering in my eyes again, but I fought them back. I had to because they were a mix of love and sorrow and because they reminded me this wasn't fair.

And that unfairness threatened to shatter any calm I'd found.

"Can I...?" Ash cleared his throat again. "Can I hold the diamond?"

My heart ached. I'd never seen him look or sound so vulnerable. Uncertain. "I don't know if you should."

His gaze shot to mine. "Why?"

"I saw things when I touched The Star. I think it's also how I know this is where your father's soul has been trapped." I smoothed my thumb over one of the points. "I saw how it was created and...how your father died."

The muscles in his shoulders bunched and tightened. "What did you see?"

I wanted to ask if he really wanted to do this, but I knew the answer. It was the same as mine would be. I would need to know.

So, I told him.

I told him everything except for the part about his mother. I just... I just didn't think he needed to know that. And then have to process the possibility that his mother had cared for Kolis, maybe even loved him once, only to be slain by him. Perhaps that wasn't my decision to make, and I was wrong for keeping it from him, but I couldn't see how having that piece of knowledge would benefit him. Maybe if we had more time, I would tell him everything I'd learned beyond what I saw in the diamond, even the claim that Eythos had killed Sotoria—something I wasn't sure was entirely true and didn't know the circumstances of.

But now? I shared with him how Eythos had tried to talk to Kolis and how he'd told his brother they could move past everything Kolis had done, saying he still loved him.

Ash's face became a cold, impenetrable mask as I spoke, and in that moment, he looked as one would imagine a Primal of Death to appear.

"Kolis didn't believe him," I continued, speaking quietly, even though no one could hear but us. "So, he stabbed Eythos with a dagger made of the bones of the Ancients to prove that Eythos lied about still loving him. He...he didn't plan on killing him."

His eyes went flat. "Bullshit."

"I don't think it is," I said, knowing that I had made the right decision not to share the piece about Mycella. "He hadn't known that Eythos had given up the last of his embers. He didn't realize how weak Eythos was."

Ash's nostrils flared. "Did Kolis claim that?"

"I *saw* it," I reminded him. "I heard it. Eythos told Kolis he knew he was capable of killing him, but he'd hoped he wasn't right. I saw Kolis cry." My eyes closed. "Kolis didn't realize I would see anything when I touched the diamond, but what I saw surprised me so much that I blurted out that I'd seen him cry." A knot lodged in my throat. "He...he knew then that I'd seen something."

"Is that what caused this?" His voice thinned with barely leashed anger, each word spoken slowly, bitten out like the flick of a whip. I hadn't heard him move, but I felt the cool brush of his fingers on my throat. "The bruises?"

That knot expanded as I forced a shrug. "He wasn't too pleased about me seeing what really happened." I opened my eyes, quickly moving on. "I think he's ashamed of what he did—ashamed of the truth."

"I don't give a fuck what he's ashamed of." Ash's hand dropped, closing into a fist. "Or that he didn't mean to kill my father. He still did it. He did everything else. He still did this to you."

"I know." I swallowed. "Kolis is..." I shook my head. "He's not exactly right in the head."

"That is by far the understatement of several lifetimes."

"True." I stepped back. "Anyway, I don't know if you'll see any of that, and I just don't want you to. You've already seen too much horrible stuff."

His head cocked. "I'm a Primal of Death, *liessa*. I've seen all manner of horrible things. Atrocities you couldn't even imagine. I've even been the one to commit some."

"But you don't need to see *this*," I told him.

Ash watched me for several moments, turning quiet and intense, leaving me feeling exposed in a way that was wholly different from how I'd felt when Kolis stared at me. "Thank you."

I frowned. "For what?"

"For caring enough to think of me," he said. "For...for loving me enough to prevent that."

For some inane reason, my cheeks warmed. "You would do the same."

Faint wisps of eather began seeping back into his irises. "I would."

And I knew he would.

So how...how could he not love? That question rose to the tip of my tongue, but there was no point in asking the pointless.

"We should probably get cleaned up," I said instead, looking back at the hot springs. "Though I feel bad for getting in there while so filthy."

Ash gave me a wry grin.

I searched for a place to put the diamond but only saw faint patches of grass peeking through the rocks. I caught sight of the relatively clean hem of my gown. I bent, carefully placing the diamond on the stone before gripping the gauzy material. I yanked, and it ripped easily.

"There are far easier ways to undress, *liessa*."

I smiled. "I know. It just feels sort of wrong to leave the diamond on the cavern floor." I tore a strip of material free, then wrapped The Star in it. "There."

There was a look to his features that I didn't quite understand as I rose. "I wish I could do what you do," I said. "And know what you're feeling."

"I'm not even sure you'd know if you had the ability because *I* don't know what I'm feeling." Ash's brows furrowed, and his gaze swept over me. "Did he always have you dressed like this?"

"You probably don't want the answer to that."

"Which means I already have the answer." His chest rose with a stilted breath, and then he was directly in front of me, his fingers gently touching my cheeks. "Everything I did was to prevent this from happening. *Everything*."

"I know," I whispered.

A faint tremor hit his hands. "Yet I still failed you. I'm so sorry, Sera."

My heart constricted as a knot of sorrow formed in my throat. "You did not fail me, Ash. You have nothing to apologize for."

"But I do. I failed you before you even took your first step into the Shadowlands."

I grasped his wrists. "How can you even say that? When you turned me down as your Consort, you did it to protect me. You made that deal with Veses to keep me unknown to Kolis. There was no way for you to know he was aware of me the whole time."

"I'm not talking about that, Sera. I'm…"

I searched his features. "Then what?"

Closing his eyes, he shook his head. "We need to get cleaned up. We'll talk more about this later."

"But—"

"Later," he insisted, dropping a kiss onto my forehead. His eyes, now open, shone like stars. "Right now, I…I just need to take care of you. Please?"

There wouldn't be much of a *later*, but he'd said please, and I couldn't refuse him. I nodded.

"Thank you."

Those two roughly spoken words made my chest squeeze even tighter. I held still as he brushed my hair over one shoulder and found the clasp of my gown at the nape of my neck. The bodice immediately loosened. Out of reflex, I caught it by folding an arm across my chest.

His fingers halted their movements. "I just want to take care of you," he repeated. "That is all, Sera. Nothing, absolutely nothing, is expected of you."

It took me a moment to understand what he meant—what he was really saying. He hadn't brought me here for any other purpose than what he claimed. To give us some time alone and to clean up. And this alone time didn't involve anything of a sensual nature. A warring mix of emotions rose inside me. There was the swelling feeling of love in response to his thoughtfulness and awareness, but there was also a feeling of…of my skin and body not being mine. A soul-deep fear that Ash no longer saw me as the Sera he knew before Kolis took me because I had no idea what he knew. What he'd been told. But he'd definitely been told *something*. He'd appeared aware of the deal I'd made to free him. Did he know about the one I'd struck for Rhain's life?

"Sera? Are you all right?"

I opened my mouth, then closed it. My toes curled as pressure clamped down on my chest and throat, more punishing than even

Kolis's hands.

"I can sense the tartness of your unease." He tilted my head back. "You have nothing to fear from me. I promise. You're safe."

I shifted from one foot to the other. Despite the warmth of the cavern, tiny goose bumps broke out over my shoulders and upper arms. I didn't want him to look at me differently. To think of me differently. I was still me. He saw that, right?

"Sera?" His gaze briefly dropped to where I held my dress. Only then did I feel the ache in my knuckles from how tightly I grasped the material. Shadows briefly appeared across his shoulders. "Would it be better if I didn't touch you?"

I blinked. "W-what?"

"It won't offend me." The featherlight press of his fingers disappeared. "I just want to help you in whatever way you need."

My heart started thumping. "Why would you think I wouldn't want you to touch me?"

"You've...you've been through a lot," he began.

And I...

I didn't hear anything of what he said next as some writhing, crunching sensation filled every part of me, and I folded my other arm over my chest. Oh, gods, what *did* he know? What *had* he been told? What did he think? Panic clawed at my skin.

"I don't know what you were told," I said, having no idea if he'd been speaking then or not. A tremor went through me, then another and another. "But Kolis and I—I mean, he didn't..." My teeth were starting to chatter. "Things didn't escalate to *that*. I swear. He didn't even really touch me." Okay, that was a lie, but the rest wasn't. "You don't have to worry about touching me. I'm still me, you know?"

"I know you're still you." His dark brows lowered. "Sera—"

"Good, because I'm not...I don't know." My face felt like it was burning and freezing at the same time. "I'm not like..."

His chest rose, and when next he spoke, his voice sounded as pained as my chest felt. "Like *what*, Sera?"

I couldn't say the words that invaded my mind. They were wrong to think, even if Kolis's assaults hadn't escalated. But had that not still happened? When he bit me, holding me as he found pleasure? It was different, not anywhere near as bad as what far too many people had suffered—even Veses, who had said it was nothing. But what happened to me wasn't *nothing*—

No.

It didn't matter because whatever Kolis did or didn't do, it didn't make me what that fucking voice in my mind whispered. I knew that. Because I didn't look at those taken in by the Ladies of Mercy as tainted. I didn't think Aios was tainted. Gemma wasn't dirty. I looked up at Ash. He wasn't ruined. They were none of those things.

So, I wasn't.

I saw Ash's lips moving and knew he was speaking, but that *thing*, the voice that had made a home for itself in the back of my mind, was firing off thoughts, one after another, leaving no room for a reprieve. It was my voice, and it was louder than Ash's, even though I knew he'd never think of me in that way. Not him. Not after what he'd lived through. But that voice questioned if he still saw me as strong. Never truly afraid. Not weak. Not someone who needed to be handled like fragile, damaged, blown glass. Treated as if they were on the verge of shattering. And was that what I was now, for whatever short time I had left? My fingers turned numb.

The embers throbbed faintly in my chest as I forced myself to breathe in, but I couldn't get my lungs to inflate. My wild gaze darted from him as I opened my mouth wider, trying to take in air, but it was thick and—

My chest rose, but I didn't think it went back down. I couldn't exhale. And that meant I couldn't inhale. I couldn't breathe—

Ash's eyes were suddenly level with mine. "Slow down." Everything about him changed in an instant. His posture. The volume and cadence of his speech. "Slow your breathing down, *liessa*," he ordered in that steady, soft way of his. "Listen to me."

I didn't understand what he was saying for a moment, and then it broke through the fog of panic creeping into my mind. It wasn't that I couldn't breathe. It was always that I breathed too fast, the breaths too quick and shallow.

"Press the tip of your tongue against the back of your upper teeth. Keep your mouth closed, and inhale through your nose, Sera." His hand flattened against my upper chest, and the other splayed across my back as I did as he instructed. "Don't exhale. Hold it for a count of four, remember? One. Two. Three. Four."

Pulse racing, I counted as he used his hands to guide my shoulders back, straightening my spine. I hadn't even realized I'd begun to curl in on myself.

"Now, exhale for the same count." He did the same, exhaling for four seconds. "Keep going. Keep breathing with me."

I mimicked him, forcing the air down my throat and into my lungs.

"That's it." He smiled, and my eyes pricked with tears. "You've got this, *liessa*."

Something beautiful.

Something powerful.

"Now, inhale again through the nose. That's good." His eyes never left mine as he went through the motions until the tiny bursts of light faded from my vision and the trembling in my body receded. "One more deep breath, okay? Keep your tongue to your teeth. Hold for four."

I did as he said, finally feeling as if my lungs were no longer being crushed. My chest loosened.

"Better?" he asked.

"Y-yeah," I whispered, my voice hoarse. "Yes. I'm...I'm sorry."

"You don't need to apologize, Sera. It's okay." He remained close, his hands on my upper chest and back, tracking my breaths. "You've got this, and I've got you."

A faint shudder ran through me as I dragged in a deeper breath, catching hints of his citrus-and-fresh-air scent.

Ash watched me for several moments. "Still feeling better?"

I squeezed my eyes shut and counted to five before reopening them. "I'm okay," I stated, voice steadier, stronger. I lifted my gaze to him. The anxiety was still there, holed up inside me, still whispering that Ash and I wouldn't be as we once were during whatever time I had left, be it days or hours—and I really didn't think it was *days*. And the only way to shut the voice up was to prove it wrong. "Ash?"

"Yes?"

"If I asked you to touch me right now, would you?" My face was definitely on fire now. "If I asked you—"

"I will do anything you ask of me, Sera." Silvery streaks of essence whipped through his eyes. "*Anything*."

"If I asked you to touch me like you did the first time I bathed in your chamber, would you?" I insisted. "Would you kiss me—?"

Ash's mouth was on mine before I could say another word, and...oh, gods, it was so apparent that he didn't see me as a fragile piece of glass. Not with the way his lips moved against mine. There was nothing gentle about his kiss. It was all-consuming and relentless. His arm came around my waist as he stepped into me, sealing our bodies together as his head tilted. He deepened the kiss as the feel of his body overwhelmed my senses: the hard coolness of his chest, the strength of his thighs, and the hard, thick press of his cock against my belly. All I felt was desire—heady, heated desire. He parted my lips and thrust his tongue into my mouth. A shiver ran through me as I released my death grip on my gown and grabbed his shoulders. My nails pressed into his flesh as I kissed him back, stroking my tongue over his—over the edges of his fangs. I felt his shudder in every part of me.

Slowing the kiss, Ash caught my lip between his as he lifted his head. Breathing hard, he said, "As I said, *liessa*, I will do anything you want. You need me to just be here? I'm here."

His hand slid from my waist, catching the flimsy, ruined gown and dragging it down, letting it slip past my hips. My breath snagged as the balmy air washed over my back.

Ash's eyes held mine. "You need me to hold you? Done." He dipped, working an arm under my knees and lifting me as if I were made of only air. He held me to his chest. "Kiss you? You already know the answer to that."

My lips felt…deliciously swollen. So, yes, I did know the answer to that.

"You want more than that?" he continued as I became aware of him walking, the ground shifting beneath us. The sound of fizzing water rose. "Want me to kiss that stubborn jaw of yours?"

Only then did he break eye contact, kissing said jaw, and then those swirling irises met mine again. "Kiss those beautiful breasts? Draw your nipples into my mouth the way I know you like?"

My lips parted as warm water swept over my feet, immediately bubbling as Ash went down earthen steps—

Wait.

He was still wearing his leathers, wasn't he?

"You want me to kiss my way down your body and then between your thighs? Or touch you there? With my fingers? My dick? *Gladly*," Ash said, and I was no longer thinking about him still having his pants on. His voice…good gods, it reminded me of silky shadows and midnight dreams as Ash lowered himself, either sitting on an underwater rock or the ground. Water rose, frothing at my waist and tugging at my hands. "I will be inside you or on my knees in a heartbeat."

"Even now?" I whispered, fingers tangling in his hair as the water teased my sides and breasts. "The on-your-knees part? Wouldn't that be difficult?"

A smoky grin appeared, one I hadn't seen in what felt like an eternity as he positioned me on his lap. "It wouldn't be impossible."

"Your head would be underwater," I pointed out as he leaned back slightly, keeping us balanced.

His eyes were like pools of molten silver. "And my mouth would still be fastened on you."

"That…that sounds really, really nice." A bolt of lust pulsed through me, causing me to wiggle a little in his lap.

Ash groaned, dropping his forehead to mine. "It sounds better than nice." His lips brushed mine. "I can practically taste you on my lips and tongue."

Tingles of desire and need pooled low as the fizzing water danced over my legs and between them.

"Anything," Ash repeated in the heated, damp air between us. "Whatever you want."

I wanted to take those promises and turn them into action. The steady, welcome throb in my core was all about it, and how his heart pounded beneath my palm told me it would barely be a heartbeat before he fulfilled what he'd promised. But…

I just need to take care of you.

That's what he'd said he needed, and these moments weren't just about assuaging my fears. The anxiety-riddled voice had quieted, proven wrong by Ash's words and what I felt pressed against me.

"Take care of me," I said. "Please?"

Ash shuddered against me, and I knew he got what I meant.

Falling silent, I relaxed against him as I watched him take one of my arms, bringing it below the water. He rubbed his hands over mine and then my arms, scrubbing away the blood. Before he moved onto the other arm, he lifted it to the narrow streaks of sunlight, inspecting his work. Once satisfied, he moved onto the next and did the same. He had me lean back so all my hair fell below the surface and held me as he reached around, gently running the strands through the churning water.

When he was done, I took his hand and brought it to my mouth. I kissed the glimmering imprint, then washed his arms as he'd done with mine. Scooping water, I bathed his chest, his face, and while his eyes were half-closed, I knew his gaze never wavered from me. Not even afterward, when he did what I asked for next.

As the hot springs bubbled and churned around us, Ash held me in the sweetly scented air.

34

"Thirty-six."

His flesh was even cool underwater.

Water bubbled around us as I lifted my head. "Were you counting my freckles again?"

"Possibly." Wet strands of his hair clung to the sides of his face and neck as he smiled at me.

We sat silently for a little while, lulled by the tinkling sound of the churning water. It was so peaceful here. I imagined the Vale was like this.

My stomach hollowed. "Can I…can I ask you something?"

"Anything."

I nibbled on my lower lip, struggling to ask what I wanted to know. It was not something I had allowed myself to wonder about.

"*Liessa?*"

Squeezing my eyes shut, I took a reedy breath and searched for courage until I found it. "What…what will happen when I die?"

Ash's chest rose sharply. "Sera—"

"I just want to know. Like will I be judged at the Pillars, or will my soul need the extra-special Primal of Death judgment?" I lightened my tone, even as my chest felt tighter. "Better yet, will I have to wait in line?"

He didn't answer.

I opened my eyes to the wisps of steam whirling above the water. "I know this isn't the greatest topic of conversation."

"It isn't even something you should be thinking about."

"I try not to, but it's hard." My fingers curled slightly. "Especially now. I just want to know what to expect." I sat up, facing him. "And I don't want to hear that I don't have to expect it."

Ash opened his mouth.

"We both know that's not true," I said before he could deny it. "And knowing just a little bit will...I don't know. Maybe it will help me."

A glow of eather appeared behind his pupils. "Will it help? Truly?"

I...I wasn't sure. "Perhaps knowing will make things worse. Maybe it won't. But it can't be worse than this."

He turned his head, and a line of sunlight glanced off his cheekbone. "I don't know."

"Ash."

"I'm serious, Sera. I cannot answer whether you will pass through the Pillars or if you'll need to be judged in person to determine your fate."

I started to frown. "But—"

"I know what I said before, but I cannot see what that journey will be. Just as I couldn't see Lathan's journey," he shared, the glow pulsing behind his pupils. "It was hidden from me. As is yours."

"Why?"

"The moment I considered Lathan a friend, my role in his eternal journey ended. It's why—"

"The Primal of Death was not allowed to form bonds with another," I murmured.

A streak of eather lashed out from behind his pupils. "Kolis told you that?"

I nodded. "If a...a bond is formed with another, the Fates balance it out by preventing the Primal of Death from knowing the journey of a soul or taking part in it."

"Yes."

"The Fates..." Thinking of Holland, I shook my head. "They're bastards, aren't they?"

His chuckle was low. "I have thought that many times."

When Kolis spoke about it, I hadn't thought it was fair, and that hadn't changed. "And none of the other Primals are subject to those rules? Say if Maia were to become close with a mortal, would she no longer be able to interfere in matters of love or fertility?"

Ash frowned. "The others are subject to the same rules. Once they form bonds with mortals or gods, they cannot influence their lives in positive or negative ways."

Irritation rose. "Kolis made it sound like only he was subject to that."

"Of course, he did," Ash said with a sneer. "He believes he is the only one who has been punished or suffered." Another swirl of eather appeared in his eyes. "But my father—the true Primal of Life? As far as I know, he wasn't held to those standards."

My thoughts flashed to the anger I'd seen in Kolis's features when he spoke about all the ways Eythos could influence the lives of those he came to care for.

"Nektas once told me it was simply because the Primal of Life was held to a higher standard, tasked with the duty to know when and when not to impact the lives of others. Or to learn when. To me, it sounded more like being constantly taunted with the ability to improve one's fate and having to choose not to."

"Gods," I muttered. "Who would want that kind of choice?"

"Kolis," he suggested. "And he only wanted it because he never had to make it."

I nodded slowly. Kolis had left out that he wasn't the only one who had to operate by those rules, but I wasn't surprised to learn that. Kolis didn't care about the other Primals. He only cared about what his brother could and couldn't do.

Settling back against Ash's chest, I returned to what had started this conversation. "Then who judged Lathan?"

"If the Pillars could not judge him, then the Arae would have."

Which meant they would likely judge me because I doubted the Pillars would know what to do with me. I wasn't sure if that was a good or bad thing or if Holland would have any say in it.

"How does the water feel?"

"Amazing." All the soreness had faded away. It had to be the heat of the water and maybe even a little of the magic of this hidden-away cavern.

Ash tucked the back of my head against his shoulder. "Better than your lake?"

"Yeah, it is." I sighed, squeezing the arm that banded my waist. As I'd noticed before, his skin was even cool under the water, which probably stopped me from overheating. "But in a different way."

His thumb moved along the flare of my hip under the water's surface, sweeping back and forth. "How so?"

My gaze flickered over the softly churning hot springs. The fractured beams of sunlight glinted off the surface as wisps of steam rose, tangling with the hanging lilacs. "My lake is...it's refreshing, but this is relaxing. Like I could fall asleep."

"Yeah. I think I could do that myself." There was a heaviness to his voice as he dipped, kissing my temple. "I wish we could."

I wished for so many things.

A knot threatened to lodge itself in my throat. I drew in a deep breath, hoping to alleviate it.

"We will come back here." Ash's lips brushed the curve of my cheek. "I promise."

My eyes shut as that damn knot expanded. It was sweet of him to promise, but we would never come back here. I hoped *he* did, though, as I opened my eyes. I looked over the glistening outcropping of rocks and the lilac-covered walls as I thought about what I wanted for him when this was all over. A life. A future. Love. I hoped he made more good memories here.

Ash's thumb stilled against my hip. "How are you feeling?"

"Good." That wasn't necessarily a lie. My stomach remained settled, and I didn't feel like I would fall over, but I *was* tired. Though I didn't think the warm water had much to do with that.

Ash was quiet for a moment. "Did I ever tell you what anguish tastes like?"

My eyes narrowed.

"It's tangy, almost bitter," he continued, straightening a delicate link on Aios's necklace.

"Stop reading my emotions."

"It's one of the hardest emotions to block out. Sometimes, it's even louder than joy, but it's almost impossible to shield from yours."

My nose scrunched. "Almost impossible?"

His chuckle rumbled against my back. "Almost," he repeated. "I'm simply more...in tune with you than anyone else."

I thought about that. Just a drop of my blood had allowed him to sense if I was in danger, even if he was in Iliseeum and I was in the mortal realm. He'd taken far more than a drop since then, so it made sense that his ability to read emotions, something he'd gotten from his mother, would also be enhanced when it came to me.

But did that mean he would feel what I felt when I…when I died?

My chest clenched. Gods, I hoped not.

I couldn't think about that, though. Only the gods knew what emotion he picked up when I did.

"I'm not sad," I told him.

"Sera," he sighed.

"It's not what you think. It's just that I wish…I wish we had more time."

"We will."

I pressed my lips together as I nodded.

His chin grazed the side of my face. "You're so brave. So godsdamn brave and strong," he whispered. "There is no one like you, Sera."

"Stop being…" I trailed off, my brows knitting.

"Stop being sweet?" Ash said. "As I said before—"

"You're only telling the truth." The skin of my shoulders pimpled. My dream came back to me in a rush. "I dreamt of you saying that."

"I know."

I stiffened, then jerked upright before twisting in his lap to face him. "The dreams—"

"They weren't normal dreams." Tendrils of eather brightened his eyes.

My mouth fell open.

"I should've picked up on it the first time," he said. "Especially when you kept arguing that it was your dream."

"I wasn't arguing."

That warm, soft grin returned. "You have such a strange understanding of the word *arguing*."

"Maybe it is you who does?"

His lips curved up farther. "Either way, everything was too damn real. The feel of the grass beneath me. The feel of you." The hand at my hip swept up my waist as his gaze dropped to where the fizzing water teased the tips of my breasts. His voice thickened. "The feel of being inside you. No dreams could replicate the beauty of that."

My heart skipped a beat as I stared at him. "Everything *did* feel real. Both times—" The skipping motion moved to my stomach. "You told me to tell Kolis that I needed you to Ascend, and to summon the Arae."

"I did. It was the best plan I could come up with," he confirmed. "I knew he would never let me leave with you, but it would've given us a chance to escape."

Ash was right. Kolis never would've allowed him to leave with me. If it had come down to it, he would've just kept Ash there until my Ascension happened.

"In the end, you didn't need me to get free," he said, pride filling his voice. My cheeks warmed in response. "You had it handled."

"I don't know about that," I said. "I never would've gotten out of Dalos without you."

"I disagree. You would've found a way." Ash leaned in, kissing me softly. "And I'm confident enough in my strength to admit that."

Liking—no, *loving*—that he didn't feel less capable due to *my* capability, I smiled against his mouth. "It was a good plan. It could've worked."

Ash kissed me again, this time longer. When our lips parted, my pulse pounded pleasantly.

"You know," I said after a moment, "I dreamt of swimming in my lake with a wolf watching over me. I dreamt that many times."

"I think that was when I was in stasis." His brows knitted. "I'm not exactly sure how, but all I can come up with is that part of me—"

"Your *nota*?"

"How do you know about that?"

"Attes told me about it one of the times he was able to get to me."

His head tilted. "Exactly how many times did he visit you?"

I rolled my eyes. "Like twice."

"And he couldn't free you?"

"You know he couldn't," I reminded him, but Ash appeared as if he were choosing not to remember that. Time to change the subject. "So, when I saw you in your wolf form, it was because…?"

"I think part of my consciousness—a part of my being—was still alert enough to find you."

My mind raced, figuring out the timing. When I dreamt of the wolf and him, it had lined up with when he was in and out of stasis, but… "That wasn't the first time I've dreamt of your wolf."

A slight frown appeared, and then his expression smoothed out. "When you almost went into stasis while in the Shadowlands." He gave me a small shake of his head when I nodded. "Damn. I thought that was a dream then, but it wasn't even the first time…"

Wait. *The first time.*

"The first dream when you weren't in your wolf form. When we had sex." I gasped. "We actually had *dream* sex?" My eyes widened. "Well, that explains a lot."

"Explains what, *liessa?*"

"Why I could, you know, still feel you when I woke up."

The tips of his fangs became visible as his smile turned almost smug. "Exactly how did you still feel me, *liessa?*"

"I could feel you—okay, all of that is possibly the least important thing to discuss right now," I decided.

Ash chuckled. "I don't know about that."

Catching the teasing note in his voice, I felt a tiny catch in my chest. Hearing him like *this* was—gods, it was too rare.

It was yet another thing I wished for: more moments like those.

I swallowed, pressing my hands flat to his chest. "I've heard stories about something like this. People who can walk in each other's dreams."

"Mates of the heart," he surmised, and I felt a twinge deep in my chest.

"I...I've heard the legends of such." I thought of my parents. "But that can't be it," I said before he could. "Then how is it possible?"

An emotion flickered across his face—too fast for me to decipher. "It could be because we've shared blood. That could be common among those who've experienced what we did."

I started to ask how he couldn't be sure, but who could he have asked? He'd still been young when Kolis killed his father, and while I thought there had been some sort of friendship between Ash and Attes, they had kept some distance between them.

"Or it's the embers," Ash added as his thumbs moved in small circles along my ribs. "In particular, the one my father took from me and put in your bloodline. That could be what allowed us to connect in our dreams."

The thing was, no one knew if that was the case or not. Well, maybe the Arae did, but what happened with the embers had never been done before. It made sense. And it also made me wonder about other ways it may have formed a connection between us. Between the blood we'd shared and this...

Tension crept into my muscles as it finally occurred to me that this was one of the reasons Ash knew something had happened when I was held captive. How I'd reacted when he said he knew Kolis had hurt me. That was how he'd known what Kyn and Kolis told him while he was imprisoned couldn't all be lies. My chest twisted as I looked up. The softness and teasing were completely gone from Ash's features as he watched me.

Shit.

I needed to pull it together, and not thinking about all of that would be the first and most important step in doing so.

Forcing my thoughts elsewhere, I thought of my lake. And Ash, watching over me. "Can I ask you something else?"

"Of course."

I smiled. "Why didn't you tell me you could shift into a wolf?"

Thick lashes lowered, shielding his gaze. "I didn't know if it would...disturb you."

"Why would you think that?"

He shrugged one shoulder and cleared his throat. When his lashes lifted, the vulnerability in his expression struck me. "Most would be at least unsettled by another's ability to change into a beast."

"Some would probably be a little freaked out by it, but I'm not most people."

"No," he murmured. "You are not."

"And a wolf is not a beast. A dakkai? Yes. That's a beast to me." I traced the line of his collarbone. "A wolf is beautiful." My gaze met his. "You are beautiful in that form."

"Thank you."

I tapped my fingers on his skin. "I find all your forms beautiful. This one. The wolf. When you go full Primal."

"Full Primal?"

I nodded, dragging my lower lip between my teeth. "When your skin resembles shadowstone, and you do that smoky, shadow thing."

Eather intensified, churning wildly in his eyes. "I think I know exactly which part of the full Primal form you find so...*beautiful.*"

My cheeks flushed as my mind immediately flashed to the night Ash had been drawn to me as I pleasured myself. Those smoky tendrils of shadow energy he controlled were definitely *beautiful.* And wicked. And highly arousing. My stomach clenched in the most delicious way, just remembering that night.

Gods, I really couldn't think of that right now, even if I was still so damn relieved and thrilled that I could. That I could feel desire. But other things needed to be handled. Important things that did not involve those scandalous wisps of eather or any of our body parts.

I squared my shoulders. "We probably need to get going."

"Yeah." He tipped his head back. "But you'll need clothing to do so."

Glancing around the cavern, I raised a brow. "I think we're out of luck when it comes to that."

"I'll retrieve some for you," he said, reminding me that he was so much younger than the other Primals and couldn't manifest clothing like Attes could. "It'll take a few minutes, if that. Enjoy a little more time here."

That meant he would shadowstep. He was going to leave. My stomach pitched, and gods, I couldn't stop the burst of panic. "I can put the gown back on."

"I don't ever want to see you in that again." The eather whipped across his eyes. "And it has nothing to do with the blood all over it. *That* is the only part of the gown I like."

"Because it's Kolis's blood?" I guessed.

He nodded.

"Savage," I murmured, my fingers pressing into his chest. "What if something happens to you? What if you don't come back, and I'm stuck here? Don't get me wrong, it's beautiful, but I don't think I can eat lilacs or—"

"Nothing will happen to me. Nor will you need to eat the lilacs—and please don't attempt that." A hint of amusement crept into his tone. "Nothing will happen. You are safe here, Sera. I promise."

I knew I was. No one even knew about this cavern. "It's not me I'm worried about."

"You don't need to worry about me, *liessa*." He brushed the backs of his knuckles across my cheek. "It is unlikely Kolis has even begun to recover."

Heart thumping, I nodded.

"It's okay to be afraid." He touched my lower lip. "But I would not leave you if I thought, for even one second, it was unwise."

"I'm not afraid," I lied yet again, and once more he knew it, because I *was* scared. Of not seeing him again. Of something going wrong. Of being alone. Of the gods only knew what else.

But I also never wanted to see the gown again. I did need clothing—preferably something that wasn't see-through. And we also didn't have time for me to have a breakdown.

"Okay," I said, but Ash hesitated, his eyes searching mine. "I'm okay." I pushed out of his lap, letting myself drift back into the water. "Go."

"Only a few minutes," he promised as he rose, rivulets running down his soaked leather pants.

The weight of the water caused them to hang low on his hips, revealing the indents on either side. I bit my lip, reminding myself that while he looked indecently erotic, he had to be so uncomfortable.

"Make sure you get something dry to wear for yourself."

One side of his lips kicked up. There was a flicker of white mist, and then Ash was gone.

Breathe in.

I looked around the dimly lit cavern. *Hold.* Other than the water, it was quiet. *Breathe out.* Exactly how far underground was I? *Hold.* Probably not the best thing to think about. Turning in the water, I nibbled on my lip as I crept forward, my heart slowing as the water gently spun around me. I stopped a few feet from the boulder Ash had pointed out. The water reached just above my chest as he'd said. I stood still, letting myself soak in the feel of the warm, frothing water. It foamed at my sides and beneath the surface, bubbles dancing wildly over my hips and legs. I looked down, realizing I had crossed my arms tightly over my chest.

Gods.

I loosened my stance as I breathed in the sweet air. Above me, I heard the faint chatter of birds, and for a few moments, I just listened to them. How long had it been since I'd heard birds? Weeks? Even longer, actually. Outside of the hawks, there was no such life in the Shadowlands.

No such life…

Clearing my mind, I searched for Sotoria's presence. I didn't necessarily feel her, but I knew she was still there. "I…I don't know what you've been aware of," I said quietly. "But I'm going to get you out of me. You're not going to be trapped."

I felt a thudding sensation then, almost like a second heartbeat. It had to be her.

"We're going to put you in something, and then…" Then what? My lips pursed as I eyed the scattered holes of light overhead. "I don't know exactly how all this will work, but I know that Attes will make sure you're taken care of, and see that you find peace again." Emotion clogged my throat. "Okay?"

I didn't hear her, but hearing her voice was rare. There was another soft, strange thud, and I took that as her acknowledging what I'd—

A sharp, pulsing ache came without warning, lancing across my face from my temples. Sucking in a gasp, I went completely still as a metallic taste filled my mouth.

Hand trembling, I parted my lips and gently prodded the roof of my mouth with a finger. I looked down. Blood dotted the skin.

I quickly lowered my hand under the water as I swallowed, wincing at the metallic taste on my tongue. The pang of pain receded to its standard dull ache.

Glancing back at the bank, I surveyed the shadows before letting myself slip under the surface.

Warm, rolling water rushed over my head and erupted into whirling bubbles all around me. I did what I always did when in my lake. I stayed underwater, my thoughts emptying until there was nothing there. This time, though, I didn't stay until my lungs started to burn. I didn't get to that point because I felt the hum of a Primal. My heart lurched, even though I knew it had to be Ash. I pushed off the ground, breaking the surface.

Ash was a few feet from the edge of the hot springs, placing a bundle on an outcropping of larger rocks near the diamond. Immediately, I saw that he'd found himself some dry pants—dark brown breeches that fit his thighs and calves like a glove, tucked into black boots.

Relief swept through me so fast that I let myself sink until the water bubbled at my chin. "That didn't take long."

"I thought to go to the Shadowlands, but I worried that would take longer than necessary," he said. "So, I went to the Bonelands."

I sucked my lip between my teeth. Obviously, he worried that I would freak out if he took too long.

"I was able to grab some breeches and a tunic for you. They'll fit and be good enough for now. No shoes yet. Bele is on the hunt for them as we speak."

"Bele," I whispered, rising from the water. I made my way forward. "How is she?"

Pulling something dark and long from the bundle, he faced me. "She's…Bele."

I laughed at that because it told me what I needed to know. She was fine. "And Aios?"

Ash went completely still. "She is okay, too. But she was not in the Bonelands." His lips parted as he watched me approaching the earthen steps. "She stayed in the Shadowlands."

"Is it safe for her?"

"Yes." His gaze moved as the swirling, frothing water dipped lower and lower, dropping first to my navel and then my hips, and then even lower as I climbed the steps.

A heady warmth gathered in my chest, moving down where he'd fastened his heated stare. I saw the tips of his fangs again. Intense pleasure darted through me, and...so did something else—something colder.

Ash's gaze lifted, the wisps of eather in his eyes stilling. My heart stuttered.

"I also grabbed a blanket," he said before I could speak. He came toward me, spreading it out. "To use in place of a towel."

"Thank you," I whispered, feeling...gods, I didn't know how I felt.

Ash was quiet as he began drying me off, wringing as much wetness from my hair as he could. I started to tell him that I could do it but then stopped. I thought maybe he needed to do this, and I enjoyed it—how gentle he was, how thorough. It reminded me of another time.

I glanced at the wrapped diamond, cringing. I really hoped his father wasn't so aware that he'd heard our earlier conversation. Or could see any of this.

Actually, it was probably best I not think about that.

"Thank you," I said when Ash finished.

He rose as our eyes met. "My pleasure."

I smiled as he turned, tossing the blanket where I'd left the gown. As he walked past them, a spark ignited the small pile. My eyes widened as silver flames washed over the blanket and gown, leaving nothing behind. Raising a brow, I looked over at him.

"I really don't ever want to see that gown again," he remarked, picking up what appeared to be black breeches.

I quietly dressed as Ash pulled on a loose, linen tunic he must've grabbed for himself. It hung untied at the collar, leaving a tantalizing glimpse of his golden-bronze skin. The breeches he brought were on the tighter side, but the shirt was several sizes too large, easily able to fit him. It fell to my knees. Honestly, it could've doubled as a nightgown.

I lowered my arms, watching the sleeves flap several inches past my fingers.

"Cute," he drawled.

"Uh-huh."

Joining me, he took hold of one sleeve and started rolling it up. "I saw Elias while I was there. Only briefly. He said Attes should be arriving soon."

"Good." I breathed out, ignoring the pulse of pain skating across the back of my head. "Do you think he found Keella?"

"I'm sure." He glanced at the diamond.

"We'll have to...release your father before anything else." I held still as Ash tucked the sleeve in at my elbow. "What do you think will happen when we do that?"

"His soul will be free." Head bowed, he moved on to the other sleeve. "He should enter Arcadia."

"Will you...will you be able to see him then? His soul?"

"I should be."

"Talk to him?"

"Souls don't speak like we do. You may hear them in your mind." He folded the sleeve up. "But I don't know what will happen."

"I hope you hear him." I pressed my lips together. "Afterward, we need to remove Sotoria's soul from me."

"I'm not sure about that."

"Ash—"

He halted halfway up my forearm, his gaze lifting to mine. "I have no idea how to remove her soul from you. We're only assuming Keella can. That means she will likely have The Star when she does it and could try to take your embers."

My brows flew up. "Delfai said the embers could only be taken if—"

"I remember what he said." A muscle flexed in his jaw. "We don't know if Keella knows that. Or if Attes does. Both could try something."

"Ash," I began. "Do you really think either of them will try something? Keella is not a Kolis loyalist."

"I'm not worried about her," he muttered. "Attes? Different story."

He finished with the sleeve. Perfect timing, too, because I crossed my arms. "You're worried about Attes?"

"Is that a rhetorical question?"

"It shouldn't be a question at all," I pointed out. "He helped us escape, and he helped me before."

"When did he do that?" Ash eyed me as I started to step back. He cupped my elbow. "Not yet."

"I know you two haven't had your little chat yet—wait, why do I need to stand still?"

Ash arched a brow as he reached on either side of my neck, slipping his hands under my hair.

"Oh." I stood motionless as he began gently working my hair from where it was stuck beneath the shirt. "Anyway, Kyn was ordered to destroy the Shadowlands to send a message and then take me. Attes intervened."

"By taking you himself." The air charged in the cavern. "To Kolis."

"It was the only way to stop Kyn from destroying the Shadowlands," I reasoned.

The look Ash gave me made it clear what he thought of Attes's interference.

"Look, your father trusted Attes," I said, trying another tactic. "Trusted him well enough that Eythos told him what he planned to do with Sotoria's soul and the embers."

Ash halted again.

"Attes has known this whole time, Ash. Wouldn't he have told Kolis about Sotoria's soul if he were loyal to him?" I said. "Wouldn't he have said I wasn't Sotoria? Because Attes also knew that whatever your father attempted did not entirely work. He knew I wasn't Sotoria, and he had no reason to keep that information from Kolis, who likely would've come to the same conclusion I did. That if The Star is powerful enough to hold and transfer embers, it would be strong enough to do the same with a soul."

That muscle running along his jaw ticked harder. "If Attes knew this entire time, why didn't he tell me?"

"That's a good question. I asked that myself."

Ash had managed to get all but a few strands of hair out from under the shirt. "I'm sure he had an answer."

"The Fates. They demanded that you never know of the plan. It was one of their ways to keep their precious balance. And, yes, that is really dumb, but Attes and Eythos feared that if they told you, it would end up turning back on you somehow."

That muscle in his jaw worked overtime as he scooped a curl from where it was plastered to my neck.

"And he didn't trust you."

"That is the first easily believable thing I've heard."

I sighed. "He didn't trust you entirely. He never knew what you really thought of Kolis, which sounds hard to believe."

"It's not." He moved on to the other side of my neck. "I told you. Even if I didn't always fool Kolis, I could be very convincing." He looked at me. "None of that means I trust Attes in this."

Frustration rose. "I sort of want to knock some sense into you right now."

"You can try." He flashed me a grin.

I ignored it. "Attes hates Kolis, and you have to know why—what Kolis did to him. To his children."

Ash's nostrils flared as he draped the last of my hair over my shoulder. "I know."

"Then do you think Attes doesn't want to see Kolis dealt with as badly as you do?"

His thick lashes lowered, shielding his gaze.

"And Attes did what Elias did," I tossed out.

The skin at the corners of his eyes creased. "He swore his allegiance to you?"

"Yeah, even did the whole kneeling and speech thing."

Some of the hardness left his features. "That's…interesting."

Rolling my eyes, I threw up my arms. "Attes has only done what Keella has, what you have. Survived while doing his best to prevent Kolis from getting what he wants," I said. "And that is not just Sotoria. It's the embers, too. He wants—or *needs*," I corrected myself, "those embers."

"So he can become a crazed, unstoppable monster?"

"Well, besides that. It's the whole balance thing. Life has to be created to keep the realms stable, and what he's doing to accomplish that is creating what he calls—"

"I know what he's created. The Ascended," he said, and surprise flickered through me. "The Revenants. He couldn't shut the fuck up about them when he came to tell me about the…" Tendons stood out along his throat. "When he came to tell me that I would be set free once my anger was under control."

I knew that wasn't what he'd been about to say. It was when Kolis went to tell him about the deal. "Why did he even bring that up?"

"Because my uncle is a boastful fuck who takes his inability to create life like my father did personally and to the extreme."

I nodded slowly, remembering how he'd reacted when he sensed that I didn't believe he could create life. "Anyway, it won't always work. He knows that. So does Kyn."

Shadows pressed against Ash's cheeks.

I quickly continued. "Kolis didn't know he couldn't Ascend me, but he still believed the whole thing would be dangerous. So, he planned to wait until I was in my Culling to take the embers. He didn't know that I had already started my Ascension. And the only reason I can figure that it didn't completely happen was because of what Kolis had Phanos do."

His gaze sharpened. "What was that?"

I told him about the ceeren and their sacrifice, and I practically saw the wheels beginning to turn in his mind. "No."

He frowned. "No to what?"

"I will not allow anyone else to give their life to extend mine. I know you're thinking that."

"Except it's not just your life you're extending, Sera. It's thousands," Ash countered. "Millions."

My hands fisted at my sides. "But only temporarily. As long as the embers remain inside me, the Rot spreads and does more damage. And…"

Ash went still again. "And what?"

"And I'm…I'm almost out of time," I admitted. I didn't think he took another breath. "I'm dying."

"No."

"I'm dying, Ash." As I spoke, I donned that veil. I hated doing it with him, but I didn't want the calmness I'd found regarding what was coming to crack and for him to feel anything from me. It would already be hard enough for him. So, I emptied myself as much as I could. "You have to take the embers, and you need to do it soon. I don't have long—"

"You don't know that." Shadows thickened beneath his flesh, quickly erasing the warmer hues of his skin.

"I do, and so do you." I cupped his cheeks. His flesh was so icy now. "My mouth—"

"Don't say it," he whispered—begged.

I had to. "My mouth has been bleeding. It was doing it just a bit ago when you left to get me clothing." When he started to look away, I stopped him, keeping his eyes on mine. "And I no longer feel the embers in my chest, Ash. I feel them everywhere. In my blood. My bones. My skin."

A shudder rocked him, and then I was in his arms, held tightly to his chest. He didn't speak as I felt his heart pounding. He didn't need to because he knew.

My Ascension had fully begun. And I was right. We didn't have much time.

We likely didn't even have a day.

The end was upon me—us.

35

The knowledge of what was to come followed as Ash and I shadowstepped into the Bonelands.

I knew the moment we arrived. The humidity and sweet scent of the cavern disappeared, replaced by a cooler breeze that reminded me of spring in Lasania.

Ash's arms didn't loosen from around me as I lifted my head. The mist started to dissipate around us as the chatter of birds faded, revealing green—*lots* of lush green foliage. I saw low, ground-hugging evergreens, bushes that bloomed with pale flowers, and trees with vine-covered trunks and sweeping limbs heavy with broad leaves.

"Huh," I murmured, holding the Star diamond in my right hand.

Ash drew up a hand, his fingers tangling in my wet hair. "What?"

"I'm kind of confused." I looked to my right, seeing more of the same. "For a place called the Bonelands, I expected to see a bunch of bones."

"Look down, *liessa.*"

My gaze darted back to him, my eyes widening. Part of me wasn't sure I wanted to, but curiosity always, *always* won out.

The corners of my lips pulled down. "All I see is dirt and grass."

"If we stood in this exact spot at the end of the Ancients' time, we'd be standing upon the remains of those who fell to them in battle," he said. "And those bones are still here, only retaken by the lands over the millennia. Nearly everything east of the Skotos to the Cove has grown from the remains of those who perished."

My upper lip curled as I resisted the urge to hop into Ash's arms. I'd seen a lot of gross things. Did quite a bit of them myself. But I somehow found this far more disturbing. "Knowing we're basically standing on the graves of the gods only know how many skeletons kind of freaks me out. And it feels a little disrespectful."

"The draken would agree with you." His fingers trailed through my hair. "They see the Bonelands as sacred."

I'd heard that. I tilted my head back. Stippled sunlight glanced over the curve of Ash's cheek and jaw. "What exactly caused the war with the Ancients?"

"One thing." His gaze drifted over my face. "And yet many things."

"That's a helpful answer."

A faint grin appeared. "The Ancients never felt things like mortals do, or even the Primals of my father's age before the first of them fell in love. They just were not...created that way," he said, sliding his hand from my hair to my chin. "But that didn't mean they were apathetic to the needs of their children or the mortals who eventually populated the lands west of Iliseeum. They were full of empathy...until they weren't."

"What caused that to change?"

"The same things that happen to any being who sees too much time pass." His thumb glided over my lower lip. "They lost their connection to those who came from their flesh and the mortals, seeing less and less of what made those who inhabited the realms beautiful over time. My father said they began to see anything not created by them as parasitic. The changes mortals made in their realm didn't help. The Ancients were particularly displeased with the disruption of land in the name of advancement. Too many forests were cut down, replaced by farms and manors. Roads replaced soil. Cities were built upon meadows. When they looked at the mortal realm, they only saw death."

"Really?" I drew out the word.

Ash nodded. "My father said the Ancients were not only able to see but could also connect to the souls of every living creation. That included higher forms of life such as you and me, but also animals and plant life."

Creases formed between my brows. "Plants have souls?"

"That is what my father said the Ancients claimed."

"So, I take it that neither you nor the older Primals can see such a thing?"

"Correct." His thumb made another sweep across my lip. "The Ancients came to believe that mortals and the lands could not coexist. They figured they had to make a choice."

"Mortals or…or the trees?"

"Mortals cannot exist without the bounty of the land," he said. "So, to them, the choice was easy. They decided to cleanse the lands and clear it of mortals."

"Dear gods," I murmured. "And they could do that?"

"The Ancients were…well, remember what was said about a Primal of both Life and Death? How such a being could both destroy the realms and remake them in the same breath?"

"Yeah." I shivered, thinking of Kolis having such power. "The Ancients could do that?"

"At first. Luckily, some realized the dangers of any being having such limitless power and took steps to lessen theirs long before the first mortal breathed. And they did that by creating offspring from their flesh."

"Primals like your father?"

"Yes. They transferred parts of their energy—their essence—into each of their children, thus splitting their abilities among them and, therefore, creating a balance of power that was shared."

Something about what he'd said struck a chord of familiarity.

"When the Ancients decided to cleanse the land, the Primals and gods joined forces with the mortals, draken, and their ancestors, to fight back." He halted. "Even Kolis fought side by side with my father. It was a different time then."

It was hard to imagine a time when Kolis and Eythos were on the same side.

The low, warbling trill of a draken drew our attention to the trees. "They're waiting for us."

"They are." Ash guided my gaze back to his. "They can wait a few more moments." Eather churned restlessly in his eyes. "How are you feeling? Honestly?"

Out of reflex, I started to tell him that I felt fine, but there was no point in lying. It also wasn't fair to him. Or to me.

I took a breath that didn't seem to inflate my lungs fully. It was a different feeling than the one that accompanied the anxiety-fueled breathlessness. This felt like a part of me simply no longer worked as well. "I'm...I'm tired."

Ash's expression revealed nothing, but his throat worked on a swallow. "How does your head feel? Your jaw?"

I wished I were still lying to him. "Just a dull ache right now."

"Okay." He dipped his head and kissed my brow. "Promise me you'll let me know if the pain gets worse."

"I promise."

Ash stayed as he was for several moments, his cool hand against my cheek, and his lips against my brow. Then he stepped back and took my left hand, moving like he planned to lift me into his arms.

"What are you doing?"

His brows knitted. "I was going to—"

"Please, do not say you were going to carry me."

"I want you to conserve your energy."

"Walking doesn't take any energy."

The scowl deepened. "Along with not understanding what arguing is, I don't think you get how the body works."

My eyes narrowed. "I can walk, Ash. I'm dying," I said, forcing my tone to be light as I swatted his chest, "but I'm not dead."

The eather went unearthly still in his eyes. "That is not something to joke about."

I sighed. He was right. "Which direction?"

"West."

"West?" I looked left and then right before turning my stare to him. "Do I look like a compass?"

His lips twitched. "This way, *liessa*."

With my hand held firmly in his, he started to our left. "We don't have to walk far," he said, his voice a little rougher than usual, drawing my gaze to his face. He stared ahead, his features impossible to read.

I squeezed his hand.

He gave me a faint smile, one that didn't reach his eyes. "Careful," he instructed. "There are a lot of small rocks and branches. I don't want you tearing up your feet."

That made me smile, and also made my heart hurt a little because he was worried about me hurting my feet. My *feet*. They could be chopped off, and it wouldn't really matter.

Okay, it would probably hasten the inevitable, but his concern was sweet and...and it felt *loving*.

With the diamond in my hand, I walked with Ash for a few minutes, him leading me around fallen branches and scattered pebbles that wouldn't pierce my skin even if I jumped on them. Eventually, slivers of white—dull white marble or limestone pillars—appeared through the trees.

"Is that a Temple?" I squinted.

"One of them." He reached up, holding a branch out of the way. "And before you ask, I'm not sure who it once honored."

"I wasn't going to ask."

A lock of reddish-brown hair fell against his cheek as he sent me a sidelong look.

"Whatever," I muttered, falling quiet for about two seconds as I eyed a fallen, moss-draped tree. "So, mortals did live east of the Skotos?"

"They did." Letting go of my hand, he gripped my hips and lifted me over the fallen tree with such ease that I couldn't help but feel dainty and delicate. "Used to live right up to the foothills of the Carcers."

"Wow." Portions of the flat, square roof of the Temple came into view. "I didn't think they ever lived that close to Iliseeum."

"Primals and gods interacted more closely with mortals then, visiting villages and spending time with them," he explained, taking my hand once more. "That was before the Primals' abilities matured, and their effects began to influence the mortals."

Ahead of us, something—no, a tall and lithe *someone* dressed in black moved between the trees, walking at a fast clip toward us.

"Who is that?" I asked.

"Bele." His lips thinned. "You don't—"

"Finally!" Bele yelled. Above us, limbs trembled as the silent birds took flight, scattering into the air. "I was starting to get worried."

My lips began to curve as Bele came more into view, her skin a light golden brown in the fractured sunlight. She strode toward us, the midnight-hued tail of her shoulder-length braid bouncing as her pace picked up.

As usual, Bele was strapped to the teeth with weapons. Daggers were sheathed at her thighs, the bands on her forearms secured smaller blades, and the hilt of a sword on her back jutted out at her waist. Over her shoulder, I saw the curve of a bow.

Bele was...she had been fierce before she Ascended, confident and sometimes a little scary. But now?

Now, she was drenched in power and strength, moving through the thicket like a predator on the hunt.

My steps slowed. She was now the Goddess of the Hunt. Or rather the Primal Goddess of the Hunt and Divine Justice. The last I'd heard, no one knew if Bele had Ascended into actual Primalhood, but that had been before Hanan's untimely demise. If she had, though, wouldn't I have felt her approach?

Bele's slightly rounded cheeks lifted as a smile spread across her face, and then she was no longer several feet away but right in front of me. I didn't even have time to gasp. Her arms went around me with such force that I almost dropped The Star, and would've toppled over backward before she steadied me if not for Ash's hold on my hand.

Bele...was hugging me. Like really embracing me, with both arms and her head buried against my shoulder.

Shock rippled through me as my gaze darted to Ash. He raised a brow. Bele wasn't the hugging type. Or really that emotional at all. She was more like the compliment-whilst-insulting-you-at-the-same-time type, which was probably why we got along. Somewhat. Both of us also seemed to thrive on irritating others.

I folded one arm around her and then my other once Ash slowly and reluctantly let go of my hand.

But he hovered close. "Take it easy on her, Bele."

Her hold on me loosened a little. I felt her chest rise. "Thank you."

"For what?" I murmured into her braid, patting her back awkwardly because I officially gave the worst hugs.

"For Aios," she whispered hoarsely, reaching between us to touch the necklace. "If I'd lost her..." A tremor went through her.

I squeezed my eyes shut, having forgotten there was the hint of something intimate between the two, something more than just friendship. "You don't have to thank me for that."

"I just did. I'm not taking it back." Her voice strengthened. "And you can't reject it."

My lips quirked. "Okay."

"Glad we're on the same page." Bele drew back then. "I hate to ruin this reunion but..." She trailed off, inhaling sharply. She dropped her arms as her mouth opened, then closed. Eather lashed across her eyes—irises that had once been a shade of hazel that leaned more toward gold but were now silver. "Please tell me you got at least one good beatdown in on that motherfucker."

For a moment, I wasn't sure what had provoked the question, but then I realized she was looking at my neck—the bruises and the wound left by the scrape of Kolis's fangs.

"She got in more than just one beatdown," Ash stepped in, taking my hand again.

Bele's chin lifted. "Really?"

"Yeah." My normal tendency to be a braggart when it came to gaining the upper hand in any fight wasn't there, which likely meant I was more tired than I realized. "He's down for the count right now."

Approval flashed across her stunning features, along with a savage smile. "I wish I'd been there to see it."

I started to smile when I realized something about her. Bele had Ascended as the Primal Goddess of the Hunt, but her arms were bare. "You don't have a cuff like the others?"

"Not yet." Bele eyed the one around Ash's biceps. "Apparently, it will appear when I'm ready." She squinted at Ash. "And exactly when will that be?"

"I am under the impression it varies. Odin didn't appear until a few years after I became a Primal of Death."

"A few years? That's annoying." Bele rolled her eyes. "Anyway, we heard that Kolis was out of commission from some god named Elias, but we didn't let him say much more before we bound his mouth."

I blinked. "Before you did what?"

"We tied him up and bound his mouth," she repeated. "Why are you looking at me like that? I don't know him. None of us does. All that we know is that Attes popped in, dropped the asshole off with his gold-painted face, and then said he'd be back before any of us could even address the fact that *that* fucker was here."

"Oh, my gods," I muttered as Ash made a noise that sounded a lot like a laugh. "Elias is not a bad guy. And Attes...I'm not explaining all that again." I shot Ash a glare. "Is Nektas here? He would know all of this."

"Nektas is doing his draken thing."

"As if he couldn't have shifted into his mortal form at any point to tell you all that Elias didn't need to be bound?" I started walking toward the Temple, where I assumed Bele had come from.

"Yeah, he could have. He didn't." Bele fell into step beside Ash and me. "Look, the god's alive. No harm. No foul."

I wasn't sure tying someone up fell under no harm, no foul.

"By the way, I apparently have even more bad news for you." Bele glanced at me. "Veses is—"

"Freed. I know. I saw her," I said. "Was anyone hurt?"

Bele shook her head. "We didn't even realize she had escaped at first. Went down there and saw that she'd basically chewed her damn arms off. I think she was more concerned with getting the hell out of there than vengeance."

So Veses had been telling the truth.

The trees thinned out, revealing more of the old Temple I now saw sat below some rocky cliffs.

"See." Bele gestured at the sweeping columns. "The god is alive."

I did see Elias. It was kind of hard to miss him since they'd tied him to the middle pillar of the Corinthian-style Temple, bound at the legs, arms, and mouth. But it was the shadows falling over the Temple that drew my attention. Two draken flew overhead, the larger of the two the black-and-gray-scaled one. Branches along the tops of the nearby trees swayed as Nektas circled the lowest cliff overlooking the Temple, while the onyx-hued draken slowed, extending his wings. He landed on the Temple's roof, his claws digging in as the entire structure shuddered under his weight.

Dust and stone rained down. My lips parted as several smaller pieces smacked harmlessly off the ground while a spiral, scroll-like ornament broke off, coming right down on Elias's head and shoulders. The god gave a muffled grunt before his body slumped.

Slowly, I turned my head to Bele. "No harm, no foul?"

Bele's eyes were wide. "He'll live."

My brows lifted.

"That is not my fault." She crossed her arms. "Not like I knew Ehthawn would decide to land there of all places."

The ache in my temples increasing, I turned back, watching Ehthawn extend his neck to lower his diamond-shaped head. He nudged the unconscious god before tilting toward us. Vertical pupils surrounded by crimson focused on me as he made a low, chuffing sound.

"He's apologizing," Bele explained.

"Uh-huh."

Ehthawn sniffed, his warm breath ruffling the strands of hair around my face. He let out a soft, almost mournful squall.

Ash's hand tightened around mine, seeming to respond to the sound the draken made. I glanced at him. Like before, his features were locked down.

Ehthawn moved in closer to me, his eyes closing. I tugged my left hand free, then hesitated. Other than little Jadis, I didn't often touch a draken in this form, but he didn't pull his head away. I lightly pressed my palm to his powerful jaw. The scales were smooth and dry, only the ridges of each rough. A trilling noise, almost like a purr, radiated from Ehthawn.

"It's okay," I told him, even if I doubted he was really apologizing. My gaze flicked over his flat, broad nose. Thickness coated my throat as I glanced at the blue, cloudless sky above, not seeing another draken. "Orphine?"

Ehthawn made that mournful sound again. My heart began squeezing. Bele had fallen silent.

"Orphine fought bravely," Ash said quietly. "She did so until her dying breath."

Fingers curling against Ehthawn's scales, my eyes closed. Sorrow rose, slicing through my chest. I wasn't sure I could call Orphine a friend or say she really even liked me, but I had been closer to her than Davina, who'd fallen in the fight against the entombed gods. I respected Ehthawn's twin, and she'd respected me. And if we'd had more time, I thought maybe we could've become friends.

Grief lodged in my throat as I opened my eyes. "I'm sorry," I whispered to Ehthawn as Ash stepped in closer to me, coolness coming off his body in contrast to the heat of the draken's scales.

Ehthawn gave another chuffing noise and then drew back. More dust fell, coating Elias's shoulders.

"Get him down from there before the whole roof collapses on him," Ash ordered.

Bele sighed. "Fine."

Ash threaded his fingers through mine as Bele stalked forward, unsheathing one of the shadowstone daggers on her forearms.

"I should've told you about Orphine," Ash said in a low voice. "With everything going on…"

"It's okay." I let out a ragged breath. "Did she…?" I pressed my lips together. "Was it quick for her?"

"I believe so." Ash tucked a curl behind my ear. "She is at peace now in Arcadia."

I wished knowing that lessened the grief. I watched Bele slice through the rope at Elias's shoulders. The god pitched forward and then crumpled to the mossy ground…headfirst.

"Whoops," Bele exclaimed, returning the dagger to its sheath. "He'll live."

I sighed.

Lips twitching, Ash led me toward the Temple steps as Bele

hoisted the unconscious god over her shoulders. Mindful of the vines trailing up the steps, we climbed the stairs, the stone warm beneath my feet. Not even halfway up, my breathing became labored, and sweat broke out across my forehead. I refused to let it show, though, forcing my legs to keep moving.

We'd only taken a few more steps when Ash stopped just above me, dipping his head to mine. "Let me help you."

My back stiffened as I stared ahead, lifting one protesting leg and then the other so I stood on the same step as he did. "I'm fine."

"*Liessa*, look at me."

"What?"

A salty breeze lifted the hair from his shoulders as he said, "There is no shame in needing help."

My cheeks warmed.

"And there is only strength in accepting aid."

"I can climb stairs," I persisted, even as my muscles screamed in denial.

"I know. That doesn't mean I can't help you." Eather spun in his eyes. "Allow me this. Please."

I swallowed a curse. "I think you've caught on to how I can't deny you when you say please."

One side of his lips kicked up. "I have no idea what you speak of."

"Sure," I muttered, but I didn't resist when he lifted me into his arms. To be honest, I wasn't sure I could've made it to the top.

And that truth didn't only make me feel pathetic.

It also scared me a little.

Ash reached the main floor of the Temple within a few heartbeats, immediately placing me on my feet as Bele strode past, dropping Elias by one of the pillars. I half-expected her to make a comment, but she said nothing, her features pensive as she stopped at what appeared to be the base of a statue that must've once stood proud. I scanned the Temple floor, seeing several blocks of marble in varying stages of ruin, leading to the far side of the Temple, where there was an enclosed space.

"Thank you," I whispered under my breath.

Ash pressed a kiss to my cheek then straightened as several figures appeared along the back columns, passing the enclosed portion of the Temple. As they crossed the floor, my shoulders tensed in recognition of most of them.

Saion and his cousin Rhahar walked together, their similar, striking features a rich brown in the sunlight. Both wore silver armor over their chests, and like Bele, all manner of weapons were visible on them.

Both drew up short, stopping at the Temple stairs. Behind them, the fair-haired god Kars that I knew as one of the Shadowlands guards appeared, along with another god I remembered seeing in the training fields.

Saion was the first to break free of the small group and approach Ash. I could've sworn the god's dark eyes glimmered as Ash moved to clasp his forearm. Saion didn't stop there, though. He pulled the larger man forward, into a one-armed embrace.

Surprise rippled through me. I'd never really seen anyone but Nektas get close to Ash, let alone touch him. And anytime they saw me touching him, it seemed like they were witnessing some sort of magic.

Ash hesitated, clearly not expecting the response. I bit down on the inside of my cheek, waiting and hoping he returned the embrace. These people. Saion, his cousin, Bele—all of them—were Ash's friends, even if he hadn't allowed himself to acknowledge that since Lathan's death. Even if he wasn't supposed to form bonds with any of them, they already had them. In my mind, not being able to see the journey of a soul or impact where they went wasn't more important than what one experienced while alive.

So, I disagreed with the Arae. Eternal afterlife wasn't more valuable.

A shudder of relief went through me as Ash finally moved, folding an arm around Saion's shoulder. "It's good to see you," Ash said roughly.

"Same, brother." Saion's voice was no less hoarse. He clapped his back. "Same."

Rhahar quickly replaced Saion the moment his cousin stepped back. I then saw Lailah making her way forward, her long braids swept back. Her lips curved into a smile, and my gaze shifted to who walked just behind her. It wasn't her twin, Theon.

It was Rhain.

Gods, he looked leagues better than when I'd last seen him. Gone was the blood and the bruised, mangled flesh.

Rhain's gaze landed on me. His steps faltered at the same moment my heart did. I looked away, lifting my free hand to Aios's necklace.

Ash was getting a lot of hugs in, so I focused on that. A faint grin tugged at my lips. I could've sworn his cheeks were a deeper shade by the time Rhain made his way to him. It was good seeing this—seeing

Ash accepting them and their obvious love for him. The next breath I took was easier and steadier.

Ash wouldn't be alone.

Breathing through a sudden slice of pain in my temples, I went to where Elias had been dumped. Kneeling beside him, I brushed a lock of brown hair back from his face. A thin trickle of blood cut through the golden paint. He was still out. Lifting my head, I looked across the expanse.

From where the Temple was positioned. I could see beyond the tips of the trees to the bumpy, uneven hills dotted with darker shades of green that led to the sandy dunes Kolis had spoken of.

There were large outcroppings of dull white rocks there, some long and slender, and others rounder. They didn't look like bones to me, but as my gaze lifted to the sparkling blue waters of the cove, I saw ships. Dozens of large vessels, their black sails down. Movement to the right of them caught my eye. On the bluffs on the other side of the cove, another black and brown draken lifted its head. Was that Crolee? Ehthawn and Orphine's cousin? I hadn't seen the other draken since I'd first arrived in the Shadowlands.

My gaze lowered to the dunes below, focusing on the deep shadows under the bluff. I squinted, seeing movement. Every so often, something silver glinted in the sunlight. Armor. *Soldiers.*

I rose and turned, swallowing a gasp.

Saion was right in front of me, bowing deeply. "Consort, we've missed you."

My grin turned wry. I didn't think he lied. I liked to believe that Saion and I had moved past the threatening-my-life part of our relationship, but the only thing the gods had probably missed was the absence of the drama my presence caused.

"We are also glad to see you here." Rhahar joined his cousin. "We knew Nyktos wouldn't return without you."

"More like *she* wouldn't return without me," Ash corrected, having appeared beside me in that silent, quick way of his.

Rhahar's brows lifted. "Is that so?"

"It was she who took Kolis down for the count," Bele chimed in, having hauled herself up onto the stone base. She was carving a...where had she gotten an apple? "Not our esteemed, fearless leader."

My lips pursed.

"Damn," Lailah murmured, her hand resting on the hilt of her broadsword. Eyeing Ash, her smile spread. "I'm going to need details."

"She also freed me," Ash told them. "I stand here because of her."

"As do I," a quiet voice added.

Kars turned, stepping to the side to reveal Rhain as he said, "I don't think many of us would be standing here if not for you."

Feeling like my face was likely the color of Rhain's hair, I shifted from foot to foot as I heard several shouts of affirmation.

"That is still something we all have questions about," Kars stated.

My gaze shot to Rhain. He hadn't told them about the deal? My grip tightened on the diamond as relief swelled inside me. Rhain hadn't been conscious when Kolis made his demands, but it would take no leap of logic to work out what it likely entailed.

"It...it was nothing," I said, unsure of what I was responding to or whom. "I only did what any of you would do."

Rhain nodded as he looked away. My gaze snagged on Ash. He watched me in a way that further confirmed my belief that he knew.

"Okay. I think we need storytime. Oh!" Bele swallowed a piece of apple. "Still haven't found any boots. Not a lot of opportunities around these parts."

"It's all right," I told her.

Ash's head cut to the right. "Storytime will have to wait."

"Got to be Attes," Bele said, frowning as she eyed the horizon. "Feels like more than just him."

My stomach dropped as Rhain asked about Attes. All I caught of Ash's response was that he could be trusted. I should've been listening, but I...I couldn't feel Attes.

There was no hum signaling another Primal's arrival.

I could still feel the essence thrumming faintly inside me, but that was probably a bad sign.

"Sera?" Ash questioned softly.

Inhaling deeply, I fixed a smile on my face and I looked up at him. Before anything could be said, Ehthawn pushed off the roof, sending plumes of dust falling as he took to the sky. On the horizon, I could make out the shape of wings—large wings stretched wide.

Rhahar and Saion stepped forward as a unit, both reaching for their swords.

"There's no need for that," Attes's voice rose from the steps. "It's only Aurelia. She will harm none of you."

"Yeah, well, can't blame my people for being wary." Ash shifted his stance so half of him blocked me. At his side, his hand fisted as there was a round of hasty bows that neither Ash nor I joined in on.

Bele didn't either.

She cut off another chunk of apple and popped it into her mouth.

I pressed my hand against Ash's back as Attes crested the top of the stairs.

"I can't." Attes glanced out to sea as his draken grew closer to Ehthawn, who rumbled a low warning. Attes's jaw tensed. "I hope your draken is just overly friendly."

Well…

"Ehthawn will not strike at Aurelia unless he's given reason to," Ash advised. "But it's not him you're really worried about."

Nektas snorted smoke from where he remained on the cliff.

Attes tilted his head. "I assume Seraphena is all right and still in possession of The Star?"

"The what?" Bele murmured.

"I am." I sidestepped Ash, looking behind him and seeing no one. "Keella?"

"She's here." Attes did a double-take as he spotted Elias. "I had her give us a couple of minutes just in case we needed them." He looked pointedly at Ash. "Hopefully, those minutes aren't needed."

"They're not," Ash replied, folding his arms over his chest. "Yet."

"They won't be needed." I shot Ash a look as Ehthawn veered toward who I assumed was Crolee.

"It's nice to deal with someone reasonable." Attes's smile softened the scars on his face.

A growl came from a much, much closer source.

Attes's smile kicked up a notch as he ignored the warning of violence building in Ash. The Primal of War and Accord scanned those on the Temple as his draken flew overhead, her scales a mix of green and brown in the sunlight.

"Um," I murmured as the draken cleared the Temple, dipping low. The end of her spiked tail skimmed the side of the cliff directly above Nektas, sending a shower of dirt down on him.

Wait. Wasn't that the draken Nektas had visited to get information from? And hadn't Reaver said he thought *Nek* was sweet on her?

Nektas grumbled, shaking off the dirt as he raised his head. Eyes narrowing, his head swiveled, thin wisps of smoke wafting from his nose. Aurelia tucked her wings to her sides, landing on a cliff above and off to the side of Nektas.

She was larger than both Ehthawn and Crolee, but Nektas dwarfed her as he rose onto all fours, baring his teeth—

Aurelia was *fast*, stretching out her neck and snapping at Nektas as the frills around her neck vibrated.

I tugged on the back of Ash's shirt. "Should we be worried about this?"

"Should we? Probably," he replied dryly. "Since this is their idea of flirting, and it tends to get a bit…aggressive."

"Kind of like how you two flirt," Saion tossed out as he strode past us.

"Rude," I muttered.

Ash chuckled, sending a little quiver of surprise through me. Normally, he would've threatened Saion, or at the very least, shut him up with a glare, but the Ash I'd first met in the mortal realm? He was more relaxed, more playful. I was seeing a bit of that now, his more teasing nature—

Nektas yelped as Aurelia nipped his neck when he got too close. He jerked back, his chest rumbling.

"Just think," Attes neared us, "if they hook up, we'll be kind of related."

"What a thrilling prospect," Ash stated.

Dragging my gaze from the two draken, I remembered the other draken Attes had spoken of. "Where's Basilia?"

"Still making sure Kolis's draken are busy," Attes answered, his smile deepening as he turned from Ash. One dimple appeared. "Lailah, it's been ages since I've seen you."

"Has it?" the goddess remarked nonchalantly.

"It has." A hint of a fang appeared as Attes strode past Kars, who gave him a wide berth. "The last time I visited the House of Haides, Theon claimed you were indisposed."

"I was." Lailah raised a brow as I saw Saion start to grin while his cousin scratched at his short, cropped hair. "I had a headache."

"A headache?" Attes repeated.

"Yes." She shifted her weight. "Strangely, it's starting to return."

The Primal laughed, and both dimples appeared. "I do believe you are insinuating that I am the cause of this headache."

"You're so incredibly astute." She blinked her wide-set gold eyes. "Perhaps you should've been the Primal of Wisdom."

"I detect sarcasm. You wound me." Attes pressed his hand to his chest. "Deeply."

"Not deeply enough," muttered Lailah.

I tugged on Ash's shirt again as I whispered, "Are they aggressively flirting?"

Ash's eyes narrowed on them.

Lailah and Theon were from Vathi. How they'd ended up with Ash was a story not yet shared with me, but the way Attes eyed the goddess had me thinking there was history there that might also involve... aggressive flirting.

Ash faced the stairs. A moment later, Keella appeared, lifting a hand as everyone started to bow again. "Not necessary," she assured the gods, but Kars and Rhain stilled bowed. She smiled at them. "I hope all is well?"

"Perfect. One second, please." Ash's head snapped to where Attes was currently circling Lailah. "Knock it the fuck off."

Attes looked up through a lock of sandy-brown hair. Quiet fell across the Temple as Keella clasped her hands in front of the pale blue cloak she wore.

"She no longer serves in your Court," Ash reminded him.

"Thank fuck," Attes replied. "I would've lost complete control of my Court if she still did."

That statement piqued my curiosity and then some.

Lailah's response didn't help. "It's okay, Nyktos. I know how to handle him."

"I can one hundred percent confirm that," Attes said, sending a wink in Lailah's direction. "With the fondest memories."

Lailah's eyes rolled.

Okay. Now, I was really curious.

"Yes." Keella lifted her chin. "Everything seems completely... perfect." She turned from them. "Attes filled me in. You have The Star?"

Blinking, I stopped paying attention to...well, whatever was going on. "I do." The moment Keella's stare landed on me, I did everything to keep from thinking about the last time she'd seen me. I lifted the wrapped diamond. "And he told you everything?"

Keella nodded as she glided forward, her sorrow-filled eyes lifting to Ash.

"So, back to the important stuff." Bele hopped off the stone, tossing her apple core toward the draken. Nektas moved to catch it, but Aurelia got there first. "What is a star?"

"I assume it's not what's in the sky," Rhahar said as the apple core—or half of it—got flung toward Nektas.

Oh, cute. They were...sharing food.

"It's something no one but the Arae should possess." Keella eyed the bundle I held. "Or should've ever created."

"I can agree with that."

"But if they hadn't, then you would not be standing here with him." Keella stopped in front of me. "There is always good in the bad." Her gaze met mine, and the intensity of her stare made me squirm. "I understood then, just as I do now."

I sucked in a short breath, knowing she was speaking of the last time we'd seen each other.

"Understand what?" Ash asked.

"That there is often good behind the bad," she said. "Are you sure of what you saw in the diamond?"

Grateful for the subject change, I nodded as I glanced at Ash. I didn't know if he wanted anyone else here to know.

Ash's gaze held mine, then flicked to the others before returning to the diamond. "It's my father's soul. It's in there."

Bele's mouth dropped open.

"Are you...?" Rhain had paled. He came forward, stopping several feet from us to stare at what I held.

"I am certain." I carefully unwrapped the diamond, letting the flimsy torn silk drift to the floor.

The milky-white light throbbed inside The Star, pressing against its edges.

"Attes told you about Sotoria?" When Keella nodded, I could practically feel the questions bursting to break free of Bele, but she remained quiet.

"It's doable, then?" Ash's chest rose with a heavy breath. "Once my father's soul is free?"

"Yes."

"And you know how that is done?" he asked. "Will I be able to do it?"

"I do not imagine it's like drawing out other souls," she said, her delicate brows knitting. "If it works like transferring the embers, then the soul could likely only be summoned by the one who placed it there."

Attes cursed, having left Lailah's side. "That's not going to happen."

"There have to be other ways."

The breeze tossed a few strands of her russet-colored hair across her jaw. "The Arae could draw the soul free."

What had Ash claimed in the dream? "You said I could summon them, right?"

Before Ash could answer me, Keella said, "Yes, but they would likely take The Star back."

Damn it.

"That won't work either." Frustration filled Attes's tone.

"There is one more way," Keella said. "The true Primal of Life can summon it."

Of course.

"Absolutely not," Ash stated.

A tremor went through my arm. "How?"

Ash stepped into me. "Sera—"

"You would simply will it, and it should happen," Keella explained as Ash cursed. "The Primal of Life—"

"Say no more," Ash growled as he blocked her. "You cannot do this."

Aware of the confusion surrounding those around us, I smiled at him. "If it's just willing it, that won't take a lot of energy."

"That's not how it works." Ash grasped my shoulders. "And you know it."

I did.

"I have to," I told him. "It's your father, Ash." Even if we didn't need to get Sotoria's soul out of me. "I need to do this."

His nostrils flared as eather briefly pumped through his flesh. "You don't need to do any of this."

"You're right." Focusing on the embers, I felt them throb weakly throughout my entire body as I joined my will to them. "I want to."

"Sera—" He went rigid, seeing something in me that told him it was too late. His fingers pressed into my shoulders. "*Liessa*…"

I felt no swell of energy, just an awareness of what I'd willed coming into creation. I looked down.

The Star heated in my palm as it started to hum and vibrate. The high-pitched whirring sound came from it again. Tiny streaks of milky light seeped out of the diamond.

Nektas let out a low, trilling sound as the light in the diamond pulsed brightly once and then twice—

Essence poured out of it, forcing Ash to stagger back a step. There were several gasps. A soft, warbling sound came from one of the other draken. Eyes wide, I watched the whitish-silver light spilling into the air between us, becoming a throbbing indistinguishable mass.

Several of the gods backed up as the light reflected off their faces. Even Attes moved away, his eyes wide.

The mass of light twisted and stretched, turning toward Ash.

His breathing seemed to halt as his father's soul hovered beside him. It throbbed and then extended, forming what appeared to be an arm, and then...

A hand and fingers.

That brushed Ash's cheek.

Ash's eyes slammed shut, his large body shuddering as he rasped, "Father."

Tears blurred my vision as Eythos's soul began to lift and drift upward.

"I understand," Ash whispered.

Understand what? Had he heard his father? I blinked, trying to clear my vision, but it didn't—

I felt my heart stutter, then speed up, beating twice in the place of one. I tried to drag in a breath, but a sudden, stunning pain ripped through my chest, taking with it my sense of sight, sound, and... *everything* else.

36

I slowly became aware of a faint taste in my mouth—a sweet, smoky, lush flavor. Decadent. Powerful. My lips tingled. So did my fingers. I stretched, enjoying the pull of my muscles as I wiggled my toes.

A body moved against mine. A sudden inhalation of breath brought a chest against my back. "*Liessa,*" a familiar, deep voice murmured—one I'd recognize anywhere, anytime. "There you are."

Ash.

My eyes fluttered open to a vivid, deep sapphire sky streaked with trailing pink and amethyst clouds. Confusion rose as I squinted. I'd never seen such a sky before. My gaze lowered to trees in an array of blues and violets that bordered on pink, reminding me of the jacaranda trees outside Wayfair.

Disjointed memories flashed. The cavern of lilacs. Arriving in the Bonelands. Freeing Eythos. Wrenching, terrible pain, and then nothing.

I stared at the surreal, brightly colored landscape. Had I…had I died? That didn't make sense. If I had, I wouldn't be in Ash's arms. He couldn't be near souls who had gone beyond the Pillars of Asphodel without risking the destruction of their souls. And wouldn't I have remembered passing through them and being judged? Despite what Ash believed about my soul, I seriously doubted I'd end up someplace as beautiful as this. At the very least, I would've been one of those souls who needed a more thorough look. Could this be that? If so, why did my temples still ache?

"Am I...?" I cleared my throat, causing the sultry taste to fade. "Did I die?"

"What?" His arm tightened around my waist. "Fates, no, Sera."

I wiggled again, feeling a soft mattress under me. We were on some sort of sofa. "Where are we?"

"The Thyia Plains." Ash shifted me in his embrace, and my head suddenly came to rest in the crook of his arm. I stared up at him. His hair was a rich, warm, reddish-brown and fell against the cut line of his jaw. The golden-bronze hue of his skin was paler, and I saw concern etched into the striking lines and angles of his face. "Keella thought you'd be more comfortable here. We're on the veranda of her palace."

My gaze inched away from his, running over the terracotta stone floor and then beyond to the cliffs that stretched out on either side. I saw Ehthawn. The draken was curled on one of the rocky bluffs, his head resting on the sun-warmed rock. I would've thought him asleep if not for the one open crimson eye and the idle twitching of his tail. I scanned the other cliffs, not seeing Nektas or the other draken.

Ash smoothed his thumb down my cheek, the coolness of his touch surprising me. It was even colder than before.

I swallowed, glancing down at my hands—my *empty* hands. My stomach twisted. "Where is The Star?"

"Keella and Attes have it," he said, and I relaxed. "How are you feeling?"

"I...I don't know. Okay?" My gaze flicked back to his. "I passed out, didn't I?"

"You did."

My mind cleared of the remaining fog, and I stiffened. "Oh, gods, I'm sorry."

His dark brows furrowed. "For what?"

"For passing out right in the middle of freeing your father."

Ash's expression smoothed out. "Sera—"

"I saw him touch you. He was talking to you, wasn't he? In a way no one else could hear?" I could clearly see Eythos's soul drifting upward. "Please, tell me you didn't focus on me when I passed out."

"I could hear him—his voice." Ash's thickened. "I didn't think I'd ever hear it again, but I did. Thanks to you."

"I really didn't do much."

"*Liessa*," he chided softly, drawing his thumb across the skin below my lip. "You did everything."

A knot lodged in my chest. "But then I had to go and pass out, ruining what was a beautiful moment. So that undoes—"

"It undoes nothing, Sera. You didn't interrupt anything. His soul was leaving this realm."

"Are you sure I didn't—?"

"I'm positive." Ash dipped his head, kissing my forehead. "He couldn't linger here. He didn't want to after all this time."

I imagined not.

Gods, I really hoped he wasn't lying to me. "What did he say to you?" My eyes widened at my question. "I mean, you don't have to tell me. I'm sure it was private—"

"He told me that he loved me." Ash drew his fingers along my jaw. "That he was proud of me—of the man I've become."

"Oh," I whispered, feeling the knot make its way to my throat. Tears pricked my eyes.

He stretched his neck to the side. "I almost couldn't believe he said that, to be honest."

"Why?" I lifted a hand, relieved that it didn't take as much effort as walking up those damn Temple steps had. "Of course, he would be proud of you."

"I've done a lot of things that no one would be proud of."

My heart ached for him. "You did things others made you do."

"I'm not talking just about that, liessa. Just in the last twenty-four hours, I've committed indisputable atrocities—killing those who laid down their swords. Those who turned and ran from me."

I frowned. "I wouldn't consider that an atrocity."

Ash raised a brow. "Such an act would likely send a mortal's soul into the Abyss."

"This is different," I reasoned.

One side of his lips tipped up. "Care to explain that reasoning?"

"Not really."

He chuckled.

I searched his features. "Do you regret killing them? The ones who surrendered or ran?"

"No."

His quick answer told me he spoke the truth. "Good."

Ash cocked his head.

"What? I would've regretted it for a whole three-point-five seconds and then moved right on. You know that." And he did because I'd shared my struggles concerning my lack of guilt. "You told me before that all of us are capable of monstrous acts, but it does not make us monsters."

"I did."

My gaze dropped to the collar of his shirt. The loose opening revealed a swatch of his shoulder and the black ink there. "One hundred and ten," I murmured, lifting my eyes to his. He may say he didn't regret taking those lives, but underneath his anger, he did. He was better than me, less monstrous. "Do not add those lives to your flesh," I said. Right or wrong, I didn't want that for him.

Thick lashes lowered, and he nodded. I felt his chest rise again with a deep but shaky breath.

"Did he say anything else?" I asked.

Ash nodded. "He told me not to forget what he said when we were near the Red River, rounding up the Shades." His jaw tensed as his thumb skated over the line of my cheekbone. "It was the last time I saw him alive."

"What did he tell you?"

"That's the thing." Ash hesitated, his eyes darting away from mine before returning. He curtly shook his head. "I don't remember."

His denial hung in the air between us, and I bit down on the inside of my lip, tasting a hint of the sweet, smoky flavor again...

Wait.

"You gave me your blood."

"I did."

"Ash." Worry spread through me like a weed left to grow. He'd been imprisoned for *weeks*, and what blood he'd taken after being freed couldn't have been enough to restore him. "You shouldn't have done that—"

"You shouldn't have used the eather to free my father," he cut in gently. "So, we both did what we believed the other shouldn't have."

"That's not the same thing."

"What you did caused you to deplete your energy and pass out," he countered, the essence in his eyes dancing. "I, on the other hand, didn't suffer those consequences."

"Passing out probably has more to do with climbing those damn Temple steps than using the eather to free Eythos."

A small smile appeared. "Sera."

"I'm serious. I hate stairs, and it's not any different. You need to conserve your energy."

Ash sighed. "I didn't give you very much blood, just enough…"

"Just enough to make sure I woke up," I finished for him. Part of me was surprised that his blood had even done that at this point. Because the pain I'd felt in my chest? I wouldn't have been surprised if my heart had imploded. "You shouldn't have done it."

"And what *should* I have done?" The softness vanished from his features. "Let you die?" His eyes narrowed when I opened my mouth. "If you say yes, so help me Fates, Sera… Because I will not let you die."

I started to sit up, but the arm I rested on tensed, and his hand curved around my shoulder. Frustration swept through me. "I wasn't going to say that."

"Really?"

"No." I struggled in his hold. "You know what you should've done."

"I did exactly what I should've done," he shot back. "And stop trying to move around. You need to take it easy."

"What is taking it easy going to do for me?" I threw up my arms, almost smacking him in the face. "The same as giving me blood? Delaying the inevitable while wasting time?"

The skin of his cheeks thinned. Shadows blossomed, thickening. "Disagree."

"Disagree?" I sputtered.

"I believe that is what I just said. You being angry with my response doesn't change it."

My eyes widened as I stared at him. "I'm not angry with you."

"Really?" he repeated dryly.

"Yes," I hissed, trying to rein in my temper. I wasn't angry with him. I was furious with *this*—the situation he'd been put in. That I was in. What couldn't be avoided. "You needed—"

"I did what I needed to do, Sera."

"You two are arguing." A deeper, raspier voice intruded. "I suppose that means Sera is feeling better."

I twisted in Ash's arms so fast I started to topple off the couch.

"For fuck's sake," Ash muttered, catching me. "Did I not just tell you to take it easy?"

My gaze swung toward gauzy turquoise curtains rippling in front of open doors and then to the tall male with long, black hair streaked with red who'd walked out. "Nektas."

I saw his lips curve slightly as he crossed the veranda, ridges of scales visible across his bare shoulders. "Hello, Seraphena."

Emotion swelled so intensely in my chest upon seeing him in his mortal form that it caught me off guard. Once again, I felt tears crowding my eyes. I had no idea why I was so freaking emotional all the time.

It probably had something to do with me dying.

But Nektas…he had always been kind to me. He'd never held what I had originally planned against me. And he…he'd told me that if I were ever not feeling okay, I could come and talk to him. That we would make sure I got back to being okay together.

"We weren't arguing," Ash said, giving up on keeping me prone. He sat up, bringing me with him. I ended up sitting half in his lap and half between his legs.

Nektas lifted a brow.

"We were having a discussion," Ash tacked on. "Where we disagreed."

Laughing under his breath, Nektas sat beside us. "You're both right and wrong."

I drew back. "You heard us."

"Anyone near the veranda heard you two."

"Oh." My cheeks flushed as I glanced at the swaying curtains.

Ash folded his arm over my waist again. "What you meant to say is that I was right, and she was wrong."

I shot him a glare over my shoulder. "That is not what he said."

He glanced down at me. "It's what I heard."

"Then there's something wrong with your hearing."

"Is this a continuation of the discussion where you two were not arguing but disagreeing?" Nektas asked.

"Yes," Ash and I snapped at the same time.

"At least you can agree on that."

"I was simply telling him that he needs to take the embers," I began.

"Not to sound repetitive," Ash said, "but I disagree."

"Oh, my fucking gods."

"Now, you're just being sacrilegious."

I glared at him.

His lips twitched.

"That wasn't even funny."

Ash opened his mouth.

"If you say disagree again, I cannot be held accountable for my actions—my extremely violent actions."

"As I was saying," Nektas jumped in again, a lock of crimson-streaked hair sliding over his shoulder as he tilted his head. His eyes met mine. "You're right. Ash cannot afford to weaken himself. *But*," he said before Ash could intervene, "he only gave you a little of his blood. Not nearly enough to have stopped this inevitability."

I snapped my mouth shut.

"I think it was more like his sheer will made it so you woke up," Nektas continued.

His sheer will?

"And is waking up in the arms of the one you care so deeply for a waste of time? There is nothing I would not give to have one more moment with Halayna."

My breath snagged at the raw honesty and lingering pain in his voice. I twisted toward Ash. "I don't think any extra time with you is a waste. I wasn't thinking."

"I know." Ash cupped my cheek.

"But Sera doesn't have much more of that precious time," Nektas said quietly. "And that cannot be denied. I can feel it." He placed a hand against the coppery skin of his chest. "Scent it."

My upper lip curled. "You can...smell it?"

"The body goes through natural changes when it begins to die. That is something we can smell," he explained. I thought about the last time he'd said I smelled like death. Had I smelled like this the whole time? "And we can sense the fading of the embers."

I looked at where Ehthawn rested and thought about the low, mournful sound I'd heard him make.

"So can Ash," Nektas continued. "So can any Primal who is near you."

Reaching down, I folded my hand over the arm at my waist.

Nektas lifted his ruby eyes to Ash. "You know what has to be done. And soon."

Ash was completely still behind me. I didn't even feel him breathe. "I do."

Briefly squeezing my eyes shut, I leaned against Ash's chest. There was so much I wanted to say, but most of it would only make things worse. I knew that.

I took a deep breath. "I'm sorry about Orphine."

"As am I."

Glancing at Ehthawn, I wished there was more I could say than that, but there truly weren't words in any language that could capture the sorrow felt after a death. "How...how is Jadis? Reaver?"

Nektas's handsome features softened. "They are good. Safe. Reaver has asked for you, and my daughter often searches for you." His smile was sad. "I think she misses sleeping on your legs."

My lips trembled, and I pressed them together as Ash folded his other arm over my chest. Would Jadis even remember that? What about Reaver? The knot tripled in size. My nose burned, and it took several moments for me to speak. "I...I've missed that," I rasped. "I miss both of them."

"I know," Nektas said solemnly.

I met his gaze and tried to say more. What, exactly, I wasn't even sure, but I couldn't get anything out. The draken's face blurred, and I tried to find that veil of nothingness because I didn't want Ash feeling any of what I was. I didn't want Nektas seeing it.

Nektas reached for me. His skin was so warm as he placed my hand between his palms. He said nothing as he drew it to his chest, pressing it over where I felt his heart beat—felt two beats, almost side by side. Then he returned my hand to Ash's. His cool fingers threaded through mine. I blinked a couple of times, letting my head fall back against Ash's chest.

Nektas turned to the doors and rose as Keella walked out onto the veranda, followed by Attes.

Icy air blasted off Ash when he saw Attes.

"I don't want to intrude," Attes announced, his steps slowing.

"But you're going to," Ash replied coolly.

"I wouldn't if I could." Attes approached us as Keella stayed back. My gaze dropped to the leather saddlebag gripped tightly in his hand. "How are you feeling, Seraphena?"

Ash couldn't be more rigid if he tried. "I'm okay," I said.

His smile was more of a grimace. "Why do I have a feeling you say that when it's not true?"

"Because she does." Ash's palm flattened against my hip. "But knowing that won't stop you."

"Unfortunately, no," Attes admitted quietly. "We need to take care of Sotoria's soul."

"I don't give a fuck about that soul," Ash snarled, shadows pressing against the flesh of the arm he had around my waist.

"But you need to care," Attes began.

Ash's head whipped toward the other Primal. "Was I not clear?" His voice vibrated with rage—his entire body did. But he held me so carefully, as if I were made of nothing more than fragile, spun glass.

"Ash," I said, twisting toward him.

"I know she's important." Attes inched closer, speaking before I could continue. "I know she's very important to you."

The churning wisps of eather stilled in Ash's eyes. He lifted his gaze from mine and slowly turned his head to the Primal. The look he gave the Primal of War and Accord could freeze a soul.

Attes was undaunted. "And I remember what that's like. It fucking haunts me," he said. I thought of the children he'd lost. "I've been told you had your *kardia* removed. In all honesty, I find that hard to believe, all things considered." He shot a pointed look at Ash. "However, if that's true, you know what will happen."

A low rumble of warning started in Ash's chest.

"And I'm sorry. I really am," Attes was quick to add. "I like Seraphena. She…" He glanced at me, his sad smile not quite reaching his eyes. "She amuses me."

The growl coming from Ash deepened.

Attes's attention shifted back to Ash. "But the soul in her is far more important."

"I'm not sure how any of that is helping right now," I said, pressing a hand to Ash's chest as his lips peeled back, revealing sharp fangs. "At all."

"What I'm trying to say is that when Seraphena dies, Sotoria will be lost," Attes stated. "And that means the only chance to truly stop Kolis dies with that soul. If that happens? Nothing will be able to stop him. And you know more than anyone, he doesn't need to Ascend into the Primal of Life and Death to wreak havoc."

"You know an awful lot about this soul, given you're the fucking Primal of War," Ash spat. "Besides that, Sotoria isn't really alive, now is she? Her soul is just an invader in Sera's body, who *is* alive."

My brows knitted. I got what Ash was saying, but… "She's alive," I whispered. Flat, chrome-hued eyes snapped back to mine. "I mean, maybe conscious is better than saying she's alive, but she's aware."

Ash frowned.

"It's true." Attes had moved closer, maybe a few feet from us. "I heard Sotoria—her voice and laugh from Sera—when Kolis first had her. It's a sound I would recognize anywhere."

My lips parted in surprise. He was talking about when Kolis had tried to take the embers. Attes hadn't shared that before.

"How would you know that?" Ash demanded.

"He knew Sotoria," I answered. "I haven't had a chance to tell you."

Attes nodded. "I met her when Kolis first brought her back. In Dalos. I was...in her presence long enough to know her voice and laugh."

"I have so many questions about that," I murmured, but something suddenly occurred to me. "Even if I were Sotoria, and what Eythos planned worked, we still can't kill Kolis, right? He is the only one with true Primal of Death embers."

"Correct." Keella drifted closer, a woodsy, earthy scent following her. "If Kolis dies without there being true embers of death in someone else, the release of those embers would devastate the realms and upset the balance."

My brows lifted. "That brings me back to the point I was making. Kolis cannot be killed."

"Yet," Keella said.

"The Star." Ash eyed the leather satchel Attes carried. "The Star can be used to transfer the embers from Kolis."

"Of course," I murmured as I frowned. "But it would be holding Sotoria's soul."

"Hopefully, not for long," Attes said. "Eythos hoped Sotoria could weaken Kolis enough for the embers to be transferred to The Star."

"But what if I hadn't found the diamond?" I pointed out. "That was a huge risk to take."

A wry grin appeared on Attes's face. "As I said, I didn't think Eythos's plan was all that great."

"Maybe it wasn't his only plan," Nektas commented. "Yes, Eythos could be impulsive, but I doubt he didn't think of all the possible ways things could go wrong. He could've had other plans and simply didn't share them."

"There's no way of knowing that," Attes said. "But what I do know is that once Sotoria is reborn, we will have The Star and can end Kolis."

Once Sotoria was reborn, she'd likely be raised as I was, steeped in death and groomed for one purpose only: to seduce and kill. Not to be her own person, with a future. My stomach twisted with nausea.

I shook my head. "What about until then?"

"Several things have to happen before then," Keella said. "Even though Eythos was no longer the Primal of Life when we placed Sotoria's soul in your bloodline, he still had the true embers of life then.

For me to do what we did again, I will need the true Primal of Life's assistance."

"So you will need Ash," I said. The subject of my statement tensed behind me. "Then what?"

Keella's gaze lifted to Ash and then returned to me, but it was Attes who said, "Then we would have to incapacitate Kolis until Sotoria can be reborn and come of age. He will be weakened by the Ascension of the true of Primal of Life. It will be our one opportunity to strike."

Ash spoke then. "You speak of entombing him. Putting him in stasis."

I now knew how that could be done—by using the bones of the Ancients.

"You speak as if this will be easy to do," Ash said. "Those loyal to him will resist. They will fight for him."

"There will be war," I whispered, looking up at Attes. "But that war has been coming."

Attes nodded. "But it won't be the kind of war Kolis would wage."

"Kolis claims he doesn't want war," I shared. "I know that's hard to believe, and only part of me thinks he spoke the truth. But that was before...well, before now. When he wakes and realizes I'm not really Sotoria, it'll be bad."

"And we will be prepared." Attes's stare moved to Ash. "We can't let the only hope we have of stopping Kolis die."

"The only person I care about not dying is Sera," Ash swore.

My heart, well, it was doing flips now. Weak ones.

"And I understand that." Attes lowered his voice. "But this is bigger than you—than Seraphena. Than all of us. You know that. Deep down, you do."

My gaze crawled back to Ash. "He's right," I said quietly. "And you know it. You might not think so now, but later? When...when all of this was for nothing?"

"There won't be a later when this was for nothing," he countered.

"Ash." A palpation in my chest—a whooshing sensation—took my breath, but only for a second. I ignored it. "This is important."

"No, Sera. That soul isn't important. You are." His whirling silver eyes fixed on the other Primal. "She is what matters. And if I have to repeat that, I will rip out your tongue."

A buzzing, bubbling sensation filled me as I stared up at the harshly beautiful lines of Ash's face. It wasn't the rather grotesque threat that made my heart swell and fill. It was the other words he'd spoken. That *I* was important to him. *I* mattered to him. I already knew I did, but I *felt* them in how he held me, tightly but gently. I heard them in how fiercely he spoke. I saw them in how he looked at me, his eyes a luminous, warm silver, and I knew them to be true.

I was important.

I mattered.

Not for what I had been born to do but for who I was.

And that realization wasn't something that came all of a sudden, only because Ash had said them. It was something I'd always known, wasn't it? I wouldn't have been so relieved all those years ago when Ash refused to take me as his Consort. I'd known then that my life mattered, despite my duty and so-called failures. I just hadn't allowed myself to accept the truth. Ash helped me see that. Accept it.

But I knew that Sotoria's soul was also important.

Leaning into Ash, I cupped his cheek. Those frigid eyes landed on me. "I love you," I whispered. "I love your protectiveness. I love that you see *me*. That I'm important to you. That *I* matter. I love you so very much for that."

A shudder went through him as the eather whirled more fiercely in his eyes. "You are the only thing that matters."

"But I'm not," I told him. "Sotoria does. Like your father, she has been trapped and doesn't deserve what will happen if her soul remains in me."

A muscle began ticking in his jaw.

"That's not fair to her. You know that." I drew my finger along his lower lip. "And I know you wouldn't want that for her. My importance doesn't cancel out hers."

Eather flared brightly in his eyes. "I disagree."

"Are you sure your *kardia* was correctly removed?" Attes asked dryly. He lifted a hand when Ash's head swung toward him. "Just asking."

"Ignore him." I guided his gaze back to me. "Look, I've started the Ascension, but I'm not going to fully Ascend right this moment. We have time to take care of this, and it's not like it will hurt me." I looked over my shoulder, glancing between the two Primals. "Right?"

"It shouldn't," Keella answered.

"That's not entirely reassuring," Nektas murmured from where he stood.

"No, it isn't." Ash's eyes narrowed on the Primal goddess.

"What we plan in regard to removing Sotoria's soul and setting her on a path to be reborn is not without risk," Keella said. "It could incite the wrath of the Fates."

"What doesn't incite their wrath?" I muttered dryly.

"Not much." Keella's brief smile vanished as she knelt beside Ash and me, her voice becoming solemn. "There is a balance to life, one that Eythos understood, but Kolis never truly could, no matter how hard he tried to. You see, if there is life, there must also be death."

Understanding crept in as I thought about Marisol and my stepfather. "If you bring someone back to life, another loses their life? That kind of balance?"

"It's more than that, Seraphena. The Fates were never fond of restoring life. Not even what I do by giving those who never truly lived a chance to do so. But reincarnation is a loophole of sorts. What Kolis has done, what Eythos and I took part in, and what we are about to do again will upset the balance."

I wasn't sure what she was getting at.

Keella leaned in, her ancient gaze fixing on mine. "There was a reason Eythos had to be careful when it came to restoring life—giving it back to one who'd passed. It cannot be done twice for the same person—mortal, god, or draken—without the Arae intervening in some fashion, becoming the checks and balances. Therefore, doing so will never end the way one intends. Either death will come for them again, or the Arae will reset the balance in some other way." Her lips quirked. "After all, look at the mess we—Kolis, Eythos, and I—have created with Sotoria." She paused. "And there is no way the Fates have not dipped their hands in this and made it even messier."

"That's...that's why Holland called the Revenants an abomination, isn't it?" I glanced at Ash. "Because they keep coming back."

Keella nodded. "Sotoria has died multiple times and was brought back in one form or another. Then her soul was reincarnated. That ceased when we placed her with the embers. She was supposed to be reborn. That did not occur."

It struck me then. "Could the Fates have been why I wasn't reborn as Sotoria and instead became a...a vessel for her?"

"I cannot answer that for sure, but if I had to hazard a guess, I would say so."

I shook my head. "So, they could do something similar again?"

"Or not." Keella tilted her head. "They could do something far more...concerning. There's no way to know, but it would be foolish of us not to consider the risk."

I studied her. "You sound afraid of the Arae."

"The oldest of us are wise enough to be wary of them." She smiled. "We may be Primals, but we are not the ultimate power."

"At this moment, I couldn't care less about pissing off the Fates. That wasn't what I was asking," Ash stated, impatience filling his tone. "Will removing Sotoria's soul harm Sera in any way?"

Keella's gaze flicked up to Ash. "No."

That was a relief. "How is it done?"

"Have you been able to sense the dual souls?"

He shook his head. "I've only ever been able to feel the imprint of Sera's soul."

"Interesting." Keella's brows furrowed and then smoothed out. "Since I have handled this soul before, I will be able to, but I need your help, Nyktos. I need you to keep your hands on Sera and concentrate on her soul."

"Is there a chance you will do something to Sera's soul?" Ash demanded.

A trickle of unease ran down my spine as Ehthawn lifted his head from where it rested. Nektas stepped forward, his arms crossing.

Keella smiled. "Not if you do as I request. You will…basically be anchoring yourself to her soul. Do you understand?"

"Yes," Ash said, and I was glad he did because I didn't. "Let's do this then."

Attes stepped forward, lifting the saddlebag. Reaching inside, he pulled out the diamond and extended his hand, his fingers opening.

The Star rested on his palm, its edges jagged and irregular. There was no milky light filling the diamond now, but every part reflected whatever light found its way to it, casting shimmering rainbow hues over my legs and across the floor.

Keella carefully took The Star. Her silver eyes met mine. "Attes said you were able to feel Sotoria's presence? Is that true now?"

Wetting my lips, I closed my eyes and concentrated. There was no hum in my chest, but there was an awareness—that presence near my heart. It was so faint, and I wondered if my being so close to death affected her. I nodded, opening my eyes. "I can feel her."

"Good." Keella was looking at Ash as Attes took a step back. "Ready?"

Ash pressed his palm between my breasts. "Ready," he said gruffly.

A moment later, Keella placed her hand just below Ash's, her pinky finger overlapping his. My lips twitched as I fought a ridiculous giggle.

Ash's head tilted down. "What are you thinking?" he asked.

"Just that it's not often I have two Primal hands on my breasts."

Nektas snorted as a dimple appeared in Attes's right cheek. I could feel Ash shaking his head behind me.

Keella's smile tipped up. "Try to concentrate on Sotoria's soul."

I nodded obediently and could've sworn I saw Attes's other dimple wink to life.

The white aura behind Keella's pupils pulsed. Tendrils of eather seeped out, swirling across her irises and into her skin. Her eyes closed as the wisps spread over her smoky-reddish-brown cheeks and moved down her throat until her entire being was awash in essence.

Ash lowered his head, pressing his cheek against mine as I concentrated on Sotoria's presence. A heartbeat passed, and then a faint coolness seeped into my torso. I wasn't sure if it was Ash's touch or more—him anchoring himself to my soul.

"Do you have Seraphena's soul?" Keella asked.

"I do," Ash confirmed, his voice rough.

I almost asked what it felt like, what it looked like, but it probably wouldn't be wise to break anyone's concentration.

Including mine.

"I feel her," Keella announced with a solemn sigh. "*Suu ta lene.*" The essence around her flared. "*Vas na sutum.*"

"It is okay," Ash translated quietly for me. "You are safe."

"*Vena ta mayah,*" she urged. I knew that one. Come to me. Tendrils of eather crackled around her. "*Illa vol la sutum.*"

"She will…she will be safe," Ash repeated.

That didn't make sense, except…Keella had told her to come to her and then said she would be safe. She wasn't talking about Sotoria. She was talking about me.

Oh, gods. Was Sotoria somehow resisting because she was worried about me?

"*Illa vol ori,*" Keella told her. "*Illa vol…*" Whatever else Keella said was lost to the sudden buzzing in my ears.

Ash inhaled sharply, and my body jerked as I felt Sotoria respond. It was like she was disentangling herself from me and suddenly moving closer to the surface. That was the only way I could describe it.

"Hold on to Seraphena," Keella instructed.

"Always," Ash responded. "Always."

My heart stuttered and then sped up as I looked down, barely able to see past the aura coming off Keella. Still, I *felt* the sudden warmth pulsing over the skin of my chest under their hands.

A soft, silvery-white light suddenly radiated from my chest. My eyes widened as Keella replaced her hand with the one that held The Star. The hard edges pressed into my skin—

I heard Sotoria then.

Heard her speaking just as her soul left me and poured into the diamond.

Keella rocked back, the essence dimming around her as she looked down at The Star. An intense, bright white light floated inside the stone.

"It is done?" Attes asked, his voice thick.

"It is." The Primal goddess rose, turning to Attes. "We will keep her safe."

"Until…" I cleared my throat. "Until when?"

"Until it's best to allow her to be reborn," she said as Attes took the diamond. He handled it with reverence, gently placing it inside the satchel. "Once we can be sure that Kolis will not be able to find her before she is ready."

Before she is ready.

A sour taste gathered in my mouth as I placed my hand on my chest. Ash asked me if I was okay, and I nodded. I didn't feel different, yet I did. The presence I hadn't been aware of for most of my life was gone, but Sotoria's parting words lingered.

We will meet again.

37

We shadowstepped back to the Bonelands, leaving Keella and Attes in the Thyia Plains.

As I stared out past the ships at sea, I wished I could've seen more of the Court. It was beautiful.

Keella had embraced me before we left. Attes hadn't. Likely because Ash would've made good on his threat to rip out the Primal's tongue. Instead, he'd placed his hand over his heart and bowed.

I'd reminded him of his promise to me as Ash said goodbye to Keella: that he would support Ash.

"I have not forgotten, Seraphena," he'd answered. "He will have my support."

"Sera," I'd corrected him.

Attes had smiled then, but his dimples didn't appear, and his eyes looked sad. I hoped he and Ash could work things out and become more than comrades. I hoped they'd be friends like those Ash spoke with now.

We will meet again.

I hadn't hallucinated the sound of Sotoria's voice, but what had she meant? Once we both passed on? That would be soon, *very soon* for me. But her?

My stomach shifted again as I thought about her in that diamond for who knew how long, only to be reborn, grow up, and be placed right back in the hands of Kolis and his obsession. It wasn't right. I should've spoken up.

I turned at the sound of footsteps, spotting Elias, who had been conscious when we returned. The golden paint had been washed from his face. It was always hard to tell a god's age, but his square-shaped face looked younger than I expected.

"Sorry about what happened when you first arrived here," I said.

"It's okay. I'd rather be seen as suspicious and ask for forgiveness than end up dead." He touched the back of his head as he glanced to where Ehthawn was now perched on the cliff Aurelia had been on before. "Though I hope I don't have any more stones coming down on my head."

"I suppose you'll need to stay out from under any draken then," I said.

Elias glanced at the sea. "Was everything a success with the diamond?"

"It was." I took in the cut of his chin. "Are you from Attes's Court originally?"

He nodded.

"Did he have something to do with you working your way up to being Kolis's guard?"

"He did. Put a good word in, but I also had to put my time in to get there." He frowned, shifting uncomfortably on his feet. "He couldn't tell you about me, you know? It was just too much of a risk."

"I know."

His gaze cut to mine. "Do you?"

"I could've used that kind of information as a bargaining tool."

"Would you have?"

I watched Ash as he spoke to Saion and Rhahar, the breeze stirring his hair. "Depends."

Elias followed my gaze. "You'd do anything for him."

"I would."

"He's a lucky man, then, to have even a day of such devotion." A brief smile appeared. "And I have a feeling I'll be a dead man if he catches me talking to you."

My lips quirked. "You'll be fine. Attes? Probably a different story."

Elias chuckled. "Attes does have a way of inciting that response in others." His eyes narrowed. "I think someone wishes to speak with you."

I followed his gaze, finding Rhain striding toward us.

"Excuse me." Elias bowed.

I nibbled on the inside of my lip when Elias departed, only to be quickly intercepted by Kars, then shifted my focus to Rhain.

He stopped about a foot from me. "I'd ask how you're feeling, but..."

"Yeah," I murmured. "Thank you for not asking."

"And forcing you to lie?"

I nodded, now the one shifting uncomfortably from foot to foot. "Oh." I reached up, unclasping Aios's necklace. I offered it to him. "Can you give this back to Aios? Or give it to Bele?"

Rhain stared at the silver chain. "You should be the one returning it to her." He took the chain.

"I would like to," I told him, glancing down at the cracked marble floor. "By the way, that's a nifty talent you have. Communicating telepathically."

The apples of his cheeks matched his hair. "Yeah, it's not something I advertise. I'm not even as good at it as Kolis believes."

I doubted that. "I'm sorry about your father and brother."

Squinting, he nodded. His chest rose. "I wanted...I wanted to thank you for—"

"You don't have to."

"But I do." His golden-brown eyes met mine. "You didn't have to intervene to save me. You didn't have to do anything. Yet, you did."

I folded an arm over my waist. "I only did what anyone else would have."

"I don't think that's true, Seraphena." He stepped in closer. "I don't know what you had to do," he said, his voice low, "but whatever it was, I will never forget what you sacrificed."

"It wasn't..." I closed my eyes, knowing it was unlikely he'd believe me if I said it was nothing. "Thank you for not telling any of them about how you were freed."

"Of course." His gaze flickered over me. "But they would not have treated you any differently if they knew. I know they would feel what I do, only regret."

"Regret?"

Rhain nodded. "For not seeing you as Ector did," he said, his voice cracking. "He saw you for what you were when you first arrived in the Shadowlands."

"Someone you didn't want to stab?" I joked.

His too-solemn stare landed on me. "Someone who has earned our respect and admiration. Especially mine." He looked away. Ash was heading in our direction. "But *he* always saw you. Always."

Ash had.

He always saw *me*, even when he was angry or disappointed.

"What are you two talking about?" Ash came to my side, and Rhain moved back several feet, followed by the others.

"I was returning Aios's necklace," I said, my gaze moving over the faces of those I might've become friends with if I had more time and missing the ones not here and those no longer with us.

I wanted to see Reaver's too-solemn and too-old eyes for such a young boy. His smile. And I wished I could hold Jadis again. Feel her weight on my chest as she slept.

Gods, it was so damn weird.

Because I wasn't sure I had appreciated that experience as much as I should've in the moment. But now? I wished I'd paid more attention. Because I imagined that if I were able to live long enough to have children, that was what it would've felt like to hold my own. Feeling their heartbeat against my chest. And knowing that I held my whole damn world in my arms.

I glanced up at Ash. He was looking down at me, and the back of my throat burned with a knot of raw yearning. I'd never really considered children. I hadn't even liked holding them on the rare occasion I'd been near one. Babes and their tiny hands and fragility terrified me. The idea of children had never been a part of my future. But as my gaze traveled over Ash's face, I would've...I thought I would've entertained that with him. He would've made an amazing father.

No, I corrected myself with a sharp breath. He *will* make an amazing father.

The tendrils of eather brightened in his irises. He dipped his head to mine, speaking low. "What's wrong?"

Everything. "Nothing."

He ran his hand up my back, slipping it under my hair. "That's not true."

I drew back, meeting his stare. "Don't read my emotions."

"Don't lie to me."

"I'm not." I totally was.

He arched a brow. "*Liessa*."

"Nyktos," I snapped, and one side of his lips kicked up.

"Are you two fighting already?" Saion asked.

Ash lifted his head. "No."

"We're about to," I muttered at the same time.

"Yeah, they are." Saion smiled at his cousin. "Told you they wouldn't make it an hour."

"Godsdamn it," Rhahar grumbled.

Saion lifted a hand. "Pay up."

Rhahar was shaking his head as he reached beneath his armor. "I need to be more cynical."

I frowned as I glanced between the two. "Did you two...?" My brows shot up as Rhahar retrieved a few coins. "You two had a bet?"

"Yep." Saion took the coins. "Rhahar believed you two would go all day without getting into it. I said you wouldn't make it an hour without arguing about something—and that was being generous."

"Wow," Rhain murmured.

I turned to Bele.

Her hands flew up. "I had no part in this." She paused. "But I do agree that Saion was being generous."

Crossing my arms, I faced Ash. "These are your friends."

His lips twitched as he eyed them. "Were."

Rhahar laughed, and Saion made some wisecrack about being friends with a Primal of Death, but I...I could barely catch my breath as I stared up at Ash.

He'd just acknowledged them as *friends*.

He had never done that before, even going as far as to claim that he had no friends.

This interaction would mean very little to most, but it was huge for him. Ash had been taught that any connection could become a weakness that could be exploited. So, he'd always kept distance between himself and everyone else—everyone except Nektas.

I tilted my head, my gaze locking with the black-and-gray-scaled draken perched on the same cliff he had been on earlier. I could've sworn he smiled. It was kind of hard to tell while he was in his draken form, but those crimson eyes looked somber.

Drawing in a short breath, I looked at the crystal-clear blue waters. There was so much I wished I had time for. I would've loved to see Ash relax around his *friends*. Share dinner or drinks with them and discuss something other than war and violence. I would've liked to see Nektas's eyes turn as blue as the sea again, and Aios, Ezra, and Marisol...

I really wished I had a chance to do some real bodily damage to Veses.

I sighed.

My gaze returned to Nektas. He was no longer looking at me but at the horizon. I turned my attention back to those before us.

Lailah was speaking with Kars, her head tilted. I wished I had gotten to know her better because I really wanted to know what in the realms was up between her and Attes. Bele stood, her arms crossed over her chest, the wind tossing her dark hair across her cheeks. The glow of eather in her eyes was almost as bright as Ash's. I thought about Aios again and wished I could say goodbye. I looked at the cousins and felt my lips spread into a grin. They were saying something to Elias, likely talking shit to the guard. I saw Ehthawn, and my heart...gods, it ached for Orphine. Her death wasn't fair.

But death rarely was.

Thinking of Ector, I felt my chest tighten as I focused on Rhain. He stood a little apart from the rest, his hair more red than gold in the sunlight. His hands were at his sides and close to the daggers strapped to his thighs. He looked my way, his gaze passing mine before darting back. I saw him swallow thickly and thought maybe he was thinking about what was to come.

The knot in my throat expanded. I wanted to linger, but we didn't have much time, and I still had to talk to Ash privately. I still needed the time Nektas said was never a waste.

I reached over, touching Ash's cool hand. His gaze came to mine. "Take me to my lake?" I whispered.

Ash's jaw immediately tensed—all traces of amusement gone.

"You promised," I reminded him.

He said nothing, but he nodded.

I took a shallow, stinging breath and turned back to those before us. Everyone had quieted. There were no smiles, and the air seemed to have thickened around us, suddenly full of tension and maybe even sorrow. They all knew what was coming. They all knew what kind of shape Ash would likely be in the next time they saw him.

I opened my mouth, but I didn't know what to say. *"Goodbye"* didn't seem adequate.

What did someone say when they knew it was the last time? I bet some people had speeches planned or eloquent words to be remembered by that would simply come to them, but I wondered how many could actually deliver those speeches or parting words when the time came. Because there were no words.

If Ector were here, he'd likely say something ridiculous. He'd make us all either laugh or curse.

I hoped he was at peace and happy.

I hoped I saw him again.

That fucking knot traveled to the top of my throat, causing my eyes to burn. I pressed my lips together.

Saion lifted his chin, a wan smile on his handsome face. "Safe travels."

I nodded. It was all I could manage. I didn't want their last memory of me to be one where I was a sobbing mess.

Rhain stepped forward, walking between the cousins. Brown eyes alight with eather locked on mine. Then, withdrawing a shadowstone sword, he crossed it over his chest and lowered to one knee, bowing his head.

I inhaled sharply.

Bele followed suit, sword in hand as she knelt. Then Lailah. What were they doing? Saion and Rhahar did the same, and I felt Ash's fingers thread through mine. Behind them, Nektas lowered his horned head to the stone and patchy grass of the cliff. Ehthawn did the same, puffing out a smoky breath.

In unison, the gods held their swords level with their chests, their other hands folding tightly over the edges of the blades. Blood dripped in front of them, splashing off the rocky soil. Then it struck me, weakening my legs. My lips parted.

They were paying me honor and respect—the same I'd seen given to knights in Lasania upon their passing.

"With my sword and my life," Rhain spoke, lifting his head. The others echoed his words. "I shall honor you." Silvery, crackling eather erupted from his fingers, spreading across the sword. The blade collapsed first, and then the hilt turned to ash. "In blood and in ash, forevermore."

38

A surprisingly cool mist dampened the air as we stood beneath a canopy of heavy branches.

The Dark Elms had quieted upon our arrival, the wildlife reacting to the presence of a Primal of Death and fleeing the woods. A few birds remained hidden in the tallest branches near my lake, calling softly to one another in the darkness.

Only fractures of moonlight penetrated the thick shadows of night. The dense thicket of elms obscured what lay beyond, but I knew I could easily find my way through the maze to Wayfair Castle. I was so close to Ezra.

To my mother.

I wanted to see my stepsister. Maybe even my mother. But what would I say to them? Even if I didn't share my true reasons for visiting, Ezra would know that something was up. She was clever, and I didn't want her last memories of me to be steeped in sorrow.

And my mother?

Any conversation with her likely wouldn't go well. It would surely end in one of us saying something terrible, which meant that Ash would probably make good on his threat to send her to the Abyss before my life even came to its end.

But I didn't have unlimited time. The last thing I wanted was to spend it upsetting Ezra or arguing with my mother.

I wanted to be with my husband.

A shaky breath left me as I lifted my gaze to him. Ash stood with his back to me, the line of his spine rigid as he stared at the still midnight waters.

He hadn't wanted to come here, but he'd promised me. And he wouldn't break that oath.

He'd been quiet since we left the Bonelands, shadowstepping us into the middle of the Dark Elms. He hadn't said a word to the others when we left. My eyes stung with the tears I held back—that I'd *been* holding back.

In blood and in ash…

In life *and* death, forevermore.

What Rhain and the others had given me was beautiful. Powerful. It was better than recognition. It was an *acknowledgment* of who I was.

A warrior.

One worthy of respect and honor.

Gods, I couldn't start crying now.

Quickly, I reached up and hastily wiped under my eyes. My fingers were only tinted red, so hopefully my face wasn't smeared with blood tears.

Clearing my throat, I stepped toward the Primal. "Ash?"

There was a long moment of silence, and then he flatly stated, "Sera?"

His tone pulled at my heart. "I know we don't have much time."

"We have all the time."

But we didn't. He knew that. If someone hadn't discovered Kolis yet, they would soon. And besides that? I was out of time.

"There's something I want to talk about," I said.

His head tilted back. "I'm listening."

Knowing this was hard for him, I succeeded in tamping down my quick temper. "Really?" I bit out. Okay. I *mostly* kept my temper in check. "You're listening, even though you won't look at me?"

Ash turned so quickly that he was a blur. "Even if I'm not looking at you, you are still all I see," he said, his features encased in harsh ice. "I see you, Sera. I always have."

Love for him surged in my chest, causing my vision to blur. "Don't do that."

His head cocked. "Do what?"

"Say things like that—nice things. Sweet words," I told him. "It'll make me cry, and I don't want to."

Some of the coldness left his face. "I don't want you to cry either."

"Then don't be nice."

His brows lifted. "Should I turn around and give you my back again?"

"No!" I exclaimed. "I'll get angry then, and I don't want to do that either."

He pulled his bottom lip between his teeth as if holding back a smile. "Then what would you like me to do, *liessa?*"

Gods.

Every time he called me that, I melted. It still melted me, but it also made me want to cry. Briefly closing my eyes, I ordered myself to pull it together. "I know you're mad."

"I'm not mad."

My lips pursed. "You're not?"

"I'm..." Ash shook his head. "Okay. I'm mad. But not at you."

"I know you're not mad at me," I said. "And I know you don't want to be here. You don't want to do what you have to do."

His nostrils flared.

"But I also know that you understand it has to be done. If there's any hope of stopping Kolis and saving the realms, stopping the Rot. This is it. And I don't want to waste what time we have left arguing over what we already know," I told him. "I want you to listen to what I must tell you."

Ash twisted his neck to the side, then gave me a curt nod.

All right, that wasn't a vocalization, but it was better than nothing.

"I want you to know I love you," I started. His eyes slammed shut, and my hands began trembling. "And I will not stop loving you. I wish I'd told you more than I have—gods, I wish I'd recognized what I felt long before I did."

"I know," he said, the two words sounding as if torn from the depths of his soul.

I stepped forward. "And I want you to know that none of this is your fault."

Ash's chest rose with a deep inhale.

"None of it," I repeated.

"Sera." He let out a scathing laugh and opened his eyes. Shadows appeared beneath his skin. "Do you know what I'd rather be doing right now?"

I could hazard a guess. "Anything else?"

He shook his head. "Not just anything else. I've thought of things."

"Like...like what?"

"Teaching you how to swim," he said without hesitation. My chest squeezed. "Showing you more of Iliseeum. Returning to the cavern—I think you liked it there."

"I did," I whispered.

"I would rather be lying in bed with you, sitting on the palace balcony together, getting you to tell me all the things you haven't shared with me about when you grew up. Training with you. Fighting with you. Even arguing with you." The shadows deepened under his flesh. "But the only reason we're standing here, having this conversation instead of doing all those things—exploring the innumerable ways I've dreamt of fucking you—is because of what I've done."

My mind got stuck on a specific part of what he'd said. "What are some of those innumerable ways?"

The change that came over Ash was swift and heady. His chin dipped, his striking features warming as the shadows disappeared. "I'd be more than happy to show you."

Heat swamped my veins, which was so not helpful at the moment. I shook my head.

"You sure?" His silky voice stretched out like a tendril of dark mist, brushing against me.

"Yes," I forced myself to say. "Unfortunately." I refocused. "Look, you made choices based on the knowledge you had. You didn't do the wrong things."

Shaking his head, he looked away. A muscle ticked in his jaw.

"It wasn't even your father's fault—not really. The Arae made it so he nor anyone who knew could tell you," I repeated what I'd told him earlier. "You didn't know any of this would happen."

That muscle worked even harder.

"I don't blame you." I inched closer. "And I know this isn't something I can convince you of. You need to come to the understanding—the acceptance. And I need you to because I want you to promise me something."

He turned his head slightly toward me.

"I...I want you to *live*," I began. "After Kolis is dealt with and you take your rightful place as King of Gods—"

"That is not my rightful place."

"Ash—"

"It's your rightful place."

My brows slammed together. "What? I'm not a Primal. I'm not even a god."

"But those embers?" Ash said. "They've become yours."

Said embers hummed faintly throughout me, but I wouldn't become *that*, even if Ash had his *kardia* and could Ascend me. The embers would likely cause my body to explode or do something else disturbing and gross. "And they will become yours."

Lips thinning, he looked away.

"And I don't want you to be alone after that happens."

The eather in his eyes went flat. "What are you saying, Sera?"

"I'm...I'm saying that I want you to live. Really *live*, Ash." I twisted my fingers together. "I want you to find a way to restore your *kardia*."

"Good Fates." He thrust a hand through his hair.

Undaunted, I pressed on and stopped in front of him. "And I want you to allow yourself to love."

His hand fell, clenching into a fist. "You have got to be fucking kidding me."

"I'm not." I looked up at him. "I want you to allow yourself to love and be loved, Ash. You're more than worthy of that. You deserve it. More than anyone I know."

"I don't give a fuck what I supposedly deserve," he snarled, shadows bleeding through his flesh. "You're seriously asking me to find a way to love another?"

"I am."

He stared down at me, his chest heaving. "I...I could *never* do that."

Pressure clamped down on my chest. "I need you to."

"I cannot believe you would even ask this of me." The shadows whipped under his skin. "Think that I would just be able to forget about you—"

"I'm not asking you to forget me. I don't want that. I don't want you to ever forget me." I placed my hands on his chest, causing him to jerk as if burned. "But you're going to live for a long time. I want you to be happy. That is important to me. Because I love you, Ash."

"Fuck," he rasped, the silver of his eyes was as bright as the moonlight reflecting off the waters of my lake, and the set of his jaw was as hard as the shadowstone beneath it.

"I love you." Fighting back tears, I lifted my hands and cupped his face. His eyes closed briefly, thick lashes fanning his cheeks. "Knowing that you will be happy will allow me to find peace because *you* will have found peace."

A heartbeat passed. Then another. His eyes finally opened. "I will find peace."

I searched his eyes. That wasn't exactly a confirmation. "Promise me you will do this for me."

"Sera—"

"Promise me you will do as I ask," I pressed, knowing that once he did, the oath would bind him. "Promise."

An array of emotions skated over his face, too many for me to even decipher. "I promise."

Before I could react or even think, his head dipped, and his lips locked with mine in a hard, fierce kiss. My mouth instinctively opened to him, and gods, the icy heat of his lips sent a sweet, hot flush through my body. The passion in his kiss was like a storm catching hold of me and sweeping me up to dizzying heights.

"That is one of the things I'd rather be doing. Kissing you. Feeling the way you melt into me. You want me to live? This is when I feel the most alive." His lips brushed mine. "Like this, with you. Live with me. I need that. I need you," he growled against my mouth.

I shuddered against him. "Time—"

"We'll make time," he swore. "We deserve that."

My fingers trembled at his jaw. He was right. We *did* deserve that. And damn it, I wanted this. I wanted him as my last act in this realm. I wanted these memories. Not the time I'd spent in captivity. Nothing to do with Kolis. Not Ash's anger and sadness. Not my reluctant acceptance of my fate. I wanted Ash and how he made me feel.

Seen.

Respected.

Wanted.

I should've had days and weeks of feeling this before the end came. I should've had a lifetime.

But I didn't.

I had right now.

And I wasn't going to waste it.

Tugging his head down, I brought his lips back to mine. No words were needed then. How I kissed him said it all.

Ash's arms came around me, pulling me flush to his chest. His hand tangled in my hair. We kissed until my lips felt swollen and my pulse thundered. Only then did his mouth leave mine, trailing a path over the curve of my chin and down my neck.

A trickle of unease pierced the heat as he nuzzled my throat, nipping gently. It wasn't even where Kolis had bitten me—and that shouldn't matter. This was Ash. My mouth dried as I forced myself to take a deep breath, drawing in his scent. Citrus. Fresh mountain air. Gods, I'd never smelled anything better than him, and I was here with Ash. Only Ash.

My eyes fluttered open as he pressed a kiss to my throbbing pulse, then lifted his head.

Lashes swept up, and molten silver eyes locked with mine. I saw an urgency in his eyes, a firestorm of need and so much want. But he hesitated. Stark need etched deep lines into his striking features, but he…he waited.

For me.

"We don't have to do this," he said, his voice thick and rough. "Having you here and in my arms, kissing you? It's enough."

Oh, gods, he *was* going to make me cry.

Even without him speaking more, I knew why he'd said that. Why he held himself back despite what I'd told him. But Ash…gods, he knew it hadn't been *nothing*. It was why he'd told me I was safe when we were in the cavern. He knew I hadn't gotten free of Kolis without gaining a few fresh scars that couldn't be seen but were embedded deep, nonetheless. He knew enough to make sure I was safe with him. And I was.

Gods, I couldn't love him more.

And I couldn't hate the realms more for taking me away from him than I did now. It wasn't fair. But if I focused on that? On any of that bad stuff? I would be sacrificing what little time we had left that hadn't already been stolen from us.

Swallowing the knot of emotion threatening to leave me a sobbing mess on the forest floor, I slid my hands down and grasped the front of his tunic. I tugged, and Ash obeyed, raising his arms. He bent, making it easier for me to tug the shirt free.

"*Liessa*," he murmured as I dropped the clothing to the ground.

Holding his stare, I lifted my hands and hooked my fingers under the borrowed shirt I wore, drawing it up. The soft, well-worn material skimmed my stomach and then my breasts. He didn't look away, not for one moment, as I pulled the shirt off, letting it fall beside his.

Ash's chest rose sharply as his icy-hot gaze traveled, inch by inch, over the flesh I'd exposed for him. My nipples pebbled against the strands of my hair as I stood still, letting him look his fill—wanting him to. I waited, my heart pounding faster than it had in days.

Slowly, he lifted his fingers, catching the sides of my hair. His stare tracked his movements along the curls as he lifted them and brushed them back and over my shoulders.

My breathing picked up as I curled my fingers around his wrist. "Touch me." I brought his hand to my breast.

Ash growled low in his throat at the contact, and my back arched, pressing me into his palm. "Like I said before, I'll do whatever you ask of me," he swore, wisps of eather spinning wildly in his eyes. He dragged his thumb over the tip of my breast. "Anything."

I knew he spoke the truth.

He would do anything for me.

My stomach fluttered as he cupped my other breast. His eyes remained fixed on mine as I moved my other hand down the cool, hard skin of his chest, inching lower. His stomach muscles tightened under my palm. Reaching the band of his breeches, I found the clasp there and undid it with slightly shaking fingers. Ash worked his feet free of his boots, and then it was he who stood still as I drew his pants down.

Kneeling, I looked up, taking in the dusting of dark hair on his thick, muscular thighs. I found faint nicks in his skin—scars I'd never learn the story behind. I'd never know if he'd gained them before he Ascended, while he learned to wield a sword, or if something terrible had created them, but I cherished them nonetheless.

I leaned in, pressing my lips to the one on his knee and then the other just above it. Drawing my hands up the outsides of his legs, I paid homage to the inch-long scar on his inner thigh.

Hearing the sharp breath he took, I smiled as I pulled back and looked up. Muscles curled low in my stomach, and I knew he had to hear the breath I took as my gaze landed on his thick, rigid cock. I bit down on my lip, remembering how he tasted, how he felt when he came against my tongue. I stretched up, started to lean in...

Ash's hand returned to my hair, stopping me.

I looked up at him. His cheeks were flushed, his lips parted. "You said anything."

"I did." His hand fisted in my hair, tugging at my scalp in a way that caused a rush of pounding heat.

"And I want you in my mouth." I clasped his thighs. "I want to taste you."

"Sera," Ash groaned. "Anything but that."

My eyes narrowed. "I didn't realize there were restrictions."

He chuckled. "I didn't either. But if you do that, I'll…"

I scraped my nails against his skin, far too pleased by the brief flash of his fangs. "You'll what?"

"I'll lose control."

My blood turned to liquid fire at the thought of him with no control. "That is what I want."

"It's what I want, too." The faint glow of eather appeared in the veins of his cheeks and throat, causing an unsteady breath to escape me. "But I want to lose control with my cock deep inside you, not when I'm fucking your mouth."

My legs trembled as a pulse of lust went straight to my core.

His head tilted to the side, causing his hair to fall across one side of his face. A glowing eye pierced mine. "You'd like that."

Nothing about him saying, "fucking your mouth" should turn me on, but I nodded. Because when he said it? I wanted him to fuck my mouth. Hard.

Ash's nostrils flared.

Had I said that out loud?

"You can have that all you want," he bit out. "After."

After.

Just a single word often taken for granted. We didn't have an after. "But—"

"*After*," he insisted, the grip on my hair firm enough to guide me to my feet.

Holding his gaze, I nodded. There was no reason to correct him. We could pretend. We had every right to. "Are there other things not included in *anything*?"

A hint of a teasing smile played across his mouth. I loved that kind of smile. It was rare. Would I remember it where…wherever I went?

"Sera," he said, softly this time.

I blinked, lifting my gaze to his.

"We're here." Both of his hands cupped my cheeks. "We're together. Right now. That is all that matters. Just us. Just right now."

Exhaling roughly, I nodded. "Just us."

Ash dipped his head, capturing my lips with a sweet, lingering touch. I trembled as the kiss deepened, as he tasted and owned me, drinking me in.

His mouth left mine once more, but he skipped my throat. I didn't know if that was on purpose—if he'd sensed that seedling of unease in me before—but his lips blazed another hot trail across my collarbone. His fingers followed his mouth, grazing over my shoulders, my breasts. They coasted over the curve of my stomach, finding the band of my pants.

Ash's tongue flicked against the crest of my breast, and then he drew the flesh into his mouth, wringing a gasp from me as he tugged the pants over my hips and then down. I stepped out of them, shivering at the soft whisper of air against my skin.

Then there was nothing between us. He moved into me, folding an arm around my waist. The feel of his flesh against mine, cool and hard against my belly, seared my skin. Holding me tightly, he carefully brought me to the ground, one hand bracing the back of my head as he laid me out on my lake's damp, grassy bank. The tenderness in how he cared for me nearly had me coming undone, and it would have if not for the sight of him.

The image of him above me, his dark hair falling against the sharp angles of his cheeks, his lips parted to reveal the tips of his fangs, and his features stark with need were the embodiment of pure lust.

His eyes glowed a luminous silver, catching mine as the soft edges of his hair teased my skin. He nipped at my collarbone. "Keep those beautiful eyes on me," he ordered in that smoky, shadowy voice of his. "I want you to see how much I enjoy the taste of your skin."

My stomach dipped and curled. "I…I won't look away."

His grin was icy-hot, and his lips maddening as he kissed his way down the center of my chest and then up the swell of one breast. His head tilted, eyes full of wisps of whirling eather as he dragged the edge of one fang over the sensitive skin. He hesitated at the tip of my breast, his cool, teasing breath heightening my anticipation.

"Watch me," he murmured.

Nothing in either realm could force me to look away. He flicked his tongue over my nipple, and my fingers pressed into the grass. I moved restlessly beneath him, shivering at the feeling of the rougher hair of his legs against mine.

Ash drew the budded flesh into his mouth, sucking deeply. He smiled as he wrung a soft cry from my lips.

I gripped his forearm, and he turned his attention to my other breast. The tip of his fang skated across my nipple. "Ash," I moaned, hips twitching.

"Mmm." He took me into his mouth and pressed his fingers into the flesh of my other breast, deftly rolling my nipple between his thumb and forefinger. "There are only a few things in this realm better than the sound of your moans."

"Like…" My breath came out in short gasps as his hand left my breast and glided down. He shifted, giving me a glimpse of muscles that dipped and rippled over his lower stomach before he grasped my hip and wedged the sleek, muscled length of his thigh between mine. "Like what?"

"The sound you make when you come. It's like a siren's song. That ranks a little bit higher," he said, the sensation of his cool lips against my hot skin tantalizing. "But you know what ranks even higher?"

Pressing my lips together, I shook my head.

He caught my nipple between his teeth, and I cried out again, rocking against him, riding his thigh.

His tongue soothed away the wicked sting. "Your voice," he said.

I was panting. "My voice?"

"Your voice," he confirmed, pressing his thigh against the damp heat between mine. "It's soft yet strong. Confident."

"Really?" I asked, not sure I sounded that soft or confident now.

Ash nodded. "Your voice is a balm."

Oh, gods.

"Another thing that ranks higher? Your laugh. You don't laugh enough, but when you do? It fucking stops me dead in my tracks."

"Ash," I whispered, chest swelling.

He groaned, gnashing his teeth together. "And *that*. The way you say my name. When you're lost to passion, and all you can do is whisper my name." He tipped his hips, pressing against me. "When you're angry with me and yell it."

I laughed. "Even then?"

"Especially then." He slid down my body and dipped his tongue into my navel, causing my entire body to jerk as sharp, pulsing sensations darted through me. "But how you say it when you're feeling sweet? When you've stripped off all the beautiful shields you encase yourself in?" Laces of eather streaked under the skin of his cheeks. His tongue and lips danced lower as his thigh shifted away from me. "When you say my name as you tell me you love me?"

I might've stopped breathing for a few moments as the seconds stretched out.

"There's not a godsdamn sound better than that, Sera. *That*, I swear." Eather pulsed in the veins of his jaw and throat. "Because it silences all the terrible shit I've had to do and see and lets me feel hope."

His words were so powerful. They soothed my soul's rough, brittle edges. "Ash." I sat up, bringing my face close to his. "I love you."

His large hand wrapped around my neck, the roughness of his fingertips scraping against my skin. A spark of energy surged from him and then through me. His kiss was a combination of dominance and vulnerability, a pull so powerful I forgot who I was for a moment. I felt it shattering barriers and undoing something deep within me.

"Ash. Gods," I whispered, tugging my mouth from his. I stared up at him. "I will always love you."

The Primal stilled against me. His body. The eather in his eyes.

Then he took me like lightning, his mouth claiming mine as he pressed me to the ground again. Everything that came next was all about us, right here and now.

When Ash's mouth left mine, he moved down, spreading my thighs with his broad shoulders.

There was no hesitation or teasing, just his cool breath, and then his mouth closing around the tight bundle of nerves.

My back arched at the intensity of the raw, pounding sensations. It was too much. I started to sit again, but his hand landed on my stomach, holding me down and in place as he feasted.

Ash devoured me.

"This?" he breathed, dragging his tongue up the very center of me before delving deep. "The way you taste? It comes in right behind my list of favorite sounds, but it is my favorite taste in all the realms."

"It is?" That was all I could manage as the tension built quickly.

"Even better than your blood," he murmured. "Sweet sunshine."

I couldn't even concentrate enough to ask what sweet sunshine tasted like to him because he *was* tasting me. Licking. Sucking. It felt like he was everywhere. His tongue. Lips. His fingers dug into the flesh of my ass, and he lifted me. All the tight, curling sensations stole my breath as my movements became almost frantic, and I rode his face as I'd done his thigh. His growl of approval burned my skin, igniting the fire.

I tried to slow the building release. I wanted to savor this, but I could feel myself rushing toward completion, and I thought that might be what killed me. I couldn't catch my breath—

Ash suddenly rose from between my legs, his mouth returning to mine before I could vocalize even a single word. The taste of him and me on his tongue was a heady mix, leaving me feeling out of control and dazed as I felt his skin harden and cool further under my palm. The way he shook nearly undid me as he gripped my thigh, hooking my leg around his waist. His mouth never left mine as he rolled his hips, pressing into where I needed him. I tilted mine, and he answered with a muffled, ragged groan.

A fine shiver rolled through me as he pushed in, my body tensing at the initial bite of discomfort from his width. He halted, but I wanted more. I needed more. Because this was it. This was what I would remember.

With my leg hooked around his hip, and my arms wrapping his shoulders, I lifted myself and pulled him down, seating him fully inside me.

"Fuck," Ash rasped, his groan half laugh. Then he said something in the Primal language, but it was too fast and low for me to pick up. He kissed me again, and these were sweet and tender. He kissed me like…like he had his *kardia* and not only loved me but was *in* love with me. Now and forever. And he *kept* kissing me as he began to move.

My body clenched around his as he pulled back until he was almost free of me and then drove back in, as far as he could go. Hot, tight shudders flooded me as he nipped my lips, my chin. The pace he set was slow and torturous, driving me insane.

"More." I grabbed a fistful of hair, and he groaned.

"Faster?" he taunted against my lips.

"Yes."

"Harder?"

I shook, lightning rushing through my veins. *"Yes."*

Ash still held back, his swirling silver eyes locked on mine as his hips punched forward, hard and deep. And I took him. I brought both knees up, hooking my legs around his waist. For a moment, neither of us moved. Our bodies were flush, hip to hip, chest to chest.

Then he moved, just like I wanted, fast and hard. I couldn't even keep up. All I could do was hold on as he took me.

"Fates, nothing feels like this," he uttered against my mouth. "Nothing feels like you."

I felt the same, but I couldn't get the words out as pleasure started to build again as he drove me to the breaking point, over and over. His mouth found mine, and he worked an arm under me, tilting my hips up.

Then I lost all sense of time. It was just the sounds of our bodies coming together and the wind above, stirring the branches. I felt him swelling and tightening with each deep, pounding thrust. The tension returned, building deep inside me until every muscle in my body tensed.

There was no slow build, no coming to the edge and then pulling back. The coil spinning inside me unfurled at a shocking rate. Crying out his name, the most intense pleasure I'd ever felt rolled over me in tight, hot waves that stretched every nerve ending.

Mindlessly, I threw my head back, but Ash's hand was there, preventing it from hitting the ground. He cradled the back of my head and ground his hips into mine, sending pulses of uncontrollable ecstasy through every nerve in my body.

"*Liessa.*" His voice was rough and low. He pressed into me, joining me in release with a hoarse shout. "Sera."

I held on to him, even as the rest of my body went limp. I just held him to me as pleasure took him in the same endless way.

"I never wanted..." Ash whispered against my skin, even as I felt him still spasming inside me. He kissed my neck, then the corner of my lips. "I never wanted until you."

39

Ash's lips coasted over mine, and his words echoed in my mind.

I never wanted.

Looping my arms around his shoulders, I held him tightly. The kiss deepened until we were drowning in each other.

I never wanted until you.

His heart pounded against mine as our lips reluctantly parted. We were both breathless and yearning—

The Primal essence suddenly throbbed intensely throughout me, causing me to suck in a short breath. Ash's head jerked up at that exact moment.

A low rumble of thunder traveled through the air, seeming to emanate from every direction, both above and below us. Tiny bumps of dread raced across my skin, and my eyes locked on his.

"Kolis," snarled Ash, shadows rapidly appearing in his cheeks as his flesh thinned. "They've found him."

"And he's conscious," I whispered.

Time…

We were out of time.

The rumble picked up, and the ground trembled, causing the trees to sway and sending several leaves falling.

I wasn't ready.

But I had to be.

I had to face the end because this was it. This wasn't a close call. There would be no tomorrows. No afters. This was it.

I stared into Ash's whirling silver eyes as a hundred—no, a *thousand*—different things rose to the tip of my tongue. I still wanted to know and say so much. All of it would take a lifetime or more, but I had mere minutes. Not even hours now.

Minutes.

Panic sliced through my chest, sending adrenaline surging through my veins.

The tendrils of eather brightened in Ash's gaze as he sucked in a sharp breath.

Oh, no. He was reading my emotions. I needed to get myself under control. I didn't want him feeling my panic or distress. This would already be bad enough for him.

Breathe in. I reached up, sinking my hands into his hair. *Hold.* I let myself feel the texture slipping through my fingers for a heartbeat or two. *Breathe out.* I willed my racing heart to slow. "I always wanted before you."

A tremor ran through Ash, and I knew it had nothing to do with the Primal rage building in Iliseeum and spreading into the mortal realm. "*Liessa...*"

"I wanted to be known," I whispered, needing him to hear this. "I wanted to be accepted."

Another shudder rocked Ash.

"I wanted to be included." I slid my hands free of his hair, drawing them down the cool skin of his neck. "I wanted to be talked to and touched."

"Sera," he breathed.

The tips of my fingers grazed the hard line of his jaw. "Most of all, I wanted to be valued, to be needed and cherished and *wanted* for who I was and not who I was supposed to be or what I could do for someone. I wanted to be *seen*." A surge of emotion clogged my throat as the ground trembled once more. "You gave me all of that, Ash. I've lived because of you."

A sound came from deep within Ash as if it tore itself free from the depths of his soul. "I will give you so much more."

Before I could process what he'd said, his mouth closed over mine. Rocking back, he rose fluidly. He cradled me to his chest, the kiss deepening, parting my lips. His tongue stroked mine, and when he kissed like this, it overwhelmed me—his scent, taste, and the cool wetness of his mouth. Our lips moved hungrily as I grasped the back of his head, soaking in all the sensations. I didn't want to forget where I was going.

I wouldn't.

Sharp wind stirred around us. The sudden shock of cold water rushing over my feet was a jolt to my senses. Ash had entered the lake, gracefully descending the earthen steps of shadowstone, the water rising and lapping over my legs and then my waist. He kept kissing me, his mouth urgent and demanding as if he sought to lose himself in it as badly as I wanted to.

His mouth only left mine when the water reached my lower back and occasionally rippled against my shoulders. "Sera," he gasped.

Calmed as I always was by the lake, my heart rate slowed. I reached up, pressing my palm to his cheek. His eyes were full of whipping silver coils of eather. "I love you, Ash."

His chest rose sharply, and each breath he took was fast and hard.

"It's time," I whispered.

The eather slowed in his eyes. His chest stopped its rapid movements. He didn't move, not even as the tremor beneath us came once more.

I cupped his jaw. "Please."

One side of his lips curled up, revealing one sharp point as he snarled, "*No.*"

Then he struck.

He was so fast I had no time to feel the unease that had threatened to take over earlier when I'd felt the scrape of his fang.

The one word he'd spoken got lost in my cry as his fangs pierced the skin of my throat. Sharp agony reverberated through my body, but the pain didn't last. What chased the sting away wasn't exactly pleasure, it just didn't hurt as his mouth latched on to my throat or maybe…maybe I couldn't feel the pleasure.

Because I knew he found none.

Ash was trembling, but he wouldn't drag this out. He wouldn't do that to me.

His fingers moved against my hip, now under the water, in slow, soothing swipes that were in tune with the deep, drugging pulls at my vein. He drank fast, taking my blood into him, and I knew this was likely killing a part of him—something that would take a long time to come back.

Sliding my hand under his hair, I moved my fingers along his neck. I hoped it brought some sort of comfort as I opened my eyes.

Stars glimmered high above us, blanketing the sky with a dazzling array of twinkling lights. There were so many. Hundreds. Thousands. And the moon? It was so big, so bright.

Ash's arm spasmed around me...or did I jerk? I wasn't sure as I stared at the moon. The embers began thrumming throughout me, at first nothing more than a minor vibration, and then a frenzied dance.

It's okay, I thought to myself, my hand sliding of its own accord to stop at his chest. My thoughts began wandering to what I hadn't allowed myself to dwell on for too long.

Where was I going?

Ash wouldn't be able to intervene. It would be up to the Arae, and I hoped they wouldn't sentence me to the Abyss. But I had taken lives when *my* life hadn't been in jeopardy. I'd killed bad people and those who happened to be enemies of my kingdom. Would I burn?

No, I reasoned. I would enter the Vale. Holland would ensure that. I had to believe it. But what would it be like? Even Ash couldn't tell me. All I knew was that it was different for everyone. I didn't understand how someone could see their loved ones if the paradise was individualized, but maybe we weren't supposed to understand it.

I wondered who I'd see. Who I'd meet. My father? That would be nice. Would I see my old nursemaid? I'd like that, too.

Would I remember?

Ash? My family? Everything? Would I be at peace? I wasn't sure how I could be if I remembered or if I forgot. Was that how spirits became...?

I sighed, losing track of my thoughts.

Dying didn't hurt.

Ash made sure of that with the cool weightlessness of my lake and the now-slower, gentle tug of his mouth against my throat.

He drew my blood into him, and my warmth... I could feel it in his body. It started in his chest and then spread down his stomach. His arms, wrapped so tightly around me, were no longer cold. My blood was doing that, giving him life. And, gods, I was so grateful to feel that again and have the chance to remember the way his body felt when it was like this. And I *would* remember.

I would.

I would.

I concentrated on the feeling of Ash's pounding heart beneath my palm. It grounded me. For a while.

But the edges of my vision started to darken—or they had been for a bit. It was another thing I wasn't entirely sure of, but I felt my heart slowing, and the rushing water was no longer so loud. It sounded muted, far away. I couldn't feel the quakes shaking the realm anymore.

But I did feel the realm slipping away as I fell into darkness.

My hand slipped again. I tried to keep it where I could feel his heart, but I was tired. Weak. My hand twitched and started to fall.

Ash caught my wrist. He didn't stop feeding, but he took my hand in his, pressing my palm flat to his chest above his heart.

He knew.

Somehow, he knew.

I felt my lips curve upward. I felt him shake, but I knew I was smiling, even though I was dying. It was happening. After all this time, there was no escaping it, and despite being in Death's arms, I *smiled*. I didn't want to die. I wasn't ready. It hadn't magically become fair. I wanted to live. I wanted life more than I ever had, but I...

I felt the warmth of Ash's skin and his mouth. I felt the strength of his heart beating beneath my palm and knew my blood now coursed through him. Ash would do more than live. He would Ascend, and he would rule as he always should have.

And I...I felt peace.

Not acceptance. Not submission. Just peace. A spasm went through my body, my heart stuttered, and the embers flared brightly in my chest—

Ash jerked his head back, his breathing still fast, hard. His features were blurred, but I saw how bright the eather was in his eyes as he stared down at me. And the embers...

They pulsed fiercely in my chest. He hadn't...

"The embers," I whispered, my tongue feeling thick and heavy.

"Fuck the embers."

Confusion clouded my mind as he placed my hand on my lap, not letting it fall into the water. "Ash." I tried to move but couldn't seem to get my body to do as I needed it to. "What...what are you doing?"

"Sera, I need you to take my blood. I need you to feed from me."

"What...?" My sluggish heart lurched as what he was doing—or *not* doing—broke through the fog of my peace. "No, Ash. No—"

"*No!*" he shouted...or whispered. I thought of how he'd said that before he'd bitten me.

I thought about how he'd refused to listen when I told him I wanted him to really live, the *after* he'd spoken of, and how he'd said he would give me more. When he spoke to me in the cavern. I thought of all he hadn't said. He'd never said he planned to take the embers—not to me. Not to Keella or Attes.

I went over everything he had said since we were reunited, and even before Kolis held me.

I will not let you die.

Ash had never planned to take the embers.

"I'm not letting you go," he said. "I'm going to Ascend you."

I felt another tripping motion in my chest. "You...you can't."

The laugh that came from him was dark and endless. "Yes, I fucking can."

"It won't...work," I reasoned.

Eather whirled in his eyes. "I'm a fucking Primal of Death. My blood is that of the Ancients, so we don't know that for sure. No one does. I don't care what Delfai or the Arae claimed. Fuck them. I'm going to try."

As his words sank in, I felt a spark of hope, but it was fleeting. When Kolis spoke of doing the same, I'd known it wouldn't work. And even if it did... "What...will I become?"

"I don't know. A demis? One of those Ascended Kolis creates?" But that...that wasn't how the Ascended worked. They were third sons and daughters. Ash knew that. Another tremor shook him. "Or the Primal of Life."

But that wouldn't happen. It couldn't.

"I don't care what you become." He lowered his wrist. "I don't care, as long as you're alive. As long as you don't leave me. I don't care. I want you however you come back to me."

Gods, I believed him.

But it wouldn't work.

Focusing on the embers, I latched on to them for strength. Faint energy buzzed through my veins, allowing me to lift my hand back to his chest, over his heart. "I love you."

His eyes slammed shut. "Sera, be quiet and don't fight me for once."

"I love you so much, but you h-have to do this."

"Shut up, Sera." He turned his head to his wrist as a line of darkness raced down his cheek.

"Take the embers. You have to. Please."

"*Shut the fuck up, Sera!*" he shouted, sending what birds remained in the elms into a frightened flight. "For the last time, I don't care about the embers or the realms. They can burn."

I shuddered, curling my fingers against his skin. "You don't...mean that."

His eyes opened and locked with mine. They were pools of still, endless silver. "I do."

"What if I still die?" I held on to my waning strength, my chest feeling as if it squeezed tighter with every word. "The embers will die, and you won't have me—"

"I know. It may not work. If it doesn't, I will lose you and the embers. I'm willing to risk it and take that chance," he said. Over his shoulder, I saw the water freeze on the rocks. "The lives of millions of mortals nor those of the gods do not surpass yours. The realms can rot into the Abyss and all life can cease." Another streak slid down his other cheek, damp and the color of midnight crimson. "I don't care, as long as you are beside me."

Oh, gods.

Blood tears coursed down his face.

Ash *cried*. "I will take the souls of those lost upon my flesh. I will gladly usher in the end, and I will do it with you beside me," he swore. "And if not? If I fail and lose you?" His voice cracked from the agony of his sorrow and remorse. My heart shattered. "The realms won't survive, Sera."

"Ash," I pleaded, hating his pain. Loathing all the regret I heard in his voice.

"If I lose you, they're already gone, as good as dead and rotted away." His forehead pressed against mine. "Don't you know that already? You do. Kolis was always right about me. He knew I would do far worse than what he could ever conceive. And I will. I will ruin the realms if I lose you. If you die, there is no hope for them—any of them...innocent or evil, god or mortal. I will destroy them all."

Ash shuddered, then kissed me hard and quick, leaving my lips numb. "So don't die."

I stared at him as he drew his head back and lifted his wrist once more. A...a weak laugh left me. "Don't die?"

"Yes. Exactly that. Don't fucking die," he repeated as if that were the simple fix. His eyes held mine. "Fuck the greater good, Sera."

"Fuck the greater good," I mumbled instead of screaming as I'd done before. The embers hummed throughout me. "Because we aren't..."

"We aren't good, *liessa*."

"But you are."

"Not without you," he said. "Not without you."

I saw his lips part. He tore into his wrist, ripping the skin open. Then I saw the shimmer of his blood coursing down his arm.

Shadows crept into my vision again, the stolen strength fading. As he brought his wrist down, I knew it would likely be the end of me—the end of the realms *and* the end of him. He would regret this. At some point, before it all ceased to exist, he would.

But his blood hit my lip, warm and tingling, igniting either the embers or instinct. My mouth opened. Sweet and smoky blood reached my tongue. There was no riot of sensations, no shock to the senses. I was too gone for that, but my body reacted on instinct. Or the embers did.

I swallowed.

His blood coursed down my throat, hot and thick as Ash pressed the gaping wound to my mouth. I drank.

I drank until my throat no longer worked. I swallowed until I could no longer feel his blood running down my throat. I...I felt nothing. Not warmth. Not coldness.

The strangest thing happened then. An unending tide of memories came at me in waves.

Me as a pale-haired child, staring at the painting of my father and finally understanding where my freckles had come from. My mother's cold stare that used to cut so deeply and then only left me feeling nothing. But then I fell into a memory of when I was...nine or ten? It had been at night, after I'd spent the day training with Holland and eating my supper alone. I'd gone into the garden to sit near the silvery-green bushes with their purplish-blue spikes of flowers. I'd liked the way they smelled because...

They smelled of Momma.

A soft footstep against the gravel had me twisting around on the bench.

Momma walked alone under the glow of the hanging lanterns, her pale hair swept up in a twist Odetta could never force mine into.

I went completely still and as silent as a spirit, just as Sir Holland had taught me. Momma didn't see me. She was too busy looking up at the sky, and I didn't think I was supposed to draw her attention when we were outside of our lessons. She never seemed happy when I did.

Momma never seemed happy.

Not even after marrying King Ernald.

King Ernald seemed happy. He snuck me chocolates when he passed me in the halls.

Squeezing my legs together, I clamped my mouth shut so I didn't breathe too loudly. I didn't want to upset her. I wanted her to be proud of me. My chin lifted. I would make her proud, but I...I wanted her to see me. To talk with me like she did with Ezmeria and Tavius. She didn't speak of duty to them. She talked about silly things like—

"I know you're there, Seraphena."

My lips came unstuck, making a popping sound as my gaze flew to her. "I'm sorry."

"You are?" She stood a few feet back, her hands clenched over her pale blue gown, and her body as stiff as mine. "What are you sorry for?"

"I..." I wasn't sure, exactly. I'd said it because I felt as if I should. I said things like that a lot.

"It's of no consequence." Her gaze shifted from mine to the flowers. The lanternlight shone off her...damp cheek. "I didn't know you came here."

Was she crying? I watched her come forward, her gown whispering silently over the pebbles and grass. "I like the way it smells."

A strange laugh left her. It sounded a little mean and sad. "You would, wouldn't you?"

I didn't know what she meant by that, and I'd learned that if I didn't know something, it was best if I said nothing.

"Do you know what they are called?" she asked after a few moments.

"Um." I glanced back at the flowers. "Lavender?"

"Close, but no." She walked past me, and I expected her to keep walking, but she sat beside me. "They are called nepeta blue."

"Oh," I whispered, fingers pressing into the thin linen of my nightgown.

She stared ahead. "Why are you out here so late?"

"Couldn't—" I caught myself. Momma liked it when I spoke properly. "I couldn't sleep."

There was no response.

"Why...why are you out here?" I tentatively asked.

"I had an ache in the temples," she answered. "Thought the fresh air and silence would do me some good."

"Oh," I repeated, dragging my lip between my teeth. Then I remembered her once telling me that was unbecoming, so I stopped. "I should leave, then." I started to rise.

"No, it's okay." Momma stopped me. "You're...you're always quiet."

Surprise rushed through me. I didn't know what to do or say. Momma never sat with me outside of our lessons. So, I did what she did. I looked at the pretty flowers.

I kept still and silent, every part of me aware of how close we were. I could almost feel the warmth of her body as the seconds ticked by, turning into minutes. I glanced at her. Her cheeks glimmered. Concern rose.

"Is your head making you sad?" I asked quietly.

"What?" She glanced down at me, her brows furrowing. "Oh," she murmured, lifting a hand to wipe her cheek as if she didn't realize she'd been crying. "No, it's not my head."

"Then what has made you sad?" I tipped closer to her, my hands balling.

"More like who," she remarked, her attention focused on me. On my face. "I swear by the gods, every time I see you..."

I held my breath. How much of me could she see? Did I wash before coming out here? Sometimes I forgot, and there was always something smudged on my face.

"You have more freckles." The corners of her lips tugged up. She smiled.

Momma smiled at me.

"Just like..." Clearing her throat, her smile faded. She turned back to the flowers. "Your father liked these."

I didn't know what to be more excited about. Her smile? Or that she was speaking of him.

"He also enjoyed their scent," she continued. "Thought they had a lighter, fresher smell compared to lavender." She shook her head. "I could never tell the difference, but he could. He thought lavender smelled like..."

I turned back to the flowers, my fingers relaxing. "Vanilla."

"Yes," she said, then sighed. "He said the same. Excuse me." She rose and left the little garden nook without saying another word.

Left...me.

I slipped from the memory with a strange sense of clarity that had never been there before. Her stares and words were never just cold; they were also full of cruel agony and heartbreak for what she'd lost and the child she could never allow herself to grow close to. Care for. Love. Because if she did, how could she honor the deal my father's ancestor made?

I fell into another memory, seeing Odetta's silver hair and her lined face softening briefly in sympathy as she shared her suppers with me. I saw myself sitting beside her at the small table in her chambers while we ate. It was before the garden. I was younger, and I...I hadn't remembered it correctly.

"Do you think Momma is proud she has a Maiden as a daughter?" I asked, toying with the fork.

"Silly child." Odetta's laugh was more of a wheeze. "Always asking silly questions."

I didn't think it was a silly question. I dropped the fork onto the table, pleased by the clang it made. "Never mind."

Odetta reached over, curling her gnarled and bony fingers around my chin. She turned my head to hers. "Child, the Fates know you were touched by life and death, creating someone that should not be. How could she be anything but afraid?"

The memory shattered. She hadn't said, "creating some*thing* that should not be." She'd said, "creating some*one*." Had she been talking about me? Or someone I would create? But I would create no one.

Holland's soft voice rose then, overshadowing mine. *"I do not fear death,"* he said as he circled me. *I was older, closer to seventeen. "I fear life."*

Frowning, I drew back my sword. "What?"

"Death can be a long-earned reward upon old age, but life?" Sir Holland spun, catching my arm and twisting, tossing me to the floor. "Life is vicious. When stolen, it can become the ruin of realms, a wrath that even Death will hide from."

Ezra replaced Holland. The air was sticky with humidity as we walked the gardens, but she wore a cream, pinstriped waistcoat buttoned to the base of her throat.

"Did you believe it?" she asked.

I looked over at her. "Believe what?"

Her attention was fixed on the book she held. "You haven't been listening."

I hadn't, so there was no point in lying.

"I was telling you what Phebe wrote about what Etris saw before she died—it doesn't matter." A breeze toyed with a lock of dark hair, sending it across her face as I wondered who in the fuck Phebe and Etris were. She looked over at me. "You matter to me."

I stumbled, nearly tripping. "What?" I laughed.

Her stare was serious. "I just wanted you to know that. You matter to me."

The smile slipped from my face. Did she know about the sleeping aid...? My chest turned to ice. How could she? Feeling my face warm, I shook my head. *"Did this Phebe write in this book to tell you that?"*

"Oh, yes. Most definitely." She grinned, the hem of her gown snapping at her ankles as she began walking.

I remained where I was, palms damp. My chest clamped down—

My chest.

I saw tiny Jadis nestled against my chest, she and Reaver sleeping soundly. The image of them dispersed like smoke, replaced by flashes of Aios and Bele. Ector's smile. Saion's deep laugh...

Ash and I in the sweet-pea-smothered passageway of the Garden District before I knew it was him.

"I did not ask for your help," I'd spat.

"But you have it nonetheless."

My heart stuttered, and then I found us here, at this very lake, my head resting in his lap, his fingers a light touch on my arm. I thought maybe I'd fallen in love with him even then. I just hadn't known. If I had...

The memory faded into a more recent one. I saw Ash and me at the coronation, looking at the golden swirls on our hands.

Ash had leaned back, one of those rare, genuine smiles on his face as he surveyed the crowd. *"The Fates are capable of anything."*

"Liessa? Sera?"

The voice jarred me from the whirling memories. "Don't leave me. Please."

It was Ash, but he sounded different. Raw. Terrified. I'd never heard him so scared. "Please," he pleaded. "Fucking Fates, I can't lose you. I can't...I love you. I do. Fates, I do. I fucking love you. How can I not? How can this not be love?" He screamed to the elms, or at least I thought he did. I wasn't sure if it was him or if it only came from my mind. "I love you, even if I cannot. I'm *in* love with you."

Then I wasn't there.

I wasn't anywhere but in death...

I love you.

Death wasn't silent.

Or peaceful.

It sounded full of feral rage.

I love you, even if I cannot.

Death was a roar of fury and agony, the sound of a soul shattering.

Of a heart breaking.

I'm in love with you.

40

I floated in the quiet darkness.

There was no pain. No happiness. No fear. No excitement. There was no sense of anything. I was just there. Who or what I was no longer mattered.

I was just an it.

A thing like every other living creature. A collection of differently shaped pieces meant to turn to ash...

Ash that would return to the earth, enriching the soil and providing for the life the lands gave birth to.

But the darkness wasn't entirely silent. There was a distant hum. A whisper. A name being called. Begging. The far-away plea tugged at me.

Seraphena, child.

I stopped floating at the louder echo. That of a...soul. One I knew, because I had been something before I was nothing—someone who made up the collection of uneven pieces. I'd had a name.

Open your eyes, girl. The voice came again—an old, worn voice that belonged to...to...

Odetta.

She was a part of the cycle now, just as I was, right?

No, child, you're not.

I cracked open my eyes. A pinprick of light appeared in the darkness, becoming a shade of swirling sapphire. Light sparked at its tail, and emerald shot out, wrapping itself around the blue. Rich brown followed, and then the three lights spun around a dark center.

In that center, there was a...a past. The past. A beginning of everything. And it started with a blast—an explosion that left small, throbbing lights behind as the raw energy rippled out, creating barren lands and mountains where there was nothing but emptiness before.

Those small, throbbing lights were stars—bright, brilliant stars. And after a time, they fell to lands no longer barren. Some fell where great winged creatures ruled while others fell to lands separated by sweeping bodies of water to the west and to the east. And those stars buried themselves deep in the ground—ground that eventually healed from their impacts. Soil that sprouted saplings, which grew into strong trees that fed what was buried deep beneath. Stars that were fed and nurtured and grown from the roots of the trees they'd given life to. Stars that stayed beneath the surface until they too were as strong as the trees, till they rose from the soil to walk as...

Ancients.

I saw them, their ever-changing eyes full of their beginnings as warmth sparked inside me. That warmth filled all my different-shaped pieces as I saw a fire in the flesh, one that created the Primals. Crackling heat flooded my limbs as I heard the names they were called, both here and beyond, in unfamiliar lands full of towering cities and steel beasts.

Then I saw the Primal of Life, whose features were so painfully familiar. He reached into soil soaked with the blood of the draken he'd spent centuries cultivating, tending to with his breath and will, and the water and fire of the realms. He lifted a small babe, red-faced and howling. The babe's eyes opened for the very first time, crimson that turned to a brilliant, stunning shade of the sky. Those eyes became a kaleidoscope of all the colors in the realms before changing to soft brown as the babe quieted upon seeing the Primal.

I saw the first mortal born, not in the image of the Primals and gods, but in the way of the Ancients, who were born of stars.

And I saw those Ancients rejoice in the continuation of life that had been shaped in their image. Then I saw that begin to change as those created in their image destroyed what came before the Primals, their very first creation—the realms themselves. And as the pulsing warmth expanded in my chest and shimmering silvery light appeared behind my eyes, I understood.

I *understood*.

The eather, the essence, had come from the stars that had fallen eons ago.

I *understood.*

Because I saw the Primals rise and the Ancients fall as my heart took its second first beat. I saw them faded into places of peace and rest. I saw many go to ground, and I saw that some remained to ensure what I now knew had to be more important than anything else.

There must always be balance, that life must always continue on. That death must always come.

I *understood.*

As the eather flowed into my fingers and down my legs, I saw the horror of what would happen if the cycle of life was broken. I heard the screams of thousands, of millions if death was vanquished, and I knew.

I knew that the Ancients who'd returned to the ground must never, ever return to the surface.

Because they were no longer the beginning of everything, the great creators, the givers of life and the balance that kept the realms stable.

They were the end that would shake the realms, erupting the tallest mountains, spewing forth flames and clouds that would consume all in its path, turning day to night. They would boil the rivers and turn seas to deserts, laying utter waste to sprawling stone kingdoms and toppling those great steel cities in distant lands.

For if they rose, they did so as blood and bone, the ruin and the wrath of that once great beginning.

As the essence of the stars hummed from within me, I saw the end.

And I *knew.*

I knew I was not a part of the cycle of life.

I *was* the cycle.

The beginning.

Middle.

The last breath before the end.

Death's steadfast companion.

I was Life.

Slowly, I became aware of a pressure in my head. It built and spread, clamping down on my lungs.

My heart seized and then sped up. A sudden burst of pain lanced my upper jaw. Teeth loosened. A metallic taste filled my mouth as a tremor started deep in the center of my chest, where the two embers flickered and pulsed, expanding with each fast-pounding beat of my heart. The embers grew, swelling inside me until the chasm that had been cracked open *splintered*.

Pure, unadulterated power poured out, spreading like roots in my veins. The essence filled my organs. Eather entrenched itself in my bones and bled into my tendons, flowing to my muscles. My body warmed.

Something tightened around me. Not something. Arms? Yes, *arms*. Someone was holding me in…in water. A lake.

"Sera?" came a ragged whisper. *His* whisper.

The Asher.

I knew that voice. I'd heard it in the darkness, hadn't I?

The One who is Blessed.

The Guardian of Souls.

The Primal God of Common Men and Endings.

The End to my Beginning.

My eyes flew open, fixing on the night sky—the stars and the moon.

"Sera," he gasped.

That name. That name. That name.

It was important, but something…something was still happening inside me. Raw, Primal energy pressed against my flesh, seeping through my pores. My skin hummed—

Time stopped. There were no sounds of water or wind. No rustling animals or distant calls. There was just him leaning over me, his silver eyes wide as he held me in his arms, keeping me afloat.

"*Liessa*," he rasped.

Eather erupted from my chest, shooting into the air in a spinning, sparking funnel. The stream of eather slammed into the sky. Time felt as if it stopped once more.

Arms tensed around me. "Oh, shit."

The surge of power throbbed, and I saw the shockwave before I heard it, rippling in waves through the air, extending in every direction. With a massive, deafening boom that shook the land in all the realms, the intense silvery-gold light rippled across the skies, stretching as far as the eye could see and beyond. That shockwave reached us—

He was torn from me, thrown back into the trees as I was lifted into the air. The water of my lake flew out and up, halting as shadowstone cracked beneath us and gave way. Tall elms groaned as they quaked, bending back and then pitching forward, their roots ripping free of the ground. They began to slide and topple, sinking into the rushing water as the eather returned to its vessel.

To me.

Essence wrapped and churned around me, crackling and spitting sparks, encasing me in its light until it was all I saw.

All I became.

41

I slept.

And I dreamed.

I was at a lake, floating in the cool water. It was so peaceful. Tranquil.

I was never alone.

A silver-white wolf sat on the bank of the lake, watching and always alert, keeping guard while I floated and...

Listened.

Someone was talking to me as I slept.

The voice was full of silky shadows and smoke. There were others, too. A raspier one. Softer, feminine tones. Quiet murmurings. But his, the voice of midnight...*his* I tuned into. It soothed me. Meant something to me.

He meant something to me.

"The first time I saw you—really saw you? You were just a child, but I didn't look like this. I'd taken my wolf form."

I looked at where the silver wolf sat. The wolf...it was him.

"Not that being in that form makes it...how did you say it?" A rough, low laugh traveled across the water, bringing a smile to my lips. "Any less creepy."

I...I'd said that?

"You were this little thing carrying your weight in pebbles, your hair a pale tangle of moonlight. When you saw me, I thought you'd scream and run away. Child or not, most sensible mortals would do that when confronted by a wolf. You did neither of those things."

I didn't think I... I was known to be sensible.

"You just stared at me with those big green eyes." There were several moments of silence, and I feared he wouldn't speak again, but he did. "It was a long time before you saw me again. Not until the night you turned seventeen, but I saw *you* between then."

I had the strange impression that the night he spoke about had once been important to me. Life-changing and haunting. A source of bitter failure that had once felt like it would never go away. But I also sensed the event no longer meant anything to me.

"I never told you about the dream I had of your lake before I even laid eyes on it," he said. "I can't even say it was a dream. It was...yeah, it was something else. But for years, I told myself that was all it was. Convinced myself until I no longer could. It was a warning, one I heeded." Heavy regret filled his voice. "But I did so in the worst way possible."

He fell quiet then, and I was grateful. I didn't want him talking about things that made him sad. I wanted him to laugh as he had before.

Time passed as I floated, and I heard other voices. Ones I didn't recognize. Some I thought I would know eventually. They talked about the past and the future. They shared ancient knowledge, speaking of magic and power until *his* voice silenced theirs.

He spoke more, mentioning the night he saw me in a Temple. He told me how he tried to distance himself from me. Talked about how he saw me again when he stopped me from attacking some gods.

It sounded like a completely insensible thing for me to try, but it made me smile.

"I already knew by then that you were brave," he said. "I just hadn't realized *how* brave you'd become. How fearless and passionate you were."

I liked that part.

"And I wasn't prepared for how much I'd feel... How I'd feel alive just being in your presence."

I *really* liked that part.

"After I had my *kardia* removed, I was still capable of feeling. Caring. I was still myself, I just didn't... I don't know." His voice sounded closer.

As I floated, I felt the ghost of a touch on my cheek. My eyes closed.

I really, really liked that.

It struck me then that I always liked when he touched me. Loved it.

"I just didn't feel things strongly. I was no longer capable of doing so," he told me. "Until you. You made me feel things strongly. Everything, *liessa*."

Liessa? Was that my name? I didn't think so, but my heart skipped at hearing it. And it wasn't a bad feeling. It was pleasant. I loved when he called me that. It had a special meaning.

"From that very first damn kiss, I should've known." He sighed.

Known what?

Better yet… I wanted him to tell me about our first kiss. I wanted to remember it.

And he did, much to my happiness. "You knew I was, at the very least, a god, and you still threatened me."

Well, that happiness was incredibly short-lived. Why had I threatened him? I had a feeling I'd been justified.

"You warned me that if I tried anything…"

Go for that weapon on your thigh again? I heard his voice—not then, but in my mind. He'd said that to me after I threatened him, and I had answered with a *yes*.

"When I shushed you, I really thought you were going to hit me," he said with another low chuckle. "I never knew a mortal to be so…wonderfully belligerent to a god. It was refreshing."

That was an odd reaction, but it still made me grin.

"I could've done so many damn things to make sure we weren't seen. Telling you to kiss me should've been the very last thing I suggested." I felt that whisper of touch again, this time on my jaw. "But your threats provoked me, and damn…it shocked me. Even before Maia removed my *kardia*, I'd learned to control my temper. To not let things rile me. I knew better."

He…he did. Because he…he'd had to learn that.

"But a few minutes with you and I was responding to your every word and every move without much thought. Just instinct. I wanted to challenge you. I didn't think you'd kiss me. I figured you'd more than likely hit me. But you did." His voice was a sigh against my skin. "And it shocked the hell out of me."

But I… My brow wrinkled as I opened my eyes to the empty, dark sky above. I had…I had bitten his lip. Then he'd kissed me back.

"Fates, *liessa*, you tasted of warmth and sunshine," he said. "Life. It left me feeling off balance for *days*. I was so damn pissed at myself for engaging you like that. I knew better. I *fucking* knew better. You didn't realize who I was to you yet, and I knew the kind of danger I was putting you in. I knew what could happen. But you were in my arms after all those years of avoiding you, and you...you...you felt like you were mine."

Mine.

Some knowledge arose that the idea of belonging to someone would enrage me, but not him. He was different. I *did* belong to him. And he belonged to me.

"I told myself it was because of what my father did. It made sense to me that I would feel that way since you'd been promised to me before you were even born."

A deal...

One made between a desperate King and a Primal to save a kingdom...and the realms.

"It couldn't be anything else, but I...I started to feel things strongly again. After that one damn kiss, I felt...I felt excitement. Anticipation. And damn, it had been a long time since I'd felt those two emotions, but everything was heightened when it came to you. Even anger and frustration," he said with a dark, rich laugh. "And when you stabbed me?"

I...I'd stabbed him?

"I even felt alive then."

What a strange man.

I smiled.

"When you argued with me. When you smiled at me. When you had that look of violence in your eyes. When it turned sensual. But especially when you laughed. I felt *alive*," he said. "But I also felt fear again. And Fates, I couldn't remember the last time I'd felt that. It was even before my *kardia* was removed, but I felt real fear when I thought about how willing you were to risk your life. Terror at the thought of Kolis discovering you."

That name...

My hands balled into fists. I didn't like that name.

I felt the soft glide of fingers over mine. I looked at where my hand drifted in the water. Slowly, my fingers relaxed, unfurling. It was his touch. It felt as if he were mapping the bones and tendons beneath my skin. He spoke of our time at the lake, and how he felt more like him-self than ever when he was there with me. He talked about how he'd finally taken me into the Shadowlands.

"That fear had me acting like a real piece of shit," he said. "And when I learned what you had plotted?"

I'd...I'd planned to kill him.

My chest seized with agony. I hadn't wanted to, but I'd believed I had to. I'd been so very wrong, though. I knew that.

"Yeah, it pissed me off."

No doubt. Who wouldn't be mad?

"But it shouldn't have angered me. I shouldn't have felt betrayed," he said, and I squeezed my eyes shut. My heart hurt. I didn't want him to have felt that. I didn't want to be the cause. "Not with my *kardia* removed. I couldn't understand why, but what I did know, even then, was that I was angrier about the risk you took than your betrayal."

My eyes drifted open.

"You wouldn't have survived the attempt. You would've died. And for what? A fucking kingdom that didn't know you existed? A mother who didn't deserve such an honor? *Fuck*," he spat.

His anger made me smile. It shouldn't. Life was important. All life was, even those deemed unworthy of such. I knew that *now*. I didn't think I'd known that then. Or cared. But it was now etched into my bones.

But so was the violence he'd seen in my eyes. Because...*life was vicious*. When stolen, it became the ruin of realms, a wrath that even Death would hide from.

And Death *would* hide from me.

Time passed as I floated in the lake, and the wolf sat on the bank, watching and waiting while the voice spoke of words we'd thrown at each other and things we'd whispered. He spoke of regrets and wants, passion and yearning. His voice always deepened then, roughening in a way that pulled forth glimpses of memories—of us, our bodies entwined and joined together. Those remembrances elicited sharp pulses of desire that left me aching, yearning to feel him against my skin and inside me so badly, I fell into those memories of him taking control.

I remembered those moments so clearly. His large body caging mine, holding me in place as he took me from behind. And I knew I only ever allowed him to dominate me and my body, and it drove me wild that I *could* do so and feel safe. That I could let go of whatever inhibitions and reservations remained hidden deep inside me and be so free. It *thrilled* me. It *empowered* me. We could make *love*. We could *fuck*. And in the end, it was I who chose.

I had the ultimate control.

I knew that.

I remembered that.

I floated some more, feeling less weightless and more solid. Later, when he spoke about his father, I *remembered* seeing the portrait of him. I recalled talking to *him*.

"Do you do that?" I asked, staring at the painting of the woman. She was beautiful, with deep, wine-red hair framing skin painted a rosy pink on an oval-shaped face. Her brows were strong, her silver-eyed gaze piercing. Piercing like his. *Her cheekbones were high, and her mouth was full. "Do you often accept the aid of others?"*

"Not as often as I should." His voice was closer.

"Then maybe you don't know if that is brave or not." My attention had shifted to the painting of the male, and I felt my breath catch then. And it did so now. *His hair was shoulder-length and black...*

But *his* hair wasn't as dark. It was a shade of brown with red undertones. A chestnut color. They shared the same features. A strong jaw and broad cheekbones. A straight nose and a wide mouth, but his was more defined than his father's. He'd gotten sharper angles from his mother.

I could see *him* in my mind now as he spoke of following his father as a child, and he was striking. Had a beauty that bordered on cruel. Perfect to me. For me.

Later, he spoke of how he used to follow his father around a large palace as a child. "He never grew tired of my presence," he said. "He wanted me with him. I think because I reminded him of my mother, even though I also resembled him. When he spoke about her, it was the only time I saw him smile—*really* smile. Fates, *liessa*, he loved her so much."

Their story was a tragic one that had ended in betrayal and jealousy.

"He was so damn strong. He never completely lost himself to the agony of her loss," he shared. His voice turned sad, and it made *me* sad. "He remained kind and compassionate, even though he'd lost a part of himself. I don't know how he did it. How he continued on for as long as he did."

A whisper of a touch brushed my jaw. "I wanted to be as strong as my father, but I wasn't him."

"It has nothing to do with strength," that raspier voice of fire joined his, and I...I felt weight on my legs.

Frowning, I looked at where my legs drifted in the water. I saw nothing, but I felt a familiar weight I knew but couldn't quite place.

"Eythos had many more years on him than you," the other voice said, and images flashed in my mind of a tall man with copper skin and long, dark hair streaked with red. "And he changed, Ash."

My heart thudded heavily. *Ash.* I knew that name. He was the nightmare that had become my dream. The calm in my storm. My strength when I was weak. The breath when I couldn't breathe. He was more than my King. My husband.

Ash was the other half of my heart and soul.

"He was never the same," the other continued. "And if you hadn't lived? He would've wasted away."

There was a gap of silence, and then, "And if I'd lost her?" Ash replied. "I wouldn't have wasted away. I would've destroyed every-thing."

"I know," the other said, the voice so heavy I felt the truth of it in my bones.

Because I *was* the other half of Ash's soul. His heart. And nothing was more powerful than that—or more dangerous.

"But that will not come to pass," the other said. "You saved her."

He had.

That other voice was right, and I knew his name, didn't I? He had once told me that *not everyone can always be okay.* He'd made me agree that if I...if I ever wasn't okay, I would talk to him. That we'd...

We'll make sure you're okay.

Nektas.

That was his name.

Tears stung my throat and eyes, his offer meaning the world to me because Nektas knew that life was worth living, even when it was often unfair and the injustices seemed to stack up. Hardships didn't always happen for a reason. Sometimes, the Fates didn't have a greater plan.

But even when it began to feel like a chore one had to force themselves to complete, life was still worth living.

Even when it was unfair and heartbreaking, dark and full of the unknown, life was still worth living.

Because rewards could be found among the chores. Little pieces of enjoyment that would come to mean something. Darkness always gave way to the light if given time, and while some heartbreaks may never completely heal, living allowed there to be space for new sources of happiness and pleasure.

Life was worth living even when it was full of unfairness and injustice. When the heart felt light and when the chest was too tight to breathe.

Because death was final.

The absence of choice.

And life was a collection of new beginnings.

Full of unending choices.

Time passed, I slept, and Ash continued to speak. His voice would grow louder and then become a whisper.

Another voice came, one that was quiet and serious—always serious. "You need to feed. When she wakes…"

When I woke, I would be…hungry.

Ash was quiet, then I felt his touch again on my cheek. His hand was cool but a bit warmer. "I never felt alive until you," he whispered, "And I should've known then what you were to me. That you were the impossible. The one thing that could return a *kardia*, scratching itself together from the wound its removal left behind. My heartmate."

Lips curving upward, I dragged my arms through the water as I smiled.

"Take as long as you need to rest," Ash told me. "I'll be here, waiting. I'll always wait for you, Sera."

42

Ash's voice faded away. The others returned for a time, calling to me, but then they, too, disappeared. Somehow, I ended up facing the bank of the lake.

The wolf was gone.

In its place was a large feline, one that resembled a cave cat, but its fur wasn't the shade of storm clouds—it gleamed like moonlight. The feline prowled the damp, mossy ground at the lake's edge.

I started to swim forward, unafraid. The cat's tail swished back and forth as green eyes spliced with silver tracked my movements. As my feet brushed the cool shadowstone, I no longer treaded water but walked forward.

The feline stepped back, its large paws sinking into the soil and grass. I saw it was a female. She sank onto her haunches as I climbed the earthen steps. Water dripped from my fingers and hair as I knelt before the stunning creature.

I reached between us, placing my hand beneath her powerful jaw. Soft fur teased my palm and threaded between my fingers. A soft purr came from the cat's chest. Movement behind her caught my attention. In the shadows, something moved—two of them. Smaller, their coats darker. My attention shifted back to the large feline. Our eyes locked, and I saw…

I saw me looking back.

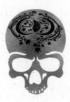

A tingling sensation started in my feet and slowly traveled up my legs, followed by a rush of heat. My fingers twitched. A leg spasmed and then curled beneath softness. I forced my mouth to part. Something scraped against my lower lip as I drew in a short breath.

A solid and…cold body shifted beside mine and a scent reached me. Fresh mountain air and citrus. I liked that smell. A lot. Brief images of silver eyes and golden-bronze skin flashed in the darkness of my mind. My throat vibrated with a soft hum.

Something touched my cheek. *Fingers.* They sent a jolt of energy through me. "*Sera?*"

That voice.

Midnight silk and sin.

Something soft and warm rasped against my thighs and breasts. A blanket? Whatever it was, my skin grew even more sensitive.

"I know it's hard waking up for the first time," the midnight voice said. "It took me hours, so don't fight it if you fall back asleep. We have time."

But I didn't want to sleep.

The fingers at my cheek slipped to my jaw, tilting my head. My back arched as that sound reverberated from my chest again—a trilling purr.

I was…I was so thirsty. Everything inside me was on fire. I felt parched and barren. My jaw throbbed, and my throat burned. I tried to swallow, but my mouth was too dry. My muscles cramped as I tried to pry my eyes open. My lids felt fused together. The trilling sound I made deepened with my frustration, becoming a raspy growl.

"It's okay. Give yourself time," the voice soothed. "I'm right here. I'm with you."

The hand at my jaw rose to the side of my face, his cool skin a brief reprieve against the inferno. I wanted to turn into the touch, press against it, but I was too weak.

I could not be weak.

Not…not *before.* And not now.

Gods, I was so thirsty. Hungry. And restless. My muscles felt unused, as if I'd slept for years, but it hadn't been years. Days, maybe. Days while I listened to a voice. His voice. The voices of others. My mind was a mess of racing thoughts, explosions of knowledge that kept coming. But I needed to move.

I needed…something.

Sustenance.

I needed to *feed*.

The throbbing in my jaw increased. I really wanted to open my eyes. Eather pulsed, first in my chest, before flooding my body with sheer will. My lashes fluttered and then lifted. I finally opened my eyes to darkness and the cool press of a body next to mine.

His body.

And it had grown still.

At first, there were just blotches of shadow, but my eyes quickly adjusted. Even with the lack of light, I clearly made out a side table holding a small wooden box. My gaze slowly moved over a wardrobe and a few chests. A table. Two chairs. That felt different, as if it had changed. Confusion and curiosity rose as fragments of memory existed just outside my reach. I spied two closed doors. Everything was spare and darkly colored. It had no life.

Except for the splashes of color strewn about a long couch. Gowns of vibrant blues and red, blouses and vests. That felt new, too. It seemed significant and—

"Sera?" The body beside mine trembled.

My hunger had momentarily gone silent as I took in my surroundings, but now it returned with a vengeance. Muscles tensed. I dragged in a deeper breath, drawing his scent into me.

My arms and legs moved at once, propelling me into a crouched position as my head whipped toward the source of the voice.

"It's okay," he repeated softly, carefully.

Through tangled, pale curls, I saw only what was inside him. My head tilted as eather throbbed in my chest and then moved throughout me, recognizing what coursed through his veins. He was chock-full of eather. It filled him. My mouth watered as he sat up more, his chest bare. I *sensed* what he was.

A Primal.

But his flesh was cold, and the part of me that now felt eons older knew what that signified.

He wasn't just a Primal.

He was the one I eventually submitted to, no matter how strong I was, how vicious and tenacious I could be. He would always win because he was the end to my beginning. He was a Primal of Death.

Mine.

The word flickered wildly through my mind, and I didn't understand what it meant. I was too hungry to concentrate, too distracted by the sudden realization that he was one of two.

And I *knew* there shouldn't be two Primals of Death. It would upset the balance, and balance must—

"Do you—?" He cut himself off with a curse. His throat worked on a swallow, drawing my attention. He lifted a hand. "Sera—"

A sharp slice of agony lit up my face from my jaw to my temples, forcing out a hiss of pain. I shrank back.

"I'm not going to hurt you," he said. "I would never hurt you."

Despite how weak I was and the threat he posed, I laughed, and the sound was throaty and warm like a summer wind. "Hurt me?" I breathed, tipping forward as I let the essence come to the surface. A silvery aura crept into the sides of my vision. "You may be inevitable, but you cannot stop me."

His brows furrowed. "I don't want... Shit." His expression smoothed out, and I saw a slight twitch to his lips as if he might smile or laugh. I somehow knew I would like that sound. "I thought I was prepared for this. Apparently, I'm not." He inhaled deeply. "Let me try again. I don't want to stop you. I don't even want you to submit to me— not now or ever."

My heart started thumping heavily as I stared at the male. His words confused me because I had to give in to him, but they also made sense because I didn't.

"Unless it's one of those times you *want* to submit." One side of his lips curled, and his scent increased with...arousal. "Then I am more than happy to oblige."

He wasn't speaking about the natural order of things. He was talking about...

An image rose of being pressed onto my chest as a large body held me down, moving behind me, inside me. My skin flamed even hotter, stoking the gnawing, aching hunger.

"You definitely remember that," he said, his voice as thick as my blood. "That's good." Hair fell against his cheeks as his chin dipped. He wiggled his fingers. "I know what you need, Sera. Me. My blood. You need to feed."

I eyed his hand as the agonizing hunger expanded.

"I am yours."

Mine.

My lips parted, and my heart thundered. There was some sense—a knowledge the other voices had shared with me... "The Primal of Life has not fed from a Primal of Death before," I said, fingers curling into fur—a blanket. "We...we are meant to be two halves of a cycle but separate."

His exhale was rough. "But we are different, Sera. Those beliefs don't apply to us." He leaned toward me, hand still raised. His scent increased until I could taste it on my tongue. Citrusy. Fresh. "I am yours. All of me. My body. My blood. My soul." His voice roughened. "My heart."

Mine.

My gaze dropped to his hand. There was something on his palm. A golden, shimmery swirl. The sight of it caused my heart to skip. Slowly, I lifted my hand and placed it in his. The contact was jarring, and a rush of energy and memories came on too fast for me to make sense of it, but I saw the top of my hand. I saw the bright, golden swirl that matched the hand beneath mine.

"That's it." He lowered his voice. "Come to me."

I watched his fingers close around mine. I lifted my gaze. He tilted his head back, exposing his throat.

My hand tightened around his. I saw his eyes close. Then I shot toward him, climbing onto his lap. He didn't react, just held himself still, vulnerable despite how much bigger he was. I clasped his shoulders as my lips peeled back. The throbbing in my jaw increased.

"Feed," he ordered.

Guided by instinct, my head snapped toward his neck. I struck, sinking my fangs into the vein in his throat.

The first drop of his blood against my tongue was an awakening.

My back arched, the shock of his taste and the strength of his essence flooding me. It was all I could think about as he cursed. It was everything. Mouth tingling, I drew hungrily, pulling the smoky yet sweet flavor into me. His blood hit the back of my throat, sparking a riot of intense sensations. His blood tasted good. He felt good against me, his coolness against my heat. But he...

His body was rigid against mine. "Release...release your fangs."

The order filtered through the hunger. I...I was hurting him. I didn't want that. We were the cycle. I was the beginning. He was the end. But we were more than that. He was *mine*. I pulled my fangs from his flesh but kept my mouth latched there. He jerked, his chest rising sharply as I took him into me. A deep moan teased my ears. He liked this now. Enjoyed it. I drank deeper, his blood coursing down my throat, soothing the burn there until it hit my hollow chest, easing the gnawing ache. But it wasn't his blood. It was the eather in him, pooling at the center of my chest, restoring my strength.

He was a Primal of Death, but his blood...his blood was life.

The Primal shifted beneath me. His arm folded over my hips, and his hand landed on my lower back. I tensed.

"Keep drinking," he instructed, his palm flattening against my skin. "You haven't taken enough."

I purred my gratitude. His hips jerked at the sound, and I felt the thick hardness pressing against me. A shiver danced through me, tight and hot. The uncomfortable heat eased, replaced by a languid warmth that spread as his hand swept up the length of my back to disappear under my hair before gliding back down. His fingers brushed the curve of my rear, making that warmth grow into a fire that didn't hurt but enflamed.

I fed at his throat, his blood filling me as he ran his hand up and down my spine. Slowly—or maybe quickly—each sweep of his hand stroked a different kind of urgency into being.

I wanted more.

Needed more of him.

I leaned forward, pressing against him. The contact of his chilled skin against mine turned the blood I drank into liquid want. My nipples hardened as I writhed restlessly against him, and they dragged against the smooth, cool surface of his chest. A heady ache settled in my breasts. His blood. His body...gods. I tingled, becoming acutely sensitive.

My fingers splayed across his shoulders as I tilted my hips forward, finding what I sought, what I needed. He moaned as I rubbed against the hard length of his cock. There was a barrier between us, Thin, soft linen. I growled my frustration.

His arm tightened around my lower back. "Fucking Fates," he groaned as I ground down.

The sound and feel of him against me was like falling into a whirlwind of sensations. Muscles low in my belly tightened as tiny darts of pleasure spread through me. I whimpered, wanting more, needing more.

His hand stilled on the center of my back. "Sera..."

Mouth latched to his throat, I moaned as I rocked against him. I wanted so much. Him. His blood. His cock.

"I know. I know what you need. Let me give it to you." His arm shifted, and he lifted me. I strained against his absence. "Trust me."

I trusted him. Irrevocably.

I stopped fighting and let him lift me from his lap.

"Keep drinking," he ordered roughly as he reached between us, shoving his pants down as he held me with just one arm. His strength…it was unbelievable. Intoxicating. "Take what you need."

Obeying, I took and took, my mouth moving greedily over his throat as I felt him cold and heavy against my heat. A wild pulse of lust lit me up. His hand returned to my hip, steadying my frantic attempts to feel him where I needed him. He guided me down, and we both groaned when I felt the cool head of his cock pressing into me.

I shuddered. That…that was what I wanted. Needed. I pushed down, moaning as I began taking him inside me. It wasn't fast or deep enough.

He sensed that, driving his hips up, stretching and filling me in one thrust. He was such an enormous presence in my body. His throat muffled my cry of pleasure as I shook. The arm at my waist lifted me and then brought me back down, causing my toes to curl as I continued drinking deeply. Ripples of pleasure washed over me in waves with each lift and fall. I was humming now, the heat spreading, his body cooling even further. I could drink all of him. Take everything of him into me.

And he'd let me.

He'd give anything for me, even himself. Instinctively, I knew I couldn't kill him like this, but I *could* weaken him, bring him to a point where his body would need to go into stasis.

I didn't want that.

He moved under me, the pace of his rising hips feverish and overwhelming, making it difficult to think about anything but satisfying the dual, brutal needs.

But he was too important, and I would *hurt* him. I couldn't do that. Because he was…he was my other half.

Body trembling, I slowed my feeding. The red haze of bloodlust dissipated, allowing my other thoughts to clear. It wasn't just Primal blood I was feeding on. It wasn't only a body giving me pleasure. It was *his*.

Ash.

My lover.

My King of Gods.

My husband, whom I was deeply in love with.

A sense of self returned to me. My name: Seraphena. Who I once was and was now. Who I was meant to become. The new sense of awareness was like a lock being turned. Memories didn't come rushing back, they just returned to me, taking their rightful places.

A tremor ran through me.

Ash…he had saved me.

I didn't know how. Holland had said the only way I could be saved was through love. And that was impossible, wasn't it?

"*I love you, even if I cannot,*" Ash had screamed. "*I'm in love with you.*"

Gods, he'd wanted so badly to love me. Had he made some sort of deal? Had the Arae intervened? I didn't know as I forced my jaw to relax. I lifted my mouth from the bite. Compelled by either the newly formed instinct or memories of Ash doing it, I nicked my lower lip. The sting of pain was barely noticeable amidst the coiling tension. Blood drawn, I kissed the wound I'd made, stopping the bleeding.

"*Liessa,*" Ash whispered.

Something beautiful.

Something powerful.

I brought my mouth to his and kissed him, knowing he likely tasted both his blood and mine on my lips. Angling my hips, I planted my hands on his chest and pushed him onto his back. It hadn't required much strength. Just a slight pressure, and he obeyed, both hands falling to my hips. He clasped them. If he wanted to fight, we'd be equally matched, and I had no idea who would win.

I couldn't wait to find out, though.

But it would have to wait.

Opening my eyes, I looked down at him and felt my chest loosen and tighten all at once. Everything about him was so much clearer, sharper now. The faint scar on his chin. The shape of his lips and their defined cupid's bow. There was another scar on the bridge of his nose that I'd never seen before. I'd always thought his lashes were impossibly thick, but now I saw just how dense they were. And his eyes? The aura of eather behind his pupils was like stars, and the wisps churning in his irises a constellation. It was like seeing him for the first time. There was so much I wanted to say—so much I knew I needed to tell him—but the powerful muscles in his chest and shoulders flexed and rolled as his grip on my hips urged me to take what I wanted.

And I did.

I rode him, my pace quickening, causing several long curls to fall forward over my swaying breasts. A sharp burst of tingles spread as I ground against his hips. My lips parted, and the sensation of the tips of my fangs grazing my lower lip was an odd one.

The tension built and built. It was like a thread being pulled too taut. The coil snapped, and then lightning hit my veins. My head kicked back as I came. Pleasure hit every part of my body, sweeping me up and away in the bliss.

Slowly, all the tight muscles in my body relaxed, and my head fell forward. Only then did I realize that Ash had stopped moving and was still hard and thick inside me. Lifting my head, I opened my eyes. Through my tangled curls, our gazes locked.

Ash shuddered and then moved beneath me, sitting up. His hand clamped down on the back of my neck, tangling in my hair. He held my stare. "You know who I am?"

His question confused me at first, but then I remembered the dreams of him speaking to me and how I'd struggled to recall his name and others. And then there was how I'd behaved upon waking. Was it possible that I wouldn't have remembered him? The mere thought caused my heart to ache. "I will always know you, Ash."

43

Ash's chest rose sharply, and then he went completely still, even the eather in his eyes.

My heart kicked as our gazes collided once more. There was an almost feral look to his stare, one that caused a whoosh to rush through my stomach. "Ash?" I whispered.

His eyes slammed shut. Shadows began appearing along his shoulders and across his chest. His skin thinned.

Oh, gods, had I taken too much blood? I moved off him a bit.

Tendrils of shadowy eather lashed out from him, coiling along my forearms. I gasped at the chill, momentarily caught off guard. My stare swept over him. Blotches of darkness appeared down his arms, his thighs, and even on his cock, where pearly white liquid beaded at the tip—

Sucking in a startled breath, my head jerked to the side as the shadows slid up my arms, brushing against the sides of my breasts like a cold winter's kiss. My nipples beaded, sending a pulse of blade-sharp desire through me.

Skin tingling, I attempted to rein in my response. Now didn't seem like the right time to be turned on, but harsh, churning lust hit my core.

A low rumbling growl echoed from Ash, snapping my attention back to him. My arousal hadn't gone unnoticed.

His lips parted, revealing a glimpse of his fangs. Dark hollows appeared in his cheeks.

"Ash," I tried again.

"I was terrified," he said, his voice thicker and guttural. "I was terrified that I would lose you."

My chest dipped. "You didn't. You saved me." I wasn't exactly sure how, but I knew he had. I knew the only reason I was here was because of him.

"Then I was terrified that you wouldn't remember me." Tendons stood out starkly as he twisted his neck to the side, seeming not to hear me. "That I would still lose you."

"You won't. Not ever," I promised, attempting once more to move closer to him.

The ripple of eather pushed down on my shoulders, pressing me onto my back. Essence pulsed in my chest, ramping up in response to his Primal display of power. My eyes widened as I saw energy spark along my skin below the throbbing mass of his shadows.

The sight of the silvery light coming from within me—light streaked with *gold*—distracted me for a second. I'd never seen it look like that before. But I...I was different now.

Reminding myself that the essence was a part of me and that I could control it, I locked the power down. It wasn't a struggle like before. In the back of my mind, I knew it was because the eather was only a byproduct of my will, and it responded immediately because I never wanted to hurt him. "Ash?"

He shuddered. "I feared I would never hear you say my name again." His body...it *vibrated*. A moment passed, and then another as he twisted his head from side to side. The tendrils of eather lifted. "When I...when I release you, you need to run."

I tensed. "What?"

"You need to run, Sera. Fast. Faster than you ever have before. You may be able to outrun me..." Another series of shudders ran through him. "You have to try. Because I...I *need* you. Your heat. Your silky tightness. I *need* to be inside you."

Another stunning pulse of desire sliced through me, causing my hips to squirm in blade-sharp anticipation. "Why would I want to run from that?"

More of the darkness became visible, nearly obscuring his skin. "I won't be able to hold on to my mortal form much longer." The shadows briefly thickened around him. "I don't want to hurt you."

"You won't. I trust in that—trust in *you*. Just as you trusted me earlier when I wasn't even all that aware—"

"This is different."

I started to tell him it wasn't, but Ash *changed*. It was him—the shape of his features, the strong jaw, and wide, expressive mouth. His high, sharp cheekbones and blade-straight nose, but he was now shadow and smoke turned to stone.

He had shifted into his Primal form, his midnight-streaked skin looking as hard as granite as moonlight wings lifted behind him, sweeping out and blocking the chamber behind him.

This was Nyktos, the Asher, the one who is Blessed, the Guardian of Souls, and the Primal God of Common Men and Endings. This was who he was at his core: an ancient predator and the giver and taker of lives.

A Primal of Death, terrifying in his power and glory…and not in control.

Even without the newly gained knowledge that had come with my Ascension, I would've known that it made him incredibly dangerous. Even to a Primal.

Even to me.

My chest rose and fell rapidly as I stared up at the Primal, still…still seeing Ash. I saw only him, and I felt no fear as more shadow-laced eather drifted out in smoky tendrils, spilling onto the bed.

"If you don't run, if I take you, I will take you like this," he warned. "And I will do so as a Primal."

"I'm here, and I'm not leaving," I whispered, willing to give him anything and everything he needed. "I'm yours, Ash. Take me."

A low, sensual rumble echoed from him, eliciting a wave of shivers from me. The swirling shadows eased off my shoulders and gathered along my forearms. They curled around my wrists. My heart stuttered as my gaze fixed on his.

Ash's eyes were pure molten silver. "I tried to warn you."

Before I could respond, the shadows yanked my arms up, pinning them to the bed above my head.

Oh, gods.

In an instant, the essence inside me strained against his display of dominance. There was no fear, though—no flashes of panic or desperation. There was no room for any of that when there was this heightened need to push back and see who would come out on top, and the twisting burst of red-hot desire.

Ash's nostrils flared as he breathed in deeply. The growl deepened as he tilted forward, curling his fingers around my ankle. My entire body jerked at the touch. I wasn't sure if it was the coldness of those fingers or the palpable tension gathering in the chamber.

Jaw clenched, he lifted my leg, pushing it to the side, exposing the throbbing heat between my thighs to the air...and to him.

Those glowing eyes left mine as wisps of shadowy eather throbbed restlessly against the bed, brushing my outer legs. The intensity of his stare was like an icy-hot brand as his gaze lowered, drifting over my heavy breasts. Between *his* thighs, his cock pulsed, and...

Was it larger? Thicker and longer?

My heart tripped as I took in the rest of him. His body was bigger—wider and likely taller. My gaze slid back down.

Dear gods.

His gaze lowered, moving past my navel and then lower still, which meant I was incapable of focusing on anything else.

Everything about him vibrated as his stare latched on to me. My legs reflexively started to close, but his grip on my ankle firmed as one of the humming tendrils rose from the bed and draped over my other leg.

The sudden cool weight of his eather caused my stomach to clench, but I still felt no fear. No unease. I never did with Ash. Not when he gave me complete control or took it for himself. I was always safe with him.

Memories of the night after the Cimmerian attack resurfaced. Would he touch me so wickedly again? I shivered. Would he do it while he knew I saw him? A rush of heat and dampness pooled where his eyes feasted.

One side of his lips curved up as his gaze returned to mine. "I can taste your need."

I shook.

His stare dropped once more as he pushed the ankle he held up, spreading my legs even wider. "So pretty," he murmured. "So wet."

My skin flushed.

"Mine," he rumbled.

The tendril on my calf started to move, drawing my attention. My heart began pounding as the swirling mass of energy rippled over my knee, leaving a cascade of shivers in its wake. I tried to slow my breathing, but it was no use. The wisp of darkness kissed my inner thigh. I couldn't look away as it crept up my trembling skin. My fingers curled helplessly into my palms as the icy burn eased over the crease in my thigh.

Cool air brushed my core.

I cried out, hips twitching as the air charged all around us. The shadow rolled against me, teasing my damp, heated skin. The mist thickened, solidifying enough that I could only see a hint of my skin beneath. I trembled at the soft, humming feel of the shadows against me, so focused on what was happening there that I didn't see the other tendrils lifting from the bed.

Thick, crackling air slid along my sides, startling me. Feeling breathless, my head tilted to the side. The tendrils flowed over my lower stomach, then spread up, kissing and licking my skin, my breasts. It felt like fingers pressing in and swirling around my nipples. My back arched—

Ash made a *tsking* sound, snapping my gaze to his. He looked utterly otherworldly in his Primal form. Primitive. Wild. "These lips are even softer."

I think I did stop breathing then as I stared at him. He had such a...a naughty mouth when in his true form.

"And warmer," he said, his tongue running along the inside of his lower lip. "I don't want my pretty pussy feeling lonely."

My pretty...

Eyes wide at his language, a laugh traveled up my throat, but it never made it past my lips. A sudden cry of shocking pleasure did as those thicker, heavier shadows pulsed, parting the softer, warmer lips he spoke of.

"Oh, gods," I cried out, hips rolling as the tendril of energy pushed inside me. My memories of this experience did not do it any justice.

My head spun as the sensations at my breasts and in my *pussy* overwhelmed me. It felt wonderfully indecent.

I moaned, twisting as the thick, churning mass moved inside me. Ash was closer, and then he no longer held my ankle. He was still on his knees, his body keeping my legs open to him and his stare. I shuddered and gasped, quickly becoming lost to the sinful pleasure. My ass lifted off the bed, and I didn't know if that was me or him, but the cool brush of air against my backside startled me.

I didn't dare move as that air slipped and slid. My hips were tilted up even farther, and I saw a thinner wisp of energy split away. Oh, gods, was he going to...? I'd never had anything go in *there*. The Mistresses of the Jade had spoken of how pleasurable it could be with the right, er, prepping, but they were speaking of cocks, not spindly tendrils of energy.

"*Liessa*," he called in a low trill.

My gaze cut to his as I felt him sliding and seeking. I didn't think my heart could beat any faster. I bit down on my lip again, either not drawing blood this time or unable to feel it as I tentatively pushed against the thrumming bolt of energy.

Eather skated across Ash's skin as his wings spread out once more. "I want to hear you say it."

His demand scorched every part of me. "Yes."

He twisted his head again, his dark, hard chest rising with a deep breath. The bead at the tip of his cock was more noticeable now. "I want to hear you say exactly what you want from me, and I want you to say it with my name."

I discovered right then that my temper hadn't improved with my Ascension. My eyes narrowed. "And if I don't?"

His snarl wasn't one of anger but of sensual challenge. The teasing presence at my rear stilled, as did the tendril inside me. "Then I won't fuck that pretty pussy and ass of yours."

Good fucking gods...

I couldn't move, think, or even breathe for a moment. He was so...shameless when in his Primal form.

And I couldn't be more aroused by it because it was *him*.

"Please," I whispered.

He cocked his head.

"Please fuck my pretty pussy and ass." I paused. "*Ash*."

The dark air between my thighs plunged forward as the sudden pressure eased into the entrance there, quickly becoming a burn—an icy, stinging burn.

Every muscle in my body locked as he held me, my lower body several inches off the bed. The pressure and fullness were...*mind-blowing*. I'd never felt anything like it. Wouldn't have imagined it possible.

Ash chuckled darkly, grasping my hip with his hand as he carefully and gently lowered me back to the bed. It was as cold and hot as the churning tendrils still inside me. The thin one didn't move, but the other...it thrust in and out as he watched himself take me that way, thin bursts of eather crackling across his skin like lightning.

"I want to see you come again," he said, his voice a whisper of moonlight as his hand urged me to move, to take what I wanted. "I want to hear it. Taste and feel it. Drown in it."

And so, I did.

I rocked against him, gasping at the fullness and the dual coils of pleasure spinning out. Within seconds, I was lost to the scandalous sensation. My hips grinding, my head thrashed. The eather at my breast pulsed, tugging at my nipples. I cried out, my body jerking.

Tension built quickly, stealing my breath and shocking me. Ash had marvelously talented...eather, but I'd never felt this kind of intensity before. Did I just feel things stronger because of the Ascension? Or was it him and these new experiences?

The wickedness of it all? I didn't know, but I couldn't even think clearly as his head lowered. Soft strands of hair grazed my stomach. His cool, slick tongue ran up the inside of my thigh.

The coil deep inside me tightened. My movements became almost frantic, the pleasure I felt bordering on painful. "I...I can't," I gasped. "It's too much."

"You can." He licked again, catching the wetness there. "You will. Because no one is stronger than you."

I wasn't sure if that was true, but I kept thrusting, my movements becoming increasingly erratic.

Tension built quickly, stealing my breath and shocking me. I screamed as a release took me hard, whirling through me in pounding waves of pleasure. And Ash...

Gods, he was relentless.

His mouth moved over me as he licked and tasted, drawing out every quiver and gasp.

The tendrils eased from me, bringing forth a ragged gasp. His eyes pulsed with eather as he rose. Power crackled across his shadowstone-hued flesh as he crawled over me.

A sharp bolt of lust lanced me. I didn't think it would be possible for me to feel anything like that after what we'd just done. Or what he had. What we'd both taken part in. Whatever.

Grasping my hip, he rolled me onto my belly. I started to push up out of reflex, but the cool press of his chest against my back only let me get so far.

One hand stayed on my hip, fingers pressing into the flesh. I trembled as his firm hold reached deep inside me, stroking that dark, wicked part of me alive once more.

Ash lifted me onto my widespread knees and then guided me so my back was almost straight. I felt him begin to press into...what had he said earlier? My pussy? I shuddered and clung to his arm.

He was...oh, gods, he was definitely bigger.

"I won't ever get tired of this," he whispered in my ear, dragging his free hand over my breast and then down my stomach to the junction of my thighs. "Especially *this*."

My hips jerked, seeking his hand, but he caught me, pushing my rear against him.

"I will never take you for granted," he promised, and my breath froze then redoubled as I felt him entering me, inch by delicious inch. "I will never dishonor you."

A spasm ran up my leg as he stretched me. The coolness of his cock was such a shock.

"I will always stand at your side, your command my will." He nipped my jaw as he went deeper. "I will never let harm come to you."

I shook, unable to even cry out as he pushed into me, to the hilt. He groaned as I stared wide-eyed at the wall. The feel of him inside me now, his cock throbbing, was indescribable.

"And I will lay waste to Primals, gods, Kings, and men if they even try to hurt you, and I will feel no remorse for doing so." His tongue soothed the skin he'd scraped. "I will give my life for yours."

My chest rose sharply. I didn't want to hear him say that. "Ash—"

His hips thrust into me, drawing out a ragged moan. He ground against me, hitting every sensitive, hidden part and then some. "And I will kill for you."

Senses whirling, I was only vaguely aware of my knees lifting from the bed, of both of us rising into the air as his arm curled around my stomach to hold me in place. He moved, pulling back until just the tip of him pressed in, and then thrust forward again until there wasn't an inch between us. My legs curled in the empty space with each hard plunge and fast retreat. I pressed the soles of my feet against his calves, trying to escape the intense sensation while at the same time trying to get more of it. The friction built a crazy storm of emotion that quickly turned into a swirling knot of deep tension that had me twisting and quivering against him and on his cock.

"You're my everything," he said, cheek pressed to mine as his hips pounded. "My world. My salvation. My redemption."

Ash drove into me, over and over, stopping between thrusts to grind against me. Pleasure licked through me like sweet flames, igniting an inferno that was somehow as intense and shattering as the ones that came before it. My feet lost their purchase as I came, his name a hoarse shout.

Things were a bit of a blur after that, and I wasn't even sure how we ended up as we were now—me on my back and Ash above me, his fingers running over my cheek and through my hair.

His eyes were full of brilliant pulses of eather. "Fates, Sera, I..." Ash's chest rose sharply as he cupped my cheek. "I love you."

44

I love you.

I didn't know how it was possible with his *kardia* gone, but in that moment, the how didn't matter. Because…

Ash had just said he loved me.

A rush of emotion hit me, stealing my breath. Those three words were so simple—a combination of just eight letters—yet so powerful. I'd never thought to hear them spoken by the one I loved.

"I don't know exactly when I started to fall in love with you," he said, smoothing his thumb along my jaw. "Maybe it started the night in the Garden District as we stood under the vines or when you plunged your dagger into my chest."

Trembling laughter escaped me. "I sincerely hope that wasn't when you started to fall in love with me."

Eather swirled in his irises. "It quite possibly was."

"If so, then that is quite demented in a…in an endearing sort of way," I told him, feeling the back of my throat and eyes starting to sting. "By the way, the stabbing-you thing was an accident."

"Sure." He drew out the word. I moved to swat his arm, but he caught my wrist. He lifted my hand—his skin warm—to his mouth, pressing a kiss to the marriage imprint. His eyes lifted to meet mine. The tendrils of eather there were so incredibly bright. "I love you."

A tremor started in my lower body, quickly racing up to my shoulders. "I-I don't know why I'm shaking."

He made a gruff sound, dropping his forehead to mine. *"Liessa..."*

My heart was beating so fast. Why was I so shaken by his declaration? I remembered what I'd heard him shout before I lost consciousness. Part of me must have known from the moment I awakened and realized who I was that Ash loved me. I wouldn't be alive if he didn't. But I had been too afraid to allow myself to believe that his love saved me. That it wasn't a desperate deal made or the Arae intervening. I just never...

"I'd thought..." I whispered hoarsely, squeezing my eyes shut. "I thought I would die without knowing what your love felt like."

Ash went rigid against me. "I couldn't allow that," he swore. "I will never allow that."

My breath caught as I shuddered. His heated oath lingered in the space between our mouths, I thought maybe I had always known he loved me, despite the impossibility of it. Because how many times had I questioned what, other than love, could fuel his actions?

Was it possible that Maia hadn't removed his *kardia*? Before I could ask if that was even possible, his mouth touched mine. The kiss was a fiery, passionate testament, proof that his words weren't hollow. I could feel the love in the gentle yet fierce way his mouth parted mine and tasted his desire in the dance of our tongues.

Ash broke the kiss, rocking back. I opened my eyes. He knelt between my legs, his thick, glistening length jutting from his pelvis.

I bit down on my lip, wincing at the brief sting caused by—gods, my fangs. I had actual *fangs*. I would need to work on being more mindful of them. But not now—definitely not now. Because his fists landed on either side of my hips, and he lowered his head. The first touch of his breath between my thighs stole mine.

"I will spend the rest of eternity making sure you never doubt what I feel for you," he promised, sliding his palms over my thighs. He parted them as he'd done with my lips moments before—gently and fiercely. "Starting now."

I held my breath, toes curling in anticipation. I didn't have to wait long. My back bowed as I felt his tongue sliding along the very center of me.

The entire realm ceased to exist. It was just him, me, and his sinfully talented tongue. All I could do was give myself over to the heat spreading throughout my body as he lapped at my wetness, driving me higher and higher. I writhed and bucked against his mouth with each stroke, every time his tongue delved into me.

His hands clamped down on my hips, keeping me trapped against his mouth. His tongue slid lower, parting me. I groaned, lifting my hips. The pleasure was so intense that it was almost painful, and he wasn't slowing down or stopping.

"Ash...please," I whispered, one leg curling, pressing into his side.

"I haven't tasted enough of you." His tongue flicked the knot of nerves, drawing a sharp cry from me. "I don't think I'll ever get enough."

Clutching the blanket beneath me, I started to shake as he rolled his tongue over that sensitive part of me once more. Then he closed his mouth over my clit. The pull and sudden scrape of his fangs sent me over the edge.

"Ash," I moaned.

His answering growl burned my skin, heightening the arousal. My head kicked back as I screamed, coming in a blinding, startling rush that I would've sworn to the gods transported me to another realm, because I had no idea how much—if any—time passed before I heard a rapping at the door.

"Is everything okay in there?" came Nektas's muffled voice.

Either Ash hadn't heard him, or he was ignoring the draken, because his answer was to flick his tongue over my heated flesh again.

My hips jerked, and my toes curled.

"I'm starting to get worried," Nektas said.

I shuddered as he ran a finger through my wetness. "*Ash.*"

He drew back just enough for me to see his glossy lips. "Everything is fine."

There was barely a chance for me to take a breath before his head dipped once more. He closed his lips over me as he worked a finger inside, wringing another gasp from me.

"Are you sure?" Nektas asked. My head turned toward the door. "I thought I heard screaming."

"You didn't."

I gripped the blanket as Ash slowly moved his finger in and out.

"I'm pretty sure I did," the draken insisted.

Ash's finger eased from me. I started to rise onto my elbows, but his hand came on my chest, just below my neck.

His eyes pulsed with eather. His other hand went to my shoulder. "I'm not done with you."

My breath caught as my gaze locked on his savage stare. I looked down where his cock remained, thick and heavy.

"What did you say?" Nektas asked.

Ash's head whipped toward the sound. "I said I may kill you if you don't get the fuck away from that door."

My eyes widened. As I took in how still his chest was as he drew his hand down the center of mine, I thought maybe he *would* do that.

"Rude," Nektas drawled. "I assume your uncalled-for threat of violence means that both of you are awake, alive, and well aware enough of each other that you're...getting reacquainted?"

Ash's head dipped, and a low snarl rumbled from him.

"I'm—" I clamped my mouth shut, muffling a moan as Ash drew my nipple into his mouth. "I'm fine."

There was a pause. "You don't sound fine."

"I swear I am." I reached down, grasping the back of Ash's head as he moved to my other breast. "But I really think you *won't be* if you don't leave."

There was a gap of silence, and then I heard a chuckle. "I am relieved to hear you are fine," he said. "Meyaah *Liessa*."

My Queen.

I gave a start, the implication of that—of what had happened—finally sinking in. What I'd seen. The voices I'd heard. My body locked up, and my lips parted.

My heart began to pound as Ash lifted his head from my breast. Somehow, I'd Ascended without the embers of life killing me. And they weren't just inside me now. They weren't even a part of me.

The embers of life *were* me.

I was the Primal of Life—the *true* Primal of Life.

The...the *Queen* of the Gods.

45

I stared up at Ash, my stomach dipping. "I'm...I'm the Queen of the Gods."

"Yes." Ash's hand slid down my side to my thigh.

My chest started dipping as he spread my legs. "And that would make you the...King of the Gods?"

"Only if you deem it fitting to call me such," he said, his gaze traveling over my body and centering between my thighs. "Otherwise, I am *your* Consort."

Him? The Consort?

No.

Hips twitching under his icy-hot stare, I swallowed. "I make you King...deem you King. Or whatever."

"Honored," he murmured, guiding my leg over his hip.

My mind raced. If I was the Primal of Life, then what did that mean for—oh, my gods, what about Kolis? He'd awakened while Ash and I were at my lake. I knew he had. I'd felt him. So, where was he? And what about the other Primals?

"Ash?"

His attention was still fixed between my thighs. "Hmm?"

I tugged on his hair, forcing his gaze to mine. "What does that mean?"

"It means the King is about to fuck his Queen."

That wasn't where I had been going with that question, but in a heartbeat, I was there completely.

Eyeing his erection, I dragged in a reedy breath. A pulse of desire echoed, surprising me. I didn't think it would be possible after the pleasure he'd already given me, but here I was.

Ash had gone still again as he stared down at me. His skin thinned. Shadows appeared across his cheeks and down his chest. Faint tendrils of mist rose behind him, seeping out from his upper shoulders to form the hazy outline of wings. I slipped my hand from his hair, letting it fall to the bed.

His eyes slammed shut as he twisted his neck to the side. Instinctively, I could sense that his Primal form was close to the surface, and he was struggling to rein it back in. I could actually...*sense* it.

Which was really weird because I had no idea how. But I could.

"I...I just need a moment to get myself under control," he said gruffly.

My fingers curled into the blanket. It would be wise for me to stay quiet and let him regain that control. Plus, there was a lot we needed to talk about. I had no idea how long I'd been asleep or what was going on with Kolis and the other Primals—or even Iliseeum and the mortal realm.

But I was reckless and unwise, even now. And all that important stuff could wait.

I rose onto my elbows, and he didn't stop me. Reaching between us, I wrapped my hand around his cock.

A low hiss of air parted his lips as his eyes flew open.

I couldn't look away from the vivid, icy burn of his stare as I drew my fingers along the length of his cock to the tip before lowering my hand to my belly. I let my knee fall to the side. "Fuck your Queen then."

There was no hesitation.

Not even a second.

Ash thrust into me, seating himself all the way. His ragged moan joined mine. The muscles of his arms tightened as he braced himself, his hips beginning to move. The rhythm he set wasn't slow or gentle. It was a torrid pace, fast and hard. Wrapping my legs around his hips, all I could do was cling to him. My fingers dug into the hard muscles of his shoulders as each plunge hit a spot deep inside me, unleashing tight waves of pleasure. His chest flattened against mine, his hips pounding into me over and over as he kissed me, lips devouring mine.

Ash did as he'd said, as I demanded.

He fucked his Queen.

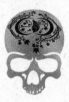

Sometime later, we lay in Ash's bed—*our* bed—facing each other, my cheek resting on his arm, and our legs tangled. In the sated silence, he toyed with a strand of my hair and kept looking at me as if I were some sort of a mirage. He barely looked away, almost as if he feared I'd disappear.

And I knew I looked at him the same way. That was why I kept my hands on his chest. As my thoughts spun from one thing to the next, I had to touch him, remind myself that we were both here.

There was so much going on in my head. I had all this knowledge in the back of my mind now. As if the essence inside me had contained it all, waiting for it to be unlocked. It was a lot, and I still couldn't quite wrap my head around the fact that I was here, had Ascended, and was now a Primal. Actually, I was *the* Primal.

Of Life.

The fangs.

Which I kept pricking my tongue on.

And I couldn't even think about how all that was possible—what it required to work. If I did, I wasn't sure if I would start sobbing hysterically or climb all over Ash.

Our bodies needed a break.

And there were so many things I needed to know—had to understand. I wasn't even sure where to start.

So, I chose one of the easier things. "Will I ever stop catching my tongue or lips on these things?"

"These *things*?" He laughed as I prodded a fang with my tongue. "You'll get used to them."

Nicking myself once more, I frowned. "I'm not so sure about that."

"You will," he assured me. "Especially since they're rather small."

My frown increased. They didn't feel small in my mouth. "Are they supposed to be larger?" I eyed his mouth, able to see the tips of his. "Did something go wrong?"

"I don't think anything went wrong, *liessa*." He smiled, clearly amused. "I imagine they're smaller simply due to your mortal birth."

"Oh." My gaze lowered. "Ash?"

"Yeah?" He dipped his head, brushing his lips across my forehead.

I smiled. "Was there a chance I wouldn't have regained my memories upon waking?"

"There was," he said, twisting a curl around his finger. "An Ascension is a powerful transition for a god. But a Primal? It's even more so. As the eather grows, changing the body while in stasis, it can affect the mind."

My stomach dipped. "Have any Primals Ascended without remembering who they were?"

"A few. Some regained many of their memories. I heard that Maia spent some time without much recollection of the years leading up to her Ascension. The same with Phanos. Attes and Kyn Ascended at the same time, but Kyn never regained his memories."

My brows shot up. "Of all the people I expected not to regain their memories, Kyn was not even on the list."

He unwound the curl of hair. "Why is that?"

"I guess because he has a twin. That it would've, I don't know, grounded him?"

"I would think the same, but Ascensions are unpredictable, especially if you go through one alone," he said, and I watched his lips move. Something about his voice was different. "If Nektas hadn't been there, talking to me, who knows if I would have remembered my years prior."

"I'm glad you did," I said, thinking it would've been terrible if he'd had no memories of his father. I dragged my finger across his chest, just below his collarbone. "So, that was why I dreamed of your voice? You were talking to me?"

"I was." He paused. "How much do you remember?"

"Bits and pieces." One of them came to the forefront. "You spoke about seeing me as a child by the lake, right? In your wolf form?"

"I did." A grin appeared, and it stole a little of my breath. "You were carrying an armful of rocks."

"I was. I don't remember why. I was a strange child." A shaky laugh left me. "I forgot to tell you this when we were in the cavern, but when I saw you in your wolf form, when you first came for me at Cor Palace, I knew it was you. I knew you were the wolf I saw as a child." I took in a shallow breath. "Thank you."

"For what?"

I almost laughed again. *For what?* "Besides the fact that you made sure I remembered who I was?"

"That's not worthy of gratitude, *liessa*."

He was...

A knot of emotion swelled in my throat. Gods, I loved him so much I felt like I would burst.

Lifting my head, I brought my mouth to his and gave him my gratitude. I poured it into the kiss.

And Ash didn't just drink it in, he gave it all back. The arm I'd been resting on curled around my waist, tugging my chest against his. He kissed me as if he wished to stake a claim to my very being. No one could kiss like that—evoke such a sensation.

Things spun from there, turning from gratitude to a near-desperate need for each other that somehow hadn't been quenched. Darts of pleasure raced through me. Every part of me became incredibly taut. His kisses could do that in mere seconds, taking me from calm to frantic with need.

Ash's hand slid down my side, over my leg. He lifted my thigh, hooking it over his hip. I gasped into his kiss as he cupped my rear, pressing me against his already-hard length.

"Yes," I whispered—begged, really. My fingers dug into his skin.

Ash groaned and then punched his hips up, sinking into me. I cried out, quickly swept up in a riot of sensations. He moved deeply inside me, slowly at first, driving me to my wit's end. And when I thought I would surely die, he rolled me onto my back. Our eyes locked. We met each other thrust for thrust, the rhythm increasing as I wrapped my legs around his waist. His mouth was everywhere, capturing a nipple as he sucked in time with his hips, then moving up to lick and nip my throat—

My stomach hollowed as my eyes flew open. I gripped his shoulders, wanting him to feed—to bite me. But I...I locked up. Confusion whirled through me as my heart started pounding sickeningly fast.

His fangs scraped my skin, and dual bursts of lust and unease— unease and *fear*—darted through me. For a moment, I wasn't there. I was in the cage, held too tightly. The reaction didn't make sense. I was with Ash. I was safe with him. Always.

"Sera?" Fingers touched my cheek. I opened my eyes, breathing fast. Ash had stilled against me. "Are you all right?"

Swallowing, I nodded as I locked eyes with him. With Ash. No one else. "Yes."

"*Liessa...*" He started to pull away, lifting his hips from mine.

A tiny burst of panic went through me as I curled my legs around him. "I'm okay. I promise." And I was. Mostly. It had just been a weird moment. One I needed to get over. *Would* get over. Reaching up, I gripped the nape of his neck. "You need to feed."

His head dipped, and I tensed, but he didn't go for my throat. He kissed me, slow and long.

When he raised his head, I was panting. "Feed," I repeated, lifting my hips against his.

Ash groaned. "I don't need to."

"I took a lot of blood—"

"And I will be fine. My body will replenish it," he assured me. "I don't need to feed."

I wasn't sure if I believed that as his mouth returned to mine, but it was okay. It was only a weird moment. I'd been fine when he bit me in the lake. I would be fine again.

Ash didn't move inside me, though. He remained still, his hard length piercing, his eyes watchful. "Sera—"

Tightening my legs around him, I made as if to roll him. He resisted for an instant but then let me shift him onto his back. I rocked, seating myself on him.

"Fates," he bit out, clasping my hips.

Planting my hands on his shoulders, I rode him, moving up and down his length. My pace picked up as I focused on him—only him—wanting every inch of him inside me. The feel of him almost made me dizzy.

His arm came around me as he drew me down. Our breaths mingled as our mouths opened. His eyes never left mine as he held me in place, grinding against me. We both came hard and fast, either one after the other or at the same time, I couldn't be sure. Then I collapsed against his chest.

Still trembling from the aftershocks, we ended up back as we had been before, on our sides with his fingers in my hair and our legs tangled.

"Fates, if we're not careful, we're going to end up exhausting you back into stasis," he murmured.

I giggled. "Is that even possible?"

"At the rate we're going? Yes." He was silent for a few moments. "Are you all right?"

"Mm-hmm."

"You sure?" Ash asked, letting go of my hair to tip my chin up. Our eyes met. His were a warm dove gray. "I wasn't gentle before or even now," he added. "At all."

"I know." I rose slightly. "You didn't hurt me then or now, and I loved both times—or all three times. Four?"

"Five," he corrected.

"So, you're counting those…" My skin flushed. "Those things you did with the tendrils of eather?"

"Those things you really enjoyed."

Feeling my breath catch, I nodded. "You seemed to enjoy it yourself."

"Enjoy it?" He dipped his head to mine. "You were drenched, *liessa*," he said, his voice turning to silk. "It's quite possible I enjoyed it more than you."

A wanton shiver rolled through me. "Good."

He chuckled deeply. Unfortunately, the sound faded much too quickly. "But your body has been through a lot. So has your mind."

I snorted. "I think my mind is somewhat calm for once."

"I'm relieved to hear that." He drew a finger down the center of my chin. "But something happened with us earlier."

Falling quiet, I debated whether to pretend I had no idea what he was talking about, which seemed very…un-queenly.

"You locked up," he continued quietly, almost carefully. "And I could taste your sudden unease."

"You really need to stop reading my emotions." I leaned back, returning my cheek to his arm.

Ash's touch followed, his fingers picking up another strand of hair. "If it makes you feel any better, it was harder than usual."

My eyes narrowed. "So, I wasn't projecting? You went searching?"

The hair slid between his fingers. "When you locked up, I was afraid I had hurt you."

The evident concern in his voice extinguished any irritation. "You weren't hurting me. At all."

He dragged the curl over my upper arm. "Then what was it?"

I gave a one-shouldered shrug. "I don't know. I think maybe it's what you said. My body—my head—has been through a lot. So, it was just a weird moment." And that was all I would allow it to be. "But all the other moments? They were amazing. Beautiful." I leaned over and kissed him. "I think I can still taste myself on your lips."

A sexy rumble vibrated in his chest. "Do not mention that." Twin silver pools locked onto me, and my body immediately reacted, curling and tensing in a delicious, heated way. "Because it makes me want to taste you again, and I have something I need to say—actually, I have several things I need to say."

"Okay," I murmured as the image of him with his head nestled between my thighs took up residency in my mind.

Ash bowed his back so our eyes met. "That also means you need to stop thinking about it."

"I'm not."

"Your arousal is so strong I can taste it." Ash nipped my lips, making my breath catch. A brief grin appeared as I pouted at him. "If you keep it up, I'm going to get myself deep inside you yet again."

Shockingly, tiny knots of coiled lust formed in my belly. "Was that supposed to convince me to stop thinking about exactly that? Because if so, you failed."

He chuckled, guiding my head back to his arm. "For some unknown reason, I'm not disappointed to learn that."

Unknown? I snorted.

"But we need to behave," he advised. "I know there is a lot we should be talking about—a lot we need to do."

There was.

Tension crept into my muscles. The moment I remembered who I was until this very second felt like a dream. One where the world didn't exist outside of this chamber. A fantasy I had never even dared to allow myself.

But the world did exist.

"We need to talk about Kolis." My stomach soured, but he wasn't the only thing we needed to discuss. There was so much more.

"We do," Ash said. "But he's not a problem."

I tipped my head back so I could see his face. "How is he not a problem? He is *the* problem."

"Right now, he's not a problem," Ash clarified. "Kolis was already weakened before your Ascension. You rising as the true Primal of Life not only has him holed up in Dalos nursing his wounds, but every god and Primal in Iliseeum felt your Ascension."

My stomach took a sharp tumble. "Why does that last part sound like bad news?"

"It is neither good nor bad." He traced small circles on my arm. "I'm sure most of the Primals are in shock and don't know what to make of your Ascension, even those loyal to Kolis."

My mind immediately jumped to the worst-case scenario per usual. "And what if they're unhappy about my Ascension once they've wrapped their heads around everything?"

"Then we will deal with that." His fingers continued making designs. "Together."

I didn't need any special, ancient knowledge to know that dealing with unhappy Primals would be violent and bloody. I could feel my chest tightening—a telltale sign of my old friend: anxiety. The corners of my lips turned down. I'd survived the impossible, Ascending into the true Primal of Life, and I *still* had crushing anxiety?

Seemed rather unfair.

"The other Primals' shock and the blow dealt to Kolis has bought us some time," Ash assured me, obviously picking up on my anxiousness. "Not a lot, but enough that they can all wait right now. Sooner rather than later, Nektas..." He paused, his brow creasing. "I have a vague recollection of him being at the door."

The corners of my lips tipped up. "He heard me screaming and was worried. You threatened to murder him if he didn't leave."

His brows lifted. "I think I owe him an apology."

Another giggle snuck free.

Vibrant wisps of eather appeared in his eyes. "Your laugh." His lashes swept down. "It's such a beautiful sound." He swallowed, letting out a ragged breath. The eather had calmed in his eyes. "I love it."

All thoughts of Kolis, apologizing to Nektas, and well...everything else vanished. Love. I would never get tired of hearing that word coming out of his mouth. Even if it was only him saying he loved grapefruit or...ripping out throats.

Ash's eyes met mine. "One of the things I need to tell you? I've never told anyone."

"Okay." I spread my fingers across his chest. "I'm listening."

He took a deep breath as he eased his hand from my hair and then curled it around my nape. "There...there was a time I hated my father for making this deal, for linking some mortal girl to me when he knew it would only bring death and horror upon her. That was before—well, before I knew why he did it. But every year that passed and the bride promised to him—and then to me—wasn't born, I celebrated."

"I can't blame you for that."

"Of course, you wouldn't." He dropped a kiss to the tip of my nose. "But then you were born, and I hated him even more." He kneaded the muscles of my neck with gentle pressure as he held me there, then let out a shaky breath. "There are things I haven't been entirely honest about."

Curiosity rose. "Like what?"

"I wasn't exactly truthful about why I refused to take you as my Consort and had limited contact with you. Part of it was to keep you unknown to Kolis, but that wasn't the only reason." His eyes searched mine. "The night you were born? I had a dream. I saw you...I saw you as you are now, in that—" He inhaled sharply. "In that lake of yours, and so godsdamn beautiful." His voice thickened. "Your hair cascaded across the dark water like spun moonlight, and these perfect, rosy lips were *smiling* up at me."

I grew still as a vague memory of what he'd told me while I was in stasis resurfaced. Something about having a dream that wasn't. When he saw my lake before he ever laid eyes on it.

"I saw you dying in that lake, and I saw myself—" He became as rigid as I was, then shook his head. "I chalked it up to my imagination, even though I sensed your birth. Just a strange dream. But then I saw you as a child, and I...I saw the lake." He shuddered. "You know this already, but I kept track of you over the years, mostly to ensure you were safe. I witnessed you slowly becoming the beautiful woman I had seen in my dream."

A tremor swept through me, and I slid my hand from his chest. I grasped the back of his neck, my heart aching at where I suspected this was headed—the story of what he'd done to himself. I wished more than anything that my suspicions weren't true because if I was right, the guilt must have...gods, it had to have been killing him this whole time.

"I did everything in my power to deny that the dream was anything more than that. Even after the first night I was to take you as my Consort."

A muscle bunched in his jaw. "Even after I sensed your emotions—the bravery that overshadowed your fear. I'd never felt anything like that before, not from generals in wars long since forgotten or gods as they faced down Kolis before their deaths. And each and every time I saw you from then on, that bravery never faltered. Not when I saw you that night in the Garden District at the seamstress's house and that damn lake. You were always so fucking brave, even when your life was in danger or you were in pain."

His lips firmed, a tangible sign of the emotions that churned within him. "And what I sensed from you, time and time again, was the same thing I sensed in that dream—fear but bravery as you died. And I could no longer deny that it was no simple dream. It was a vision. It didn't show me how you died or why, but I believed Kolis had to be involved. So, I was determined to keep what I saw from coming true. At least that's what I told myself. But in reality, Sera? What I saw—what I *felt*—in that vision? It terrified me." His jaw flexed. "So, I had my *kardia* removed right before I brought you into the Shadowlands. I was still healing from it the first few days."

My breath stilled in my lungs. I was right. Worse yet, I clearly remembered accidentally walking into him after having supper in the dining hall. His hiss of agony had stayed with me. Tears dampened my lashes. Somehow, knowing that he'd had his *kardia* removed after growing to know me made it all…it made it even more tragic.

He briefly closed his eyes. "I never should have done it. I should've been more like you—afraid but courageous. Instead, I was a coward."

"No," I denied, rising onto one elbow. "You've never been—"

"I was, Sera."

Tangled curls fell over my shoulders as I sat up, the ends brushing against my legs. "You're no coward."

"I appreciate your denial. I do." He rose at the waist, shifting his weight to the hand next to my curled knee. "Your life could've been so fucking different. Your family never would've punished you. You wouldn't have had to feel as if you were alone—never allowed to experience what most take for granted. You wouldn't have felt like a monster. My apologies were and will never be enough. I could've—"

"Stop," I pleaded. "Listen to me. I'm not going to lie, Ash. I wish you'd made a different choice, but the one you made doesn't make you a coward. It makes you stronger than anyone I know."

His mouth opened.

"It does," I insisted. "You sacrificed so much to protect me. More than I think you even realize."

A lock of hair fell over his cheek as his chin lowered. His eyes closed. "You're too understanding—accepting. Under all that toughness, you're too kind."

"I don't know about all of that, but what I do know is that you're not a coward. You did what you believed was best with the knowledge you had. It isn't your fault." I flattened my hand against his cheek. "If the Fates hadn't decreed that no one could speak of what Eythos did, you would've made different choices. All of us would have."

Ash nodded slowly. As I eyed him, I sensed there was more. What? I didn't know. In all honesty, I wasn't sure how I even knew there *was* more. Like before, it was almost like the knowledge or awareness simply formed in my mind. It reminded me of…

A shaky breath left me. What had Kolis said about Eythos? About the Primal of Life? That he had foresight? Intuition. Ash's father hadn't been born with it. He'd received it upon his Ascension.

Holy crap, did that mean I was now a know-it-all? Because if so, I would be way more obnoxious than ever.

But none of that mattered right now.

Ash did.

I drew my fingers along his shoulder, letting the unknown knowledge of there being more to what Ash said come to me. It wasn't hard. I just didn't think about what came to mind. I spoke it instead. "Did…did that dream or vision show you anything else?"

He cleared his throat. "It showed me what happened after you died. I saw the realms die—both mortal and that of the gods, and they…" His eyes met mine. "They died at my hands."

The words he'd spoken right before he Ascended me… I knew he'd been speaking the truth then, and I heard that truth even now. Felt it.

"I had my *kardia* removed because I knew you were the one who would one day wreck me," he rasped. "And only one thing could cause such agony, such destruction from a god or a Primal of Death." His eyes searched mine. "That vision showed me that I'd fallen in love with you, and that it wasn't Kolis who ended the realms. It was me. I ended them because I lost you."

"Ash," I whispered.

"And I thought removing my *kardia* would save you and the realms." A harsh laugh punched out of him. "But in reality, it brought the realms within mere minutes of destruction. And maybe I read that vision wrong. Maybe it was trying to warn me not to do it. I have no idea. But…" His eyes glimmered. "But I still fell, Sera. Hard and fast. Irrevocably. Even without my *kardia*, I fell in love with you."

"You did." A tremor went through me. "Now, there is something I want to tell you. When I said I thought I'd die without knowing what your love felt like? I was wrong. Even if I *had* died—"

Eather pulsed in the veins of his cheeks. "I don't want to talk about you dying."

"I know, but what I'm saying is that you've proven to me, many times over, that you love me," I said. "It was in every one of your actions, even if you never spoke the words. I knew when you held me in the lake that if what you felt wasn't love, it was something even stronger—better. We just didn't know it was possible."

"It shouldn't be." He pressed his lips to my cheek. "There is only one thing I can think of that would make it possible. We're of the same soul." He drew back, leaving our faces inches apart. "It's the only thing that could've made removing the *kardia* utterly meaningless."

"Of the same soul?" I sat back. "Like mates of the heart?"

Ash nodded.

With everything that had happened, I'd totally forgotten about the dreams. "That was how we were able to walk in each other's dreams?"

"Why I could connect in some way to you while in stasis. I think so." His lashes swept down. "It wasn't the embers or that you'd fed from me."

"I know we talked about this in the cavern," I said, "but I never knew if it was true or not."

"To be honest, I didn't either." He drew his bottom lip between his teeth. "Mates of the soul—or of the heart—are even legend among us. Something rare the Fates were supposedly involved in."

The Fates... A memory or piece of knowledge flickered through my mind, moving too fast for me to grasp at the moment. I shook my head slightly. "What do you mean?"

His brows furrowed. "It's said that when the Arae look upon the threads of fate and see all the many different possibilities of one's life, they can sometimes see what may come of the love between two or more souls. And in that union, they see possibilities that can reshape the realms by either creating something never seen before or ushering in great change," he explained, running his thumb over the golden swirl on my hand. "And when they see that one thread, they are forbidden to intervene in the affairs of those souls, as they believe the bond between them cannot be circumvented. So, not even death of the body or the heart and soul—the *kardia*—can break such a connection." His gaze returned to mine. "And the joining of our souls has brought up something never seen before. A *Queen* of the Gods."

My lips parted. If what had been said about mates of the heart was true, then it explained how Ash could love.

How he'd been able to love me this whole time.

Something Holland said floated through my mind. "Love is more powerful than the Fates," I murmured. "If the Arae are not supposed to meddle in the affairs of mates of the heart, then how was Holland allowed to interact with me for so long? And do what he did?"

Ash's lips quirked up. "I have a feeling Holland really likes to push that fine line he walks between interfering and casually observing."

"Yeah." Something tugged at my memories, but whatever it was existed on the fringes. "I hope I get to see him again."

"*Liessa*," Ash drawled. "If you want to see Holland again, you can. You're the true Primal of Life. You can summon the Fates, remember? There will be little you cannot do."

"Little I cannot do?" My eyes widened. "That…that's actually kind of scary."

"Yeah." Ash grinned. "Yeah, it is."

I started to laugh, but something struck me—something huge. The essence of life had been fully restored, ceasing the slow death of the embers that had started the moment I was born, along with the consequences of placing them into a mortal bloodline. That meant…

Even though that odd, uncanny sense of knowing told me the answer, I needed to see it for myself. I jerked upright and scrambled off the bed.

"Sera?" Concern filled Ash's voice.

Heart pounding, I raced past the sofa and made a beeline for the balcony. Shoving the heavy curtains aside, I threw open the doors. My gaze shot first to the sky as I walked outside, the stone cool beneath my feet.

It was a shade of gray, full of vivid, shimmering stars, but it was different. The gray wasn't as flat as I was accustomed to and seemed to carry faint strokes of lighter streaks, tinged in purple and pink. It reminded me of the brief moments of dawn.

"Sera," Ash repeated, having joined me in his silent way. "Is there a reason we're both naked as the day we were born on the balcony?"

As the Queen of the Gods, I should probably be more concerned about my nudity, but I couldn't give that much thought as I went to the railing and looked down at the courtyard's barren, packed earth.

My lips parted as a faint tremor ran through me. The ground wasn't as I remembered either. Patches of green had sprouted every few feet, replacing the dull, dusty dirt.

"Grass," I whispered hoarsely. "I see *grass*."

"You do." Ash came up behind me, closing his arms around my chest. "Nektas told me it began before I even returned to the Shadowlands with you."

I lifted a trembling hand to my mouth. "That means…"

"It means you did it." Ash dipped his head, brushing his lips over the curve of my cheek. "You stopped the Rot, *liessa*. Here and in the mortal realm."

46

I lay on my back, eyes closed, and my hand resting on the bed beside me, the space still cool from where Ash's body had been.

After confirming what I already knew—that the Rot had been stopped—Ash had drawn me back into the bedchamber, hopefully before anyone spotted me standing out there, completely nude.

That wouldn't make for a great first impression as Queen.

The Rot had stopped.

Lasania would be saved—well, at least for now. There was still Kolis and…whatever I might have done to the kingdom during my Ascension, but the Rot would not be its destruction.

I truly hadn't failed.

I'd ended the Rot.

A small laugh bubbled out of me as my fingers curled into the sheet. Ash was currently out in the hall, speaking with Rhain, who had also swung by to check on us. Instead of threatening the god's life like he'd done with Nektas, Ash had stepped out into the hall, likely to assure Rhain—and therefore everyone else—that I was not only okay but also knew exactly who I was.

Ash had only been gone a handful of seconds, not even a minute, and I missed him.

Which was silly.

But it was a good kind of silly.

Opening my eyes, I rolled onto my side and stared at the closed doors. I didn't want to get out of bed again. Despite what Ash had said about us having time, I had a feeling I would have to face the reality of, well…everything that existed beyond those doors if I rose again—whether naked or clothed.

I wasn't ready to stop being happily silly, with the knowledge that the Rot had been ended. Where I was just a wife, and my only problem was missing my husband. I could spend an eternity as that.

But I knew I couldn't.

At least not now.

Once I got up and *handled* things, then I could have that eternity.

I *would* have it.

My gaze wandered to the small nightstand. There was a clear pitcher, and two glasses turned upside down. Reaching for the water, I stopped, instead focusing on the small wooden box.

Glancing at the door, my curiosity got the best of me, and I rose onto my elbow and picked up the container. It had small silver hinges and was surprisingly lightweight, almost as if there was nothing inside it. Sitting up, the thin fur blanket pooled at my waist as I traced the delicate lines carved into the lid, my finger following the etchings. The markings were the vine scrollwork I often saw on the tunics of those in the Shadowlands and the doors to the throne room.

Who'd made this box? Ash? Possibly his father? Nektas? Someone else? Whoever it was, the time it must have taken to craft such intricate lines made me think it was something one would use to store important items.

Knowing I was being a complete snoop, I cracked open the lid. My lips parted as I peered inside. The realm seemed to hold its breath for a moment. As did I. A slight tremor went through my hands as a mixture of disbelief and elation swept through me.

I didn't know what I'd expected to find, but it wasn't—in a hundred years—the answer to where all the hair ties had gone after Ash unbound my hair.

Now, I knew.

They were all in this box. I didn't know why that delighted me so. Why it felt as important as learning the Rot had been stopped. But there was no suppressing the wide smile that spread across my face. For there to be so many stowed away—about a dozen of them—it had to mean that he had been keeping the ties since the very first time he gently unwound the braid in my hair.

Even when he was angry.

Actually, I knew why this moved me so.

A Primal of Death had been collecting my hair ties, treating them as if they were prized possessions—treasure.

It was such a small token, something most probably wouldn't even think twice about. But these little hair ties had belonged to me, and Ash had sought to keep them close to him—to keep a part of *me* close to him.

A rush of tears hit my eyes as I quietly closed the lid and returned the box to where I'd found it. I lay back down, blinking the dampness from my lashes.

Those hair ties…they were further proof that Ash had been falling in love with me long before my life was truly on the line—long before I'd been willing to admit that I'd been falling in love with him. They were further proof that our hearts, our *souls* were truly one.

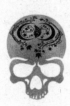

When Ash returned from speaking with Rhain, he immediately joined me. Bracing himself with one knee on the bed, he caught the back of my head and brought his down to mine. His lips tasted of desire as he claimed my mouth in a languid and tender kiss. Every touch of his lips sent shivers down my spine.

"I think you missed me," I said when we parted. I felt a little breathless.

He trailed his fingers across my cheek. "I did."

Thinking about the collection of hair ties, I smiled against his mouth. I didn't doubt for a second that he spoke the truth.

"Did anyone see me naked?" I asked.

"Lucky for them, no,"

I shook my head. "Is everything okay, then? With Rhain and everyone?"

"It is." A lock of hair fell across his face. "Rhain was a little concerned after Nektas told him I threatened his life."

I grinned.

"I have a feeling that amuses you to no end."

"It does." I nodded for extra emphasis.

"Knew it." Ash kissed me again and then pulled back. He cupped my cheek, tilting my head back. His gaze met mine.

"Your eyes are beautiful, *liessa*."

Feeling my chest warm, I smiled. "Thank you."

Ash settled onto the bed beside me. His hands roamed over my body, running down my sides and then back up over my breasts. I moaned softly, aching for him.

"I still have things I want to talk about." His hand slid over my hip, cupping my rear. He tugged me closer to him. "And you're being distracting."

"Me?" I shivered as the tips of my breasts grazed the cool hardness of his chest.

"Yes, you." His fingers pressed into the flesh of my ass.

"You're the one who kissed me," I reminded him, drawing in his fresh, citrusy scent as I worked a leg between his. "And you're also the one groping my ass."

"That's only because I don't want your ass to get lonely." He nipped at my lower lip. "I'm just being thoughtful."

I laughed, loving this rare, playful side of him. "So incredibly thoughtful."

He murmured an agreement that was lost in the sigh he drew from me as his lips found mine once more. This kiss was just as slow and sweet as the one before, an unhurried dance that spoke volumes of love and longing. We were *both* breathless this time when our lips parted, our hearts pounding.

"Remember when I said I needed to tell you several things?" he said, tucking some strands of my hair back.

I nodded.

A moment passed, and when he spoke again, there was a change in his tone—a richer, fuller timbre I wasn't sure I would've picked up on before. "I love you, Sera."

My lips immediately split into the same wide, goofy smile that seeing the hair ties had provoked.

"And you love me."

"I do." I wiggled an inch closer.

His stare caught and held mine. "You're my wife."

"Hearing you say, 'I love you,' has become my favorite three words of any I've heard you speak," I told him. "'You're my wife' is a close second. Or maybe they are tied?" I wrinkled my nose. "No. I love you is my favorite."

"Stop being cute." He kissed the bridge of my nose. "It's also distracting."

I grinned, flattening my hand against his chest. "Sounds like that is one of those *you* problems you're continuously having."

"One you're currently not helping with," he pointed out, letting go of my hair to place his hand atop mine. It was his left and my right. Our imprints touched, and I could've sworn our skin hummed. "I'm your husband," he repeated. "You're my wife. And I know I don't have a whole lot of experience in this, not even secondhand…"

Neither did I. Even though my mother had remarried, their marriage had been more of a necessity. I wasn't even sure she and King Ernald loved each other. Maybe they simply tolerated one another.

If I were honest with myself, my stepfather carried more than just a fondness for my mother but she…she was still in love with my father.

That made my heart ache as I focused on Ash.

"And even though I never allowed myself to consider what it would be like to be in love with another and be married, I know what kind of marriage I want." Ash drew his lower lip between his teeth. "Or I know what kind of marriage I want with you."

My heart started doing that skipping thing again.

"I want us to trust each other," he began.

"I trust you," I told him. "Irrevocably."

A small smile appeared, softening his features. "I know, but this…I think this is a different kind of trust, one that allows us to share everything with each other. The easy and the hard—especially the hard." Only a faint glow of eather pulsed behind his pupils. "The kind of trust where we know we can be honest and feel comfortable knowing that anything we share will not change how we see each other."

My stomach hollowed as my gaze fell to where his hand still rested atop mine. I looked at the imprint.

"We have that kind of trust already, don't we?" Ash asked, his breath cool against my forehead.

I nodded, my throat thickening. "We do."

"So, you know that, no matter what, I will always see you as being as strong and brave as you are clever and fierce." His fingers pressed between mine. "That my attraction, my need and want of you, will never be lessened, no matter what happens." He paused. "Or what has happened."

My lower lip trembled, and the edges of my fangs scraped against the back of my lips as I pressed my mouth closed.

"I know *who* you are, Sera, and *what* you mean to me. And that is everything because you are everything to me." He pressed a kiss to my forehead. "And that will never change."

A shudder went through me.

"It would be impossible for that to happen." He shifted so his forehead rested against mine. "Because even if we weren't mates of the heart, what you made me feel from the moment you stood in the Shadow Temple years ago to every moment between then and now, would've still made me fall in love with you. Your courage and strength, your beauty and utter fearlessness, your humor, and most of all, that softness of yours you share with me. It would've made sure my *kardia* somehow came back. I believe that—I *know* that—because you're the first person I have ever felt has truly accepted me, no matter what I've done in my past or what has been done to me. You're the first to refuse to allow any more drops of blood to be inked into my flesh. You were the first to ever make me feel anything that mattered," he swore. "You're...you're simply my first, Sera, and you will be my last."

My eyes stung with tears. "You're going to make me cry."

"I'm not trying to." His hand squeezed mine. "But it's okay if you do. I wouldn't think less of you if you did. There isn't anything that could make me think less of you."

"I know," I whispered hoarsely. And I did. The reasonable, logical, and unfortunately very small part of my mind knew. "And I know what you're getting at. I do. You're talking about my time with Kolis."

"I'm talking about things in general," he said. "And about that."

"It was nothing," I said in a rush, my insides twisting, causing my breath to catch.

It was nothing.

Veses had said the *same* thing. She had spoken the *same* lie.

Ash's lips brushed the curve of my cheek, and then he pulled his head back a few inches. His hand left mine. A heartbeat passed, and I felt the tips of his fingers on my chin. He tilted my head back. "I want you to know that when you're ready to talk about everything, whether it's nothing or not, I'll be waiting. I'll be ready."

I squeezed my eyes shut so tightly I saw white for a few seconds. A flood of words crawled up my throat, but a wall of emotion and sheer will as strong as shadowstone choked them off.

Veses had lied.

I didn't.

I *wasn't.*

"By the way," Ash said, his gruff voice reaching me. "Rhain is going to gather some food for us. He's positive you're starving."

Gods, the way he'd changed the subject and the moment he chose to…

I loved this man.

I would always love him.

Counting the beats between each breath, I opened my eyes. "That's nice…" I cleared my throat. "That's nice of him. Which is kind of strange, isn't it? Rhain being nice."

Ash arched a brow. "Rhain is known as one of the kindest gods in the Shadowlands."

"I'll have to take your word for that." My eyes widened when I saw an icy hardness creeping into his features. Shit. "I mean, Rhain had a reason not to be all that welcoming toward me."

"I'm not sure I agree with that."

"Rhain is loyal to you—"

Eather seeped from behind his pupils, stirring the energy inside me. "He is loyal to you," he stated in a low growl. "His Queen."

"Okay, he is loyal to both of us," I amended, half-afraid for Rhain's safety. The other half of me was, well, kind of aroused by Ash's protectiveness. "But before, he was loyal to you. And since I *had* been planning to kill you, his initial response to me was completely understandable."

Ash said nothing to that, but I could practically see him plotting out his next…conversation with Rhain.

"Don't say anything to him about it," I stated.

"I won't."

"I'm serious. If he still harbors any ill feelings toward me,"—which I truly didn't think he did—"or if anyone does, I will handle it. I need to. Especially if I'm going to be their Queen."

"If?" Ash chuckled. "*Liessa,* you are their Queen."

My stomach dipped. Gods, I was having a really hard time processing that.

"You're right, though. You need to handle it," he said as he picked up my hand. "I won't say anything. "

"Wow," I murmured, surprised.

"But if you handling it doesn't actually handle it? And they still show you disrespect?" Wisps of eather churned through his eyes. "I will fucking destroy them."

I blinked.

"No matter who they are," he promised.

My lips twitched. I didn't think smiling would help, nor would telling him that his fierceness when it came to me had to be more potent than radek wine. For once, I listened to that voice of reason.

"Speaking of Rhain," I said after a moment. "Thought projection? That's a nifty talent of his I was completely unaware of."

"Many don't know he can do that. You weren't told about—"

"There was no reason for me to know then," I interjected, understanding that sharing that kind of knowledge with me, who in the past had sought to betray Ash and hadn't shown much interest in ruling the Shadowlands alongside him, would've been a risk. "So, all those times I could've sworn Rhain was communicating with you, even though I didn't hear him speak, he was?"

One side of Ash's lips quirked. "He probably was."

Smiling, I watched him trail his finger along the golden swirl.

The *imprint*.

The direction of my thoughts immediately shifted as it occurred to me that perhaps it *wasn't* me who had blessed our union. Maybe it *had* been the Fates. Or perhaps it happened because we were mates of the heart.

And maybe…maybe the fact that such a thing was real, meant that what I believed about my parents was also true. It explained why the agony of my father's loss embittered my mother so deeply and how their union was important since it brought me into—I gasped, my head jerking up.

"What?" Concern filled his eyes.

"Holland saw this. He must have. All of this. Remember when he and Penellaphe came, and you were off to the side talking to her while Holland and I spoke? You asked me what he said, and I—well, I lied."

"Shocker," he murmured, the eather in his eyes twinkling. It struck me then what about his voice was different. It was lighter.

He was lighter.

My chest burned with emotion, causing Ash's brow to pinch. The gods knew I'd probably just projected that emotion at his face. I had to suck it back down to speak without crying all over him. "*Anyway*, he said that broken thread of mine was unexpected and that fate was as ever-changing as the mind and heart. He was speaking of *your* heart. He told me that love is more powerful than the Arae can imagine. It was like he was trying to tell me not to give up hope." My nose scrunched. "Because he knew…he knew you could love me."

"He likely knew I was already in love with you, Sera."

Hearing that made my heart skip. "And he couldn't have told us any of this?"

"I think that would be obliterating that fine line he likes to walk," he replied, lips turning up.

I rolled my eyes. "He could've at least been a little less vague. Like, I don't know, randomly mention mates of the heart surpassing a *kardia* or—" Feeling the essence stir, I stopped what would surely be a lengthy tirade. "Okay. I'm just not going to think about that."

His smile spread.

"So." I drew out the word. "Why do you think you had the dream?"

He raised a brow.

"What? I mean, you had a vision. That's kind of important." I sat straight. "Do you think it was the mates of the heart thing? I…" I trailed off, letting that odd sense of knowing fully form without interruption.

It was the one thing more powerful than the so-called Arae.

It was that unexpected thread.

Unpredictable.

It was the unknown.

The unwritten.

Powerful.

It was something not even the Fates dared to predict or control.

The only thing that could disrupt fate.

It couldn't be found.

It could only be accepted.

It was even more powerful than what coursed through the veins of the Primals and their creators. Equally awe-inspiring and terrifying in its selfishness. It could snap a thread unexpectedly and prematurely.

It could extend a thread of life by sheer *will*, becoming a piece of pure magic that could not be extinguished.

It was true love of the heart and soul.

"It is because we are…we are *heartmates*." I nodded smugly. "I feel very clever for answering my own question."

"You mean figuring out the very obvious answer?" he suggested dryly.

I swung at him again, and like before, he caught my wrist. "Fuck," he groaned, pushing me onto my back and bracing his weight on his forearms as he leaned over me. "I love you."

There was so much we needed to deal with—so much uncertainty. There was Kolis. The other Primals. All the other stuff that kept popping into my head whenever it went quiet. The things those unknown voices that I knew were as old as this realm said to me while I was in stasis. What I saw. What I *knew*. A lot of it was disjointed, making little sense, but I suspected all the scattered pieces would come together if given time. Then there was how my...my Ascension affected Iliseeum and the mortal realm—the latter something I was almost afraid to ask about because I suddenly recalled the blast of power that had left me, hitting the skies above Lasania. There was Sotoria's soul, and the plans surrounding it—things that left me uncomfortable.

Plans I was empowered to change.

But right now, the only thing that mattered was Ash. Us. This miracle of a second chance. The first opportunity for both of us to truly be able to *live* and have complete control of our lives.

"Say it again," I demanded.

Ash kissed my brow. "I love you, Sera."

The essence hummed, as did my heart, my soul. "Again," I whispered.

Laughing, Ash cupped my cheeks and kissed me. "I love you, *liessa.*"

I clasped the back of his head, feeling my chest swell. "Show me."

He did.

There were no more confessions or whispered truths. We came together once more, but this time...this time, we made *love*.

From #1 *New York Times* bestselling author
Jennifer L. Armentrout comes the thrilling
conclusion to her beloved Flesh and Fire series...

Born of Blood and Ash
Flesh and Fire, Book 4
Available May 7, 2024

VISIONS OF FLESH AND BLOOD

A Blood and Ash/Flesh and Fire Compendium
Available in hardcover, e-book, and trade paperback.
Coming February 20, 2024

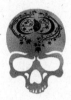

VISIONS OF FLESH AND BLOOD: a Blood and Ash/Flesh and Fire Compendium is a comprehensive companion guide for background, history, reader-favorite information, art, and reference materials. Combined with original short stories and scenes from some of the world's most beloved characters, as well as never-before-seen visual enticements, it's a treat for the senses.

Told from the point of view of Miss Willa herself, the compendium acts like research material but reads like a journal and cache of personal notes, allowing the reader to revisit the characters and history they so love yet view things in a different way.

VISIONS OF FLESH AND BLOOD by Jennifer L. Armentrout with Rayvn Salvador is a must-add addition to the series that any Blood and Ash/Flesh and Fire fan will enjoy.

DISCOVER MORE
JENNIFER L. ARMENTROUT

From Blood and Ash
Blood and Ash Series, Book One
Available in hardcover, e-book, and trade paperback.

Captivating and action-packed, From Blood and Ash is a sexy, addictive, and unexpected fantasy perfect for fans of Sarah J. Maas and Laura Thalassa.

A Maiden…

Chosen from birth to usher in a new era, Poppy's life has never been her own. The life of the Maiden is solitary. Never to be touched. Never to be looked upon. Never to be spoken to. Never to experience pleasure. Waiting for the day of her Ascension, she would rather be with the guards, fighting back the evil that took her family, than preparing to be found worthy by the gods. But the choice has never been hers.

A Duty…

The entire kingdom's future rests on Poppy's shoulders, something she's not even quite sure she wants for herself. Because a Maiden has a heart. And a soul. And longing. And when Hawke, a golden-eyed guard honor bound to ensure her Ascension, enters her life, destiny and duty become tangled with desire and need. He incites her anger, makes her question everything she believes in, and tempts her with the forbidden.

A Kingdom…

Forsaken by the gods and feared by mortals, a fallen kingdom is rising once more, determined to take back what they believe is theirs through violence and vengeance. And as the shadow of those cursed draws closer, the line between what is forbidden and what is right becomes blurred. Poppy is not only on the verge of losing her heart and being found unworthy by the gods, but also her life when every blood-soaked thread that holds her world together begins to unravel.

A Kingdom of Flesh and Fire
Blood and Ash Series, Book Two
Available in hardcover, e-book, and trade paperback.

Is Love Stronger Than Vengeance?

A Betrayal…

Everything Poppy has ever believed in is a lie, including the man she was falling in love with. Thrust among those who see her as a symbol of a monstrous kingdom, she barely knows who she is without the veil of the Maiden. But what she *does* know is that nothing is as dangerous to her as *him*. The Dark One. The Prince of Atlantia. He wants her to fight him, and that's one order she's more than happy to obey. *He may have taken her, but he will never have her.*

A Choice…

Casteel Da'Neer is known by many names and many faces. His lies are as seductive as his touch. His truths as sensual as his bite. Poppy knows better than to trust him. He needs her alive, healthy, and whole to achieve his goals. But he's the only way for her to get what she wants—to find her brother Ian and see for herself if he has become a soulless Ascended. Working with Casteel instead of against him presents its own risks. He still tempts her with every breath, offering up all she's ever wanted. Casteel has plans for her. Ones that could expose her to unimaginable pleasure and unfathomable pain. Plans that will force her to look beyond everything she thought she knew about herself—about him. Plans that could bind their lives together in unexpected ways that neither kingdom is prepared for. And she's far too reckless, too hungry, to resist the temptation.

A Secret...

But unrest has grown in Atlantia as they await the return of their Prince. Whispers of war have become stronger, and Poppy is at the very heart of it all. The King wants to use her to send a message. The Descenters want her dead. The wolven are growing more unpredictable. And as her abilities to feel pain and emotion begin to grow and strengthen, the Atlantians start to fear her. Dark secrets are at play, ones steeped in the blood-drenched sins of two kingdoms that would do anything to keep the truth hidden. But when the earth begins to shake, and the skies start to bleed, it may already be too late.

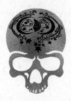

The Crown of Gilded Bones
Blood and Ash Series, Book Three
Available in hardcover, e-book, and trade paperback.

Bow Before Your Queen Or Bleed Before Her...

She's been the victim and the survivor...

Poppy never dreamed she would find the love she's found with Prince Casteel. She wants to revel in her happiness but first they must free his brother and find hers. It's a dangerous mission and one with far-reaching consequences neither dreamed of. Because Poppy is the Chosen, the Blessed. The true ruler of Atlantia. She carries the blood of the King of Gods within her. By right the crown and the kingdom are hers.

The enemy and the warrior...

Poppy has only ever wanted to control her own life, not the lives of others, but now she must choose to either forsake her birthright or seize the gilded crown and become the Queen of Flesh and Fire. But as the kingdoms' dark sins and blood-drenched secrets finally unravel, a long-forgotten power rises to pose a genuine threat. And they will stop at nothing to ensure that the crown never sits upon Poppy's head.

A lover and heartmate…

But the greatest threat to them and to Atlantia is what awaits in the far west, where the Queen of Blood and Ash has her own plans, ones she has waited hundreds of years to carry out. Poppy and Casteel must consider the impossible—travel to the Lands of the Gods and wake the King himself. And as shocking secrets and the harshest betrayals come to light, and enemies emerge to threaten everything Poppy and Casteel have fought for, they will discover just how far they are willing to go for their people—and each other.

And now she will become Queen…

The War of Two Queens
Blood and Ash Series, Book Four
Available in hardcover, e-book, and trade paperback.

War is only the beginning…

From the desperation of golden crowns…

Casteel Da'Neer knows all too well that very few are as cunning or vicious as the Blood Queen, but no one, not even him, could've prepared for the staggering revelations. The magnitude of what the Blood Queen has done is almost unthinkable.

And born of mortal flesh…

Nothing will stop Poppy from freeing her King and destroying everything the Blood Crown stands for. With the strength of the Primal of Life's guards behind her, and the support of the wolven, Poppy must convince the Atlantian generals to make war her way—because there can be no retreat this time. Not if she has any hope of building a future where both kingdoms can reside in peace.

A great primal power rises…

Together, Poppy and Casteel must embrace traditions old and new to safeguard those they hold dear—to protect those who cannot defend themselves. But war is only the beginning. Ancient primal powers have already stirred, revealing the horror of what began eons ago. To end what the Blood Queen has begun, Poppy might have to become what she has been prophesied to be—what she fears the most.

As the Harbinger of Death and Destruction.

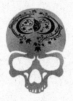

A Soul of Ash and Blood
Blood and Ash Series, Book Five
Available in hardcover, e-book, and trade paperback.

Only his memories can save her…

A great primal power has risen. The Queen of Flesh and Fire has become the Primal of Blood and Bone—the true Primal of Life and Death. And the battle Casteel, Poppy, and their allies have been fighting has only just begun. Gods are awakening across Iliseeum and the mortal realm, readying for the war to come.

But when Poppy falls into stasis, Cas faces the very real possibility that the dire, unexpected consequences of what she is becoming could take her away from him. Cas is given some advice, though—something he plans to cling to as he waits to see her beautiful eyes open once more: Talk to her.

And so, he does. He reminds Poppy how their journey began, revealing things about himself that only Kieran knows in the process. But it's anybody's guess what she'll wake to or exactly how much of the realm and Cas will have changed when she does.

#1 New York Times bestselling author Jennifer L. Armentrout revisits Poppy and Casteel's epic love story in the next installment of the Blood and Ash series. But this time, Hawke gets to tell the tale.

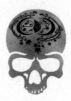

A Shadow in the Ember
Flesh and Fire Series, Book One
Available in hardcover, e-book, and trade paperback.

#1 New York Times bestselling author Jennifer L. Armentrout returns with book one of the all-new, compelling Flesh and Fire series— set in the beloved Blood and Ash world.

Born shrouded in the veil of the Primals, a Maiden as the Fates promised, Seraphena Mierel's future has never been hers. *Chosen* before birth to uphold the desperate deal her ancestor struck to save his people, Sera must leave behind her life and offer herself to the Primal of Death as his Consort.

However, Sera's real destiny is the most closely guarded secret in all of Lasania—she's not the well protected Maiden but an assassin with one mission—one target. Make the Primal of Death fall in love, become his weakness, and then...end him. If she fails, she dooms her kingdom to a slow demise at the hands of the Rot.

Sera has always known what she is. Chosen. Consort. Assassin. Weapon. A specter never fully formed yet drenched in blood. A *monster*. Until *him*. Until the Primal of Death's unexpected words and deeds chase away the darkness gathering inside her. And his seductive touch ignites a passion she's never allowed herself to feel and cannot feel for him. But Sera has never had a choice. Either way, her life is forfeit—it always has been, as she has been forever touched by Life and Death.

A Light in the Flame
Flesh and Fire Series, Book Two
Available in hardcover, e-book, and trade paperback.

The only one who can save Sera now is the one she spent her life planning to kill.

The truth about Sera's plan is out, shattering the fragile trust forged between her and Nyktos. Surrounded by those distrustful of her, all Sera has is her duty. She will do anything to end Kolis, the false King of Gods, and his tyrannical rule of Iliseeum, thus stopping the threat he poses to the mortal realm.

Nyktos has a plan, though, and as they work together, the last thing they need is the undeniable, scorching passion that continues to ignite between them. Sera cannot afford to fall for the tortured Primal, not when a life no longer bound to a destiny she never wanted is more attainable than ever. But memories of their shared pleasure and unrivaled desire are a siren's call impossible to resist.

And as Sera begins to realize that she wants to be more than a Consort in name only, the danger surrounding them intensifies. The attacks on the Shadowlands are increasing, and when Kolis summons them to Court, a whole new risk becomes apparent. The Primal power of Life is growing inside her, pushing her closer to the end of her Culling. And without Nyktos's love—an emotion he's incapable of feeling—she won't survive her Ascension. That is if she even *makes* it to her Ascension and Kolis doesn't get to her first. Because time is running out. For both her and the realms.

ON BEHALF OF BLUE BOX PRESS,

Liz Berry, M.J. Rose, and Jillian Stein would like to thank ~

Steve Berry
Doug Scofield
Benjamin Stein
Kim Guidroz
Chelle Olson
Hang Le
Chris Graham
Tanaka Kangara
Jessica Saunders
Malissa Coy
Jen Fisher
Stacey Tardif
Laura Helseth
Jessica Mobbs
Erika Hayden
Dylan Stockton
Kate Boggs
Richard Blake
and Simon Lipskar